The dead girl, her skin glowing with a bluish pallor, comes toward me, and the crowd between us parts swiftly and unconsciously.

They may not be able to see her but they can *feel* her, even if it lacks the intensity of my own experience. Electricity crackles up my spine—and something else, something bleak and looming like a premonition.

She's so close now I could touch her. My heart's accelerating, even before she opens her mouth, which I've already decided, ridiculously, impossibly, that I want to kiss. I can't make up my mind whether that means I'm exceedingly shallow or prescient. I don't know what I'm thinking because this is such unfamiliar territory: total here-be-dragons kind of stuff.

She blinks that dead person blink, looks at me as though I'm some puzzle to be solved. Doesn't she realize it's the other way around? She blinks again, and whispers in my ear, "Run."

Praise for **The Death Works Trilogy**

"I enjoyed this book right from the first page. Jamieson opens with a literal bang as his main character starts getting shot at and it's quickly paced from that point on."
—sfrevu.com

"The world-building is complicated and interesting, the descriptions of the underworld are fantastic, and Steven de Selby is a charming bumbler."
—*RT Book Reviews* (4 Stars)

"The story itself is fresh and utterly gripping—I've read a lot of urban fantasy...and I've not come across anything that tells a story like this one."
—*Australian Speculative Fiction in Focus*

"A br[illegible] o be an enthralling series."
—*Bookseller + Publisher* (Australia)

"Terri[illegible]
—alternative-worlds.com

By Trent Jamieson

THE DEATH WORKS TRILOGY

Death Most Definite

Managing Death

The Business of Death

THE DEATH WORKS TRILOGY

THE BUSINESS OF DEATH

TRENT JAMIESON

www.orbitbooks.net

The characters and events in this book are fictitious. Any similarity to real persons, living or dead, is coincidental and not intended by the author.

Orbit
Hachette Book Group
237 Park Avenue, New York, NY 10017
www.HachetteBookGroup.com

First North American Edition: September 2011
Death Most Definite and *Managing Death* originally published in paperback by Hachette Australia: 2010

Orbit is an imprint of Hachette Book Group.
The Orbit name and logo are trademarks of Little, Brown Book Group Limited.

LCCN: 2011925277
ISBN 978-0-316-07801-6

10 9 8 7 6 5 4 3 2 1

Printed in the United States of America

For Diana

CONTENTS

BOOK ONE

DEATH MOST DEFINITE

But lo, a stir is in the air!

Edgar Allan Poe, "The City in the Sea"

Brace yourselves.

Old RM Humour

PART ONE

THE SCHISM

1

I know something's wrong the moment I see the dead girl standing in the Wintergarden food court.

She shouldn't be here. Or I shouldn't. But no one else is working this. I'd sense them if they were. My phone's hardly helpful. There are no calls from Number Four, and that's a serious worry. I should have had a heads-up about this: a missed call, a text, or a new schedule. But there's nothing. Even a Stirrer would be less peculiar than what I have before me.

Christ, all I want is my coffee and a burger.

Then our eyes meet and I'm not hungry anymore.

A whole food court's worth of shoppers swarm between us, but from that instant of eye contact, it's just me and her, and that indefinable something. A bit of *deja vu*. A bit of lightning. Her eyes burn into mine, and there's a gentle, mocking curl to her lips that is gorgeous; it hits me in the chest.

This shouldn't be. The dead don't seek you out unless there is no one (or no thing) working their case: and that just doesn't happen. Not these days. And certainly not in the heart of Brisbane's CBD.

She shouldn't be here.

This isn't my gig. This most definitely will not end well. The girl is dead; our relationship has to be strictly professional.

She has serious style.

I'm not sure I can pinpoint what it is, but it's there, and it's unique.

The dead project an image of themselves, normally in something comfortable like a tracksuit, or jeans and a shirt. But this girl, her hair shoulder length with a ragged cut, is in a black, long-sleeved blouse, and a skirt, also black. Her legs are sheathed in black stockings. She's into silver jewelry, and what I assume are ironic brooches of Disney characters. Yeah, serious style, and a strong self-image.

And her eyes.

Oh, her eyes. They're remarkable, green, but flecked with gray. And those eyes are wide, because she's dead—newly dead—and I don't think she's come to terms with that yet. Takes a while: sometimes it takes a long while.

I yank pale ear buds from my ears, releasing a tinny splash of "London Calling" into the air around me.

The dead girl, her skin glowing with a bluish pallor, comes toward me, and the crowd between us parts swiftly and unconsciously. They may not be able to see her but they can *feel* her, even if it lacks the intensity of my own experience. Electricity crackles up my spine—and something else, something bleak and looming like a premonition.

She's so close now I could touch her. My heart's accelerating, even before she opens her mouth, which I've already decided, ridiculously, impossibly, that I want to kiss. I can't make up my mind whether that means I'm exceedingly shallow or prescient. I don't know what I'm thinking because this is such unfamiliar territory: total here-be-dragons kind of stuff.

She blinks that dead person blink, looks at me as though I'm some puzzle to be solved. Doesn't she realize it's the other way around? She blinks again, and whispers in my ear, "Run."

And then someone starts shooting at me.

Not what I was expecting.

Bullets crack into the nearest marble-topped tables. One. Two. Three. Shards of stone sting my cheek.

The food court surges with desperate motion. People scream, throwing themselves to the ground, scrambling for cover. But not me. She said run, and I run: zigging and zagging. Bent down, because I'm tall, easily a head taller than most of the people here, and far more than that now that the majority are on the floor. The shooter's after me; well, that's how I'm taking it. Lying down is only going to give them a motionless target.

Now, I'm in OK shape. I'm running, and a gun at your back gives you a good head of steam. Hell, I'm sprinting, hurdling tables, my long legs knocking lunches flying, my hands sticky with someone's spilt Coke. The dead girl's keeping up in that effortless way dead people have: skimming like a drop of water over a glowing hot plate.

We're out of the food court and down Elizabeth Street. In the open, traffic rumbling past, the Brisbane sun a hard light overhead. The dead girl's still here with me, throwing glances over her shoulder. Where the light hits her she's almost translucent. Sunlight and shadow keep revealing and concealing at random; a hand, the edge of a cheekbone, the curve of a calf.

The gunshots coming from inside haven't disturbed anyone's consciousness out here.

Shootings aren't exactly a common event in Brisbane. They happen, but not often enough for people to react as you might expect. All they suspect is that someone needs to service their car more regularly, and that there's a lanky bearded guy, possibly late for something, his jacket bunched into one fist, running like a madman down Elizabeth Street. I turn left into Edward, the nearest intersecting street, and then left again into the pedestrian-crammed space of Queen Street Mall.

I slow down in the crowded walkway panting and moving with the flow of people; trying to appear casual. I realize that my phone's been ringing. I look at it, at arm's length, like the monkey holding the bone in *2001: A Space Odyssey*. All I've got on the screen is Missed

Call, and Private Number. Probably someone from the local DVD shop calling to tell me I have an overdue rental, which, come to think of it, I do—I always do.

"You're a target," the dead girl says.

"No shit!" I'm thinking about overdue DVDs, which is crazy. I'm thinking about kissing her, which is crazier still, and impossible. I haven't kissed anyone in a long time. If I smoked this would be the time to light up, look into the middle distance and say something like: "I've seen trouble, but in the Wintergarden, on a Tuesday at lunchtime, c'mon!" But if I smoked I'd be even more out of breath and gasping out questions instead, and there's some (well, most) types of cool that I just can't pull off.

So I don't say anything. I wipe my Coke-sticky hands on my tie, admiring all that *je ne sais quoi* stuff she's got going on and feeling as guilty as all hell about it, because she's dead and I'm being so unprofessional. At least no one else was hurt in the food court: I'd feel it otherwise. Things aren't *that* out of whack. The sound of sirens builds in the distant streets. I can hear them, even above my pounding heart.

"This is so hard." Her face is the picture of frustration. "I didn't realize it would be so hard. There's a lot you need—" She flickers like her signal's hit static, and that's a bad sign: who knows where she could end up. "If you could get in—"

I reach toward her. Stupid, yeah, but I want to comfort her. She looks so pained. But she pulls back, as though she knows what would happen if I touch her. She shouldn't be acting this way. She's dead; she shouldn't care. If anything, she should want the opposite. She flickers again, swells and contracts, grows snowy. Whatever there is of her here is fracturing.

I take a step toward her. "Stop," I yell. "I need to—"

Need to? I don't exactly know what I need. But it doesn't matter because she's gone, and I'm yelling at nothing. And I didn't pomp her.

She's just gone.

2

That's not how it's meant to happen. Unprofessional. So unprofessional. I'm supposed to be the one in control.

After all, I'm a Psychopomp: a Pomp. Death is my business, has been in my family for a good couple of hundred years. Without me, and the other staff at Mortmax Industries, the world would be crowded with souls, and worse. Like Dad says, pomp is a verb and a noun. Pomps pomp the dead, we draw them through us to the Underworld and the One Tree. And we stall the Stirrers, those things that so desperately desire to come the other way. Every day I'm doing this—well, five days a week. It's a living, and quite a lucrative one at that.

I'm good at what I do. Though this girl's got me wondering.

I wave my hand through the spot where, moments ago, she stood. Nothing. Nothing at all. No residual electrical force. My skin doesn't tingle. My mouth doesn't go dry. She may as well have never been there.

The back of my neck prickles. I turn a swift circle.

Can't see anyone, but there are eyes on me, from somewhere. Who's watching me?

Then the sensation passes, all at once, a distant scratching pressure released, and I'm certain (well, pretty certain) that I'm alone—but for the usual Brisbane crowds pushing past me through the mall. Before, when the dead girl had stood here, they'd have done anything to keep away from her and me. Now I'm merely an annoying idiot blocking the flow of foot traffic. I find some cover: a little alcove between two shops where I'm out of almost everyone's line of sight.

I get on the phone, and call Dad's direct number at Mortmax. Maybe I should be calling Morrigan, or Mr. D (though word is the Regional Manager's gone fishing), but I need to talk to Dad first. I need to get this straight in my head.

I could walk around to Number Four, Mortmax's office space in Brisbane. It's on George Street, four blocks from where I'm standing, but I'm feeling too exposed and, besides, I'd probably run into Derek. While the bit of me jittery with adrenaline itches for a fight, the rest is hungry for answers. I'm more likely to get those if I keep away. Derek's been in a foul mood and I need to get through him before I can see anyone else. Derek runs the office with efficiency and attention to detail, and he doesn't like me at all. The way I'm feeling, that's only going to end in harsh words. Ah, work politics. Besides, I've got the afternoon and tomorrow off. First rule of this gig is: if you don't want extra hours keep a low profile. I've mastered that one to the point that it's almost second nature.

Dad's line must be busy because he doesn't pick up. Someone else does, though. Looks like I might get a fight after all.

"Yes," Derek says. You could chill beer with that tone.

"This is Steven de Selby." I can't hide the grin in my voice. Now is not the time to mess with me, even if you're Morrigan's assistant and, technically, my immediate superior.

"I know who it is."

"I need to talk to Dad."

There are a couple of moments of uncomfortable silence, then a few more. "I'm surprised we haven't got you rostered on."

"I just got back from a funeral. Logan City. I'm done for the day."

Derek clicks his tongue. "Do you have any idea how busy we are?"

Absolutely, or I'd be talking to Dad. I wait a while: let the silence stretch out. He's not the only one who can play at that. "No," I say at last, when even I'm starting to feel uncomfortable. "Would you like to discuss it with me? I'm in the city. How about we have a coffee?" I resist the urge to ask him what he's wearing.

Derek sighs, doesn't bother with a response, and transfers me to Dad's phone.

"Steve," Dad says, and he sounds a little harried. So maybe Derek wasn't just putting it on for my benefit.

"Dad, well, ah..." I hesitate, then settle for the obvious. "I've just been shot at."

"What? Oh, Christ. You sure it wasn't a car backfiring?" he asks somewhat hopefully.

"Dad... do cars normally backfire rounds into the Wintergarden food court?"

"That was you?" Now he's sounding worried. "I thought you were in Logan."

"Yeah, I was. I went in for some lunch and someone started shooting."

"Are you OK?"

"Not bleeding, if that's what you mean."

"Good."

"Dad, I wouldn't be talking to you if someone hadn't warned me. Someone not living."

"Now that shouldn't be," he says. He sounds almost offended. "There are no punters on the schedule." He taps on the keyboard. I could be in for a wait. "Even factoring in the variables, there's no chance of a Pomp being required in the Wintergarden until next month: elderly gentleman, heart attack. There shouldn't be any activity there at all."

I clench my jaw. "There was, Dad. I'm not making it up. I was there. And, no, I haven't been drinking."

I tell him about the dead girl, and am surprised at how vivid the details are. I hadn't realized that I'd retained them. The rest of it is blurring, what with all the shooting and the sprinting, but I can see her face so clearly, and those eyes.

"Who was she?"

"I don't know. She looked familiar: didn't stay around long enough for me to ask her anything. But Dad, I didn't pomp her. She just disappeared."

"Loose cannon, eh? I'll look into it, talk to Morrigan for you."

"I'd appreciate that. Maybe I was just in the wrong place at the wrong time, but it doesn't feel like that. She was trying to save me, and when do the dead ever try and look after Pomps?"

Dad chuckles at that. There's nothing more self-involved than a dead person. Talking of self-involved . . . "Derek says you're busy."

"We're having trouble with our phone line. Another one of Morrigan's 'improvements'," Dad says, I can hear the inverted commas around improvements. "Though . . . that seems to be in the process of being fixed." He pauses. "I *think* that's what's happening, there's a half-dozen people here pulling wiring out of the wall." I can hear them in the background, drills whining; there's even a little hammering. "Oh, and there's the Death Moot in December. Two months until everything's crazy and the city's crowded with Regional Managers. Think of it, the entire Orcus here, all thirteen RMs." He groans. "Not to mention the bloody Stirrers. They keep getting worse. A couple of staffers have needed stitches."

I rub the scarred surface of the palm of my free hand. Cicatrix City as we call it, an occupational hazard of stalling stirs, but the least of them when it came to Stirrers. A Pomp's blood is enough to exorcise a Stirrer from a newly dead body, but the blood needs to be fresh. Morrigan is researching ways around this, but has come up with nothing as of yet. Dad calls it time-wastery. I for one would be happy if I didn't have to slash open my palm every time a corpse came crashing up into unlife.

A stir is always a bad thing. Unsettling, dangerous and bloody. Stirrers, in essence, do the same thing as Pomps, but without discretion: they hunger to take the living and the dead. They despise life, they drain it away like plugholes to the Underworld, and they're not at all fond of me and mine. Yeah, they hate us.

"Well, I didn't see or sense one in Logan. Just a body, and a lot of people mourning."

"Hmm, you got lucky. Your mother had two." Dad sighs. "And here I am stuck in the office."

I make a mental note to call Mom. "So Derek wasn't lying."

"You've got to stop giving Derek so much crap, Steve. He'll be Ankou one day, Morrigan isn't going to be around forever."

"I don't like the guy, and you can't tell me that the feeling isn't mutual."

"Steven, he's your boss. Try not to piss him off too much," Dad says and, by the tone of his voice, I know we're about to slip into the same old argument. Let me list the ways: My lack of ambition. How I could have had Derek's job, if I'd really cared. How there's more Black Sheep in me than is really healthy for a Pomp. That Robyn left me three years ago. Well, I don't want to go there today.

"OK," I say. "If you could just explain why the girl was there and, maybe, who she was. She understood the process, Dad. She wouldn't let me pomp her." There's silence down the end of the line. "You do that, and I'll try and suck up to Derek."

"I'm serious," Dad says. "He's already got enough going on today. Melbourne's giving him the run-around. Not returning calls, you know, that sort of thing."

Melbourne giving Derek the run-around isn't that surprising. Most people like to give Derek the run-around. I don't know how he became Morrigan's assistant. Yeah, I know *why*, he's a hard worker, and ambitious, almost as ambitious as Morrigan—and Morrigan is Ankou, second only to Mr. D. But Derek's hardly a people person. I can't think of anyone who Derek hasn't pissed off over the years: anyone *beneath* him, that is. He'd not dare with Morrigan, and only a madman would consider it with Mr. D—you don't mess with Geoff Daly, the Australian Regional Manager. Mr. D's too creepy, even for us.

"OK, I'll send some flowers," I say. "Gerberas, everyone likes gerberas, don't they?"

Dad grunts. He's been tapping away at his computer all this time. I'm not sure if it's the computer or me that frustrates him more.

"Can you see anything?"

A put-upon sigh, more tapping. "Yeah...I'm...looking into... All right, let me just..." Dad's a one-finger typist. If glaciers had fingers they'd type faster than him. Morrigan gives him hell about it all the time; Dad's response requires only one finger as well. "I can't see anything unusual in the records, Steve. I'd put it down to bad luck, or good luck. You didn't get shot after all. Maybe you should buy a scratchie, one of those $250,000 ones."

"Why would I want to ruin my mood?"

Dad laughs. Another phone rings in the background; wouldn't put it past Derek to be on the other end. But then all the phones seem to be ringing.

"Dad, maybe I should come into the office. If you need a hand..."

"No, we're fine here," Dad says, and I can tell he's trying to keep me away from Derek, which is probably a good thing. My Derek tolerance is definitely at a low today.

We say our goodbyes and I leave him to all those ringing phones, though my guilt stays with me.

3

I take a deep breath. I feel slightly reassured about my own living-breathing-walking-talking future. If Number Four's computers can't bring anything unusual up then nothing unusual is happening.

There are levels of unusual though, and I don't feel that reassured by the whole thing, even if I can be reasonably certain no one has a bead on me. Something's wrong. I just can't put my finger on it. The increased Stirrer activity, the problems with the phones... But we've had these sorts of things before, and even if Stirrers are a little exotic, what company doesn't have issues with their phones at least once a month? Stirrers tend to come in waves, particularly during flu season—there's always more bodies, and a chance to slip in before someone notices—and it's definitely flu season, spring is the worst for it in Brisbane. I'm glad I've had my shots, there's some nasty stuff going around. Pomps are a little paranoid about viruses, with good reason—we know how deadly they can be.

Still, I don't get shot at every day (well, ever). Nor do I obsess over dead girls to the point where I think I would almost be happy to be shot at again if I got the chance to spend more time with them. It's ridiculous but I'm thinking about her eyes, and the timbre of her voice. Which is a change from thinking about Robyn.

My mobile rings a moment later, and I actually jump and make a startled sound, loud enough to draw a bit of attention. I cough.

Pretend to clear my throat. The LCD flashes an all too familiar number at me—it's the garage where my car is being serviced. I take the call. Seems I'm without a vehicle until tomorrow at least, something's wrong with something. Something expensive I gather. Whenever my mechanic sounds cheerful I know it's going to cost me, and he's being particularly ebullient.

The moment I hang up, the phone rings again.

My cousin Tim. Alarm bells clang in the distant recesses of my mind. We're close, Tim's the nearest thing I have to a brother, but he doesn't normally call me out of the blue. Not unless he's after something.

"Are you all right?" he demands. "No bullet wounds jettisoning blood or anything?"

"Yeah. And, no, I'm fine."

Tim's a policy advisor for a minor but ambitious state minister. He's plugged in and knows everything. "Good, called you almost as soon as I found out. You working tomorrow?" he asks.

"No, why?"

"You're going to need a drink. I'll pick you up at your place in an hour." Tim isn't that great at the preamble. Part of his job: he's used to getting what he wants. And he has the organizational skills to back it up. Tim would have made a great Pomp, maybe even better than Morrigan, except he decided very early on that the family trade wasn't for him. Black Sheep nearly always do. Most don't even bother getting into pomping at all. They deny the family trade and become regular punters. Tim's decision had caused quite a scandal.

But, he hadn't escaped pomping completely; part of his remit is Pomp/government relations, something he likes to complain about at every opportunity: along the lines of every time I get out, they pull me back in. Still, he's brilliant at the job. Mortmax and the Queensland government haven't had as close and smooth a relationship in decades. Between him and Morrigan's innovations, Mortmax Australia is in the middle of a golden age.

"I don't know," I say.

Tim sighs. "Oh, no you don't. There's no getting out of this, mate. Sally's looking after the kids, and I'm not going to tell you what I had to do to swing that. It's her bridge night, for Christ's sake. Steve, how many other thirty-year-olds do you know who play bridge?"

I look at my watch. "Hey, it's only three."

"Beer o'clock." I've never heard a more persuasive voice.

"Tim, um, I reckon that's stretching it a bit."

There's a long silence down the other end of the phone. "Steve, you can't tell me you're busy. I know you've got no more pomps scheduled today."

Sometimes his finger is a little too on the pulse. "I've had a rough day."

Tim snorts. "Steve, now that's hilarious. A rough day for you is a nine o'clock start and no coffee."

"Thanks for the sympathy." My job is all hours, though I must admit my shifts have been pretty sweet of late. And no coffee *does* make for a rough day. In fact, coffee separated by more than two-hourly intervals makes for a rough day.

"Yeah, OK, so it's been rough. I get that. All the more reason . . ."

"Pub it is, then," I say without any real enthusiasm.

I've a sudden, aching need for coffee, coal black and scalding, but I know I'm going to have to settle for a Coke. That is, if I want to get home and change in time.

"You're welcome," Tim says. "My shout."

"Oh, you'll be shouting, all right."

"See you in an hour."

So I'm in the Paddo Tavern, still starving hungry, even after eating a deep-fried Chiko Roll: a sere and jaundiced specimen that had been mummifying in a nearby cafe's bain-marie for a week too long.

I had gone home, changed into jeans and a Stooges T-shirt—the two cleanest things on the floor of my bedroom. The jacket and pants didn't touch the ground, though, they go in the cupboard until I can get them dry-cleaned. Pomps know all about presentation—well, on the job, anyway. After all, we spend most of our working day at funerals and in morgues.

I might have eaten something at home but other than a couple of Mars Bars, milk, and dog food for Molly there's nothing. The fridge is in need of a good grocery shop; has been for about three years. Besides, I'm only just dressed and deodorized when Tim honks the horn out the front. Perhaps I shouldn't have spent ten minutes working on my hair.

Getting to the pub early was not such a good idea. Sure, we avoided peak-hour traffic, but my head was spinning by the first beer. Chiko Rolls can only sop up so much alcohol—about a thimbleful by my calculations.

"Why bulk up on the carbs?" Tim had declared—though I'm sure he'd actually had something for lunch. "You need room for the beer."

I end up sitting at the table as Tim buys round after round. He comes back each time a little bit drunker. His tie slightly looser around his neck. A big grin on his face as he slides my beer over to me. "Now, isn't this perfect?"

We've always been like this. Get us together and the drinks keep coming.

He's already bought a packet of cigarettes. We used to sneak off at family parties and sit around smoking whatever cigarettes we could afford, listening to the Smiths on cassette. Things haven't changed for Tim. If Sally knew about those cigarettes he'd be a dead man. To be honest, I'm not that keen on them either. The last thing you ever want to do is pomp a family member.

"Look," he says, well into our fifth pint. He nurses his beer a while, staring at me like I'm some poor wounded pup. "We're worried about you. Look at you there, all miserable."

"Yeah, but I don't get shot at every day. This is new."

"You know that's not what I'm talking about."

"Don't you mention her. It was three years ago."

"Exactly."

"I'm over her."

Tim drops his glass onto the table. It makes a definitive and sarcastic crack. "If Sally were here she'd be laughing right now. Just because we've stopped setting you up on dates doesn't mean we agree with you." He raises his hand at my glare. "OK. So how about work? Is that going well? I hear there's been a few issues lately."

"What are you fishing for?"

"Nothing—that's Mr. D. He's been away the last few days, fishing, hasn't he?"

I raise an eyebrow. "I didn't think these were work drinks. You trying to claim this on your tax?"

Tim shakes his head. "Of course not. I suppose I just get a bit nervous when Mr. D is away for so long. The whole department does."

"Shit, you *are* fishing."

"Not at all."

"You're going to have to be more subtle than that. Morrigan doesn't like you that much, Tim."

Tim's face darkens. "It's not my job to be liked. Besides, he doesn't like your dad all that much, either."

"Morrigan loves my father. He just never agrees with him. That, my dear cousin, is the very definition of a friendship. Mutual admiration orbiting mutual contempt."

Tim grins. "Certainly what we have, eh? And may it always be so." He raises his pint glass. "To immortality."

I crack my pint against his. "Immortality." We're both aware of how ridiculous we sound. Grow up around Pomps and ridiculous is all you've got.

I want to tell Tim about the dead girl but I can't quite bring myself to. Truth is, I'm a bit embarrassed. I'm not sure if my feelings for her show that I'm finally over Robyn or that I'm in deeper than ever. Besides, it's just not the done thing. You don't fall for a punter. No one's that unprofessional. No one's that stupid.

By mid evening there's a pretty decent cover band belting out versions of pub rock standards from The Doors to Wolfmother. They've only started into the first bars of Soundgarden's "Black Hole Sun" when I see the dead guy. I look at Tim, who's just ducked back from a smoke.

"That's odd," I say, all the while wondering how sober I am.

Tim raises an eyebrow. He's not a Pomp but he knows the deal. He can recognize the signs. And they're very obvious in a crowded pub. Some people reckon that Black Sheep know the deal better than anyone, because if you're from a pomping family you don't choose to become a Pomp, you choose not to. "Punter?"

"Yeah." I tap my phone with beer-thickened fingers. Is this thing broken? I wonder.

"Maybe it's someone else's gig," he says, hopefully, looking from me to the phone and back again.

I shake my head. "No. The schedule's up. Nothing about a Pomp being required here. Second time today."

"And you neglected to tell me this?"

"I thought this wasn't a work meeting."

"See what I mean?" Tim says, pointing at the space where the dead guy stands. "This is why we worry when Mr. D goes fishing."

I throw my gaze around the room. The last time this happened someone started shooting at me. Can't see that happening here.

"Something's not working," Tim says. "Shouldn't you...?" He nods toward the dead guy.

"Yeah." I put down my beer and roll my shoulders. There's a satisfyingly loud crack. "I've a job that needs doing."

I get up, and an afternoon's drinking almost topples me. I grip the table, perhaps a little too desperately.

Tim reaches out a steadying hand. "You right?"

"Yep. Yep." I push him away. "I'm fine."

There is no way I should be doing this drunk. I could lose my job. I'm sure it's somewhere in my contract. But technically this isn't supposed to happen. There's a dead guy here, and no one to facilitate his next step. It's a crowded pub, and yet there's this empty space—empty to everyone but me. If it didn't piss me off so much it would be funny to watch. Anyone who gets close to the dead guy frowns then darts away.

If only that space was near the bar.

The dead guy's head jerks in my direction. His eyes widen and he blinks furiously: a look that would be almost coquettish if it wasn't so familiar.

"It's all right," I say.

It isn't, he's dead. But there's nothing that can be done about that. Whatever could have been done wasn't or failed. We're past that. Pomps don't deal with the dying but with what comes after. We're merely conduits, and gatekeepers. The dead pass through us, and we stop the Stirrers coming back. But this—this dead guy in the Paddo, and me—is too reactive. Someone should have been sent here by head office. He should be on the schedule. But he isn't. And that leaves a very bitter taste in my mouth; I do have some pride in my job. Death is the most natural thing in the world but only because we work so hard to make it look easy.

I look around. Just in case... Nope, no other Pomps in the building. Should be able to feel one if there is, but I *have* had a lot to drink.

"Sorry," the dead guy says, his voice carrying perfectly despite the noise.

"Nothing to be sorry about." I'm wearing the most calming expression I can muster. I know he's scared.

I reach out my hand, and he flits away like a nervous bird, and brushes a bloke's arm. The poor guy yelps and drops his beer. Glass shatters and the circle around us widens, though people don't realize what they're doing. I can feel eyes on me. This must look more than a little crazy. But the gazes never linger for long—looking at a spot where a dead person is standing can be almost as uncomfortable as bumping up against one. The average human brain makes its adjustments quickly and shifts its attention elsewhere.

The dead guy steps back toward me.

"What's your name?" I ask him, keeping my voice soft and low. His eyes are focused on my lips.

"Terry."

"You want to talk, Terry?" A name is good. Morrigan would describe it as being of extreme utility. It's a handle, a point of focus. Terry's eyes search my face.

"No. I—this isn't right. I've been wandering, and there's nothing. Just—" He blinks. Looks around. "What is this place? Shit, is this the Paddo?"

"You shouldn't be here, Terry," I say, and he's back, looking at me. There's more confidence and less confusion in his eyes.

"No shit. I haven't been back to Brisbane in years. I—do people really still listen to grunge?"

"What's wrong with grunge?"

Terry rolls his eyes. "Where to begin…"

I take another step toward him. "Look, it doesn't matter, Terry." This is inexcusable. Someone has majorly screwed up, and I'm certain I know who. But that's for later. I need to stay calm.

"Terry, you know where you need to be," I say gently, as gently as you can above the cover band's rendition of Nirvana's "Smells Like Teen Spirit."

He nods his head. "I can't seem to get there."

"Let me help you, Terry."

I reach out. This time he doesn't dart away. I touch him. And Terry's gone, passing through me, and into the Underworld. There's the familiar pain of a successful pomp, a slight ache that runs through me. I take a deep breath. Then, between blinks, all that space around me fills with people. I elbow my way toward my table none too gently; I reserve softness for the dead. I'm fuming with a white-hot rage, my body sore from the pomp.

Derek's in trouble, now. If he's messed up the rostering this badly, what else is he doing wrong? I'm filled with a righteous (and somewhat enjoyable) anger. I'd call him right now, but anger isn't the only thing I'm filled with and it's decided to remind me in no uncertain terms.

I make a dash for the toilets, stand at the urinal, and it's a sweet relief. I glance over at the mirror; the hair's looking good.

"You're in danger," a familiar voice whispers in my ear, and I jump. It's the dead girl. She smiles that mocking smile.

"Jesus! Where the hell did you . . . What do you mean, in danger?" I'm a while framing that question.

She shakes her head, her eyes a bit fuzzy. She blinks. "I'm not sure." Then there's some clarity in her gaze. "Still trying to remember. You're really taking this people wanting to kill you thing very well. Or maybe not . . . Hmm. How much have you had to drink?"

I'm pretty unsteady on my feet, and I'm still peeing. So, a lot.

"I . . . Would you mind turning the other way? I don't think *people* want to kill me, that was just some crazy guy with a gun."

The dead girl's face creases. "A crazy guy who just happened to take potshots at you?"

"Which is why he's crazy. I mean, why would anyone want to blow my brains out?"

Someone's walked into the toilet. The movement catches my eye.

I turn, free hand clenched, a move I know is hardly intimidating, particularly while I'm pissing. I sway there a moment.

"Not him," she says.

"How do you know?" I demand. "You're hardly a reliable source of information, what with the dropping in and dropping out."

The poor interloper hesitates for a moment, looking at me, looking at the urinals, and feeling the presence of a dead person pushing him anywhere but here. He heads straight to a stall and locks the door.

And I'm suddenly feeling a whole lot more sober. The dead girl stands far enough away from me that I can't pomp her. It's not like I'd touch her before washing my hands anyway.

"Are you really dead?" I zip up. The room's swaying a little, which can't be good.

She nods. "The real deal. And you need to get out of here, there's stuff I have to tell you, I think." She looks down at her hands, and there's something about the gesture that makes me ache. "It's much harder keeping this together than I expected. And the urgency, I'm trying to hold onto that... But I'm remembering." She looks up at me. "It's getting a little clearer. That's something, right?"

I wash my hands, studying her in the mirror. A dozen contradictory emotions dance across her face. All of them legitimate, and every one of them adding to her confusion. And here I am leaden with drink. This demands sensitivity. I want to help her but I'm not sure if I can. Maybe the best way, the most professional way, is by pomping her.

But I'm also angry. She's scaring me, and that's not supposed to be the way this works.

"Good," I blurt, "because I really want to know why someone was shooting at me."

The dead girl scowls. "Maybe I should just let you die."

I shrug, drunkenly belligerent. I'm not the dead one after all. "Maybe. Then at least we'd—"

That's when the beer, the I've-been-shot-at-and-lived-to-tell-the-tale beer, has its effect on me, and I'm running for the nearest stall, the one next to the poor guy I scared off the urinal. When I am done, after a series of loud and desperate sounding hurls, I feel utterly wretched. I look up at her, because she's followed me in. "Bad Chiko Roll," I explain, half-heartedly.

The dead girl grimaces at me. But her eyes are more focused. The mere act of talking, of a person's interest in her, has helped ground her.

She even smiles. Nothing like a spew as an icebreaker. "Do people even eat those anymore?"

What is it about the dead today? Everybody's talking back. "Yes, and they listen to grunge."

"What?" She rubs her chin thoughtfully. "Though that might explain it."

"It was a legitimate movement."

"The stress is on the *was,* though." She's looking more coherent, almost concrete.

"Name's Steven," I say, and I instinctively reach out toward her. It's my job after all. She darts back, a look of horror on her face.

"Watch that!"

"Sorry, it's just habit." My head's feeling clearer.

We stand crammed in the grotty stall for a moment, just staring at each other. There's a tightness in my throat, a ridiculous sense of potential in a ridiculous place. Whatever it is, it passes. She nods, taking another step back, so that she's almost out of the stall. She keeps an eye on my hands.

"Lissa," she says. "Lissa Jones."

Which sounds a hell of a lot better than Dead Girl.

I open my mouth to say something, anything, but she's gone. And again, it's nothing to do with me. She's just gone. I'm suffering an altogether unfamiliar hurt, and it's awful.

4

Tim is far too drunk to drive me home. But sober enough to get me a taxi with what appears to be some sort of magic gesture. It's as though he plucked the car out of the night.

Tim presses the packet of cigarettes into my hands. "Hide the evidence, eh. And look after yourself."

"You too."

He gives me the thumbs up. "'S all good!"

And I know that he'll be at work *sans* hangover tomorrow, which brings a slight wave of resentment to the top of my rolling-drunk thoughts because my day off isn't going to be nearly as pretty. I watch him pluck another taxi from the ether.

"Where to?" the driver asks me. I mumble directions. Tim's taxi is already off. His driver probably knew where to go before Tim had even opened his mouth.

The taxi ride home is just swell, though a couple of times I nearly hurl again: seems my stomach has found more than that Chiko Roll to challenge it. Both times the driver is just about ready to push me out the door. I swear, one time I feel his boot on my back. But we make it, and he's happy enough to take my money, and happier still when I wave away his vague, and extremely leisurely, attempts at giving me change.

The taxi pulls away and I stare at my place. It's all a bit of a blur really, except for the brace symbol marked above the door. It's glowing: there must be Stirrers about. Not my job, though, the night shift will be dealing with those.

As I unlock the front door Molly's greeting barks are gruff and accusatory. She may be the most patient border collie in the world, but even she has limits. I realize that I hadn't fed her before I left. I make up for it, nearly falling flat on my face as I scoop dog food into her bowl, then walk into the bathroom and splash my face. I hardly feel the water. The space around me seems packed in cotton wool. I poke my cheek and it's as though I'm touching something inanimate. For some reason that saddens me. There's a few of Robyn's things still in the bathroom cupboard. A small bottle of perfume, a toothbrush. Three years and I've not managed to throw them out.

Molly pushes her black and white snout against my leg; she's wolfed down dinner and needs to go outside. There's an impatient gleam to her eyes. I think she's just as sick of me mooching over Robyn as everyone else, and Molly never even knew her. I bought her after Robyn left. Yeah, rebound pet ownership—real healthy.

"Sorry, girl."

She's on my heels all the way through the house to the kitchen and the back door, rushing past me as I open it. The refrigerator hums behind me.

In the backyard the air is cool. It's a typical spring evening and the city is still and quiet, though I know that's a lie because it's never really still or quiet. People are always sliding away to the Underworld, and things are always stirring. But I can imagine what it would be like to believe otherwise. I sit on the back step, smoking one of the cigarettes that Tim bought—yes, I'm *that* drunk—and wait for Molly to finish her business, thinking all the while about Lissa. I'd helped Terry easily enough. Why couldn't I help her? She's the most striking girl I've ever seen, but that shouldn't matter. I'm already feeling the remorse that no amount of alcohol can shield you from, because drinking is all about remorse.

Molly trots up next to me and I scratch her head. "What's wrong with me, eh?"

She's got no answer to offer. She's happy, though, to receive the scratching. I yawn at last, get up and leave the unquiet city outside.

I'm drunk and exhausted but I'm restless as all hell. I walk about my house, not really connecting with any of it. All the stuff I've bought. The useless shit, as Dad calls it. The posters, the DVDs, and CDs: some not even out of their wrappers. None of it plants me here. None of it means anything. I might as well be a ghost. I wonder if this disconnect is how it feels to be dead. I'll have to ask Morrigan—if anyone will know, it'll be him. Molly follows me for a little while but can see no sense in it, or just gets bored, and wanders off to her bed. I drop onto the couch in the living room, and sit on my cordless phone. The damn thing beeps at me.

I press the talk button and hear the familiar rapid blipping dial tone: there's at least one message on my voicemail.

I ring through to check. Two missed calls. The alcohol steps politely aside for a moment. One of the calls is from Morrigan: too late to call him back. Besides, if it had been really important, he would have tried my mobile.

There's a message, too. The phone crackles, which means either there are Stirrers about or we've hit a period of increased solar flare activity. Both mess with electrical signals.

"Steven," Dad says. "Hope you haven't been drinking." He doesn't sound too hopeful. "Thought I'd call to let you know you were right, it wasn't a coincidence. The police released the name of the gunman. Jim McKean."

McKean...

McKean...

The name's familiar. Dad fills in the blanks. "McKean's a Pomp... Was a Pomp. Sydney middle management; didn't show for work yesterday. I've heard he was doped out: on ice, that's what they call it these days, isn't it? Out of character, completely out of character."

Of course, McKean!

I remember him. A quiet guy. Always seemed nice, and a little bookish. We'd actually talked science fiction at a Christmas party a few years back. He was a real Heinlein nut, not that I'm saying anything, but...

"Morrigan's using his connections, digging into the why, but—whatever the reason—McKean is behind bars. You don't need to worry."

But I am. The guy came after me with a gun. Even with Molly the house seems too...empty.

"Give me that phone, Michael." It's Mom. "Steven, your father was less than speedy in passing on to me the details." Mom stresses the last word. "Your rather worthless father said you'd had a tough day. He neglected to tell me that you'd been shot at. You'll be having dinner with us tomorrow night. No excuses. Now, I hope Tim hasn't gotten you too drunk. We're all rather worried about you."

The message drops out.

I've a dinner invite for Wednesday, and I'll be there. Mom and Dad are excellent cooks. I might have inherited the pomping career but the culinary skills seemed to have skipped me. I might even have made enough peace with my stomach to be hungry by then.

I play the message over, twice, just to hear their voices. It grounds me a little. The dead aren't the only ones who like to feel that people care. I check my mobile but no missed calls, no texts, and the schedule hasn't changed.

I switch on the television, and flick through the channels.

Two of them are running stories about McKean. Shots of him being taken into custody, backlit by a frenetic clicking lightshow of camera flashes. There's something not right about him but I guess you could say that about anyone who decides that today is a good day to start firing a rifle into a crowd. No one was killed, thank Christ, but not all of that is luck: he wasn't gunning for anyone else. There's nothing in the story linking him to me. Nothing about me at all.

The sight of him draws a rising shudder of panic through me that even the weight of alcohol can't suppress. I guess it has affected me more than I care to admit.

I turn off the television and switch on my Notebook, hook into Facebook, and the Mortmax workgroup—Morrigan set that up—and there's Jim McKean in my network: looking his usual awkward self, and nothing like a killer. I check his profile. His life/death status is up as dead. Morrigan installed that morbid little gadget a year or so ago. Pomp humor is very much of the gallows sort.

Peculiar, as McKean *isn't* dead. But that slips from my mind in an instant, because there's Lissa's face in his friends list. I click on her profile photo.

She worked for Mortmax?

I bang my head with my palm. Of course she had. Lissa Jones. Melbourne agency. It's all here, and I must have met her before. Her green eyes mock me. Her status though, according to this, is living. Something's wrong with that gadget of Morrigan's.

I open Dad's profile. *Dead.*

Then Mum's. *Dead.*

I open my own profile. Status: *Dead.*

Then I'm opening all the Brisbane pages. And every single one of them, including Morrigan, is the same.

Something prickles up my spine.

I switch to Mr. D's profile. It has his usual picture, a crow on a tombstone. His is a dry and obvious sort of humor. But Regional Managers are like that. Death, after all, is the reason for their existence. His status: gone fishing.

Nothing peculiar there. Our RM loves to fish—most of the

Orcus do. I've heard he has a boat docked at the piers of Hell, and that Charon's own boatmen run it. I've seen the photos of the things he's caught in the sea of the dead—the ammonites, the juvenile megalodon, the black-toothed white whale with old mariner still attached.

Regardless, the timing is odd. I get the feeling that there's something I'm not seeing, but there's a thick and somewhat alcohol-muddied wall between the truth and me.

I switch off the Notebook. Then look at my watch. There's no one I can reasonably call about this. So I call Dad.

"Do you know what time it is?"

I don't realize that I'd been holding my breath until he answers. Morrigan's gadget is wrong, thank Christ. "Sorry, Dad, but..." I mumble something drunkenly at him about the Facebook accounts.

Dad lets out a weary breath. "*That's* what this is about?"

"Yeah, it's, I—"

"We'll discuss this tomorrow, when you're sober."

"But Dad—"

"Get some sleep."

There's a long moment of silence. Dad sighs again. "OK, there's some sort of glitch on the server. If we'd kept to the old ways... well, I wouldn't be answering a call from you in the middle of the night. I tell you, Steve, it's been a hell of a week." Which is saying something, as it's only Tuesday night. "Just a wonderful one for Mr. D to take off. Morrigan's looking into it. Now, go... to... sleep." Dad sounds like he is already, which is good or I'd be in for a lecture.

"Sorry," I say.

"'S OK," he says. "I'm just glad you're not hurt. We'll talk about this tomorrow." He hangs up, and I'm left holding the phone.

Dad said I'm safe, earlier. I can't say that's how I see it.

It's a weird world. A weird and dangerous world. When you're a Pomp, even such a low level one as me, you get your face rubbed in it. Robyn couldn't handle it. I don't think she believed in half of what I did. I don't blame her for leaving, not one little bit, nor for the hole she left in my life. She didn't grow up with all this, hadn't seen some of the things I've seen, or witnessed some of the deaths I've attended. Still, until today I'd never been shot at.

I walk around the house checking the locks, and then double-checking the front and back door. Then I'm looking in cupboards, even under the bed. It's a drunken, shambling sort of scrutiny. And when I catch myself stumbling to the front door for the third time I snort.

"Ridiculous."

Molly, who's been watching all this from her mat with a bemused tilt to her head, stares up at me.

"Ridiculous," I say again, and scratch behind her ears.

She grins at me.

"Safe as houses, eh, Moll?" I stumble to the bedroom, and crash onto the bed, after flipping my shoes across the room where they land with two dull thwacks against the wardrobe mirror. My reflection shivers at me.

"Buffoon," I whisper at it.

The bed begins a wobbly spin, even as I'm slipping into sleep. I stare at the window to steady that roiling movement. It works, but I know I won't be awake for much longer.

One drawn out blink, and then another, and I'm sure Lissa's face is pressed against the window or through the window. Then it's just the moon, full and blue. "Luminous," I whisper, at the pale light.

The moon says something, but I can't read her lips.

The window rattles as a car mutters in an eight-cylindered tongue down the street. Exhaustion has its hooks in me, and I'm too far gone, and full, to find a pause from my fall into slumber.

No wakefulness. No dreams. Just dark, dark sleep: that's where I'm headed. And Lissa, the moon, and all the questions rushing around me like Mr. D's crows, cannot follow me there.

5

My status on Facebook isn't the only thing that's dead. Someone has jimmied open my skull and poured highly flammable liquid migraine directly into my brainpan. I can taste stale vomit, a night's worth of spewing crusted to the roof of my mouth. I open my eye a crack and admit a jack-hammering Brisbane morning light that ignites all that potential pain at once. I shut my eye again. The room, windows closed, smells delightfully of sick and ashtray.

The phone rings, and I'm immediately regretting the decision to have a handset in my bedroom. The ringing is an ice pick swinging into my forehead.

I ignore it. Let it ring out. A second later my mobile starts up. Fucking ice pick all over again.

I open my eyes. The light is merciless as I scramble around hunting for my mobile, and it keeps ringing and ringing and ringing. This has to be some sort of cruel and unusual punishment. Sliding out of bed, I realize that I'm still half in my jeans: the other pants leg has the pocket with my phone in it.

I snatch out the mobile, consider hurling it against the wall, then see the number and moan.

Mortmax. And whoever's calling has disengaged the message service, which gives me more than a clue as to who is responsible.

I flip the phone open. "Yes."

"Steven," Derek says, "we need you in the city. No later than ten."

He hangs up.

Yes, king of bloody small talk. And do I have a thing or two to talk about with him! Starting with Lissa, and ending with Terry. Derek's messed up a few too many times in the last couple of days.

I look at the clock. 8:30.

Shit! I can't imagine this hangover leaving before late afternoon. It has teeth and cruel hangovery hands that are less than gently clenching my stomach, engendering an argument over which end of me is most likely going to be needing to evacuate the evils of the evening before. There are good odds it could be both at once. It's a finger-in-all-pies sort of hangover.

How do I get myself in these situations?

My phone chirps with a text. Tim. *Hope you're feeling OK :-)*

Prick.

Just chipper, I text back. Even texting is painful and nausea inducing.

I fish through cupboards, and drawers, until I find something strong for the pain. I manage to keep it down. Molly's waiting, eyes lit with a weary impatience, to be let out the back door. Opening it only lets in more of that brutal morning light. I wince, leave the door open for the dog, and make the trek to the bathroom.

Oddly enough Molly follows me. I shrug at her. "Suit yourself."

There's blood in the bathroom. On the walls; a little on the mirror. I wrinkle my nose at it. Molly sniffs at the walls, doesn't bother licking them. This ectoplasmic blood is mildly toxic. The first time she encountered it, gobbling down what she obviously thought was a marvelous, if peculiar, free feed, she had diarrhea for two days. Now *that* was pleasant for the both of us. Whenever there's an increase in Stirrers this happens. These sorts of portents come with the job. I do my best to ignore the sanguine mess. Cleaning is for post hangover.

The shower, alternating hot and cold, helps a little. I even manage to think about Lissa, wondering where she is and how horrible that state of limbo must be. Her having been a Pomp at least explains some of the why of it. She's got the know-how. Though I don't understand how she's managing—but maybe she isn't, maybe she was pomped last night. I finish my shower with that disturbing thought, and reach for a towel. The movement sets my head off again. It's as though the shower never even happened, except I'm dripping wet.

This is hell, self-inflicted or not. I stand still for a while, taking slightly pathetic little breaths. Then get dressed, moving like an old, old man in a particularly didactic anti-alcohol advertisement.

Molly barks from the backyard. I stumble out, and she's there with her mini-football in her mouth, wanting a game. One look at me and she changes her mind, dropping it to the ground with an expression that breaks my heart.

"Sorry, girl," I say.

I step back from the door, into the kitchen and I consider breakfast, and then ruefully laugh that idea off. Besides, I've run out of time. I fill a bottle with tap water.

Molly isn't too happy to come back inside, but she does. I pat her on the head, tell her how sorry I am, that I'm such a lousy fella, and make a mental note to take her for a long walk tonight, no matter how awful I feel.

People go on about the quality of light in Brisbane. Whatever it is, there is far too much of it today. My sunglasses only cut it down by the barest fraction; the migraine ignites again. If I had a better excuse there's no way I'd be going in today. But I don't. I still have all my limbs, and I'm not dead.

Now, Derek and I have our differences, but there's one thing I'm sure we'd both agree on: if I don't make it to the office, I'm gone for sure. I look at my watch. 9:30.

Half an hour's cutting it fine, but I manage to catch the next train. It's crowded for this time on a Wednesday morning. Someone's mp3 is up so loud that we're all getting a dose of Queen's "We Will Rock You." That pounding rhythm is pretty much in time with my headache. I glare at the culprit but he isn't looking in my direction.

Derek's been hunting for a reason to fire me for a while now, and I've never been a favorite of the other states' administrators either. I do tend to get into a bit of trouble. I can't help it if people don't get my sense of humor. Really, how can that be my fault?

The only thing that has kept me in the job is that I'm good at it, and that Morrigan likes me. Morrigan's influence as Ankou can't be denied. Mr. D's close working relationship with Morrigan tends to piss off the state admins mightily—and Derek cops that because Morrigan is a person you don't want to cross. All of which pleases me no end, because Morrigan is virtually family.

Morrigan and Dad rose through the ranks together. Dad, a traditionalist; Morrigan, an innovator. Dad coordinates the cross-state linkages, pomps, and helps oversee Mortmax's non-death-related industries—the various holdings in supermarkets, petrol stations and other businesses. He used to run the scheduling too, but a couple of years ago the side businesses expanded to such a degree that he had to let that slide. Morrigan had been pushing to stop him pomping as well but Dad prefers to keep his hand in.

I'd like to think that I could have taken over the scheduling. But a desk job's dull. Derek, on the other hand, loves it. Too bad he's doing such a miserable job.

I glance at my watch. It's going to be close. Not showing up for a meeting is the fastest route to unemployment. Punctuality, under all manner of stress and duress, is an absolute necessity in the pomping trade. A hangover doesn't even begin to cut it as an excuse.

I'm pretty sure I can make it, even riding what seems to be the slowest train in existence, but whether or not I can avoid spewing over Derek's desk is another matter. But it would be a pathetic vomit at best: the last thing I ate was that Chiko Roll.

Anyway, getting into work is going to furnish me with some answers. There's just been too much weirdness in the last couple of days. Too many things are unsettling me. If I wasn't so miserable, they'd be unsettling me even more.

I get off at Roma Street Station, ride the escalator up and out onto George Street, taking small sips of unsatisfying water as I go.

I don't notice anything is wrong until I touch the front door to Number Four.

I push, and the door doesn't give. So I push harder.

Nothing but my knuckles cracking. The door doesn't even draw its usual drop of blood. That's the way it is with Pomps. You need blood to close certain doors, and blood to open them. But not today.

Number Four is locked up tight and toothless.

My first thought is that this is Derek, that he's getting his revenge. Except the two wide glass windows either side of the door are dark. Not only that, but the brace symbol above the door has been removed. That symbol, an upside down triangle split through the middle with a not quite straight vertical line, keeps away Stirrers. It has to be refreshed every month or so, redrawn with ink mixed with a living Pomp's blood. Now it's gone, and that's crazy.

The door should have opened. The lights should be on inside. But they're not. I peer through the window to the left of the door, or try to. It's totally dark beyond. My reflection stares back at me.

I touch the door again. There should be a buzz, a sort of hum running through me on contact, but there's nothing, no sense at all that this is a point of interface between the living world and the dead one. It's just a door. A locked metal door. I glance around, there's no one I know standing around ready to tell me this is all some sort of joke.

The door leads into the vestibule of the building. There's a desk at the front. Some chairs, a couple of prints, including Mr. D's favorite painting, Brueghel's "Triumph of Death." Beyond the desk is a hallway leading to old-fashioned elevator doors, lots of brass, glass and art nouveau designs. The elevator has twelve floors marked, but our building only has eight storeys here. The other four are in the Underworld. That linkage between the living world and the dead should have me buzzing. Hell, standing this close to Number Four should have *anyone* buzzing.

It's the reason we don't get a lot of hawkers.

I reach toward the door again, then hesitate. Because in that moment it... changes. The door suddenly possesses a sly but hungry patience: as though it's waiting for me to touch it this time. *Just put your hand up against me, eh.*

Instead, I press my face against the window to the right. Again, nothing but darkness. The hair rises on the back of my neck. Then something slams against the glass.

I get a brief sensation of eyes regarding me, and of blood. A soul screams through me. It passes, as though thrown, so fast that I don't even get a sense of who it is I've just pomped. I stumble back from the window. They may have moved fast, but they'd been holding on. Their passage a friction burn, I'm seared a little on the inside.

I don't tend to get the violent deaths but I've pomped enough to recognize one. Someone has just died, savagely and suddenly. Someone I know. Maybe Tanya behind the desk, or Clive from records. Brett was always down there, too—had a thing for Tanya. "Jesus."

And then there's another one. The second death is so quick on the back of the first that I moan with the fiery biting pain of it, then retch a little. Another violent exit, another desperate but futile clawing at survival.

"Get out of here, Steven." The voice is familiar.

My mouth moves, but nothing comes for a moment. I turn toward Lissa, fight my almost instinctive desire to pomp her. At least that would be normal. But the urge passes in a wave of relief. Here she is, at last. How can she do this to me, this rising excitement, even now? But she does.

"What?"

"You have to get to Central Station," she says, sliding around me, slipping out of hand's reach, then darting in to whisper. "You need to get as far away from here as possible."

I blink at her, expect her to disappear, but this time she doesn't. In fact she seems much more together than I have ever seen her—a layer of confusion has been sloughed away and replaced with a desperate clarity.

"Hurry. We don't have much time. Someone is killing Pomps." She smiles at that, then frowns, as though the first expression was inappropriate. "You're the first one I've managed to save. And I'm getting tired of repeating myself."

The door picks that moment to open. Just a crack. A cold wind blows through it, and it's not the usual breath of air conditioning. From within comes the distant rasping of the One Tree, the Moreton Bay fig that overhangs the Underworld. That sound, a great sighing of vast wooden limbs, dominates the office. Hearing it echo out here in the street is disturbing. Christ, it terrifies me. It's as though Hell has sidled up next to the living world and has pulled out a bloody knife. I hesitate a moment. I know I should be running but those two pomps in quick succession have scattered my thoughts. And this is meant to be a place of refuge. There's a gravity to that doorway, born of habit and expectation.

Lissa swings in front of me. "Don't," she says. "You go through that door and you're dead."

And I know she's right. It's like a switch finally turns off in my brain.

I sprint from the doorway, glancing back only when I'm at the lights (fighting the urge to just run out into the traffic, but there's too much of it and it's moving too swiftly) to see if anyone, or any thing, has come through the door after me. I get the prickling feeling that someone's watching me.

I blink, and the door's shut again, and that sensation of scrutiny is gone. I take a deep breath.

"Roma Street Station's better," I say, trying to keep focused, even as my head throbs. This really is a bitch of a hangover.

"What?"

"Central's too obvious. If I was looking for someone trying to get out of the city I'd go to Central."

Lissa appears to consider this. "You're probably right."

I know I'm right. Well, I hope I am. I need to have some semblance of control, or I am going to lose it right here in the middle of the city.

We're on George Street, heading to Roma Street and the train station, stumbling through late-morning crowds: all the business and government types up this end of the city, heading out for their coffees, oblivious to what's going on. People are being killed. My people. It can't be happening. Part of me refuses to believe it, even now, but those violent, painful pomps tell me otherwise.

I could feel resentful, but that's going to serve no useful purpose. The further I get away from Number Four though, the better.

To the left are the council chambers, reaching up into the sky, looking like a Lego tower of Babel constructed by a not particularly talented giant infant who nonetheless had *big* ideas. Just to my right is Queen Street Mall where, only yesterday, I was running for my life. Who'd have thought it would become something of a habit? Behind me, the state government building looms shabbily, a testament to, or rather an indictment of, eighties' architecture.

Tim works in that building.

"Where are you going?"

I turn around heading toward Tim's building, hardly realizing I'm doing it.

Lissa's in my face, hands waving, sliding backward to keep out of my reach. "Are you stupid? This is the wrong way."

I stop and stare at Lissa. How do I even know I can trust her? But there's something there, surely. Something in her gaze that tells me I can.

"No, it isn't."

"I don't want you to die."

"I know," I snap. "That much I get." And I don't want to die either, not with her around.

Her face creases with irritation. "You're making the concept easier for me, though." She slides to my right. Turns her back on me. I'm almost relieved; the fire in that gaze would consume me. She passes into a patch of light and is almost completely devoured by it. But then she's out and staring at me.

"Well? Aren't you going to keep moving?"

We cross George Street, pass the stately sandstone edifice of the Treasury Casino. The street's not as crowded on this side, away from the shops. There are a few buses coming and going and people are heading toward the government building, or office towers; suits and skirts of the power variety. The Riverside Expressway is a block away, and a cool breeze blowing up from the river carries all that traffic noise toward me. Traffic, not the creaking of the One Tree.

I get to the glass doors which front the government building and stop. A couple of blocks down, the door to Number Four is waiting. My skin crawls—that sense of being watched again. Still, I hesitate. I reach into my pocket, pull out my phone.

No, I can't draw him into this. Not yet. I put the phone away.

I have to figure this out. On my own, or with the help of my kind. This isn't Tim's problem, he's a Black Sheep—government liaison or not—and my best friend, and there's no way I'm going to drag him into whatever this is. He made his choice not to be involved in the business years ago, and I'm going to honor that. Besides, I doubt there is anything he can do.

I turn around, walk back down the street in the direction of Roma Street Station, keeping to as much cover as I can. Lissa's presence makes me stand out in a crowd—to those who know how to look, anyway.

I think about that damn disconcerting door, and whoever it was I pomped. The pomps had been too fast for a visual, but the souls seemed familiar somehow. Perhaps Morrigan, or Derek? I can't imagine either of them dead.

The day's warm but I'm shivering in my suit.

Lissa looks at me. "It's going to be all right. Take some deep breaths. Try and calm yourself down, Steven."

"You really think this is going to be all right?" I growl. She looks away. "How the fuck is this going to end well?"

"You have to believe it will, or you might as well just sit down now, and do nothing. Wait for whoever it is to find you, if you want. Let me tell you now, they won't be gentle."

"I'll get home, and we can sort this out."

"No," she shakes her head stridently, "you don't want to go home. They'll be there. I went home, and it was the last mistake I made. I can't tell you how angry it makes me, to have died this way."

I look at her more closely; she's starting to fade a little. I need to bring her back. "Why didn't you tell me that you were a Pomp, Lissa? I found you on Facebook last night."

"I'm surprised it took you that long," she says.

"Well, what with the shooting, and the running, and your appearing and disappearing... I'm a Pomp, not a detective. And then I had a lot to drink." The hangover's circling again and, in the busy street, everything's starting to tilt into the surreal. Lissa gives me a look that could pass as sympathetic but for the edge to it. Her gaze holds me and, stupid as it is here and now, I'm thinking how beautiful she is. My kind of beautiful—and I'd never really been aware that I'd had a kind of beautiful before I met her. Why now?

"I'm sorry," she says, "but death is...confusing. Painful, scary, everything moves so fast. I was shifting from Pomp to Pomp. With the first one I was fine, not that it helped him—knife to the back, horrible. But by the time I got you—and I wasn't controlling who I ended up with—I was rather...scattered."

"But how did you shift from Pomp to Pomp in the first place? That's not possible is it?"

"Look, I was desperate, and dead, Steven. Who knows what's possible?"

"How long has this been going on?"

"I know about as much as you. Two days at least. You saw me those first times. I was confused. You grounded me." She swings her face close to mine. I could just...I mean I want to...Those lips. There's a charge shooting up my spine. An ache I thought I'd never feel again.

Enough.

"That's my job. You know how it is," I say, and step away. She doesn't. How could she? Lissa is so far out of my league. I'm actually feeling a little lousy about not recognizing her from the start, because I *did* know her. Not personally, but enough that I realize that I recognize her. There aren't that many Pomps working in Australia. "You work in Melbourne."

"Um, I *used* to work in Melbourne," she says slowly. "No one does, now. They're all dead. There's a whole Night of the Long Knives thing going on."

I must be looking at her blankly because she slows it down even more. "You know, the Night of the Long Knives? Hitler gets an out-with-the-old-and-in-with-the-new attitude and kills his Brown-shirts' leaders—"

I clear my throat. "I know about Nazis. I've got the History

Channel, watch it all the time. You think this is an inside job? It doesn't make any sense."

Lissa regards me with those striking green eyes of hers, and I'm feeling stupid. "Think about it, Steven."

How can I think about anything when she's looking at me that way?

"Anything else doesn't make sense," she says. "Whoever's doing this has to understand our communication system, our computers. We don't outsource any of that."

We stop at the corner of George and Ann, waiting for the lights to change. Big trucks and maxi-taxis roar by, dragging curtains of dust and diesel fumes. I don't hear the phone, just feel it vibrating in my pocket. Number Four, the LCD says. I show it to Lissa. She looks from the little screen to me, and back again.

"You better answer it."

I don't know what I'm going to hear, don't know if I want to hear it. I lift the phone to my ear. "Yes?"

"Steven?"

Finally, someone I know. "Morrigan, thank Christ." In the background, above Morrigan's voice, the One Tree creaks. Morrigan is definitely in Number Four.

Words pour out of me. "I tried to get into work. The door was locked, wouldn't shift, and then the door was something else." I sound like a child, reporting to their head teacher. Lissa watches me and my face burns, though there's no judgment in her expression.

"It's lockdown in here," Morrigan says. "Only we haven't done the locking. I don't know who it is. There's three of them. Stirrers from the feel of it, but not like any I've encountered before. For one, they're using weapons. They've not yet made it into the main offices. You're lucky you couldn't get inside, believe me. Everyone in the vestibule is dead."

"Do you want me to come back?" Something shatters. A gun fires. Even down the phone the sounds have me flinching.

"No, that would be... unwise." Morrigan's voice lowers to a whisper. "We're holed up here. I'm trying to get some word out. Just keep away. Derek's here. If we can keep them out of the main office, I can still keep track of people."

I hesitate. "I'm not far away... I could—"

"You'll do no such thing," he snaps. "You keep away, Steven. Keep moving. You did good running. They'd have just gotten you too. We're losing Pomps."

"I know, Lissa told me."

He's silent for a moment. Then, "Lissa—Lissa Jones is with you?"

"Not exactly."

"Oh." I can hear the sadness in his voice. Morrigan knows everyone. He may be based in Brisbane, but he has a lot of influence in the other states, too. You don't get to the top without knowing the people beneath you. "You listen to her, Steven. This is worse than I thought. If Lissa's gone, Melbourne's gone, too, probably Sydney as well. She'll help you. I need you to stay out of this. Tell her, I'm sorry."

"Maybe Tim—"

"No, keep him out of it. The last thing we want is the government involved. If they trample over this the whole country's going to circle the drain. He's your cousin, Steven, but he's not one of us. He made his decision."

"OK, no Tim."

"Good lad. Steven, I should have seen it coming."

"Seen what?"

"I'd found references in some books, though I never believed—"

The phone dies, there's nothing down the end. I smack it with the palm of my hand.

"That's not going to do anything," Lissa says.

"Makes me feel better." I jut out my lower lip, and scowl. Just how petulant can I be? My face reddens again but Lissa's ignoring the show, considering the problem like I should be. After all, I'm the living one here.

"Is there some drift?" she asks.

I shake my head. "No, the signal's strong." I show her the phone. "The under and upper worlds are in sync. They're almost rubbing up against each other."

"Maybe that's why all this is happening. All this death. All these murdered Pomps."

"It's not murder," I say. "It's assassination."

And then I have a terrible thought.

Something so obvious that the realization hits me hard and cold.

"Gotta call Mom and Dad."

"Too late, Steve," says a voice at my ear.

It's Dad, and Mom is with him.

"Been too late for at least half an hour," he says.

6

This is the moment I've dreaded all my life. I'd always imagined it differently. But here it is, as it is for civilians: unexpected, sudden and utterly terrible.

Dad's in his usual attire—pants, and a light tan sports jacket. All of it crumpled. He's even wearing his favorite fedora, hiding his thinning hair. Pomps are well dressed in the main. Most of the time we're in a suit, black, of course; comes from going to so many funerals. But Dad could get away with wearing a pink Hawaiian shirt to a funeral. Charisma, I guess. He dresses sloppy, but it's charming sloppy. I've never really understood it but people tell me it's there. Everybody loves my dad.

"It's not your fault, Steve," Dad says. His face is lined, but those lines were drawn by smiles. It's a generous face, though he's already losing that—the emotions are slipping away to the One Tree. He frowns. "Did you have a big night last night? You sounded like it on the phone."

I shrug: avoid eye contact. Standard guilty son response. "I may have... indulged." Parents, even dead ones, know how to push the right buttons.

"Look at me, boy. That's better. Son of mine, I worry about you." And he does, it's in his face, even if it is fading. It shames me a little.

I want to hold him. I want to hold Mom. But I can't. The moment I do, they will go. "Dad... What happened? How?"

He coughs. The spirit clings to these old habits. "It was fast, didn't even suspect, until it was over. We hadn't even finished breakfast. Just don't go over to our place. Promise me that."

I nod my head, feeling sick to the stomach.

"Same happened to me," Lissa says, and Dad turns toward her.

"This is Lissa," I say.

"Ah, Melbourne isn't it? The Joneses?" Dad asks, and then he catches me looking at him. "Never forget a face."

"Particularly a young woman's," Mom says. She's as I remember her, in a sensible woolen jumper and pants, both mauve, both as neat as Dad's are crumpled. She's wearing (technically projecting) her favorite brooch: a piece of Wedgwood. There's a clarity and a calmness about her that she'd never had in life. That's over for her now, only the One Tree waits. There's still enough life left, though, to bring up these age-old arguments.

Lissa turns a remarkable beetroot red.

"Now, that's not exactly fair," Dad says, hands raised placatingly. "The Joneses are an old pomping family. Hardly any Black Sheep, too, I might add."

"Not *that* old," Mom says. She looks at Lissa. "I was very sorry about your loss last year. Both parents, and so quickly."

"It's all right," Lissa says. "We of all people know that."

"Still—"

"Leave off, Annie," Dad says. "She obviously doesn't want to talk about it."

"I'm trying to be compassionate here, and you start on this. You're just uncomfortable talking about your feelings. And look at what that did to your son."

"Please," I say wearily, though I really don't want an end to this. Mom and Dad can argue for as long as they want if it means I can still have them here. "This isn't the time or place."

But there's no time, and only one place for them, and we all know it.

"Sorry," Dad says.

Mom nods. "Yes, he's sorry."

Yet again, I'm waiting for the lights to change, on the corner of George and Ann Streets, the edge of the CBD. I can't move. Dead people who no one else can see, though their presence must be raising some hackles, surround me. I don't care. I don't want to share this space with anyone. There's a huge black dog barking madly across the road, its eyes firmly fixed on my posse and me. It strains on its leash, the dog's owner shaking her head with embarrassment, doing her best to stop it pulling her across the road.

The living are stepping around us as though I'm stinking of urine and praising some cruel deity at the top of my voice, a vengeful one, obviously.

The lights have changed a half-dozen times at least, but I'm not ready.

I'm dazed.

Various cousins and aunts and uncles, well their spirits at any rate, keep dropping by. Uncle Blake dressed in his golf clothes shocks me with how calm he is, dead or not. There's none of the bluster, the fire that made a lot of the de Selby Christmas parties so interesting. He just seems resigned. Aunty May grabs my arm, perhaps in shock at her death, and is pomped at once. There can't be that many Pomps left in Brisbane. The conversations are mainly like this.

"Steve, oh, they're—"

"Did you?"

"Boyo, be careful."

"Who's that? Oh—the Jones girl." (Am I the only one who doesn't know this girl and her family?)

"Love, be careful."

It's my younger cousins that hurt me the most. Too young, all of them. Too young. They sigh and moan as they pass through me.

My Aunt Gloria looks at me sadly. "Just call Tim, will you? Promise me that. Let him know that Blake and I love him and that we always will."

I think about what Morrigan told me. Maybe calling Tim isn't such a good idea. But I can't keep this from him. "He knows that already, Aunty G. He knows how much you love him."

She gives me a look—the family look—a mixture of stern disapproval and dismay that only someone who truly loves you is capable of, and that engenders a kind of cold, chemical, panicky reaction in my stomach.

"I'll call him. Once I sort this out." That last bit has become something of a refrain. But I don't think I'm ever going to sort this out. Then she pomps through me, and is gone.

The lights change but I hover on the corner. All of this is really starting to sink in. I'm in serious trouble, half the Pomps I know are dead, and most of those are family. Now my entire living family consists of poor Tim and an aunt in the UK.

"Are you all right?" I ask Mom, and she's looking at me with the eyes of a dead person. There's love there, but it's a love separated from life. I'm regretting that I haven't been around to see them outside of work in a while, and now I've promised to not see what is left.

She blinks, looks at Dad, then back at me. "It didn't hurt, if that's what you're asking."

"Absolutely," Dad says. "Whoever did it was a professional. Quick and painless."

Of course it hurt, but they're trying to spare me that. I try and respect their pretense and play along, but I can't. Quick death is always painful, always dislocating.

"Mom, I need to—"

"You don't *need* to know at all. You *want* to." Her voice hardens.

"Steven, you know the deal, we all do. I'm not happy with this, but it's happened."

"But why? Why has it happened?"

"If either of us had any idea, we'd be telling you," Dad says. "But we don't. You're going to have to find out, and even that may not save you. I had no inkling of this in the office, and I thought I knew everything."

I think about the phones, the rise in Stirrers. Something had been coming. Maybe I'd even felt it before I first saw Lissa. It's easy to see that with hindsight. But that isn't going to help now. I will get to the bottom of this. If this is death most definite then I'm determined to understand it. I just—I just wish I felt a little more capable.

Mom and Dad smile at me. Part of me is missing them already, and another part of me is so damn mad that I could kill someone. But there's no one, or thing, I can direct my anger at. Not yet.

"We'll come with you for as long as we can," Dad says. "But..."

"I understand," I say, though I wish I didn't.

There's more dead coming through. Pomps and regular punters, drawn to me because the number of living Pomps is shrinking. I'm giddy with it and feeling sick at the same time. I've never had this many people to deal with.

Pomping hurts. Each pomp is like a spider web pulling through my flesh. The silk is fine, but every strand is crowded with tiny hooks that snag and drag until they're through. It's more of a discomfort than a hurt, but with enough of them things begin to ache. I'm raw with the souls I've pomped.

I've heard stories about the world wars, about the Pomps there, how it nearly killed them. So many dead rushing through. I lost a lot of great-uncles, most to the meat grinder of the front, but some to the job itself. I don't want that to be me.

The lights change. Time to get moving.

I'm moving down Roma Street, up and over the overpass, heading toward the Transit Centre, the underbelly of which is Roma Street Station.

"You know I love you," I say to my parents. I'd said it nearly a dozen times in the walk between Ann Street and the overpass. I knew I didn't have much time; they couldn't stay with me forever.

"Course we do," they say in unison, and like that, in the blinking of an eye, they're gone.

The last contact I get is their passage through me. Such a swift pomp. I'm never going to see them again. I try to hold on, to keep their souls with me, but there's nothing I can get a grip on. All it does is draw out the hurt.

The grief is almost paralysing when it hits.

I'm right out in the open, not yet at the escalators sinking down into the station. I stop and hunch over, because this is agony. I'm not numbed by their absence, I'm hurting. A coughing sob shudders through me. I'm going to lose it.

Just because I know what goes on in the afterlife doesn't mean I'm not missing my parents. I need time.

But there isn't any.

"Hey. Hey," Lissa says.

"You're still here?"

I look at her, and even that hurts me. She's beautiful, and I won't get a chance to talk to her in the flesh. My mourning tugs me this way and that. Have to slap myself. My cheek stings.

Doesn't help.

Lissa looks at me as though I am mad. There's pity in her expression as well, and that makes me more than a little angry: mostly with myself.

She isn't gone yet. I'm not quite alone.

I walk into the station.

"Hey!"

I spin on my heel, cringing. When's the bullet coming?

"Your ticket!" The guard at the gate frowns at me, looking through Lissa, though I know how uncomfortable that must make him. It doesn't help that she then swings a tight circle around him. His face twitches in synchrony with her movements. At any other time it would be amusing to watch.

"Yeah, right. Sorry." I dig my pass out of my wallet.

He takes it from me. Nods. "Next time think about what you're doing." He pushes it back into my hand.

I nod, too, smile stupidly, and walk through the gate into the underpass that leads to the platforms.

"You have to be more careful than that," Lissa says. "You have to stay focused. Something like that may get you killed."

"I'm doing the best I can."

She's clearly not happy with my answer. But it's all I've got.

I know where I have to go. The only place that I might possibly find some answers.

It might also kill me. That's on the cards anyway. In fact, I imagine that's where this will all end up. I'm a Pomp after all. Death is what it's all about. Death is what it's always about.

So I keep moving.

7

"Are you sure this is a good idea? I mean the Hill..."

I'm sitting in the train heading west along the Ipswich line, out of the city, my forehead resting against the cold glass of the window. People sniffle and cough all around me. The carriage is heavy with the odors of sickness: sweat and menthol throat lollies duke it out. It's flu season all right, I can feel something coming on myself—or maybe it's the last remnants of the hangover, combined with the ache of all those pomps.

I pat my suit jacket. "At least I'm dressed for a cemetery. Do you have any better suggestions?"

Lissa shrugs. I know she wishes that she did. So do I.

"The Hill's the only place I might get some answers," I say. Problem is, the answers I'm after are just as likely to kill me as save me.

I try Tim's work number. Can't get through. His mobile switches straight to voicemail.

How do I tell him? I need to warn him. I need to tell him that his mother and father are dead. His voicemail spiel ends and I'm silent after the beep, working my mouth, trying to find words.

Nothing comes. The silence stretches on. Finally: "Tim, I don't know what you know. But I'm in trouble, you too, maybe. You have to be careful. Shit, maybe you already know all this. Call me when you can."

I hang up.

Lissa stomps up and down the aisle. People shudder with her passage, burying themselves in their reading matter or turning up their mp3s. She's oblivious to it, or maybe she is taking a deep pleasure in the other passengers' discomfort, the dreadful chill of death sliding past life. I don't know. Our carriage is emptying out fast, though. I find her movement hypnotic. Her presence is tenuous and vital all at once. I've never seen a dead person like this. Nor a live one, if I'm honest.

She catches me looking at her. The grin she offers is a heat rushing through me. My cheeks burn and for a moment my mind isn't centered on life or death. I'd thank her for that, if this was going anywhere but Hell.

I've fallen in love with someone I cannot have. Someone who isn't really a someone anymore. How bloody typical. But even this misery is better than the ones that crowd around me, grim and cruel, on that train. At least it's bittersweet rather than just bitter.

The train rolls into Auchenflower. The Hill's presence is already a persistent tingle in my lips like the premonition of a cold sore. Every place has a Hill, where the land of the living and the dead intersect. In Brisbane it's Toowong Cemetery. I know the place well. Used to picnic there with the family. Lost my virginity on its grassy slopes when I was seventeen. Mary Gallagher. Didn't last. None of my relationships ever had. I'm thinking of Mary as the train stops at the station. I don't even know what happened to her. Married, I think, maybe has a couple of kids. Robyn was just the last in a long list of failures.

I get off the train, Lissa with me, and I'm sure everyone in the carriage behind me breathes a sigh of relief. The train pulls away, leaving a few people on the platform. All of them walk in the opposite direction to me. I'd find it funny, but the nearby Wesley Hospital distracts me. My perception shifts. There's an odor as unsavory as an open sewer coming from there. Something's going on in the hospital's morgue.

Lissa drifts that way. Face furrowed.

"You sense it too?"

"It's not good." She coughs as though clearing her throat. "Something smells well and truly rotten, wouldn't you say?"

"Stirrers, I think." I wonder if they're like the ones Morrigan described, different.

"Nothing you can do about that now."

Yes, but I don't like it. The air around there is bad and a kind of miasmal disquiet has settled into the building's foundations: an unliving and spreading rot. *Someone hasn't been doing their job*, I think. *Who's left to do it? Who's going to sort this kind of stuff out?* These things can get quickly out of control and then you're rushing toward a full-blown Regional Apocalypse. Think Stirrers and death in abundance. Civilizations tend to topple in the wake of them.

I try not to think about it. Lissa's right, there's no time. I head in the opposite direction; take the underpass beneath the station and away from the hospital. If I get a chance I'll come back. I push the hospital to the back of my mind, where it settles uneasily. Nothing good can come of this day.

My head is pounding again. Then a caffeine craving hits me all at once. It's a deep, soul-gnawing pit in my stomach. I'm tempted to swing into Toowong, casually order a coffee—a nice long black—and sit on the corner of High Street and Sherwood Road and watch the bus drivers try and hit pedestrians; tempted till it's a throbbing ache. Now, I'm hurting. The last time I remember talking to my living, breathing mom was over coffee. Both of us had been real busy, like I said—flu season.

We keep moving through inner-city suburbia, up and down the undulating landscape of Brisbane, swapping the disquiet of the hospital for the jittering energy of the Hill. We reach Toowong Cemetery in pretty good time, though I have to catch my breath. Squat, fat Mount Coot-tha rises up before us like the great dorsal fin of a whale. My eyes burn as though there is suddenly too much fluid within them. Something else is straining to inhabit my vision.

This close to the Hill, Pomps get flashes of the Underworld. I can hear the great tree creaking. I can even see it. This is why Mount Coot-tha and the cemetery were once called One Tree Hill. For a moment this other view stops me—the tree, a Moreton Bay fig, is spectacular, all sky-swallowing limbs and vast root buttresses. Then Mount Coot-tha's silhouette returns, marked only by blinking rows of transmission towers.

A traffic chopper is flying low over the Western Freeway like some predatory bird hunting snarls and head-ons. As we climb the undulations that lead to the hill there's a hint of the city to the east, gleaming red in the afternoon sun. We're out in the 'burbs, the beginning of a vast carpet of houses that stretches almost to the granite belt in the west. Hundreds of thousands of homes. But here, it's old city, Brisbane's CBD isn't too far away. It's close to sunset and I'm still not sure what it is I'm doing. I circle around the base of the Hill, keeping clear of the open areas, and staying as close as I can to the trees among the tombstones. The Hill has multiple nodes: connection points with Number Four. The Mayne crypt is one, but that's too obvious, with its ostentatious white spire and curlicues, and it's big and toward the top of the Hill—we'd be too easy to spot. I'm heading to a quieter node, near the place Tim and I used to sneak off to, to smoke.

"Listen," Lissa says. She spins around me, gesturing at the lengthening shadows. I'd almost forgotten she was there. We haven't said a word since we edged into the cemetery. "I'm serious, listen."

"I'm listening," I say.

She shakes her head. "Not to me. To this, the cemetery."

And then I'm *really* listening. I've never known a place to be so quiet. Where are the crows? Where are the chattering, noisy myna birds? There's not a sound, not an insect clicking or buzzing. Even my footsteps in the dry grass seem muted.

"Maybe this wasn't such a good idea," Lissa says, right into my left ear.

I jump. "I never said it was a good idea, but it's the only one we have."

"The only one that *you* have."

"What's your idea?"

"Head for the hills, not the Hill."

"I promise, I'm being careful."

"Is that what you call it?" She darts away from me. Runs up the hill and back again. In this light, she's a blue-stained smear of movement. She's back by my side in a breath.

"Didn't even break a sweat," she says.

"See anything?"

"Nothing. But that doesn't mean they're not closing in."

"You're making me paranoid."

She swings her face close to mine, her eyes wide. "Good."

I find the right tombstone halfway up the hill, a David Milde, RIP 1896. It's been a while since I've done this, but the spot recognizes me. The stone shudders, becomes something more than a mere memorial.

"Watch yourself," Lissa says.

I glance at her. This close to a node, her form is losing some of its clarity. "Maybe you should too."

She raises a hand toward her face. "Oh."

The node would take her to the Underworld, if it could. But I'm in control here. I wait until Lissa steps back, and then I reach over and settle my fingers on the rough stone, wincing at the electric shock that strikes my fingers on contact. My teeth clamp shut, and I taste blood.

The cemetery is gone. I'm in Number Four. And it's not pleasant.

The air is alive with exclamations: bullet hard. The last thoughts of the dying, before the mind and body scatter.

There are other Pomps here. Not just Morrigan and Derek.

The first thing I feel are their deaths.

Each one smacks against me, and I try to hold onto them, and work through these errant memories. But it's no good. There's nothing there. Nothing of use anyway, merely pain, the unsuspecting howls of the executed. Jesus, I've been lucky to get even this far. For a moment I envy those gone, that it's over for them, that they're not left flailing in the dark. I concentrate, move through the muddy haze of dying minds and then: There are upturned desks, reams of paper scattered around them like the shattered stones of a stormed castle. Mainframes have toppled. And there's blood, every-fucking-where. My heart's doing 160 BPM easy. I almost drop out of the node then.

There's a man bent over, hacking up blood onto his yellow tie. He's wheezing, "Fuck. Fuck. This is. Oh—"

Blood crashes in my vision as a bullet makes a crater in his chest. He lifts his head, and there's a moment of recognition, just a moment. The bastard even manages a scowl.

"Derek," I say. Poor old officious Derek.

But he's dead; he falls almost gracefully onto the floor.

There are no answers here. I have to get out.

Then a head peers over the desk. Morrigan looks over at me, his eyes wide with terror. "Steven, what on earth?"

"I needed to find out what was happening," I mumble.

"Jesus, Steven, get away from the Hill!"

"Who's doing this? Can I—"

"There's nothing you can do. We're being slaughtered. They hit us hard, more people than we first thought, and at the same time as I called you." He pats his arm, there's a bloody wound there. Shrapnel scars his cheek. "Steven, you need to get moving. Get away from the Hill and keep away from Number Four."

"I need to get moving? What about you? I can get you out."

Morrigan scowls at me, the facial equivalent of the stone you'd throw at Lassie to get her to run away.

"There's a Schism—maybe one of the other regions, wanting to muscle into our space. I don't know, but they're good." He fires a pistol over his desk. Someone fires back; woodchips explode from the table he's hiding behind. "I can't get to Mr. D. He's closed himself off. Don't trust anyone, Steven. Leave your phone on. I'll call you if I can."

Still, I hesitate.

"Steven, you will go *now*! GO!"

I break contact with the tombstone and reality whoomphs around me. I shake my stinging fingers, my heart pounding in my chest, blood streaming from my nose. Everything's moving too quickly. I drop to my haunches, gulp in air, try and slow my breathing down.

"Steven? Steven?" Lissa's voice pulls me out of it. I blink and look up at her.

"We have to get out of here," I say. "Number Four's gone, or soon will be. Morrigan's wounded. He told me to run, that he'd try to get in touch with me. I can't see him making it. Lissa, there was blood everywhere." I peer around the tombstone, careful not to touch it again. There's nothing, just Lissa and her ghost light. "Morrigan thinks it might be one of the other regions trying to take over."

Lissa glares at the tombstone, as though this was its idea. "That's unheard of. Why would anyone want to shut a region down, Steven? Because that's essentially what a take-over would do. Regional Managers can be ruthless, but that would be stupid, it's too much extra work for no gain. And what about the Stirrers?"

"Maybe something's changed. Maybe the Stirrers are just taking advantage of the whole thing."

"No, things don't change that much. You don't understand the system at all if you think otherwise. There's no advantage to a Regional Manager if they take another region. And then there's the increased Stirrer activity. That's been happening for weeks. They're in on it, somehow. Mr. D would know."

I shake my head. "Morrigan's been trying hard to contact him. No luck. Maybe he's in the dark as much as we are."

"Now you're scaring me," Lissa says.

"I'm scaring both of us. We have to get out of here."

Lissa nods.

"And quietly," I say.

"I'm dead." Lissa gives me a dark look. "I can't make any noise."

"I was just trying to remind myself."

We're as silent as a pair of ghosts as we come down the hill. Easy enough, I suppose, when half of the couple is a ghost. And we're moving pretty quickly, which is why I almost stumble upon them, and why they don't see me.

And this is the first time my fear turns to something else. *No fucking way!*

My parents are weaving around the tombstones ahead.

Not my parents, just their flesh. They're not moving like Mom and Dad, and that's the oddest part of seeing them. Mom and Dad, *my* mom and dad, but they're all wrong. The creatures that inhabit them haven't got the hang of the real estate yet. Dad holds a rifle, Mom is speaking into a phone.

"Stirrers," Lissa says and I roll my eyes at her. Of course they're Stirrers—zombies, I suppose, in the common vernacular. The second part of our jobs as Pomps, the things we're supposed to stop stirring. These aren't your "Grr, brains" zombies. Nah, that shit doesn't happen. These are more perambulatory vessels. My parents aren't infected or blood crazy; Stirrers inhabit them.

It's the only way that Stirrers can exist in our world. They were long ago banished from the land of the living, but they want back in any way they can. I've heard that if they tip the balance—inhabit enough bodies, get more than a toehold—they might just be able to return in their real form, whatever that is. If that ever happens, we're all screwed.

These aren't my parents. They're just the place of death. My parents have gone over into the Underworld.

I'm taking it pretty well. My blood is only partially boiling, I'm only clenching my fists until they hurt, not until they draw blood. I groan as another soul passes through me, another Pomp. Real pain. Someone is hurling souls at me.

Normally we're directed to a specific location to physically sight and sometimes touch a spirit. But now, maybe because there are so few Pomps left, or because most of the dead today have been Pomps, they're actually hitting me wherever I am. These are really violent deaths, and they're coming hard and fast.

Those spider webs are starting to grow more hooks. It's like having a cold, and a constant need to blow your nose—at the start the tissues are soft, but by the end they're more like razors wrapped in sandpaper—except that the razor burn runs through my whole body.

On top of that I can now sense the Stirrers. And if I can feel them...

"Shit," Lissa says.

I do a double-take. I look at Lissa—and then to Lissa. "That's—"

"Somebody has to pay for this." She covers her face with her hands, but the rage and the hurt radiates from her.

Stirrer Lissa strides down the hill, away from the tall white spire of the Mayne crypt, talking on a phone. And she's walking toward me.

"The Hill is compromised," I say at last.

"No shit, Sherlock," Lissa says, and I'm already backing away. There's a distant clattering sound, like someone hurling ball bearings at a concrete wall.

Great, we're being shot at. It's my dad with that rifle. He fires again. I wait for the bullet to hit me, but it doesn't come. His aim is out, still not used to the body, I suppose. A tombstone a few meters away cracks, exhaling shards of dirty stone.

"Run," Lissa yells, and once again, I'm sprinting.

8

Two blocks away from the cemetery, after a dash through suburbia—streets filled with jacarandas dripping with blooms, and with enough cars parked on the road that we have some cover—we come across a bus shelter.

Miracle of miracles! There's a bus pulling in, on its way toward the city, but I don't care where it's going, I just need to be heading somewhere that isn't here. I'm on it. It's the first time in my life that a bus is exactly where and when I want it. With what little sense of mind I have left, I realize I still have my pass and I flash it at the driver. He looks at it disinterestedly, and then I'm walking to the back of the bus, past passengers all of whom assiduously avoid eye contact. Ah, the commuter eye-shuffle. I must look a little crazy. I certainly feel it.

I'm breathing heavily. Sweat slicks my back, and is soaking through my jacket. It's only the middle of spring but the air's still and hot. For the first time in about an hour I'm aware of my body, and it's telling me I'm tired, and hung-over. The adrenaline's not potent enough to keep that from me forever. Sadly, I feel like I could do with a beer.

Lissa looks as fresh as the first time I saw her, if you discount the bluish pallor. You're never fitter than when you're dead.

Finally we've time to talk with no rifles firing.

"So why are you back there? And how?" I ask beneath my breath, but it still comes out too loud. People turn and watch.

"That's not me!" Lissa is furious, and I can understand. I wouldn't want someone wandering around in my body, either. But I'm also wondering why she's so worried. Worry's a living reaction; it's not like she needs that body. She is acting most unlike a dead person, but then she has from the start. "That's not me," she says again. "Don't you *dare* think of that as me."

I raise my hands. We're tripping up on semantics here. "Your *body*... Why was your *body* back there?"

Lissa looks out the window. "I—I don't know. Whoever's doing this is using Number Four and shipping Stirrer-possessed Pomps around via the upper offices. And they're using my body. Shit, shit, shit."

I really want to hold her and tell her that this is going to be OK, but I can't do either, because I really don't believe it, and the Lissa I might possibly be able to hold without pomping is behind us somewhere, and she would kill me without hesitation.

This relationship is complicated.

"The upper offices? Can you really do that?" I think about Number Four, and those labyrinthine upper floors.

"You can if you know what you're doing. It's dangerous if you're not an RM, but people do it from time to time—saves on airfares. I've heard that you can enter any one of Mortmax's offices through them. It's probably how the Stirrers got into the Brisbane office. They could have come from anywhere."

"We'll work this out," I say.

She glares at me. "How, Steve? Just how the hell are we going to work this out? I'm dead. My body's walking about the Hill, inhabited by a bloody Stirrer. It's not enough that I've been killed—whoever is doing this is rubbing my face in it. You were right, as much as I didn't like it, the Hill's the only place we had a chance of finding out what's going on."

"Which was exactly why it was being guarded," I say. "They knew we had to get there. And my parents were there, too. This isn't just about you."

Lissa shakes her head. "Who deals with Stirrers? It's freaking insane! You can't deal with Stirrers. They've nothing to offer but hatred and hunger."

Apparently someone has, and quite successfully. I don't understand it any better than Lissa does. The idea chills me and I'm even more afraid about this whole thing. But at least it explains why Jim McKean was shooting at me. I couldn't work out how I might have pissed him off. There are others with whom it almost wouldn't have surprised me (Derek being one of them) but Jim hadn't made any sense.

"We just need to keep moving," I say.

"No point in running." The voice startles me, coming from behind. It's all rather too pleased with itself. I jerk my head around.

There's a dead guy sitting on the rear seat. He looks at me, and then at Lissa. When he sees her the wind comes out of him. "Sorry, darl," he says, "they got me too, just out of Tenterfield."

That's it. I'm dead. I don't see how I stand a chance.

The guy with us is Eric "Flatty" Tremaine, state manager of the Melbourne office, which puts him almost as far up the ladder as Morrigan. He's a friend of Derek's—maybe his only friend—and another paid-up member of the Steven de Selby Hate Club.

I notice the way he's looking at Lissa, and the way that she's looking back. There's definitely a history there. I catch myself; I'm not going to survive this if all I'm really thinking about is Lissa and her previous relationships. But it does no good. Jealousy, wearing Eric Tremaine's smarmy face, has brought matches and it's lighting them up inside of me.

"So what's going on, Flatty?" I ask, and for the first time Eric seems truly aware of me, even though my presence must have drawn him here. He gives me a wide, almost manic grin, and slaps his knee.

"Steven de Selby. Wonderful, so you've managed to stay alive. I wouldn't have put money on it. You never really struck me as the sharpest knife in the drawer."

"Enough of that," Lissa says. "Play nice."

"Who's behind this?" I demand. I don't have time for point scoring, even if I am still hunting for some sort of witty comeback.

Eric shrugs. "I don't know. All I can say for sure is that they're very good at their jobs, and they know a lot about ours." He glances significantly at Lissa. "Why the fuck are you hanging with this loser?"

"You tried to call Mr. D?" I ask, ignoring the insult. After all, he *has* just died.

"Of course I have." Eric nodded. "Line was busy, which makes sense for a couple of reasons."

"Yeah, everybody would be trying to call," I say. Though, to be honest, I really hadn't thought of it. Thinking about Mom and Dad had been occupying my mind more—that, and the running. Besides, Mr. D is... difficult. I take a deep breath. "Maybe I should try him. Can't be too many Pomps left."

Tremaine makes an ineffectual grab at my arm—his hand passes through my flesh and he's nearly dragged through me with it. His face strains as he struggles to stay in this world, and part of me can't help laughing at such a basic mistake. I have to respect his strength of will, though, because he pushes against the pomp, his form solidifying.

"No! You don't want to do that!" he says, once he's managed to stabilize his soul. "I tried to call him just out of Tenterfield. The buggers got me there on the New England Highway. They're obviously using the phones to find us. Please don't tell me you've got yours on."

"Oh." The blood's draining from my face. I switch off my phone, and then slide it into my pocket.

Eric gives Lissa an "I told you so" look. His gaze, when it returns to me, is condescension stirred with pity. He doesn't expect me to live much longer, either.

"You're going to have to talk to Mr. D, but not now," he says. "I suspect he's out of the loop somewhat. He has to be, I can't believe that he'd let this happen."

"Someone has," Lissa says.

"Yes, and I have my theories, but they're just theories. Steve, you're going to have to talk to him face to face. Draw him out of wherever he's hiding, or being held."

"You think he's being held?"

"He's hardly on a fishing trip now, is he?" Tremaine says archly. "He's too intimately connected to all of us. Every death must be filling him with pain and anger. For something like this to succeed you'd need to remove the RM as quickly as possible, before you start trying to kill Pomps. You know how Mr. D is. He knows when one of us dies, and he's always there. Let me tell you, he wasn't there for me. This has to be an inside job."

He lets that sink in.

"Then how am I going to be able to talk to him?"

"There are ways that can't be stopped. If you know what you're doing." He looks at me.

I take a deep breath. Maybe I should just pomp the prick. I'm a little threatened by the thought of one-on-one time with Mr. D. I've only ever met him a few times, and they were with my dad.

"Mr. D's not that bad, really," Lissa says, and I realize that she is almost touching my hand with her own. At the closest point her form is wavering. It must be uncomfortable for her, but she holds the position. I'm the one who pulls away in the end. Tremaine gives her a look, and I smile like the cat who got the cream.

"If you say so. I've just never had much to do with him."

"Regardless, you're going to—and soon," Tremaine says with all the nonchalance that a recently dead person can muster. "Maybe too soon." He points out the rear window.

There's my dad's body, driving his red Toyota Echo, not too well, but well enough to be gaining on the bus. But this is the least of my worries because Mom's body is on the passenger side, and she's scowling in a most un-Mom like way and pointing a rifle at me.

"Shit!" I drop to the floor behind the seat as the rear window explodes.

9

There is a carpet of gleaming glass before me. I'm sure I'm breathing the smaller fragments of it into my lungs. It doesn't help that I'm almost hyperventilating. Another shot blasts a hole in the back seat next to my head. I'm feeling like a cartoon character. I know the double-take I give that burning hole, stuffing everywhere, must look almost comical. I'm surprised I haven't shat myself, but of course there's still plenty of time for that...

The bus driver brakes: all that commutery tonnage comes crashing to a halt and we've got a whole domino effect, of which I'm painfully a part, passengers tumbling and screaming. Then the red Echo slams into the back of the bus. I'm thrown forward onto the broken glass from the window. It's safety glass, but those little beads still hurt when you fall on them.

Metal screams and I'm yelping as the back seat deforms inward. The rear side windows shatter. There's glass and seat stuffing everywhere.

The Echo's horn is droning in an endless cycle like a wounded beast, and there's the sharp, stinging odor of fuel. I shake my head. I try to slow my crashing breaths. I want to rub my eyes, but there's no telling what I'd be grinding into them.

I reckon I've got about thirty seconds, maybe a minute, before they're out of that car. It's going to take much more than a collision with a bus to stop them. There's bits of glass in my hands but no deep cuts; it hurts like a bastard, though, which is actually a good thing since it distracts me from the headache regrouping in my skull.

"Are you all right?" Lissa asks.

"Can anyone in that bland suit be all right?" Tremaine says.

I'd be better if he shut up. I've never been a fan of Tremaine, but then again, he's never been much of a fan of me or my family, either. He sees us Queensland Pomps as a bunch of slackers and, sure, I may have gotten drunk at a couple of training sessions, but the guy's about as boring as they come.

"You and your taste." Lissa shakes her head.

Tremaine gives her a smug smile. "Darling, it *was* yours for a while."

"We all have to regret something, Eric."

I glance at these two—Lissa scowling and Eric giving her the sleaziest, most self-satisfied smile I've seen outside of a porno. Bastard. *Oh God, Lissa and Flatty Tremaine!*

I'm jealous: bloody burning with it. But there's no time for this. I scan the bus; people are slowly recovering from the shock of the collision. I was the only one who had a moment's warning, and I'm still as shaky as all hell. There's a few nosebleeds, but that seems to be the worst of it. I have to get out of here fast, or someone is going to die. It may not be me, but it's sure as hell going to be my fault. I run for the front door of the bus.

"Have to get out," I say.

The driver's on the radio, calling it in. No one seems to know a rifle was involved. Everyone is shaken but not as disturbed as they should be. The driver waves at me irritably. "No, you're staying on the bus until I say so. Council policy."

Fair enough, but not today. I reach over, turn the release switch. The door sighs open.

He grabs my arm; I tug my arm free, and bolt for the exit.

"What? You! Get back—" I hear him slamming down on the switch.

I'm almost through and the door closes on my leg. It's a firm grip and I'm hanging, suspended by the door. I yank my leg like some sort of trapped and clumsy animal, and something gives because I'm dropping onto the road, the ground knocking the breath from me.

"Smooth," Tremaine says.

"Screw you," I manage, which is stupid because I shouldn't be wasting any of the breath in my lungs. Blobs dance in my vision.

"And ever so charming."

I give him the finger. Tremaine raises an eyebrow. Lissa's watching the bus.

"Get up," she says. "Get up, get up."

Winded, I lie there on the side of the road. Even with the adrenaline coursing through me that's about all I can manage. I stare blankly at the looming city with its skyline of genuflecting cranes. I'm on the verge of slipping into manic, gasping chuckles. The sky is lit up by the city, everything's calm . . . and I've been shot at—twice—by my parents.

"Get up," Lissa says. "Now."

At last, after what really can't have been more than a few seconds, breath finds my lungs.

"I'm trying." I get very unsteadily to my feet. Which is when the bus driver comes crashing through the door and tackles me.

I'm back down on the road. More cuts, more bruises.

"Get the fuck back in the bus!" he growls, his arms wrapped around my legs.

"No, I can't!" I scramble, kicking and twisting and flailing, to my feet.

We circle each other. He's taking this personally, his face beet-red, his hands clenched into fists. The driver is a big man. I'm not, just tall and thin. He also looks like he might practice some particularly nasty form of martial art that specializes in snapping tall, thin people in two.

"I don't want to have to fight you," I say, mainly because I don't want to have to fight him.

"Then get back in the bus." The way he says it suggests there's no gentle way of getting back into the bus.

He advances, his eyes wild, obviously in shock, or just extremely, extremely pissed off. I lunge to the right, then sprint around the side of the bus. He crashes after me, swearing at the top of his lungs. There's not much room to move—we're hemmed in by traffic, though none of it is moving that quickly, on account of the accident and the show we're putting on. We get around twice; I've got the edge on him, speed-wise, which is kind of meaningless because all I'm going to do is end up running into his back.

There are cars pulling up everywhere. Some industrious and extremely helpful guy has stopped and is directing traffic, and there's a woman over at the crumpled, smoking Echo. She sees me and starts waving at me to come over, maybe to help. I yell at her to get away. Someone is moving in the car, and I suspect that someone is going to have the rifle. Every passing second improves his or her hand-eye coordination.

The bus driver's boots crunch on the gravel behind me. "Get back here, you prick!" the bus driver yells. I glance around to see how close he is. He catches a mouthful of smoke and bends over, coughing. The air is positively toxic. For a moment I worry that he might just drop dead. But at least he's not running after me anymore.

"This is all going so wonderfully," Tremaine says, startling me. I ignore him.

I pull my sunglasses over my eyes and sprint-sneak over to the helpful guy's car, a green hatchback. I feel like an absolute bastard. The keys are in the ignition, which is a relief. I start up the car, and shoot down Coro Drive, fishtailing around the bus, and nearly smash into oncoming traffic. I straighten the hatchback at the last minute, not knowing where in Christ I'm going.

In my rear-vision mirror the bus driver is roaring away at me between coughs, the helpful guy with him. He's not looking that helpful now, and I don't blame him. I feel awful, like I've mugged a nun.

"Was that wise?" Tremaine is grinning at me, now also in the rear-view mirror. I've never seen a dead guy looking so full of himself.

"Shut the fuck up."

"It's so nice to see that you can keep your cool in a crisis."

Tremaine's lucky he's dead already. "Well, only one of us is still alive," I snarl.

Low blow, but true. Tremaine is a prick, and being cruel to him is the least of my crimes today.

"What the hell else was he supposed to do?" Lissa asks him.

They flit around each other in the back seat of the car, two aggressive and luminous blurs.

"Not breaking the law might have been a good beginning," Tremaine says prissily.

Yeah, I could have fled the scene on foot. Not having the police chasing me as well as Stirrers would have been a good idea. But the Stirrers would have caught up with me for sure. I needed to get out of there fast, even if that meant stealing the Good Samaritan's car. I glance back at Tremaine. "Next time we'll follow your plan. Which was... Hey, didn't we already ascertain that you were dead?"

"You're *deadest.*" Tremaine clenches a fist in my face. "That's what you are. Which really doesn't surprise me, you bloody hick Queenslanders."

"Come a little closer, and I'll fucking pomp you, dead man."

"Oh, shut up," Lissa says. "Both of you shut up."

Four blocks later, and heading back into Paddington away from the city, I ditch the car (leaving whatever money I have on me in the glove box for the owner's trouble) hoping that there are no CCTV cameras around. There's nothing to connect me to it. I should be safe, particularly when I shave off my beard, which I am going to be doing very soon. Clean-shaven, I'll look like a different person; certainly not the kind of guy who would steal a car, anyway.

OK, so that's the story I'm running with, because I have to believe *something*.

I walk another four blocks looking for the right bus. I must be a sight: bloody hands, torn pants and edgy as all hell, glancing up and down the streets, ducking for cover at the slightest noise. Any second I expect a bullet to come driving into my brain or worse, into my back, driving me to the ground where I'll writhe like road-kill. If I'm going to be killed I want it to be as quick and painless as possible.

Finally, the bus I'm after is trundling down the street. Why does public transport travel at such glacial speeds when people are trying to kill you? I flag it to a stop, flash my pass and get on board. The driver barely gives me a second glance.

"Where are you going?" Lissa asks.

"My question exactly." Tremaine's voice drills into my skull.

"Home," I say, keeping my voice low and spinning toward the dead couple. "Is that all right with you two?"

Lissa slaps her forehead disdainfully, and looks at me like I'm an idiot. "Surely you wouldn't be so stupid as to—"

"Exactly. Surely I wouldn't be," I say. "There's a back way—well, it's actually someone's yard. They're not going to expect me to go home, anyway. They're going to expect me to go to Mr. D."

"He has a point," Tremaine says, which immediately makes me suspect my own logic. "Besides, you can bring Mr. D to you."

"I don't like it." Lissa frowns.

"Any more than you don't like being dead?" Tremaine winks at me. He's certainly taking a bipartisan approach to pissing people off.

"Hey," I say. "That's below the belt."

Tremaine shakes his head, even manages a laugh. "Boy, you've got it bad."

Lissa is looking at me, with that mocking expression I'm getting to know so well. I feel about two inches tall. "He does, doesn't he?"

"Yes, he does, and he's not going to get far with that. And if he thinks so then he's as big an idiot as any of the Queensland crew."

"Stop talking about me as though I'm not here." I glare at Tremaine. "Just tell me how I bring Mr. D to me."

"All right, it's difficult, and location specific, but not... Oh—"

And then he's gone. But not smoothly. Eric struggles in a way that I've not encountered before. As though he's trying to take me, too. I grit my teeth, feel dizzy, shout, "Not yet, you bastard! Not yet."

Half the bus is staring at me, or trying to ignore me, but I can't afford to give that too much consideration. Finally he releases. I feel it as a sort of shocked sadness, as though he can't quite believe it. I have to admit, the man had stamina.

Lissa groans. I look over at her, she's getting hazy. Fading out.

Eric's passage through me must have opened the door a little, or left a sort of wake. It's threatening to take her, too.

"Keep your distance," I say, teeth clenched. I close my eyes and try to find some sort of center to the chaos of Eric's passing. It hurts to delve so deep into the process, like shoving your fingers in the guts of a machine while it's ticking over. I find something.

Yes. There's a calm space there. The door closes, the wake subsides. Now, that wasn't pleasant. Not one little bit.

I open my eyes a crack, Lissa's still here, looking more substantial than she did a moment ago. I'm beginning to wonder why she's sticking around. What exactly it is that's holding her here? She reaches toward me, and then pulls back at the last second.

It taxes her, or whatever it is that is left of her. My body is trying to draw Lissa in, and no matter how much I don't want it to, I can't switch it off. I don't even want to consider the effort it must be taking for her to resist the pomp. She grimaces and sits a seat away from me. The two nearest seats are empty.

"Your nose," she says. "It's bleeding."

I grab a tissue from my pants pocket and wipe my face. Blood, and plenty of it. "Shit. Eric even pomps roughly. You OK?"

Lissa nods. "I'm OK. I'll be joining him soon enough."

"Both of us," I say. "I've lost my one chance of getting in touch with Mr. D."

"Not at all. I know how to bring Mr. D to you," Lissa says. "It's not very pleasant, and will be rather painful."

Of course it will. Messing around with death offers that as a given.

"I need to go home first." And I do. Dangerous as it is, I have to. "I can't keep wearing this suit, and I can't be walking around with this beard." I lift my bloody paws. "And these need seeing to. There's no way I'd be any safer at a hospital."

I remember Wesley Hospital and shudder.

Lissa gives me one of her disapproving stares. "I don't think you should."

"I've got no other choice."

And whether she thinks it's a good idea or not, she has nothing to say about that.

10

The back door hasn't been broken down or even tampered with, as far as I can tell, which is a good sign. And the brace symbol above the door is whole. Another good sign, literally, though it's glowing even brighter now, but that's to do with the increased Stirrer activity. I take a deep breath and open the door.

There's another reason I had to come home, and she almost knocks me off my feet. That's how pleased she is to see me, though not half as happy as I am to see her. I crouch down and give Molly a hug, scratch behind her ears, and apologize for her horrible treatment. She's forgiving.

"Lovely dog," Lissa says.

Molly is sniffing at my heels. She glances up at Lissa, isn't fussed by her being dead. Seems if she's good enough for me, she's fine with Molly. I get Moll to sit then throw her a treat. "She's my best girl, my Molly Millions girl," I say, and rub her behind the ears again. She grins her big, border collie grin.

Lissa snorts. "Molly Millions, hah. You *are* a geek."

"So, I like *Neuromancer.* Who doesn't?"

"But, Molly Millions . . ."

I glare at her, then smile down at Molly. "I just had to make sure she was OK," I say.

And I'm thinking of the time when I brought her home, the tiny bundle of fluff that she was then. Puppies, particularly bright ones, can be trouble but she never was. She grins up at me again, and I grab another treat from the bucket by the fridge. She catches it in one smooth motion, then crunches it between her teeth.

We walk through my place and Molly sticks to my side. I know it's because she can sense how unsettled I am. I can tell no one has been here—there are no unfamiliar presences, and there's certainly no stench of Stirrers. And Molly isn't acting too weird. I stop in the living room.

There's a photo of Dad and Morrigan on my mantelpiece.

Those two have been pomping as long as anyone at Mortmax, other than Mr. D. Both had graduated from Brisbane Grammar and both had had something of a reputation as hellraisers in their day. The stories I had heard from each about the other, and *always* without implicating themselves, were told with relish, and were usually accompanied with a lot of eye rolling from Mom.

Morrigan is family in the best sense: family you choose. I feel a twinge of worry for him. But that's all I allow myself, I can't wallow in grief and fear. There are walls building inside of me. I don't know how sturdy they are, but I'm unwilling to push them too hard. At least I know that there's an afterlife.

Dad and Morrigan both came from a long line of Pomps; they could trace their line back to the Black Death, but Dad's focus had always been family. Not so Morrigan, death had been his life, and he'd risen in the ranks faster than any other Pomp in the business. He knew more about the processes than anyone except, of course, Mr. D.

But where Mr. D was aloof and, let's face it, creepy as all hell, Morrigan was extremely hands-on. He'd set up the automatic payroll, all from Mortmax Industries' accounts. Before then Mr. D had paid Pomps with checks, and those bastards always took a week to clear, partly because Mr. D's handwriting was so bad, but mostly because banks like to take their time with other people's money.

Morrigan had also set up the phone network. Sparrows had been used prior to that. We still used them on occasion but only in trials and ceremonial events, and mainly to humor Mr. D who is decidedly old school. None of us enjoyed the sparrows that much, because they were bad humored at the best of times, and the process involved a little pain—a short message for a drop of blood, a longer one for an opened vein. Blood and pomping go hand in hand, from the portents to the paint used in brace symbols. And without blood you couldn't successfully stall a Stirrer. But the sparrows were different. They insisted on taking it for themselves, and they were pretty savage about it. Like I said, old school.

Above all, Morrigan had actually done something that no other member of the organization had ever achieved: turned Mortmax into a profitable business. There's no money in pomping, and it was the side businesses, the companies that Mortmax owned that made the money—a couple of fast-food chains, a large share in a mining collective. Once Morrigan had started working that side of the business our pay packets had all increased rather dramatically, which is how I can afford to live the way I do. It's not that extravagant, but I can certainly afford to pay my mortgage and eat takeaway once—well six, maybe seven, times—a week.

Dad never really approved of the changes, though he was happy to take the pay rise. He used to say that pomping was for Pomps and business was for arseholes. I think he was quite shocked by how good he was at the business side of things. Mom often said he was merely proving his axiom.

"Great music," Lissa says, and I lift my gaze toward her in the corner of my living room, checking out my neat racks of CDs. "The Clash, Dick Nasty, Okkervil River. Shit, you've got all the Kinks' albums, and Bowie's. Don't you ever get your music as downloads?"

"Yeah, I'm eclectic," I say as she follows me into my bedroom. "And I don't like downloads, I want my CD art and liner notes."

"I see, so you're not quite geeky enough to do everything as downloads, and not quite cool enough to buy vinyl."

Lissa is already digging around the bedroom. "And it's a relief to see a little mess. Walking through the rest of your place I was beginning to worry that I was hanging out with a serial killer. A serial killer obsessed with peculiar bands, and science-fiction DVDs. A geek serial killer."

"Thank you," I say. "You really know how to charm a fella."

Lissa grins and shrugs.

I grab a backpack and start throwing clothes from my floor into it. A cap, T-shirts, socks, underpants and jeans. Most of them are clean. There's a bottle of water on my bedside table and I throw that in, too.

"What I like about you," Lissa says, peering under my bed, "is that you don't leave your porn stash lying around. Clothes, yes, but not the porn. Can't tell you the number of dates I've—"

"This isn't a date. Could you get out of there... please?" Her face is buried in my cupboard, and I'm trying hard not to admire her from behind. *She's dead. She's dead, you idiot. And people are trying to kill you. Now look the other way, dickhead.*

Yeah, my inner monolog is pretty brusque. Sometimes it's like a crotchety Jiminy Cricket; you know, a conscience that doesn't whistle or sing, and is all bent up with arthritis and bitter at the youth of today. My inner monolog would write letters to the council and the local paper, complaining about apostrophe use. Heaven help me if I ever live to anything approaching a ripe old age. I'll be a right pain in the arse.

I try to ignore it most of the time.

Lissa keeps checking through my stuff. "Aha! I knew you kept them somewhere, how polite."

"I'm a real gentleman," I say. Though my face is burning, I'm also wondering if Tremaine kept his stash lying around, and why I've never thrown mine out, because I can't remember the last time I looked at it, other than yesterday. "Could you stop perusing my porn . . . please?"

"A real gentleman who likes *Busty Trollops*, eh?"

"That isn't mine." I push into the closet and Lissa steps out of my way. I reach past the DVDs and grab a thick roll of fifty-dollar notes.

"Hmm, you leave that much cash lying around? What, you expected to run into trouble?"

I shrug, but maybe I had, or maybe I just like the idea, and the somewhat philanthropic notion, that anyone who breaks into my house and makes it past the porn will get a lovely surprise. "Glad I did, though. Now, what else do I need?"

"For one, you're going to need a knife—a sharp knife, sharper than the one you use on the job. A scalpel would be perfect. And you're also going to need a pen, with the thickest nib you can find."

"How about a craft knife? Got new blades and everything."

Lissa raises an eyebrow. "What do you need a craft knife for?"

I shrug. "Crafty things." I'm not going to start explaining my scrapbooking. Even I'm a bit embarrassed about that.

"Crafty things, hah! And this place is so neat, admittedly not the bedroom—but who has a neat bedroom? Even your dog looks neat. Just who are you, Mr. de Selby?"

"What are you talking about?"

She shrugs. I smirk back at her.

I'm packed—clothes, craft knife, pen with a thick nib (yeah, scrapbooking again), even some brace paint, which is my blood mixed with a couple of small tins of something I bought at a hardware store. After seeing those Stirrers on the Hill, I suspect I might need it.

I risk a shower, Molly standing at the door, a grinning sentinel. The pressure's crap, and the hot and cold are sensitive, but I've mastered it over the years to the point that showers with regular pressure seem odd to me. Within a minute I'm enjoying the heat. Washing away a little of the terror. I even clean the morning's blood from the glass. It's an empty gesture but it makes me feel a little better.

I have a pair of tweezers in the bathroom cabinet, and under the steamy shower I pick the beads of glass out of my palms. There isn't a lot of it, thank God, but it hurts. The blood washes away down the drain.

I don't know how long I'm standing there beneath the water but I'm back to thinking about my family, and that starts to put me in a spin.

"Nice tatt." I look up, and Lissa's there leering at me. "Never got one myself."

"Yeah, I live the cliché." Most Pomps have tattoos. Mine is on my left biceps, a cherub with Modigliani eyes. It's bodiless, with wings folded beneath the head.

It's a cherub, but it's a menacing, snarling cherub. Actually it's downright creepy looking. I know it's wanky; I had it done when I turned nineteen, had far too much money and way too much to drink. The bemused tattooist wouldn't have let me do it except, well, Tim was there. Actually I think the whole thing was his idea. And he can be so persuasive. Thing is, I don't remember him ever getting a tattoo.

That was before I decided on the path of single-income home debt, and I was heavily into Modigliani. And I liked the irony of it, drunk as I was. Despite what you see on Victorian era tombstones, cherubs have had nothing to do with pomping in centuries.

Most Pomps go for the hourglass, with all the sand at the bottom, or butterflies. Depends on how old you are, I reckon. We like our symbolism. Morrigan has a small twenty cent coin-sized skull tattooed on his forearm, and a flock of sparrows on his back, which extend to sleeves over his biceps. But he can do things with his that

I'm incapable of—they're genuine inklings. I've seen them break the cage of his flesh and go flying around the room.

Mom and Dad had been horrified at my ink. Going against the trend, neither of them had even a hint of iconography in their house, let alone on their skin. They'd always been a bit suspicious of my own interests in that area. Morrigan had talked them out of disowning me. After all, he had tatts too, so it couldn't be too bad.

Thing is, Lissa isn't looking at my tatt. I feel my face flush.

"A little privacy please," I say.

"But we've already bonded over your porn collection. And Molly's sitting there."

"Out," I say. "Both of you."

"But you look so happy to see me. Well, I hope that's because of me." And she's gone. Oh dear, part of me misses her, even if it's rapidly deflating. She is dead after all. Molly turns tail, too, and I get the feeling that she's laughing at me.

I rinse off the soap and begin the process of shaving off my beard. I only cut myself twice which means that my hands aren't shaking as much as they were. Once done, I dry myself down and dress, quickly and somewhat timidly, feeling decidedly self-conscious. Once dressed I take a few deep breaths and work on my hair. My hands sting, but they're glass-free.

No one's come crashing through the front door. I'm careful not to pick up my phone. Maybe coming home was reckless, but I had to recharge. I needed this—I'm hungry, and I'd kill for a cup of tea. I boil the kettle on my gas stove, cupping my hands over the flame.

It's gotten cold. I hate the cold, and I've put on a duffel coat that Lissa says makes me look like a thief. I'm tired; I can't be bothered explaining that the coat was my father's. He gave it to me when I was little. It used to be twice my size, then—height and width. The first time I could wear it without tripping over its hem was one of the happiest of my life. While I have this coat, I've still got something of my dad.

I set two cups down and ask Lissa if she takes milk or sugar. It's an automatic gesture. She shakes her head.

"I'm not a tea drinker," she says, and we both laugh. I open the pantry door, take out a Mars Bar, and start gulping down its various essential nutrients. I realize the last thing I ate was a Chiko Roll. I may actually manage to kill myself with my diet before someone gets me with a gun.

"One thing I can't stand is noisy eaters," Lissa says. "If you're going to inhale that thing, at least do it quietly."

"Anything else you don't like?"

"I never really liked my job."

I'm impressed by her segueing. "Well, quit."

Lissa glares at me. "Aren't we Mr. Glib."

I'm feeling a little better. The kettle's boiling, I pour the water into my cup. Mom loved her tea. The thought that I'll never have a cup with her again takes the breath from me. I'm not sure I want it anymore. I put it back down and step away.

Lissa's giving me a worried look, now. Is this the best that I can get? Concern from a dead girl? Someone who was lost to me before I even got to know her, someone who should be receiving that concern from me. What's wrong with me? And here I am having a cup of tea.

"You're scaring me a little here," Lissa says.

"Mom," I say, gesturing at my cup.

Lissa frowns. "Well, she wouldn't want you to stop drinking tea, would she?"

I shake my head. I need milk for the tea. I drink my coffee black, but I take milk with my tea. Mom was very particular about that, even with tea bags—boil, then steep, then milk, but no sugar. Don't get me started on that. I open my fridge.

"Shit."

There's a bomb in there. A mobile phone, wrapped in a tangle of wires that is buried in a lump of explosive like a cyber tick on a C-4 plastique dog. And the phone's LCD is flashing.

Lissa screams, "Run!"

I'm already doing it.

"Molly," I yell, as I grab my bag in a reflex action that may just get me killed. I hurtle out the back door, down the steps and into the backyard. "Moll—"

I'm consumed by brilliance. A wave of heat comes swift on its tail. I'm lifted up and thrown into the bamboo that lines the back fence. Behind me the house is ablaze. A few moments later, the gas tanks beneath the house detonate. Molly, where's Molly? I throw my arm over my face and weep. My house, the one I've been paying off for the last six years, is all gone. Fragments of my CD collection are part of the smoldering rain falling on my backyard.

I crawl back through the bamboo. It's digging into me, there are shards of wood that are actually stuck in my flesh. I wrench myself out of the thicket, dragging my bag. Something whines.

"Oh, Molly."

She's broken. Her back is twisted at an angle that makes me sick with the sight of it. She tries to rise, even manages it for a moment. She moans and slumps back to the ground. There's blood all through her fur.

I'm running to her side, and she looks at me with her beautiful eyes, and there's terror and pain there. *This isn't fair. It isn't fair.* She doesn't understand what's happening. She tries to rise again. "It's OK, girl," I say, and I rest my hand on her head, and her breathing steadies a little. It's the only comfort I can offer her. "Molly."

I don't know what to touch. I don't know how to hold her, what's not going to hurt her anymore. She's shivering, and I stroke her head. "Molly, good girl."

What's left of my house burns, flaring up when something particularly flammable catches alight. My face is hot, and I stroke my dog's head. *Shit. Shit. Shit.*

Molly takes one more shuddery breath, and is still. And she isn't my Molly anymore. Something passes through me, gentler than a human, but it hurts regardless.

I look up and Lissa's watching me, her eyes wide.

"I was going to get Tim to pick her up," I whisper, as though I have to justify this. Christ, what if Tim had opened the fridge?

"Oh, Steve. I'm so sorry."

"It's OK," I say. "It's OK." But it isn't.

Molly is dead. There's only her ruined body, and even now it's growing cold, and it doesn't look like her anymore, because with Molly it was always about the way she was thinking. The way she moved. She really was a clever dog. She didn't deserve this. She put up with so much. She never got enough walks. Molly's gone, and I can't make it up to her.

Lissa's gaze stops me. Her eyes, green as a hailstorm now, are serious, and they're focused on me. For a moment they're all I see. Lissa saves me with that stare. I don't know how to explain it. It's as though she's always been a part of my life, as though she knows exactly what to say or do to comfort me.

I'm in an alternate universe, though, and one far crueler. One where Lissa and I never connected when we were alive. Never had a chance to tumble into love, and all its possibilities. Her gaze saves me, but it also makes me bitter because I'm never going to get that chance. She's dead, and my parents are dead, and Molly's dead.

And that fills me with something hard, cold and resolute.

"We have to get out of here," I say.

"Yeah, we do."

One last look at Molly and I jump the fence behind the burning bamboo into the neighbor's backyard. The sound of sirens is building, filling the suburbs as they rush toward my home. People are heading toward my house but I'm running in the opposite direction, and it has to look suspicious. My house is going to be on the news tonight. My face is going to be there, too, and beard or no beard, the people on the bus are going to remember that face, and the guy whose car I stole. But I try not to think about that. And while I need it, desperately need it, I have no space for strategy, except this.

I have to stay alive now.

Someone has to pay for what has been done to me and mine.

11

We're halfway down the block when the pale blue sedan pulls up alongside us. Its headlights flash. I flinch, wondering whether or not this is it. There's nowhere to run, just the road to my right, and tall fences to my left. No one pays this car much attention besides me but that could well change if someone starts firing rounds out of it. The passenger-side door opens.

"Get in," Tim says.

My jaw drops.

"There's no time to explain, just get in!"

"Can you trust this guy?" Lissa demands.

I'm already in the car, shutting the door behind me. Tim races down the road. I can sense Lissa's displeasure emanating from the back seat of the car.

"This isn't your car," I say. The car smells of cigarettes. Tim has the radio on and we have a background of inconsequential jokey disc jockey chatter. It's somehow calming where I would usually find it irritating. Bad radio hints at normalcy, and this is seriously bad radio.

"Do you think I'd be stupid enough to drive my own car?" Tim looks terrified, and wounded, like a man who has lost his parents. I recognize the look I had seen in my own face earlier. He takes a deep breath, slowing the car down to the speed limit.

"Didn't think about that," I say. "I haven't really been thinking about anything."

"Shit. Steve, what the fuck's going on?" Tim lights up a smoke, waiting. Suburbia streaks by. My house is the only one that's exploded, but everything looks wrong, feels wrong. The lens of losing everything has slipped over my eyes and I wonder if I'll ever see the world in the old way again.

Tim keeps swinging his gaze from the road to my face and back again, as though it or I have answers. I'd put my money on the road. "I don't know. I don't know. How did you..."

"I got a call. I don't know who from, just a male voice, it was all very confusing. They said you were in danger, and that I needed to get to your place right away." Tim smiles, it's a weak, thin thing, but a smile all the same. "They also said not to drive my car, that people might be looking for it. I borrowed this. It's a neighbor's. When I got to your house it was in flames. I saw you leap the fence."

He sighs. "Why didn't you call me again? That message you left, what the fuck was that?"

"I didn't want you to get dragged into—"

"Jesus, I'm always going to be part of this. You Pomps, you snooty bastards. I'm a Black Sheep, but that doesn't mean I can't be some help. Shit, my parents are dead. They were murdered, so were yours."

I turn to Lissa. "Why didn't I...?"

She shakes her head. "The day you had, Steve. It's lucky you're not dead."

"I'm sorry," I say to Tim. "I really am."

"Yeah. At least you're OK."

As if this can even remotely be called OK. None of us are.

"Who's in the back there?" Tim asks.

"It's a dead girl. She's been following me around."

I hear a loud humph, at that from the back. "Following, well, I—"

"You two have a thing going?"

I shrug. "She's dead, Tim."

"She's also right here," Lissa says. "Like, hello!"

I frown at her. Then turn back to Tim. "Someone's killing Pomps. She's a Pomp, she knows how to trick up death a bit. She warned me."

"Mom's dead," Tim says. "Dad, too. The family. She couldn't have warned them."

"I was just lucky, I suppose. Just lucky," I say, and I know that's not quite right but I can't think of anything else to say.

Tim jabs a finger in my face. "The next time you call me, fucking be a little more specific, eh." He glances toward the road, just in time to swerve out of the way of a fire engine, its lights blazing. "Maybe I could have done something."

"It was already too late then," I say. "If there'd been anything I could have . . . Christ, Tim, you weren't the only one to lose family."

Tim slows the car.

"They're all gone. Your mom said that she loves you. Tim, you and Sally, and the kids, you have to—"

"I'm not going anywhere," Tim says. "Sally, the kids, they're already on a flight to London."

"Aunt Teagan?"

"Yeah. Steve, we have to get you out of here. I'm safe, they're not going for Black Sheep. I've checked the register. Not a single fatality in six weeks. You're the only one in danger here. Not me, certainly not the dead girl."

"Lissa," I say. "That's her name."

He looks at me, shakes his head. "You've never made it easy on yourself. The ones you fall for."

My cheeks are burning, so there's no point in denial. Tim pretends to ignore it.

"I'm sure Lissa doesn't want you dead. It's crazy that you don't run."

I raise my hands in the air. "I know, but I'm staying. I need to get to the bottom of this. Maybe after this is done, whatever it is that needs to be done. If I live long enough. But if I stop now, and think…" My eyes start to well up. There's a dark wave of loss towering over me, but I can't acknowledge that now. I wipe the tears away with my thumb.

A couple more fire engines race past us. "Jesus, Steve, you've put on a show," Tim says.

"I can't have you driving me around," I say. "Even in this car. It's too dangerous. I'm a target. Every moment you're with me puts you in danger. I don't care what the guy on the phone said. I need you to stay out of this."

"Fuck that."

"Tim. I can't be responsible for your death. I just can't. You've got kids. A wife. You have to think of them, mate."

Tim's shoulders tense. "That's bullshit," he says. "Here we fucking go again, just because I'm a Black Sheep. Because I didn't become a Pomp."

"No, it isn't, and you know it. Shit, if you were a Pomp, you'd probably be dead by now." I take a deep breath. "You need to be safe. Promise me you will."

Tim glares at me. There's an anger there that I'd never seen before, and it hurts me to see it. Then the more methodical part of his brain starts reining in his rage. "OK," he says at last. "Where do you want me to take you?"

I give him an address, not very far away. We're there in a couple of minutes. No one follows us: the streets are almost empty. Tim pulls the car to the side of the road.

"Thank you," I say. "If you can, get out of town. I think this is going to get worse before it gets better—if it ever gets better. Stay at a friend's place for a few days."

Tim nods, though I know he's just going to go home and try and deal with what's going on. "Be safe, you bastard," he says, then turns and speaks to the back seat. "Take care of him. He's all the family I have left, even if he is a Pomp." I don't have the heart to tell him that Lissa's already out and standing on the side of the road.

"You be safe, too." I get out of the car.

Tim glances at me, and all I see are the wounds that he's carrying, the hurts that I recognize because they are the same as my own. It almost brings me to my knees. He slips the car into gear and shoots off down the street.

"Interesting guy," Lissa says. "Now, tell me, why are we here?"

"My car's round the back." I point at the nearby garage. "It's supposed to be fixed." I jingle my keys. "We're going to be on the road in no time."

We're just turning into the mechanic's—the place is closed for the night, just the cars waiting to be picked up—when there's an almighty explosion. A wave of heat strikes me. I smell what's left of the hair on my arms.

"Don't tell me," Lissa says.

"Yeah."

Bits of my car fall from the sky. A dark shape streaks out of the flame toward me. It's a crow—a big one—and its wings are aflame. It races toward my head, a shrieking, flapping comet. An omen if I've ever seen one. I cringe and duck, throwing my hands up before my face. But it's already gone.

I swing around to Lissa, her pale blue face lit by the fire coming from my car, her mouth open. She looks as horrified as I feel.

"What the hell does that mean?" Lissa asks.

"It means that wherever we're going, we're walking for a bit." I look around at all that flame, and the dark sky filling up with smoke. My environmental footprint has broadened considerably this evening. "Maybe we should start running again."

Things can't get any worse, except I'm certain that they will. It's the first new law of the universe according to Steven de Selby's life: things *always* get worse—and then they explode.

12

So I'm dead," Mike says to me and blinks, his eyes wide.

The newly dead blink a lot.

It's more from the memory of the flesh than any brilliance in the afterlife. There's no walking into the light or any of that nonsense, their eyes are just adjusting to a new way of seeing the world. It's a doors of perception sort of thing.

I have an inkling of what that feels like now, because my world has had its doors and its walls blown open, one after the other with all the ruthlessness of a carpet bomber. I'm feeling a little more than angry. Which isn't the kind of thing you want to bring to the job, it's wildly unprofessional. If this is even a profession anymore.

"Yeah, Mike." I glance around, not sure if anyone is following us. "I'm sorry to say it but, yeah, you're dead."

"Well, this wasn't what I was expecting." He's a bit hesitant. I can't get near him, maybe I'm not helping that much. I'm not really in the mood.

Mike is the fourth dead person who's found me since my car exploded, and that was only an hour ago. Two others were Pomps, the third a punter like Mike. I hadn't seen the Pomps since last year's Christmas party; one of them had gotten a little amorous with the bar staff. Poor bastard—that stuff sticks to you—even dead he couldn't look me in the eye. With them gone I'm probably the only Pomp in the city. Maybe the only Pomp in Australia. And every dead Pomp means more work for me, more of that dreadful pain.

"I'm sorry," I say again to Mike, and I really am.

"Don't be. I'm OK with it," Mike says, shrugging. He's not a Pomp, just a punter, a regular dead guy. "It was hurting at the end. This is much better. I'm really OK with it."

"Good." I'm not OK with death, but I'm trying to cling to my flesh and bones. Shit, I catch myself, I'm being so unprofessional.

"So who is she?" Mike points a thumb at Lissa.

"I'm dead too, Mike," Lissa says, even manages a smile.

Mike nods. Lissa lets this sink in. He blinks, looks her up and down. He obviously likes what he sees. Once again I feel a little tug of jealousy. "You cool with it?" Mike asks.

Lissa sighs. "What you gonna do, eh?"

Mike laughs. "Yeah."

I reach out a hand, pat his wrist and he's gone. I grunt with the pain of it, hunched over. Then I cough.

Every one of these is getting worse, and there's only ever going to be more of them. Souls always take the path of least resistance. As the number of Pomps fall, the souls of the dead are going to go to the closest Pomps they can find, and they're going to come in hard and fast. Sure, some will use Stirrers but if I had a choice of a nice well-lit hallway or a cave dripping with venom, I know which one I'd pick. Doesn't mean I like it.

"I'm doing your job for you," Lissa says, as I straighten with the slow and unsteady movements of the punch-drunk. It seems a long way up to my full height. And there's blood in my spit: a lot of it. My mouth is ruddy with the stuff.

"What the hell do you mean by that?"

"Some punters need talking down. That guy didn't even need it and you still couldn't manage to be professional."

I raise my hands. "Whoa, you're being much too hard. For Christ's sake, I don't even know if there's a job now."

Lissa flits around me. "As long as they keep coming to you, you do your job." Her eyes are wide and set to ignite. "You didn't want this? Well, neither did I, boy. But we chose this, nonetheless, when we chose to do what our parents did. Without us, without you, things are going to get bad and fast. So do your job."

"Yeah, well, easy enough when you're not experiencing each pomp." I can feel the sneer spreading across my face. "I'm bruised on the inside. My job is going to get me killed." One way or the other it will, I'm certain of that now.

"Maybe, maybe not," Lissa says. "But you've got to keep moving, and you've got to keep sucking it up. Death doesn't end."

"What the hell do you think I'm doing?" I demand, while not moving at all. My hands are on my hips, and I've a growl stitched across my face, my jaw bunched up so tight it hurts.

"Stopping, wandering aimlessly, a little bit of both." Lissa counts out on her fingers. "Oh, and I could throw in some misdirecting of anger."

She's right of course, but I'm not going to admit it.

I'm walking toward the river—there, that's a destination, everything in Brisbane leads to the river, eventually—through the pedestrian and cyclist underpass near Land Street, concrete all round. The traffic of Coronation Drive rumbles above. Cyclists race past me, all clicking gears and ratcheting wheels, thunking over the seams in the concrete, each thunk jolting me into a higher level of stress.

All these people are in a hurry to be somewhere. Going home, they're the last wave of the working day, the sunset well and truly done with. Until yesterday I was one of these restless commuters, my phone always on, hoping that it wouldn't ring with a change of schedule.

"You know, I had a home once," I whisper. "Had four walls, a dog and a bloody fine CD collection. Shit, I didn't care about the CDs or the house, but Molly. Molly."

"We've all lost things, people we care about," Lissa says. "I've got feelings, too. It's all I have. If you give in to your losses you may as well give up."

I walk around in front of her. She stops, and we hold each other's gaze. "What was your place like?" I ask.

"It was nice, near the beach, not far from a tram line. Oh, and the restaurants." She stops. "Bit of a pigsty, though. Never really got into the whole house-frau thing."

"No one's perfect."

Lissa smiles. "Would have driven you mad."

"I'm sure." I want to say that I would do anything to be driven mad by her. But now's not the time.

I pull my duffel coat around me. The evening's grown a gnawing chill. A wind is funneling through the underpass, lifting rubbish, and it swirls around us like this is all some sort of garbage masque. For a moment it passes through Lissa's form, spiraling up almost to her head. She blanches, shifts forward, and the rubbish topples behind her, leaving a trail of chip packets, cigarette butts and leaves.

"Well, that's never happened before." There's something delightful about her face in that moment, something starkly honest that hurts me more than any pomp. I want to touch her cheek. I ache for that contact, but all we have are words.

"Look, I'm sorry about before," I say, startling a jogger, one of the few I've passed not listening to an mp3. He looks at me oddly, but keeps running.

"So am I," Lissa says. Suddenly a part of me wants to take another jab at her, because maybe it would be easier if she hated me. After all, I'm going to lose her. But I clamp my jaw shut.

I reach the river end of the underpass. There's a seat there and I slump down into it and stare at the water, the city's lights swimming like lost things in the restless dark.

"I think that little fellow wants you," Lissa says.

I look up. There's a tiny sparrow perched on the ledge behind me.

I look at it more closely. It's an inkling. One of Morrigan's. Its outline is an almost ornate squiggle of ink.

The little bird regards me with bright eyes, its head tilted, then hops closer. It coughs once, strikes its beak against the ledge and coughs again. I put out my hand, flinching slightly as the sparrow jumps quickly onto my finger. Its squiggly chest expands and shrinks in time with its breathing, and all the while its eyes are trained on me, unreadable and intelligent.

There is a tiny roll of paper clipped to its leg. I reach for it, and the sparrow pecks down hard on my arm, drawing blood. An inky tongue darts out.

"Shit." I'd forgotten about that, mobile phones are a sight easier than this stuff. The sparrow needs to know that it has the right person, and there's also a price. Blood's the easiest way. Satisfied that I am the correct recipient, the tiny roll of paper falls from its leg into my open palm.

The sparrow looks at Lissa and starts chirping angrily, fiercely enough that it's almost a bark, surprisingly loud from such a small creature. Lissa glares at it and the sparrow gives one final growl of a chirp, launches itself into the air, and is gone into the night.

"I don't think it was too happy to see me," Lissa says. "In fact, I know it wasn't."

"Why?"

"Because I've outstayed my welcome, I shouldn't be here. The world wants me to go."

"I don't want you to go."

Lissa crosses her arms. "Steven, you haven't been acting like it."

"I—"

"Just look at the note, would you?"

I unfold the paper. Morrigan's handwriting is distinctive: all flourishes and yet completely legible, even when it's covered with bloody fingerprints.

Still alive, Steven. You're not the only one. Don's in Albion, Sam is too. Get there if you're able. Your best chance is together.

Be careful.

M

I read it aloud. Lissa frowns as she looks from the note to me. She shakes her head. "Steven, this doesn't feel right. It could be a trap."

"Everything feels like a trap, though, doesn't it? Every street's a potential ambush. If we keep this up, whoever our opponent is will have won." I heft up my backpack. "Morrigan's alive. I have to cling to some sort of hope."

Lissa's lips tighten, she's not happy at all. "But there's hope and then there's insanity, Steve."

I look her squarely in the eyes. "I've got a bit of both, I reckon. And anyway, besides you and the contents of this pack, it's all I've got."

I'm also much happier following Morrigan than trying to get Mr. D's attention. Lissa has explained the ritual, and why the craft knife is necessary. Anything else has to be worth trying first. Lissa knows that. It's hanging there in front of us, this secondary truth. Drawing Death the old way scares the shit out of me, and I can understand why most Pomps would be unfamiliar with the process. There's too much pain. It's one thing to have people wanting you dead, another entirely to take yourself to that place.

Now all I've got to do is get to Albion. It's a northern suburb, about twenty minutes away. Once I'm there I'm sure I can find Sam and Don. Pomps can sense each other—it's an innate thing, hard to describe, but you know when they're near and, if you know them well enough, you can tell just who is about. I haven't sensed any Pomps since the Hill and I'm a little hungry for it. There's a loneliness within me that is completely unfamiliar.

I realize that all my life there have been Pomps around and now there seems to be nothing but the polluting presence of Stirrers. I need my own kind with a desperation that is almost painful.

And I'm terrified that they'll be dead or gone by the time I get there.

13

"I can't believe I'm asking this, but, are you going to steal another car?" Lissa asks.

I have to laugh. The thought had crossed my mind. "I might be mad but I'm not stupid." Besides, actually finding an unlocked car with its keys in the ignition in this part of the city looks like it would be impossible. I'd like to think I could hot-wire a car after breaking into it, but I can't.

I run up the steep stone staircase, two steps at a time, that leads from the river onto the jacaranda-lined traffic of Coronation Drive, and jog to the nearest bus stop, Lissa pacing me all the way. Behind me, a CityCat glides down the river toward the Regatta pier. I stare after the big blue catamaran's flashing lights as a bus comes to a halt. I clamber aboard, and show my pass like I'm just going to Albion for a curry or a pizza. How I wish I was, and with Lissa, too. But the truth is I'm probably going to Albion to die.

"Got a clear run at last," the bus driver says. "Some idiot messed up a bus, then stole a car." I doubt he'd be so friendly if he knew I was the one responsible, which then makes me distinctly uncomfortable with the idea of traveling in a bus. Bad memories surface. Perhaps I should have stuck it out and found a car.

"Yeah, some people, right?" I say.

I sit in the middle of the bus nearest the exit. The driver's already put the bus into gear and is nudging into the traffic on Coronation Drive. From this angle I have a view of the west and I can see a thin trail of smoke darker than the night coming from the direction of the garage. All that's left of my car is blowing in the wind.

The bus rumbles toward the city then takes the Hale Street exit, peeling away from the skyscrapers to the right of us, heading toward the inner-city bypass and Albion. It's also how you get to Royal Brisbane Hospital, and the airport. I'm familiar with the hospital, most particularly the morgue, but it's been a long time since I've been to the airport, and that was only to pick up friends and family. There was a time I'd dreamed of traveling, just never got around to it. Wish I had. I catch myself at that thought—I've indulged in more than enough self-pity. I look at Lissa.

"What?" she asks.

"So tell me about Lissa Jones," I whisper. No one seems to notice that I'm talking to thin air.

Lissa rolls her eyes. "Gorgeous, single, thirty-something."

"Something being?"

"Thirty, and only just. It was my birthday yesterday."

"You could have told me earlier."

She snorts. "What, so you could buy me a cake?"

"Well, happy birthday, Miss Jones." I dig the bottle of water out of my backpack and take what I reckon is a suitably celebratory swig.

"Never wanted to be a Pomp," Lissa says.

"Really? I know you said it, but I thought you were joking."

Lissa raises an eyebrow. "Joking, eh? Because the last day has been such a barrel of laughs."

"Sorry." There's a bit of silence, and it's only going to deepen unless I dive in. "For me it was always something I was going to be." And it was. My parents had never said anything outright banning me from considering anything else, but they'd never really encouraged me to explore my options, either.

Lissa chuckles. "I studied event management," she says, and her smile widens. "I certainly learned a lot about staging a good funeral."

"Your parents used to take you to them?"

"Didn't yours?"

I laugh. "I actually used to think that wakes were just something that people attended every day. I had a black suit from about the age of four."

"Bet you looked cute."

"Yeah, and none of that past tense, thank you." I smile, though there's part of me still demanding that I stop flirting with a dead girl. I know I'm being unprofessional, and she knows I know but, then again, after what has happened to my profession, it hardly seems to matter anymore. "I remember Dad stopping a stir in Annerley. The body was actually twitching, and Dad went up to the coffin and slapped the corpse on the face. Stalled it then and there. People were looking at him as though he was mad, and I was just grinning, proud as punch.

"Dad did most of the hospital gigs, the staff knew him. Doctors and nurses, particularly the nurses, they see all the weird stuff. They understand why our job is so important. So they were always polite around him, respectful. I liked that."

Lissa smiles. "Dad's boy, eh? I didn't want the job. I didn't want to spend my life going to funerals and morgues. But the job picks you, and it sticks in the blood. Anyway, in my family it does, whether you want it or not."

I'm not sure if she's making fun of my family's rather high Black Sheep to Pomp ratio—Aunt Teagan, my late Uncle Mike, Tim—so I just nod, and go along with it. "It makes sense, though, could you imagine pomping cold? Shit, that would really screw you up."

It was different in the old days, there was something of a cultural scaffold. If you started to see weird shit, everyone knew what it was. Well, it's not like that anymore. Without family guidance those first few pomps would be nightmarish. I wonder how things are going to work now, who's going to pass on all this information to the next generation. Surely not me.

"I was stubborn, though," Lissa says. "Finished my degree."

"Good on you," I say.

Lissa glares at me. "Anyone ever told you you're a patronizing shit?"

"Yeah, but I'm serious. I only got through the first year of my BA—if you can count four fails and four passes as getting through."

Lissa shakes her head.

"Neither do I."

"You can always go back." I love her for saying that, talking as though there might be some sort of long-term future.

"Nah, I'm scarred for life." The sun's been down a while now and the city's luminous, a brooding yet brilliant presence to our right. "Which isn't going to be too much longer, anyway."

"Don't say that," Lissa says. "You can't think that way. You mustn't."

"Well, it's true. You spend your life around death like we do, pomping and stalling Stirrers, and it tends to make you numb. Hell, it numbs you a lot. You know it does. I have plenty of free time, and what do I do with it? I accumulate things. Not ideas, just things, as though they're ideas. Shit, half the reason I gave up at uni was that I decided it was easier *not* to think.

"And when you decide it's easier not thinking then you're only a short step away from deciding it's easier feeling nothing. I can't remember the last time I cried before today."

"I remember my last tears," Lissa says. "Like I said, I never wanted to do this job. I cried whenever I thought about that too much."

"See, I envy you your pain," I say.

"Don't." Her eyes hold mine in that electric gaze of hers.

"But at least you strived for something, even if you failed at it. That's incredibly heroic, as far as I'm concerned," I say.

I tried my hand at non-Pomp work, the regular trades as we call them. I gave up the mobile and the pay packet, and it just didn't fit.

Honestly, though, I really didn't try that hard. What I did learn was that I wasn't really a people person—I'm too much of a smart arse for one thing. Anyway, you get hooked on the pomping, the odd hours, the danger. It's certainly more exciting than working in retail: it didn't matter if your clientele weren't always cheery as there was no follow-up, you didn't have dead people coming to see if their order had arrived, there weren't any secret shoppers, and you never had to clean up the mess (a blessed relief in some cases).

For me, pomping was the perfect job. There was no real responsibility, and it was good money. I had few friends, other than family, and a few people whose blogs I read. There I was, walking and talking through life, not having much impact, not taking too many hits either.

The problem with that is that it doesn't work. The universe is always going to kick you, and time's waiting to take things away. If my job hadn't made that obvious, well, I'd deserved what had happened to me.

In my case it had taken everything at once. And put in front of me the sort of woman I might have found if I'd actually been in there, living.

I realize that I've been staring into her eyes.

"Don't fall in love with me," Lissa says.

Too late. It's far too late for that.

"You've got tickets on yourself," I say softly. "Fall in love with you? As if!"

I look up. The bus driver's staring at me. Half the people in the bus are. I didn't realize I'd been talking so loudly. Talking to myself, as far as they can tell.

"I'm serious." Lissa turns her head, stares out of the window.

"Too serious," I say, not sure that she is even listening. We sit in silence for the next few minutes until we're a stop away from the heart of Albion. I jab the red stop signal like it's some sort of eject button. The bus pulls in, the doors open and I'm out on the street, in a different world. Restaurants are packed to the rafters with diners. The place is bustling.

That's not where Don and Sam are, though.

"Aha," I point west. "I can already feel them."

We wander down the street, a steep curve, the traffic rushing by, desperate for whatever the night has on offer.

There are some nice parts of Albion. On the whole it's a ritzy part of Brisbane, but no one's told this bit of the suburb. The restaurants are behind us now, and we're descending from the urbane part of suburbia to the sub. It's no war zone but there's a burnt wreck of a bikie club a few blocks down, and a couple of brothels nearby. You can smell petrol fumes and dust. The city's skyline is in front of us, high-rises and skyscrapers bunched together, lighting the sky. You can't see Mount Coot-tha from here but I can feel One Tree Hill, just like I can feel Don and Sam. They must be able to do the same.

They're holed up in an old Queenslander which would have been nice, once, with its broad, covered verandah all the way around, big windows and double doors open invitingly to catch afternoon breezes. Not anymore, though. You *could* describe it as some sort of renovator's delight—if they had a wrecking ball.

"Absolutely delightful place," Lissa says. We both have a little chuckle at that.

The corrugated roof dips in one corner of the front verandah like a perpetually drooping eye, as though the house had once suffered some sort of seizure. Some of the wooden stumps the building's sitting on have collapsed. It's a dinosaur sinking into itself.

"Still looking at about half a million for it I reckon."

"Real estate, everything's about bloody real estate," Lissa says. "That's the problem with the world today."

"Well, it's a prime location."

Lissa grimaces. "If you want easy access to pimps and car washes."

"The train station is just up the road, don't forget that."

"And what a delightful walk that is."

I make my way gingerly up the front steps. One in every three is missing. The front porch has seen better days, too, and that's being generous. The wood's so rotten that even the termites have moved on to richer pastures, and whatever paint remains on the boards is peeling and gray, and smells a little fungal.

As I reach for the door, something pomps through me, another death from God knows where. Not again. There's more of that far too frequent pain, and I'm bent over as the door opens a crack. I'm too sore to run, so I push it and find myself staring down the barrel of a rifle. I know the face at the other end of the gun, and there's not much welcome in it.

"Hey," I say. "Am I glad to see you."

"Stay right there," Don growls.

"Don't be stupid, Don," Sam says from the corner of the room. I can just see her there. She's holding a pistol and not looking happy. "It's Steve."

"How'd you find us?" Don demands.

"Morrigan," I say. "He's alive."

"Of course he is," Don says, his face hardening. "He's the bastard who betrayed us all."

14

Don has old-school Labor Party blood running through his veins. Broad shouldered, with a big jaw that the gravity of overindulgence has weakened somewhat, he looks like he should be cutting deals with a schooner of VB in one hand and a bikini-clad babe in the other. He has the dirtiest sounding laugh I've ever heard. The truth is he's a gentleman, and utterly charming, but two failed marriages might suggest otherwise. After a couple of beers, he slips into moments of increasing and somewhat embarrassing frankness. "They were bitches, absolute bitches."

And after another couple, "Nah, I was a right bugger." And then, "Don't you ever get married, Steven. And if you do, you love her, if that's the way you butter your bread. You *do* like women, don't you? Not that it matters. It's all just heat in the dark, eh? Eh?"

Yeah, charming when he wants to be. Which isn't now. To suggest Morrigan is behind all this is ridiculous. Even I'm not that paranoid.

Don looks ludicrous with a rifle, even when the bloody thing is pointed at my head. Maybe it's the crumpled suit or the beer gut and his ruddy face. But he's serious, and he hasn't lowered the gun yet. No matter how silly he looks, he can kill me with the twitch of a finger.

He stinks of stale sweat and there's a bloody smear down his white shirt. There's a hard edge to his face, and I recognize it because I'm sure I look that way, too. It's part bewilderment, part terror and a lot of exhaustion. We three have probably been doing most of Australia's pomping between us for the last twelve hours.

Sam, on the other hand—even in her cords and skivvy, with a hand-knitted scarf wrapped around her neck, and a beret that only a certain type of person can pull off—looks like she was born to hold a pistol. Sam is what Mom would call Young Old, which really meant she didn't like her. I couldn't say what her age is, maybe late fifties or early sixties. Her pale skin is smooth, except her hands—you can tell she has never shied away from hard work. She grips her pistol with absolute assurance.

Interestingly, it's aimed at Don.

We've gone all *Reservoir Dogs* in Albion, and I almost ask if I can have a gun, too, just to even things up a bit. I'm also wondering if I can trust anyone. Don certainly doesn't trust me.

"Jesus, Don, put the bloody thing down." Sam jabs her pistol in his face. This could all go bad very quickly. "There are enough people trying to kill us without you helping them."

"You put yours down first," Don says sullenly. I open my mouth to say something, then glance back at Lissa who shakes her head at me. She's still outside, and out of sight of Don and Sam. There's no need to complicate this stand-off any further. I close my mouth again, partly to stop my heart from falling out of it. It seems I'm getting more familiar than I've ever wanted with the actuality of guns—and it's not getting any more pleasant.

"On the count of three," Sam says.

Don lowers his rifle immediately. He's not much of a conformist. "You're right," he says. "I know, Sam. It just got under my skin a bit... the whole damn situation."

"I have a tendency to get under people's skins," I say.

"So do ticks," Lissa whispers, but I'm the only one who hears her, and I don't even bother flashing her a scowl.

Don chuckles. "That's what I've always liked about you." He

reaches a hand out to me, and pulls me into a sweaty bear hug. At the human contact I struggle to hold back tears. "Sorry, Stevo. Christ, I've just had a bad kind of day."

"We all have," I say as he pulls away.

Sam runs over to me and her hug is even more crushing. She smells a lot nicer though, mainly lavender and a hint, just a hint, mind, of some good quality weed.

"I'm so glad you're all right," she says.

If you can call this all right, then you're way more optimistic than me, I think. Still, I hug her tight, and this time I can't quite hold back the tears.

"It's all right," she says. The bloody Pomp mantra: It's all right.

Does she think Morrigan's responsible? Surely not.

"You want a cup of tea?" Don asks, looking a little embarrassed. He nods toward a Thermos in the corner of the room sitting somewhat incongruously next to a sledgehammer, a new one, its handle coated in plastic.

"Tea?" I say, wondering at the hammer.

Don smiles ruefully. "I'd get you a beer but, well, I haven't had time to run to the bottle shop."

Too busy worrying about Morrigan, I think.

"Tea would be great," I say.

"I'll have one, too," Sam says, then blinks, staring out the open door. "Lissa? Oh, I'm sorry."

Does *everybody* know this girl? So I wasn't a member of the Pomp Social Club, but Jesus, how did I never meet her?

"Don't worry, Miss Edwards," Lissa says. "It was quick. I've had time to adjust."

"Miss Edwards?" I'd always known her as Sam, and this throws me.

"Some people are more polite than others. In your case, most people," Sam says to me. "You were lucky she found you."

I nod my head. "Lissa's the reason I'm still alive."

"No surprises there," Don says. "You couldn't piss your way out of a urinal."

Well, isn't this the Steve de Selby support group. I'm about to say something narky but I notice that Don's hands are shaking, enough that I think he may soon spill the tea. I take the cup gently from his grip.

"No arguments from me," I say, even if I'm grinding my teeth slightly. "How did you two make it?"

"They got a little over-enthusiastic," Don says. "I was finishing at a wake—no stir, oddly enough—when some bastard just starts shooting. They missed, and I could see something wasn't quite right. Turns out he was a damn Stirrer. That in itself was peculiar, because I should have felt him. Then I realized he was a Pomp . . . well, used to be. I recognized him, but didn't know his name, though I've since seen a few I do. I blooded up and touched him, too quick to get some answers, and then all I had was a still body and a rifle. Then I got the hell out of there, once I'd made sure." His fingers brush at his blood-smeared shirt.

It has to be touch, and it has to be blood to stop them. Death is intimate, and bound in life. And blood and death are entwined. Think about all those ancient tales that mix them up, like vampire myths. Stirrers don't feed on blood, but life, and a Pomp's lifeblood is the only way to shut the gate.

Death is up close and personal and we're all staring into its face. Which is why pomping can hurt, though death is less traumatic than life. If every pomp was as painful as childbirth, the world would be crowded with dead people desperate to cross over to the Underworld. And they'd damn well want to be paying us more.

"I got lucky, too," Sam says. "I saw the Stirrer before it saw me, stalled it, took its pistol and got in touch with Don."

"We were both lucky," Don says.

Sam wraps an arm around his waist. I look at Lissa, she smiles at me. I didn't know that these two were a couple: one of the many things on the list of stuff that I don't know about my friends, family and colleagues. Don bends down and gives Sam a kiss.

"I'm sorry about your parents, Steve," Don says. "But there was nothing you could have done."

I don't know how to respond to that. *Was* there something I could have done? I run the options through in my mind. I was just as much in the dark as anyone.

Don changes the subject fast. "So you said that Morrigan's alive?" He looks over at Sam as though to say, I told you so.

"Doesn't prove anything," Sam says. Aha! So Sam doesn't agree with Don!

"Last time I saw him, via the Hill, he was in Number Four, and he was wounded," I say. "Then an hour or so ago, a sparrow got a note through to me. I suppose he had a fair idea where I might be. Sparrows are good hunters."

"A sparrow. One of those inklings of his?"

I nod. "Yeah."

Don and Sam exchange looks. "He sent you here?" Don asked.

"Not here, exactly, just the general direction." I don't know where he's going with this, but I'm starting to not like it.

"We haven't spoken to Morrigan."

"Do either of you have your mobiles on?" Lissa asked.

Sam pales. She pulls her phone out of her handbag, it's a hot-pink number. She flips it open. "Shit."

"Turn it off," I say.

It starts ringing, and Sam jumps. We all do. She hurls it at the ground and stomps on it with her purple Doc Martens until it stops ringing and is nothing but bits of plastic and circuitry. But still it looks sinister somehow, and puissant, because we know it's too late.

Other than Morrigan, we're probably the last three Pomps in Brisbane, the lucky ones, and now we're clumped together. If Morrigan is behind all this... "We have to get out of here, right now."

And then a dead guy appears in the middle of the room. We're standing in a rough circle. He's tugged this way and that by our individual presences.

He blinks at us. "Um, where am I?"

We all look at each other.

"Queensland," I offer.

He shakes his head, and looks about the squalid room. "Shit, eh? Queensland. What's this? Am I...?"

"Yes," we all say.

"Well, what does it all mean?" He scans the three of us, as though looking for a point of egress. He's about to make a break for it. But I'm not anxious to pomp him, my insides are feeling tender enough. Don gestures furiously at me to do it, but I'm pretending I don't notice him.

"I don't know what it means. But it's all right," Don says. He winces and then gently touches the dead guy on the back. The fellow's gone.

"We're all playing our A game today," he says, looking from me to Sam and back again. When we say nothing, he shrugs. "I'll check the back."

I feel like an absolute shit, but I'm so glad I didn't have to make that pomp.

Don's at the back door, peering out, his rifle held clumsily in one hand. He stiffens, closes the door softly and backs away down the long hallway to the living room. "There's someone out there." Don's pale as a sheet. "Couldn't see them, but I could feel them."

Now that he's said it, I can too. It's similar to the darkness that I had felt around the Wesley Hospital. The air is slick with an unpleasant psychic miasma. It's catching in the back of my throat like smoke. Don is looking worse and I'm not surprised: he took that last pomp.

"Time to use the exit plan, I think," he says, glancing over at Sam.

She nods and lifts up the sledgehammer from the corner of the room. She looks like some weird combination of Viking god—blonde plaits hanging from beneath her beret—and hippy grandma.

Sam passes it to me and I grunt, the thing's heavy. Its plastic grip crinkles in my hands. I look at her, confused. How is *this* part of the exit plan?

"Steve, would you mind smashing a hole in the floor?"

"Not at all."

She points to the middle of the room. "About there would be good." Then she runs to the window, peers out and fires her pistol into the dark.

It's surprisingly easy to make a hole in the wooden floorboards—they're rotten—though every time I strike the floor, the whole house shakes and I wonder if I'm going to bring it down around our heads. Once the hole is big enough, even for Don, I step aside for the others.

Don drops down first, grunting as he hits the ground. Sam motions for me to go. I hesitate and she grimaces.

"Steve, I've got the gun. You go, and now."

I'm down and running at a crouch. Someone fires, and I'm not sure if it's them or us. I look back and watch Sam drop neatly through the hole. Her pistol flashes. Lissa's with me, and I don't think she could look more worried than she does. She darts away into the dark and is back in a heartbeat.

"There's three of them. Stirrers."

The moment she says it, their presence floods me. A foulness stings the back of my throat. "At least three," I whisper.

The house is musty and muddy underneath, and I'm getting mouthfuls of spider web. No spiders yet. I follow Don through a scrubby little garden and onto the road.

We don't stop running for three blocks, until we reach Don's brown transit van. Don's bent over, and having a spew. It's the perfunctory vomit of a heavy drinker. I wonder if I'm heading that way, too, since I've been hitting the drink pretty hard of late. Well, that's the least of my worries. Don straightens, wipes his mouth, and jabs his rifle butt at the van.

"In the back," he says to me, as Sam catches up to us.

I slide open the side door and scramble onto the hard bench seat inside. Sam's behind the wheel, Don beside her, and we're off with a squeal of tires. Sam takes the first corner so tightly that I'm thrown out of my seat and hit the corrugated metal floor with a grunt.

"Put your seatbelt on," Sam says. I clamber back into my seat and pull the seatbelt across my waist.

A car horn honks at us as we shoot past, and Sam gives it the finger.

"Keep out of the fast lane, ya dickhead!" Don yells.

Lissa's laughing. "Old people these days."

"You watch who you're calling old," Don says, "or I'll come back there."

Sam concentrates on the road.

"I hate driving in the dark." Don reaches over and flicks on the headlights.

"Don't you say a word," Sam growls.

We take another corner like we're a bunch of drunken hoons on a Friday night, and even with the seatbelt on I nearly slide off the bench again. Sam knows how to drive fast, but this van is hardly handling like it's on rails.

"So you really think Morrigan's involved in this?" I ask Don, as much to distract myself from Sam's driving as for my pressing need to know. The Morrigan argument seems absurd—I saw him wounded and I've known him for as long as I can remember. He talked me out of the nightmare of my break-up with Robyn, he's sat at the table for Christmas dinner. He's walked Molly—possibly more often than I did.

"He's about the only one who could pull it off. The man knows everything, runs everything. And we let him," Don says. "It's probably not a good idea to trust anyone at the moment."

Yeah, which is exactly the right thing to say to someone stuck in the back of a van while the two people up front both have guns. Then again, if they had wanted me dead I suspect that I'd be a corpse by now.

"One thing is certain," Don says, "we need to split up. Morrigan—or whoever's hunting us—wants us to stick together."

"Here?" Sam says.

Don nods. "Yeah, here will do." He smiles back at me. "Milton, not a bad suburb to dump you in. At least it's near the brewery."

Sam swings us off the road, and slams to a halt. Another car beeps its horn as it flies past, but Sam ignores it. "Sorry, Steve. I know you don't want to hear this, but Don's right. Together we're a bigger target."

Of course she was going to side with Don. They're lovers. "Are you two going to split up as well?" I ask, a little petulantly.

Sam nods her head, and I've never seen her look so sad. "That was the plan all along. We just wanted to see each other, before—"

"Before we sort this thing out," Don breaks in, "and make the bastards, whoever the fuck they are, pay." Don's out of the van and is sliding the door open. "Keep breathing. I'm going to try and get in touch with Mr. D. I don't think he knows about this."

"If he does," I say, "then none of it matters, we're all dead."

Don nods. "That we're still breathing makes me believe he doesn't. Mr. D has much more elegant tools at his disposal than guns."

Which is absolutely true. Death stops hearts, and stills brains with a breath. He could have killed every single Pomp with a thought. After all, he is disease, he is misadventure, and he is just stupid bad luck, almost all of which I've encountered in the last thirty-six hours.

"Speaking of which..." He digs around under the front passenger seat. "Aha!" Don passes something to me. A pistol. "Be careful with that, it's loaded."

I look at it like it's a scorpion. Sam rattles off some details about the weapon, which bounce just as rapidly off my skull. All I know is that it's a gun. You point it and squeeze the trigger.

"...You got that?" Sam asks.

"Yeah, um, yeah. Of course."

"We have to go." Don shakes my hand roughly and I wince. There might still be a piece of glass in there. Then he pats me on the shoulder. "You'll be fine."

"Good luck," I say, and wave at Sam. The faux smile she gives me is matched for false cheerfulness by the one I'm wearing. We're chimps surrounded by lions, grinning madly and pretending that the big cats are not circling ever closer, and that it's not all going to end in slashing claws and marrow sucked from broken bones.

"We'll be all right," Sam says. "You take care, and keep that Lissa with you." She glances over at Lissa. "And, you, look after this guy. He's one of the good ones."

"I will," we both say.

Don's already back in the van. I step out and slide the door shut.

Sam's off, crunching the gears and over-revving the engine, leaving me coughing on the edge of the road in a pall of black smoke.

15

"Think she needs to get that gearbox seen to," Lissa says. When I don't reply she looks at me more closely. "Are you OK?"

"I think so." Twin bars of tension run up my neck. I roll my head to the right and the crack's loud enough to make me jolt. I'm edgy all right. If this keeps up I'll be jumping at my own shadow, which might be sensible.

"Just you and me again, kiddo," Lissa says.

"There's worse company." My voice cracks a little. "Much worse. You've—I don't know what I'd—"

"Don't," she says, taking a step away from me, and I know what she means. There's no future for us. There can't be. That's not how this works. No matter what else has happened, she's dead, and I'm alive. The divide is definite.

But it's bullshit isn't it, because she's still with me. I'm not keeping her here. In fact my presence should be doing the reverse. She's a dead girl, and she shouldn't be here, but she is. That has to count for something.

"I hope they make it," I say, all the while wishing that Lissa had made it too. Though if she had, I'd probably be dead.

It's hardly a comforting thought, but there aren't any of those that I can find anyway.

We get a little further away from the road, closer to the rail overpass at Milton. A black car hurtles past, one of those aggressively grille-fronted Chevrolets that must burn through about five liters a kilometer. Its engines howl like some sort of banshee. I cringe, and drop to the ground. The bad feeling—mojo, whatever—coming from the car is palpable and all I can hope is that, at the speed they're going, they don't feel me. And they mustn't, or at least they don't stop. Maybe I'm not seen as a threat.

"Stirrers," I say, "a lot of them." I don't mention that one of them looked very much like Lissa.

Another car follows in its wake, likewise crowded, and this one driven by the reanimated corpse of Tim's father, my Uncle Blake. He's in his golf clothes, and would look ridiculous if his face wasn't so cruel, his eyes set on the road ahead. Once they've passed, I get to my feet and watch them rush up and down the undulations that make up this part of Milton Road.

In just a few moments they've run two sets of lights, nearly taking out a taxi in the process, and are already passing the twenty-four-hour McDonald's and service station, shooting up the hill past the Fourex brewery, leaving mayhem in their wake. Cars are piled up at both intersections, their horns blaring, shattered windscreens glittering.

"Their driving's almost as bad as Sam's," I say. Lissa drifts between the road and me. She looks tired and tenuous, her skin lit with the mortuary-blue pallor of the dead, and I wonder how much longer I'll have her with me. Not too much, I reckon. I ram that thought down, push it as deep as I can.

"Sam was flying, wasn't she?" Lissa says.

"Don't you mean, 'Miss Edwards'?"

Lissa's eyes flare, but she doesn't take the bait. "She and Don should be at least a couple of suburbs away by now."

I hope Lissa's right, but it's out of my control. "We need to keep moving," I say. Then, in the cold and the hard inner-city light, I'm suddenly dizzy. I stagger with the weight of everything; all those pomps. The ground spins most unhelpfully.

"You right?" Lissa's hand stretches out toward me but she doesn't touch, of course.

I take a deep breath, find some sort of center, and steady myself. Shit, I need food, anything. A Mars Bar is not enough to keep you moving for twelve hours, and I'd been running, hung-over, and on empty all day. Could I have picked a worse night to get so damn drunk?

"Yeah." I've started shivering, I am most definitely not all right. "I need to sleep." Exhaustion kneecaps me with an unfamiliar brutality. I almost convince myself that I could stumble down to the service station, or the McDonald's—both are open—but it's too soon on the tail of the passing Stirrers. Besides, those few hundred meters seem much, much further now. I need some rest, and a bit more time.

I look at my watch. It's 2:30. Dawn is a long way off. I walk under the train overpass, find a spot hidden and away from the road and try to ignore the smells of the various things that have lived and died, and leaked down here. Then I curl up under my coat, with my head on my bag, which makes a less than serviceable pillow.

"If I don't wake up," I say, smiling weakly, "well, see you in Hell."

"If you don't wake up, I don't know how I'm going to get there," Lissa says.

"You're resourceful, you'll find a way."

I slip—no, crash—arms flailing, into the terrible dark that I have no doubt will fill my dreams for the rest of whatever short fraction of life I have left. There's only sleep and running for me now. I'm too tired for self-pity, though, so that's one blessing at least.

I wake to the sibilant bass rhythms of passing traffic, with the bad taste of rough sleep in my mouth, and a host of bleak memories in my head. This is the first day that my parents weren't alive to see the dawn. I stamp down on that wounding thought as quick as I can.

My watch says nine, and the light streaking into my sleeping pit agrees with it. On the other hand, my body feels like it's still 2:30 am and I've been on a bender. I stretch. Bones crack in my neck and there's drool caked on my coat collar. How delightful.

"That was hardly restful," Lissa says.

"For you or for me?"

"I wouldn't call this resting in peace, would you?"

She points at the space around me, and there is blood everywhere. Portents. Stirrers. I'm not surprised but it's unsettling to see all that gore drawn here from the Underworld. It's a warning and a prophecy. Well, I've seen blood before, even if it's usually in the bathroom, or my own, curling down my fist, potent and ready to stall a Stirrer.

"I slept. That's one thing, no matter how poorly. How's my hair?"

"You really want to know?"

"You're chirpy."

"What can I say? I am—I *was*—a morning person."

"Well, you'll be pleased to know I was once a person who hated morning people."

"What changed your mind?" Her face draws in close to mine, well, as close as she can comfortably get without me pomping her. I'm treated to the scrutiny of her wonderful eyes. My cheeks burn.

My stomach growls. There's nothing like a stomach gurgle to change the subject—and this one is thunderous, a sonic boom of hunger. I rub my stomach. "I really need to eat."

Lissa gestures at all the blood. "Even with all this?"

I nod. "I can't help it. I *have* to eat."

Which is how we end up at a dodgy cafe in Milton, eating a greasy breakfast with black coffee. It's busy, but then again it's Thursday morning. The whole place smells like fat—cooking fat, cooling fat and partially digested fat being breathed out in conversation. That's the odor of the twenty-first century. I grin and bite down on my muffin.

The city's covered with a smoky haze. There have been grass fires around the airport. Spring's always dry and smoky in Brisbane—storm season's a good month off—and my sinuses are ringing. Everything about me is sore and weary, and even the sugar and coffee isn't doing much to help that. But it's something. Just like my snatches of nightmare-haunted sleep were something.

My head's buried in the *Courier-Mail*, partly because my face is on the cover. It's not a great picture, and I'm bearded in it, but it's enough. The article within is brief and speculative in nature. It doesn't look too good, though. I've been around too many explosions of late and too many people connected to me have died. I'm wanted for questioning. There's no mention of Don, Sam, Tim or Morrigan and there are suggestions that this is all part of some crime war. They've got the war bit right at least.

I give up with the paper. I need to think about something else for a moment, before the crushing weight of it all comes back.

"Could be worse," Lissa says. She's sitting opposite me.

"How?"

"You could be reading that in jail."

"Thanks."

"And you're really not that photogenic, are you."

"What the hell do you mean by that?"

"I mean, you're much, much better looking in the flesh."

"You're far too kind."

"Where did they get that photo anyway?" She peers at it.

"Facebook."

"Well, then, it really could have been worse. You've never dressed up like a Nazi obviously, or they'd have chosen that for sure."

I stare at some kids playing in the courtyard of the cafe, working out their weird kid rules, which generally seem to be about making someone cry while the rest look on, or shuffle off to their parents.

"You want to have children?" Lissa asks.

"Not really. OK, maybe, but look at me. I'm sleeping under bridges... I'm twenty-seven years old, with only a small chance of living more than a few hours. Not exactly great parent material." I shake my head, and my neck cracks painfully, again. I feel sixty-five today. "Did you ever want to have kids?"

Lissa shifts into the daylight, maybe so that I can't see her face.

"I don't know, maybe, I never felt settled enough. Wasn't much of a nester."

"Robyn—my ex—wanted kids," I say. "She just didn't want them with me."

"Then it was lucky you broke up." She doesn't come out of the light.

I wonder how Don and Sam are going. I haven't felt them pomp through me, so I hold onto the slim hope that they're alive. I mean, *I* am, and those two are infinitely more capable. They managed to rustle up a hideaway and some alone time. All I'd done was arrive in time to see my house, and then my car, explode.

After breakfast, I stand in the car park, looking at all those cars, wondering if that's the answer. I certainly need to get moving. A little further up Milton Road squats the bulk of the Fourex brewery. The whole suburb smells of malt and smoke, like a poor-quality whiskey, and though it was only yesterday that I had the mother of all hangovers, I surprise myself by actually desiring a beer.

I consider mentioning this to Lissa then think better of it. I'm sure she already thinks I have a problem.

"You've got a visitor," Lissa says.

The sparrow has been looking at me for some time, I feel. It gives an exasperated chirp. So Morrigan has found me again. I'm a bit nervous about that, thanks to Don. But I bluff it.

"Hey," I say. "Sorry, little fella." I have to remind myself that being patronizing doesn't improve an inkling's mood. I've never seen a sparrow glare before.

I reach out my hand and it jumps up, pecks my index finger hard, much harder than is necessary, drawing blood. It'd be a hell of a lot more pleasant if the buggers just needed a handful of seed.

The sparrow drops its message, then gives my arm another savage peck and strikes out at the air with its wings. I curse after it, then my jaw drops as two crows snatch the bird out of the sky and tear it in half before it can even shriek. It forms a small puddle of ink and brown feathers on the ground. Then, with a black and furious crashing of wings, the crows are gone. It looks like human Pomps aren't the only ones doing it tough.

The message is brief.

Phone.

M.

I hesitate, then look at Lissa, who shrugs. "What have you got to lose?"

We both know the answer to that. But there is so much more to gain, even if it's just clarifying who my real enemy is.

I switch on my phone, holding it like it's a bomb.

It rings immediately. I jump, swear under my breath, then pick up.

"Steven," Morrigan says.

I can hear a background rumble of traffic. "Where the fuck are you?" I ask. He's not the only one who can skip over small talk.

"Look, we don't have time," he says. "The phones, they can trace them. And the sparrows, well, I'm running out of tattoos. Something's attacking them as well."

"Crows," I say. "It's crows. I just saw them then."

"If someone's using Mr. D's avian Pomps, they're more powerful than I'd thought. This just keeps getting worse."

"Yeah, it does," I say. "How do I know you're not in on it?"

There's a long silence down the other end of the line. "The truth is you don't. But how long have you known me?"

I don't answer that one.

Finally Morrigan breaks the silence. "Steven, you have to trust me. I'm telling you, Mr. D has a rival. They need to kill all the Pomps, then they can start up their own outfit. There's going to be absolute chaos. Because while that's going on, there's no one to stop the Stirrers. In fact, I believe whoever is behind this is actually dealing with the Stirrers."

I could have told him that.

"Which is why we need to get together. If enough bodies stir, the balance will tip. We're talking end of days, Regional Apocalypse. It's not far off."

That chills me. The idea had already crossed my mind, but I hadn't really wanted to consider it. I may not have the greatest knowledge of Pomp history, but I know about this. Every one of the thirteen regions has experienced one or two of these down the ages. Death piled upon death. Stirrers outnumbering the living. It's a vast and deadly reaving. And there hasn't been a Regional Apocalypse in a long time.

Sure, there's been some bloody, terrible crap that's gone on in this country, all of which could be considered that way—genocides and wars—but this would be an end to life. *All* life. Stirrers don't stop at people. They don't even start at them, it makes sense to start at the bottom. Everything from microbes up would go. And it wouldn't be like a motion picture zombie apocalypse, or remotely close to an alien invasion—they're a walk in the park compared to a Regional Apocalypse. Stirrers don't bite their victims, they don't need to touch an unprotected person, they don't even need to be that close to them after a certain threshold point is reached. They're like a black hole of despair, and once they've taken enough joy and light, their victim is gone and there's another Stirrer getting about, snatching even more energy from the world.

"I don't know if I believe you. Maybe you're trying to draw me out." I feel terrible because I might as well be saying this to Dad. Before last night and Don's comments I would have trusted him with my life.

Morrigan sighs. "Who are you going to believe? Look, how can I be certain that you're not in on this somehow? Steven, you need to trust me."

Well, if he's actually the perpetrator he'd know.

"We're running out of time," Morrigan says. "Meet me at Mount Coot-tha, the cafe there. One o'clock." He hangs up on me.

I look at my watch. It's 11:30 already. I explain what's just gone on to Lissa.

"I don't like it," she says, which is beginning to sound like something of a running joke.

"Neither do I. But he's right. If enough bodies stir, things *will* tip, and there'll be nothing left within weeks." And I'm not being melodramatic. Where Pomps are conduits to the Underworld, Stirrers are gaping wounds—they're the psychic equivalent of blowing out the window in a pressurized plane, only instead of air, you've got life energy torn out of this world and sucked into the Underworld. One or two Stirrers is bad enough, but that would be only the beginning if we didn't stop them.

I remember seeing my first Stirrer when I was five, shambling away from my father, its limbs juddering as it struggled to control the alien body which it then inhabited. I remember the horror of it—the weird weight of its presence as though everything was tugged toward it—Dad squeezing my hand and winking at me, before pulling out his knife and slicing his thumb open; a quick, violent cutting.

He walked over to the newly woken thing and touched it, and all movement stopped. It was the first time I'd ever found a corpse—all that stillness, all that dead weight on the ground—comforting.

"Not so bad was it?" Dad had said.

The first one gave me nightmares. After that... well, you can get used to anything.

Stirrers are drawn to the living and repelled by Pomps. Well, they used to be, they've been attracted to them lately, which suggests they've realized that they've got nothing to fear.

But what it means is, whether I trust Morrigan or not, I have to get to Mount Coot-tha.

16

Mount Coot-tha is broad and low, really little more than a hill, but it dominates the city of Brisbane. Inner-city suburbs wash up against it like an urban tide line but the mountain itself is dry and scrubby, peaked with great radio towers, skeletal and jutting in the day and winking with lights in the evening.

I have two options.

I consider climbing the mountain, approaching the lookout and the cafe from the back way, up the path that leads from a small park called J. C. Slaughter Falls, but decide against it. If it's a trap, that way will be guarded, though our competition has shown a marked disregard for subtlety. Besides, I'm exhausted; the pathway is too steep, and the name is far too bleakly portentous for my liking.

So I take another bus, in my sunglasses, my cap jammed firmly on my head, with Lissa sitting next to me not at all happy with my decision. I don't blame her, I'm not too happy with it either.

I arrive at 12:58, check the return bus timetable then head up to the lookout cafe. Morrigan is hyper-punctual, as usual. He is sitting at a table sipping a flat white and looking at his watch. The cafe is crowded with tourists. I slip off my glasses and cap, glad my coat is in my bag. The evenings are cold but, even here on the top of Mount Coot-tha, midday is too warm for anything more than jeans and a T-shirt. My shirt's damp and clinging to me already.

Seeing Morrigan actually centers me a little. In fact, I'm surprised by how relieved I feel. Here's something I know, despite Don and Sam's suspicions. Here's a much-needed bit of continuity. I'm desperate for anything that might bring me back to some sort of normalcy. Morrigan's gotten me out of trouble before. I can't help myself—I grin at him.

He doesn't grin back, just nods, and even that slight tip of the head is a comfort. Morrigan isn't one to smile that often though we've been friends for a long time. His face and limbs always move as though contained and controlled, and never more than now. There's a rigidity to him that is at once comforting and scary. Morrigan has always been a bit of an arse kicker, expecting everybody to lift to his level. A lot of people have resented him for this trait; some have even resigned over the years because of it.

Morrigan and I share very few traits, if any. I've never met a more disciplined man. He jogs every morning and lifts serious weights, though he has the lean, muscly build of a runner. His gaze is usually as direct as Eastwood's Man With No Name, only harder.

But for all that I have never seen him look so old, or so fragile. The last couple of days have wounded him, but there's no surprise there. The job is Morrigan's life in a way that it has never been mine. I doubt if Morrigan has ever made a friend outside of the pomping trade. This must be tearing him apart, almost literally if he's experienced as many pomps as I have recently. The front of his shirt is streaked with dark patches that can only be blood.

But he's alive. Can't say that about many of my friends these days.

"You're late," Morrigan says, looking up at me and wincing with the movement. And all at once I am unsettled and back on the defensive.

"Not according to my watch," I say, and stare at him with as much suspicion as I can muster.

"Enough of this bullshit. You don't trust me. I don't blame you."

Morrigan coughs and wipes his lips with a handkerchief. Blood dots the material. He looks in pretty bad shape, his face colorless, his hands shaking as they bring his cup to his lips. "Yeah, I was winged," he says, in response to my expression. "I've got a cracked rib at the very least, and every time I lose a sparrow, I lose more than a sparrow."

He pulls up a sleeve. Bloody outlines of sparrows track up his arm. The neat Escheresque pattern of birds is ruined. One of the sparrows has lost an eye and dark blood scabs the wound.

I whistle, remembering the brutal efficiency of the crows. "How did you escape?"

"Luck, I suppose. They hit Number Four hard and fast. We're not a military organization." He nods to the bulge at my hip. "We're not killers. Jesus, Steven. I'm so sorry. Your parents. If only I'd seen this coming. But I didn't. The only one who could have was Mr. D, and he's gone."

Tears come—well, try to—and I stanch them. Now's not the time for crying. We have a Regional Apocalypse to stop. "You've got nothing to be sorry about," I say. "And there's no time. What's going on?"

"A Schism."

"A what?"

"I didn't believe they were real. There are records but only a few. When a Schism is successful, there's not a single Pomp left to record anything. As far as I can tell, once they got Mr. D, they left Queensland until last. We were deemed the least threatening of the states that make up the region, I suppose.

"Look at us—two days and there's only you, me, Don and Sam left. And the other regions would stay quiet about it. These things can spread."

"So you're saying someone has their eye on Mr. D's window office?" Lissa says, and I can tell from her tone that she has a fair idea who is to blame, and that he's sitting directly in front of me.

"Good afternoon, Lissa," Morrigan lifts his gaze to her, shielding his eyes from the sun. I realize that Lissa has chosen the spot where she's standing in order to make it difficult for him to see her. It's not helping me, either, her body doesn't really cut out the sunshine, rather it is filled with it. She's not the wan beauty I'm used to but a luminous, translucent figure that stings the eyes.

"Miss Jones, thank you." Her arms are folded. Well, I think they are. Her voice suggests it at the very least. "You don't deserve such familiarity."

Morrigan shrugs. "Miss Jones, if that's what you want."

"I don't want to be dead. I don't want to see my body parading about, inhabited by a Strirrer."

"Oh," Morrigan says. "I'm sorry, I can't even begin to understand how that must feel."

"It doesn't feel good."

"Feelings are all you have, Miss Jones. And you're right, it is my fault. If only I had been more focused."

No one says anything and the silence is long and awkward, until a coffee arrives.

"I took the liberty of ordering you a long black—asked them to bring it over when you arrived," Morrigan says.

I thank him and sip at it, then grimace. The coffee's burnt and bitter, but it's still coffee. "So what do we do?"

"We need to get to the morgues. We need to get to the funeral homes. We have to stop the stirring. If we can contain it here we might stand a chance."

Morrigan's phone rings. He jumps, then flicks it open. "Yes... No... If you must, but there isn't much time... All right."

He hangs up. Lissa and I are both looking at him suspiciously.

"Don," he says. "I spoke to him, too. He took some convincing, but he's swinging around to Princess Alexandra Hospital. Sam's on her way to Ipswich. I'm going to use the Hill and get to the

North—Cairns and Rockhampton. If we want Queensland to keep going we need to do this."

"What about the rest of the country?" I ask.

"I'm trying to arrange some support from other RMs, Suzanne Whitman in the U.S. for one, but there's a hell of a lot of trouble getting calls out. It's not easy, but I don't think anyone wants a Regional Apocalypse. That doesn't matter—I want you to do Wesley Hospital."

A prickle runs up my spine. The place had tasted terrible yesterday. It's not going to be any better now.

"You'll be a target," Lissa says to me.

"Weren't you listening, Miss Jones? We're already targets." Then Morrigan grabs my arm. "Be careful."

"I always am," I say, and almost believe it.

We part company, I don't know how he's going to make it down to the Hill. It's probably better that I don't. I look at my watch: five minutes until the next bus.

"I still don't trust him," Lissa says.

"That's your call."

"I want you alive. I want to see you through this. It's all I've got left."

"You don't know the man."

"Neither do you."

That hurts a little. I think of all the parties, the time he got me out of jail for some stupid misdemeanor involving beer and a fountain in South Bank. "Yes, I do."

I'm walking toward the bus stop when another voice stops me.

"Mr. de Selby, I need you to come with me."

"Shit," Lissa says.

Shit indeed.

"There doesn't need to be any trouble," the police officer says.

17

He's a young guy, no older than me, and tall, though hunched down, maybe self-conscious like me about his height, or maybe because he has a bad back. But I don't care either way because he is an officer of the law, and here I am on Mount Coot-tha, my house a smoking pile of wood, having stolen a car (well, borrowed a car, and only for a little while) and my own car having exploded. Oh, and I'm *not* happy to see him, that *is* a gun in my pocket. Shit, I'd forgotten about that. I consider my options.

"Just why do you need me to come with you?" Maybe I can talk my way out of this.

"I think you know why."

Honesty seems the best policy. At least the one most likely to end without bloodshed.

"I have a gun in my pocket," I blurt out. His face immediately tenses. "I'm going to lie down on the ground. You can take it from me, I'm not going to put up a fight."

"Just pass it to me," the officer says. "Handle first. Slowly."

I do what he says, I'm in enough trouble already. It's all I can do to stop my hand from shaking.

"Do you want to handcuff me or something?"

"Do I need to?" He's got a no-bullshit sort of expression. I shake my head.

Well, this is about the worst thing that could have happened. At least I don't have to wait for a bus. Every cloud, right?

I'm bundled into the back of the police sedan. It smells like pine disinfectant. The seat is immaculately clean, though someone has still managed to scrawl phalluses deeply into the headrest.

The car starts up.

"Hell of a day, eh," he says, passing me back the gun. I hold it uncertainly. This is not how I expected it to go down. "I put the safety on your pistol, Mr. de Selby, I'm amazed you didn't blow off your foot. Do you even know how to shoot that thing?"

"I—"

He doesn't seem to care that much, just keeps rolling on. "Don sent me. I'm Alex."

"Don sent you? Thank Christ! You know Don? You know about Pomps?"

"Half the force does, mate." He glances back at me through the wire. "So who's the bastard trying to kill my old man?" I didn't know that Don had a son. Another Black Sheep.

Lissa laughs. "Oh, he's Don's boy! Heard he was cute. Now the rumors have been confirmed." I look at her in disbelief and she winks at me lasciviously.

"You're not out of the woods though," Alex says. Glancing at him through the rearview mirror, I can see a lot of Don in him. The lantern jaw, the brilliant blue eyes. He's the sort of person who should be going through all this, and probably would have gotten to the bottom of it by now. Me? All I have is a passing acquaintance with mortality and a crush on a dead girl. "Stealing that car wasn't the brightest thing you could have done."

"Someone was trying to kill me."

"Yeah, like I said, not the brightest thing, but ballsy, all right. Find out who's behind this and we can make it go away. Right now, though, you're on your own, and pretty much regarded as Brisbane's, if not Australia's, biggest sociopath."

"I stole the car, yes," I say, "but that's it. I didn't have anything to do with the rest."

"I know that, Dad's told me. It's going to take time for people to cotton onto what's happening. And none of it's been helped by most of the bodies disappearing. Regardless, there's nothing we can do about this. This is your domain, and totally beyond our jurisdiction."

"But people have died. They're after your dad, too."

"Yeah, I know, which is why I'm going to help you—though this is entirely unofficial."

"I don't have much time," I say.

"I know," he says. "So where can I take you?"

I tell him, and five minutes later we're there. I get out and thank him.

Alex grins. "Don't worry about it. Just remember to keep the safety on that pistol—until you need to use it."

I watch the car pull away. "First break of the day," I say. "And it only took until 2 pm."

"Yeah," Lissa says, as we walk through the hospital grounds, heading straight for the morgue. It almost feels like coming home. "But what are we heading into?"

We both have a fair idea. The Wesley's feeling even worse than it did yesterday. Bile's rising in my stomach. My body's already reacting to this place and the creatures it contains.

And it gets worse as we get closer.

A park borders Wesley Hospital on one side, the train station on another. Coronation Drive is nearby, I can see the tall jacarandas that line the river. The Wesley is a private hospital but a big one, with new works always being constructed. Cranes and scaffolding generally cover at least one side of the building.

It should feel like a place of healing, not this sick-inducing death trap.

"Thank God," says an orderly, a fellow I recognize. His eyes are wide and wild. I can smell his fear. "Where have you lot been?"

"Busy, John. Busy." I don't have time to go into the details.

"At least we have these," John says. He lifts his sleeve, there's the bracing symbol tattooed on his arm. It's a good idea. Most orderlies working the morgues and mortuaries have them. You only need to see one Stirrer, and feel its impact on you, to change your mind.

"How many?" I ask.

"Seven."

I swallow uncomfortably. I've never seen that many Stirrers together in my life. This is bad, really, really bad. It's one thing to hear Morrigan talking about Regional Apocalypse, it's another, much more visceral experience, to face it alone.

"We've got them tied down. But someone is going to hear the screaming. You've got to—"

"I know what I've got to do," I say, a little shortly. I don't really want to do it, but I have no choice.

Dealing with seven Stirrers strapped to gurneys is not something I'm looking forward to. The first thing I encounter are their screams. Another orderly comes at us. "You need to do something!"

"That's what I'm here for," I say.

I walk into the room. Lissa follows me in, though she keeps her distance from the gurneys. A Stirrer could draw her straight through to the Underworld. I don't want her here with me—it's too dangerous—but, Christ, I'm glad she is.

Their presence (or absence) is choking. It's like stepping into a room with no air. It's freezing in here and condensation has turned to ice on everything, a sort of death frost. The Stirrers are flailing on the gurneys, held down tight, but not tight enough for my liking. I look at Lissa. She shrugs. She hasn't seen anything like this either.

I've heard about the world wars, how these things were common at the front where there was so much death gathered in one place. But this is inner-suburban Brisbane.

I sigh. Take out my knife and slice open a fingertip. Once the blood is flowing I reach out toward the first one.

"Can't stop us," it whispers, and then the others are taking up its cry, their voices not quite right. More gurgle than chant.

"This isn't good," Lissa says.

I look at her. "Tell me something I don't know."

"Just thought I'd say it."

"Can't stop us," the Stirrers chime in.

Yes I can.

I press my bloody finger to each Stirrer's hand. They still for good.

But the last one, a bulky fellow, snaps a hand free of its constraints. His fingers clench around my wrist. Bones creak and I wince. I yank my hand free and swing my blood-slicked fist at his face.

"Can't stop us!" he howls, then is gone, my bloody touch stalling him. I get out of that room as quick as I can.

That took more blood than it should have. The Stirrers are getting stronger.

I glance at John. "These won't stir again, and I'll return if I'm alive." I don't tell him how unlikely a proposition that may be when charted against the days—no, the hours—ahead. "But there will be more. I rather suspect that everyone who dies will be... reinhabited."

I incline my head at his tattoo. "You might want to brace as many rooms as possible with this." I give him a tin of paint. There's a few drops of my blood in it and it should provide some limited protection for the hospital at least.

John frowns, as he pockets the paint tin. "And where will you be?"

"If I can come back, I will. I'm just not sure that it's an option."

I'm still a bit shaky as we walk out of the hospital. Stalling takes a lot out of you. One or two is bad enough, but seven is off the chart. Morrigan was right, we're nearing some sort of tipping point. The Stirrers can sense something is wrong. I can imagine the queues of Stirrer souls just crowding around waiting to get into newly dead bodies. Humans have become prime real estate in a way that hasn't happened since the darkest days.

A basketball center's to the right of us, on the other side of the train line. There must be a couple of games going, I can hear the screech of shoes, the indignant shriek of whistles.

"We need to get the system up and running again," I say to Lissa.

She shakes her head. "Sorry, *you* need to get the system up and running."

"Well, running might be a good idea," says a familiar voice. Don's ghost is standing by Lissa. They circle each other.

"Where's Sam? Is she alive?" I demand.

Don shakes his head. "I don't know."

"I'm sorry, Don. Really, really sorry," Lissa says.

Don fixes her with a stare. "You know how it is."

His form flickers. He blinks.

"What the hell happened?" I ask.

Don grimaces. "I feel stupid." His irritation is without much edge, though. He's already sliding away into the land of the dead, though he manages to fix me with a stare. "It's Morrigan."

"I knew it," Lissa says. "All that polite bullshit. All that sympathy. What an absolute dickhead."

"The bastard tried to pomp me, too. But I managed to—" he glances at Lissa. "Christ, how do you keep this up?"

"It gets easier."

Don shakes his head like he doesn't believe her. "Morrigan's decided he doesn't need to hide now. And there's something you need to know: every time a Pomp dies, he becomes more powerful. Whatever presence or energy they have, well, he gets it. That's something he let slip."

Which means he must be pretty powerful now if there's only him and Sam and me left.

"But I was speaking to Morrigan this morning, at Mount Coot-tha," I say, feeling the blood drain from my face. Then I do what anyone would do in that situation—start with denial. "It can't be him. He didn't look powerful at all. He told me—"

"Well, he's a fine actor. Must be, to have pulled all this off. Steve, the bastard shot me," Don snaps. "How much more of a definitive delineation of betrayal do you need? We have to get you out of here, out of the city. Morrigan's holding off on killing you now."

"I met Alex," I say. We're running out of the car park and onto the road, then around under the train tracks and into the basketball court's car park. My head is spinning. I really thought I could trust Morrigan. It had been a good feeling, having a central point in all of this, the idea that someone was guiding the ship again, and now...

Don grins. "My Alex, a good boy. Total Black Sheep. I love the kid. Was going to go to the footy with him on Sunday. Broncos match. Hate the Broncos, but the boy's dead keen." Don shook his head. "I couldn't believe it, about Morrigan, I mean. I started trusting him when you made it alive down off Mount Coot-tha. I think that was the plan all along. No offense, Steven, but Morrigan reckons he can kill you off when he likes, when the rest of us are done with. But he doesn't count—"

Don's gone with a soft sound like the ringing of a tiny bell, a sparrow cutting through him, pomping him, its wings whirring. I'm still blinking at the sight of Don sliding out of non-corporeal existence, trying to understand why Morrigan might be keeping me alive. The bird flits past me.

It's one of Morrigan's sparrows. The inkling twists sharply in the air and hurtles toward Lissa.

I'm running at her, trying to get in between her and the sparrow. If it gets there first then I'm alone. I just make it, the sparrow hits my chest hard enough to hurt. It thumps off and onto the ground, and I stomp down. Little sparrow bones crunch beneath my boot. And then it sinks away into a tiny puddle of ink and feathers.

Hope that hurt you, Morrigan.

And then there are more of them. And more.

Someone slows in their car beside me, and then picks up speed. I don't blame them, I must look insane thrashing and swinging at the little birds. I dance around as one sparrow, then another and another and another, descends. They're all around us. I can't do anything about it.

But something else can. Crows crash from the sky, like the eagles in *Lord of the Rings*. If someone had started yelling "*The crows are coming! The crows are coming!*" I would have cheered. The black birds are cawing and crying, snatching sparrows out of the air with their dark beaks in a maelstrom of wings above and around us.

Then the crows are gone and the only remnants of the melee are inky puddles.

"That was... interesting," Lissa says.

"Wasn't it just," I say.

We look at each other. There's another player in the game. The sparrows are Morrigan's; the crows, they belong to Mr. D. So maybe he's not as in the dark as we believe.

I'd seen Morrigan form an inkling once, at a party. He was charming then as usual. We were talking about tatts, comparing our ink. My cherub had gotten a few appreciative comments, newly cut. Then Morrigan, one never to be outdone, had said, "That's a fine tattoo, boy, but can you do this?"

He'd pulled up his sleeve to the first Escheresque tangle of sparrows that ran from his sinewy biceps and over his back. He whistled then, a shrill, short note, and a bird pulled free of his flesh. "Inklings are quite simple once you get the hang of it."

The sparrow flew around the room, picking up snacks and bringing them back to him.

It had appeared effortless, until I saw him later, coming out of the bathroom. He'd been a bit shaky on his feet. I could smell the sweat on him, even over his cologne. I didn't want him to have a stroke, still, I'd respected his pride and just quietly helped him to a chair. If only I had known what it would come to . . . Well, I would have kicked the legs out from under him.

That had been one sparrow, now we had seen tens of them. And he was using them to pomp the dead. Don was right, Morrigan's powers had increased incredibly.

18

"So what do we do?" I ask, staring at the ink-stained ground. "I can't see how I can keep you safe."

"First we're going to need cover," Lissa says, and heads back toward the hospital car park. I follow, hurrying to keep pace.

"You're going to have to bind me to you and this realm," Lissa says.

"I'm unfamiliar with the process. I've heard of bindings, but never seen it done."

"There's a reason for that. OK, a couple of them, the first being that it's old. You wouldn't have come across it unless you're particularly interested in the history of pomping. And there really isn't much written about Pomps. It takes quite a bit of research." Lissa smiles, a little too mockingly for my liking. "And, no offense, you don't exactly strike me as the studious type."

I take immediate offense at that. "Morrigan never exactly encouraged it."

Lissa nods. "Well, we know why now. Anyway, people don't talk about this stuff, in the specific. You have to really dig. The process is... It's a little confronting." She flashes me another smile. "But if we don't do it, I'm worried that Morrigan will pomp me, and you need me." She's so right, but I rail against that a little. She can see it in my face, and her laugh is both affectionate and mocking. "Don't you try and suggest otherwise, laddy."

We're under the cover of the car park. "OK, so how do I do it? How do I bind you? It sounds pretty kinky, you know."

Lissa reddens, just a little, and I get the feeling that she's more embarrassed for me than anything else. "Well, it sort of is."

"What do you mean?"

"Most of these types of ceremonies involve blood, but in this case that's not enough, because you're not pomping, you're binding." Her eyes seem to be having trouble meeting mine. "You're going to need semen. Your own semen."

"Here?" I turn in a quick circle. There's no one about, but this is a car park. Of course I'm sure there's been plenty of that here, but not mine. "I'm supposed to—"

"This is no time to be squeamish, or prudish," Lissa says impatiently. "There might be a whole flock of bloody sparrows on their way."

"Pressured is the word that comes to mind, actually."

"Performance anxiety, eh? Well, I'm dead, it'll be our little secret. Besides, I've already seen you naked."

"Well, there's naked and then there's naked." I am utterly exposed out here, and it's cold. The odds of me being able to ejaculate are pretty grim. Lissa leers at me. That doesn't help.

She rubs her hands together. "Well? Pants down, prong up."

"Could you look away?"

"I'll look away," she says. "Just think about some of those busty trollops and you'll be OK."

Wicked woman!

There's got to be cameras around here somewhere. I imagine the image as I, um—present—another addition to the caseload against me.

"Hurry up," Lissa hisses at me. "I can hear a car coming."

OK, deep breaths: a half dozen of them. I know that I have to do this, that there's nothing else to be done, but I'm feeling very peculiar about it. In fact, I'm feeling very dirty-old-mannish. Friction isn't enough. Nor is strength of will.

It has to be done. It has to be done.

And it is. And at the moment of ejaculation, a quick hard orgasm, I see Lissa's face.

I open my eyes, and I'm looking into Lissa's face. Oh. My. God.

"You were supposed to look the other way," I grumble, my face burning.

"Good work," she says, ignoring me, though she seems a bit flushed, too.

I've got the semen in a handkerchief. I'm not sure if I've ever been more embarrassed in my life.

"Can I have a look at your, um, handiwork?"

I comply, careful to keep my distance.

She frowns, looks like she's doing maths in her head. I'm not exactly sure how the dead perceive the world but she couldn't possibly be counting the little swimmers. "That should be enough."

"It better be."

The car drives slowly past. I give it a wave. Nothing to see here, now.

19

Crouching down like some maniacal Gollumesque creature, I scrape with a stone the Four Binding Elements (as Lissa called them), basically four triangles, each containing a circle on the cement of the footpath. Lissa stands in the middle of my esoteric squiggling.

"You need a drop of your doings for the center of each circle," Lissa says.

I mark each one, then step back.

"Now, look at me. We need eye contact, and total concentration."

I take a deep breath and gaze at her. It's not gazing, it's grazing, I hunger for her stare. I could look into those eyes forever, they are a fire in my chest and in my stomach. Lissa holds my gaze. I don't know how long we stand that way; it's intense but pleasurable, how my orgasm should have been. The air around us pushes in. I feel the weight of all that sky, and I am bound in a kind of leaden warmth. And then it bursts. The pressure is gone in an instant. And it's just me and Lissa, and the car park. The air is cold. I let out a breath.

Lissa stumbles back from the circle of triangles, her eyes wide. She looks at me, her lips moving soundlessly. Whatever moment we shared has passed. She smiles. "Well, you've bound me. I cannot be pomped on this plane, except by an RM, and we haven't seen too many of those about lately, have we? It won't last forever, but for the next few days it should do."

A few days are probably all I have, anyway, though I keep that thought to myself. I've already shared far too much with Lissa in the last half-hour.

She winks. "Naughty, isn't it?"

"Easier than I thought," I say.

"Well, I *was* thinking that about you," Lissa says.

"So what do we do now, have a cigarette?" I'm shaking a bit, my face is still burning with the intimacy of the ceremony.

"If only... but what we have to do is get you out of Brisbane. We need time to think. To get Morrigan on the backfoot."

"I'm not so sure. Tremaine said we should contact Mr. D."

"Let me tell you about Eric Tremaine. He's a bit of a tosser but, of course, you know all about that." She chortles. "I don't know if you can totally trust anything he has to say. Me, on the other hand..."

Tremaine must have really had it in for me. Sure, I'd let down the tires on his car at a convention last year, but it had just been a bit of fun. Maybe that was one of the reasons; other people had found it a lot of fun too. After all, it was how Tremaine had gotten the nickname, Flatty. "One of my reasons for breaking up with him was that he was too negative."

"It's hard to be upbeat when you've just been killed," I offer. I can't believe I'm coming to the guy's defense.

Lissa glares at me. "You're telling *me* that?"

Yeah, that's me, Mr. Sensitive. "I'm sorry," I say.

"I still agree with Don," Lissa says. "You need to get out of here. Out of Brisbane altogether. And out of mobile range. This is Queensland, there's got to be lots of places like that. Morrigan knows he can't let the Stirrers grow in serious numbers. He wants to be the new RM, and if he's going to become part of the Orcus, he needs to keep the Stirrers in check. Leave it up to him. I think you have to take yourself out of the picture for a while."

"I know a few places that—"

"No, they have to be places you don't know, towns that Morrigan isn't going to look."

She's right. And Queensland *is* perfect for that. I could jab my finger at a map of the state with my eyes closed and find a hundred of them. Once you get out of the south-east corner or away from the coast, most of the country is hot and dry and empty.

People get lost there all the time. Often they're never seen again.

I find some cover after sunset, and try and rest while Lissa keeps guard. I wake from bad dreams to the dark.

"I have to call Tim," I say.

We stop at a pay phone in a park near the Regatta Hotel. I grab the handset and pause, disturbed by what I'm feeling in the air.

They're out there in the dark. Stirrers, stumbling through the night. At first they'll gather in the deserted places, the quiet places, and when there are enough of them together they won't bother hiding.

If Morrigan doesn't get on top of this soon, there will be a lot of suicides over the next few weeks, a lot of unexplained behavior. Bodies will disappear from morgues, people will see their deceased loved ones walking in the street, or wake with them in their bed. And there will be no joy in the occasion, because they are not loved ones, just something that possesses their memories: an imperfect and deadly mimic.

Stirrers are voids. They will turn a house cold, and they will swallow laughter. They are the worst aspects of time only sped up and grown cruelly cunning. Bad luck follows them.

They'll keep their distance from me, if they can. If they have a chance they'll try and kill me, from as great a distance as possible, with a gun or in a hit and run. They can sense me, but I can sense them as well. And I'm more practiced at it, and I've only just had to face off seven of the bastards in the Wesley. You could say my palate was refined.

Which was why I could tell that the man pushing the swing in the park was a Stirrer, even from a few hundred meters off.

I slide my knife across my palm, wincing a little. And then I come up on him casually, trying not to look like he's where I'm heading. It works for a while.

He finally feels my approach and turns, but now I've got up quite a head of steam. The Stirrer runs from the swing set toward me, but he doesn't quite inhabit the body properly. After all, people spend the first couple of decades of their life coming to terms with their bodies. It's one of the most obvious ways of telling them apart.

Their flesh will be bruised, the nails and hands will often be dirty. The longer they stay in the body the less clumsy they become, but there are limits. They will never attain the kind of grace that even a relatively clumsy person has—this isn't their universe.

The Stirrer slips, then gets to his feet. I grab his back, and he wrenches away, so I tackle him, a perfect round-the-legs tackle. My hand brushes cold flesh.

The Stirrer rushes through me, and it is like swallowing glass. I push myself away from the motionless body, my chest heaving.

"Rough stall?" Lissa looks at me with concern.

I nod, some stalls aren't too horrible and some are like a punch to the stomach. This was the latter. Jesus. Normally I would have called for a pick-up, someone to take the body and dispose of it, but that's not an option, now.

The Stirrer opens its eyes, sits up: sees me. Its panicked expression is almost comical. It lets out a groan and struggles to its feet, legs shaking. The blood on my hand must have dried too much to have a permanent effect.

I reopen the wound, fresh blood flows.

The Stirrer stands there, unsteadily. Its eyes dart left and right of me, looking for some sort of escape route.

"Fuck off back to the Underworld," I growl, and slap my hand against its face. The body drops. This stall doesn't hurt as much. The Stirrer hadn't inhabited the body long enough to get a good hold on it, but there's more pain to it than there ought to be.

"That's not good," Lissa says. And it isn't. That was way too fast.

The Stirrer's eyes flicker. And I do it again, this time sitting on its chest while I get out my knife.

I slice open one of my fingers, making a fresh wound, and touch the Stirrer's cheek. There's a definite finality to that stall, like a door slamming shut. The body stills for good. Nothing will get through now, as long as I stay alive.

I get to my feet. We have to keep moving.

"The world's gone to hell," I say as I dash across the park, Lissa by my side.

"Not yet," she says.

And I know she's right. Things can get a whole lot worse, and they probably will.

"I have to see, Mr. D," I say. "There's no way I can leave Brisbane with this going on. It's obviously getting out of Morrigan's control."

"And I'm telling you that's not going to help anymore—at least, not now, maybe later. You just need to stay alive for a little longer, get out of Brisbane. Come back later."

"But if that's what Morrigan wants—"

"I think he wants you in Brisbane. But regardless, I want you alive. Neither of us know enough about Schisms to hang around, except I can guarantee this much: all the other regions will have closed down communication. They don't want word of this spreading. Something like this could see a whole heap of madness. No, you need to keep moving, and Brisbane's not big enough for that to work."

I head back to the pay phone on the edge of the park and dial a number I know off by heart.

"I thought it would be you," Tim says. His voice is strained, the kind of strained that the last few days will engender. I look at my watch: it's three-thirty in the morning.

"Not getting many calls?"

"Too many, but I just thought it would be you. I'm glad to hear your voice."

I'm glad to hear his as well. "We need to meet," I say.

"The Place?"

"Yeah, that'll do. I have to get out of Brisbane." It's not far away, I can easily walk it.

"I'm going to have to organize a few things," Tim says. "You going to be safe until mid morning?"

"Yeah. I think I can manage that." I'm not sure if I can, but Tim knows what he's doing.

"You OK?"

"No. You?"

"Not at all."

Honesty is such a wonderful thing.

20

Delightful," Tim says, glaring at a gob of spit on the ground by his foot. It's fluorescent green and ants have encircled it like a besieging army, a boiling hungry black mass. "That your handiwork?"

I shake my head, thinking about some of my recent handiwork. "If I start spitting that sort of stuff you'll know I'm not long for this world."

I doubt I'm long for this world as it is, but neither of us goes there. I'm feeling very rough this morning. The souls have kept coming, and the drain I slept in last night was hardly salubrious. I reckon I've slept maybe three hours in the last twenty-four. I know I don't smell that good.

The first thing Tim did was throw some clothes at me. I've got my backpack with me, but it doesn't hurt to have some more. They feel better than what I was wearing, not exactly a perfect fit. The jeans are OK, a little loose around the waist, but my wrists jut a good ten centimeters out of the sleeves. I'm rolling them up as Tim gets to work on his third cigarette.

We used to smoke cigarettes here, when we'd first got our licenses. Or sometimes a little weed, but not for a long time. Tim offers me a cigarette, but I decline. "Yeah, stupid idea." But he lights one up and has a puff.

"The Place" is a small park in Paddington. Very suburban, but old-Brisbane suburban. Big weatherboard Queenslanders surround us, all of them in far better condition than the one I'd belted my way out of in Albion, but essentially the same design. Their verandahs are empty. No one is that interested in being outside.

Tim has driven here, in yet another car that I don't recognize. I apprise him of the situation in detail that I didn't want to disclose over the phone. Tim's opinion I trust, though he doesn't need to know anything about the binding ceremony. Lissa corrects me often enough that, even though Tim can't hear her side of the conversation, he laughs. "You're sounding like your parents."

I glare at him. "Cute. Real bloody cute."

"Schism, you think," Tim says. "I've heard of them."

"Really?"

"You'd be surprised how much the government's got on you. Think about it, Steve. Technically you don't exist. And what are the rules binding government in dealing with things that don't exist?"

"If this goes wrong everybody dies, Tim."

"Which is why we think there should be tighter state controls."

"Do you really think that?"

Tim grinds his cigarette out beneath his boot. "Look at what's happening. Do you think we could fuck this up as badly?" Tim sighs. "But fuck that. Other than Sally and the kids, you're all the family I've got left. You know that me and Aunt Teagan don't get on."

"Who does?"

"Lots of people, just not her family."

"Have you talked to Sally?"

"As much as I can. I don't trust the phone lines either. She says she's sorry. We all are."

"Yeah."

"If locking you up in a room would keep you safe, I would, but you'd find a way to get into trouble." Tim knows me better than I know myself sometimes. "I can understand this is as scary as all hell.

But I agree with Lissa, you have to get out of town. I've spoken to Alex, did that after I got off the phone with you. He'll be here soon."

"You know Don's son?"

"You really need to be more sociable, Steve. Maybe it's guilt or something, but we Black Sheep stick together."

"That's a bit ironic."

Tim ignores me. "I've talked to Alex, and he's got a car for you. You take that, and you get the hell out of here until it all cools down, or whatever it needs to do."

I don't think it will cool down. Not in the way Tim means or hopes. "What about you?"

"Some of us have to work for a living," Tim says, and now he's the one trying to sound all casual. He snorts. "Look, don't you worry about me. I can take care of myself. It's what I do for a living. Anyway, you think my minister could take a crap without me?"

That's policy advisors for you. "Maybe I will have a cigarette." But it's a mistake, I'm coughing after the first puff.

"Smoking never took with you," Tim says wryly, picking out his fourth cigarette in half an hour. "Lucky bastard."

Alex pulls into the park flashing his headlights. Lissa shakes her head. "You call that a car?"

"Hey, don't diss my wheels." I'm not sounding that convincing.

Even Tim laughs. "I can't remember the last time I saw one of that... um... vintage on the road."

Alex opens the door and gets out of the multi-coloured, mid-seventies Corolla sedan. It's a patchwork of orange, black and electric green. He looks from me to Tim, who is actually laughing so hard he can't breathe. I'm not far behind my cousin. It's the first time I've laughed like that in—well, in a long time.

"What's so funny?" Alex demands.

21

"There's a full tank of petrol. That'll get you on your way. Wherever that is." Alex chucks me a phone, and a handful of sim cards. "You'll get one call with each of those, I reckon. Probably more, but better safe than sorry. They've probably got the network tapped. Morrigan doesn't do anything by halves. Chuck them away when you're done."

"I will. I'm sorry about your father."

Alex stops me with a look. "I know you are. Let's just keep you alive, eh."

He tosses me the keys. I unlock the front passenger door and put the phone on the seat.

God knows where Alex got the car from, probably the same place as the various other bits of contraband sitting under the blanket behind the front seat. I've got a feeling that if I open the glove box I'll find half a kilo of something or other. I open it. There's a yellowing service manual, which looks like it should be in a museum, a wad of cash that must come into thousands of dollars, a charger for my mp3 player, and a pair of aviator sunglasses. What the hell, I slip the sunnies on.

"Well, I'll be your wing girl, Maverick," Lissa says, flicking me a salute.

"Shut up, you."

I look at all that money. With that and the money I took from my place I have an alarming amount of cash. "If any cop stops me, I reckon I'm in trouble."

Alex shakes his head. "If any *officer of the law* stops you, you get them to call this number." He hands me something he's written on a Post-it note.

"They call this number, and I'll be fine?"

Alex grimaces. "It's by no means a Get Out of Jail Free card. If you drive carefully no one's going to stop you."

"Don't worry, Officer, I don't intend to get any traffic infringements."

Tim chuckles, but Alex doesn't. He looks at his watch. "I'd wait an hour or so before heading out of the city. Go with the traffic. You'll be harder to follow."

"Harder to tell if I'm being followed, too."

Alex shakes his head. "Nah, these guys are pretty obvious. You'll know if someone's following you."

"And what do I do if they are?"

"You drive, as fast as you can."

Lissa snorts. "Which won't be very fast in that car."

I thank Alex for everything including the number, which I slip into my wallet. Alex's eyes follow the movement.

"I just hope you don't have to use it," he says.

My face is raw. The only razor I could get my hands on was as blunt as a toy pocketknife, but I need to look clean-shaven. My stubble marks me more obviously than anything else, though I can't say I like the bare face beneath. At least the hair's looking good. I'm wired on adrenaline and cups of strong black coffee, and driving an old bomb out of Brisbane, following the Western Freeway. It's the fastest route out of the city if you want to head toward the low mountains that make up the granite belt.

Up in the mountains, as low as they are, the air will be cool, even this late in spring—and the mobile reception should be terrible.

The car is older than I am, though Alex assured me it would run like a dream... Yeah, a patchwork dream. Lissa's already calling it Steven's Amazing Technicolor Dream Car. And I must admit that the car *is* running smoothly. Corollas from this era are about as unstoppable as the Terminator, and every bit as ugly.

"Any tunes?" Lissa asks.

I try the radio. Only AM. We get a couple of stations playing classical, and a talkback radio show, all leavened with a fair bit of static. Lissa sticks her head through the front windscreen, which is quite disconcerting.

"That explains it," she says. "The aerial's been broken off."

The stereo itself is fairly new. I link up my mp3 and we have music. Radiohead, intercut with Midlake, is a perfect soundtrack for my mood.

The sun's setting. Brilliant in its suspension of red dust, it's the starkest, most beautiful sunset I've ever seen, and I'm driving into it like some character out of a movie, crashing into the apocalypse. Number Four and the Hill are sliding away from me. And while that should be some sort of relief, all it does is leave a bad taste in my mouth. I'm deserting my city, and this is no movie.

We stop at Stanthorpe, about 200 kilometers southwest of Brisbane. I get a single room on the ground floor of a boxy old hotel, best for a quick exit. The carpet is about the same era as my car, a combination of curlicues and some sort of vomit-colored flowers—why were the seventies all about vomit colors? It's the ugliest thing I've ever seen, almost hypnotically ugly. But it's a survivor; you can barely make out the cigarette burns, which is something you can't say for the bedside table or the tablecloth which, while perfectly clean, is dotted with melty holes. There's a no smoking sign on the wall by the door.

The first thing I do is mark the doors and windows with a brace symbol.

The second thing is open a beer from the fridge.

I'm sitting there, in my underpants and a T-shirt, counting the cigarette burns on the tablecloth when I look up and into Lissa's eyes. "What do you do when I'm sleeping?" I ask her.

"Look at you," she says, and I laugh.

"Seriously?"

"Seriously. I look at you and I think. You'd be surprised how patient you can be when all you are is thought."

Thought is so fragile. A strong wind could blow it away like a dandelion. That fills me with a dreadful sorrow.

"How long's this binding going to hold?"

"I don't know. Do you want to break it?"

"No!"

"Are you sure about that? You've only had grief since I came along."

"Less than some of my girlfriends," I say.

"Girlfriend, eh?"

"It's more of a marriage. After all, we're bound together."

"Well, at least you haven't started nagging me yet," Lissa says, giving me a dirty look. "And the only sex we've had resulted in your orgasm. You didn't even expect me to fake one. So I suppose it's a marriage all right."

"Ha! I'll have you know we de Selbys are extremely generous lovers. Besides, you're a ghost."

"I still have my urges," Lissa says, a little defensively.

"Well, I wish you had more corporeality," I say.

"So do I."

We stop ourselves there. Our eyes meet, and we both turn sharply away.

I finish my beer, then walk to the bathroom and clean my teeth with a finger and some salt. I wonder if I'm being a dickhead. Probably. More than probably. I know it with deep certainty, and I'm suddenly ashamed. This girl brings out the best and the worst in me.

I've experienced more with Lissa, and with more intensity than with anyone else I've known, including Robyn—then I catch myself. It's the first time I've thought of her in what feels like days. Well, that's something at least. And here we are in this old hotel room which smells of smoke and cheap instant coffee, the traffic rumbling outside, the road's endless breath. It's the lovers' cliché, this.

I step out of the bathroom and look at Lissa. Those amazing green eyes hold me again. This time she doesn't turn away.

"You can have a quick wank if you want," Lissa says, and smirks.

I grimace. "I'm going to sleep."

After switching off the light there's half an hour of restless tossing and turning on a mattress that's firm and soft in all the wrong places.

Lissa chuckles. "Go on. You'll feel better for it," she whispers in my ear.

"Shut up."

22

I never sleep well in strange places, and that's all I've had these past few nights. At least the hotel is better than a highway underpass or a stormwater drain. My sleep is light and dream-fractured. There's a lot of running. I keep seeing the faces of my family and they're yelling at me, but I can't hear what they're saying. All I get is the urgency. And then there are a couple of nightmares on high rotation. I'm dreaming of:

Bicycles. They're tumbling from the sky.

Wheels spinning, gears shifting, and when they strike the ground they make skullish craters, the orbits of which cage vivid green eyes. Every death's head skull stares at me with Lissa's eyes.

It's not that far away, a voice whispers.

A bicycle strikes me hard. Gears grind down my arm. I drop to a crouch, cover my head with my hands. Warm blood trails from my wrist.

Duck and cover doesn't work anymore. It never really did.

I recognize the voice, it's—

I remember the first time I saw Mr. D. I was about ten and Dad had taken me to work. Even then I had a clear idea of what my parents did. Death was never such a big deal in my family. Cruelty, unfairness, rugby league—these were often spoken of—but not death, other than in the same way one spoke about the weather.

So I guess I was in something of a privileged position. Most kids my age were just starting to realize that such a thing as their own demise was possible, where I already considered it a natural part of existence.

Dad had told me it was time, but I hadn't really understood until he took me into Number Four. There was Morrigan, who scruffed up my hair. Number Four tingled around me with all the odd pressures of multiple worlds pulling and pushing at my skin like ghostly fingers. It was a peculiar sensation, and unsettling.

Then I saw Mr. D and he terrified me.

"Is this your boy, Michael?"

Dad nodded. "This is Steven."

"My, he's grown."

I realized that he must have seen me before. Well, I knew that I hadn't seen him—how could I forget? His face, it shifted, a hundred different expressions in a second, and yet it was the same face. He crouched down to my height, and smiled warmly.

"You were just a baby when I saw you last. Have you had a good life so far? Do you want to be a Pomp like your father?"

I nodded my head, confused. "Yes, sir," I said.

"Oh, none of that. Mr. D will do fine. The age of formalities is deader than I am." He looked up at Dad. "He's certainly your boy," he said. "Very brave."

I didn't feel brave at all.

He looked back at me, and I saw something in his eyes, and it horrified me. There, reflected back at me, was a man on his haunches, face covered in blood, howling. And a knife: a stone knife.

I let out a gasp.

Death held my hand, his fingers as cold and hard as porcelain in the middle of winter, and he squeezed. "What's wrong?"

"N-nothing."

"Not yet, anyway," Mr. D said, and he smiled such a dreadful and terrible smile that I have never forgotten it.

And I dream of it still, even when I don't realize that's what I'm dreaming of. Shit, that grin creeps up on me when I'm least expecting it. There was a bit of the madness of Brueghel's "Triumph of Death" in it, though I didn't know that at the time, and something else. Something cruel and mocking and unlike anything I'd ever seen.

I have spoken to Mr. D since, and nothing like that has happened again. Of course, it doesn't matter anymore, but it did then, and it haunted me for over a decade. It's true, isn't it? You drag your childhood with you wherever you go. You drag it, and it sometimes chases you.

I wake, and then realize that I'm not awake. The sheets cover me, and then they don't. I'm naked, standing in the doorway, and they're out there, a shuffling presence, a crowd of wrongness rapidly extending through the country.

You need to hurry, Steven. I can feel every single one of them. They shouldn't be here. But of course they are, there's no one to stop them.

You wait out here, and it will be too late.

You have to call me.

I turn to see who is talking, and I know, and am not surprised.

Mr. D is a broken doll on the floor. He's a drip in the ceiling. A patch on the floor. He's smiling.

And then Lissa's there and she's gripping an axe. The smile on her face is no less threatening than Mr. D's, and it's saying the same thing. Death. Death. Death. In one neat movement the axe is swinging toward my head. I hear it crunch into my face and—

I wake to dawn, feeling less than rested. My face aches and I know I've come from some place terrible.

"Not a good sleep?" Lissa's looking down at me.

The image of an axe flashes in my mind. It takes a lot not to flinch.

"What do you think?" I rub my eyes and yawn one of those endless yawns that threatens to drag you back into sleep. It's early, no later than 5:30, but I don't want to return to my sleeping. I don't want to slip back into those dreams.

"You talk a lot in your sleep, you know," Lissa says.

"I have a lot on my mind."

"And you drool all over your pillow."

I wave feebly in her direction, then drag myself out of bed and stumble to the bathroom. There's a hell of a lot of blood in there, more blood than any portent has given me before.

I don't know where the blood comes from, even now. I've never found a satisfactory answer, which is fine, when most of the time it's only a splatter here or there. But this bathroom has more in common with an abattoir. I almost throw up.

"Come and have a look at this," I say.

She's by my side in an instant. "Oh, that's not good."

"What the hell is going on?"

"I don't think Morrigan has everything under as much control as he would like."

That's an understatement. I grab the showerhead and start hosing the blood away. I feel like some mafia hitman cleaning up after a brutal kill, only there's no body, thank Christ. It's gone fairly quickly but the stench remains and, with it, the feeling of things coming. A dark wave on the verge of breaking.

I shower, soap myself down, rinse and do it all again. Maybe fleeing the city wasn't such a good idea after all. But if that portent is correct there is a stir happening somewhere near, a big one.

"I have to do something about it," I say.

"He may be able to track you, if you do."

"My job is to facilitate death," my voice sounds high and unfamiliar in my ears, "not to allow murder, and if I don't stop this stir, I'm a party to it."

"How many stirs do you think are happening now, right around the country?"

I glare at her. "I know, but I'm near this one."

23

I get dressed and take a drive.

It's easy to sense, more than ever. The Stirrer's presence is a magnet, and I follow the line of least resistance toward it. It's as though the car has a mind of its own. I barely have to turn the wheel.

Lissa's silent the whole way, and I don't know if she's angry with me or worried, maybe a bit of both.

We end up at the local hospital, almost in the center of Stanthorpe.

The staff there let me through when I raise one hand to reveal the scars criss-crossing it. They look harried and frightened. I guess that there have been a lot of things going bump, and then murderous, in the night lately.

One of the senior doctors meets me near the reception desk.

"I'm here to deal with your problem," I say.

"Thank Christ. We've never had to wait this long."

I can tell. Everyone here is strung out and weak. The Stirrer is drawing their essence away. There's a vase of dead flowers by the reception desk. The doctor looks at that.

"Not again," he says, tipping the dead things into a bin. "Keeps happening."

And there's no stopping this, until I do something about it. Soon, the sicker, older patients will pass on, and more Stirrers will appear, and more life will be drawn out of the world. It's reaching tipping point and I'm gripped with a sudden urgency to get this thing done.

"Where is it?" I ask. I hardly need to, I can feel it.

"The Safe Room," he says.

Out here in the regional areas it can take a day or so before someone is available to pomp a Stirrer. They don't make a big fuss about it, but most regional hospitals have ways of dealing with their Stirrers.

We walk through the hospital, descending a level by way of a narrow stairwell. With every step, the sense of wrongness increases. The air closes in, grows heavy with foulness.

Another senior doctor's waiting by a door. He mops at his sweaty brow with a handkerchief.

"We've had to lock the lower room," he says, relieved as all hell to see me. "This one is a bit more active than usual."

I nod, hoping that I look more confident than I feel.

"This is too dangerous," Lissa says again, though her eyes say otherwise. I'm doing the right thing, the only thing.

The door is marked in all four corners with the brace symbol. My Pomp eyes can see them glowing. They're lucky, Sam made these markings.

"Sam's alive," I say to Lissa.

The doctor looks at me questioningly. He can't see Lissa, of course. "Sam's one of my workmates. She's in trouble."

This guy doesn't know the least of it. "Yeah, we all are."

My fingers brush one of the brace symbols. I swear and yank my hand away from it. "Hot," I say, blisters forming on my fingertips.

The Stirrer has pushed its will against this door for quite some time. The sort of will that can generate friction is unnerving. Actually it's downright terrifying. A muscle in my left thigh starts to quiver, fast enough to hurt. *Suck it up*, I think. *You're here to do a job.*

I turn to the doctor. "The moment I'm through, lock the door and refresh those symbols. The brace is weakening." I toss him a little tin of brace paint. "Don't open this door until I ask you."

He nods. I look over at Lissa. "Don't go in there," she says.

"I have to." She looks away, but just as quickly turns back to me. "Don't let it hurt you."

The doctor glances at me.

"Sorry," I say. "Nervous tic."

"Just watch who you're calling a nervous tic," Lissa says.

I open the door, and it closes behind me. Maybe I should just turn around, head back out and think this through. I can't see the Stirrer, but I can feel it. I realize that with all that talk of trouble and doom, I'd forgotten to ask who was in here, or how big they might be.

Then it grabs my legs with its hands. Huge hands. They squeeze down hard.

Big mistake. My touch stuns it, but not enough. I slice open my palm and stall it, but it's painful, rough as all hell. This Stirrer's grown fat on the energy it's drawn from the hospital. I can feel its pure, wild hatred as it scrabbles through me like shards of glass, or knives slicing, cutting inside me. Almost the moment it's gone there's another Stirrer within the body. I stall that too, an easier stall since the soul's not been as long in the body, hasn't put down roots. I reach for my knife. I need more blood to do this properly. The next Stirrer to inhabit the body crash tackles me, knocking the breath from my lungs. The knife flies from my hands and skitters along the floor.

I scramble toward it, knocking over a tray of instruments. Sharp things tumble on me, stuff sharper than my knife. I feel around, both hands scratching over the tiles. Who the hell puts blades in a "safe room"?

The Stirrer is up. It's clumsy but quick, stomping toward me. One of its boots crashes down on my hand and words slur in its unfamiliar mouth: "Not this time." Then I see the flash of a blade, a cruel, hideous looking mortuary instrument.

I howl as the Stirrer's boot grinds down on my knuckles. It's a purer pain than that of a stall. I clench my teeth. All I can smell is blood, and death. Things have never been so clear. It lifts its boot up to put in another grinding stomp and I drive my shoulder into its leg, hard. Something snaps—I pray that it isn't my collarbone—and there's another swift stall. Then I'm cutting my hand on the nearest knife I can find . . . hell, there's a dozen cutting edges scattered across the floor. I slam my bloody palm against the Stirrer's face, just as its eyes open.

"Not this time," I say, my voice barely a whisper.

Pure hate regards me, then all life, and un-life, slips from its features and it's just a dead body.

I limp out of the room.

"Steven, Steven," Lissa says. "What did they do to you?"

I look at her. I realize just how frightened I was that she wouldn't be here when I came through the door, but here she is. Relief flows through me. I find myself shaking.

"I'm OK," I say. "I'm OK."

The doctor frowns at me.

"Sorry," I say, "just mumbling to myself again."

He drags a chair toward me. "Sit," he demands.

I look at the door out of here, then the chair. Gravity decides for me. Before I know it I have a blanket over my shoulders and a cup of tea in my good hand.

"You're not going anywhere until I look at that hand."

"And when will that be? I have to keep moving."

"When you finish that tea."

As determined as I am to get out of here, it takes me a while to drink the tea. It's sweet and too milky, everything I hate about tea, and it's the most delicious cup I've ever had.

"Nothing broken," the doctor says. "You were lucky. Now let's look at that palm."

He winces. Even Lissa winces. "Any deeper and you'd have needed stitches."

"Yeah, I was in a bit of a rush. I'm not usually so amateurish."

He looks at the scars that criss-cross my palm, and shakes his head. It's all part of the job these days, it seems, deeper and deeper cuts, more blood.

I get slowly to my feet. I'm still a bit shaky. "I have to go," I say, and nod back at the open doorway to the morgue. "Burn the body. As quickly as you can, and any other body that comes down here. These are strange times."

"It's going to get worse?" he asks.

"I think so."

"Jesus, it's real end-of-days stuff."

"Regionally, yes," I say, and when he looks at me questioningly, I shrug. I don't have time to explain Pomp jargon. "I have to go. Someone will be coming for me, it may be too late already."

"Thank you," the doctor says.

I wish I could do more. But I'm only one person, and I've got my own problems. I get into the Corolla and head out of town.

"They know where to look now," Lissa says.

"I don't know how long we can stay out bush."

"A few more days," Lissa says. "We'll come back when he least expects it."

And then what? A few more days for things to get worse, for more horrible dreams? "I think he's going to expect it whenever I go back to Brisbane."

"Maybe. Maybe not."

I drive up north, inland across the dry plains. The land is flat and vast, but it doesn't feel anywhere near big enough to hide me.

We find a caravan park in a small country town, as far from anywhere as I've ever been. I pay cash for a couple of nights. The owner doesn't look at me, just my money.

It's hot and dry during the day, and cold at night, with a sky clear enough to see the wash of stars that make up the Milky Way. You can lose yourself in that sky. Morrigan certainly couldn't get me there.

If I sense a Stirrer—and I do, even if it's hundreds of kilometers away—I go to it. And every night I use a different sim card and try and call one of the other regions. No one answers. The Regional Managers know what's going on, Lissa's absolutely certain of it, and they're not going to help.

They don't want this spreading across the sea. They don't want this in their backyard.

24

It's the third day in the same town and we're on our way to the local supermarket—Lissa and I have agreed on some music, Simon and Garfunkel, which is better than the Abba she suggested, and I just knew she wasn't in the mood for Aerosmith—when I notice the black car following us. I don't like the way it feels.

We pass the supermarket and start heading out of town. Lissa glances at me.

"We could be in trouble," I say.

Lissa looks behind us. "That's one way of putting it."

"Country towns, eh? You go out shopping and this happens."

The car's going fast, even for the straight stretch of road we're on, and it stinks of Stirrers. I put on a bit more speed but the Corolla doesn't have too much to give. We take a corner, way too fast, and the wheels slip a bit. The car shudders, but we stay on the road. The stereo hisses with the Stirrers' presence, the music rising and falling in intensity.

The black car's closing the gap between us, and then I realize I've seen it before. It's the Chevrolet Lissa and I had watched race down Milton Road after Sam. Its grille is dark with dead bugs. It's been driving all night.

I put the pedal to the metal, squeezing every bit of speed out of the car, my knuckles white around the steering wheel. But in every moment that passes I get a clearer, closer view of our pursuers. Don and Derek! At least Lissa's not there. The Chevy's V8 engine is soon drowning out my sputtering four cylinders.

Don neatly swings the car into the next lane and it roars up beside me. The stereo's breathing nothing but static now.

Derek smiles at me. There's a rifle in his hands and a predatory look sketched across his face that somehow combines the Stirrer's hatred of life and Derek's almost palpable dislike of me. His shirt flutters in the wind and I can see the gaping hole where his chest should be.

He fires through the window. I've got the windows open—the only aircon you can get in a '74 Corolla—so there's no explosion of glass. The bullet misses me by just inches. I'm so glad Stirrer Derek isn't using a shotgun or most of my face would be missing now in a red spray of shot.

The road narrows up ahead. I smack my foot down on the brakes and the tires smoke. The Chevy shoots past. I'm already spinning around, my foot hard on the accelerator, choking on the smell of burning oil and smoke. Lissa's yelling, I'm yelling—shrieking, really. Various forces that I'd understand more about if I'd listened in my high school physics classes tug at us as we turn, and it's a near thing between rolling the car, colliding with a tree and getting back on the road. We make it, somehow, judder up to speed and head back the way we'd come. Simon and Garfunkel crackle back into life.

"Thank Christ," I say, though my relief's short-lived. In the rear-view mirror the Chevy turns neatly, far more neatly than I could ever have pulled off, and tears back after us. What else was I expecting?

"Steven!" Lissa's pointing frantically in front of us. That's when we nearly collide with a police car, head on.

It's only through luck that we both veer to our left.

I keep going, and the cop performs a textbook handbrake turn.

Then the Chevy clips the back of the cop car and hurtles through the air, flipping over. It slides down the road on its roof.

I bring the Corolla to a shuddering, squealing, rattling halt. I can't leave the cop with these Stirrers, even if the Chevy is totaled.

He's a target, and if they take him they've just got another agent for their cause, and a cop car. Time to put an end to their aggressive expansion.

I take a deep breath and turn the Corolla around. This would be all so very *Mad Max* if I was driving a V8, and if it wasn't me. Lissa doesn't say anything until I stop the car off the road by the smoking wreck. She knows what I have to do. I swing open the door. Lissa follows, staying back, the Stirrers' combined presence pulling at her.

Only one of them is getting out of the car. Don. I slide my knife across my palm.

But that's bad enough. I'm gagging at the sight of him. Most of his chest is crushed against his back and his heart flutters beneath the wreckage of his meat and bones. He's the perfect picture of a Romero zombie, except the bastard is lowering a rifle to point at my chest. I'm thinking about the standoff at Albion, only this time Don *is* going to shoot me.

Why couldn't the gun have been totaled in the crash?

"Hey!" the cop shouts.

Don spins and aims the rifle at the cop. I sprint toward him, grab the Stirrer by the arm and feel him slide through me. But almost at once there's another one in the body. It stalls through, too, and then another one. Every stall is rough and breath-snatching. The Stirrers are getting stronger, and the rate at which they are re-entering bodies is rapidly increasing. I feel each one's rage at its too-swift passing, and there's so many of them.

Lissa's frantic behind me. There's nothing she can do. We both know that. But it doesn't make it any easier.

Stirrer Don is a bloody spinning door, and I'm standing on the precipice of a vast and horrible invasion. The body jerks and I grit my teeth against the motion. Each Stirrer gets a single movement in. They're orchestrating it, each entering spirit moving in sync with the previous one. Jesus knows how they're doing it, but I'm getting an elbow in the head. The movement is little more than a series of stop motion convulsions, but the elbow is no less persuasive. And every stall is tearing through me, so I'm hardly at my best.

This is going to kill me. I let go, and the gun rises up again. But I've not stopped. My knife is out again. I slice open my hand, deeper this time.

The Stirrer snarls at me, the rifle against my chest. He fires. The bullet must just clip something, blood's washing over my face. I swing my head hard against his and with that bloody contact the body drops to the ground.

The cop has his gun aimed at me.

I lift my hands in the air, then remember the weapon, and let the knife fall.

"Don't shoot!" I'm almost screaming. I don't want to die like this. The car is now an inferno behind me, and my back is hot. I'm dripping with grimy sweat and blood's sliding down my wrist and face.

"Get down," the cop roars. He hits the ground, covering his face with his hands.

I'm on my chest with a bone-juddering dive. The Chevy explodes. And there's more heat striking me, and bits of car spilling from the sky in a heavy metal rain. I stay there a moment, coughing with all that smoke and dust, then slowly get to my feet.

The cop is already up, peering over at the corpse.

"He's dead," I say. "He was before I touched him."

"I know. That body's been dead for a couple of days at least," the cop says. His eyes widen at something behind me. He shakes his head. "I've seen some flaming weird shit lately. But this, you've got to be kidding me..."

The second Stirrer has pulled itself from the car. Derek's body is burning, but it doesn't stop it from shambling toward us: another rifle raised. Shit, give dead people firearms and soon enough it's all they know. Shoot this, blast that.

The cop doesn't hesitate. He fires twice, both scarily accurate headshots. "Supposed to work on zombies, isn't it?"

"Only in the movies," I say. "Slows them a little though."

The Stirrer hasn't done more than stumble though there's barely anything left of its head. It shoots, and misses. If it still had eyes it wouldn't have. And its presence is offending me, driving me mad. This isn't Derek, but this is as close as I'm going to get. I know what I need to do.

I rush at the flaming body. My knees almost hit me in the chest I'm running so hard. My shoulder slams into Derek's stomach, tipping him onto his arse, and he lands with a grunt. I drive my bloody palm against his flesh, and then roll away, extinguishing flames as I go.

Not well enough, obviously, because the cop drenches me with a fire extinguisher.

"My hair! How's my hair?" I demand, and the cop laughs, and then we're both laughing the crazed laughter of the utterly terrified.

"You're insane." He stretches. Joints crack, and he looks from the corpses to me, and back again. "Sorry about this, mate, but you're going to have to come with me."

"I've got a number for you to call," I say, and I can't quite hide the desperation in my voice.

He raises an eyebrow. His shoulders tighten belligerently almost instantly.

I give Alex's special number to him. The cop walks away and when he comes back, holding two shovels and some gauze, he's pale.

"You've got some very powerful friends," he says. "He said to tell you that it's getting bad in the city. And not to use that number again. Oh, and you're to help me, so dig."

After I bandage my hand (the wound in my scalp has stopped bleeding) we dig two holes for the bodies. My back's screaming by the time I'm done. I'm a Pomp, not a gravedigger. My hand's not much better.

"You all right?" the cop asks, wiping sweat from his brow. We've worked in silence, though I can see there's a good dozen or so questions he's desperate to ask me, and that he can tell I have no intention of answering them.

"Not really," I say. "About as good as you'd expect."

He laughs at that. "Yeah. You seem to have a complicated life."

"You don't know the half of it."

The cop goes back to his sedan. The back end is dinged up badly but it still looks driveable. The radio's already screeching with something or other. He says a few things into the handset and looks set to drive away, but doesn't. He comes back to me and shakes my good hand.

"Good luck." He looks at me, grimly. "Yeah, and I'd prefer it if you didn't come back through my town again. Not if you're bringing this kind of trouble."

"No problem," I say. "Trouble's probably going to come anyway."

"Thought as much. Anything I can do?"

"Run, if you get the chance."

He nods. He doesn't look like the sort who would run.

Lissa's waiting in the car. "That was close."

"You're telling me." I start the engine. God, how I want to kiss her, but that's not going to happen.

We drive for hours, heading to the coast, me pushing the car as hard as I dare. I'm running but I'm not sure where.

I stop at a deserted truckstop. While I'm washing my hands, and splashing water on my face, cleaning off as much of the sweat and blood as possible, I think about what needs to be done. I have to bring this back to Morrigan somehow. I can't keep running, and Morrigan is sure to find me eventually. If that prick were here right now, I'd—

I look up, and Morrigan's walking out of a cubicle. I blink and he's still there. I scramble for my gun.

"You really should think before you start wishing for things, my boy." He's wearing a short-sleeved shirt. The tattoos of sparrows on his arms are no longer bloody. The last time I saw him—wounded and frail—couldn't be a greater contrast to this Morrigan before me. I have never seen him looking so strong. He almost glows. Wholesale murder does wonders for the complexion, it seems.

On the other hand I'm pale, washed out, and what fingernails I have that aren't broken are dirty and black with blood. I wave the pistol in his face. "Get out of here!"

"Why are you so frightened? If I really wanted to kill you right now, you'd be dead. All in good time."

I steady the pistol, aim it at his face. It's one thing to know that he's behind all this, another entirely to hear it from his lips. I hesitate.

He blinks. "Are you going to shoot me with that?"

I pull the trigger. Nothing happens. Morrigan laughs dryly. "You always were such a stupid little fuck. You will see my messenger soon, just so you know how serious I am."

He's gone before I release the safety. I feel Number Four—I feel the Underworld—open then close.

Lissa's through the wall, her gaze swinging this way and that. "You're shaking."

I am, fear's running through me. I want to cry. I want to hit something. "Morrigan was here. How the hell did he do that?"

Lissa grimaces. "Morrigan is Ankou. He can shift."

"Shift where?"

"Anywhere he wants to."

"I thought that was an RM thing."

"It takes some effort, but Ankous can do it, too. Besides, his powers are increasing. That bastard really kept you in the dark. And I didn't feel anything, not until he was gone. He must have been waiting. You should have called for me."

"And what could you have done except put yourself in danger?"

Lissa shrugs. "I could have been here."

I try Tim's phone. No answer, it just switches through to his voicemail. I don't leave a message, there's no point. He's in trouble, he has to be. Lissa suggests that he might just have his phone switched off, but even she looks worried.

We head down the coast, driving until I'm too exhausted to drive anymore which is far too soon, but I know that I'm going to wake up with the car wrapped around a tree if I don't stop. I pull into the first motel in Noosaville with a vacant sign, not caring that I look a sight, though the bored teen at the counter hardly glances at me as I pay for a room.

I'm exhausted, but manage to have a shower.

Steam fills the room. Tim's in trouble, he has to be. I've been out here for days and I still know so little, except that Morrigan doesn't seem to have a lot of difficulty finding me. If I stay out here, there's no one to help Tim. How could I ever face Sally again?

The truth is, Morrigan can kill me whenever he wants.

It's three o'clock in the morning and I'm standing in the doorway, shaking, after another dream of bicycles. Even here I can feel it—the Stirrers building in the west and the south. I've had as much rest as I'm going to get.

"We have to go back, now. I can't spend another moment out here."

Lissa nods. "This was never going to be easy, Steven. But what do you really know?"

"That this has to stop. I'm learning nothing out here, except that Morrigan can get me."

So much for escape, it really was a bad fit. I'm a Pomp, death is calling me, and the rough madness of the Stirrers. Maybe that's what Morrigan expected, maybe he knew I couldn't keep away for long. "We have to finish this."

"It's going to be tough, going back."

"Yeah. But what else can I do?"

"I'm worried about what it's going to do to you," Lissa says. "I don't want to see you hurting."

"Hurting more than I am now?"

Lissa nods at last. "I guess you're ready. It's time to find Mr. D."

I grab my backpack—it's already packed—and open the door.

Lissa stands there. The Stirrer.

"We need to talk," she says.

25

My knife is in my belt. I can get it out in a moment. I look Lissa—I mean, the Stirrer—up and down. It doesn't seem to be armed.

"Well?" it asks.

I can either fight and run, or step back from the door.

I let the Stirrer in. She/it is unarmed and walks quickly by me and sits on the bed. The room shifts with her presence—the life in it starts bleeding away. I can feel all those poor microscopic creatures that fill any space on the earth dying. A silent shriek fills the room.

Lissa fumes at her body, and the Stirrer either ignores her or can't see her.

My eyes dart between the two of them. My Lissa, and this facsimile. Its presence startles me. This is a first, a Stirrer not trying to kill me. Just having her here is unsettling enough. They're Lissa's eyes, but they're not. The mocking wit has been replaced by a hatred that is at odds with her words.

"Morrigan wants you back in Brisbane. The killing's over with. He says it's time you returned."

This immediately rings false. I have no position of power to negotiate from.

She must read this in my expression. "He needs you back, Steve." The informal address is wrong and its callous eyes narrow. "He says it has to stop, for the sake of the region."

"I don't believe her," Lissa says.

Neither do I. Her presence itself is a continuous nexus of death. As long as this Stirrer and its ilk exist, the dying cannot stop—it can only accelerate.

"I don't believe you," I say to Stirrer Lissa. I can see that this is going to get confusing very quickly. I'm so used to waiting for Lissa's opinion. And that's just what he's given me, a deal dressed in the most persuasive face possible for me. The bastard has wrong-footed me.

"He wants to negotiate?" I don't know why, but my words send a shudder down my spine. I move toward the door.

"Yes." Then Stirrer Lissa realizes what I'm doing. She gets up from the bed, but it's too late. "You little prick!"

I dash over the threshold and slam the door shut then mark it with the brace symbol. At once it's hot to touch. It will take a while for her to break through.

She's swearing on the other side of the door. But not as much as my Lissa.

Then I'm in the car, rattling down the road. Heading away from the motel as fast as I can.

"I couldn't stall her," I say.

"Why not?"

"Because it's you."

"It's not me," Lissa says. "It isn't. Everything that it remembers, everything that it knows—that I knew—contains nothing of the me that you know."

"I know, you're right. But it's you."

"Oh, Steven. I could kill you."

Well, I couldn't kill her. Not even a malevolent copy of her. Not ever.

We're on the road to Brisbane. Stirrer Lissa was right, it's time to negotiate, but not with Morrigan. No matter the pain, it's time to talk to Mr. D.

We drive south down the Bruce Highway, heading through the lightening landscape toward Brisbane. The flat plains on either side of us are broken only by the warty ruptures of ancient volcanoes, now silent. It's a tired country, and an old one, and I know what it feels like.

My brain is somewhat similar, my thoughts worn down, broken only by the sudden adrenal jolt that I'm actually doing this, crashing toward the last place any sane person would want to. There's a fair bit of traffic going the other way, people already starting to flee the city. I shake my head at the folly of that, even if it's a lesson I've only just learned. You can't escape death. It has a habit of following you.

We're in Brisbane early in the morning before peak-hour traffic—before even its first suggestion, just trucks and taxis on the road—and I get the feeling that it's not going to get too busy. The souls of the newly dead are hitting me: an altogether different and unwelcome traffic. They're stale and prickly and every one of them turns my stomach. Each has felt the touch of a Stirrer. I wonder if Sam is still out there, and how she might be feeling, having had to deal with all this urban pomping virtually alone.

I head to the inner-city suburb of Toowong. It wasn't so long ago that I fled from here, though it feels like an absolute age. I park the car in a side street, under a drooping poinciana tree, slip on my backpack then walk to the CityCat terminal on the river and wait for a ferry. This is the most convenient place, Lissa tells me. I don't want to telegraph my movements too much, though I already suspect that Morrigan has more than a good idea about where I am.

As we sit on the dock waiting, I sketch an upside down triangle on the bench, pick at a scab until it bleeds and mark the triangle with my blood. Anything to make a Stirrer uncomfortable.

"Bugs Bunny or Daffy Duck?" I ask Lissa, because there's never a moment that's too dark to talk cartoons.

"Mickey Mouse. I can't stand Warner Brothers cartoons."

"Shit, are you serious? You can't be serious." So those badges aren't ironic. *You can never tell.*

"I love Mickey Mouse," she says, tapping the badge on her sleeve. "Finest fictional creation of the twentieth century."

"Finest creation of the—Oh my, you seem to have forgotten Batman, not to mention Superman. What's Mickey Mouse got besides a whiny voice and big ears?"

"Universality," Lissa says. "No Mickey Mouse, no Disney, no manga, no anime. Besides, he rocks."

"He's a bloody wimp. I can't believe anyone actually likes Mickey Mouse, well, anyone above the age of four. Now, I'm a Bugs Bunny man. He's like some sort of trickster god."

"He's just Brer Rabbit."

"That's like saying *Firefly*'s Mal was *just* Han Solo. He wasn't."

Lissa rolls her eyes. "There's no point in having this conversation with you. You're too much of a nerd."

I'm just nervous as hell, that's what I am. There's a CityCat coasting in, the pontoon rocks with its approach. The blue and white catamaran's engines hum; its forward lights blink. "At least I don't like Mickey Mouse. Next you're going to tell me you don't like the Simpsons."

"Well... Nah, just kidding."

The CityCat docks, and we get on. I nearly buy two tickets—even now it's hard to escape the habit, the belief that she's actually there. It's early and the CityCat's almost empty, but there are still some passengers, all of them looking a little startled by the hour, which is odd. People up at this time tend to be annoyingly bright and chirpy. I wonder if they're feeling what I feel. Being this close to a Regional Apocalypse it would make sense. Unprotected, even the chirpiest of the chirpy would start to present with symptoms of fatigue and despair. I sit out front, and the cat pulls away from the pier. It slides toward the city, the skyline brightening in the distance.

It would almost be a normal day except there are bodies floating in the river. As I watch, someone topples from the edge of the CityCat and what's left of their soul burns through me. No one even notices.

Lissa points to a metal tower on the side of the river across from Toowong. It looks like a lighthouse but is actually an old reconditioned gas-stripping tower. It was used to clean coal gas for the city, stripping it of impurities, but now it's just a landmark on the West End side of the river. "That's where we need to go to get at Mr. D," she says. "I can feel it."

And looking at it, I know she's right. The tower has a sort of gentle gravity—it draws the eye, like Lissa draws the eye. This is why we had to come back to Brisbane. There's a certain density of souls in the city that the rest of Queensland doesn't have. The population here is big enough to make such a place possible. I can't believe I've never noticed it before. Now I find it hard to look at anything else. It's the tower or Lissa. Both entrance and terrify me.

"Why are you sticking around?" I ask. She tilts her head at me. "I mean, *how* are you sticking around? You should be gone already, even with the binding. Everybody else is gone."

"The Underworld is pulling at me all the time," Lissa says, "but I don't want to go. I'm a Pomp, and I know what I'm doing. I know the tricks, there's all manner of stalls. The binding is just one of them."

I'm wondering how I don't know this. I wish I'd never bought into Morrigan's philosophy. There was so much I just didn't bother learning. I'd been too busy doing nothing, earning money, not really caring where it had come from, and moping after Robyn.

"But that's only part of it," she says. "There are two things holding me here. Hate—I really want to get the bastard who did this to me—and something else."

"What's the other thing?" I ask.

"You."

The city has never looked more beautiful than it does now. I smile, and Lissa's smiling too. She's never looked more gorgeous. Ah, I tumble so fast, but this is different. I want to hold her hand, but I can't. I want to wrap my arms around her, and I can't. She's all I want but to touch her would destroy her, and take away the little that we have. This perfect moment is nothing but a lie.

Lissa coughs. "You've got that whole geek–cool thing going on, like Cory Doctorow or—"

"Who's Cory Doctorow?"

"Science-fiction writer, and cute."

I don't know what to say about that. So I just say nothing, pull my jacket tight about me, shove my hands deep in its pockets and wait until we get to our stop.

We turn our backs to South Bank and head toward the tower in West End. There's hardly a soul about, though someone's swimming at the little fake beach there by the river. The tower's a half-hour tramp along the bank and it's still a good walk away when it starts to rain. And it's not just rain. I can't believe that I didn't see this coming.

Brisbane is beautiful in the rain, and it doesn't rain nearly enough. The city's been drying up for decades, so I feel kind of mean-spirited cursing it, but this rain is something else. It's the fiercest downpour I can remember. The sky's so dark, and my vision so limited, that it could be the middle of the night. But even then I'd see more clearly, because there would be streetlights.

The wind builds quickly as we walk, growing from breeze to gale to something else, the river churns past us, black as the sky. Storm-tossed things crash past us: outdoor furniture, rubbish and signage. Every step toward the tower is a struggle.

"This isn't normal," Lissa says.

I look at her. "It used to be. This is about as close to a Brisbane storm as I've seen in years. But it feels wrong."

We just grin and bear it, and I find myself almost knocked on my arse on several occasions, but it isn't enough to stop us.

"So they've built a fence around it," I say. "A high, rattling, shaking in the wind, fence."

There are Moreton Bay figs thrashing in the wind behind the fence, which looks like it could take off into the air at any moment.

"You can climb over it." Lissa is already on the other side, a broad smirk on her face. "It's hardly a fence at all. Hardly any barbed wire."

"Yeah," I say uncertainly. I hadn't actually noticed the barbed wire. The rain is streaming off the figs that rise up behind the fence, their root buttresses like knuckles bunched above the ground. I remember reading about this now. They're the reason this tall, portable (possibly too portable) fence has been erected—the trees are unsafe. The tower just happens to sit directly behind them. Metal spotlights shudder stupidly in the wind, making shaky shadow puppets of everything.

It seems some sort of fungus has gotten into the roots of the trees. It's visible even as I near the top of the fence, a dark stain penetrating the wood. I wonder what that might be like if it ever affected the One Tree. The fence can't support my weight, it wobbles, creaks, and then slams onto the muddy, but hard, ground. I'm face down in it, and winded.

"Well, that's one way to do it."

"Yeah, really elegant. I'm a bloody Pomp, not James Bond."

I get to my feet, slowly. Nothing seems to be broken. I check the straps on my backpack and wipe mud from my jeans. *Great, just great.* I take a couple of deep breaths, then consider the tower. "So how do we do this?"

Lightning strikes the tower before us. I'm momentarily blinded, my ears ring. There has to be a better way—with less thunder and great balls of fire. Lissa's unaffected by it all, and I'm reminded again that she's not of this world anymore. The storm, the lightning, all of it is an inconvenience.

Then a Stirrer drops from the nearest tree and comes barreling toward us.

"Steven!" Lissa shouts, and she's suddenly in front of me but, of course, it crashes through her. If I hadn't bound her to me she'd be gone.

I don't have enough warning to do more than tense as its shoulder slams into my stomach. I crumple over its back then hit the muddy ground again, with a groan.

"You should never have come here." I recognize the voice, Tremaine. The Stirrer looms over me. "But I'm glad you did."

Hatred breeds hatred. Stirrer Tremaine has it in for me far worse than the living one ever did. "Morrigan will be here soon, but I can kick the shit out of you before that."

"Have a go, Flatty," I say, hardly from a position of strength.

Tremaine swings a boot at me and I grab it, catching it mere centimeters from my face. The kick jolts through my body. He yanks his foot, but I'm holding on tight and I've got a good grip. I push him hard. He's on his back. I stagger to my feet, I have to finish this quickly. I need to get into the tower before Morrigan arrives. I kick him, then bend down. I slap my hand against his face and realize that he's wearing some sort of mask. I feel his smile beneath it.

"Not so easy is it?"

My hand yanks the mask free. He punches me in the stomach and I throw up all over his face.

Seems that blood isn't the only way to stall a Stirrer. He gasps then shudders, and is still.

"Christ," Lissa says from behind me. "You're an innovator."

I'm too shaky and sore to be embarrassed. The rain is crashing down with even greater force and my stomach is an ache that extends all the way to my mouth. And I know what I've been fighting for—just another gateway to pain. To make it even worse, a soul pomps through me. People never stop dying. The taste of blood is added to the delightful mix of vomit and terror.

"We have to get this over and done with," I manage.

"Follow me, mud boy," Lissa says quietly, her voice carrying easily above the storm.

We circle the tower once. It's metal, a rusty red. Up close it looks even more like a lighthouse than anything as industrial as a gas stripper.

"Follow you where? There's no way in, besides it'll be full of baffles and gas-stripping stuff. Maybe we need to do this outside?" I've decided I really don't want to go in there. I'm feeling sick with fear. "Yeah, out here would be better."

Lissa shakes her head. "Put your hand against the wall."

I brush a hand across the cold metal, hesitantly. "See, nothing." I'm lying though, there's a definite buzz to the metal, and the moment I touch it I can hear bells tolling in my skull.

Lissa gives me her darkest grin. "I'm sorry, Steve. But this isn't that easy. You know it isn't. Keep your hand on the wall. And you're going to need the craft knife."

I pull the knife from my pocket.

"There's a reason why this is so hard to do."

I understand that. We can't be encouraging people to cross over into the Underworld, even to the edge of the Underworld. It's easy enough to enter Number Four. Sure it requires a little blood, but only a pinprick, because that is an entranceway sanctioned by Mr. D. This is something else. This is a back doorway and its lock is much more complicated, much more demanding.

Lissa points to a spot on the back of my hand. "There," she says.

I know what to do. I drive that craft knife right through to my palm. I tear my throat with the scream.

The tower jolts and I leap back, my hand burning. The wound has healed, but darkly, and where the wound was is now a smoking scar. And where my hand was there is now a door. It opens inward with the force of the wind, clanging against the inside of the tower.

"Go the magic and shit," I growl.

"You always this cynical?"

I nod, peering through the doorway. It's dark in there. "Sometimes, but mostly only when I'm half frozen to death and covered in mud, and I've just driven a knife through my hand. After you."

Lissa walks through and I follow, closing the door behind me. It's an effort against the wind, but when it shuts it stays shut.

26

So what do we do now?" I shrug the pack from my shoulders.

We're in the gloom of the tower, in a space that shouldn't be. We're somewhere between worlds—a bubble of time and space, its surface marbled with possibilities, and far too many of them are grim. Whether I succeed or fail has never mattered more than now. The walls of the tower are marked at regular intervals with glowing brace symbols. No Stirrer could enter this place.

The air is rank with a back-of-the-throat burning odor of cat piss and vomit. Magic door and what not, it still bloody stinks. There's crushed up fast-food wrappers and soft-drink cans cluttering the floor, and a used condom opposite the door—hardly a clinical place for what I imagine is about to be done. But then maybe that's the point of it. Maybe it has to be rough and raw, and there's certainly something in the air, a little like the quiet expectancy of the doorway to Number Four.

The rain is loud against the metal walls, and the trees outside sound like they are thrashing in the storm as though the riverfront's become some giant's moshpit. Inside the tower, everything rattles and creaks and groans. What's more, there is a bell tolling in the distance: really bloody portentous. I feel like I'm on some sort of carnival ride, one that is exceedingly fast and poorly maintained.

"It's going to hurt," Lissa says. "More than the knife through your hand."

"I know it's going to hurt."

"No, you don't. You just think you do."

"Look, are you trying to talk me out of this? If that's the case I would have been more open to persuasion before we made our way through the storm, before I fell in the mud and was nearly struck by lightning, and before being almost kicked to death by Tremaine. And just where else are we going to go anyway?"

"Have you got that marker and the *craft* knife?" Even now in the dark, with me scared and sweating, she can't help but smirk. Somehow, it helps.

I dig around in my pack and pull out the marker. The knife is clenched in my hand.

"So you're a Pomp, right," she says. I nod. "Well, you're going to have to be your own conduit. You're going to have to pass through yourself into the land of the dead. Well, to its edges, anyway. You don't want to go too far in—the further you go, the harder it is to come back."

"I'm going to the Underworld? I'm sure every Stirrer I've faced could have sent me there much less painfully."

"And much more permanently," Lissa says.

"Then how am I going to draw Mr. D out? If he's still around."

"He'll be around; he's trapped or hidden somewhere. This ceremony will not only bring you firmly into the Underworld, it'll also break through whatever's holding him. It's essentially a summoning ceremony, but one where you show a *real* commitment."

"Mr. D won't be happy. You know what he's like."

"Yeah. But trust me, he *will* be impressed. Do you have a handkerchief or tissue?"

I feel in my pockets. Nothing.

"Then you'll have to use your shirt. You're going to need to soak it in blood."

"All right then." I take off my shirt.

Lissa whistles and I give her a look. It's not like she hasn't seen it all before. But it breaks the tension, and then she's all business.

"You need to cut here and here." She points to two points on my shoulders. "It's absolutely necessary that you sever the arteries there, and only *those* arteries. They're the portal wounds. I'm sorry, Steve. You've got to bleed for this to work. Profusely. Mark those points with your pen."

I shiver, my skin is all gooseflesh. She reaches out a hand to touch me, and stops just before contact. I look into her eyes and can see her recognition of my fear.

"You'll be all right. The binding ritual went perfectly. Just don't forget that shirt."

The binding had been a quick wank—a little messy, but hardly fatal. I've never felt as close to death as I am now. The precipice is before me and I'm the one who has to step off it. If I look too intently at the edge I know I'm not going to do it.

The adrenaline from the fight and the stabbing of my hand is fading. All I have to do this with is me, terrified and tired me. If I die, at least it'll be on my own terms. That has to mean something.

I mark the two spots Lissa has pointed to. The first one is going to be easy, if driving a knife into your own flesh is ever easy. I click the knife blade free of its plastic sheath. It glows dimly.

Everything is silent. I can't hear the storm. My entire universe has narrowed down to this. There's such a thrumming tension running through me that I could snap. Then all of a sudden my head is pounding, beating time with my heart. This is more horrible than I could have thought, and I haven't even started. *Calm down. Calm down. Calm down.*

I take a breath, and push the knife into my flesh. It's hard to apply the right amount of pressure. My hands don't want to do it, and a lot of me agrees with my hands. Most of me in fact.

But, shit, I *need* to.

I push and cut. At first there is no pain. That doesn't last.

"Oh, God." Blood spurts, ridiculously and vividly. I drop to my knees.

"Breathe," Lissa says, as though I am giving birth, somehow. I feel naked before her, stripped down to my essence. "Breathe. I'm here with you, Steven. I'm here."

I never realized just how far blood could jet from a wound, and its bursts are fast and forceful because my heart is racing. I'm shaking. Part of me is wondering just how much time I have before I lose consciousness, but that isn't going to get me anywhere. I clamp down on my thoughts with whatever will I have remaining, because there's only one action left to me.

I drive the knife into the shuddering meat of my other shoulder, my hands sticky and slippery with my own blood.

"The shirt," she says.

I've dropped it. Christ, I've gone and dropped it!

A bell is ringing. *Ha!* The voice of Eric Tremaine is rattling around in my head. *How the hell did you survive this far?*

I swing my head left and right, searching for the shirt. I'm clumsy, drunk with the loss of blood and the pain and the shock. My vision is spotting, narrowing down. There it is! Away from the mess of my wounds, untouched by blood. Definitely unsanguine. *How the fuck did that happen?*

It's you, Tremaine says, buried in my head somewhere, a new voice for my own self-loathing. *You.* Derek's there too, and they're both laughing, having a right old time, slapping each other on the back like the old chums they are. *See you in hell.*

I scramble desperately toward the shirt, through the blood that was once part of me and that is still pouring from me, though with less and less urgency now. *The well is dry, gentlemen. The well is dry.* I reach out one bloody paw and grab the shirt. "Lissa—"

Darkness smothers me like death.

PART TWO

THE ORPHEUS MANEUVER

27

You come out of that sort of dark and you know you're done. You're dead, or you've brought the Underworld to you—and there's not a lot of difference between the two states.

Lissa's looking at me, her gaze heavy with something—pain maybe, or relief. We're in the tower. Only we're not. We've made it through to the fringes of the Underworld. I can feel it, not just in the silence, because there is no storm on this side, but in my flesh, just as I do when I'm at the office, only this is purer, darker and more terrible.

"I'm—" That's all I manage, my body is startling me. It's not how I remember it: except it is. The wounds are gone.

And there is no blood. Anywhere. Not a single drop of it within the curved space of the tower. I open my hand and there is the shirt so, yeah, there is some blood. The material is dark and dry with it. I fold it up and put it in my pocket. My backpack is next to me. I grab another shirt and slip it on.

I'm whole, and hale, except the cherub tattoo on my biceps is burning, as though it has only just been inked. I ignore it. Quite frankly I've experienced much worse in the last few days. The air, too, is fresh. No cat or drunk has ever marked this place.

"You did good," Lissa says. "For a moment... I thought you did too good."

And I want to kiss her. Her lips lack their usual blue-tinged pallor.

In fact, her cheeks are flushed. There's not even a moment's hesitation. It's the only time I'll ever get the chance. I reach over and I touch her face, and it's warm against my fingers.

"Jesus," I say, and I can feel the pupils of my eyes expanding so fast they hurt.

"Here," she says, "in this place, we can touch. Here, we're the same." She holds my hand against her face. That contact of warm skin against warm skin is electric, and her beautiful eyes are wide. "But I don't know for how long. Steve, I can feel the One Tree calling me. I've denied it for so long."

I pull her to me, hardly hearing her.

"I—"

Then we're kissing. And I'm on fire. There is part of me railing against this madness. We're in the land of the dead. There is no time for this. But, really, my sense of time is gone. It has been since I drove the knife into that first artery. In a heartbeat such reservations burn away, and all I want is her.

Lissa pulls at my shirt, and I'm tugging at her blouse, and trying to get my jeans off at the same time.

I stumble out of them, awkward as all hell, but it doesn't matter. Nothing does except her. Her skin is soft against my chest. My lips find the hollow of her neck, my arms find an aching rest against her back, and there's a synergy, a perfect motion between us. I kiss her gently, then slide down, my lips grazing her skin, feeling her shudder through my lips.

I'm on my knees tugging at her clothes, then burying my face in her, rough and soft and wet. I'm tasting her, devouring her with a hunger that I never knew I had, that I never believed I could deserve.

"Steven," she breathes.

I am so hard. How can I have an erection here? How can I feel this way? The questions fall from me. They have to, because I want this so much.

I slide up against her. My body feels like it's fused with hers, that we've somehow melded together. I can feel her heart beating beneath her breast. It's crashing and pounding like mine, and here, in this gateway to the Underworld, it dazes me. Then I remember that we're not yet one, and then we are. And that should be enough to bring me to orgasm, the long lack of such sensations, the liquid heat of it. But I don't and I don't and when we do it's an epiphany of fire.

"Oh, my," she says.

"Oh, my," I say right back. My body is sore, but it's a good sore.

I kiss her so hard my lips hurt. I run a thumb along her cheek, then hold her head gently, staring into her eyes, trying to peer into the green-gated glory of her soul.

She smiles at me, and it's a different sort of smile. Not sardonic in the least. I feel for the first time that I've gotten past the armor, that I'm really seeing her.

Still there's part of me that's thinking, *Well, only one place to go from here, can't beat that,* and another part is yelling, *Shut up, shut up, shut up!* and there's another part that's just beaming, grinning like crazy. My head's become an awfully crowded, complicated space.

Sex with a dead girl. That sets a new low for Pomps. Except we're both sort of dead now.

And, here's the thing: I don't care.

I open the door.

There's a cold wind blowing, strong and smelling of rain, a memory of the world I had just left. I shiver and pull my duffel coat about me.

The ritual was a success. We're somewhere, and I have the means to bring Mr. D to me and, perhaps, find a way to end Morrigan's Schism. And, hell, I'm in love. Totally in love. I almost spin. Buried in all this dreadfulness, I've found a perfect moment. I'm happy for the first time in longer than I care to admit.

I glance around.

We're in Death's neighborhood, but not George Street. We're in the park in the Underworld equivalent of West End—the tower is behind me. The river's flowing in front of me, but has a dark luster more like licorice than water. It's Brisbane but not Brisbane. There are gaps, places where the wind whistles through from... There's one near the tower, between it and the river, and I peer into its depths. Someone stares up at me and there is a jolt of recognition. I'm looking at my face. It winks at me, and then is gone, and I'm staring into a dark space as deep as the one I fell into to get here. Why the hell am I down there?

I look up, my eyes taking a while to adjust to the light. Across the river are the Underworld versions of the suburbs of Toowong and Auchenflower. In the living world the Corolla is in Toowong, in Auchenflower my house is nothing more than a pile of smoldering wood. Traffic is congested along Coronation Drive, and behind it all Mount Coot-tha rises, and it's there that the dead gather. Here the mountain is topped by a tree, a Moreton Bay fig, that reaches into the sky, its lower branches extending over the inner suburbs, its roots sliding all over the mountain, and descending into the city in great blades of wood.

The One Tree is a blazing cynosure above the city: the death tree where everybody in Australia goes when they die. The Hill squats beneath it, its stony surface blazing with a red fire. I've never seen it burn like that. Usually it's a dim blue light like something you'd expect in a public toilet to dissuade junkies from shooting up. I wonder if Lissa has any idea what it means.

"Lissa, you might want to see this." I walk back to the tower and poke my head in the door. "Lissa?"

She's gone. There's just the empty tower.

I feel her absence like a punch to the stomach. Now I understand what Lissa meant when she said we didn't have much time. She'd held on to me longer than she should have as it was, binding or not. Coming this close to the Underworld was going to draw her away from me faster than anything else. I should have realized that, but then I've been distracted of late. It's not much of an excuse. And it is no salve to my pain.

I take a deep breath, pull the blood-soaked shirt from my back pocket and drop it on the ground. Nothing happens. There is no sense of change or a magical burst of power. There is no sudden rising darkness that takes the form of Mr. D. It's just me looking at my blood on my shirt.

"What the hell are you doing, idiot?" Morrigan is standing on the edge of the road. He looks pale, almost ill. "I can't believe that—"

"Well, you wanted me dead."

"Do you not know how difficult that ceremony is?" And it's almost the Morrigan of old, the mentor, the one I've known since I've had memory.

"I know it intimately," I say.

"Bullshit," he snarls. "That ceremony has worked just once in three generations, and the man who did it then was raving mad. It's not supposed to work. You're mad, crazy." He's sounding crazy himself. Spit flecks his lips.

I shrug. "Maybe, but it worked."

"You're the luckiest man I have ever met." Then he wrinkles his nose. "I can smell the sex on you. Where's your sense of propriety? You did all this to get into Lissa's pants? I'm quite disappointed." And he sounds disappointed, genuinely dismayed.

"Lissa—"

"She's gone." He nods to the tree behind and above us. "You know how these things go. You're quite welcome to join her. Yes, there's an open invitation for you, care to take it up?" He looks hopeful, and I'm thinking maybe that's the way to go. With all this running around, I was heading in that direction anyway. But there's also a part of me that wants to wipe that smug grin off his face.

"Nah. Not just yet."

Morrigan rushes toward me, his hands clenched. Something cracks in the air, a thin sound, like a tire iron scraping over concrete. Morrigan backs away.

A shadow forms, coalesces, out of the air.

Morrigan pales. "You."

"Yes, me. Richard, you should go." The voice is dry and quiet, little more than a whisper. "This is still my kingdom, and you do not have a clue what you have set in motion... Not really."

The man standing between us doesn't look like he should be particularly imposing. His suit is conservative, even a little threadbare, and his hair is parted neatly to one side. But he's imposing all right. And his anger fills the air with a dull and steady buzz. It makes my stomach roil, and he isn't even looking at me.

There is a soft exhalation, and Morrigan is gone. It's just me and the RM. Mr. D looks at me with such a wild expression that, for a moment, I wish I was with Morrigan. Then he grins warmly, though that's not all I see. There are too many faces for that.

"I've wanted to do that for days, but Morrigan is canny. It took your summoning to free me from the place he'd thrown me into. A broom closet, would you believe? Of all the bloody places, and not even a magazine to read. Steven, you've gone to rather a lot of trouble to see me. Shall we walk?"

It is a peculiar sensation talking to Mr. D. The man is slight and rather handsome, but also vast and power-hungry and grinning. He moves slowly, carefully, and sometimes he doesn't move at all, and yet he's shambling, racing, rushing around you, and checking and peering, like a doctor on speed doing an examination or a spider binding its prey in its web.

"How bad is it, Steven?" Mr. D asks.

"Well, I'm here aren't I?"

"You have a point. I would have expected Tremaine, your father, or even Sam."

"I can't tell you about Sam. But Dad's gone. Tremaine, too."

"So everyone senior?"

"They're dead," I say, and Death nods.

"I felt them, but I couldn't be sure. Everyone dies eventually. Call me biased, but that's what life's about. Even I can die, and without my Pomps, my position here is... tenuous. Morrigan knows that. He knows that my power is at an end—the prick."

I clench my jaw. "It isn't fair."

Mr. D laughs. "Nothing's fair, Steven. Not in the games we play."

I catch a movement out of the corner of my eye. An engine roars. And then an SUV strikes Mr. D from behind.

It nearly takes me too, but I'm just that little bit closer to the gutter, and Mr. D's hand pushes out precisely at the moment of impact, throwing me to one side. Death slides under the wheels. Bones crack like thunder. The SUV pulls away and shoots down the street.

I run to Mr. D's side, I try and help him. I didn't know Death could bleed, but he's bleeding all right. His clothes are sticky with it. There's blood leaking from his ears, and his lips and teeth are rubicund. I start dragging him off the road.

"Get away, Steven," he says, and pushes my hands from him. He's still strong—I'm flung from the road, the breath knocked out of me.

Mr. D stands, his legs shaking, his face messed up. One of his eyes has closed over. "Perhaps you should run," he says to me.

But I'm stuck to the spot. The SUV has come back and it hurtles into him. This time it turns in a tight circle and hits him again, then again. Morrigan's behind the wheel, smug as all hell, and by the time he's done, Mr. D is a lump of blood and rags on the ground. Finally I regain the will to move.

"Don't even think about it." Dad steps from the passenger-side door and points a rifle at my head.

"Dad, I—"

"How thick are you, Steven? I'm not your father," he says in my father's usual irritated tone. How can I think of him as anything but my dad? But the moment my eyes meet his, there can be no doubt. There's a wild, tripping madness there, and a vast alien hatred. His skin glows with a lurid, sickly light. Stirrers shouldn't inhabit the Underworld this way. Its true form is slowly burning through his flesh.

A week ago this was my father, though that animated spark has gone and has been replaced by the enemy. Still, if you're going to die, die pissing something off. "Dad—"

He swings the rifle at my head.

"None of that," Morrigan says, sliding out of the SUV.

The rifle butt stops just centimeters from my skull.

Morrigan rolls Mr. D's body over with his foot, and smiles. "So it's done. Death be not proud and all that," he says, rubbing his hands gleefully. This is Morrigan as I have never seen him. So damn happy. He terrifies me, more than Mr. D ever did. "Death is dead."

"Why?" I demand, and Morrigan wags a finger in my face.

"Need to know basis only, I'm afraid. And you know too much as it is. But don't be too sorry for him. The bastard deserves every last instant of pain." Morrigan glances over at Dad. "End it."

Dad fires.

At the same time cold fingers run over my flesh. Everywhere. They're brushing everything. I'm smothered in a rushing, tapping, piercing density of ice.

A voice whispers in my ears. "The rules are changing, Steven."

Then I'm in that dark space again, and the last thing I hear is Morrigan's weary voice.

"Oh, fuck," he says.

28

Crack!

That's how I wake, with a jolt and a deep gasping breath, as though I've been drowning.

Crack! The door nearby shudders.

Crack!

Dust, centuries old, spills from the top of the bookcases that line one wall.

Crack!

Mr. D sneezes. "Don't worry, I made this office with my own two hands. The doors are reinforced with my own blood, and the blood of my enemies. There's a bit of strength in them yet. Do you take milk?"

I nod my head as Mr. D pours my tea into a fine china cup. I've been here once before, so long ago that I'd almost forgotten about it. It's the inner sanctum, the throne room. Mr. D's big chair is up at the other end of a long wooden desk, and it's covered with carvings of figures running, fighting, dying, all of them gripping daggers, and is utterly incongruous with the metal, plastic and leather business chairs that face the desk. Morrigan covets that deathly throne. It shivers and sighs and seems to stare back at me. I feel the intensity of its regard. How can an inanimate object have such a tangled scowling presence? I can't imagine anyone ever wanting to sit in such a thing.

The desk is submerged in paper—scrunched up balls of it, rough teetering piles of it, and all of it covered in Mr. D's dense scrawl. Post-it notes fringe one side of the desk.

Mr. D catches me glancing at the papery chaos. "I never bothered with a computer for the real work." He lifts a hand and Post-its flutter like jaundiced butterflies from the table toward his wrist. "Who needs one, eh? Though I do like my Twitter." He reads the notes that he'd called to him, and frowns. "There are too many names I know on these things."

I'm quick to forget about that, though. Something else has grabbed my attention. Mr. D really does have the original "Triumph of Death" on his wall. There are all those skeletons getting jiggy with the damned. Mr. D has always seemed a little too smug about this picture for my liking, but here it is, in all its splendor.

I walk up to it and shudder. Looking closely, I don't see the Orcus in those skeletons, or Pomps, I see Stirrers. And I'm thinking about that impending Regional Apocalypse.

"Quite a piece of work, isn't it?" Mr. D says. "I, um... procured that for myself a long time ago. One of the benefits of this job. Well, it was."

"What the fuck is going on?" I ask, turning away from the picture. It's bigger than I expected, and I can feel all those mad eyes staring at the back of my neck.

Mr. D sends the Post-it notes fluttering back to the desk. "Death and death and death, I'm afraid."

There's an almighty crack and the door behind him shudders. We both jump.

"Well, that was a big one." Mr. D passes me my cup and saucer. His mind is already wandering to a new topic. It's not just his face that jumps around.

"There are other spaces, other places, and they proceed endlessly, universes and universes. One day, death may not be needed. But we're a long way from that." Death sips his tea casually, even as the door and bookcases shake. "I keep up with my reading. I like physics, I like the possibility that one day death will be irrelevant. After all, death is merely a transitional state. The body is devoured, and made alive again in all the creatures that devour it. And the souls of those gone are absorbed into the One Tree, sinking through it to eventually track across the skies of the Deepest Dark.

"Death's job, Steven, is to shape the Underworld, to bring to it a neatness, a less savage afterlife. And that's all I've ever done, managed my little alternate universe. Other RMs do it differently, but we're all here to provide a peaceful transition, to make sure the dying continues as it should, and to stop the Stirrers. That's the position Morrigan hungers for."

I'm still a couple of steps behind. I think I always will be. "He killed you. How are we even here?"

"Think about it." Mr. D taps his skull.

"I'm a Pomp—"

Death nods, and takes a loud slurp of his tea. Lissa would hate him. He also takes sugar. Mom would have hated him too. "Exactly. You pomped me here and I took you with me. Things are different for RMs—the manner of our deaths—particularly in such situations as this. We're given some leeway. You being a Pomp meant I could use you as a portal to get us here. When that door they're so desperately trying to break down does, things will become a little more... final. The rules are changing, Steven. I'm not the first RM of Australia, nor will I be the last unless, of course, we have come to that time when death is made redundant." The door jolts, metal shrieks. Mr. D considers the door. "I'm quite certain that we haven't reached that point yet, not even close. For one, you're still breathing." He finishes his tea and gestures toward mine, frowning. "You haven't touched yours."

Crack!

Mr. D turns toward the sound. "Don't worry, we've time enough, believe me."

The dark carried me here half an hour ago and Death made tea with all the speed of a man who has no idea of the concept of the word "hurry" or "apocalypse."

I wish I could say that I share his lack of urgency, but I want out of here. And I want answers. "So what is Morrigan planning? To become the new RM?"

"Morrigan has always been extremely diligent in the application of his duties. It was only a matter of time before he wanted my job." Mr. D shakes his head ruefully. "Something much easier to recognize with hindsight, of course."

"So what can I do?" I look down at my cup.

"The first thing would be to get young Lissa Jones down from the tree."

"But the rules..." I have no idea how I can even reach the One Tree, let alone rescue Lissa.

But if there's a way... Mr. D better not be messing with me. I want Lissa back. I need her.

"Everything comes to a close, even the efficacy of paradigms, Steven. And besides, you must realize the rules are remarkably flexible. After all, you're here having tea with me, aren't you? Well, you would be if you actually had a sip."

I can't drink the tea. I'm too keyed up. "This hasn't happened before, how can Morrigan—"

Mr. D laughs and regards me with his affably vicious eyes. "Of course it's happened before. When these... Schisms occur there are no survivors, not if the new RM is doing his job. And let me tell you, I did my job most thoroughly."

"Oh."

Mr. D isn't quite the friendly fellow he was a moment before, and I wonder who or what I am really locked in this office with. If you scratch the surface of any business you start to find dirt, I guess. But it's disappointing. "So you..."

Mr. D nods his head. "Don't feel sorry for me, de Selby. But I am pissed off. I didn't see this coming. I knew it was inevitable, of course, but that hardly means I was expecting it, and certainly not from Morrigan. He was just too good. A stickler for the rules. A fellow always creating new efficiencies. I was lulled, Steven. I thought he had my back, not a knife pointed at it. I'd forgotten how it goes, you see." He grins at me. "I was a very nasty man, Steven."

Mr. D moves close and pats my back. "I still am, though I'd like to say I was an idealist, and I can assure you that I never dealt with the Stirrers. Morrigan is opening doors that should never be opened.

"Pomps are the front line in a war that has been going on since the Big Bang, between life and the absence of life. Ultimately it's a war that we probably have no chance of winning. Our enemy is powerful. You don't give Stirrers an edge, you *never* give them an edge. And certainly not now.

"Morrigan is very likely to discover that he won't be RM for very long. Once enough Stirrers are through there won't be anything living to bring over. Morrigan's made death too efficient for his own good."

I'm still a couple of steps behind, but I have to bring something to the conversation. "If you hadn't sent those crows I wouldn't have survived, and I would have lost Lissa sooner than I did."

Mr. D turns his changeable face toward me. "Crows? I didn't send any crows. I've had no control over my avian Pomps since Morrigan pushed me in the broom closet."

"Well, if you didn't, who did?"

"Crows like to see things out to their own conclusion. Perhaps they wanted to even things up a little. After all, my Schism may have been brutal—and it was, believe me, it was—but Morrigan has taken it to a whole new level. You shouldn't deal with Stirrers. I don't know if I can stress that enough. Absolutely no good can come of it."

"So what do I do?"

"Well, first things first, be careful: you can die here. Morrigan is going to want to stop you, and his influence in the Underworld is strong. You need to find Lissa. Love's far more powerful than you can believe, and you are going to need allies."

He's suggesting an Orpheus Maneuver. I thought they were impossible. They've certainly never worked before, as far as I know. Otherwise they'd have been named after something other than their most spectacular failure.

You can't just go to Hell and back whenever you choose. It exacts a price. It demands pain and suffering. Bringing someone else back is even harder. Orpheus failed and he was the best of us. I can't see how a Brisbane boy is ever going to better that.

My face burns. "What about my parents, would they make powerful allies?"

His eyes flare, and he jabs a bony finger at me. "Are you trying to bargain with an RM? Believe me, it doesn't work."

"Paradigm shift," I remind him, and I feel pretty cool, eye to eye, with Death. Is he really Death anymore?

Mr. D chuckles. "Now that's the spirit, but it would take a greater paradigm shift than anything we're capable of to bring them back. Bigger than that of the Hungry Death of old." My jaw drops at that. I'd always thought the Hungry Death was a myth, a scary story. "I'm sorry Steven, but they're too far gone."

"Thought it was worth a try."

"Everything is. The Boatman Charon, now he's the one you want to make a bargain with. Indeed, you'll have to. Or Neti, Aunt Neti, but no, she's probably best avoided for now."

The door cracks, louder than ever before. We both swing our heads toward it. Fragments of the frame tumble to the floor. There's not much left in it.

"One more thing. You're going to need this." Mr. D hands me a key. The metal is warm and oily, in fact it feels disturbingly livid. "It's my key to Number Four. The iron was shaped around the finger bone of the first death—the Hungry Death—so they say. I can't be sure of that, but it's old and powerful. Keep it on your person and Stirrers won't feel you. Morrigan won't change the locks. He can't, not until every Pomp is gone. Make sure he's never able to, Steven."

The door cracks explosively and splinters strike us both. Dust fills the room—serious dust, the dust of the dead, and it's heady stuff.

Mr. D's grinning and then he coughs. "Take a deep breath, Steven. I'm sending you to the place beneath the Underworld, the Deepest Dark. It's a short cut to the One Tree. You'll feel it drawing you. There will be a bicycle there. I like bicycles. Just keep riding until that breath gives out."

The mention of the bike startles me. I hope this one isn't going to fall on me. Mr. D sighs. "There's much about the nature of a Schism that Morrigan doesn't understand. That's about the only advantage you have. Once you find Lissa, you're not going to be able to run anymore." His shifting gaze settles on me, his face swims in the dust. "Things are going to get very nasty before the end, de Selby. And you're going to have to approach them head on. I'm sorry, but you've not seen anything yet."

I don't know what to say to that. I *try* to say something, but my lungs fill with dust, and all I manage to do is cough.

Mr. D pats my hand, and smiles. "Finally, lad, for what's ahead it's best not to think about it too much. We all die in the end."

And then I'm gone again.

29

The Deepest Dark is loud with the creaking of the limbs of the One Tree, but the sounds are carried to me through an air more viscous than air has any right to be. The vibrations of the One Tree judder through me. I am in the underbelly of the Underworld.

I'm crouching on ground knotted and ridged with questing root tips. Dripping from them like a luminous fluid are the souls of the dead, their time in Hell done. They slide into the air, first just as balls of light, but soon they take a roughly human shape—a life's habit, a life's form, is hard to undo.

Here, down is up and up is down. Above my head is the great abyss that all souls rise/fall into. What happens after, I'm not sure. Souls coruscate across the dark like stars, heading to places our words cannot encompass, because no stories come back from there. Nothing comes back from there.

For a while, despite my urgency, I am held by that sight. Captivated. The time will come when I'll know it intimately—maybe soon—but not now.

The air crackles with the whispers of those long dead, coming down through the roots of the tree.

"It was only a cold. A passing that became passing."

"Miss her."

"Miss her."

"Sorry, never finished before I finished."

"And... And... And..."

"Sometimes it rains, and all I am is the rain. Can you feel me?"

"Here... Here..."

It is a tumbling cacophony of bad poetry. Maybe that's what people are, ultimately. These chattering final thoughts, crowded and messy.

I lower my gaze and try and shut out the sound.

Here in the dark, I reach out, and my questing fingers find the bicycle that Death has somehow left me. "Yes."

Yes, yes, the bicycle echoes. *Ride. Ride.*

I clamber onto the seat. I haven't ridden a bike since I was twelve, but you never forget. OK, maybe you do. The bike shakes beneath me and I wrestle with the handlebars.

Care. Care, it whispers.

Once I start pedaling, I'm in the groove. Easy. Sort of.

I ride in the darkness, the bicycle wobbling between my legs. The dark is a deep cold liquid pressure around me. My ribs complain, everything feels like it's going to implode. My breath grows stale in my lungs. Suffocation looms.

I make the mistake of looking up into the dark again and see the souls there, drifting slowly, spinning and orbiting one another. Some are twitching but most are still, and they extend into the weightless abyss above.

I get the sense that, if I look too long, my flesh, or whatever this is that inhabits this space, will hollow and lighten, and I will lift and rise into that dark. It's already starting to happen, and it's not altogether unpleasant. I've stopped riding. The bike tips, and I fall on my side. It doesn't hurt. I get to my feet, and I realize that my grip is tenuous. I've also noticed that the urge to breathe has disappeared. I'm starting to get awfully casual about the whole thing.

A crack has opened up before me, and I peer down. Light spills from it and I'm gazing into my own stupid mug. It's a bemused face, a little sleepy, an I-just-had-sex face. Then I remember why I'm doing this: Lissa. I don't know what future we have together, but I want to create the possibility of one.

I wink at myself, clamber back on my bike and keep riding. There's a long way to go.

I follow my instincts, taking one narrow road, then another, rising up one hillock then down the next. I pick up speed as my confidence returns, and I start to accept my surroundings rather than gawking at them. This isn't so hard.

Slowly the darkness becomes something else. A green glow reveals the streets of some under-under city. And it's the first time I start to have any serious doubts. There's a familiar wrongness about the place. It shouldn't be here. The root tips that extend over this part of the Deepest Dark are dying—curling up and blackening. The air is foul and choking. But it's where I need to ride.

There's a hall in the middle of the city and a door is open. Something vaguely humanoid slips through it. Its eyes are huge, its face narrow, and its long mouth opens to reveal teeth. There are rather a lot of them, and they look sharp.

Then I realize where I am.

I've never seen one in its natural form, but I know what it is immediately. The hate-filled eyes glare at me. If looks could kill…I'm staring at a Stirrer. And this is the city Devour. I'm in the heartland of Stirrers. I'm a dead man.

The Stirrer sniffs at the air, and takes a step toward me. How the hell do you stall a Stirrer in the Deepest Dark?

It takes another step toward me.

The bicycle shudders between my legs. *Flight,* it whispers. *Haste.*

Good idea.

The Stirrer howls. It's a shrill and horrible sound that tightens my skin, and I pedal faster.

Not much time, the bicycle says.

I know what it means. The world closes in as I pedal through the streets, clumsily jumping gutters when I need to. The whole place is lit like the radium dial on an old watch. The sky above here is absent of souls, it's a patch of utter darkness. A wind crashes down from the dark, and it's frigid. I'm really not meant to be here. This place is telling me that in no uncertain terms.

A quick glance over my shoulder reveals a dozen Stirrers loping after me. They're making ground. The under-under world increases its pressure against my flesh. I start pedaling as hard as I can. And then the bike stops, just jolts to a halt. Unfortunately I don't, and I'm flying over the handlebars. I flip in the air, then land on my back. I open my eyes, all my breath gone now.

The Stirrers race toward me, their great mouths widening. I look at all those teeth. They grab my bike first. It lets out a shrill scream. The air closes about me like a vice. The fastest Stirrer grabs my leg and I—

I can breathe again.

The Deepest Dark is gone, and I'm... well... I'm in the Underworld again. The familiar smells of rosewater, rot and doughnuts fill my nostrils, the odor overpowering everything else, but for the dim hint of Stirrers. Here I am as deep in the Underworld as I have ever been and it is shockingly familiar.

I'm standing and shivering at the top of Mount Coot-tha—well, the Underworld equivalent. It's actually quite crowded here. But whether these people are dead or, like me, just visiting, I'm not sure. I think about what it takes to reach this place if you're not dead, and I doubt they're like me. But then there are tourists to every realm. Even Everest can be crowded at this time of year. People are gathered at Mount Coot-tha's lookout, built in the gap between two mighty root buttresses, gazing idly down on the city.

A baroque, brass curlicue-covered CityCat—looking like something a cartoonist might draw after a couple of tabs of acid, all flourishes and shadows, everything either sharp-edged or ridged with flowers—piloted no doubt by one of Charon's many employees, is cruising the black coils of the river below. Shadows clamber over it. The Brisbane River is one of the many tributaries of the Styx, and if you blink you can see, momentarily, the multitude of other rivers intersecting it so that the river below looks less like a cogent single stream and more like the vascular and shifting fingers of a delta or the veins of a lung.

The suburbs below, stretching out to the city and south to the Gold Coast (well, their Underworld equivalents) are, for the same reason as the river, a difficult thing to look upon. Buildings are fused together, different histories fold over each other. If you blink, sometimes the city isn't there at all, just a great forest. Only the sky is a relative constant, and the constellations that mark it are those that I know, though the dark is a little more crowded. Shapes stream through the spaces between the stars—spiraling ropes of birds and bats, or things that look like birds and bats, their cries distant and shrill, and meaningless.

The land of the dead is actually a little more happening than I guessed. We don't see this side of the world from our offices. Absurdly, I wonder, can people have mortgages here? What are the interest rates like? Have those fragments of the living clung onto that much?

But then I stop thinking about that because my left biceps starts to burn with a horrible liquid fire, more than the stinging ache that had bothered me by the tower. I grab it, and the flesh twists beneath my fingers. My tatt is taking a three-dimensional form: a nose and face pushes out from my skin. I try to push it back, and tiny teeth nip my palm. I snatch my hand away with a yelp. The tattoo draws a deep breath. The sensation of air entering my arm isn't pleasant.

Tiny eyes roll up in its cherubic head to meet my gaze.

"Shit." My voice is a whisper.

"You're telling me," the cherub says. It stretches its wings, which is a truly disconcerting feeling, as though someone is moving rods beneath my flesh. "What the—? I'm stuck on your arm. Oh, and where's my body?"

"You're just a symbol," I say, thinking, *I've grown a bloody inkling.*

The cherub squints at me. "One pissed off symbol. This is Hell."

"I'm sorry, I never thought about giving you a body."

"No, I mean, what are we doing in Hell? You're not dead, yes?"

I shrug. "I guess. It's complicated."

"No, it's not. Don't you sound so damn uncertain. That sort of uncertainty is going to keep you here."

"But here's the thing. I *am* uncertain. I've got no bloody idea what the fuck it is I'm doing here. Or even how to start getting Lissa back."

"You need a guide. Call me Virgil."

"You worked for Dante, I suppose."

"Ha. Maybe we should get a coffee first." The cherub says, and I don't argue. "The name's Wal."

"I thought your name was Virgil," I say.

"Don't get cute on me, buddy."

"What kind of name is Wal?"

"Better than Stevie wouldn't you say?"

We reach the cafe and I sit in pretty much the same seat that I sat in not so long ago when I was rendezvousing with Morrigan in the living version of this place. A lot's happened since then. The creaking of the tree dominates, louder than I have ever heard it. It's calling me, I realize. This is truly what it must feel like to be dead. There's a mesmeric quality to the sound and it generates a hunger in my chest.

I've pomped all my adult life, but I've never felt this before. This is what I'm going to have to fight against, if I ever want Lissa back.

I run through the coffee choices.

"Sweet Jesus. All I want is coffee. What the hell is a flat white?" Wal peers at the crow growing out of the barista's neck. "What do you recommend?"

The crow cocks its head.

"Just get him something easy," I say.

The barista sniffs. "You saying we're not up to the task? Saying we can't make good coffee?"

"No, I—"

"We'll make you good coffee," the crow says. "You'll like it. Now what do you want?"

"Long black, no milk."

"Ah, typical," the barista sneers. "Fucking tourist."

The tree creaks like it's ready to tumble. Should it fall, the whole weight of it would surely break the thin shell of the earth and drive the city into that chill abyss beneath. I realize I've heard that creaking ever since I sliced open my arteries with the craft knife. It's a background noise that has lifted startlingly in volume, shocking me when I least expect it.

I sip my coffee out of a paper cup. It's cold and tastes burnt and a little ashy, but no matter, I'm still getting over the fact that my money is good here.

I look at my change. The money is subtly, slyly different. The plastic of the notes is a bleached white. The faces printed on it are the same, but the flesh hangs loose, the eye sockets are empty, and the expressions contained within change every time I glance at them. They shift from mute terror to mad laughter in an eye blink. Except for the coins and the five-dollar note—there the Queen's face is serene and motionless. She's still alive, I guess.

The cherub grins at that. "I can't believe that after a century of federation, you're not a bloody republic yet."

Wal grips a chai latte in its wings, taking loud sips every few minutes that disquietingly warms my left biceps. I don't understand why *my* coffee is so cold.

I'm not terribly comfortable with the whole thing, but he seems to be enjoying his latte. "Haven't had a cup like that since, well, I can't remember. I do remember old Vic was still queen, and it wasn't as milky."

"Nor was it chai, I'd wager. Which hardly makes it coffee."

Wal grunts. "Maybe we need to keep going."

"How familiar are you with the Underworld?"

"I've been here a few times, day trips mostly. Been a long time between visits. So you're a Pomp. It explains a lot. The Underworld's different for you guys. It doesn't like you lot messing around. It gets you out of the way as quickly as possible. You can't change the order of things around here, mate. Your girlfriend will be up in the tree, and if she's been fighting her death like you say, then it may be faster for her."

"What'll be faster?"

"Assimilation. The tree's going to want to absorb her."

I'm looking at him, not comprehending at all.

"By your blank look, it seems to me that you are a pretty typical Pomp." I'm immediately defensive. But Wal doesn't allow me time to respond. "I don't know how you've lasted so long. What do you think a tree does?"

I shrug. "Grow."

"Nah. Well, yes, but *how* does it grow? It absorbs stuff, and it leaches stuff, too. This tree's just a wooden sieve. It separates the soul, and puts it where it belongs.

"It's the memory of the world, and a reflection, distorted of course, by the memory of it, because memory distorts everything. And it's the resorption of all that psychic energy, all those souls. The tree does that. Without this place, you'd have souls running amok everywhere, and Stirrers. Shit, there'd be so much confusion they could just walk in and take everything. Which is, from what I've heard, exactly what's been going on."

"So Lissa's being absorbed?"

Wal grimaces, his eyes lifting toward me. "Slow on the bloody uptake, aren't you? Yes and, like I said, it's going to be quick. As far as the tree is concerned, Lissa's been dead too long already."

And then I notice the armed Stirrers walking through the crowd in the lower section of the lookout. Stirrers here? How brazen.

I have to get going before they spot me. I know they can't sense me because I'm holding Mr. D's key, but they'll find me soon enough if I stick around here. They approach the barista. Great. He points vaguely in my direction, with an arm and a wing, and the Stirrers head my way.

I move as quickly as I can, hopefully without drawing attention to myself, to the base of the tree trunk. Once there, I can see stairs carved into the wood. The stairs stop at each branch after winding a lazy, but steep, circle around the tree. I start taking the stairs three at a time. It's a long way to the first branch, and even longer to the top.

"Slow and steady, eh," Wal says. "You'll wear yourself out at this rate."

"I don't have time," I gasp at him.

By the third circuit I'm hunched over, my hands gripping the rough bark of the One Tree, and I'm throwing up my coffee.

"You right?" Wal peers up at me.

"Fine, just some bad coffee."

"Just try not to get any of it on me."

Several times I pass dead folk heading where I'm heading, though none of them seem in any hurry. They look at me disinterestedly. There are a few I recognize, like John from the Wesley morgue, who nods at me. The sight of him disturbs me. But we don't talk, there's no time for that. All of us are too focused on our respective destinations. And I'm too out of breath.

There is only one person who passes me.

Mr. D comes silently from behind. He doesn't look at me as he goes, his shoulders hunched, his face set. The RM just walks higher and higher into the tree, and though he hardly seems to be walking at all, he's soon out of sight.

So he's finally gone. I'm seriously without allies.

"There's a place for all the Deaths—for the whole Orcus—high, right at the top of the tree. It's called the Negotiation," Wal says.

"What's up there?"

"Something you don't need to consider right now. One thing at a time."

And that one thing for me is these steps, one after another, over and over. It could be worse. I could be carrying a rock above my head.

As I climb, Hell unfolds beneath me, attended all the while by the creaking branches of the tree and the cold fingers of wind blown in from the sea. It's a beautiful sight, awe-inspiring in its vastness, the colors muted but varied. It's city, forest and sea. It's a sky streaked with blood-orange clouds. It's every sunset I've ever seen, every first glimmering star. I'm determined not to get used to it.

This place is death to me. Beautiful or not, that's all this kingdom is about.

30

I reach the first branch, and know at once that it's not the right one. It's a sensation buried in the meat of me, a certainty that is almost comforting, because it suggests that I might know where I'm going.

A little further up there is the scent of familiar souls, of family—cinnamon, pepper, wood smoke, a faint hint of aftershave and lavender. Maybe it'll be the next branch, or the one after that.

I stop to catch my breath and peer along the wooden limb. It's a gently swaying woodscape, and all along it there are people. Most are lying down, some stand, but the tree is absorbing all of them. Wood sheathes their flesh. It's a macabre yet somewhat serene vision. There is no pain here, just a slow letting go.

Then I see the Stirrer. A big one. It'd take two of me to fit in it. It's walking between the dead, peering at this body or that. Above its head heat shimmers, but that's not what catches my eye.

In one hand the Stirrer's holding a machete. It looks at me and grunts loudly. Shit. Mr. D's key means it can't feel me, but it certainly recognizes me. I lingered here too long.

It runs toward me, along the branch, and I don't wait around. I start up with a stuttering, desperate sort of run. I get back to the next set of stairs.

By the first circuit up from the branch it's obvious that it's going to catch up with me, and soon. My legs are burning, I don't have much pace left. I pass one then another of the dead, making my way around them as quickly as I can on the vertiginous stairway. The Stirrer isn't far behind me. I hear him push them off and their screams echo up to me.

"The bastard," Wal says. "They're going to have to do that climb again."

It's hard to find much sympathy for the dead, the worst has already happened to them. I know how resilient souls are. Me, on the other hand... I'm doing my best to avoid that outcome. I get flashes of the machete and the easy way the Stirrer holds the weapon in its hands. The thought of it slicing into the back of my legs is about the only thing that's giving me any strength.

I manage to reach the next branch, and I don't have any climb left in me. I stagger-run out onto its flat, windy, shuddering expanse. I'm panting and dripping with sweat, my legs rubbery. The edge is too close. I stare around me. In the distance a helicopter circles, looking for something that I suspect is me. I don't know what I'm going to do, but I need to do it here.

I only have a few moments to catch my breath.

"Stirrers are different here," Wal says.

"How so?"

"The Stirrers here must still inhabit bodies, but in this place between the living world and their city in the Deepest Dark, the bodies are tenuous things. The Stirrers don't fit well. There's a kind of friction of wrongness that exists between the bodies they inhabit and the Underworld."

"That's good, right?"

"Not really, they're stronger. The Underworld is much closer to their element and their true form will struggle to escape the flesh."

Wonderful. Exactly what I wanted to hear.

But there's no time to worry. The Stirrer's here and it comes at me, waving its machete in the air. Its host body is smoking, overheating.

Flesh bubbles almost hypnotically, and ectoplasm the color and consistency of mascara streams down its cheeks. I'm fighting a zombie Robert Smith.

"You don't belong here," the Stirrer says in a sing-songy sort of voice.

"Neither do you. Morrigan should never have brought you here."

The Stirrer shakes his head. "Come the Negotiation he will be the new RM. This will be his kingdom to rule."

So it hasn't happened yet.

The Stirrer swings the machete at my head, and I duck. My legs, weak from all that stair-climbing, shake beneath me, but they still have enough spring in them for me to swing up and drive the palm of my hand into its chest. It grunts and something shifts beneath its skin: the true Stirrer within. The form within the form strikes out at me. Its little claws or teeth rend its host's flesh. I tear my hand away. The Stirrer's skin is hot and there's a stinging red welt across my palm.

It's not what I was expecting. The Stirrer hasn't gone anywhere.

"Oh, yeah. Stalling won't work for you here," Wal says.

Now he tells me.

But the Stirrer is regarding me cautiously, and where my hand touched its flesh is a palm-sized black hole. It backs away. I've hurt it somehow, and I need to press the one advantage I have. I charge the Stirrer.

It hurls the machete at me, an easy, brutal gesture, and the pommel strikes me hard in the sternum, knocking me off my feet. The Stirrer looms over me and Wal's wings are a desperate blur to my left, as though he's trying to lift me through wing power alone.

"Get up, get up, get up," he urges, and I try, but it's too late.

The Stirrer grabs me and lifts me above its head. Smoke streams from its points of contact with my flesh. I can smell myself cooking, but I'm not the only one suffering—bits of its undead fingers are falling away like wet sponge cake and slopping onto the branch.

It stumbles and curses in an alien tongue, then something collides with it. The Stirrer stops, shakes its leg. Its fingers loosen their grip now, just when I don't want them to. We're a long way up, and the edge of the tree is so near. I can see the city and the dark beyond. I'd very much like to stay up here rather than go hurtling down.

There's an oddly familiar growl coming from the Stirrer's ankles. I look down and there is Molly. Her jaws are wrapped around the Stirrer's ankles. She looks at me and her expression is like, *Well, come on, help me out here!*

I slam my fist into the Stirrer's temple, hard enough that my knuckles crack. It shudders, releases its grip on me, and I fall. I swing out at the branch, grabbing as I go, but my grip is slippery at best. I slide over the edge until I'm holding on by my fingertips, my feet dangling over all that empty space. I get the feeling that if I fall I won't be climbing back up as anything living. Wal's wings are a hummingbird blur again; as though that's going to do any good.

Molly grabs at my wrist, as gently as she can, and pulls. Together we get up onto the branch and I lie there panting. I reach up and hug her. "Molly," I say. "Molly, I'm so sorry."

The Stirrer stays back. Bits of it have fallen away, and whatever's left has slipped so that it looks like a poorly made human collage.

Molly's smiling that beautiful grin of hers. She stays by my side for a moment, then crashes toward the Stirrer, barreling into its legs. The Stirrer topples forward, sliding past me and over the edge of the branch. Its slide slows and Molly leaps onto its back. She starts to burn, but she's everywhere, snarling and biting. The Stirrer's eyes are wide with terror or rage, Molly snapping at its neck. It reaches out for the branch, and gets a grip. Then, with the sound of wet paper tearing, wrist and hand separate. And they're gone.

I stumble toward the edge.

I watch Molly and the Stirrer fall away like some sort of flaming comet, rushing to the dark earth beneath us. The earth opens up, or low dark clouds scud in, because they are suddenly out of sight. Besides, I can hardly see at all. My eyes are wet with tears.

"Molly," I say. "Molly Millions."

I stare down at the dark where they fell. I'm beginning to understand this place better and what it means to come here. In essence it's just a way of losing what you love a second time. "Maybe I should have let Lissa go," I say.

Wal's head turns up toward me. "Ah, bullshit," he says. "Think of all the people who have suffered to get you here. Everyone suffers to get here. And you're ready to give up."

"Maybe."

Wal sighs. "That's just the Underworld talking. It's going to get worse, but if you want Morrigan to rule here, if you're happy to have him get away with all the killing, then who am I to argue? After all, the best I can get is living on your arm. It's *not* inhibiting at all."

Wal's right. I give myself a few more moments at the edge and then I climb again, following the stairs up into more crowded branches. Here, the stairs and the branches intertwine. We climb a tight bundle of fleshy tendrils, and we follow wooden handholds, hammered into the trunk of the tree, sticky with sap. Upward, always upward, and soon we're on another broad branch.

And, there, I see my parents.

The tree has begun to wrap around Mom and Dad's legs with woody vines rising from the trunk. Mom looks up, her eyes are dull. Death is already settling down her humanity, letting her sink into the tree and the universal thought or whatever it is that exists beyond the flesh and the memory of flesh. Soon she and Dad will be nothing but whispers and light dripping from the roots of the tree.

It's always faster with Pomps, maybe because we have an idea of what to expect, and we're cool with it. Slipping into some sort of universal truth is so much better than spending your eternity in heaven or whatever. Still, when Mom sees me her eyes widen and the dullness fades away.

"Steven. Oh, no. I was hoping that—"

"It's OK, Mom. I'm not dead."

Mum gives Dad a significant look. She might as well be giving him the crazy signal. Dad frowns.

"Seriously, both of you. I'm not."

"Then what in the seven bloody hells are you doing here? The living aren't meant for this place, Pomp or not."

"I'm looking for Lissa."

"Oh, the Jones girl! An Orpheus Maneuver, eh?" Dad gives me an extremely wicked look. "You know where she is, love?"

Mom has always had a greater sensitivity to the dead. We both look at her. Mom lifts her head and breathes deeply. "Oh, but there are a lot of Stirrers on the tree! They're like termites. They're going to be hard to get rid of, and it makes it difficult to... Yes! I can feel her. She's on the next level. She came in fast, which means she'll leave fast. If you weren't here I'd think you were with her." She glances over at Dad. "He was certainly all over her."

I redden at that. "Yeah, well..."

Dad winks at me, and Mom sighs. "But Steven, if you *are* here, it's not bad. It's marvelous, in fact. I've not felt... It's... Well..." Finally she shakes her head.

I know what she means. It is terrible and marvelous at once. The things I've seen getting here, things not even hinted at from our vantage point at Number Four. It's the sort of stuff you're not supposed to know until you're dead.

I don't know what I am here in the Underworld, except I'm not that. Definitely not dead, not yet. I kiss Mom's forehead. Her skin is cold against my lips. I'm finally getting the chance to say goodbye, but it isn't any easier.

"I love you, Mom."

"I love you, Steven." She blinks. "Get out of here as quickly as you can."

Dad nods. "Go get her, Steve," he says. "She's a good one."

"I could try and send you back," I say, and there's a slight pleading tone in my voice.

"No, I've died once. That's enough for me, Steve. I'd like to say I miss you but that's for the living, and your mother and I, well, we're not living anymore." He smiles, looks over to Mom, and she nods her head—wow, they actually agree on something. "Get her, Steve," he says. "And then, stop Morrigan. I can feel what he's doing even here. He's an idiot. You can't deal with the enemy and not expect grim consequences."

I look at them one last time, then clamber up the interconnecting branch.

"Oh, and I'm glad you got rid of that beard!" Mom shouts after me.

31

I look down and notice that, not too far below, there are Stirrers with machine guns. One of them points up at me. I hear a distant crack, crack, cracking and the wood near my feet explodes. I get out of the way, quick smart.

Even more worrying is the helicopter racing over the city toward this branch.

I don't know how long I've got, but I can hear the chopper drawing nearer. It's a peculiar looking thing, with huge, flat tear-shaped blades that look as though they're made of brass. But the Stirrers in its cockpit are grim- and melty-faced and all of them are carrying guns—old AK-47s. Morrigan's ambitions are huge, but he's still obviously working on a budget. One of the chopper crew points in my direction.

"That can't be good," Wal says, less than helpfully.

All I can do is try and climb faster.

The wind is picking up: salt driven on the air. A storm rushes along the surface of the sea, pelting toward the city. I grin into the wind, feeling somehow recharged by it. Out there beyond the edge of the city the great dark sea is crashing against the shore. Even here things rage and swell and live a kind of life, and my cares fall away from me all at once.

I'm wearing that smile on my face when I see her, but it doesn't last.

The One Tree has bound itself around her with rough fingers of bark. Lissa's eyes are milky with death. There is no recognition there. I might already be too late.

One of her fingers wiggles.

I touch it, and feel the slightest warmth, just the barest hint of life.

I don't want to be here and, above all, I don't want her to be here. If I could tear down the Underworld I would. But I don't have that power, just my love and my will. I'm terrified of failing, I'm terrified of succeeding. The only thing I don't doubt are my feelings for her.

The branch fights me all the way. It grows thorns. It snaps at my fingers with little teeth. I bleed pulling the bark off her, and maybe that's what does it, because the tree gives her up at last. I lay her gently onto the branch.

I touch her face. There's a flat warmth to her flesh that is almost worse than the cold I was expecting. Her eyes are dull, barely green at all, and nowhere near the startling, quick to fire color that I remember.

I hold her in my arms. She is still. I can't feel any more warmth. I lower my lips to hers and a force, a presence, a fire passes through me in a brief, agonizing flash. The tree shakes. Something howls, the light dims and I get a vague sense that the whole Underworld has paused. Even the storm seems to be waiting.

Then Lissa coughs and shudders. Her eyes widen. "Steven?"

"Lissa." *My darling Lissa.*

Her face wrinkles. "Steven, this isn't some sort of cruel joke, is it?"

"It better not be." I'm grinning again, a smile so wide that it hurts. My hand rests on her cheek; her skin is warming. And her eyes, they're no longer as flat, as lifeless. Shit, of course that could just be wishful thinking—that's gotten me here as much as anything else, even if Wal doesn't believe it.

"So how do we do this?" I ask her, and she frowns.

"Do what?"

"I'm taking you back."

"There's no... You can't. Not an Orpheus Maneuver," Lissa says. "You'll get yourself killed."

"That's been on the cards for about a week now," I say.

"No, you have to leave me here. You can't."

"Another bloody optimist," Wal says. "How do you two get out of bed in the morning?"

Lissa's eyes regain some of their gleam. "Who's your little friend?" she asks.

"Little friend!" Wal snorts. "This woman lacks sensitivity. Throw her back, Steve. There's more fish in the sea."

"Hmm, I don't like him either," Lissa says. "He's much better as a tatt."

Introductions are quickly made above the increasingly vocal wind. The dark clouds bunching up near the horizon are sliding toward us fast.

"I'm getting you out of here," I say.

"But the thing is that Orpheus Maneuvers always fail."

"Paradigm shift," I say, then kiss her.

She kisses me back. Her flesh warms, then burns. I feel her excitement. Her hands are getting busy at the back of my head, pulling me in closer, and I'm holding her face. When we finally pull away she looks into my eyes.

"I love you, Steven. Find me," she says.

There is a sudden blinding brightness.

I'm on the One Tree alone. Lissa's gone. I'm not sure where, the Deepest Dark or back to the land of the living. I stand there looking out at the Underworld, and stare at all those bodies closest to me, wrapped in tree. Most of them are Pomps. The nearest one is Don.

"How about a kiss then," he says and grins lasciviously.

I roll my eyes.

"Good to see you, de Selby," he says, though he's already slipping into that post-caring dead state. "Morrigan. Did he send you here?"

"No, Mr. D, after he died. Morrigan tried though, and he's going to pay."

"You make sure he does. I'd just paid off the place in Bulimba and Sam had moved in. Not bad, eh? I spent my childhood in a bloody caravan in Caboolture, and there I was with a classy lady like Sam. She's still alive, isn't she?"

"Yeah, I haven't felt her here."

"Good."

"He'll pay, I promise." I feel that sense of urgency winding up in me again. I need to find Lissa again. And then we'll make Morrigan pay for what he's done.

"Good on you, kid," he says. "Now get going, there isn't much time."

There are cries in the distance. Stirrers. I walk to the edge of the tree. Peering over it, I can see dozens of them rushing up the stairs. Bodies tumble everywhere as the Stirrers push them out of the way.

"I'm not sure how I get out of here."

"There's really only one way," Derek says. He's standing behind me. The tree has yet to take him. "Make sure you get Morrigan." The bastard has his hand in the small of my back. He hardly has to push at all.

I tumble off the tree. There are cries, I hear gunshots, but they can't hurt me now. I'm moving too fast. I spin in slow circles as the ground rushes up. It's terrifying, my stomach is a dozen flips behind me, and I think it's so unfair that, even here, my body holds on tight to vertigo.

"Sorry," Wal says, "sometimes this doesn't work."

"Now you tell me."

The ground beneath me opens its great earthy maw and I'm enveloped in loamy darkness, and then I'm out, and once more in the whispering Deepest Dark.

Lissa's soul is a brilliance in the dark. It coruscates, and I recognize it immediately with a certainty that only years of pomping, and true love, can provide. Oh, how I love her. She's my Lissa, and I'd go through Hell a thousand, thousand times to find her. And if I lost her I would do it again.

I reach for her soul and it bites me, bites and scratches in a way that no light should. I yowl into the void, but I hold on. The soul is chaos in brilliant form. It is all that is love and hate, it is all that is passion and hopelessness, and madness. It is so definitely madness. But so is what I'm doing.

I am holding her essence.

I bring it to my chest and Lissa's soul passes through me. It's a fierce liquid pain, and one I've never known before, but there's also a rightness to it and an intimacy that goes far deeper than what we shared when we made love. It spreads through my flesh, seeps into my bones.

A Pomp is a gateway, a conduit, and that doorway can extend back to the living world. I don't fight it, just let it happen. Until it's over.

At last, I release my breath.

She's gone. Again. I look up into the sky, where all the souls are flickering like stars, shining and waiting, waiting perhaps for the love that is life to call them back again. And I realize that this is what we're fighting for, this aching brilliance. This is what the Stirrers want to destroy.

And suddenly I'm scared, because it seems so fragile. I felt the essence of Lissa, held it in my hands, though already the clear memory of it is fading. My flesh cannot hold it, shouldn't hold it. Life is longing, it isn't certainty. That is what is most wonderful, and awful, about it.

I take a deep breath in the cold. It's time I went home. Time I faced Morrigan.

32

Do you think that did it?" I take a few jumping steps, to try and get the blood flowing. Dust lifts in a fine silvery cloud into the air.

Wal sighs. "Hard to say. You're mixing up the natural order of things, and while I'd be the first to say that nature and supernature could do with a kick in the teeth sometimes, it can be difficult."

"You're saying that after everything I've done—after being macheted at, shot at, pushed off the branches of the One Tree and falling, falling, falling—that I still may not get home?"

"That's exactly what I'm saying, Dorothy," Wal says. "You're not even wearing any slippers, and if I remember correctly there is no place like your home, because it blew up. As I said, it can be difficult."

"Sure is," whispers a dry old voice. I turn toward the sound and there is Charon. At last.

He's the tallest—why is everybody so tall in the Underworld?—gauntest man I have ever seen. Bones are barely contained by his skin and jut like bruised wings from his hollow cheeks. His fingers and wrists seem to contain a fraction too little flesh to enclose the meat and skeleton beneath.

"Been waiting for you," I say. You can't pull an Orpheus Maneuver and not expect to talk to the Old Man. "Where's the boat?"

"That metaphor really isn't appropriate anymore. Besides, I've got staff. They drive the hydrofoils, the UnderCityCats, for me."

"So how do I get back?"

"My, you are a tubby bugger," he says, swinging his hand faster than my eye can follow. He pinches my stomach with fingers hard as stone.

"I'm not fat," I say.

"You're a regular bloody buddha." Charon shakes his head, and lifts up one of his wrists. "This, my matey, is size zero. You don't get any leaner. Well, perhaps there are a few fashion models who do, but they're on a fast track to this place. The world's gone to fat, particularly the bits of it that exist on the back of the other bits. When did you last go hungry, Mr. de Selby?"

I shrug. I'm starving now, in fact. I can't remember the last time I ate.

Charon isn't one for silence, I suppose he gets plenty of it. "Yes, well, you'd know if you ever really had—"

"So how do I get back?" This could go on for a while.

"Hmm, it was *you* who interrupted me." He frowns. "I had a peek at your dossier. It's highly unusual for you, but these are highly unusual times. The Negotiation is going to be very interesting, I think, more interesting than any of those dickheads upstairs expect." He pulls a packet of Winnie Blues from his pocket and picks out a cigarette. "Want one?"

"I don't smoke. Not when I'm sober, anyway."

The Boatman grimaces. "C'mon, this is the Deepest Dark. Indulge yourself."

I shake my head, and he puts them away. "Let me tell you though, you will—and sober too, that's a total one hundred percent prophecy—or maybe you won't. Now, back to the question. You don't leave—"

"I have to. I have to get out of here, there's unfinished business."

"Funny, I meet a lot of people who say that here. It's as though life owes you a neat ending," Charon says flatly. "And once again you interrupt. You don't leave, not all of you. You have to leave something of yourself behind."

"I'd not heard of that condition."

"Probably forgotten. It's been a while since anyone's done this—kudos to you on that, too, boyo. Think about it, even The Orpheus left something of himself when he tried to escape the Underworld."

"Eurydice," says Wal somewhat irrelevantly.

"Yes, your little arm face is right. Though obviously back in the day, Hell was all about cruel and unusual punishment. The Orpheus left his heart behind and so do you."

The Boatman coughs, and thumps his chest with a bony hand. The sound echoes loudly in every direction, booming back at us. I imagine that whatever beats beneath those ribs, if it beats at all, is dusty and ancient and probably needs the occasional jolt.

"Well, not exactly your heart," he says, once he gets his breath back. "I'm obviously getting metaphorical, you know, figuratively speaking. The Orpheus looked back. It saved his life though, because I can tell you if he hadn't left Eurydice behind he wouldn't have gotten back himself. The fellow was far too cocky."

"Cold comfort though, isn't it?" I say.

"This is Hell, this is the flaming capital of cold comfort, mate." The Boatman looks down at his feet. He's wearing rubber thongs. They're huge, but his feet overhang them by a good three or so inches, and his long toes end in nails painted black. He crouches, picks at something beneath a toenail. "Besides, if you go back, what are you going back into? That blocked artery is still going to be there, or that embolism. It's a revolving door for most people. Even Deaths aren't afforded the privilege of immortality, just a very, very long existence. Until Schism time, that is. That's how Deaths work."

I'm not in the mood for a long lecture. "Can I nominate what stays behind?"

"No." Charon lifts from the crouch and looms over me, bending down to regard me with eyes dark and dangerous. "Crikey, that's just being cheeky."

I hold his bleak gaze. "So it can be anything?"

"Yes."

"Like, say, the left ventricle of my heart?"

"Always getting back to the heart. You're heart-centric. There are a lot of other organs that are essential now, aren't there? And, each of them, including the heart, would be covered under the word 'anything,' though it would hardly be in the spirit of the deal. Look, it's a risk. But we can't have the living, not even Pomps, coming here and expecting it to be easy."

"I never expected it to be easy." The truth is, I hadn't really had a clue about what to expect or, until Mr. D gave me the option, that it would be possible.

"You're in the Underworld, Steven. You're not on *The Price is Right,* or jumping a fence." He scratches his head. "Well, it's exactly like both, only the price of losing is death—the fence is fatally electric, probably has skulls painted all over it, or it's made out of skulls."

Wal looks up at me, and rolls his eyes. "You've got to hope for the best, mate," he says. His little wings flutter in that disturbing way that scrapes the bones beneath my flesh.

"Yeah," I say, "because everything's been working out well so far."

"You sent Lissa back, didn't you? And you're still alive—well, sort of, if we ignore technicalities." I look down at him, unmoved. "The other option, of course, is that you stay here," Wal huffs.

"In that regard," Charon says, rubbing his long hands together, "we can be very accommodating. I'm much happier bringing people here than taking them back. It seems wrong. In fact, it doesn't just seem wrong, it *is* wrong. That whole natural order of things, you know."

He's right. There's no point in arguing. I nod my head. "OK. Send me back, take what you will."

He grins. "That's my job. Now, you know the deal."

"The giving up something?"

"No, the other one."

"Which is?"

"Don't look back . . . and run."

And I want to argue the logic of that. After all, we just spoke about The Orpheus and his looking back, but it's too late. Charon claps his hands, once. There is a deep booming sound that reverberates through my body so that I feel as though I'm some sort of living bell.

Charon's gone.

The air feels and smells different, at once fresher and fouler. The scent of newly turned dirt. A warm breeze blows against my skin. Then all that's gone and I'm walking down a metal corridor lit with the blue lights of the Underworld, my footfalls ringing loudly. I'm not walking toward the light, but through the light.

I can smell doughnuts again, then something like burning tires.

"What do you reckon, Wal?" My voice carries uncertainly through the air.

The cherub is remarkably silent. I consider staring at my arm, but I'm not exactly sure what constitutes looking back. These rules can be extremely loose and terribly precise.

Then something chuckles, and it's not Wal.

I remember Charon's other advice. I run all right. The Underworld never lets you get too casual with it. I put on as much speed as I can, but it doesn't seem to do any good.

I run through hot and cold spaces, wet and dry. The air alternately clings to me or pushes. This is the edge of life and death, both forces are tugging at me, even as I go. I'm hoping for some sort of tidal shift, that life will start to grow more potent, and soon.

There are noises. Liquid, horrible noises, and scurryings, and more laughter.

The blue lights flicker.

I know not to look back, but that laughing... Something is drawing nearer, every footfall louder than the last one, every step faster than my own, and I'm no longer running, but sprinting, crashing down the hallway. Strobing blue lights line the walls. It's as though I'm racing down a long, halogen-lit disco, only whatever is behind me is more terrible than anything a disco ever produced.

It slobbers and howls. For a moment I think of Cerberus, the Hound of Hell, but then it's cackling, and dragging bones or bells along the ground.

I want to look back. I want to know what it is that will have me, to see if I've actually put any distance between us. The want is burning a hole between my shoulders, my skin is tight. The hairs on the back of my neck rise. But I keep my head down, keep sprinting until the tendons in my legs tear, until the muscles in my flesh burn.

And then I trip over, and I'm sliding on the floor.

It's on top of me and over me, and it's sliding into me, crashing into my mouth, my ears, my pores.

I don't scream until I'm back in the tower, but by then it's too late. I'm standing woozily, naked and blood-stained in the cold.

I know now why you can't look back: you see what's chasing you, and you may as well give up, may as well not bother running, because it is terrible and remorseless. Life, the living world, was what pursued me down that hallway. And it caught me, wrapped me in the mad vitality of its arms and flesh and showed me that it was as cruel as death ever is.

And here I am, back in the land of the living.

33

I don't even get time to laugh, because a moment later souls start rushing and scraping through me. They're zeroing in on me. It doesn't hurt as much as it once did, maybe because I've been to Hell and back.

All of a sudden I know that, other than Morrigan, I'm the last Pomp alive in Australia. Sam—well, her spirit—is here, looking extremely pissed off.

"The bastard got me too, Steve," she says. "They'll be coming for you now. All of them."

"I'm sorry," I say.

"Don't be sorry, just get moving. He was fast. I was driving through the outer suburbs around Logan, heading toward the PA hospital. He shifted right into the fucking car."

I nod my head. "Apparently he can do that now."

"He said to tell you he has what you want. That's all. Then he shot me. And here I am."

"Yeah, I'm so sorry, Sam." I'm not sure what I'm sorry about. Everything, I suppose. But the words catch in my throat. Sam doesn't deserve to be pomped by me, she should be the one still alive.

"So am I," Sam says, "but it had to happen. Mom died from a stroke, a series of them. I swore that I'd never die in bed but I never expected Morrigan to fulfil my wish. He was my friend. I've known him for nearly thirty years."

"He was everyone's friend," I say. "Don's waiting for you."

"He bloody better be." Sam frowns. "There's something different about you." She looks around the tiny interior of the iron tower. "Where's Lissa?"

Her words are little more than a breath, then Sam's gone, too. I call Lissa's name. Nothing.

There is no one in the tower except for me now. The place stinks of old blood, and there is indeed blood everywhere—my blood. Oddly enough I feel remarkably sanguine. Whatever I had lost was replaced, though that doesn't mean I am without wounds.

Where I had cut to reach the portal arteries there are two thick nuggets of scar. They have healed, but they ache, and when my fingers find the rough cicatrices of my knife work, I have to grit my teeth with the pain. The tattoo of Wal is gone as well, and where it was there is nothing but pale skin.

I'm shivering, and naked. My backpack has come with me but it and its contents are coated with mud—a final residue of the Underworld, perhaps. I scrape off what I can and quickly get dressed. My clothes are a little stiff, and my every movement hurts. I manage it. The cold has seeped into the fabric, and now it is pressed up against me. I feel like I've dragged myself out of icy water onto an icy shore.

"Lissa." I can't feel her, and if she was anywhere nearby I would be able to.

There's nothing.

I've lost her. I almost had her. We almost got a chance at a life together. I failed her and I failed my future. I sit in the tower, my knees pulled up to my chest, and sob.

Finally, I get up, wipe my hands on my jeans and step out of the tower. There's only so much grief I can allow myself. I am alive and I am still hunted. The storm's passed, gone on to drench someone else, or has dissolved into the ether. And it must have passed a while ago. The air is dry again.

By the tower is a bike, and on the bike, a note.

If you're reading this then you are most probably alive. Welcome back, Steven. Now ride.

They'll be coming for you.

D

My watch says it's ten o'clock in the morning, Sunday. I've been gone since Friday. It's one of those beautiful days when the sky is so eye-searingly bright that it's almost beyond blue, and there's a warm breeze coming in off the river. I want to take pleasure from it, but I can't.

Besides, there's little pleasure to be had. I can taste Stirrers, they're filling my city. It's as though the air has thickened with some sort of grease. A bleak psychic cloud smudges the city as heavily as any stormfront. Tomorrow, if not tonight, things are going to tip into Regional Apocalypse. But that's not my biggest concern.

I quickly run through my possessions.

I've got Death's key to Number Four and my knife. I've still got an mp3 with about two hours worth of charge, as well as my phone, around $2000 in hundred-dollar notes and a couple of twenties. Oh, and a bike.

The world isn't exactly my oyster, but I've looked Death in the face and that counts for something. Well, I'm going to make it count for something. This is going to hurt Morrigan.

I ride out from under the cover of the trees and over the fallen-down fence, putting the iron tower behind me, then cycle into West End. It's an inner-city suburb, but leafy and crowded with shops and cafes. Made up of detritus and dreams, there's a vitality to West End, a sense of community. It's old Brisbane with tatty finery and make-up. Maybe that's why some of the shops are still open. People cling to whatever normalcy they can when the world falls down around them.

Two Stirrers walk down Boundary Street. Both smile at me while

I slide my knife down my palm. "It's not going to make any difference," one says.

I stall them. It certainly clears the air here, though.

I walk into the nearest cafe and order a long black from staff who may have served more disheveled customers, but not many. The coffee is scalding and it strips away a little of the cold within me. It's far better stuff than they have in the Underworld.

Lissa's gone. There's nothing I can do about that, except get angry.

Coffee done, I buy a new shirt and a pair of black jeans, then a hat and sunglasses, to avoid attention and the increasing glare of the sun. I slip my old clothes into a bin.

Then I insert a new sim card into my phone and call Tim. There's no answer. I try his home number, it rings out. So does his work number. Morrigan has Tim without a doubt. I try Alex.

He answers the phone in a couple of rings. "Steve," he says.

"He's got Tim."

"The prick," Alex says. "The whole bloody city's going to hell here."

"Yeah," I say, "Regional Apocalypse."

Alex snorts. "Never liked that Morrigan. Always seemed too smug if you ask me."

"Listen, I'm sorry to pull you into this."

"Don't give me that shit. You're not pulling me into this. When my father died, Morrigan dragged me into it, willing or not," Alex says. "You've got nothing to be sorry for. As far as I see it, you're the only one who can stop this."

"Maybe, but I'm sorry anyway." Still, that realization makes it easier to ask him for the things I need.

Alex sounds a little surprised by the time I'm through with my list, but his voice is resolute. "I can get all of that. I'll see you at four. The Place?"

"Yeah."

I throw out the sim card and then ride as fast as I can to the Corolla in Toowong, hoping it's still where I left it. To my surprise it is, obviously not an attractive enough vehicle for anyone to steal. I open the driver's side door and sit down behind the wheel. The car feels so empty without her.

Working as a Pomp, you have a pretty good idea of the forecast, even if you don't know the specifics. But I'd never really understood until I'd failed Lissa so badly. There's always pain coming. There's always loss on its way. That's a given. Doing this job, you know it more than most. It makes you appreciate the little things all that much more. Sometimes that's worse, because the more you hold onto something the harder it is to let it go. Life and death are all about letting go.

That's the one lesson the universe will keep teaching you: that until you stop breathing, until you let go, life is loss, and loss is pain. Sometimes though, if you're lucky, you can find some grace. I'd seen it enough at funerals, a kind of beaten dignity. Maybe that's all you can hope for. Maybe that's all I can hope for.

I'd promised my parents that I'd do my best to go on, and that drove me, hard. Jesus, I'm lucky I had a chance to say goodbye, most Pomps don't even get that. Shit, I'd only managed because of Lissa. And now she was gone.

Alex is waiting for me. He smiles, though I know he really wants to tell me that I look like shit. It's one of the ways he's different from his father. Don would have told me straight up.

"You got that aspirin?" I have a headache, but that's not what it's for.

He nods and passes the packet to me. I take a handful of the pills and swallow them.

"You sure that's a good thing to do?"

"It's not a good thing at all. But aspirin's the quickest way I know of to thin my blood," I say. "Have you got the suit?"

He nods. "Oh, and I got something else." He chucks a heavy black vest at me. I catch it with a grunt.

"What's this?"

"Something you didn't think of. It's Kevlar, the best I could manage."

"Good work."

"It won't protect your head, but it's better than nothing."

It's *far* better than nothing. The suit and the vest are even the right size. I don't ask how he managed it. I just change. The suit's an affectation really, ridiculous. But if I am going to my own funeral, if I am doing the work of a Pomp, then I want to be in a suit. I look at myself in the car door window. If it's at all possible I look thinner than I've ever been, but the suit fits well, partly because of the bulletproof vest. I almost look good. Even my hair.

Alex has managed to get me everything else I wanted. "Thanks. You did good."

"The CBD's virtually deserted." He grimaces. "I had to do a little bit of looting. For the greater good, I kept telling myself, for the greater good."

I shove everything in the sports bag (another item on the list) and dump that on the front seat. Alex is standing there, formidable as always, waiting. But probably not for what's coming.

Suddenly I'm telling him about Lissa. It's pouring out of me, and by the end of it Alex, Black Sheep or not, is looking at me sternly.

Then he grins, and chuckles. "You fell in love with a dead girl. Even I know that's unprofessional." Alex shakes his head. "But then again, Tim said you were always getting into trouble."

I laugh even though there are tears in my eyes.

Alex grabs my arm, and scowls. "Steve, if you have any chance of getting through this, and believe me when I say I want you to, you're going to have to put everything aside, or Morrigan's won. You're not dead yet, and that's got to count for something, don't you think?"

"I've let stuff slide all my life," I say.

"Yeah, but that's different. Stuff was never going to get you killed. Morrigan murdered my dad, Steve. He murdered your parents, too. Now we both know the score when it comes to death, but it still hurts. I'm still not even sure how I feel about it. But there's one thing I do know—Morrigan's trying to kill you, and he'll succeed if you lose focus." He pats my arm. "Maybe Lissa's out there. Shit, man, you've been to the land of the dead. You went there and you came back. Just stop and think about that for a minute before you face the end of days, eh?"

"It isn't," I say.

"What?"

"It isn't the end. I'm not going to die." We both know that this is unlikely, but we both know that I have to try.

Alex grins. "Yeah, bloody right, you're not."

"Maybe you should think about leaving town for a while."

"And extend the misery a little longer? No thanks, mate. If this doesn't work, I'm going to the Regatta to drink till I want to die. You think Tim's alive?"

I shrug. "I haven't pomped him, but that doesn't mean anything. Morrigan could have, or his spirit's been left wandering. I'm sure there's plenty of souls in that position."

Alex takes a deep breath. "Let me come with you," he says.

Christ, I wish he could. Alex is a thousand times more capable than me. For one, he managed to get everything that I needed. I reckon he could storm Number Four in his sleep.

I shake my head. "There's too many Stirrers." I point over toward the center of the city. Their presence is a choking foulness in my throat. "Even you must be able to sense them now. You wouldn't last a minute being so close to so many. I could brace you, but if I go under, you're gone. I don't want to have that on my conscience."

I don't know if he looks angry or relieved. But I'm sure I've made the right decision. Alex is a Black Sheep, and a cop. He knows what I'm up against—and so do I. I'm trying not to think about it too much, because I need to believe that I might have a chance. I desperately need to believe that.

"Well," I say. "It was nice knowing you." I hand him a tin of brace paint. "This will keep you safe for a little longer."

Alex nods then slides the tin into a pocket and we shake hands, which seems at once ridiculously formal and apt.

"Good luck," Alex says.

"You too."

We stand there awkwardly, then the moment passes and we head to our respective cars.

Number Four is waiting for me. Morrigan is waiting, and I'm going to give him what he wants.

It's time to end this.

34

Number Four is on George Street, so I park in the Wintergarden car park. The big car park is empty but for a couple of deserted cars—all nicer than the Corolla, but it hasn't let me down yet. I'm less noticeable as a pedestrian, and I can reach George Street and Number Four directly from here. It's only a few blocks away and there's a nice circularity to it—though I only think of that once I've parked. The last time I was here I could have convinced myself that my life was normal. I yearn for that time. But it's lost to me now.

I pass through the food court where I first met Lissa and fell in love or lust or whatever it was at the beginning, just before she told me to run—in the other direction. Even then I knew to avoid Number Four, even if it was for all the wrong reasons.

Everywhere I look I see Lissa, the places she filled. I struggle to stop the rising anger that it brings, a bleak force that threatens to overpower me as much as any Stirrer.

It's now late in the afternoon and normally the CBD would be crowded with Sunday shoppers, but it's a virtual ghost town as I walk up Elizabeth Street, past empty boutique stores and bus stops. None of the pubs and clubs are open, their doors are dead mouths gaping, their windows blank eyes staring. There are so many Stirrers in the city that my senses burn with them. What I'm feeling is far worse than the Wesley Hospital. It's a deep and sickening disquiet. Get too many Stirrers together and people sense the wrongness of the situation, in the same way they could sense Lissa on the bus seat next to me. The buses and trains would have been crowded this afternoon but people have stayed away, shops have shut early and no one would have been able to explain why.

It feels as though most of the Stirrers in the city have gathered here. Better near me than out in the suburbs.

As I approach Number Four, the key starts tingling in my grip, then it begins to burn. For all its heat I refuse to let it go. I'm not Death, and the key knows it, but that's the thing, there is currently no Regional Manager. I'm hoping that I haven't set off alarms, I just don't know.

But when I turn into George Street, that's the least of my worries.

Stirrers have gathered around Number Four. There are at least a hundred of them, and that density of death is going to kill. A void of that magnitude is going to drive people away if it doesn't just swallow them up before they get a chance to run. Of course they don't just consume people. The trees along the street are wilting, birds are falling out of the sky. As I watch a possum tumbles from a tree.

A hundred Stirrers at least and they're not scared of me. I cut both of my hands, deep and hard. It hurts, but I am so used to that sort of pain now. And I'm angry. I don't know if I've ever been angrier. The things Morrigan has stolen from me. The important pieces of my life. All I am now is pain and anger.

At their front is Jim McKean. It's appropriate that this should end with him. At least he doesn't have a shotgun now.

"Out of my way," I snarl.

"Try and stop us," Jim says. He's in a suit, not as nice as mine, but pretty stylish. I grab him with my weeping hands, and the Stirrer passes through me.

"It's my job." I let the body fall. The Stirrers pull back, wary of my blood.

Then someone points a gun in my face. I duck as it fires. I'm rolling. The Stirrer aims again, and then its chest implodes. It staggers back, dropping the gun, then steadies, looking for the weapon. There's a distant crack and a moment later the Stirrer's head is gone, too, and the body falls. I stall it before it has a chance to get up.

I throw my gaze around the street. Alex, it has to be Alex. He's ensconced himself in a building somewhere nearby. I've a sniper at my back. The Stirrers hesitate. There's another crack; another head explodes. I stall that one, too. They know they have no choice now. The circle closes.

And they're on me. It's worse than any rugby scrum, grabbing and gouging. But I'm stronger than any of them. I'm a Pomp, and I'm damn good at my job, and I've got nothing to live for, nothing to fear. Because I've seen the other side—shit, I've ridden a bicycle down its boulevards! They couldn't get me then and they're not going to get me now.

I tear the Stirrers away from their hosts, one after another, and I pay for it in my blood and my hurt. By the end I'm hoarse with screaming, but there is an end. Unbelievably, impossibly, there is. I lie there amongst the dead, my breathing ragged, until I have the strength to pull myself out of the mass of bodies. Blood streams from wounds all over my body, but that doesn't bother me. All it says is that I'm alive. Besides, I've experienced worse in the past few days. And I know that this is only the beginning.

And then a new wave of Stirrers pours around the corner and I'm striking out with fists coated in my own blood, and every time I connect another body stalls.

I recognize these faces. Most of these people were Pomps. It's terrible work, but I know that they would have done the same, that I'm honoring their memory, however desperately and clumsily. There are tears in my eyes, and an ache in my chest.

By the time I'm done there is a pile of corpses on George Street, but that's not my problem. I know that this mess will be cleaned up, if I succeed. And if I don't, then the region is doomed anyway.

This close to Number Four the building tugs at me, drawing me in. The big Mortmax Industries sign is winking, as though unable to hold a charge. The ground hums beneath my feet, and it's not due to passing traffic. There is none. The city is empty.

We recognize each other, Number Four and I, and it recognizes the key. I've never felt this connection to Number Four before. Remarkably, the thing I sense coming from it most is sympathy.

I peer through the window. It's no longer dark. There are more people I know in there with clipboards, on mobile phones, a few are working in front of laptops. But when I say people, I mean they were people once. They're not anymore.

I've known this for some time but to see Morrigan actually working with the Stirrers still makes me shiver. Of course it makes sense. Stirrers, after all, are pure Pomps, even if they're otherworldly Pomps. It sure beats training new staff. We've been economically rationalized. Imperially screwed, as Don would have put it, a step up from royally fucked.

And here's the thing: his replacements haven't kept up their end of the bargain. We Pomps are not only easing the passage of the soul into the afterlife, we're also fighting an invasion, and Morrigan's not only sold us out, but he's sold out the whole continent.

Morrigan's pure eighties' Brisbane, never too frightened to tear down the old for the new. And I can see him getting ready to push this idea internationally as a more efficient facilitation of the pomping process. Morrigan's always been an early adopter, and the other regions' Ankous keep an eye on what he does, and, generally, take it up quickly.

I wonder how many other Schisms he's set up. These could be tripping through the world, Schism after Schism, Regional Apocalypse after Regional Apocalypse. It may explain why not a single RM has answered my calls. No region's that parochial, and the various RMs are, in most cases, happy to step in when a takeover is liable to occur.

This time it's as though the rest of the world is holding its breath, waiting to see how this plays out. Well, they don't have to wait too long, damn them all to Hell. The landscape of death and life has changed for good. I know that, but I'm after some payback.

The door before me no longer emotes any of that odd sense of knowingness. It's just a door. There's no hunger there, or maybe my own hungers are matching it, somehow canceling it out. Maybe I just don't care anymore.

I pull out my pistol, release the safety—yeah, I'm learning—and then insert Mr. D's key in the lock.

The door opens. I step through it.

35

The first Stirrer I see is Mom. She's standing there by the front desk. I grab her with one bloody hand and the Stirrer evacuates her flesh. Her eyes widen and her body drops with a soft sigh. I've no time to lay it down gently. Though it hurts me deeply, I let it fall.

There are so many Stirrers in here. They're a dull scratching behind my eyes, an infection of all my senses. My only hope is that Mr. D's peculiar key is doing what he promised and dulling my presence to them.

I sprint down the hallway past a half dozen Stirrers. There's one at the desk, my Aunt Gloria, Tim's mother. That almost stops me in my tracks, but only for a moment. I hope Tim's somewhere ahead of me, and that he's unharmed. If he isn't, I've failed her.

Aunt Gloria's body doesn't notice me until I've leaped over the tabletop and grabbed her arm with my bloody fingers. It's another hurtful but final stall. Aunt Gloria's body slides from her chair.

The elevator door opens. It's empty. Stirrers are coming down the hallway after me.

I jab the button for the eighth floor. If Morrigan is anywhere it will be there. The door shuts and up I go.

The elevator door pings open. My cousin Jack sees me and his eyes widen. He comes at me with a ring binder. I dispatch Jack quickly.

"Could you please stop neutralizing my staff?" Morrigan asks. He's standing at his desk, his fingers resting on a glass paperweight of the world. He picks it up and puts it down. My gun is trained on him.

"Don't listen to the bastard," says a familiar voice from a corner of the office.

Tim's alive! I look over at him. He looks a little disheveled but is otherwise all right, even if he is tied down to a chair. I see where Morrigan has marked him with a brace. He's proofed against the Stirrers. That's a relief.

"You OK?"

He nods his head. "Better than expected."

"My staff haven't harmed him," says Morrigan.

"Your staff? These are Stirrers. They don't work for you." I glare at him.

"You're wrong there, Steven. We have an agreement, and it is to our mutual benefit. I don't think you understand how powerful I've become."

"Powerful or not, you can't trust them, surely?"

"It's not about trust," Morrigan says. "They do exactly what I tell them to do. They are under the strictest controls. My controls. You see, there's always a problem when you try to fuse an organic process with a bureaucratic one, Steven. Everything is open to corruption, but nothing more so when there is an ill fit, when two separate processes collide."

"Tell me about it," I say. "People start getting murdered in their beds. Friends turn on friends and family. It's definitely a flawed system. You should just kill everyone, then everything's smooth and simple."

Morrigan ignores me. "But I've managed it. Efficiencies will be improved. The Stirrers are much better than human Pomps. You keep them under enough control and everything works well."

"So what you're saying is that death works best without the living to screw it up?"

Morrigan nods his head. "All those noisy rituals, all those dumb beliefs drawing us away from the truth, and shaping the Underworld until it's a mess. You've been there, Steve. You can't tell me it works."

The truth is I can't, because if it had, I'd still be back there, drawn into the One Tree. "So, it has some problems," I say.

"Problems, Jesus!" Morrigan hisses. "I'm steering us toward uniformity here. My region will be like no other, and then the others will slip into line. There will be new efficiencies."

"You're trying to control Stirrers here. They don't care about your efficiencies."

"Poppycock," Morrigan says. "Total bullshit. You want to know what I did? I dragged Mortmax Industries up by the bootstraps. Turned it from a small family business into a well-oiled machine. I may have been born into pomping, Steven, but I chose this path. I didn't just drift around, expecting everything to fall in my lap.

"Have you ever worked a proper day's work in your life, Steven? Have you ever sat there, planning, setting out the future?"

We both know the answer to that, and there's a small part of me that's blaming him. It's not like he ever encouraged me to apply myself. "But I also never planned on killing everyone, never decided that the way forward was fucking contingent on slaughtering my friends."

Morrigan jabs a finger in my face. "We work for the Orcus! The way forward was always going to involve death. You're not a child, stop acting like one."

I step back. "Yeah, then what about the Stirrers on George Sreet? The Orcus would never allow that. Remember what this job is about?"

"You don't know what you're talking about," Morrigan says, but he doesn't seem as certain as he did. And he's shuddering, the bastard is as worn out by all the pomping as I am. And that shouldn't be happening if the Stirrers were actually helping him and not just waiting to devour Australia.

"I wish I didn't. I've pomped a hundred people today. All you've done is remove the people who held back the Stirrers. But it isn't too late. We can stop this. God knows it'll probably kill us, but we'd be halting a Regional Apocalypse."

Another Stirrer comes near enough for me to touch and I do. It takes the breath from me. Every time I do this, my heart tears in my chest. "You know it's true, Morrigan. We can do this. The Stirrers are older than life itself, and they want this universe for themselves. And you've let them in. You've opened the door wide and I don't even know if we can close it now."

"Steven, the moment I killed Mr. D, I put into motion something that can't be stopped. And I don't want it to."

"But maybe—"

There's a dark flash of pain, and I'm down. I hear my gun clatter to the ground. I'm not long after it.

My eyes open slowly. I don't know how long I've been out. Not that long, I think. The big glass paperweight of the world that struck my skull is next to me on the floor, and there's blood all over the thing. *Oh, the prick.*

"Good, you're awake," Morrigan says. "Now kill him, darling."

I look up. Blood is pouring into my eyes from the deep cut in my head, but there's Lissa's body. The evidence of all my failures. Not her, why did he choose her? She's holding a rifle.

She swings the gun up and fires.

The bullet strikes Morrigan in the chest. He stumbles backward a step, and then another. He stares at the wound in disbelief, then falls to the ground silently, his arm outstretched toward me.

"You're alive," I say, somewhat obviously.

She runs toward me and wraps her arms around me in what is the most wonderful embrace I have ever known. She's all hard breath against my neck. I kiss her.

She's alive. She's alive! I didn't fail her. I'm woozy, bleeding, possibly dying, and I can't stop smiling.

"Don't you ever do that again," Lissa says. "Don't you ever pull me out and leave me alone."

"I won't, I won't," I say. She pulls back and I drown in those eyes. "I thought you were gone. Jesus, I thought I'd lost you."

"Where else did you think I would be? My body was here. I'm so sorry, I've been doing my best to keep away from Morrigan, and the Stirrers, but trying to look like I'm not. It's exhausting, let me tell you."

"It's OK. We've made it." The words come slowly. I'm just so happy to see her.

Lissa shakes her head. "I don't think so. Look where we are."

But at least we're together again, I think, smiling. "How do I look?"

"Like shit, not a good impression at all. I thought you were dead." Lissa grabs my face gently, it hurts. "When you slipped away from me, or I slipped from you, there were all those Stirrers and their guns. I couldn't see how you'd survive that, but I thought if you did survive, you'd come here, and if not, the Stirrers could take me again."

"Have you managed to stall any of them?"

"Steve, I'm not a Pomp anymore. I died, remember? You brought me back. I don't have those powers, and there's no RM to give them to me. I'm not even sure I want them back. If I hadn't stolen some of Morrigan's brace paint I'd be dead."

"Good for you," I say. I'm really bleeding a lot. My vision's fading.

"You patronizing shit. Now, hold on, you're going to be OK."

I touch her oh-so-serious face. "It's a Regional Apocalypse. There are Stirrers everywhere. If you're powerless, you need to get out of here. As far away as possible."

"You're going to be OK," Lissa repeats.

"I really don't think so," Morrigan says. He's on his feet and looking as bad as I must, maybe even worse. We're mortal, even here in Number Four. Being Pomps we have no excuse for forgetting that. I don't want to die, but I know that's what's about to happen.

Morrigan lifts his rifle and aims it at me.

With whatever strength I have left, I push Lissa away from me, except she's already off me and rolling, her gun swinging up toward Morrigan.

And Morrigan's rifle fires, almost at the same time as Lissa's.

36

Well, I did my best. There's that howling wind again, rising through the dark, promising a storm. I'm dead. The One Tree is a siren call in my skull. I know where I am before I even open my eyes. Still, I don't expect to see Death looking down into my face. I bite back a yelp. The pain is gone, I'm whole, and shocked to the point of shuddering, then even that's gone. I'm just lying there beneath that prickly, various gaze.

"What are you doing here? You're dead."

"Dead, but still existing." Mr. D smiles. "Hi, Steven, I kind of hoped you'd kill each other, it brings you to the Negotiation on an even footing. So there are only two of you left, eh? All my wonderful employees, all of them gone."

"And Lissa, there's three."

Death shakes his head. "She's not a Pomp anymore, unless she chooses to take that role up again, and only if the new Death offers it to her. It's just you and Morrigan."

Lissa's got to be happy with that, but then I think of her there, cradling my body in her arms. Oh, Lissa. Yeah, it was never going to end well. But then nothing does. Everything is jagged at the end, truncated and cruel, love most of all, like a branch of the One Tree snapped off.

"Why am I here?"

"Because you're dead and Morrigan's dead, and you're the last two Pomps. And here you'll get to decide who gets to live again. The Negotiation always comes down to this. Morrigan vanquished me and he chose you as his opponent."

I notice Wal, hovering behind Mr. D. The cherub winks at me. He's in possession of a body now, chubby and bewinged, and I'm seeing far too much of his package. He flits this way and that, with a speed and grace that surprises me.

"It always comes to this," Mr. D says. "Start a Schism and it ends here on the uppermost branches of the One Tree, the point where all the Underworlds connect and the laws of living and dying are more flexible."

Then I see Morrigan off to Mr. D's right. His sparrows lift into the air and hover behind him like some winged cowl. Blinking, Morrigan pats his chest, then grins. The injuries we'd sustained are gone.

Around us in a ring are all the other RMs in their ceremonial garb. No corporate gear, just the long dark cloaks of the Orcus. The thirteen regions, the thirteen Deaths. I'm waiting for them to start chanting, "Fight. Fight. Fight."

Suddenly the Stirrer helicopter is lifting into view. Half a dozen machine guns fire. The Orcus laugh.

"Cheat!" Mr. D roars. He flicks one hand casually at it, as though it is nothing more than some sort of annoying insect.

The chopper tips, then plummets away. A few minutes later there is a distant popping sound.

A savage smile is stretched across Morrigan's face. I can tell he didn't expect the helicopter assault to work, but Morrigan is the sort of person who will try anything once. He rubs his hands together. His sparrows spin off in two braids of shadow. They loop around him, with the precision of a troupe of stunt jet pilots, then return to their position behind his head. I look over at Wal, he gives me a jiggly shrug. I really wish the little guy was wearing pants.

"So this is it," Morrigan says. "The Negotiation."

"Yes," Mr. D says. "And don't think I've forgiven you for running me over. It's a most terribly ignominious way to die. A bullet in the back would have been preferable, or even a knife across the throat—at least that ends with an ear-to-ear smile—but you've never been one for the up close and personal, have you Morrigan? Everything is automated, everything is done at a distance. I don't understand that."

"Which is why your time is past." Morrigan moves in. "It's my time now. Things will run smoothly."

Mr. D swells. He broadens across the chest, and his limbs lengthen until he towers over Morrigan, and his face is all faces. It is ruptured meat and broken bone, and the furious swelling of flies and worms, and the quiet that comes after. Then it is Mr. D's face again, marked with a silent rage, and he's his usual stick-thin size. "Not just yet," he says. "I stay to see this out. Those rules remain. This, as you said, is a negotiation, The Negotiation. But not between you and me, that has already played out. Between you and him."

He's pointing at me.

"At last." Morrigan's grin keeps getting bigger and bigger.

"This isn't fair," I whisper. Why is Morrigan looking so cheerful?

Mr. D spins to face me, and I see there's a measure of anger in all that rage just for me. "When is life or death fair?"

"Can we just finish this? I've had enough of your talk, years and years of your bloody talk," Morrigan says. "I have a lot of work to attend to."

"Of course you do," Mr. D snaps. "The creatures with which you have made your curly, crooked deals will ensure that. You were the one who started rolling the knuckle bones, Morrigan. But it is up to me to bring it to an end. I cede, I was outplayed, one by one you have gained my powers...but I wonder if you haven't outplayed yourself."

Morrigan sighs. "This is exactly why I began this in the first place. I'm tired of this slow, slow bureaucracy. You were never fast enough, nor efficient enough. I know I can do better. Just let me start. Just let me get it done."

Mr. D is having none of that. "The cleverest thing, of course, was that you left the weakest Pomp till last."

The penny drops. *Ker plunk.*

I realize how I've been manipulated. I glance over at Wal, and he shakes his head. Seems the idea's just struck him as well.

Everything was done to drive me to this place. I would have died a week and a half ago if Morrigan hadn't wanted it to end up here. He shaped everything, probably even Lissa's ability to stay in the land of the living. I don't know how I know that but, here, on top of the tree, I'm certain of it. Lissa came and went too conveniently. Now I understand why Morrigan looked so shocked to see me in the Underworld, and why he had grown so angry at me attempting the ceremony. It hadn't, as I'd thought, been a remnant of avuncular concern. If I had died then, he'd have been forced to fight one of the other more capable Pomps. And he'd counted on me. Of course, he'd adjusted quickly. He'd known I would pomp Mr. D on the side of that road, and had even hurried it along by getting my Stirrer father to fire at me.

I understand now why Mr. D hadn't known about the crows. By that stage Morrigan even had control over them. And why Lissa survived "unnoticed" around all those Stirrers. I was never meant to die, just to believe I was going to, until he had me where he wanted.

I think about all those other Pomps better able to challenge Morrigan physically or experientially. Morrigan was behind every step I've taken and, looking at it, I can sense his smiling presence in everything. He's known me all my life, knows how I think.

The dickhead even used me as bait.

"You did this because you thought I'd be the easiest one to beat," I say.

Morrigan looks over at me like I'm a pet he's extremely fond of. "Steven, you were my best choice. Why do you think you've managed to keep your position as a Pomp all these years?" He shakes his head. "Even then, you nearly ended up killing yourself a half-dozen times. Why did you go home? That bomb wasn't meant for you, just to keep you away so you wouldn't have a chance to regroup. I needed you running, not thinking, because even *your* brain starts to consider things eventually."

Morrigan planted that bomb there himself. Now I know why Molly hadn't seemed worried when I got home. She knew Morrigan, he'd actually taken her for a few walks a couple of weeks ago. My hands clench to fists.

Mr. D motions for me to stop. "Not yet, boy," he whispers. Then, more loudly, he says, "Of course, Steven is quite different now. Your attempts at engineered mayhem were perhaps a little too realistic. I rather think you underestimated him. Now, you have to face the consequences."

Then it sinks in. What this is all about. The heat of my rage chills.

"I don't want to be RM," I say, and it sounds a little whiny. "That's never what I wanted. I was just trying to survive, that's all."

There's a gasp from all the attendant Deaths. It's as though they can't understand why anyone wouldn't hunger for this job. Mr. D did and Morrigan does, but they have known me in one way or another since I was child. My ambitions have never been as focused or as cruel.

Honestly, I hadn't even thought about it. Maybe I'd had some hazy idea that after beating Morrigan (not that I'd ever really believed that I could) all the other Deaths would gather together and vote on a new Regional Manager. But I'd really only been thinking about the corporate veneer, not the rough and callous beast that lies beneath it.

OK, I'm screwed.

Mr. D brings his bleak eyes to bear on me. "You want to give all this to him? You want Morrigan to get away with everything he's done, and become the new RM?"

I don't say anything. My gaze slips from Mr. D to Morrigan. There's a bad taste in my mouth that has nothing to do with Stirrers. Bloody Morrigan. He knew I wouldn't want this.

Morrigan smiles. "Then it's easy. The Negotiation's done. I desire this, I have the will, and I most definitely have applied the way. Send me back," he says to Mr. D.

Our old boss shakes his head; he even waggles his finger. "That's not how it works," he says. "No, we're talking about death here. And death is brutal."

"No," I say. "I'll do what it takes, but I don't want to be Regional Manager."

Mr. D sighs. "Look, Steven, it's time you grew up. You've drifted along, cashed your checks and done your job, but little more. If this job hadn't existed, you'd be a video-store clerk, getting angrier and more bored. Sometimes the world hands you something and you have to take it."

"You don't have to," Morrigan says. "We can negotiate."

Mr. D nods his head. "Of course you can. The problem is that this Negotiation is done with knives. And it has begun."

The other Regional Managers draw in close, their black cloaks flapping in the wind like a murder of crows. There is a deep and awful sense of anticipation. Blood lust glints in their eyes, brighter than hair in a shampoo commercial. This is the moment they've been waiting for, the reason calls have remained unanswered, why Australia hangs, teetering on the brink.

I look down at my feet where a stone dagger, the length of my forearm, lies. The damn thing wasn't there a moment ago. It shivers with a hungry anticipation that is palpable and more than the sum of the gathered RMs'. The only one not hungry for this is me.

Morrigan fits in here. He knows this game, he will excel at it.

"You either pick it up, or there's no resurrection for you, Steven," Mr. D says, impatiently. "Hurry."

Morrigan has already snatched his dagger up from the ground and is running at me. All right then. I get the feeling that this isn't one of those cases where, if I die willingly, I get the job and Morrigan is hurled into the depths of Hell.

Do I want this?

Do I really have any choice?

I crouch down quickly and snatch the blade up. It's heavy but well balanced, as though it wants to cut, its point dipping and rising, seeking out Morrigan's blood. The hilt's cold, with a spreading iciness that runs up my arm and envelops my flesh. Morrigan is already on me, swinging his dagger down. Out of the corner of my eye I can see Wal, up against Morrigan's flock of sparrows. He's snatching at them, but they're fast. His skin is already flecked with tiny wounds.

A storm explodes about us as I meet Morrigan's strike. It's a violent raging gale, cold and laden with stinging raindrops. Morrigan has attacked me with such force that I stumble. Somehow I'm meeting his next strike, then I realize that the dagger is guiding me, because there's no way I should have been able to block that blow. There should be a stone dagger jutting from my windpipe. My knife is already slicing through the air, cutting off another jab.

Oddly enough, and this is the hardest thing, winning this is going to be a matter of trust. If I fight against the dagger I am going to slow my response time. I realize that I'm not exactly going with the flow when Morrigan's blade draws a red line across my chest. I pull away just in time. The cuts mark my skin millimeters above my nipples.

It burns like hell. I'm lucky that this competition isn't to the first blood. By the end of it there's going to be so much of it. Our hearts are pumping and the knives slice deep.

I back away.

A sudden gust hits the branch and it flexes. Now it's wet and slippery, and I stumble backward and fall, which is what saves me as Morrigan slashes out. My cheek flaps open, a raw line of pain across my face. Better that than my eye.

Morrigan's hungry for it and I'm just me—I'm hesitating, fighting the blade. It's only going to be a matter of time. My death is imminent and Morrigan knows it. The bastard is grinning like the Cheshire Cat.

I think of Lissa, everything that she has had to endure, and just what Morrigan might do to her if he wins. I want her. I want to be with her. My lips curl, and my cheek tears a little more. Salty rain rushes into the wound, splashing against my teeth. I get back on my feet.

Fucking Morrigan.

He swings up and under at my chest and I grab at his wrist and catch it before the blade strikes my skin. I don't even know where that move came from, but I hold his wrist and twist, muscles juddering in my arms.

He winces, and I loosen my grip, though I'm still holding on too tight for him to pull away. I duck away from his flailing free hand, but not before it strikes me in the side of the head.

His eyes narrow. "That's the story of your life, Steven. Do you really want this?"

"I want to live. I want my family back."

"Neither is going to happen. So just give it up."

He punches down on my wrist and snatches his hand from my grip, but as he pulls away, my knife hand is swinging around and it catches him in the middle of his palm.

I yank the blade toward me, tearing flesh. "How's it feel?" I growl. "Hurts doesn't it?"

He kicks up and catches me hard in the crotch. I stumble back again, the tree shaking beneath my feet. Mr. D looks on, his face expressionless. The other Deaths are motionless, captivated. Each face is a rictus of pleasure. There's blood in the water and the sharks are circling—their eyes might be blank and cold, but their jaws are working, widening into that most devouring sort of smile.

I slide on my arse away from Morrigan. The stone blade is slick with rain and blood but I hold it tightly. All I can taste and smell is the iron scent of my beating heart. Morrigan casually kicks me in the chest, and ribs break. I'm nothing but pain, and searching eyes.

"You really drew this out, de Selby," Morrigan says. "Just like your bloody father, he never knew how to get to the point. It's only fair that I draw it out now, at the end. And to think you took up the blade. You even considered that you might be able to make it as one of the Orcus."

He kicks me again. And my chest is on fire, a liquid fire that has me gasping. "Look at them, boy! Look at them! They'd eat you alive in under a minute."

Then his boot finds my mouth, once, twice. I spit out teeth.

My mouth can barely contain all the blood in it. I can't catch my breath. All I'm breathing is ruddy and choking. My vision spots as Morrigan transfers the blade from one hand to the other. My brain is empty but for the pain. I can't even move.

He drives the knife toward me. I weave—well, fall—to the right. Oh, the pure broken-ribbed agony of it. Surely there's not much life left in me, there can't be. But there's something, a wild and raging vitality, and it burns inside me. I can barely see, my eyelids are swelling with blood, everything is torn and battered from the toes up, and it doesn't matter. This is what death comes to. This is what it is all about.

Morrigan scowls. "Just die. It's over, don't you get that? It's over."

Wal's in trouble too. He's a blur in the near distance, hemmed in by all those sparrows. He's snatching them out of the sky, and hurling them down. But there's more than he can handle. Inky wounds streak his flesh. Sparrows are snapping at his wings. One breaks, and he falls. The sparrows are all over him, smothering him, pecking, devouring.

I scramble backward, trailing blood, and spit out another tooth.

Well, fuck it. It's over.

I smile. Nothing else. Just that broken grin. Morrigan charges at me, driving down toward my chest with his stony knife.

My breath roars in my head. My mind goes blank. I duck away from his blade.

Morrigan stumbles, and in that moment—in the absence of my own will—my own stone knife guides me, subsumes me, so that all I am is something cutting and deathly. There's a force, ancient and hungry, bound by its own cruel covenants, and it propels my hand. The blade glides forward, almost languidly, and it slams into Morrigan's left eye with a wet detonation.

He screams and I push the knife in further. I get to my feet—I don't know how, but I do—and he stands with me. Morrigan and I are one thing, swaying, unsteady, joined with a dreadful intimacy by the bloody length of the knife.

"Not enough," he mumbles, but there is no force in him, just the soft exclamation of a dying man. "Not enough."

I don't know if he is talking about him or me. His words mean nothing. He's carried on my blade, blood bubbling from his eye. I wrench his knife from his loosening grip and slash it across his throat. I'm screaming. All I am is death, violent, terrible death. There is no room for me, just this.

It scares me. I see the edge and somehow step back. I let go of the knives. And it's me again, and I'm horrified.

Morrigan's body spills blood as it topples to the broad limb of the tree. It shudders once, then is still. And he lies there, an old man, bent and broken and bloody, and I killed him. The Negotiation is ended. Jesus, how did it end up this way?

"Good work," Mr. D says.

"No, it wasn't." That's all I can manage. My breath is whistling through the hole in my cheek. Every heaving breath is agony, and it feels like I'm leaking fluids from every pore and orifice. As the rain lightens and the storm heads out, deeper into the Underworld or out of it altogether, I'm ready for death myself.

Mr. D pats my back, and the touch is gentle, but even that hurts enough to send a painful shudder through me. "Yes, it was. You know, you're the first person to ever win a Negotiation who hadn't engineered it in the first place. I don't know what that means, but—"

"Some fucking negotiation!" I spit blood. It splatters across the rough bark of the tree.

"It's not finished yet. You've won the right to exist, to be RM, to sit upon the throne of Death, to have the high six-figure salary."

Mr. D's fingers drive into my back. Agony runs through me. It's jagged and dirty and I scream. Then the deeper pain melts from me. Ribs shift beneath my chest. The torn cheek knits closed. I'm almost a whole man again, except I'm more than that. Something passes from Mr. D to me, a coiling and vast prescience. Mr. D is diminished and I, well, I don't know what I am anymore.

"So it's over?"

Mr. D shakes his head. "Steven, it's only beginning."

Go the cliché, but he's right. Oh, is he ever right. There's no sense of closure, merely a cruel momentum. When am I ever going to get a chance to stop, to mourn?

37

The other Regional Managers crowd around. They're quick, as management always is to recover from shock outcomes, each one slick and ready to engage in damage control. It's all I can do to stop scowling at them. Not a single one of them stepped in to help while my family and workmates were being slaughtered. But is there any point railing against death?

I'm going to find out, but not today. Healed or not, I'm exhausted.

I look up and Wal winks at me, then winks out of existence. I glance at my arm, and he's back there, a motionless 2D inky presence, smiling benignly. This job has some perks after all.

The sparrows are all gone.

No one else seems to have noticed either event. New Zealand's Regional Manager, Kiri, nods at me, then grins a huge grin. The sort that shows far too many perfect teeth, all of them sharp. At least he doesn't go for Mr. D's theatrics, his face keeps the one terrifying visage. "Good one, eh mate." He slaps my back warmly. "Never liked Morrigan. He was a prick as far as I'm concerned."

Still, you didn't help, now, did you? There might be no point in remaining bitter, but I damn well intend staying pissed off about this for some time.

The UK Death smiles, as bloodthirsty as a lion. "I was hoping for Morrigan, I'm afraid." *Well, thank you. Let's let bygones be bygones, eh.* "But I'm sure you'll make a wonderful Regional Death." He doesn't sound sincere, but at least he's honest, and I realize what a minefield it is I've stepped into. A ruthless minefield built on countless little dirty deaths. They're all murderers, they're all ambitious, and they all see me as a new player, a new way of getting one over the others.

Africa's Deaths look on. There are three of them, all in suits well out of my price range. The only one that is less than eons old is South Africa—Neill something or other. I can tell their ages, now, just by looking at them. Some of these Regional Managers, particularly in Europe, are "only" a few hundred years old. The next youngest to me is only a hundred. But in each and every one of them I can see, suddenly and vividly, the sharp memory of the violence that was their Schism, their rise to power, and it sickens me, because none of them would have it any other way. And I can see in each Schism each poor idiot like me who was put to the knife. Already this is mine, this knowledge, this seeing, and I hate it.

Perhaps that is what needs to be done, perhaps only people who hunger for this can handle the job. Well, we'll see. I have a problem with perceived wisdom.

"Excellent," says Suzanne Whitman, the North American RM. She smiles warmly at me, and that grin is hungry and cruel at the same time. "Morrigan was too ambitious. I trust you'll still be organizing Brisbane's Death Moot in December?"

I look over at Mr. D. Death Moot? Shit, I'd forgotten about what amounts to the APEC for the Underworld, all those RMs in one room together for two days. And we're holding it in Brisbane this year. Mr. D nods his head.

Suzanne's still waiting for some sort of response, even as the One Tree gives me an image of her stabbing her own opponent in the heart, in her Negotiation.

"I suppose so," I say. God, I'm actually RM. I'm not even sure what that entails, but I know that I'll find out.

She shakes my hand and grins another deathly, horrifying grin.

"Mr. de Selby, you are perhaps the luckiest person I have ever met. It's good to have you on board."

"Yeah, thank you," I say. "Every single last one of you."

"You're welcome," she says warmly and without the slightest hint of irony.

And then they're gone, and it's just me and Mr. D and Morrigan's body.

"You don't want to be offending your fellow RMs, Steven. In their defense, though none of them need defending, I wouldn't have stepped in to help any of them. In the event of a Schism you don't. It's bad form, and there are rules to be followed. That said, I wouldn't trust a single one of them, and they certainly won't trust you." Mr. D looks at me sternly. "You don't get to be RM unless you're prepared to kill everyone you love for it. Well... until now. And that's the worrying thing. Steven, you represent a change, and don't for a minute believe that any of those RMs won't try and exploit it. You've more sensitivity than all of them combined, and that means more chinks in your armor."

He leads me away from the Negotiation and all those bloody battles, enacted over and over again. "But I'll be around for a while, to ease the transition. It's traditional, and I can't tell you how glad I am it's you and not Morrigan that I will be advising. If you need me, you know where I'll be."

Mr. D motions at a treetop nearby and a small platform there which looks much more cozy than it ought to. There's a pile of books on a small table by an old wooden rocking chair. Classics, mainly. I even spy Asimov's *Foundation* and a few of P. K. Dick's. "I'm going to catch up on my reading, and enjoy the aspect, not to mention watching what you might do with it all."

The view's both fantastic and terrible at once. The city stretches into the distance, and then up rise the mountains of the Underworld like the shoulders of some mad beast, vaster and more enduring than the One Tree. At the mountains' base crashes the sea, its waves a raging, dizzying vastness. They slam into the stony cliffs and rise up hundreds of meters, their spume blown on the winds over the city. It's a mixture of salt and ash and fire.

Mr. D catches my gaze. "You really should go fishing there one of these days, once everything is sorted out. I'll instruct you, it's very relaxing." I wonder how a sea that huge and wild could ever be relaxing. "And the fish... Tremendous. Certainly a marvelous way to celebrate your victory."

I'm not really ready to celebrate anything. I'm not even sure if there is anything worth celebrating. I'm the new RM of Mortmax Industries, Australia, I've lost all my workmates and replaced them with the twelve most bloodthirsty people on the planet, and my only advisor is as bad as the rest of them. Don't trust anyone, Mr. D had said. Yeah, well, I'm starting with him.

I look at Morrigan's body, and I'm crying.

I'm angry and sad. And that's not exactly what I'm weeping about. It's more for the other things that I've lost, and so swiftly. The man's died twice to me. Ambition had proven as bad as a Stirrer, possessing him cruelly and completely. But he had chosen that path. I think about how long he must have been planning it all, working side by side with the people whom he intended to kill.

It explains why he had been so easy on me over the years. He needed a patsy, someone he could manipulate. My, but he did a good job. I don't know how I feel about that right now, but it isn't good. I still can't believe that it came to this.

Less than a fortnight ago, Morrigan was as close to me as my parents, I was just heading back from a funeral, and I had no idea what it was to be in love. Things change so quickly. This job should have taught me that. All we have are moments and transitions. You never know what's going to come next.

Morrigan's body dissolves, and all I'm staring at is one of the creaking upper branches of the One Tree, marked with the faintest memory of Morrigan, one shadow hand, its palm outstretched.

I glance over at Mr. D. "Where did he go? I mean, am I going to have to worry about him coming back?"

"Good heavens, no." Mr. D jabs a finger at the branch and Morrigan's shadow. "Morrigan's nowhere and everywhere. He took the most deadly lottery in the world and he lost. Morrigan's soul has been as close to obliterated as anything can be in the universe." Mr. D snaps his fingers. His grin is chilling and satisfied, extremely satisfied.

I don't know what to say, or whether I'm pleased that I didn't know that I was fighting for, not just my life, but my afterlife as well. Who am I kidding? Like Mr. D told me, what feels like months but was just a couple of days ago: It's best not to think about it.

If I had known what I was probably going to lose, I'd never have been able to empty my brain. Not even that close to death. Killing is an emptying, and an absence of fear, an absence of empathy. It's also a state I never want to experience again.

"This is all going to change," I say. "It can't stay this way."

"You're the new Death, that's your prerogative," Mr. D says, with a generous shrug. "You can do what you want."

"Paradigm shift," I say, and I like the sound of that.

"The Underworld's your oyster, de Selby."

"Thanks a lot."

"You're welcome."

Then it hits me, worse than anything that Morrigan ever managed to throw at me. "Lissa's not a Pomp anymore."

"That's right."

"And she's surrounded by Stirrers."

Mr. D frowns. "Yes, you better do something about that." Like I said, Mr. D has no real sense of the pressing nature of certain events.

"How?"

"Oh, I think you'll find a way, de Selby." Mr. D waves a hand airily, then he is gone. Though I know he hasn't gone far from this empty triumph of death, I want him gone forever. But the truth is, I'm more terrified of his absence than I'm prepared to admit. Better the Death you know. Except I'm Death now, and I don't know anything.

I glance around me, at the great branching Moreton Bay fig that devours the hill below in rolling roots as wide and as tall as monstrous pyroclastic flows, and around which teems the suburbs of the Undercity of Brisbane. Cold salty air crashes against me. This place is as much mine as anyone's. It can bend to my will, but all I want is to get back to Number Four.

Easy, right?

38

What do you know, *it is*. Even if, as Wal once said, I have no ruby red slippers and my home is a smoldering wreck.

It's easy and painful. Shifting tears at my limbs. My flesh feels raked over. I scream. So much for an element of surprise. Every gaze is on me.

Lissa is in trouble, Stirrers surround her. Not that she's too worried. My girl appears to be pretty handy with a rifle. But, there are so many of them. And Tim's still stuck in his chair, though he's worked one hand free. He smiles at me.

"Hey," Lissa says, and she sounds so very, very happy. "You made it."

"Yeah. Where did all these guys come from?"

"Pending Regional Apocalypse," she says, matter of fact, and shoots another Stirrer in the head.

"Not anymore." I lift my hands, a motion perhaps too cinematic, too contrived, but I'm new to this shit. "Get out," I snarl at them, and my voice is louder and stronger than I remember it.

The Stirrers turn toward me, and they howl. It's a cry of distilled rage, a sound too much like the one I made in my fight against Morrigan. They are many, but I am Death here. I am the master conduit of this region, and I understand what that means at the most visceral level. I really do, and that almost shocks me to a stop. But the momentum's still building, and it's that momentum that takes me.

One of the Stirrers, Uncle Blake, still in his golf gear, raises a gun and fires. The bullet passes through me. It hurts, but then the hurt is gone.

"It's too late for that," I say. "Far too late. You didn't get what you wanted. You got me."

Oh, and they have *my* Pomps. I call them now and they come crashing down George Street, where another wave of Stirrers has gathered. The crows are pure death, as powerful as anything I have ever encountered. *We are here. We are here,* they caw. They beat at the sky with a thousand midnight-dark wings. For a moment I'm viewing the world through thousands of eyes, hearing the whoosh-whoosh of wings finding rough purchase in the air. Amazingly, I'm dealing with the vertiginous vision easily.

The crows descend in a storm of claws and beaks, and every Stirrer they touch is stalled.

It's hard keeping them under control. These aren't human Pomps, they're easily distracted, and the way they stall these bodies is different, more violent. It is a steady tearing of flesh from bone. But there are so many that the Stirrers can't keep up, they can't fill bodies fast enough. And the crows are taking their toll.

I can taste the meat, feel it pulling away from dead bones. It should turn my stomach but it doesn't. These crows are mine. I am so intimately connected to them that this act, this devouring, seems natural. I wonder if this is what Mr. D had referred to as the Hungry Death.

But it isn't enough. Number Four is full of Stirrers, and the region itself, from the Cape to the Bight, is far worse than that. There are hundreds of them throughout the country. I look over at Lissa.

"So, are you open to becoming a Pomp again?"

"I want a raise," she says without hesitation. "A big one."

"Sounds good to me." I grab her hand, and transfer my essence into her, my fingers tingling as energy runs down my arm. For a moment I feel like I'm not just touching her flesh, but her soul again. It's frighteningly intimate. And the transfer is two-way, I feel something of her in me, something that gives me strength.

"Hey," Tim says, free now. "I want to help, too."

I raise an eyebrow. "Are you sure?" I'm not sure I really want to share that experience with anyone else, just yet.

"Just do it. Now. Do whatever the hell it is you have to do before I change my mind."

I glance at Lissa. She nods. We're going to need all the help we can get.

I reach over and hold his arm. The ability slides into him. He seems to fight it for a moment — a lifetime of Black Sheepdom I suppose — then gives in to it.

There's usually much more ceremony than this, not to mention contracts to be signed — and a bit of gloating, after all he *was* a Black Sheep — but we don't have time. Now, I have two Pomps. It's hardly an army, a once-dead girl and a Black Sheep, but I feel my strength increase, and the Stirrers are pausing, staring at us with their flat, undead eyes.

I open myself up to the Stirrers in Number Four, and I pull them through me. It is like nothing I have ever felt before. It is terrible and gorgeous at once. It is life, and it is life's ending, and there's so much wonder, so much pain, so much joy. Because death-like life is the contradiction and the certainty. It is the terror and the inescapable truth. And I embrace it.

I blink.

The Stirrers in Number Four are gone. The bodies are gone. *Is that it?* I think. *Surely that can't be it.*

And then it tears through me, worse than any pomp I've ever performed, because there are hundreds of souls, not just from here, but from all across the country, carried to me by the force and the will of the crows, the souls of Stirrers and people. Lost souls, angry souls, souls desperate for absolution, souls gripped in terror or madness, and I take them all because I am Australia's Death. I direct that raging torrent to the Underworld. I realize why a Regional Manager needs all his Pomps, and why he is so fragile without them. This is hard and awful, and utterly necessary.

I've stopped a Regional Apocalypse, but at a cost. People all across the country have paid with their lives. The Stirrers worked as fast as they could to turn people. There are hundreds more dead than there should be. Now I'm paying, because this dying business stops with me.

How could anyone want this? How could anyone kill for this?

Tim and Lissa grow paler by the moment, their lips bloody and cracked, but I'm taking most of it. I have to. This could kill them, and it may yet.

The Stirrers come first and each one is rough, a howling soul hurled into the abyss. But they're soon gone, all of them banished from my region. After them are the usual deaths. The misadventures and illnesses, the pointless tragedies as slow as cancer or as abrupt as a gunshot. It's all that dying darkness which the world holds up at the end though, of course, it's not the end. Not by a long shot. There's so much more. Every stage is precious and discrete, I understand that now. But there is continuity, and the responsibility of that begins and ends with me. I infiltrate the worlds of the living and the dead in a way I can hardly believe is possible.

And it's a dreadful agony.

Then I'm in a different space. If still feels like Number Four only it's different, somehow. Darker, colder, the only light a sickly green.

Stirrers surround me in their true form, narrow-faced, saw-toothed. Their vast emptiness is palpable and insulting, and all of a sudden I know them a little. Better than Morrigan ever could, deal or no deal.

I enter the dialog of their existence, see their world and ours through their eyes. They are old, older than death itself. I'm slammed with an epiphany. To them, the *living* world is the aberration, the new thing. They are not so much invaders but the usurped. Their time passed so long ago, but they refuse to acknowledge it. I could almost respect them for it if they didn't hate so desperately.

They cannot think of anything but our destruction. For two billion years at least they have focused on it. And we are but the latest opponent in what has been such a long campaign for them.

This is just the beginning.

Now I know why they were so eager to deal with Morrigan, why they sought such a disruption to the order of things, and that it wasn't just to cause mayhem.

Something is coming. Something big and dark—rising out of the darkest depths—and it was ancient before life began. I know at once that the Stirrers worship it and fear it in equal measure. It is drawing near, and I know that it has been here before.

In that moment of utter clarity, I look up, and it is not the ceiling of Number Four I see, but a space, an inky desolation through which howls a wind as cold and bleak as any I ever encountered in Hell. My body clenches, reacting against this place. My newly possessed power slides around me, sheathing me from this realm's touch, but even that is not enough to take the cold from it, nor the terror from what I see.

An eye the size of a continent rolls toward me in its orbit.

Its vast bulk strains against the dark and I cower beneath its alien scrutiny. There is a part of my brain that starts to lock down, a part of me that wants to curl up into the smallest ball it can and never look into that dark again.

But I hold its gaze for a fraction of a moment. The god's endless hatred and cruel hungers crash against me, but I do not quail, even as every bit of me chills. This is the creature that the Stirrers serve, the beast that their death and destruction feeds. Why have I not been told about this? It's one more thing to add to the misinformation that is my life.

The Stirrers call to it, and it shrieks back, a long sharp cry that sets reality rippling. Although I can see it clearly, the god is still so far away that my mind cannot fathom it. I am Death, but I am nothing compared to this. And it is coming.

But it isn't here. Not yet, not today.

I snap back into the land of the living.

I'm not sure how long I've been gone but when I wake, Lissa's looking down at me and squeezing my hand.

"Where were you?" Lissa asks.

Tim's not far behind her, looking sick with worry and exhaustion. "You right, Steve?"

Maybe I should be asking him that.

I blink. I feel like I'm newly born or newly dead. Everything is tender. But that's not all of it. The world itself is clicking along at a slightly different pace . . . or am I? "I went everywhere," I say. "And I saw what's crashing toward us and it's terrible." I realize that I'm on my knees. There's a lot going on in my head, so many thoughts spinning tight orbits around each other, so many terrors. And there's so much to do.

For Christ's sake I'm holding a Death Moot in December. What the hell do you do, or even wear, at a Death Moot? But that is for later. Right now I can stop running. "It's done. For now. We've won, I guess." I touch Lissa's face. I could never get sick of that contact. "You're alive. We did it. We made it."

Tim clears his throat. I glance over at him.

"Mom, Dad. Did you see them?"

I shake my head. "They were gone."

Tim nods his head. "You tried though?"

"I didn't have much time."

"Yeah."

"Morrigan's gone," I say. "He paid for what he did. I made him pay."

Tim seems satisfied with that, and it's all I can give him. Lissa helps me get to my feet. I'm not that steady on them. She lets me hold her, and it feels good. Everything about her feels good.

"You're even cuter alive, you know," I say.

Lissa arches one eyebrow, her lips twitch. "Do you ever take anything seriously?"

"My hair. I take my hair way seriously."

"I hate to say it, but I think you're thinning on top."

Tim snorts. "She's right, you know. I didn't want to say anything but..."

"Really?" Shit, I know that baldness is hereditary, but I'd been doing so well.

Lissa glances over at Tim, then me. "Nah... Maybe."

"You are such a bitch." These two are going to be trouble.

"Aren't I adorable?"

And she is, and I'm staring into those green eyes, and there's still all that *je ne sais quoi* stuff going on, and I think there always will be, if we get a chance. If this job, and everything else, gives us a chance.

I hold her face in my trembling hands, and then I'm kissing her. There's so much to be done. So much to absorb, to rage against and mourn the passing of. All of that confusion is inside me, churning madly, demanding attention, and I can't pretend it isn't.

But I get that moment, that kiss. And it's a start.

ACKNOWLEDGMENTS

You only ever get one first book. And, being the first book, I could fill it with a book's worth of people to thank. So here's the stripped-back version.

Off the bat, I'm in no way the first to play with Death. This book is very much a fusion of my love for Fritz Leiber, Terry Pratchett and Neil Gaiman's Deaths, and Charon from *Clash of the Titans*, not to mention Piers Anthony's *On a Pale Horse*. All of these have left a wonderful and, no doubt, influential impression.

Now to the people I know.

Thanks to Marianne de Pierres for getting the ball rolling. Thanks to Travis Jamieson and Veronica Adams for reading early drafts, and to Deonie Fiford for pushing the book to the next level, and giving support at the right time.

And of course, there's my brothers and sisters in writing, ROR. They're the best writing group you could ever want, really.

For the last stages, a big thank you goes to my publisher Bernadette Foley, my structural editor Nicola O'Shea and my copy editor Roberta Ivers. You've helped make this book better than I thought it could be.

And a thank you to every bookstore I've ever worked in, and the wonderful people I have worked with. Thanks to everyone at Avid Reader Bookstore (and the cafe) for being amazing, and for putting up with the least available casual staff member in the universe (particularly Fiona Stager and Anna Hood). And a massive thank you to Krissy Kneen, and to Paul Landymore, my SF Sunday compadre.

Oh, and there's Philip Neilsen at QUT, my mate Grace Dugan, and Kate Eltham at the QWC, and the SF Writer's group, Vision. And the city of Brisbane, with which I have taken some liberties... I really better stop—well, not yet.

Thanks to my family, always supportive. And finally, to the one who puts up with everything, and who has never doubted me, Diana, thank you, my heart.

BOOK TWO

MANAGING DEATH

I heard a fly buzz when I died;
The stillness round my form
Was like the stillness in the air
Between the heaves of storm.

EMILY DICKINSON

PART ONE

THE SHIFT

1

There's blood behind my eyelids, and in my mouth. A knife, cold and sharp-edged, is pressed beneath my Adam's apple. The blade digs in, slowly. I'm cackling so hard my throat tears.

I jolt awake, and almost tumble from the wicker chair in the bedroom. And I really didn't have that much to drink last night.

Dream.

Another one. And I'd barely closed my eyes.

Just a dream. As if anything is *just* a dream in my line of business.

These days I hardly sleep at all, my body doesn't need it. Comes with being a Regional Manager, comes with being Australia's Death.

And I'm a long way from being used to it. My body may not need sleep, but my brain has yet to accept that.

But it wasn't the dream that woke me.

Something's happening. A Stirrer... well, stirring.

Their god is coming, and they're growing less cautious, and more common: rising up from their ancient city Devour in greater numbers like a nest of cockroaches spilling from a drain.

Christ.

Where is it? I scramble to my feet.

Unsteady. Blinking, my eyes adjusting to the dark.

Stirrers, like their city's name suggests, would devour all living things.

They're constantly kicking open the doors between the lands of the living and the dead; reanimating and possessing corpses in the hope that they can return the world to its pristine, lifeless state.

It's the task of Mortmax Industries, its RMs and Pomps (short for Psychopomps) to stop them and to make sure that the path from life to death only heads in one direction. We pomp the dead, send them to the Underworld, and we stall Stirrers. Without us the world would be shoulder to shoulder with the souls of the dead. And Stirrers would have much more than a toehold, they'd have an empire built upon despair and billions of corpses.

But sometimes the serious business of pomping and stalling can get lost in all the maneuvering, posturing and backstabbing (occasionally literally) that modern corporate life entails.

Work in any office and that's true. The stakes are just a lot higher in ours.

My heart's pounding: fragments of the dream are still making their rough way through my veins.

For a moment, I'm certain the monster's in the room with me.

But it's a lot further away.

Lissa's in our bed: dead to the world. I don't know why I'm surprised at that. After all, me wandering in here drunk an hour ago didn't wake her.

She's exhausted from yesterday's work. That's the downside of knowing how things are run, of having the particular skills she has. I feel guilty about it, but I need her to keep working: finding and training our staff. As well as pomping the souls of the dead, and stopping Stirrers from breaking into the land of the living.

Lissa's heart beats loud and steady. Fifty-five beats per minute.

But it's not the only heartbeat I hear. They're all there, wrapped inside my skull. All of my region's human life. All those slowing, racing, stuttering hearts. They're a cacophony: a constant background noise that, with varying success, I struggle to ignore. Mr. D says that it becomes soothing after a while. I'm a bit dubious of that, though

I've discovered that stereo speakers turned up loud can dull it a little; something to do with electrical pulses projecting sonic fields. Thunderstorms have a similar effect, though they're much more difficult to arrange.

Someone dies.

It's a fair way away, but still in Australia. Perth, maybe. Certainly on the southwest coast. Then another: close on it. The recently dead souls pass through my staff and into the Underworld, and I feel a little of that passage. When I was one of the rank and file it used to hurt. Now, unless I'm doing the pomping directly, it's only a tingling ache, an echo of the pain my employees feel. So that I can't forget, I suppose.

At least Mortmax Australia is running smoothly. Though I wish I could take more credit for that. Our numbers are low after the bloodbath that occurred just two months ago. But with my cousin Tim being my Ankou, my second-in-command, master of the day-to-day workings of the business, and Lissa running our HR department and leading the Pomps in the field, our offices have reopened across the country. It seems there are always people willing to work for Death. And we've found many of them. Some from the old Pomp families, distant relatives or Black Sheep who've decided to come back to the fold. But most of them are just people who had heard things, whispers, perhaps, of what we're about.

Who'd blame them? The pay's good after all, even if the hours can be somewhat . . . variable.

It used to be a family trade. Used to be.

I leave Lissa to her sleep, stumble to the living room, down a hallway covered with photos of my parents: smiling and oblivious to how terribly it was all going to end. My feet pad along a carpet worn thin with the footsteps of my childhood and my parents' lives. This was their home. I grew up here, moved out, then my house exploded along with my life. Now I'm back. They're dead. And I'm Death. It's pretty messed up, really. *I'm* pretty messed up.

My mobile's lying next to a half-empty bottle of Bundaberg Rum.

I grab my phone and flick through to the right app, marked with the Mortmax symbol—a bracing triangle, its point facing down, a not-quite-straight line bisecting its heart. I open up the schedule: the list of all deaths to be in my region. Technically, I don't need to look anymore; all of this comes from within me, from some deep knowledge or force gained in the Negotiation. Regardless, it's reassuring to see it written down, interpreted graphically, not just intuitively.

It was definitely a death in Perth. One of my new guys, Michio Dugan, is on the case. There's another, in Sydney, and two in Melbourne. A stall accompanies one of those. The stir that necessitated that was what woke me.

I close my eyes, and I can almost see the stall occurring. The Stirrer entering the body: the corpse's muscles twitching with the invader's appropriation. Eyes snapping open, my Pomp on the scene—another new one, Meredith—grimacing as she slashes her palm and lays on a bloody hand.

Blood's the only effective way to stall a Stirrer (though I once used vomit), and it hurts, but that's partly the point—we're playing a high stakes game of life and death. No matter how experienced you are, a Stirrer trying to reach into the living world is always confronting. And my crew are all so green.

I feel the stall that stops the Stirrer as a moment of vertigo, a soft breath of chilly air that passes along my spine.

The Melburnian corpse is just a corpse again.

I dial Meredith's number. I have all my staff's numbers, though I rarely call.

"Are you all right?" I ask before she can get a word in.

She's breathing heavily. My breath syncs with hers—it's part of the link I have with my employees. "Yeah. Just surprised me."

I wonder, though, if she isn't more surprised that I rang her. I know I am. I must still be a bit drunk.

"Stalls get easier," I say, though in truth they do and they don't: a Stirrer is always a bugger of a thing to stop. "You didn't cut yourself too badly?"

"No... Maybe... A little."

They all do when they start out. There's a good reason why we call our palms Cicatrix City. The scars that criss-cross them chart our passage through this job.

"Get to Number Four and have it seen to," I say.

"I'm a long way from the office, maybe—"

"No maybes." I've seen the schedule. Meredith's a ten-minute drive from the Melbourne offices, at most. Every state and territory capital has an office, a Number Four, and medical staff on call. "I pay my doctors far too much not to have them see to you."

"OK," she says. "I will."

"Good work," I say, then worry that I'm sounding patronizing.

"Thanks," I can hear the smile in her voice—maybe I'm not. "Thanks a lot, Mr. de Selby."

"Mr. de Selby? That's what they called my dad, and he didn't like it either. Steven's fine."

"OK, Steven."

"Now get to Number Four." They're all so new. It's exhausting. "If I hear that you decided to tough it out I'll be very pissed off."

I hang up. Slip the phone in my pocket. Then open the bottle of Bundy and sip my rum. I'm all class, Dad would say.

Another five pomps and one stall, across the country, in quick succession. All of them done in time.

Five heartbeats gone from the pool. And another monster stopped.

It's nothing, right? But I hear them all. I ache with their urgency and their passing. There are always new heartbeats as well. One of those falters after a few minutes.

Another successful pomp.

Life's cruel. Life's what you have to fear.

Death. All we do is turn off the lights and shut the door and if we need to bolt it, that's none of your concern.

I briefly consider going into the kitchen, making a cup of coffee. But I don't like spending time in there at all. Mom and Dad loved to cook; somehow the skill passed me by. And that space drives it home. Lissa and I eat a lot of takeaway.

What's more, my parents were killed in the kitchen. That was where most of the blood was. I miss them so much. I miss their guidance, their laughter. I even miss their bickering. Their bodies, Morrigan's Stirrers inhabited those. The last time I saw my parents as flesh and blood they were being used to try and kill me. That was how far Morrigan had fallen.

Yeah, the bastard was a regular puppet master. He still haunts my dreams. He was directly responsible for starting a Schism, and the deaths of almost every Pomp in Australia. Nearly killed me too. I wish I could say I'd survived because of my tenacity and bloody perspicacity. Truth is, I was lucky. Lucky to have Lissa around. Lucky to have brighter, more able friends.

Sure I'd beaten Morrigan at the Negotiation and become RM—on the top of the One Tree, the heart of the Underworld, where his and my future, our very corporeal and non-corporeal existences were decided—but even that had been more through luck than design.

Two months ago I was just a Pomp—one of many—drawing souls into the afterlife.

Now I'm so much more, and I hate it. Morrigan even killed my border collie, Molly Millions. Until very recently, I imagined seeing poor Moll out of the corner of my eye, several times a day. And every time I did, it knocked the wind out of me. Another casualty in the minefield that is my life.

I could try and sleep. But even if I did, I'd wake just as weary.

And the nightmares. They drive into me even when I'm awake. I close my eyelids for more than a second and there they rush, blood-slicked and cackling. I'm clambering and running over screaming faces. Torn hands clawing and scraping, and these aren't the dead, but the dying, and they're dying because of me. More often than I care to admit, I'm enjoying the madness: reveling in it. Sometimes there is the scythe, and I'm swinging that thing, loving its heft and balance, its never-dulling edge, and laughing.

No sleep. No rest. Not when that's waiting. And a man shouldn't wake with an erection after such a dream. How can that arouse me?

I dig out something doleful and rumbling from my CD collection. A little Tindersticks, some Tom Waits. Let the music dim down the roar of a nation's beating hearts. But no matter what I choose tonight, the volume refuses to drown out the sound—and I don't want to wake up Lissa. I sit there restless, Waits crackling along like bones and branches breaking.

I work on finishing the rum.

What the hell, eh? Drinking's easy at any time once you start. Easier if the right music's playing. Tim once told me that music was the perfect gateway drug. He's not wrong. Finally the rum and the music start to work. Not a lot, but enough.

Twice I stumble into the bedroom to check on Lissa, and to marvel that I didn't lose her when I lost nearly everything else, that she's sleeping in my bed. All I want to do is hold her. There was a time that I couldn't, when to touch Lissa would have banished her from me forever. I went to Hell and back to find her, I pulled an Orpheus Maneuver. Not even Orpheus managed that one, but where he failed, I succeeded. If one good thing has come of this, it's Lissa.

She snores a little.

It's endlessly fascinating the things that you find out about your partner when you can't sleep. The sounds, the unaffected routines of their bodies. The way a person's eyes trace their dreams beneath their eyelids. There's more truth in slumber. Perhaps that's why I feel so unanchored. It's a space lost to me.

What a whiny bastard I've become.

Sometimes Lissa wakes screaming from her own nightmares. She never tells me what they are, claims she can't remember them, but I can guess.

There's not much of the Bundy left come first light. And there's been seventy-five more deaths, two of them followed by Stirrers stirring.

Seventy-five more successful pomps and two stalls and the day hasn't even properly started.

I never wanted this. Nor was I supposed to have it.

For Death, it never stops. It's a twenty-four-hour, seven-day-a-week sort of thing. When I was a Pomp, out in the field, I had thought I understood that.

Well, as it turns out—as it turned out for a lot of things—I'm completely clueless.

2

I'm making coffee, trying not to think about my parents (where they were sitting, what they were saying) when Lissa stomps into the kitchen. She's dressed in her usual black: a neat blouse, a shortish skirt, and a pair of purple Doc Marten boots, at once elegant and perfect for kicking in the heads of Stirrers. Around her neck is a silver and leather necklace from which hang rows of black safety pins leading to a Mickey Mouse charm at the bottom. Early *Steamboat Willie* Mickey, grinning like mad. I can't help but roll my eyes at that. Only Mickey's smiling, though.

"Do you know what time it is?" she demands.

I shrug.

"Seven," she says. "Someone switched off my alarm."

I pass her a cup. Surely you can't stay mad at someone who's just made you coffee. I lean in to give her a kiss. Lissa screws up her face. "Christ, Steve. Just how much did you have to drink last night?"

I wince, slipping on a pair of sunglasses. It's bright enough inside the house, and the cruel sun of a Brisbane summer waits outside. "Maybe more than was good for me."

"More than was good for the both of us. Again. Try not to breathe in my direction, will you?"

Seven in the morning. The sun is already high and bright, the air-conditioning throbbing, like my head, though the hangover's fading. One of the upsides of being RM is that I heal faster than I used to.

Regional Managers are considerably harder to harm or kill than your average Pomp, though I've seen it happen. My predecessor, Mr. D, died beneath the wheels of an SUV, but by then he had lost the support of his Pomps. Most of them murdered. He looks pretty good considering all that, but you have to go to the Underworld to see him. I try and avoid it if I can.

I grab the car keys from the bowl on a table next to the front door. Lissa snatches them from my hand.

She glares at me. "Don't even think about it. Turn off the aircon and clean your teeth. I'll be waiting in the car."

I'm quick about it. Lissa looks very pissed off. For no good reason, as far as I can tell. Hey, I haven't been drinking *that* much lately. She offers the barest hint of a smile as I get into the car, hardly waits for me to sit down before we're going. The little multi-colored Corolla's engine bubbles along. This car predates air-conditioning. There's a bead of sweat on Lissa's lip that I find endearing. I reach over to touch it with my thumb, and she pushes my hand away. Ten minutes of silence. Out of the 'burbs and onto the M3 Motorway.

"You really should be practicing your shifting." Lissa says at last. The traffic's already creeping, the highway burdened with even more cars than usual; it's a matter of days until Christmas.

"Yeah, but I like coming to work with you." That's only partly true—certainly not today.

Shifting hurts, I really haven't mastered it yet, and I don't like the pain. I'm sure I could handle it if it was the same sort of agony each shift, but it's not. Sometimes it manifests itself as a throbbing headache, others as a kick to the groin, or a hand clenching my guts and squeezing. There's usually a bit of gagging involved.

Lissa grunts. Changes lanes. I reach over to turn on the stereo and she slaps my hand again. This is the real silent treatment.

"What did I do wrong?" I shake my stinging fingers.

"It's what you haven't done," she says, and that's all I can get out of her, as she weaves her way through the traffic.

What the hell *haven't* I done? It's not her birthday. And we've only been together for two months, so there's no real anniversary to speak of. I try to catch her eye. She ignores me, contemplating her next move. Changes lanes again.

We cross the Brisbane River on the Captain Cook Bridge, crawling as the Riverside Expressway ahead becomes anything but express: choked by a half-dozen exits leading into and out of the city. I can feel the water beneath us, and its links to the Underworld and the Hell river Styx—all rivers are the Styx and the Styx is all rivers. When I was a Pomp it was just murky water to me, a winding thread that bound and separated the city, east from west, north from south. Now it hums with residual energies, it's like stepping over a live wire. My whole body tingles, the hangover dies with it—down the river and into the Styx, I guess. A smile stretches across my face. I can't help it.

Lissa doesn't seem to appreciate the grin.

She clenches her jaw, and swerves the Corolla into a gap in the next lane barely large enough. A horn blares behind us, Lissa holds the steering wheel tight, the muscles in her jaw twitching.

I settle in for one of the longest fifteen minutes of my life. The only noise is the traffic and the thunk of the Corolla's tires as it passes over the seams in the unexpressway. I can't find a safe place to look. A glance in Lissa's direction gets me a scowl. Looking out over the river toward Mount Coot-tha earns me an exasperated huff so I settle on staring at the car directly in front of us, my hands folded in my lap. It's as contrite a position as I can manage.

At last Lissa belts into the underground car park of Number Four, off George Street, pedestrians beware. She pulls into a spot next to the lift, turns off the engine and stares at me. "So, even after that drive you've got nothing to say for yourself?"

"I—" I give up, look at her, defeated. I can feel another grin straining at my lips. That's not going to help. Lissa's eyes flare.

"Look," she snarls, "we've all lost people that we care about, but you—"

"I've what? What do you think I've done?"

"Oh—I could just—no, forget about it." Lissa yanks her seatbelt free, storms out of the car and is already in the lift before I've opened my door.

I have to wait for the lift to come back down. The basement car park's full. I can see Tim's car a few spots down. I'm last to work, yet again.

I could shift up to my office from here. But I don't reckon it's worth the pain.

The lift takes me straight up to the sixth floor. Everyone's a picture of industry when the doors open, and no one gives me a second glance. Which worries me. Where are the usual hellos? The people wanting to talk to me? Why hasn't Lundwall from the front desk hurried over to me with a list of phone calls that I'm not going to bother returning? I look around for Lissa. Nowhere. No one meets my gaze.

"OK," I mumble. If that's how everyone is going to play it...I mean, I haven't come to work drunk in over a week.

I amble over toward the coffee machine in the kitchen. The tiny room empties out the moment I walk in. I don't hurry making my coffee, then stroll into my office, taking long, loud sips as I go.

"Nice to see you've made it," Tim says. Tim's trying so hard to hold it all together. I used to be able to tell, with a glance, what he was thinking. Now, sometimes I can't even meet his eyes. He's developed movements, tics and gestures, which are wholly unfamiliar to me. He's sitting on my desk—his bum next to the big black bakelite phone—carefully avoiding the throne of Death. I understand why. It exerts a pull. I'm sure he feels it, too. How it does it is beyond me, it shouldn't. It's not particularly imposing, merely an old black wooden chair. There are thirteen of these in the world, made for each member of the Orcus. Just a chair and yet so much more. I cannot stand in here without feeling the scratching presence of it. I know I could lose myself in it, that I'm perhaps losing myself already. Sometimes I wonder if that wouldn't be so bad. Then I wonder if that's what the throne wants me to wonder. If a chair can really *want* anything.

In one hand, Tim's clutching the briefing notes that I should have read about three weeks ago.

"Yeah, isn't your office across the way?" I ask.

Tim folds his arms, says nothing.

"So who's stealing paper clips this week?" I force a grin. Honestly, that *had* been a major issue last month. Paper clips and three reams of A4.

The door bangs shut behind me. I jerk my head around, and Lissa's standing there, her arms folded, too. Ambushed!

"What the hell is this? Look, those Post-it notes on my desk are all accounted for."

She's not smiling. Neither is Tim. Christ, this is some sort of intervention.

"Do you know what today is?" she asks.

"The 20th of December." Sure, I have to look at my desk calendar for that.

Tim snorts. Pulls the bookmark out of the briefing notes. A bookmark whose movements have been somewhat fabricated—damn, I thought he'd swallowed that one. He slaps the notes. "If you had actually read these, you'd have an idea, you'd probably even be prepared."

"Look, I've got work to do. The Death Moot's on the 28th and I—"

"Absolutely. What do you need to do?"

I shrug.

In a little over a week the Orcus, the thirteen Regional Managers that make up Mortmax Industries, will be meeting in Brisbane for the biannual Death Moot. With just two months in the job, I'm expected to organize what my predecessor Mr. D once described as a meeting of the most bloodthirsty, devious and backstabbing bunch of bastards on the planet.

"You've got no fucking idea, have you?" Tim says.

Lissa touches my arm. "Steven, we're worried about you."

Tim doesn't move. His eyes are hard. I can't remember seeing him so pissed off. "Mate, I like to have a drink as much as anyone, but I have responsibilities. And you do, too. To this company, to your staff and your shareholders, and to your region. You're an RM. You're one of the Orcus!"

"I know, I know," I say. How the hell did I ever become one of the Orcus? Me being RM was just a massive mistake, a joke played out by the universe. I'd fought for this role, only because I'd had no choice. Death for me, and death for my few remaining friends and family—or fight and live. I'm about to mention my call to Meredith when Tim laughs humorlessly. My cheeks burn.

"Then start acting like it," he says.

I walk past him, drop into my throne. For a moment, there is no argument. Lissa and Tim fade away. It's just the throne and me. The throne deepens and broadens my senses, brings the living/dying world even closer to the fore. In this chair I touch not only the land of the living but the land of the dead as well. Traffic is moving nicely in both zones, which is really rather remarkable. The throne is opiate, CNN and 3D extravaganza rolled into one. I have to concentrate to manage that sensory overload. Part of me doesn't want to; the effort of it burns a little behind my eyes like the seed of a migraine. How the hell am I expected to handle all this? And it's not getting any easier.

I open my eyes. Oh, yes, the "interventionists" haven't left. How much have they seen?

"You don't have a clue how hard I work," I say, but they do, and they're right.

"That's just it," Lissa says. "You're working so hard at avoiding everything that you're going to avoid everything out of your life. You've come unstuck, you're drifting, and you haven't even noticed it."

Tim's nodding. I glare at him.

"Steve, you're even more disengaged than you were when Robyn left."

Now, that's just too low. Robyn's my ex. She couldn't handle me being a Pomp and it took me years to get over that. It took Lissa, and the loss of nearly everything that I cared about. Surely I'm not... "That's bullshit!"

"What's bullshit is the amount of work Lissa and I have had to do to cover for you. When was the last time you spoke to another RM?"

I'd initially tried really hard to keep in touch with them. To start a discussion about a global response to the Stirrer god. Nothing, silence. The global response had been for every RM to ignore my emails and my calls. If they weren't going to speak to me, I wasn't going to speak to them. "They're all pricks and backstabbers," I say.

Tim nods. "Exactly, and you've left us to deal with them. The whole Orcus, and no RM to bat for us. Thanks a lot, mate."

"Well, you're my Ankou."

Tim nods. "And I'll watch your back. But I'm not here to wipe your arse. If this keeps going on... we're both out of here."

Lissa's face is as resolute as I have ever seen it. "Do you know how hard I've been working? Hunting down new staff in Melbourne, Perth, Mount Isa, Coober Pedy? I've run around this country, God knows how many times, trying to find you people who at the very least have a chance of not dying on the job. And you're hardly interested. Have you spoken to any of them after their interview? Have you made yourself available to any of them?"

I open my mouth to speak: what about Meredith? But once, just once, isn't enough of a defense. They're right. I know they're right, but if they could sit in this throne...dream my dreams...They're right. "So what do you want me to do?"

"Today?" Tim asks. "Or from now on?"

"Both."

Tim beams at me. "That's what I want to hear. A bit more enthusiasm would be nice, though."

I lean back in my chair. "All right. All right. Where do I start?"

Lissa unfolds her arms, walks to the desk and takes up another chair. "The Death Moot. Let's start with that. The business we can get to, but the Moot is a priority. You've got to find the Point of Convergence."

"Can't we just book a hotel?"

"Ha! This is Mortmax Industries," Lissa says. "Things don't work that way. It's revealed through some sort of ceremony, although I'm not sure what it entails. And Tim can hardly go and ask anyone else. How do you think the other RMs would take that?"

"Bad. It would be bad," I say.

She pats the black phone on my desk. "You're going to have to speak with Mr. D. And after that you're going to have to start paying attention to the business of being RM."

I pick up the heavy handset. "Do I have to call him now?"

Lissa starts to fold her arms again. Tim's face is settling into a scowl. "It has to be done. And today," Lissa says. "In some ways we've been as bad as you. We should have done this sooner. Today's the last day you can perform the ceremony."

More than a twinge of guilt hits me at that. They've been putting this off and putting this off, hoping I'd come good on my own. I can't help feeling I've let them down. The business I don't care about, but Lissa and Tim are the center of my world.

Yet there's part of me wondering how they could have let this get so far. Ah, more guilt! I put the phone to my ear.

"I was wondering when you would call," Mr. D says, without the slightest pause. There's a large quantity of affront in his voice. Maybe the bastard has some feelings after all. I certainly didn't witness them when he was alive.

"Are you in on this, too?" I ask.

"Mr. de Selby, I have no idea what you mean."

"I need to talk to you."

"Yes, you should have been talking to me for some time, but you haven't. Oh well, it's never too late to start." He chuckles. "Until it's too late. And you are running out of time."

"I'll be there soon."

"Don't keep me waiting."

I put the handset back in the cradle. "There," I say.

Both Tim and Lissa stare at me.

"Don't you two have work to attend to?"

Tim smiles thinly. "Of course we do." He's out of my office without a backward glance.

Lissa stays a moment, touches my arm. "It had to be done," she says. "I'm sorry."

"Don't be. You're both right." I grab her wrist as she pulls away, and squeeze it gently. Flesh and bone. I doubt I'll ever get used to being able to touch her. "I'm just happy that you care enough to do this." I'm not sure that I sound all that convincing. I've got to see Mr. D. I've suddenly got work to do.

Lissa bends down and kisses my cheek. "Dying isn't the only way a girl can lose someone," she says.

I want to ask her if that's a threat, or a fear, or a promise. Talk of Robyn has got my head in something of a spin. I could do with a drink.

Instead, I get to my feet, prepare myself for my shift into the Underworld and say, "Don't worry, you haven't lost me yet."

I let go of her wrist and, looking into her eyes, I disappear—or she and the office do. I'm not sure which it is. One reality is exchanged with another, the air folds around me, changes density, and taste. Light, sound, all of it is instantly different. I'm bathed in the red glow of the Underworld.

The shift is hard. This one makes me sick, literally. Mr. D pats my back until the vomiting stops. "You do understand that it gets easier the more you practice?"

I wipe my mouth with the back of my hand. "Yeah, but it's the practice that's so hard." He passes me a glass of water, obtained from a small tank by his chair. I gulp it down, and take in my surroundings. This is Hell of course, but what a view. I'm standing on one of the uppermost branches of the One Tree. The Underworld equivalent of the city of Brisbane is beneath us, suburbia stretching out to the dark waters of the Tethys, the CBD's knuckles of skyscrapers constrained as Brisbane is bound up in a ribbon of river. The air is loud with the creaking of the One Tree. It permeates everything in the Underworld. The One Tree is the place where souls go to end their existence. It draws them here from across the Underworld and absorbs them, down into its roots and into the great secrets of the Deepest Dark. It's a Moreton Bay fig tree, bigger than any city, with root buttresses the size of suburbs. It's also where my old boss hangs out. Dead but not dead, he waits here to act as my mentor in all things RM.

There's a cherub by the name of Wal fluttering about my head. He looks a little plumper than I remember him, but I wouldn't say that to Wal. He's rather sensitive, comes from spending most of his existence as a tattoo on my arm. In fact, it looks like he's already pissed off. His Modigliani eyes are narrower than usual. It's been a good couple of weeks since I was in the Underworld, and it's only here, or close to it, that he can manifest. He gets rather shirty if he can't spread his wings. I do my best to ignore him. I only have enough strength for one intervention today.

"You know why I'm here?" I ask Mr. D.

"It's the 20th of December. Must be getting hot up there. I was always fond of Christmas in Brisbane. Are the cicadas singing? Have they put up the Christmas tree in King George Square?"

"Yes, but—"

"It can be very lonely in Hell," Mr. D says, and his face, which notoriously shifts through a dozen expressions in a second, grows even more furious in its changes. "Particularly when you are in someone's employ. Specifically to advise that someone. To steer them through the roughest channels of their job away from the snares and the rocks of Orcusdom. To save them making the same mistakes you did. And yet, they never visit you. Never call. Never ask for advice." He nods to his armchair, the single piece of furniture on the branch, and the stack of old science-fiction novels beside it. "I'm running out of things to read, and without you I can't even go fishing. When did you last drop a mercy pile of books down here? When did you last reply to one of my invitations on Facebook, or comment on an update? You're not even following me on Twitter."

"He really is rubbish, isn't he?" Wal says to Mr. D. "I can't fly, can't do a thing when I'm stuck on that arm. And would it hurt to use a little deodorant, mate?" He lands heavily on my shoulder. Talk about the weight of opinion. And I'm not too happy about being that close to all that pudgy nakedness.

I raise my hands in supplication and defeat. This all would have been a lot easier if I'd had something to drink beforehand. "You're right. Both of you are right. I'm sorry. I'll do better. I have to."

"I forgive you," Mr. D says, grinning a dozen various but magnanimous grins. "But you owe me."

I clench my jaw, try not to make it obvious. "Yeah, I owe you. But, finally, I'm here to make you work."

Mr. D dips his head knowingly. "Yes. You need to find the Point of Convergence. Without it, you can no more have a Death Moot than you could hold the Olympics *sans* stadium. And without the Point of Convergence you cannot engage the Caterers."

"I thought we could just hire someone from a restaurant."

Mr. D chortles, exchanges an amused glance with Wal. "And they would be able to enter the nexus between the living and the Underworld, how?"

Wal's laughing too, holding his belly. "Oh, he's beyond bloody naive!"

"Yeah, beyond naive," I say, feeling sick. Which is either the residue of the shift, my embarrassment at not knowing this and the fear of all the other things I don't understand, or just possibly the throbbing filament of rage that is firing up in my brain at all this mockery. "And I will continue to be beyond naive if you do not educate me."

"Right," Mr. D says, "the Point of Convergence is revealed through a ceremony. This is what you need to do..."

By the end of his instructions, I'm less than pleased.

He gives me a hearty pat on the back. "You'll be fine, son. Be careful with those Caterers, though. You don't want to piss them off. Oh, and the canapés, you want them to do the canapés—they have this thing they do with an oyster..."

Son? Mr. D never calls me son.

Maybe boy, or Steven, or de Selby. Just what is he up to? This is why I've barely used him as a mentor. Too many riddles, too much in the way of diversion—and I don't think he even realizes he's doing it.

He hands me a piece of paper and a pen. "Oh, and I need you to sign this."

"What is it?"

"A release. A legal and magical document. It allows me at least a modicum of movement. Sometimes I would like to be able to visit my friends. Aunt Neti is down there, as are the markets. How am I supposed to sample the Underworld if I am trapped here on the branches of the Tree?"

Seems fair enough. Maybe a little *too* fair.

I glance at him suspiciously and he smiles, almost looks innocent, but for the tumble of faces that follow. Mr. D can never settle on just one.

Still, out of guilt at my neglect of him, I sign it.

"Don't be a stranger," he says, and looks at his watch. "You better get going. I can't believe you've left it so late."

Neither can I. The one thing I don't want to mess up is a Death Moot. Ruin this, and I'm on my own. And that Stirrer god is approaching. The End of Days is approaching, and it seems I've gotta jump through a whole lot of bloody hoops to stop it.

"Oh, and next time? Some books, please," Mr. D says. "Now shoo!"

Another shift.

Back in my office.

I take a deep breath. Maybe it is getting easier. Then I throw up in my wastepaper bin, noisily and messily. *Bloody shifting*. I rinse my mouth out with cold coffee, put the bin as far away from the desk as possible, to be dealt with later, and walk out into the open workspace of Number Four. People are busy coordinating pomps, getting the right people to the right place. The floor beneath us would be just as hectic, though they deal with the business end of Mortmax: the stuff that finances all of this. Our shares are doing quite well at the moment, so Tim tells me.

I knock on Tim's door.

"Enter," he says somewhat officiously.

I poke my head in. Tim's having a smoke. He juts his jaw out, daring me to comment. I don't take the bait.

"Lissa out on a job?" I ask.

"Yeah. There's a stir expected at the Wesley Hospital." I remember the last time I was there. Seven Stirrers and me, one of the few Pomps left alive in Brisbane. Still gives me the shivers.

"I miss her when she's not around."

Tim snorts at that. "Ah, young love. Give it time. The missing goes, along with all the sex. Believe me." Yeah, right, I know how much he misses Sally. Young love, indeed.

"OK, I just wanted to tell you that if anything goes wrong with this whole Convergence Ceremony thing it's your fault."

Tim stabs the cigarette butt into his ashtray. "That bad is it?"

"I have to see Aunt Neti."

Tim smiles wanly. Aunt Neti freaks him out. Maybe it's the eight arms, or the murderous glint in her eyes. "You going now? Do you want someone to come with?" It's the least earnest sounding offer I've ever heard. But no surprise there. Our first meeting had been rather memorable, Aunt Neti's predatory eyes focused on the both of us as she recounted tales of particularly bloodthirsty Schisms. She'd been very annoyed when Tim didn't finish his scones. His joke about avoiding carbs had fallen curiously flat, and the air in Neti's parlor had chilled considerably. I thought she was going to tear his head off.

"Yeah, I'm going now. Better to get it over and done with, obviously. And thanks, but I need to do this one alone. I want to." At least I can manage to sound like I mean it.

"OK." Tim can't hide the relief in his voice. "On the plus side you've only got a short walk."

A short walk to Hell; well, a particular part of it. "I'll talk to you when I get back. I'm going to need your help with the ceremony," I say. "I'm sorry. I didn't realize how badly I'd let work slip."

That's not true. I knew, but I just couldn't find a way out. Can't say that I have yet. But at least I'm trying.

"We were never going to let you fall too far," Tim says. "We love you too much. Now be safe."

"I will." I shut the door behind me. If I really wanted to be safe there's no way I'd do what I'm about to do.

There's a doorway—and though its door is very heavy, it's never closed—that leads to a hallway, which in turn leads to Aunt Neti's parlor.

Every region's headquarters has one. As I walk toward the portal, conversation in the workspace dies down. I straighten my back, check my hair in a mirror near the door. I sigh. It'll have to do. Still no one has said a word. I turn around: a dozen pairs of eyes flick this way and that.

"Don't you all have work to do?"

A phone rings. Someone starts typing away furiously. A stapler snap, snap, snaps.

I enter the hallway, suddenly I need to pee. But I can't, I have to stay on the path.

No turning back now.

3

The hallway creaks and groans, echoing the One Tree. Two, three steps in and the sounds of phones ringing, the beating of hearts, the snap of staplers grow muted. Then there's just silence, but for that creaking and groaning. The brown carpet ripples in sympathy with a floor that buckles with the stress of keeping a link between dimensions. It's hard to stay on your feet here, but I do my best, and I don't need to grab a wall to steady myself.

My right biceps starts burning. I take a few more steps and Wal pushes his way out from under my shirt sleeve. He flaps his wings and grins at me.

"Hello again," he says, then his eyes widen. His little head swings from left to right. "Bugger, wasn't expecting this." His voice is low and quiet.

Neither was I. The last time I walked down this hallway, about a month ago, Wal didn't appear. Something's happening that shouldn't. Just another thing to disturb me. At least I have company. Wal settles down on my shoulder and considers the walls and the rippling floor, his face pinched with distaste.

The closer I get to Neti's door, the heavier Wal gets. There's a subtle hint in the air of scones freshly baked; of butter, jam and cream. Aunt Neti's expecting company.

I reach her front door and lift my hand toward the brass knocker which is shaped like a particularly menacing spider.

The door swings open.

"Good morning, dear," Aunt Neti says. Her eyes dart toward Wal, and the little guy almost topples from my shoulder. "Oh, and you've brought a friend with you, and not your rude Ankou, this time. How sweet."

Seeing Neti is like looking at an iceberg and knowing there are immeasurable depths beneath it. More than nine-tenths, I'm betting. And she's terrifying enough as it is. Aunt Neti is all long limbs and bunches of eyes—eight of each. A purple shawl is wrapped around her shoulders. She straightens it a little, with a spare hand or two, and bends down to peck me on the cheek. Her lips are cold and hard, and the peck so swift and forceful that I'm sure I'll have bruises tomorrow.

Aunt Neti bustles me inside, all those hands patting and pushing and pulling at once, so I'm not quite sure what she's touching, just that I'm being moved from doorway to parlor and that my pockets hold no secrets from her. Her nails are black and sharpened to points, and they click click click with her pinching and prodding. It's all done before I can even put up a struggle. I've gotta say it's not that much of a stretch to imagine that's how a fly would feel as it's spun and bound in spider's silk.

She shuts the door behind her. Wal's keeping away from those hands, though at least a couple of her eyes follow him. And I'm making the decision that you always have to make when you're talking to her: which eyes do you look at? I choose a bunch in the middle of her face. The ones with the most smile lines. They're crinkling now.

"Sit down, sit down." Neti gestures toward one of a pair of overstuffed chairs set across from each other, a low table between them.

As we sit in her parlor, I keep to the edge of my seat—as though that would save me. The room is tiny and cozy, the walls papered with an old damask design. The paper's peeling in one corner and a tiny spider has webbed the gap between wall and curling edge. I can't shake the feeling that it's staring at me. And those eyes are no less hungry than Aunt Neti's.

There are two plates on the table. On both there are crumbs, and butter knives, covered with jam as red as arterial blood. And my seat is warm. Someone was here, only moments ago. I look around, wondering if they've really gone. But there's no one. I look down at the plates. There's no hint there of whoever I've displaced, just crumbs and jam.

Aunt Neti picks the plates up and slides away to her kitchen with them, saying, "Plenty of visitors today, my dear. But none as special as you."

Wal raises an eyebrow at me. Neti is one of the two caretakers of the interface between the living and the Underworld. The other one is Charon. Both have their unique ways of running things. Charon with his boats; Neti with her residence, which, like a web, is connected to everything. She lives in these few rooms: a parlor that intersects every office of Mortmax in the living world. Like Charon, Aunt Neti's an RE, a Recognized Entity.

And despite appearances, she's not that fond of me at all. Mr. D tried to explain why a few weeks ago. Something about the Orpheus Maneuver that I pulled to get Lissa back from the Underworld, and how I should have gone through her, not Charon. At the time I thought I'd had no choice. Seems I did, and it's made me an enemy—no matter how unknowingly on my part.

Aunt Neti comes back into the parlor, walks past me to a tall cabinet. It's covered in scrollwork and seems to be carved out of the same black wood as my throne. Several of her hands apply pressure to different bits of the cabinet, a palm in one corner, a finger tapping on a carving, another hand applying pressure at its back.

A door slides to one side. Aunt Neti reaches in and pulls out two stone knives that I'm all too familiar with. She grins at me, revealing a mouth full of crooked black teeth, and drops the knives on the table before me.

"You'll be needing these," Aunt Neti says.

I pick them up. They're perfectly weighted and heavy. They mumble and hum.

I used these on the top of the One Tree in a place the Orcus call the Negotiation, to "negotiate" my way into the position of RM. It had been a bloody reckoning between me and Morrigan—once a family friend, a man as dear to me as any uncle. These knives had slashed his throat and blinded his left eye. They'd cut his soul away from existence itself.

I need these knives for the Convergence Ceremony but seeing them, holding the damn things in my hands, is terrifying.

"Now," Aunt Neti says, laying down two clean plates, "be careful for goodness sake, or you'll cut yourself. That's for later."

I hold them away from me gingerly, my hands tight around the stony handles. Until this morning, I hadn't expected to see them again for a very long time, had hoped that it would be even longer than that. They whisper to me.

Hello.

Hello.

"Put them down," Neti says, and slaps my wrists. "Put them down."

I drop them back onto the table, cracking one of her plates with a knife hilt. My breath catches. The stony knives grumble.

"That'll cost you." Neti's laugh is shrill and horrible. "Oh, it starts with plates, and before you know it, you're putting a vast crack in the world."

"Sorry," I say.

"Never you mind, Mr. de Selby. Never you mind. Was just having a joke at your expense. I've a room," she jabs a thumb at a door to the left of us, one of many, "a big room crammed floor to ceiling with others, just like them. I make them from the bones of the dead—it's a hobby. You'd be smashing plates from dawn till dusk for a century or more before you'd put a dint in the size of my collection. And how many have I used in all these ages? Just a dozen or so." She smacks her lips. "Now I trust you will indulge me, and have a scone."

I do, and it's delicious. As long as you don't think too much about where it's come from. There's something too sanguine about that jam. But it's sweet, and it's no real trouble to have another one.

Neti looks at the knives. "You know what you have to do with those?"

I nod. "Yes, I have been given instructions."

Neti sniffs at that, and I wonder if I haven't fucked up again and offended her. "You'll have them back before three, thank you."

"You could always come with me." It doesn't hurt to offer an olive branch.

Neti grins wryly. "Oh, to walk the streets of Brisbane again. To terrorize and shop. Hm, what sort of parasol is in fashion these days?"

I start to frame an answer and she laughs. "Mr. de Selby, these rooms and my gardens are enough. But I appreciate the offer. Besides, what you need to do is a private thing, and best shared only with your Ankou. That is, if you trust him."

"Of course. Absolutely."

Neti swings a set of eyes toward the grandfather clock that takes up a large chunk of wall space between two doors. "You're best away. You don't have much time."

I wipe my lips with a linen napkin on which little black spiders have been stitched, far too realistically. I stroke one for a moment, and I swear its legs flutter. I drop it, pick up the knives and leave Neti to her parlor. I feel every single one of her eyes watching me as I walk back down the hallway.

"She's not kidding," Wal says, his eyes fixed on the Knives of Negotiation. "You be damn careful with those."

"I will," I say, but he's already a tattoo on my biceps again. And it's just me and the knives.

I walk through the offices, the naked blades in either hand. I've got nowhere to put them and they're certainly not the sort of thing you slip in your pockets. My staff keep their distance. Maybe it's the slightly manic expression on my face. No, it's definitely the knives. It gives the concept of staff cutbacks a certain, well, edge. I feel every eye on me and I try not to look menacing, but with the Knives of Negotiation it's impossible not to. The knives, too, seem curious. They're mumbling and somehow staring at everyone and everything. I can feel that rapt attention running through my wrists. They want to jerk this way and that. I don't let them. Though part of me wants to. Part of me knows how easy it would be to re-create my dreams of blood and cuts.

Once ensconced in my office, I take a deep breath and call Tim.

Tim regards the knife in his hand with a look that tells me he's wishing he was back working in the public service. "So, how do we do this?"

We're standing in the middle of my office. My back's to my throne, but I can feel it there, the bloody thing a constant presence.

"I know you haven't done a lot of pomping, but the cut has to be shallow and long. Just like you would if you were stalling a Stirrer."

Tim hasn't stalled anything since we faced off against Morrigan's Stirrer allies in these very offices a couple of months ago. I've kept him away from all of that. He's much better at administration, at getting people to do what needs to be done. Lissa's the opposite. She leads by example; people follow her because she gets down and does it, too. I've fallen down on the leadership front, but that's going to change now.

Tim's knife hand shakes.

"I wouldn't ask you to do this," I say, "if I didn't need you, and believe me there are much more confronting ceremonies than this one in a Pomp's repertoire." I remember the binding ceremony I'd once performed with Lissa's ghost. That had involved arcane symbols and a few good dollops of semen. "From what Mr. D says, the knives will guide us."

For a moment I feel sorry that I've pulled Tim into all this. But then he grins at me, and it's just like old times.

"Fuck it, let's do this now."

I find myself grinning back. "Pub afterward?"

"Absolutely."

As one we slice our hands. My cut burns, a flaring burst that wrenches its way up my arm. These are the Knives of Negotiation, after all, they are edged in a multitude of ways and all of them are cutting. The blade bites deeper than I intended. Blood flows thick and fast. Tim reaches out his bloody hand, and I grip it.

And then.

Tim's eyes widen, in sync with mine, and we realize what we are about to do. Both of us struggle, but the ceremony is driving our limbs now. There are no brakes that we can apply to this.

We slam the knives point first into each other's chest.

4

I die for a heartbeat then.

So does Tim. I can feel it.

I cry out, but my lips don't move. The air tightens around us. The One Tree's creaking becomes a roaring. Great dark shapes loom and cackle. Then, out of nowhere, I see the Kurilpa Bridge. Its tangle of masts and wires. Mount Coot-tha rising in the northwest. Lightning cracks, a luminous finger trailing down.

And then the knives are back in our hands, bloodless. The wounds gone.

Sometimes I would like a job that involved less stabbing.

Tim coughs, his fingers scramble desperately over his chest. "What the fuck was that?" He waves the stone knife in my face. "Christ. Christ! *Christ!*" I snap my head backward to avoid losing my nose.

Then he seems to realize what he is doing, breathes deeply, slowly, in and out, and puts the knife down carefully on my desk, as though it's a bomb.

And it is, I suppose. I follow suit, and the knives mumble at the both of us. They sound happy.

"Shit, I don't know," I say. "It wasn't what I was expecting."

"Wasn't what you were expecting? What the hell were you expecting?" Tim's looking down at the front of his shirt.

There's no blood. I haven't bothered checking, I'm an old hand at these sorts of things now.

"No one told me that would happen, believe me. Not Mr. D or Neti."

"I can see why." Tim drops into one of the chairs at my desk. He grins a little though, surprising me. "It was a bit of a rush."

"So Kurilpa," I say.

"Yeah, the new pedestrian bridge."

Kurilpa Bridge sits on the curving Brisbane River just on the edge of the CBD. It's a wide footbridge; steel masts rise from its edges like a scattering of knitting needles, and between them are strung thick cables. You either love it or hate it.

Can't say that I love it.

"How do you hold a Death Moot on a bridge?" I move to sit in my throne, shaking my head. The moment my arse touches the chair the black phone on my desk rings. I jump then look from the phone to Tim.

"Well, I'm not answering it," he says.

I snatch it up.

This is no regular phone call. Down the line a bell is tolling, distant and deep. I keep waiting for some slamming guitar riff to start up.

Instead a thin voice whispers, "You have engaged us, across the peaks and troughs of time. And we will serve you."

There's a long pause.

"Thank you," I say at last.

"We are coming," the voice says. "The bridge has been marked with your blood. The bridge has been marked and we are coming. Oh, and there will be a set menu. And canapés."

The line goes dead.

"They're coming," I say, looking at the handset.

"Who?" Tim looks at me blankly.

"The Caterers."

"Excellent," Tim says, taking this whole being-stabbed-in-the-chest thing very well.

"Oh, and there will be canapés."

"As long as there aren't any of those little sandwiches, then I'm happy."

"But when do these guys arrive? I forgot to ask."

"That I know," Tim says. "Four days from now. We'll take them out to the bridge then." He gets to his feet. "Well, that's that. The Death Moot has begun. Pub?"

I shake my head. "You and Lissa are right," I say. "I need to start actually being here. I need to make sure that I'm ready." I pick up the knives. "And I need to get these back to Aunt Neti. They're much too dangerous to leave lying around."

Tim grins at me. "Nice to have you back."

There's an angry bruise on the horizon when I get home. It's six o'clock and a storm is coming. I feel virtuous, and pleased that, after two visits in one day, I won't have to speak to Aunt Neti for some time. The Knives of Negotiation are safe. The Caterers are on their way, and the Death Moot has a venue. Not bad for a day's work. I've texted Lissa, told her I'll be waiting at home.

I'm determined to show her I can do this. That I'm not dropping out, and that she isn't losing me.

She's right, I do need to practice my shifting, and I want to read as much of Tim's briefing notes as I can before she gets home. Here, where I'm relatively free from distractions. I've been drifting. Dad once said that pomping is for Pomps and that business is for dick-heads. Of course, it didn't stop him being very good at both. Pomping's all I've ever known, but managing a business is uncomfortably new to me. I like people, but I'm not sure I can tell them what to do.

After all, I spent a lot of my time as a Pomp arguing with management. The shit I gave my immediate superior Derek... I almost miss the guy.

Tim's last words to me this afternoon, after a very quick beer, were: "Meeting tomorrow morning at 8:15. Cerbo. Do not be late. And you would be better off for reading my notes." Faber Cerbo is Suzanne Whitman's Ankou. I've not had much to do with him. I wonder what he wants?

Tim's notes are extensive, and amusing. He knows his audience, I guess. And I can understand why he might be hurt that I haven't read them yet. He's obviously put a lot of work into making it de Selby digestible.

By the time Lissa pulls into the driveway, I'm a third of the way through the notes and aware of various allegiances within the Orcus or, as Tim has subtitled his report, Who Hates Who. The most prominent allies on the list surprise me: Neill Debbier, South Africa's RM, and Suzanne Whitman, the RM of North America. Between them they seem to wield the most influence.

It's fascinating. As is the fact that Cerbo is Mortmax's resident expert on the Stirrer god. I should have been pushing for a meeting earlier. Tim's notes suggest that now, with the Death Moot so close, the lobbying is going to start in earnest. Hence my meeting with Cerbo, I assume.

I watch Lissa get out of the Corolla. Her face is pinched with the weight of a day's work. She pomped five souls today. I felt them all, as I did the stall she performed at the Wesley Hospital.

There's a bandage wrapped around her hand, and she's bending over to pick up some groceries. I leap down from the front steps and run to carry them for her.

"You don't have to," she says.

"Bullshit." I take the bags from her. "Let me look at that hand."

"It's nothing. Dr. Brooker's seen to it. Says to say hi."

Dr. Brooker's the Brisbane office's medico. He's tended to that office since before I was born.

I take her bandaged hand and kiss it, gently. Wrap my arms around her, and hold her tight. Just liking the way she feels. The corporeality of her.

The storm's coming, dark clouds boiling, dogs howling and barking in response to bursts of thunder. The rain sighing, exhaled from above and beating down on a thousand suburban roofs not too far away. The air's electric and, with it, my region's heartbeats are shed from me like a cloak. Steam rises from the road.

Bring on the lightning. Bring on this moment of peace.

"Let's get inside," Lissa says.

And we do. Just before it starts pissing down.

I lug the groceries to the kitchen and I'm a few minutes putting stuff away. Looks like there's cooking going on tonight. For the first time that feels all right. I grab a Coke from the fridge for Lissa and a beer for myself, and we sit out on the balcony. It's too hot inside.

Lissa holds my hand and we sit there, drinking our drinks, sweat cold against our skin, and watch the rain fall.

Storms build slowly but pass too quickly, and soon the pulse of the world is back.

"What are you cooking for dinner?" I ask.

Lissa arches an eyebrow.

"What are *we* cooking for dinner?" I offer.

"You'll find out."

"I'm sorry I've been such an idiot lately."

"I think the correct word is dick," Lissa says, and kisses me hard. Apology accepted.

After dinner I walk into the bathroom and my good mood evaporates at once. The walls are covered with blood. It's a typical portent for a Pomp but this is the worst one I've seen in a while. A stir is coming, and a big one.

We need unity in the face of the Stirrer god, and that's not going to happen unless my Death Moot goes off without a hitch. With the exception of the odd alliance, regions keep to themselves outside of these biannual meetings, partly because the work load for each Death is phenomenal and mainly because most of the RMs don't trust, and/or actively hate, each other. I need the Death Moot to succeed.

I try to be quiet about it, cleaning furiously at the walls—all tiled because my parents were Pomps, too, and no one wants to make work for themselves—but Lissa catches me in there.

"Oh, no," she says.

"Yeah."

She looks so tired. I don't let her help, she's worked hard enough today, and she needs her sleep.

Bad shit's on its way. That's what this wall is telling me. The blood dissolves easily enough with soap and water and scrubbing. It's not the real stuff, but an ectoplasmic equivalent. Regardless, it takes me a good half-hour to clean it all away, and clean myself up.

When I finally get to bed, Lissa's asleep.

I lie next to her for a while, but don't close my eyes. I wish I could follow her, but I can't. I've no desire for nightmares tonight. After all, I've already faced some of them today, and been reminded of others.

People die as I lie there. Heartbeats stutter and fail.

Then my eyes shut. *Wham*. I'm back in that madness of knives and laughter. And then the scythe. My hands clench around its snath, the blade humming at the other end. Two hundred people stand before me, their eyes wide, their mouths small Os of terror. And I start swinging.

I jolt awake. Only a moment has passed.

I pull myself from the bed, pick up Tim's notes and finish them off.

I also started on another bottle of Bundy.

5

I open one eye a crack. There's half a bottle of rum settling uneasily in my stomach. I'd fallen asleep again. Well, I don't know if you could call it sleep, but I was definitely unconscious. My mobile phone's ringing.

The clock radio gives out a hard red light: 2:30 in the am. Bloody hell. Lissa nudges me with an elbow, soft, then not so. When did I come back to bed?

"Going to answer that?" Her voice is a late-night mumble, with just a hint of edge to it.

It's the first night in two months that I've actually fallen asleep—totally by accident, Lissa's head on my chest—and someone calls.

At least they dragged me from that cackling nightmare. The swinging scythe, though in this version it was in time to Queen's "We Will Rock You." Maybe I was awake before the phone started ringing, just trying to pretend I was asleep. Either way, I'm awake now.

If this is Tim calling, drunk and doleful, from the Regatta in Toowong, there are going to be serious words. Particularly after his and Lissa's intervention.

Another elbow nudge. She's going to crack a rib at this rate. "Well?" Lissa says.

The sheets tangle as I try and get up. Lissa grabs a handful, tugs, and I'm free enough of the sheetly bonds to move. I scramble for the phone on the bedside table. It's the brightest (loudest) light source in the room, so it's easy to find. Still, 2:30! And it keeps on ringing. Who'd have thought a Queen medley ring tone could get annoying?

Not Tim. Caller ID sets me straight on that.

Suzanne Whitman.

Mortmax Industries' North American Regional Manager. What the hell is the U.S. Death doing calling me now?

"Hello," I croak.

"I'm sorry, did I wake you?" She sounds surprised. Sleep is hardly de rigueur in the RM crowd.

I pause, long enough to get my game voice on—sort of. "Not at all. Just came back from a run."

"At 2:30 in the morning?"

"My personal trainer's a bloody bastard. What can I do for you?"

Lissa sits up next to me and mouths, "Who is it?" I shake my head at her. She frowns. If there's one thing that Lissa hates, it's secrets. She'll have to wait.

"It's not what you can do for me, Mr. de Selby, but what I can do for you—and it's quite a lot," Suzanne says, somehow sounding both threatening and sexy at once. "Meet me in the Deepest Dark in an hour."

"An hour?"

"I assume you're going to need a shower after your run." She hangs up.

I drop my phone back on the bedside table, and pull myself completely out from under the sheets. Lissa's bedside light switches on.

She looks at me intently. "So... who was that?"

"Suzanne Whitman."

Lissa's face tightens. "Her. Why now?"

"She wants to see me in an hour, in the Deepest Dark."

"Death Moot?"

"What else would it be?" The ceremony has set more than just the Caterers in motion.

"You want me to come?" Lissa asks.

"You know you can't go there. There's no air, for one, none that you can breathe, anyway." I drop back down next to her, rest my chin on my hand. "Are you concerned about me spending the wee small hours of the morning with another woman?"

Lissa purses her lips. "No, of course not, but the Deepest Dark's a bloody odd choice."

Lissa's been there. She wasn't alive at the time. I don't know how much she remembers, but she certainly doesn't look too keen to return.

I shrug. "It was her decision."

"Don't let Suzanne Whitman make your decisions for you."

"I won't. No one makes decisions for me but me. You're starting to sound like you don't like her."

"I don't."

"And why's that?"

Lissa rolls away and pulls the sheets over her head. Then reaches out and switches off the light. "I need to sleep," she says.

The shift to the Deepest Dark is a blazing supernova of agony in my skull.

It's *really* that bad.

I arrive bent over and coughing. Desperate as I am not to show any weakness, it's as good as I can do.

It's a moment until I'm aware of my surroundings.

The creaking of the One Tree permeates everything because, in a way, the One Tree *is* everything in the Underworld and the Deepest Dark. The sound rises to us through the dark soil beneath our feet, it builds in my bones. To say that it is loud is to emphasize one aspect of it to the detriment of everything else. It is a sound against which every other sound is registered.

And this place is hardly silent. The dead whisper here, a breathy, scratchy, continuous whispering. They release their last secrets before ascending into a greater secret above.

Up and down are relative in the Deepest Dark. Around us, through dust and soil that comes directly from the Underworld, wend the root tips of the One Tree: each is the width of my thigh. In the Deepest Dark we are beneath Hell itself. The air smells of blood, ash and humus. It's a back of the throat kind of bouquet. Not the best thing when you're already gagging.

Suzanne doesn't speak until I'm standing straight, and I've wiped a hand across my mouth. "You're late."

I make a show of peering at the green glowing dial of my watch. "I'd hardly call thirty seconds late." I'm being deliberately provocative. I find it helps when people think you're stupider than you are. It's about the only advantage I have.

Suzanne smiles thinly. Her dark eyes regard me impassively.

Suzanne's got a Severe—yes, with a capital S—sort of Southern Gothic thing going on. Her hair is cut into a bob. A black dress follows sharp lines down her lean body. Pale and muscular limbs jut from the sleeves. It's certainly not sensible garb for the cold fringes of the Underworld. She could be going out for the night, or about to chair a meeting. If she could get away with it in the Deepest Dark, if it wasn't so dark, I guess she'd be wearing black sunglasses. She glances at the tracksuit pants and tatty old jumper I'm wearing beneath my dad's old duffel coat, and sniffs.

"So, Suzanne, just what is it that you can do for me?"

She smiles condescendingly. "I chose this place because it is important to you."

Above us the sky is luminous with souls, glowing faintly red, heading out through the ether to wherever souls go once life and the Underworld is done with them. It should be peaceful except there's a great spiraling void, like a photo negative of a galaxy, eating up one corner of the sky, and it's getting bigger. The Stirrer god.

In the distance, maybe a kilometer away, is Devour, the Stirrer city. Its high walls glow a color very similar to my watch. I rode a bike through there a few months ago, fleeing for my life and for the life of the woman I love.

That Stirrer god, though, is hard to ignore. It's a sinister dark stain on the pants front of Hell and it's getting bigger. Sometimes it's a great eye, as I remember it, sometimes a million eyes, staring down. Leering at the Underworld.

I've felt the weight of the god's vast and angry gaze upon me, and I've stared back at it. So I've a personal stake in all of this, but then when that god arrives, life itself, from bacteria up, will be under threat. It's amazing, though, just how much people are pretending that it isn't going to happen. RMs, my colleagues. People who should know better.

"You chose this place because you knew it gives you an advantage over me," I say.

"What a cynic."

"I prefer to call it realism." I point toward the dark god in the sky. "Maybe it's just too big. Maybe it's something that we can't do anything about at all. But we have to try."

"What do you know about that thing up there?" she asks.

"That the Stirrers worship it and that it's drawing closer. What else is there?"

Suzanne waves her hand dismissively, as though the Stirrer god was nothing more than a buzzing insect. "Look, I want to offer you a deal. Think about all the resources you would have at your disposal. My offices, my staff—they're much bigger than yours. And that difference in staffing is even larger now after your little problem."

The "little" problem she's referring to, the one that led to my promotion, wiped out Mortmax's Australian offices and, almost, due to a minor Regional Apocalypse, Australia's living population. Workplace politics can be genocidal in my line of business. And when things get that way they have a tendency to spill out into the world. The Spanish Flu, the Black Death—they were both preceded by "problems" in my industry.

"You let that happen, too." I glare at her. None of the RMs stepped in to help. In the end it had been left up to me. "All of you are guilty of that."

Suzanne's eyes narrow just enough that I know I've got to her. "You know the rules," she says, "our hands were tied. Morrigan manipulated us."

Morrigan manipulated me more than anyone. But I'm not going to let Suzanne get away with her comment. "Excuses aren't going to save the world. Morrigan was small time compared to *that*." I point at the Stirrer god amassing on the horizon.

Suzanne raises her hands placatingly. "I have my best people working on it," she says. I open my mouth to speak but she jumps in first. "But that's not why I'm here. You need me."

"Like a coronary." My turn for a condescending grin.

Suzanne grimaces, though I can see that I've amused her, which makes me a little grumpier. "Try not to be so aggressive. Yes, this is scary for you, Steven, I understand that. You're a newly negotiated RM, in the process of building up your Pomps. It's going to be years before you're at full strength. You're vulnerable. You can barely shift without throwing up."

Fair assessment so far. But I can't let it lie. "I'll get better."

"Of course you will," she says, "but I can help you. I can ease the transition. I can lend you more Pomps, for one thing." She reaches out, squeezes my hand. Her fingers are warm. I pull away, and Suzanne frowns, but not with anger. She dips her head, even manages a smile. "I understand exactly what you're going through. I can guide you."

"I've already got Mr. D for that."

Suzanne's face tightens, her smile attenuates, whatever humor there was in her eyes leaves with it. I'm familiar with that expression—I tend to bring it out in people, and Mr. D was even better at it than me.

"Mr. D was never one of us," she says. "You want a second-rate mentor? You stick with that idiot. I'm giving you a chance." She bends down, grabs a handful of the dust which coats everything here, and lets it fall. Only it doesn't. The dust drifts around her lazily, glowing in all the colors of a particularly luminous acid trip. It spirals around her head creating a halo, and beneath it she's all shadows, sharp angles and full lips. The darkest points of her face are her eyes. When she smiles, her teeth are white and straight. "No one understands this place, this job, like I do. Just consider it. That's all I'm asking."

"And what do you get out of it?"

"I get an ally, Mr. de Selby, and one who is aware of his powers and limits, one who doesn't go off rushing madly into things, making it difficult for everyone. Mr. D isolated himself. He never really bothered with us. Sometimes I think he delighted in making enemies. When you think about all the people who died—all that you've lost—remember who let it happen. Morrigan had the schemes, but Mr. D allowed him to flourish in your branch."

She has a point.

"Steven, I liked your family. Michael and Annie were good people. The things your father did for Mortmax... He even lifted our profits in the States."

I can imagine Dad rolling in his grave at that. He'd always been slightly embarrassed by his business acumen. All he'd really wanted was to be a Pomp. Now Dad, if pressed, would have made a great RM. Mom, too. I wish they were here. I wish I knew what they would do.

Suzanne shivers. It's cold here, and I doubt she would ever show such vulnerability willingly, but my father raised me this way: I shrug out of my coat and put it around her shoulders. She's wearing Chanel No. 5, my mother's favorite perfume. I remember coming home, after my parents had died. The house had smelled of it and it was the first time the reality of their deaths really hit me. It was also the first time that I wondered if moving into their place was a mistake.

I pull away. Suzanne doesn't notice, or pretends not to, though she does look at me oddly. "You are a gentleman, Mr. de Selby."

I open my mouth to speak, but she's already gone. "Hey! What about my coat?"

All I have to answer me is dust falling to the ground again. I crouch down and scoop up my own handful. In my palms it's just dust, gritty and gray. I open my fingers and it drops. Only the souls in the sky, and the nearby city of Stirrers, offer any light.

My right biceps tingles, then burns. Ah, finally. Wal crawls out from under my shirt and stares up at me.

"I don't trust her," Wal says. No surprise there, that's Wal's standard response, though it's been proven remarkably accurate.

"Where were you?" I ask.

"Stuck to your arm," he says, looking more than a little chagrined. "She stopped me, I don't know how. But she did it well."

I grin at him cruelly. "Ah, so there are things, very *useful* things, she could teach me."

Wal slaps me across the face with all the force of a handful of tissues. "You shut your mouth."

He actually looks hurt.

A dim hooting comes from the city of Devour—like a parliament of malevolent and fractious owls. Bells ring and, all around us, the dead whisper their brittle, final whispers before drifting out of hearing and further into the Deepest Dark.

The air chills. Both of us feel it. I don't have my coat anymore, but Wal is the only one who is naked.

He shivers. "I don't like this place."

He's not the only one.

6

"I can't believe I'm going to be late!"

Most of my clothes are in piles in the bedroom. But my suit, one of eight I own, hangs in the wardrobe. A Pomp never leaves their suit on the floor. Never. And I'm RM now, I have to set the standard. I slip into it like a second skin. It's Italian, and cost me three weeks' salary—and that's my current salary. This meeting with Cerbo is formal; tracksuit and jumper just isn't going to cut it. Lissa watches, then hits me with the most deafening wolf whistle. I can't understand how she finds this body attractive. OK, maybe a little, I do work out. And the suit looks pretty fine. But still, I feel my cheeks flush at Lissa's scrutiny.

I knot my tie, straighten everything, and even I have to admit that I look good.

Though not nearly as lovely as Lissa. I want to be back in bed with her. We never seem to spend enough time together. A moment apart is an ache in my chest. Tim might be right, new love and all that. But I never felt this intensely for Robyn. And Lissa is the only woman I have ever pursued to Hell.

"Maybe I should call off this meeting, spend the morning with you. You're not working till late, I've seen the schedule. We could..."

Lissa appears to give this some serious thought. "No, Tim would kill you, and me. Not after all we've done trying to get you engaged with the business again. The Moot's a week away. You've got to—stop that!"

She doesn't push me away, though, as my lips brush her neck. Then—I feel her body stiffening with the effort of it—she does, and I'm backing off the bed, away from the intoxicating smell of her. "You'll crush your suit, or, at the very least, stretch the front of those pants."

"Oh." I look down. "I see what you mean."

And I'm blushing once more. Lissa grins at me wickedly. I straighten my suit again.

Yeah, new love. Such new, new love.

"How do I look?"

"You're the bomb," she says.

"The bomb?"

Lissa laughs at me. "Just get out of here. Or your cousin will have an aneurism."

"How's the hair?"

She squints at me. "Still thinning."

"I hate you."

"No, you don't."

I kiss her again, and then I shift to Number Four.

It's another body punch of a shift. I miss my office by about fifteen meters. End up at the reception desk. Lundwall blinks at me.

Number Four. This is Australia's Pomp Central, and the major node in the southern hemisphere's Underworld–living world interface, which makes the architecture interesting in a multi-dimensional kind of way. Outside one part of the building, Brisbane is in the middle of a boiling, sweating summer. And outside another part, Hell is going through a rather mild spring. The seasons rarely correspond. In here, the air is loud with the hum of air-conditioners and the creaking of the One Tree.

Phones ring throughout the office. People are working busily and trying hard to ignore me and my clumsy entrance. I get the feeling that Tim has been doing a fair bit of storming around this morning. Tim is great at his job, but you don't want to get him mad. He says it doesn't help that I'm so casual about the whole thing. Well, I think we balance each other out perfectly.

But I *would* think that.

I stumble over to Tim's office and open the door without knocking. He's stubbing out a cigarette when I appear and looks guilty.

"Gotcha," I say.

"What if I was having a wank or something here?"

I smirk. "Hardly. If you had to choose between smokes and masturbation there's no contest."

"Ah, your deductive capabilities astound me, Holmes."

Other than the ashtray heaped with cigarettes, Tim's room is as neat as an anally retentive pin. I'm more than a little envious of his work ethic. His inbox and out are emptied throughout the day and there's a well-marked year-planner on one wall. Seven days from now, on the 28th of December, the Death Moot begins. He's circled that day, and the two that follow it, in thick red marker. I've a year-planner somewhere under the mess on my desk.

This was once Morrigan's office. Tim hasn't changed it that much, apart from the photo of Sally and the kids next to his keyboard—I bought him the frame. He's even using the same daily desk calendar, the one with the inspirational quotes. Everything from Dorothy Parker to Sun Tzu is in there. He and Morrigan shared a deep commitment to work, a fastidiousness about everything in their life, and a love of beer, though Tim has never tried to kill me. But the way he's looking at me, maybe that's all about to change.

Then the pain of the shift hits me in a residual wave.

Tim waits politely until I finish dry heaving before he starts taking strips off me. "Jesus, mate! Could you at least have a shower before coming to work?"

I shrug. No point telling him how hard it was to leave Lissa this morning. Then I see the bandage on his left hard. "Not like you to be out with the Stirrers. Was it a hard stir?" Sometimes a Stirrer will require more blood than usual to stall it.

Tim shakes his head. "I wish, it'd mean I was out of the office more. No, the door's being particularly demanding today." Number Four may be the only place that demands—well, not so much demands, but takes—a blood sacrifice of its staff on entry. RMs are exempt, most of the time, something I'm pleased about. For me, it's usually only a tiny pricking of the thumb, and weeks may go past where it asks for nothing. I wonder if the ferocity of Tim's sacrifice has anything to do with the massive portent I spent part of last night cleaning from the bathroom.

Tim throws me a small spray can of deodorant. I manage to catch it before it hits my head. Then he hurls a pack of breath mints. Not so lucky with those, they skitter all over the desk. I scoop up a few of them.

"I'm guessing you didn't clean your teeth before you headed over here," Tim says.

"You guessed wrong. Anything else?" I pop a handful of mints into my mouth, regardless.

"Oh, I haven't started yet." His hands rest on his hips. "You cut it this fine again, and you can find yourself another Ankou."

"Where am I going to find one as good as you?"

"Exactly. Which is why you are never going to do this again. Now, I've been thinking about this Death Moot—"

"Is Cerbo here?" I interrupt.

"Not yet. Wonder of wonders, we've actually got five minutes."

"Good. I had a meeting with Suzanne Whitman last night."

"And you have only told me this now because . . . ?"

"Look, it was late. I didn't want to wake you. At least you can sleep."

"Still having trouble, eh?"

"Shit, Tim, I've been whingeing about this for a month."

"Pardon me if I've been too busy to notice." And as if to prove his point, his mobile starts ringing.

He looks at it. "It's only mildly urgent," he says. "I'll call them back."

Tim slips his phone into his pocket and smiles at me. "Now, this is interesting, *really* interesting. If the U.S. RM is so keen to negotiate, the others can't be too far behind. What did she want?"

"She said she wanted to help."

Neither of us successfully choke down the laugh that follows.

"Said I could do with an ally."

Another snort.

Tim checks his watch. "We'd better get to your office. Cerbo will be there in a minute." We walk past the desks of Pomps and the hallway that sits in the middle of the office, the one that leads directly to Aunt Neti's parlor. She's baking scones or muffins or biscuits; the smell drifts down the hall. Probably expecting a visitor. I can't help wondering who.

My office is a bit stuffy. I switch on the lights and the aircon. It's your basic sort of corner office, except for Brueghel's painting, "The Triumph of Death" against one wall (not a copy, the real thing, all those skeletons bringing on the apocalypse, herding the living to Hell) and the throne, of course.

I drop into the throne, and my region immediately grows more vital around me. The beating hearts, the creaking tree.

Sitting in my throne I feel what Tim's reports can only tell me. We're stretched painfully thin. My Pomps are struggling out there. It might be a picture of industry in the offices, but it's little more than a veneer painted over chaos. I've been ignoring this for far too long.

"We need more staff," I say to Tim.

"Lissa's doing the best she can," he says irritably. "It's not exactly easy to advertise for Pomps. There's a whole bunch of stages that we have to steer people through. I think it's remarkable that we have as many staff as we do."

"We've got to do better."

"You could take a more active role. That might help," Tim says sharply.

"I'm doing the best I can," I say, mimicking his tone.

Tim groans, shakes his head. "How about a unified front?"

"Yeah, how about it?"

"Sometimes you piss me off, de Selby."

I grin at him. "That's what family is for."

"Maybe that's why I decided to become a Black Sheep."

"Nah, you can't escape it no matter what you do. As long—" and I stop myself there. I was going to say as long as there is family left, but there isn't that much family remaining. There are some things neither of us are ready to joke about.

I'm almost relieved that Faber Cerbo shifts into the foyer at that moment. Apparently Ankous can do that, if their RM is sufficiently skilled. Morrigan could, and it didn't seem to hurt him, either, the prick. Cerbo's appearance is presaged by a slight pressure in my skull. His heartbeat, a sudden addition to my region, is loud—like you'd expect from an Ankou—even louder than Tim's, and at a steady sixty beats per minute.

I glance at my watch. He is exactly thirty seconds late, and I can't help feeling that Suzanne is making a point. Lundwall—heartbeat ninety-three bpm, up from seventy, now that Cerbo has appeared at his desk—leads him into the room.

Faber Cerbo, like any self-respecting Pomp, is in a suit. We all are, here. As though Death was truly like any other business. Well, we can pretend. The real reason is the vast number of funerals we attend and morgues and mortuaries we visit. In those places a suit makes you virtually invisible—even in Brisbane on a forty degree day.

Unlike Tim and me, Cerbo is wearing a hat, a bowler. That, and the pencil-thin mustache, make him look like a mash-up of a British accountant from the thirties and the filmmaker John Waters, and are completely at odds with his Texan accent. I've never liked wearing hats, they mess up my hair. But it suits him, somehow. Gripped in his left hand, his nails coated with black nail polish, is a brown leather folder.

Cerbo doffs his bowler, and rolls his shoulders. Bones click with the movement.

I don't get up from my throne, in fact I make a point of swinging back on it, looking as casual as I can. After all, here I am in the seat of my power, so to speak. It is poor form to neglect it.

I nod at Cerbo and gesture to one of the chairs in front of the desk. He gives a swift and slightly mocking bow—well, I think it's mocking, and if I can't be sure, the odds are high. My rise to RM was something of a shock to a lot of people—myself included—and I'm not treated as seriously as I could be. But then again, it fits into my tactic. Just grin and let them think you're stupid.

Tim shakes his hand. Cerbo gives him a warm smile then sits down, so lightly it's as if he's hardly sitting at all. He puts the folder on the table.

"My mistress says she met with you last evening, Mr. de Selby." He gives Tim a pained look, and Tim nods sympathetically. I wonder what Ankous say about their bosses when they're not around. Hell, Morrigan ran over Mr. D with an SUV. Maybe we push them to it.

"Yes, we had an interesting chat."

"Unfortunately, since I have not been apprised of your *chat,*" another pained look in Tim's direction, "I can only tell you what it is that I was briefed on, and hope that our topics of conversation are in some way sympathetic."

He opens his folder, extracts a single sheet of paper, and slides it toward me, pushing aside a half-dozen unopened envelopes, a Mars

Bar wrapper, and a scrunched up packet of salt and vinegar chips. We all jump back a little when a cockroach scurries out of the chip packet. Tim whacks it with a packet of envelopes, misses, and the insect's off and running toward a distant corner of the room. Tim glances at me. OK, so I need to clean up a little. Cerbo doesn't say a word (his pursed lips and raised eyebrows are enough) and deposits the sheet of paper in front of me.

The number 10 is written across the sheet in black marker.

I look from it, to Cerbo, then to Tim, then back to the paper. I shrug. "And this means what? You're shifting to the metric system?"

Cerbo gives out a rather theatrical sigh, as though it's painfully obvious what the number represents. "That, Mr. de Selby, is the number of Pomps Ms. Whitman is willing to add to your ranks from her own."

I raise an eyebrow and lean across the desk, my elbow crunching down on the chip packet. "And what is expected of me if I accept?"

Cerbo clears his throat, makes a little nervous gesture with his hands as though he's shooing away flies. "Time, Mr. de Selby. You are to give her your time. An hour for each Pomp. Ten hours, in total, of your undivided attention, before the Death Moot begins."

"It's a generous offer," I say.

Cerbo's lips curl in a grimace. "It is more than generous. Ms. Whitman doesn't want you to fail in your work. Power vacuums are something of a danger in this business."

"And what do you think the odds are of that?"

Cerbo doesn't answer.

"I'll consider it," I say.

I get the feeling that he was expecting a response, and an enthusiastically positive one, at that. But I'm not ready to answer, and Cerbo can tell. He's disappointed, and not all of that seems to be about going home to his RM empty-handed.

He dons his hat. Slips his folder beneath his arm, and stands.

"Don't be *too* long in considering it. That may be regarded as an insult."

I nod. "I am aware of that. Believe me, I've no desire to put anyone's nose out of joint. But this is my region, and I'll take as long as I need."

He glances at Tim. Tim shrugs and gives him his most "my boss is crazy" look. Cerbo sighs again. "Good day, gentlemen."

He shifts, and there's nothing but air filling the space he's left. The sheet of paper flutters on my desk, the Mars Bar wrapper falls to the floor.

"How the hell did he do that?" Tim asks enviously.

"I don't know." I throw my hands up in the air, and the throne tips. Both it and me end up on the ground.

Tim laughs.

My face burning, I get to my feet. The chair looks very smug. Bloody throne. I drop back in it, heavily. "You told me you'd do the talking."

"Sometimes listening is better than talking."

I want to say that he knows nothing of listening, that he knows nothing of the things I can hear, of the things bodies tell me—beating hearts and closing veins, the stealthy drift of a clot toward the brain. But I'm just not that petulant.

"You did good, I think," Tim says. "The game's started. Opening gambit, all that shit."

"Whose game are we playing?"

"It was never going to be ours, at the beginning. Someone else had to make the first move. We're too new. We don't even know what pieces we've got, or what the game is."

"Ten Pomps. We could do with ten Pomps," I say.

"But they wouldn't really be yours. They'd be doing her bidding."

"But they'd *know* what they're doing."

Tim gets to his feet. "That's what worries me." He glances at his watch. "Shift change. Things are about to get crazy. We'll discuss this tonight, eh?"

"Yeah. Holding off until tomorrow is long enough to piss her off, but only a little."

"Annoying people isn't the greatest tactic, Steve."

I grin at him. "You use what gifts you're given."

"Oh, you use that one all right, and it's a rough instrument." He closes the door behind him.

"I didn't get this job because I was subtle," I say to the door. "I got it because I was stupid."

The chair beneath me shivers, as though it is dreaming. Three people die in a car accident. Someone clutches at his chest. His heart beneath races, shudders, halts. I look at the corner where the cockroach ran. There's been enough death already. I let it be.

I'm Death, not an exterminator.

7

With Tim and Cerbo gone I get to work.

Well, I try to.

First I pick up the chip packet and toss it in the bin. The chocolate wrapper goes the same way. I straighten a few papers, open some letters, but I'm not really reading them. I switch on my MP3 and listen to some Black Flag. Henry Rollins gets me in the right headspace today.

Complacency's a killer, Morrigan used to say. He should know. He used it to kill most of Australia's Pomps. But it took him down, too, in the end. He certainly hadn't expected me to win the Negotiation.

If I'm honest, neither had I.

Here I am sitting in the throne. An RM with all the responsibilities that entails. Staff beneath me, a region and a world to save from Stirrers, as well as a commitment to good returns for our shareholders.

I think about those ten Pomps and just how helpful they would be, not to mention Suzanne's knowledge. The black bakelite phone sits there. This is the sort of thing Mr. D could advise me on. But I need to start making my own decisions. I'll talk to him this afternoon, once I work out exactly how I feel about this offer.

I type up a couple of emails, then text Lissa: *Interesting morning, how about you?*

No response. So I send another one, creaking backward and forward in my throne: *Wish you were here. Naked.*

No response. I play the crossword in the *Courier-Mail*—only cheat half the time.

Then I consider the paperwork on my desk. There's a whole bunch of stuff I sign off on.

A car accident on the Pacific Highway chills me with eight deaths. It's just a gentle chill, but their deaths come so suddenly—I worry that there is no one there to facilitate their way into the Underworld. That there is, and that it is done, brings a tight smile to my lips. A seventy-five-year-old woman in her garden in Hobart clutches at her chest and tumbles among her rhododendrons. Two children jump off a bridge in some northern New South Wales town: only one surfaces. Someone takes a hammer to their husband, claw end first. Death. Death. Death. And my people are close by at every one.

It sounds terrible. But there's life before those endings, and existence after. It's not the world ending, but lives. The world's ending, though... I need to find out more about that Stirrer god.

Still no response from Lissa, so while I work I follow her via my Avian Pomps.

A crow witnesses her stalling a Stirrer in the Valley—the corpse had somehow escaped the Royal Brisbane Hospital. She lays the body gently against a bench and makes a call. An ambulance will be along soon. They'll ship the body back to the morgue and it will be as though it never happened. She binds the wound in her palm quickly and efficiently.

A sparrow watches as she eats a kebab for lunch, sitting in a mall, just a few streets from where she laid the body down. I can almost smell the garlic. I want to reach out and touch her, and the sparrow, misinterpreting this desire, flies at the back of her head. I manage to convince it otherwise an instant or two before contact.

An ibis ostensibly digs in a bin as she attends an open-air funeral service and pomps a soul, that of an elderly gentleman, whom she charms utterly. I can see his posture shift from scared, to guarded, to a chuckling disregard as she reaches out to touch his arm. He is gone in a flash—I feel the echo of the pomp through me. And Lissa is standing there, on the very fringes of the funeral service, alone.

Lissa's the ultimate professional. She talks to the dead so easily. Knows how to bring them around from loss to acceptance. She is the best Pomp I've ever seen.

After a while, she walks up to the ibis. I stare at her through its dark eyes. "Steven, I love you, but this is creepy. Don't you have work to do?"

I'm out of there in an instant, my face flushed.

I get out of my chair and, as I do every day about this time, pull open the blinds to the rear windows. These face the Underworld. My office is immediately lit with a reddish light. The One Tree isn't far away. Down below, the traffic of the Underworld moves slowly, in a stately reflection of the living world's traffic. The various bends of the river that I can see are busy with catamarans and ferries. Traffic, cars and buildings are almost identical to the living city, except everything is that little bit ornate. Mr. D says that's his fault. I haven't bothered to change it, yet. I'm not sure how, but I'm certain it's a lot of work.

With the blind open, the sunlight and unlight battle it out over my desk. They're equally matched. Where they strike my desk there's a patch of gloom, neutralized only when I turn on my lamp. I've read that the living and the dead worlds occupy the same place, but I don't really understand how that's possible. I prefer to think of them as two skins of the same onion.

A shrill screech startles me. I flinch, then glance over at the window leading to Hell. Someone's hanging from a harness and cleaning the glass from the outside with one of those big plastic squeegees. He's slowly sinking into view. This is a first. He's a big fella, pale skin, long black hair pulled back into a ponytail, a strong jaw marked with stubble. The harness digs into his shoulders. What is a living person doing in Hell?

He waves, I wave back.

Then he pulls out a gun and fires. It's such a casual movement that I hardly notice it. Don't even react until it's done. My stomach flips, I throw my hands in the air, and stumble backward, then catch my balance on the back of a chair.

The window stars, but doesn't implode. You have more than double-glazing when your office faces Hell.

Through the fragmentation of the glass, I see the "cleaner" frown.

I look at the door; I'm much further from it than the window. If I run that way I'll probably get a shot or two in the back and, while I'm at it, lead him into the office. Enough people have died in here this year already. It seems clear that he's only after me—and if this is about me, I want to keep it that way. Besides, I've taken bullets before and survived them easily. I lift up a chair. Not the throne, that weighs a bloody ton.

He fires again. The window shatters this time, glass going everywhere. The bullet thwacks against the wall behind me. Alarms sound throughout the building and the One Tree's creaking intensifies to a dull roar now there's no glass to block it out. Hell has entered the building.

My arm tingles, then burns. Wal extrudes from my flesh. He pulls the most impressive double-take I have ever seen, his wings fluttering madly.

"What the hell?"

"Gun!" I shout. "Assassination attempt!"

"Right, then. Shouldn't you be running the other way?"

"Shut up and help!" I yell.

I charge toward the gunman, the chair gripped in my hands as though it's some sort of medieval weapon. Here's a guy with a pistol, and me with something that I bought from IKEA. My boots crunch over glass, a big chunk of which slides through the side of my shoe and into my foot. It should hurt more, and it will, I'm sure, but right now all it does is make me angry.

I jab the chair at his head. He leaps back with all the grace of a gymnast. Fires again.

Misses.

But not quite, my ear stings. I resist the urge to slap a hand over the wound. It hurts more than the last time I was shot.

Wal's already buzzing around the bastard's head, and the gunman slaps him away easily, but Wal is back just as fast.

The gunman arcs out on the end of the rope, a pendulum packing a pistol. As he hurtles back in, I hurl the chair at him. He struggles to weave out of the way and the backrest hits him in the head with a sickening crunch. He swings in, then out, and in again, hanging limp.

I hobble over to him and reach out, but suddenly he falls, a long tail of rope following him. I peer down into the Underworld and watch him tumble, his limbs twitching. It's a bit of a mess when he hits. The mess itself is gone a moment later, back to the living world. He wasn't from the Underworld, that's for sure. Someone's just received a very nasty, splattery surprise.

"Watch it!" Wal yells. "There's someone on the roof!"

Who the hell is that? I swing my head up—stupid, stupid, that's the best way to lose your face, but I have to look—and someone ducks for cover. But I catch a glimpse of the stork-like beak of a plague mask.

I jerk back in from the window, and shake my head at Wal, who grimaces and then shoots up past me, hurtling toward the roof. He's gone a moment, before swooping back. He tears past me and hits the carpet hard, but is back in the air almost at once.

"Shit," he hisses. "That hurt. Not enough Hell here for me to fly properly."

"Did you see who it was?"

"Oh, yeah, I'm all right. And no, I didn't, they were gone."

Then the first bastard's soul arrives, lit with the bluish pallor of the dead. I'm the nearest entity capable of pomping him. I should have expected him.

He blinks—like the dead do, and his death was more sudden than most—surprised, perhaps, at who he's ended up with. He snarls at me, his every movement a blur, as though he can't find traction here. There's a terrible weight of anger in him. It's holding him here where his lack of flesh can't. I try to use it to my advantage.

"You're not going anywhere until you tell me who sent you."

"You'll find out soon enough." His voice is quiet, controlled, and then he's running at me, a final act of defiance, and one I'm not expecting. I can't stop the pomp from happening. He tears through me, a scrambling fury of claws. This fellow didn't expect to die, and he's mad about it, but not enough to betray his boss. In fact, I can tell he blames me. After all, I didn't die and I was supposed to.

Well, he doesn't have my sympathy.

The pomp is painful, but fast, then he's gone, and I'm left standing, feeling dizzy. Rubbing at my limbs. No one should die with such rage inside them. It leaves me hurting, and angry. Dissatisfied on every level.

"You really should clean up in here," Wal says, picking up another chip packet.

"Don't you start," I growl.

My mobile chirps. I drag it from my pocket. It's a text from Lissa: *Of course you do.*

What?

My office door swings open and Wal slips from air to arm. The ratio of earth to Hell has shifted in earth's favor. There are shouts, another ringing alarm, and Tim and a couple of the bigger guys from the office rush in. They look at me then at the broken glass. All this mess. It's the first time I have a real excuse for it.

"Naked." I lift the phone up in the air. "Of course!"

"What the—Steven, are you right?" Tim demands, then his eyes widen. "What the fuck happened to your ear?"

Oh, I'd forgotten about that. I reach up and touch it. My fingers come back bloody. I'm aflood with wooziness. *Jesus.*

"Someone just tried to kill me. And a second someone killed them, from upstairs, on the roof—Hellside, but you should check the real roof, just in case..."

Tim looks at the men with him, nods, and they run off. Leaving him, me and the phone.

I sway near the broken window. Perhaps I should move away from that drop. "Sorry about the mess." And then I remember the glass in my foot.

"Watch your step," I say, as darkness swallows me.

8

I'm rushing through the creaking, mumbling dark. Knives whisper and flash around me, winding and slashing at each other. In their wake, smoke trails and bodies fall where there were none—as though the knives have knitted their victims' existence and demise in the same instant.

My boots crunch on ash and bone.

A man gibbers on the hill. He sees me, comes rushing down. I stand and wait, uneasy, my belly cold. But I will not run. I recognize him at last.

Morrigan.

"You didn't think you had it that easy, did you?" he says.

The earth is a mouth, a great swallowing mouth. Morrigan tumbles and is gone.

I am rushing through the dark. The knives a circle of stone around me.

A hand closes on mine and I can't get free.

Another hand, and then another grabs me. Someone pulls out my index finger, and cuts. Severs the digit from the palm.

"One by one. That's how it works." It's Morrigan again. He brings his face close to mine. "You never should have won. The job's too big for you. Your feet are too small for the boots you're clomping in."

I push him away. He slashes out with a whispering knife. Another finger falls.

I'm awake. I check my fingers.

All there.

Someone is stitching up my foot. There's that uncomfortable

sensation of skin being pulled tight, without the pain. Not that I want the pain, but my body is all too aware it's going on somewhere, that trauma is being had whether I can feel it or not.

I'm lying on a bed in Brooker's room, which has to be the best fitted-out sick bay in any workplace in Australia.

"I don't remember Mr. D ever getting into this sort of trouble," Dr. Brooker says, looking at me over his glasses. Brooker's work as Mortmax Brisbane's physician usually means the occasional bit of stitch work, a few prescriptions and a lot of counseling. He's very rarely in Number Four—which is what saved him during Morrigan's Schism—but he's available most of the time. I've known Dr. Brooker since I can remember, before memory, in fact. He was the attending doctor at my birth. Yeah, and I get about as much sympathy from him as anyone in my family would have given me. I suppose I could take that as a compliment. I called him the "good Doctor Brooker" once and got a cuff under the ear. His mood hasn't exactly improved since.

I grimace. "Mr. D had been doing this a century or two before you were even born. He'd gotten the trouble out of his system."

"Nevertheless... you really need to concentrate on your job, not this messing about with guns. People always get hurt." He jabs a gloved finger at my foot. "You're an RM. You're not about hurting people."

"*He* had a gun. *I* had a chair, and believe me, he ended up much worse than I did. Ouch!"

Brooker harrumphs and pulls a stitch tight. "Keep still. You were much better when you were unconscious. You'll be all right. Quite frankly, I don't know why anybody even bothered trying to shoot at you. Waste of time—you can't be killed that way."

"Maybe they just wanted to see if they could hurt me?"

"Well, they can hurt you all right." He smiles broadly. "But not as much as me if you don't keep still."

"Where is everybody?"

"Does this look like a party to you?" Brooker rolls his eyes and finishes his stitching with a neat knot—he's done an awful lot of those over the years. "They're waiting outside, where I told them to wait."

Yeah, I might be RM, but in this room Brooker is king.

I clear my throat softly. "Can I ask you something?"

Brooker looks at me. "Shoot. No pun intended."

"Did Mr. D ever talk to you about his dreams?"

Brooker shakes his head; I can tell he thinks the question has come out of left field. "Steven, I hardly ever spoke to him at all. Don't tell me you thought otherwise. He was a peculiar man." Brooker squints at me. "To be honest, I like you much more."

I don't tell him that Mr. D is still very much around.

I remember how Mr. D died. Bones crunching as the SUV rolled over him. He certainly ended up in a lot of trouble. But then again for the majority of us that's all we can expect. Time and the world are hard and grinding. Bones and flesh are soft.

"Now, these dreams..."

I sigh. "They're nightmares really. Nasty as hell nightmares."

"Everyone has bad dreams," Dr. Brooker says. "Particularly in your job, and mine."

"That's not the problem," I tell him. "It's just that I rather like them." My face flushes.

"How much?"

My face is burning. "A lot."

"Hmm." He squints at me like I'm some kind of thermometer. I don't know what sort of reading he gets but after a while he turns away. "Don't get caught up with dreams. Sometimes that's all they are."

We both know that isn't true. Brooker looks worried. "See me in a day or two—this really isn't my specialty. Now isn't the best time, you've been through a bit of trauma. And I'm sure that hasn't helped."

"It'll heal," I say looking at my foot.

"I wasn't talking about that. The way all this happened—the way you became RM, and the betrayals you faced—none of it was good. Steve, I lost a lot of dear friends that week. You lost more than that. It takes its toll."

But is that really a good enough excuse for the number of times I've shown up at work drunk? Or just not bothered to show up at all? When you don't sleep there's an awful lot of time you can spend drinking, even if it's not filling up the hole left by all that loss, and the guilt that I'm letting those nearest to me, and equally wounded, down. Which, of course, leads to more drinking. It's how I've dealt with all the major dramas of my adult life.

Home and work, everywhere I look there are gaps. Reminders of friends and family gone, snatched away by the chaos of Morrigan's Schism. And as for the work itself, I don't know how to lead people. Where do you learn that? Where do you pick up all the arcane and complicated tricks required in the running of a business like mine? Despite Tim's notes there's no manual. I have Mr. D, but I don't know what questions to ask, and he isn't that great at answering the ones I do. I'd suspect him of being deliberately evasive, except he's always been that way.

And Lissa. Where do you go after what we've shared? Surely happiness of the forever-after sort is deserved. I'd settle for a few years of it, but there's no prospect of that. We've a dark god coming.

Suzanne's offer is looking very attractive. Maybe it's not too late to fix this. To be what I need to be.

Brooker works in silence for a while, cleaning then binding the foot. "All done," he says at last. "You'll need to sit on your chair for a while."

"My throne?"

"Don't start putting on airs and graces. When I was a kid we called the shitter a throne." He sighs. "But that's the one. It'll heal you much faster than you can on your own."

There's shouting outside. It's an achingly familiar voice, an achingly familiar heartbeat, even if it is racing. My ears prick up. Dr. Brooker grins. "I'll just get her for you."

The door flings open and nearly bowls him over. Dr. Brooker doesn't even bother calling her on it. He knows better than to get between us. She's in her usual black get-up: a Mickey Mouse brooch on one collar of her blouse. I don't get the appeal of Walt Disney characters—give me Bugs Bunny any day—but I'm so happy to see her.

"Are you OK?" Lissa asks. She grabs me tight enough that my ribs creak.

"Yeah, I am." I groan in her embrace. "Well, I think I am."

Brooker nods. "He's fine." He's already packing up his bag: good doctors are always in demand. "As far as I know, nothing can really hurt him, just slow him down a little."

"Define hurt. My foot's throbbing!"

"Well, the glass was part of Number Four, I'd say that's why it hurts you so much." He rubs his chin thoughtfully. "Or it could be that your body is still getting used to what it has become. The pain may just be old habits dying hard."

I wish they'd die a little more easily.

Lissa pulls back, looks at me, and winces. Oh, I'd forgotten about the ear. It starts to sting, but now no more than a scratch might. The top of the ear is already growing back.

Tim peers through the door. Dr. Brooker delivered him as well. "He OK, Dr. Brooker?"

"Nothing a bit of rest won't fix. He's an RM: both wounds will heal quickly, not like the rest of us idiots." Dr. Brooker looks at me. "Just be careful."

His phone chirrups, signaling another emergency, or a game of golf. He merely looks at it, grunts, and with a curt nod, leaves the room.

I glance over at Tim. "OK, we're six hours into the working day and I've already been shot at. I want to know why, and I want to know now."

"I'm already on it," Tim says, pulling his phone out. "I'll call Doug at my old department." Doug Anderson is a good choice. The man has more fingers in more pies than anyone we know. He took up Tim's role as policy advisor and head of Pomp/government relations. "The last time this happened..."

Call me a pessimist, but I have a terrible certainty that this is going to be worse.

And why's Morrigan in my dreams again? He's gone, and there's no coming back for him. As Mr. D said, after the knife fight of the Negotiation, Morrigan's soul was obliterated.

I can't be feeling guilty about that, surely?

9

Seems I'm stuck in my office. Despite her concern, Lissa couldn't stay long. Her hand is bandaged again, another cut, another stir. And she's always on the hunt for potential Pomps. That's hard work. Like Tim said, we advertise, of course, but that's not easy either. The job titles are deliberately vague, the interview process detailed and convoluted. None of us earlier generation Pomps ever had to interview for the job. Our families had all worked for Mortmax for generations, probably since the last Schism.

There's just too much work to be done. People never stop dying, and there are not enough of us to make sure the transition is smooth.

For all its healing attributes, the chair itself really isn't that comfortable. Not enough lumbar support or something. I'd rather sit in a recliner, but no recliner I know is going to knit me back together as quickly. A fella could go mad with all this sitting, *Rear Window* style. I'm used to being on my feet, out and about: pomping the dead, and stalling Stirrers.

I keep having to remind myself that that is in the past now. The first thing I can do is check on my staff. Make sure I'm not letting them down anymore.

I close my eyes; connect with all my Pomps, the 104 people that I have working around the country. My other Pomps, my Avians—the sparrows, crows and ibis—work as good eyes but they are hard to control and their "process" in stalling a stir involves a considerable amount of pecking. I find directing them gives me a migraine which makes practice somewhat unappealing. Generally they're left pomping the spirits of animals, those big-brained enough to cage a soul.

The window's already repaired, and the floor has digested the broken glass. I wonder what else it might just eat. The building is self-healing; the glass had apparently grown back within a few minutes of me blacking out. Looking at it, the glass appears thicker—dark filaments line it, some sort of reinforcement, I guess. Number Four has grown paranoid.

A familiar face pokes around the door wearing a big grin that fails to obscure the concern behind his eyes.

"Don't people knock anymore?"

"What a mess," Alex says.

"No, this is what my office usually looks like bar the blood and paper." I glance around; the glass has already gone. "In fact it looks a little neater than usual."

Alex is dressed in his uniform. He is a Black Sheep but, unlike Tim, I couldn't lure him back into the fold. He lost family like the rest of us in the Schism. His father Don saved my life and Alex kept up the tradition. He got me out of town when the worst of the Schism was going down. He saved me later, too, when I came back from Hell, thinking I had failed in my Orpheus Maneuver, and lost Lissa. Without his help, Australia really would have sunk into a Regional Apocalypse. I feel a bit guilty that I haven't been keeping in touch with him nearly enough. But seeing him always reminds me of Don, and my parents, and Don's girlfriend Sam. I can't help wondering what he thinks when he sees me. He's my link into the Queensland Police Force. I trust him almost as much as I trust Tim.

"So this is the first time this has happened?" he asks.

"Well, not exactly." I glance at Alex, we've been through a few bad times together. He knows that I've been shot at before. "Not since October, and the Schism."

"Two months." He shakes his head.

"Yeah, no wonder I was getting used to not being shot at."

"You're understandably shaky."

"No, I'm pissed off. It happens whenever people start shooting at me. Bloody hell, Alex, don't pull this shit on me. I don't need you telling me I'm all right feeling nervous. I need to know what's going on."

Alex sits down. "I'm more worried about this than you could believe. People shooting at you tends to lead to scary places." Right now, the way Alex grits his jaw brings Don back to me. I miss the old bugger. I miss them all. "You've an alarming tendency to draw trouble to you, Steven."

"I'm trying not to make it a habit."

"Yeah, I know. I want to help you with this but I've been told explicitly that this isn't my area. They've got someone else in mind. The moment Tim called for help—"

"What? Tim called who?" He was only supposed to call Doug. I guess he's just used to thinking for me.

"Me, but once he did, I had to alert my bosses. Major incidents are flagged, and someone trying to kill the current RM is a major incident, now." Alex sighed. "I know you like to sort out your disputes inhouse. But after Morrigan... Well, you know, the rules have changed."

"So who are they sending in?"

"A new group, federal not state. Still police, though. I hadn't heard about them until about an hour before I came over here." Alex scowls. "They're called Closers. Seem to know an awful lot about you."

So, another government department. I'll get Tim to do some digging.

There's always someone poking around here. Unofficially, of course, because the work we do at Mortmax can't be official.

Unofficially we could tell them to piss off, but unofficially they could cause a lot of trouble for us.

"I hate this," I say. "Bloody governments."

"They're not too fond of Mortmax, either. Look, the paint hasn't even dried on this department yet. None of them will have much experience in dealing with the things that are dumped on their desks."

"So why aren't people like you involved?"

"Why do you think?"

"You're regarded as compromised? Guilt by association." I frown. "Don't they trust you at work anymore, Alex?"

Alex scowls. "If you were doing your—"

"What? If we were doing our jobs properly? Is that what you're saying?" I look at my ruined office, the blood, the paper blown everywhere. He kind of has a point. "I'm not here to bend over for every government department."

Alex grins. "Not every department, mate. Just one from now on." His face grows more serious. "Steven, be careful. People aren't over the moon with what's happening here. I've been hearing things."

"You can't be serious. Morrigan was responsible for all of it." I fix him with as severe a stare as I can manage. "What sort of things?"

"Nothing specific. Just that no one was happy to have a Regional Apocalypse at their doorstep. They're blaming you."

"I had nothing to do with it." I straighten in my throne, slam my foot down on the floor and remember why I'm sitting here in the first place. *Fuck, that hurts.*

"Doesn't matter, Mortmax did, and you're running the Australian branch. You're responsible as far as people are concerned. And they don't think you're doing such a great job."

"If they want to have a go at running death, let them." My bluster is just that, though, and Alex knows it.

"Perhaps you shouldn't be so bloody glib, mate."

"Yeah, well, I've got eight stitches in my foot, and a bit of my ear is missing. Inappropriate glibness is all I have." We glare at each other.

There's a knock on the door.

A man peers through at Alex and me. An Akubra hat obscures his features. Most people can't pull that look off, but he manages it, somehow. It's the broad shoulders, the skin just on the flesh side of leather. He doffs the wide-brimmed hat, scratches his head. The hair beneath is clipped to within a breath of shaved; a band of sweat rings it. Dark eyes peer at me through thickish metal-rimmed glasses. I can't tell what he's thinking, but his heart beats slow and steady.

"Can I join the party?" he asks, and smiles warmly.

Alex glances at me, gives me a we'll-talk-later kind of face.

"Yeah, absolutely," I say. "There's room for everyone. Once I know just who they are."

"Of course, of course. I thought you knew I was coming. Detective Magritte Solstice," he says. "I'll be running this investigation." He shakes my hand. It's one of those firm but slightly threatening grips that suggests a lot more strength could be applied—if needed.

"Can't say I'm pleased to meet you."

Solstice's laugh is warm and deep. "No one ever is under these situations." He looks over at Alex. "That's all for now, Sergeant."

"Yes, Sergeant," I say. "It's time for the grown-ups to talk."

Alex nods, gives me a little (and very ironic) salute and gets out of there.

Solstice shuts the door behind him. The smile slips a little. "Now, to get the shit out of the way before it stinks up the room, if you have any problems you call me. I know he's your friend, but this isn't Alex's specialty." Solstice hands me a card with his name and number on it, and a symbol of three dots making an equilateral triangle. It reminds me of the brace symbol we use to block Stirrers. "My group runs these investigations."

"You're the Closers?"

Solstice blinks at that. I'm happy to wrong-foot him a little. "Yeah, it's our job to close doors that shouldn't have been opened in the first place."

"A bit poetic, isn't it?"

Solstice grimaces. "I didn't come up with the name. Our job is to work with organizations like yours, off the public record, of course."

"Well, off the record, what do you really think you're doing?"

"Fixing your fuck-ups."

"That's good to know," I say. "Puts everything into context."

"All right. So where did it happen? Scene of the crime and all that."

"You're looking at it," I say, waving at the room. Solstice lifts an eyebrow.

"I'm sorry, but the window's self-healing. The body's missing, too. It went back to wherever it came from. It was a professional hit, but it didn't work out too well for the professionals."

"At least no one was hurt."

"Much," I say.

He looks at me.

"No one was hurt *much,*" I say.

"What's wrong with you?" Solstice asks. "You look fine to me."

"Yeah, now I do."

"Stop your complaining."

I frown at him.

"Oh, sorry. Stop your complaining, *sir.*" Solstice walks around my desk and stares at "The Triumph of Death." It was Mr. D's particular obsession: death at war with life, a vast wave of skeletons breaking over the world. Mr. D said he found it soothing. I don't know about that, but it is something. "Isn't *this* a bit much?"

"Look, I didn't buy it." (Actually, I don't think Mr. D *bought* it, either.) "But you have to admit it's funny in this context."

Solstice peers at all the mayhem on the panel. "If you say so." He walks to the window and pushes his face against the glass. "So the body fell . . . ? Where am I looking?"

"That's Hell," I say, pouring myself a glass of rum. "You're looking into Hell."

Solstice blinks. "Remarkable. It's not exactly what I was expecting."

"It never is." I offer him a drink.

He shakes his head. "On duty, and all that." He goes back to peering out the window.

He jabs a thumb down. "So the body struck the ground and it disappeared?"

"Yeah, someone cut the rope a few moments after I'd knocked him out."

Solstice looks at me. "You knocked him out?"

"I got lucky."

"Very lucky." He scrawls something in his notebook. "So someone cut the rope. Are you sure you weren't that someone?"

"Very sure. I wanted to know what he was doing. Why he was there, and how."

"Couldn't you have just asked his ghost? Maybe killing him was an easier, safer way of getting the information you required."

I shook my head. "It doesn't work like that, not as neatly anyway. I pomped the soul, and the body returned to wherever it was when it entered Hell."

"You didn't think to ask the spirit any questions?"

"Oh, I tried, but with a death that violent, the soul just usually blazes through. I didn't get much more than rage and anger at being betrayed, I guess, and then I was losing consciousness myself."

I hobble over to the window beside Solstice. Stare down. "What I want to know is how a living person ended up out there."

"Is it really that odd? I mean, I'm here right now, aren't I?"

"It's remarkable, all right," I say. "In here you're not really in Hell, just a point that juts into Hell, and even that involves quite a bit of power. Two worlds are mixing here, and it's not a very good mix. A lot of people have trouble with this room; they get all sorts of migraines, dizzy spells. It's why we do our job interviews here. If you can't cope with the energies in this room, you really shouldn't become a Pomp. You're handling it very well, Detective."

Solstice rubs the bridge of his nose. "Hm. I do have a bit of a headache, but that could be just the condition I suffer from."

"What's that?"

"Hypochondria."

Yeah, funny guy. I point down at the footpath. "Down there. To get down there with the possibility of returning involves serious pain. The Underworld doesn't like life, just afterlife. Its barriers are permeable, but not without incredible effort, arcane knowledge, and a lot of blood."

"Blood?"

"Yeah, you need to die and not die. It's about as easy as it sounds, believe me."

Solstice's pen gets to work again in his notebook. He has a swift, neat writing style—a dot-the-"i"s-cross-the-"t"s sort of thing. "Well, he didn't stay living for long." Solstice scratches the bridge of his nose. "But then that seems to be something that happens to people who spend any time with you, doesn't it?"

"What are you implying?"

Solstice grins. "Nothing at all."

"I honestly don't know how you're going to uncover anything," I say. "There's no body that we could find. Who knows where it is? Number Four is healing itself, and we've never used closed circuit TV here."

"You leave that to me," Solstice says. "There's a body somewhere. And there will be a gun."

"I don't know about that—oh, sorry, Detective, just a condition I suffer from."

"Yeah, and that is?" he asks.

"Pessimism."

"I like you already," Solstice says, patting me on the back. His rolled-up shirt sleeve slips back to reveal a rather large tattoo.

I get a good look at it before Solstice pulls down his sleeve in what must be an automatic gesture. I'm not sure how they regard tatts in the force.

"You'd make a good Pomp," I say, nodding at his arm.

"What? Oh, yeah." Seeing no point in hiding it, he grins a little crookedly and pulls up his sleeve to reveal more. A dragon extends all the way along his forearm, the tail disappearing under the fabric. Its scales are a luminous green, narrow red eyes stare at me, and a tiny puff of smoke curls from its nostrils.

"Nice work isn't it?" Solstice says. "Guy who did it won a lot of awards."

"Yeah. Your own design?"

Solstice dips his head. "A little bit Tolkien, a little bit Chinese. I call it Smauget."

I'm not about to compare tatts. Wal isn't quite as fierce, and his creation was less considered, more alcohol-fueled.

Solstice peers at his phone. "No bloody signal."

Closers certainly don't have access to a phone network as good as ours.

Solstice reaches over to the black phone in the middle of my messy desk. "Mind if I make a call?"

"Not with that, you won't." I lift up the tattered end of the phone cord, bits of rusty wire jutting out.

"What is it then, a paperweight?"

"Internal line," I say with a lame grin. I'm not about to tell him it's a direct line to my old boss, Mr. D. The fewer people who know, or even suspect, that he's still about, the better.

Solstice nods his head and glances at his watch. "I'm going to have to leave. Believe it or not we have more than one case."

"You Closers," I say, "you're a big department?"

"Big enough."

"Why haven't I heard of you until today?"

"You've never needed to." He glances at his card on my desk. "You call me if anything happens."

"I will."

He slips on his Akubra. "And try not to give us any more work."

10

Tim and I meet at a park in the leafy suburb of Paddington, near enough to some decent pubs if we feel so inclined. It's a meeting place that we use if we want a little privacy. And I'm not sure whom I can trust in the office right now; most of my staff are brand new. But last time we met here I was on the run for my life and Lissa was dead, so things could be much worse. Silver lining, right?

After two months of me being ignored, the afternoon had seen a flood of RM visitors. I'm not sure if it was because I've finally peformed the Convergence Ceremony, or that I was shot at by an unknown assassin, but they certainly didn't talk much about the latter.

China's RM, Li An, was the first to visit. He surprised me; just sat down across from me and didn't say a word. His eyes fixed on me.

I didn't know what to say, I just stared right back. Finally, after twenty minutes, his lips just hinting at a smile, Li An nodded his head and stood. I shook his hand. It was dry, and just a little cold.

"I think she made the right choice. It was a pleasure getting to know you, Mr. de Selby," he said. Then he shifted out before I could ask him what he was talking about.

East Europe's RM, Madeleine Danning, came and gave me a pot of daisies. "They'll look good in the corner, over there. But you mustn't forget to water them. I always thought they'd cheer this place up."

England's RM, Anna Kranski, wanted to talk early Hitchcock films, and was mortified that I hadn't watched *The 39 Steps.*

No one suggested any deals. Not Kiri Baker from New Zealand. Not Devesh Singh from India. No one made any offers. I didn't know how to take it. This was the Orcus. These were the Deaths of the world, and I was treated with nothing but the utmost politeness.

Those who did talk were anxious about the Death Moot. Had the Caterers hinted at what they were doing this time? Was the bridge prepared? Which bridge was it exactly?

The fact that it was a footbridge seemed to impress Japan's RM, Tae Sato. "A good omen," he said. "You'll find it to be a good omen."

Charlie Top, Middle Africa's RM, was also pleased.

All this RM happiness. And there I was with that image in my head of them at the Negotiation: the hungry gleam, bordering on naked bloodlust, in their eyes.

The only two RMs who didn't visit were Neill Debbier and Suzanne. I didn't know what that meant, but by the time I was ready to leave my office I was tired and didn't really want to know.

"You're one of the club now," Tim says leaning back on the bonnet of his car. "It's a good thing."

He passes me a beer, and I twist off the cap. "Yeah, but none of them wanted to talk about the attempt on my life."

"Maybe it's more common than you think."

"No, Mr. D would have mentioned it." *Or would he?*

The sun's set, but the night is slow in cooling, the air close and thick. We used to sneak off to this park and smoke. Tim's furiously working his way through a packet of cigarettes between mouthfuls of VB. I'm not such a fan of the beer—I like my Fourex—but at least it's cold. Our stubbies are beaded with beerish sweat. I could do with something stronger though.

"So who do you think's responsible?" Tim asks. "Stirrers?"

"No, I'd have sensed them if it was. We all would have."

Tim nods. You can smell and feel a Stirrer from a long way off. Their presence pulls at the throat, burns the nose like a bad chemical. There's been enough Stirrers rising to get us far too used to the sensation.

"I've been dreaming about Morrigan, lately. Maybe..."

Tim leans in toward me, eyes hard. "No, he's gone. You told me that yourself. He's deader than dead." His voice is strident, but he looks like he needs reassurance.

"Yeah, I saw him die. He's gone. Would have been easier though, knowing it was him."

Tim shakes his head, jabs his beer in my face. "Morrigan was a devious, murdering prick. Don't you dare wish him back on us!"

I draw back at his vehemence. "No, they were just dreams. That's all, they can't be anything else. So where does that leave us?"

"One of the Orcus, then?" he suggests.

"But which RM wants me dead? All the RMs are capable of it, but I don't think it's one of them. And certainly not after this afternoon. It's in the Orcus's interests to maintain stability. And I think if one wanted me dead, well, they wouldn't screw it up so badly, and they wouldn't be so underhanded about it." I glance at Tim. "Do you think Solstice will have any luck?"

Tim shrugs. "Those guys know less about our organization than we do."

I fix him with a stare. "How long have *you* known about these Closers?"

"Not too long. Actually, I thought they were a bit of a joke." Tim takes a slow mouthful of beer. "What they've done is built on an idea I had years ago at the department—a group to actually work in tandem with Mortmax, to help out if the Stirrers ever became too much of a problem. I thought it would be a good thing, maybe increase the flow of information between both sides, and reduce some of the fear. But they've started it too late."

"You didn't think it worth your while to give me a heads-up about it?"

"Like I said, I thought they were a bit of a joke, though I've changed my mind, now. A scared government is a dangerous government."

I glower at him. It's bad enough feeling the scrutiny of the Orcus without knowing the federal government is looking into us, too. There was a time when no government would even consider questioning our actions. Trust them to decide otherwise when I'm in charge.

Something crunches in the undergrowth close to us. Tim and I spin toward the sound.

"Down," I say, and Tim drops behind his car.

I can hear a heartbeat. It's racing, and it's not Tim's. I grab the only weapon at hand, my stubby. The heartbeat is coming from behind a nearby tree. Taking a deep breath, I rush toward it and catch sight of a dim shape there, a large figure, hunched down.

There's a flash. I hurl my stubby at the form. Beer splashes back at me. Glass shatters.

There's no detonation of a gun firing. No bullets penetrating my thick skull. The heartbeat is gone. I scramble around the tree.

Nothing. Just a torch, its beam directed at my feet—the source of the flash, I guess. I can feel the residual warmth of a body from where it had leaned against the tree, and the slight electrical residue of a shift. It's less than the memory of a ghost post-Pomp.

Whoever was here is good. They know how to hide their movements, even if they're heavy on their feet.

"It's all right," I yell at Tim, holding the torch in the air.

He gets up and curses. Seems he threw himself onto his packet of cigarettes. Every single one of them is bent or broken.

"At least you're not drenched with beer," I say.

Tim grins staring at the mighty stain spreading across my trousers. "Are you sure that's beer?"

I give him the most sarcastic smile I can. "Who the hell was that?"

"Now, *that* could have been one of the RMs, or an Ankou. Spying on us, maybe wondering why the hell we were out here."

"They know how little we know then, if that's the case."

After another drink we've relaxed a little, and the beer down the front of me has evaporated. I might smell like a brewery but at least I'm dry. I've had two texts from Lissa, asking where I am, and I'll respond to them soon.

"We're going to need someone to watch your place," Tim says. "You'll want Lissa close."

"What about you?" I ask.

"I'll organize some security for us all." He straightens a cigarette.

"Just how effective can security be if whoever is after me can shift?"

"Look, we don't even know if these two incidents are connected. If they were, why didn't they just shift into your office this morning? A bit of protection is better than nothing. And trust me, the guys I've got in mind are *far* better than nothing. They're prepared for this sort of thing."

"Really?"

"You're so used to dealing with this through Mortmax that you've forgotten that other people work to fill the gap. These guys are like this. I've used them before—my old department had the occasional bit of trouble."

"If you say they're good enough. I trust you. I just wish—"

"What are wishes going to get you?" Tim asks. "This is happening. You are who you are, and you have to act appropriately."

"Sorry," I say.

"For what?"

"For bringing you into whatever the hell this is."

Tim shakes his head. "Steve, you didn't bring me into the last Schism. This is as much a part of my heritage as it is yours. I may have turned my back on it, but it wasn't you who forced me to return. That bastard's dead, dreams or no dreams." He pats my arm. "How are you coping?"

I want to tell him that I'm not, that I'm drowning in my responsibilities and inadequacies, and now someone is trying to kill me as well. That when I close my eyes, dreams pound into me like the laughing waves of some gore-soaked sea.

"I'm doing OK." I grin. "Hey, I'm head of an Australia-wide branch of an international company, and a profitable one at that."

"Yes, we're living the dream," Tim says sardonically. He picks out the least damaged cigarette. "God help us." He lights up. "I've got to get going. Sally has bridge tonight, I have to look after the kids."

"Be careful," I say.

"If the last few months have taught me anything, it's exactly that." He smiles. "I'll be careful, and you, too. Don't go running into anything without letting me know—and even then, maybe think before you run."

11

Tim's bodyguards stand outside my parents' place. Dad wouldn't have tolerated this. Mom would have laughed, maybe made a reference to Whitney Houston and Kevin Costner.

They're two burly guys who Lissa tells me are called Travis and Oscar. Both of them arrived about twenty minutes before me. Tim doesn't mess around. I rather suspect he had this organized well before he broached the subject with me. They are armed and stationed at opposite ends of the house. Oscar's at least my height, and nearly that wide, but it's all muscle. Travis is even bigger. I'm not too sure about all this, having guns in and around the house—they're nothing but trouble. Dr. Brooker's right about that much.

I've drawn enough souls, who were killed by guns, to the Underworld, been nearly killed by guns myself. But this time I suppose they're a necessary evil. Doesn't mean I have to like it.

We've just finished dinner, and I'm on my third beer, helping with the washing up (Dad didn't believe in dishwashing machines) when Lissa fixes me with a peculiar, disappointed stare. "When were you going to tell me about Suzanne's deal?"

I lift my foot with exaggerated care, even groan a little, but it doesn't cut it as a sympathy maker. Lissa's hands are on her hips now, and she's scowling at me.

I drop the scrubbing brush into the sink and stop myself from asking who told her. "Look, I've been a little distracted of late."

"I know, but this is big. You're talking about the most influential member of the Orcus. What does she want with you?"

"She's going to give me ten Pomps to supplement our numbers, and all I have to give her is ten hours of my time."

"I don't like it. Suzanne could do a lot with ten hours."

"Not nearly as much as you, my dear." I know I've said the wrong thing at once. I narrowly avoid a tea towel in the eye.

"She has a reputation, you know."

I feel my face flush. "You've got nothing to worry about."

"Don't tell me what I do and don't have to worry about."

"Hang on, you wanted me to get involved, to work harder. And that's what I'm doing, isn't it?"

"I don't trust her, and you shouldn't either. The woman's a scheming bitch!"

That vehemence in Lissa's voice gets my attention. *What has Suzanne done to her?*

"Think about it," she says. "They're pushing so hard. The phone call at 2:30 in the morning. The meeting in the Deepest Dark. Cerbo's offer—and then someone starts shooting at you."

"Lissa, they're Americans. They're brash, they're proud."

"Exactly. And who loves guns more?" She hangs up the tea towel.

"No, I'm willing to accept that they're playing at something, but the shooting, it's got to be a coincidence. Maybe it's something to do with the Death Moot. Maybe it's something to do with the Stirrer god—perhaps it has other agents here. What I know for certain is that we need more Pomps. Look at what it's doing to you. Look at your palms."

I know how much they must hurt. When Morrigan started his Schism, and as the Stirrers stepped up their invasion, my hands became open sores. And then there was the consequence of pomping itself—the psychic pain and damage. With every pomp it built until you felt as though you were being scratched from the inside out. Things weren't that bad, but they could be better.

"I'm all right," she says. "Things are improving."

I lean in to kiss her but she pulls away.

"I don't think you should do it. Just tell her to piss off."

"I'll take that into consideration," I say.

Lissa scowls at me. "RMs are devious, and she's worse than all of them combined."

I need those Pomps. Ten more workers could make a real difference. Lissa can obviously see me thinking this; I'm certainly not one of those devious RMs. She takes a deep breath.

"Look, I'm serious, that woman slept with my father. It's all I can do not to hit her when I see her. It didn't stop Mom."

"*What?*" Seems Lissa's just as good at keeping secrets as I am.

"It's a small world in any corporation. It happened twelve years ago, at a Death Moot in San Francisco. Steven, it nearly destroyed my parents' marriage. It certainly scarred it. I don't want that woman having anything to do with you."

"But you can't think—"

Lissa glares at me.

"I mean, I love you. I'd never do anything to jeopardize that. But—"

Lissa's glare burns into me like the light of a very attractive but blazing sun. I'm withering beneath it.

"OK," I say. "I promise I won't agree to her offer without letting you know."

That seems enough for now. I hobble to the couch with her and we snuggle and watch a DVD. She's asleep before the first scene is even finished. I stroke her hair for a while, she snorts in her sleep, and I ease myself out from under her. I'll wake her in an hour or so. I switch off the DVD, surprised that the sudden silence doesn't drag her from her dreams.

I'm in trouble. I need those Pomps and I need what Suzanne can give me: her experience. Mr. D isn't enough, already he is distanced from the game, and from what I've read, and Suzanne's comments, he was always a little isolated. If I don't know what I'm doing, and why, there's no way that I'm ever going to run my region well.

But I don't want to hurt Lissa. She stirs in her sleep, frowns as though my plans are already upsetting her. My heart twists in my chest. There has to be a way I can keep this from her, and reduce the capability of Suzanne's Pomps to spy on me. The new ten could service some of the regional areas, with a couple more surreptitiously inserted into the Sydney and Perth offices. Those are the two that Lissa knows least of all. If I can keep them out of Brisbane I should be all right.

And Lissa has been on at me to keep practicing my shifts. It's not as though she can tell where I'm going. With the preparations for the Death Moot, I'm going to have to be moving about.

Yeah, I think I can do this.

I grab my mobile, fast, before I can change my mind and text Suzanne: *Yes.*

A text hits my phone.

Suzanne Whitman.

No time 2 waste. We might as well start now.

"I can't see why not," I say out loud.

"I thought you'd say that," Suzanne says from behind me.

What? I spin and face her. Her presence strikes me hard, burns into my skull.

I glance over at Lissa—still sleeping on the couch, thank Christ. In fact, she's rolled away from Suzanne like a sleeper might from a cold draft.

"Get out of here, now," I hiss, nodding toward Lissa.

Suzanne smiles. "Keeping secrets, eh?"

"Deepest Dark, ten minutes."

Suzanne is gone.

I walk over to Lissa, crouch down and shake her, gently.

Her eyes open.

"I have to go out for a little while. Didn't want you to panic if you woke up and I wasn't here."

She yawns. "What?"

"I have a meeting."

"With who?"

"Cerbo." Well, that's almost the truth.

"What does he want?" Her eyes narrow.

"That's what I'm going to find out. It'll be about Suzanne's offer at a guess."

She purses her lips. "Don't trust her, or him. Never trust another RM or their Ankou. There's always a bigger game at play."

"I know."

I lift her up gently, she rests her head in the hollow of my neck. All I can smell is her hair. How does it always smell so good?

"I love you," she says into my shoulder.

"Love you, too," I whisper. She's already asleep, poor tired baby.

I carry her to the bedroom, pull the sheets over her, and set the ceiling fan on high. After a quick peck on her cheek I direct a crow to circle above, to monitor the front and the back of the house. Oscar and Travis are still there. Neither seem to have noticed Suzanne's sudden appearance. I really wonder how effective they are going to be.

At least the contact with my Avian Pomp hasn't given me a migraine this time. Must be getting better. Of course I'm probably heading into a much bigger headache with Suzanne.

12

The Deepest Dark is just as cold as the last time we met here. We're a little closer to the city of Devour. Lights are flashing there, and it's toward them that Suzanne is staring as I arrive. This shift is a particularly bad one. I'm a few minutes catching my breath. But at least there's no vomit. Gotta love that.

"Something's happening over there," Suzanne says. She's wearing my duffel coat. I can't quite bring myself to ask for it back.

"That's usually a good thing isn't it?" I watch the lurid fires burn. "If it's happening here, it's not happening in the living world."

"You'd think so, but their focus is only on our world. Anything happening down here has consequences for up there."

"What do you think it is?"

Suzanne shrugs. "I have my spies and, of course, I will inform the Orcus of anything that they uncover."

"Spies?"

Suzanne smiles. "This is your first lesson, I suppose. The Underworld is more permeable than you might think. Stirrers can enter our world through the agency of a corpse. Well, we can enter theirs, too. It doesn't always work, but I have received some very good information before my spies have been discovered. And they always are. Just as a Stirrer takes a while to get used to a human body, a human takes a while to get used to a Stirrer's."

"You're telling me they actually enter a Stirrer body?" All bony limbs, cavernous eyes and sharkish teeth; what would it be like to inhabit such a form?

"Yes, remarkable isn't it? And you're already learning something."

"What's it like?"

"Horrifying. It changes people. The ones I've managed to bring back, anyway. They're different, life becomes less appealing to them, more wretched. Let me just say that they don't tend to stay in the organization for very long."

I try and imagine how it must be, trying to make a life in that city. Being so deep undercover that the very smell and essence of life disgusts you. Does the reverse happen? Do Stirrers learn to love life as we do? I've not seen it.

I wonder if she mightn't also use those spies for assassination attempts. Say, on RMs. I'm starting to feel a little uncomfortable out here in the open. If keeping face weren't so important I'd be away in a shot.

"And what happens when they're discovered?" I can't imagine ever sending anyone down there.

"The ones we get out? Well, they survive. But the others..." Suzanne shrugs. "Something horrible, I suspect. They don't get to make a report afterward, Steven. This is the Deepest Dark, after all. You don't play around down here unless you're hungry for pain or retribution." Suzanne touches my arm. "You should understand that."

"Is that what you do?" I ask. "Play around down here?"

"It's much more serious than that. I'm as concerned by the Stirrers' plans as you are. Things are in motion, believe me. But we'll leave that for the Death Moot, not now."

Where her fingers touch me is the only warmth in this place, and she leaves them there too long. I pull away, but perhaps not fast enough. Hell, I shouldn't be worrying about what is fast or not. I should be focusing on her conversation. She's watching me, waiting for a response. And I already feel outplayed. "I'm not one for waiting."

"Six days isn't very long." Suzanne's tone suggests she's talking to a five year old, any more patronizing and she'd be handing me a lollipop. "Now, let me say how horrified I was to hear of the attempt on your life." She closes her eyes a moment. The air glows, dust swirls around us, becoming a round table and two chairs. She gestures at one of the chairs. "Sit, sit."

I touch the chair tentatively. It feels solid enough. I sit down and it takes my weight. I want to ask her just how she does this, but now isn't the right time. There are more important things before us.

"Steven, you made a lot of enemies when you performed that Orpheus Maneuver of yours."

"I had a lot of enemies already."

"But these are of greater consequence. You broke rules, you performed the impossible, and that scares people. Does the name Francis Rillman mean anything to you?"

Rillman. Where have I heard that name? "It sounds familiar."

Suzanne nods her head. "It should. He was Australia's Ankou before Morrigan, and a major embarrassment to Mr. D. His disgrace is an important, some might even go so far as to say tragic, part of your corporate history. It's what allowed Morrigan to do what he did. Certainly gave him ideas."

"Maybe that's why his name only sounds familiar. Morrigan didn't like to share information, not the important stuff anyway."

"Yes, well, he was partly involved in Rillman's downfall. And his downfall certainly led to Morrigan's rise." Suzanne sighed. "Francis Rillman, like you, performed an Orpheus Maneuver after his wife died. Only he failed, utterly and terribly. I thought he was dead, but the name's been surfacing lately. And more often than not it's been around you." She sighs. "I rather believe that Rillman wants you dead."

"Why? Why would someone I don't even know want me dead?"

"Because you did what he couldn't, and Rillman is a bitter creature."

"I'll dig around in the files," I say.

Suzanne clicks her tongue. "I hate to say it, Steven, but Mr. D should be educating you more thoroughly. Take this to Mr. D. He's the only one 'alive' in your organization who knows the full story."

The next hour or so is taken up with a series of lessons echoing Tim's briefing notes: short histories of my fellow RMs, things I should have known, things Mr. D should have taught me. I'm wary though, this is only Suzanne's perspective. After the Moot, when I have time (ha!) I'm going to talk to each and every RM, draw out their stories, and put what Suzanne has told me into context.

The lesson's interrupted by a cry from the Stirrer city. A packed-stadium sort of roaring—if a stadium was full of meth-addicted berserkers. Suzanne and I both turn toward the sound.

Suzanne shakes her head. "OK, looks like class is over for the night. Do you want to check that out?"

"Why not?" We get up and the table and chairs return to dust.

She holds my hand. "Don't pull away," she says. "I thought I would spare you the pain of a shift."

"I can do it myself." But we're already there.

So that's how it should feel. I think I can copy that, model my own shifts on it. Suzanne nods at me. "Get the basics right, and everything else will follow."

We're at a point just outside Devour's walls. The city didn't have these when I was last here—riding a whispering bike on my way to find my lost love—but the Deepest Dark, like the Underworld, changes fast.

I place a hand against one of the huge stone blocks. It's cold and shuddering in time with the Stirrers' yells. I realize Suzanne's still holding my hand. I try and pull away. "Not yet."

Another shift. We're on the walls, all that juddering stone beneath us.

We crouch down and stare into the city, which is really the wrong term for the spaces open before us, though there are structures analogous to our cities. It's more of a nest, a nexus of hunger. Below us, hundreds of Stirrers have gathered in a circle, their teeth-crammed mouths chanting in utter synchronicity. They're as identical in appearance as ants, which is why the Stirrer in the center of the circle stands out. Its face warps, or unwarps, grows human. It is a face wracked with agony.

Suzanne squeezes my hand.

"One of yours?" I ask.

She nods.

I look around for some way to get down to her spy and for a possible escape route once we do. "We have to get him out of there."

Suzanne shakes her head. "We can't do anything, not here. Not now." She lets go of my arm. "You need to leave."

"What are you going to do?"

"Bear witness." She glares at me. "Go."

The man in the center of the circle screams, and I feel a force push at me: Suzanne. I give in to it. But not before seeing the man's long limbs torn from him and thrown out into the crowd. The Stirrers howl.

The shift to my parents' living room is easier than I was expecting, but I bring that howl with me. I blink, let my eyes adjust to the light, and slump into the couch.

Poor bastard.

Oscar's standing out the front. I can hear Travis's heartbeat coming from the back. The pair's heartbeats tell me all I need to know. Nothing has happened since I left. Still, I go and check on Lissa.

She's sleeping.

Then I call Tim.

"Do you know what time it is?" he grumbles.

"Yeah, I'm sorry, but I've got a lead."

"And Lissa's obviously sleeping." He yawns. "So what's this lead?"

"Francis Rillman. Mean anything to you?"

"Not a thing." He sighs. "Actually... It does sound familiar."

"It should. He used to have your job."

"Ministerial advisor?"

"No, your job here." I run through what Suzanne has just told me.

"Really? Shit. *Now* I remember the name. Something my dad used to say when I was grumpy. Don't chuck a Rillman. Never understood what it meant. Let me Google him." He sighs again. "So how do you spell Rillman?"

"The usual way," I answer.

Tim groans. "Don't be a smart-arse."

I spell it out. "Anything?"

"Nothing, but give me some time. If he's out there, I'll find him. Keep safe."

"You too."

I hang up; make my way back to the bedroom.

I need Lissa. Right then I need her more than anything. I kiss her. Gentle and hard on the lips, her mouth responds. Her tongue searches mine. I slide a hand down her neck, slowly, and she pulls me in close. Eyes opening.

And for the first time in what feels like weeks, we really connect.

"What was that about?" she asks when we're finally still, sweat-drenched.

"I love you."

"Well, duh." She stretches, and I can't help but stroke one of her breasts gently with a fingertip. She pushes my hand away—after a while. "How was your meeting?"

"Informative."

"And Suzanne's offer?"

"I don't know." The lie sticks in my throat.

"Suzanne is like that. She has a way of confusing the issues." Lissa clicks her tongue. "Are our heavies still outside?"

"Yeah."

"How long is this going to go on, Steve?"

"A while, I think. I've got a bit of a lead though, someone by the name of Francis Rillman."

"Did you say Rillman?"

"Yes."

"It can't be him. I pomped him two weeks ago."

"Are you sure?" I slide out of bed, disappointed. Rillman looked promising, and I want this over with.

"We had a chat. He's an interesting character. You know he tried an Orpheus Maneuver once. His wife, he lost his wife. And he failed to bring her back."

"I'm aware of that."

"Maybe, but did you know he failed because Mr. D stopped him?"

I nod toward the kitchen, slipping on some boxers. "Coffee? I think I need to be properly awake to get my head around this."

Lissa laughs. "You're supposed to offer that *before* the lovemaking." She gets up and pulls a dressing gown around her shoulders.

The kitchen is quiet but for the heavy breathing of the espresso machine. I pour two cups. Why is Suzanne so sure it's Rillman if he's dead? Where does that leave me? I've got two suspects as far as I can see: Rillman who is dead, and Morrigan who is beyond dead. It's easier to believe that Suzanne is trying something.

Shit, I am so bad at this!

Lissa watches me as I set the cups down on the table.

"So Rillman, what'd he look like?" I ask, pushing her cup toward her.

She brings it to her lips, sips contemplatively. "Nothing much. Bland, unmemorable. I know that sounds glib, but..." She furrows her brow. "Tired, he looked tired, washed out. His hair was short, parted to one side. Wait a minute, there was one thing." She reaches up and touches my nose. Her fingertips are warm and I blink at the contact. "His nose was broken, not badly, but you could tell someone had given him a mighty whack once."

"Maybe Mr. D?" Though I can't imagine Mr. D ever hitting anyone.

"Yeah, possibly. He asked about you. Seemed very interested in what you did. Hey, I might have a photo!"

Lissa runs out of the kitchen. I hear her digging around in the bedroom, then a cry of triumph. She comes back holding a photo album, open to a page. "Here, here they are! Mom, Dad and Rillman."

Lissa's description is apt. He's plain, all right, not unhandsome, I suppose. But in this photo he's smiling, and there's not a glint of murderous intent. His arms are around another woman, tall, dark hair down to her shoulders. She's smiling, too. Happy days.

"Is that his wife?"

"Yes," Lissa says. "I can't remember her name."

No one remembers names, just the tragedies. What must it be like to fail at an Orpheus Maneuver? Not just fail, but be stopped? I understand him a little, I think. Suddenly I have to hold Lissa. I kiss her hard.

"What was that about?" she asks when I let her go, but I know she gets it too. She has to, right?

I look back at the photo. "Did he seem angry at all?"

"No, more resigned. I got the feeling the angry part of him was long gone. And you know how souls are, they're a bit insipid, bloodless."

I reach across the table and touch her arm. "You weren't."

Lissa smiles. "But that's just me, I'm special."

"You are. You don't know how much you are."

Lissa shakes her head, but she isn't one for false modesty. "I should have paid more attention to him, but it was a busy day. I think I must have pomped eight people that afternoon. Rillman was the last."

"I'd have been the same. Strange, though—everything that I've been hearing seems to suggest Rillman could be behind the attack."

"Where'd his name come up?"

"Something Mr. D said," I lie, and it's easier than I thought it would be. Like shifting, I'm getting better with practice.

"Really?"

"Yeah, why not? He's *supposed* to be teaching me something."

"It's just... Mr. D doesn't like to talk about Rillman. It's a generational thing, none of them did. Rillman apparently put Mortmax Australia about ten years behind the rest of the world." She grins. "Oh, yeah, he also ruined a Death Moot."

"I like the sound of this guy."

"It was quite the scandal."

"Well, the chances of it being Rillman are pretty slim," I say. "You don't come back."

Except we both know that isn't true. It makes me uncomfortable to consider it, but somehow Rillman's death, his interest in me, make me certain he is the one responsible. That he has come back somehow. It feels right. It terrifies me. Before tonight I didn't know that humans could inhabit Stirrers. What's a little moving between worlds compared to that? Like Suzanne said, the Underworld is more permeable than I had thought. Who and what else might be coming through?

Lissa picks up her coffee cup and walks it to the sink. I can see her thoughts in the slope of her shoulders as she rinses the cup.

"It's OK," I say, kissing the back of her neck.

"I'm so sorry." She places the cup in the drainer. "Sometimes I think all this is my fault. If I hadn't—"

She's mirroring my thoughts. This isn't her fault, it's *mine*. I think about what Suzanne said. About the enemies I've made, and all because I fought to stay alive and honor the memory of my family, and because I loved someone enough to chase them through Hell and bring them back.

We saved each other. Whether it was the right thing or not, it was the only thing either of us would have done. And hang the consequences.

13

The office is quiet, predawn. I've a stack of files before me: Rillman, everything I could find on him. Which is virtually nothing. Who the fuck is Francis Rillman? What did he become?

Solstice had left a message on my phone, asking just this question, which is worrying and encouraging. Solstice obviously knows his job—and mine.

There's another half-bottle of rum sitting in my stomach. My head's spinning a bit. The throne might heal my wounds but it doesn't seem to do too much with alcohol until I stop drinking. I'm in my suit, my second-best one. I keep telling myself the drinking's not a problem when you're in a suit.

Fifty-nine people have died across Australia in the last hour. My ten new Pomps have taken some of the workload off my crew—Suzanne was exceptionally quick about organizing that—but the work is still constant. People are always dying.

And the phone calls have been pretty steady, too. RMs or their Ankous. All of them wanting a piece of me, some favor, or their seat moved in the grand marquee of the meeting room.

I look at the calendar on my desk, pushing the rubbish off it. The Death Moot's drawing ever nearer. The catering's organized at least, and the location.

Of course, I could be dead by then.

I grab a sheet of paper, write *Francis Rillman?* in thick black pen. Then scrunch the sheet up and hurl it at my bin.

I'm going to have to go to the source for this one.

I pick up the handset of Mr. D's phone. Even though the line's dead I can feel the presence listening in on the other end. I play with the phone cord that spirals down to nothing, kind of a nervous thing.

"We need to talk," I say.

No response, but I know he's heard me.

"Now. We need to talk now."

"My boat," Mr. D says, his soft voice coming through like a slither of ice in my ear. There's slight irritation in his tone and I know that I've interrupted his reading. Well, too bad. His novels will be waiting for him when he gets back.

There's a click, and silence again. Seems I'll be fishing, literally and figuratively.

I send Lissa a text, tell her where I'm going. Then I take a deep breath, close my eyes and shift to Mr. D's boat.

Mr. D raises a hand in frustration as I throw my guts up over the edge of the rail—the other is gripping his fishing rod. "You're not practicing. You've got to keep practicing."

"I'm not enough of a masochist."

"Really?"

I hobble over to Mr. D across the broad wooden deck of his boat, the *Mary C.* My foot's throbbing. The wound's healing fast, but it still seems to be a case of my mind catching up with my body. My nose burns with the salt of the sea of Hell, which is better than the taste of vomit. "And I have been practicing!"

"Yes, well, this is the second time you've seen me in three days. One would think you were having troubles." He hands me a fishing rod. Wal's already holding his, knuckles white. He got it almost the moment he peeled from my flesh, seems to be enjoying the novelty of it all.

"Suzanne's made me an offer."

"An offer, eh?" Mr. D's eyes narrow as he connects the rod to a belt around my waist.

"I've taken it. Ten Pomps for ten hours with her. Ten hours of mentoring, of course. Nothing else, completely above board."

Mr. D stares out at the choppy water. I can't tell if he's hurt, or being melodramatic. His shifting face doesn't help either.

"We're stretched to capacity," I say.

"I don't need your excuses and you don't need her advice."

"Where the fuck am I going to get it?"

Mr. D rounds on me. "That hurts. That really hurts. I've been an endless fount of—"

"Bullshit."

Wal shakes his head at me sternly. Since when did these two become so pally?

"Sometimes I could just slap you, de Selby," Mr. D says.

"It doesn't work. Believe me, mate, I've tried it," Wal says.

"I'm not surprised," Mr. D says.

Yeah, the Steven de Selby fan club is in session. "Look, I don't really have time for this," I say between teeth so tightly clenched they're squeaking a little round the molars.

Wal rolls his eyes. Considering he doesn't really have any, it's impressive. "Christ, Steve, would you look at where we are?"

A long way from shore, I think.

Mr. D casts his line into the sea of Hell. The sinker plonks and plunges down, down, into what Mr. D calls the deep tract depths. Great shapes roll out of the luminous water: proto-whales and megalodon mainly, long ago extinct, but this is Hell, and Hell teems—there's really no other word for it—with such things.

Extant memories, the seething echoes of other ages. I just wish that all the teeming stuff wasn't so bloody huge.

Mr. D assures me we're safe. After all, I'm the big boss around here. "Unlike those above, these seas are yours."

One of the perks of being RM. Nothing in Hell can touch me. But I'm not about to go for a dip. Wouldn't if you paid me, wouldn't if you gave me a cage to swim in.

I glance back across the bay toward the coastline, salt still stinging my eyes and burning my lungs. The One Tree rises on the distant shore, its great branches extending like a leafy mushroom cloud over the entire Underworld echo of Brisbane. But out here I can almost imagine that it's just a regular Moreton Bay fig in the distance. I peer over the edge of the boat, my free hand gripping the icy stainless steel rail.

A great sharky eye looks up at me. I swear it winks as it glides past.

I step away from the rail. "Um, pass me a beer... and maybe a bigger boat."

Mr. D digs around in the esky. "How many times do I have to tell you, de Selby? You're perfectly safe here on the *Mary C.*" He slaps a cold one in my hand.

"You think you should be having that?" Wal asks, his lips pursed.

I shrug. "Hair of the dog."

Wal casts his line into the sea, his tiny wings flapping furiously. "Hair of the dog, my arse."

As usual I can see rather too much of his arse. His chubby baby fingers grip his fishing rod, and he hovers like an obese hummingbird. How's he going to cope if a fish takes the bait?

This is all looking like such a bad idea. I take a mouthful of whatever brew Mr. D could get on sale in Hell, some sort of generic brand that I've never heard of—Apsu Gold. It goes down pretty rough and bitter and tastes of ash in my mouth. Still, it's beer.

The boat rocks, shivers, judders, messes with my already impaired sense of balance. I swear it's moving in a dozen different directions at once. One of Charon's pilots is behind the wheel. Even he's looking a bit green. Of course, he's used to river traffic.

Mr. D has returned to his chipper and annoyingly distracted state. He sips on his beer politely and eats tiny sandwiches, cut into triangles. His rod is lodged casually under his right armpit. I've never known a more capable man who somehow manages to look like he doesn't have a clue.

Something tugs and I let it feed out, give it plenty of line. Mr. D doesn't mess around with his fishing gear. His beer might be cheap, but this is top-of-the-line Underworld equipment.

"So what has she told you? What has she said that has led you to me, your old boss, your *current* mentor?" Mr. D asks. I'm almost shocked by his directness. Finally.

"Francis Rillman," I say. "The name keeps cropping up."

Mr. D shakes his head. "That is one person I will not talk about."

"But he—"

"That bastard crossed me. He tried to tear down everything I had built and all... all for a woman."

Mr. D had a terrible track record with his Ankous. After all, Morrigan followed Rillman.

"I think he's trying to kill me. Suzanne says it's because I managed to pull off the Orpheus Maneuver."

Mr. D checks his line. "It may have drawn his attention to you, but Rillman, I doubt it. He's an idealist."

"And what does he want?"

"An end to death itself," Mr. D says as though it's the most amusing and obvious thing in the world. "And, ironically, me dead. I told him at the time that he couldn't have it both ways." I can see him inhabiting that moment. Something passes across his faces, an old hurt—a bitterness—and the amusement is replaced with an emotion more resolute. His lips tighten, he plays out more line. "That is all I will speak of him."

An end to death! As if that is possible, or even preferable. Death is pervasive and necessary: it is the broom that sweeps out the old and allows the new to flourish. Sure, I would think that, but I can't see why Rillman would want this.

My fishing rod dips. I let out a little more line.

And then something is more than tugging—there's a wrenching, hard against me. "Hey, I—"

And then I'm plunging into that brimming-over-with-monsters sea. The line didn't feed, and that line is connected to me. I'm being dragged down.

The water's cold and slimy. It snatches the breath from me. I'm tangled in the rod, and I'm going fast. Already the water pushes hard against my ribs.

Should be no problem. I should be able to shift myself out of here. Only it isn't working. What should feel like an opening out, a broadening of perspective, mixed with the snapping of a rubber band against my back brain, is nothing but a dull ache. I can't shift. Interestingly, my hangover's gone. You've gotta take the good with the bad.

I look up. The *Mary C*'s hull is a tiny square on the surface. It winks out of sight; something big has passed between the boat and me. Something huge. It's several seconds before I can see the bottom of the boat again, and it's barely a square at all now.

I think I see a pale shape dart in the water, but it's more likely the spots and squiggles dancing before my eyes. I'm still going down, and fast. I grab the pomping knife from my belt, start cutting at the line. It should be easier than it is, but I'm not surprised that it isn't. Finally the line snaps. My lungs burn. Great dark shapes are circling.

I feel a pressure on my shoulder, sharper than the water, and ending in five points, each digging into the muscle of my shoulder.

I whip my head around—no one, nothing—but the grip, if anything, grows more certain.

A whisper, straight into my ear, no wet gargles. Just a voice as sharp as that grip: "You're in danger."

No shit.

I thrash in the dark. The last bubbles of my breath escape my lips. This shouldn't be happening. This is no earthly sea. This is *my* domain. Damn it, I'm the RM of this entire region of the Underworld. Nothing should be able to touch me here. But something has—is. And not just touching, but squeezing. I wonder for a moment if this isn't some elaborate initiation ritual.

No breath now. All I have is a mild discomfort, a soft dizziness running through me, and that insistent voice, and it's permeating me more completely than my blood.

"You fall, but not alone, and in the falling, darkness waits."

Darker than this? I doubt it.

"And then you will be alone. Everything dies, by choice or reason. There is meaning in the muddle. There is blood and crooning in the mess."

I'm not finding much sense in the mess presented. I struggle in the grip, but it's unyielding.

"Oh, but there's a long drop for you."

"Let. Me. Go." I swing my head toward the voice, concentrating, throwing everything at it: which isn't much. Things tear within my psyche. A sickening sensation of my thoughts, of me, ripping apart. My muscles clench in sympathy. And for a moment, I catch a glimpse of something. A face. A grinning shadow, a mirror reflection, but so much more varied.

"Such a long drop for you. Such a long fall."

Then the pressure's gone, and I'm rising. A tiny, chubby pale hand is clamped around my index finger. We shoot toward the surface.

Then out of the darkness a great maw opens. Teeth the length of my forearm loom over and under us. Wal looks at me. I shrug.

This is not a good day.

But this I can deal with. The megalodon's rough teeth brush my arm, but here I cannot be hurt and certainly not by something dead.

It's odd, but for a moment I'm curious. A slight objectivity clouds my fear, or burns it away. This is what it is to be an RM: to be endlessly curious, to endlessly count down the hours, to peer at the life around me and not be involved in any of it other than the taking. It's with almost a sense of ennui that I consider the rows of pale teeth flexing in the meat of the megalodon's mouth.

Wal's hand tightens around my finger. His lips are moving but I can't make out the words, just the panic and I remember where I am.

The force that dragged me down has gone. I squeeze Wal's hand with my thumb, concentrate on the boat and then we're there, coughing and spluttering on the deck. I reach around and clutch at my shoulder where fingers had dug so deeply in, and dry heave out my pain.

Mr. D is waiting with towels. He chucks one at me, and then Wal. "What took you so long?"

"I thought I was safe here."

He shrugs. "You're not dead, are you? Not even bleeding."

"It grabbed me, the damn thing grabbed me, and then it spoke." I'm still spluttering.

Mr. D stops still. "What spoke? What did it say?"

"That I would fall. That I would be alone."

Mr. D's eyes widen. "What do they have planned for you?" he whispers.

"Who? Who has what planned for me?"

"Nothing. I'm sure it's nothing. Sounds like the All-Death — the death that exists outside the linear, the now and the then. I wouldn't worry about it too much. It likes to grab and mutter. Most of the time it doesn't make any sense."

"Like an oracle?" I ask, thinking back to high school and Year Ten Ancient History.

Mr. D shakes his head. "It's more like a drunk old uncle at Christmas time, or a senile great-grandfather. Just nod your head sagely and listen, but don't take it too seriously. I've not known it to actually have much of a handle on reality. It may even have you confused with someone else."

"OK," I say, wanting to take some relief from this.

"Yes, but it is a little disturbing." Mr. D doesn't know me all that well if he thinks that's going to offer any comfort.

"So what do I do?"

"Wait and see."

Wait and see; it's always wait and see! I glance at my watch. "I have to get back to work."

Mr. D smiles. "You're Regional Manager, you're one of the Orcus. You never stop working, whether you want to or not."

Which is exactly why I feel like an impostor.

Wait and bloody see? I already know what's coming. I don't need Mr. D or the All-Death to tell me. No matter how hard I try, it's never going to be enough.

14

Home.

The house is silent, but for the last few drops of water dripping from my suit. Boxes are still stacked against one wall. The place smells a bit musty; some windows haven't been opened since we moved in. The air-conditioning's been off for a while and I'm sweating before I take my first step. Everything is lit with hard Brisbane summer light.

Lissa's left a note on the kitchen table: *You know where I'll be. Oh, and one of us has to get milk. Hope you enjoyed the fishing.*

I don't know about "enjoyed." In fact, I feel more confused than ever. How could Rillman bring about an end to death itself? It's impossible. Life is built on death, the passing on of things, the dreams and devourings. Take out Mortmax and all you have is chaos and a Stirrer-led apocalypse. Rillman can't want that. It makes no sense.

Out of the living room and into the bedroom. I drag off my wet clothes; fabric making sucking noises as I tug first pants then shirt and underpants from me. My hair's plastered to my forehead.

This All-Death disturbs me. A dim echo of its voice scratches away in my ears. And I can tell it worried Mr. D as well. He couldn't have got me away any faster if he tried.

A quick shower, a little product for the hair, and a dry suit and I'm looking... well, I'm looking better. I'm head of Mortmax

Industries in Australia and I look the part at least. Very funereal, but classy funereal, I reckon.

I look at my watch, Lissa should be at work by now.

I shift. This time I feel like I can hold it together. Maybe it is getting easier. Lissa jolts as I appear behind her in Number Four. Oscar and Travis jump, and I get the feeling that if I'd appeared any closer to Lissa I'd have received a fist to the throat.

I don't care that there are two burly men surrounding her. I wrap Lissa in my arms, and I kiss her hard.

"What was that for?" she asks when she is done kissing me back.

"Sorry to leave you alone this morning," I say, once I catch my breath.

Lissa smiles. "I'll live."

I don't want her to just live. But I can't say it here. I hug her again, tighter. Stopping only when someone behind me clears their throat.

Lundwall from the front desk hands me my messages. "I've emailed the details to you."

There are phone calls from Sydney and Perth. Tim is down in Melbourne, sorting out some issues there, and I don't expect to see him until the Christmas party tonight. People look to me for advice and I'm not sure what I need to give them: certainly more than I'm actually capable of. I sometimes pity my staff, looking up to me as though I know what I'm doing. Poor bastards.

Lissa follows me into my office. I sit down in the throne and it whispers a greeting that only I can hear.

Her phone plays the "Imperial March," confirming an app update. Ah, the schedule's running through, being reconfirmed now that I am sitting in the throne, and all the multitudes of variables are factored in. She lifts her eyebrows as she takes in her jobs for the day.

"Busy day?"

"You should know."

"We'll do something tonight, I promise."

"Of course we will," Lissa says. "It's the staff Christmas party."

Then she's out of here.

Oscar clears his throat. He's standing at the door. "A word if you please, Mr. de Selby."

"I know, I'm sorry I left you in the lurch."

Oscar shakes his head. There's a sort of sternness in his eyes that I've not seen in anyone since Morrigan died. "This will work much better if you do what we tell you . . . and you keep us informed of your plans."

"My plans tend to change from moment to moment."

"Just keep us updated. That is all I'm asking."

"Did you see anything last night?"

Oscar shakes his head. "Other than the RM who visited you? Nothing."

They're a little more on the ball than I thought. Well, that's good, right?

Oscar watches this work its way across my face.

I clear my throat. "I'll keep you posted on my . . . um . . . movements. I'm sorry, if I forget. Just let me know, though—what exactly is the difference between what you're asking and being a hostage?"

Oscar grins. "Unfortunately very little, other than the very large sums of money you are paying us for the privilege of our protection."

Talking of being a hostage, I wave at the huge amount of paperwork in front of me. "Yeah, I've got stuff to do."

He nods. "I'll be at the door. My replacement will be here in half an hour."

"What? You're telling me you need to rest?"

"Only if you want to live."

Everyone's a comedian.

I sign off on a couple of investment suggestions. Read the latest data from Cerbo on the approaching god, which isn't much, but I know I'm going to have to contact him soon.

The lack of information I have at my fingertips is frustrating, so I flip through Twitter.

Death@MortmaxEuro: *Ah, plague so wearying.*

Death@MortmaxUS: *Train wreck@Festival LA. More B-list stars, but one A. Expect a thousand tedious retrospectives.*

I resist the temptation to read the online news, then check my email again. There's one from the South African RM, Neill Debbier.

Mr. de Selby,

While I am aware that you are no doubt busy with all things Death Moot—not to mention the attempts on your life—I would be appreciative if you were to visit my offices. My diary is flexible today. You are welcome at any time.

Regards,

Neill

It's a change from Suzanne who seems to want everything now, now, *now.*

What the hell. I look at my desk with its teetering piles of paper. No time like the present.

I don't shift directly into his office—well, I try not to at any rate—that would be rude. And in these times, when RMs—OK, only one RM, but we're all a team, aren't we?—are being attacked, it could induce a panic.

I'm not sure what a panicked Neill would do, but I don't really want to find out. I'm only beginning to understand my own abilities and RMs are notoriously closed mouthed. There are more secrets within our organization than I would have believed just a few months ago—secrets, like landmines waiting for me to inadvertently stomp on them. But then again, what's a landmine anyway, but a really, really nasty secret?

The shift is relatively painless this time. "Yeah!" I punch the air a little.

Neill's Ankou, David, types away for a moment or two, pointedly ignoring me.

I cough.

He looks up, feigns surprise. "You're early," he says.

Why does everyone seem to know what I'm doing better than me? "When were you expecting me?"

"Based on your movements, around your lunchtime, so very early morning here."

Based on my movements? I wonder just who it is who is watching me. I don't have anyone spying on the other RMs, maybe I should. Yeah, as if I could afford to lose more staff.

"Are you ready to talk to the boss?"

"Of course I am."

I get what looks to me like a smile of pity. David presses down on a somewhat prehistoric intercom, a big brown box as clunky as all hell. I get the feeling they don't bother with Bluetooth here, but then again, Mr. D used to use sparrows as his main form of communication, and his "data-storage" consisted of scrunched-up balls of paper and Post-it notes.

The intercom buzzes a moment before Neill picks up.

"Yes?" The voice is warm.

"Mr. de Selby's here."

"He's early. Excellent."

Neill's through the door almost at once, his hand out, giving me a professionally firm handshake that lasts one or two seconds too long.

"Come in," he says gesturing at his open door. "We have a lot to talk about, you and I."

The door is heavy, the windows barred. Like my office, he has views of both the living and the Underworld. But the bars obscure it somewhat. All I can see are street lights. It's late here, does Neill ever go home?

"As you can see, we are quite secure here."

I want to say something about how needing such security doesn't suggest security at all. But I bite my tongue.

Neill's throne is almost identical to mine. The wood is a little paler, the carvings a little different, perhaps telling a story of an older continent. After all, the Orcus had its origins, like all human life, in Africa. Although some of the carvings definitely aren't of humans.

Neill sits down and sighs. His skin brightens, flushes a little as he leans back in his chair. I wonder if that's how I look. I know I've grown somewhat dependent on my throne.

Neill pours, then passes me a glass of twenty-year-old scotch. Without even bothering to ask if I want one. The bottle of scotch is the only thing sitting on his desk, other than a couple of sheets of paper, over which he has made notes in an extremely neat hand. I try not to look but I think I can see my name. Neill slides the papers away and into a drawer under his desk. I almost expect him to pull out a gun. See what a paranoid state I'm in?

"There are some things you're better off not reading," Neill says. "Besides, my spelling is atrocious."

I sip my scotch. It's good stuff. I compare this with the beer Mr. D has been foisting on me. My old RM has sunk a long way. "I think you need a mentor, Steven. Hope that doesn't make me sound too much like a wanker. But Mr. D, he was never the best of us, had a habit of making enemies."

"I've already made a deal with Suzanne Whitman." Not that I trust her in the least.

Neill's expression hardly changes. "I wouldn't trust her. Suzanne is many things, but trustworthy is not one of them."

Is this bugger reading my mind? "And why should I trust you?"

Neill smiles. "Mr. de Selby, there really isn't anyone you should trust. Not friends, nor family. Everyone can betray you. Why, you can betray yourself—and that's the worst sort of betrayal, isn't it?"

"You're telling me that trust is pointless. Then why bother making any deals at all?"

"They're no guarantee against betrayal, but they do, with the right amount of paranoia, make it harder. It's as much about information. Sharing."

"What do you want from me? You seem to know everything anyway."

"Not at all. I know less than you think. But I do have something for you. Rillman—I have heard that he's causing you trouble." Neill sighs. "You're not the first. Rillman is a pain, and your Mr. D should have stopped him years ago. Do you know that he regularly crosses the boundary between the land of the living and the Underworld?"

"What?" Well, that explains a lot. The bastard's got a passcard to Hell. I'm not sure whether I feel relieved he's back on the table as a suspect or horrified by the implications of what he can do.

Neill's eyes crinkle with the slightest of smiles. "Death holds no dominion over him. You might want to ask just who is letting it happen."

"Do you have any idea?" He can't give me this and not have an idea!

Neill shrugs. "Perhaps your new *mentor* knows. She has promised you much. The Orcus has plans for you. You would do well to ask just what they are."

"Why don't you tell me now?" I want to bang my fist on the table.

Neill grins. "If I could. Yes, but then she would know. This, I can get away with. This, you should have been able to guess yourself. You're new, of course the Orcus would fit you into their strategies. But if I tell you any more I risk... Well, it would not be good."

"I'll think about your offer." I finish my scotch and force a smile, wondering if he's being genuine, if I can even trust the information about Rillman that he's given me. I've seen Neill's Negotiation, just as I've seen all the others: one nasty gift I wish I'd never received.

You see someone decapitate their foe, you think differently of them.

"Yes, please consider it carefully."

The phone rings. He glances over to it. "I need to take this call."

He stands up, shakes my hand. "Be very careful, my friend."

I nod and shift out of there.

There is a knock at my office door, almost at the same second I arrive back. I'm a little woozy, but otherwise OK.

"Come in," I say, trying to hide the irritation from my voice.

A giant of a man walks into the room. At first I think it's the New Zealand–South Pacific RM. He's at least this big, but it's not Kiri Baker. I feel guilty—another couple of movements I haven't let the security crew know about.

The big guy blinks. "Just thought I'd let you know there's been a shift change." His lips move a little oddly, as though they're scarred. I know I shouldn't but I stare at them, trying to work out just what is wrong.

He comes toward me, his hand out. "Jacob. I'm Oscar's replacement."

"Thanks," I say, standing up to shake his hand. "I really appreciate what you're doing. And I've promised Oscar that I'll be good."

His hand encloses mine. And I catch the movement of his other hand far too late: it's not open.

Jacob's fist slams into my head. I see stars, literally all sorts of unnerving constellations. *Aquarius—today you will have the shit beaten out of you, dope. Dress for wet weather, and probable death.*

"You're welcome," he says, swinging another fist at my head. I sense him changing. Shrinking somehow, or maybe it's just that the room is spinning. "You're so welcome."

Shift. Got to shift. Close my eyes. Focus on anywhere but here!

But that's the end of me. Five shifts in such close proximity was never going to happen. I'm on the floor, stunned, one nostril sheathed in a bubble of blood that's expanding and contracting with my breath. He lifts me up easily, and the bloody bubble bursts. I'm shaking my head, trying to stop the ringing in my ears. All I can see between long blinks is the carpet, and my blood splattering in Rorschach patterns.

I try to speak, just manage a couple of grunts. And then we shift. It doesn't feel like far, but I've no way of knowing. For a moment my assailant's heartbeat races.

More carpet, a familiar color. A door swings open, and we move into another room. I'm tossed into a chair. The door clicks shut. Darkness. A chance. I've got a chance.

I try to get up, legs hardly like springs, and the Hulk punches me down again. "Not yet, we've a way to go," he says, in the dark. "I've just started with you."

15

My head's clearing. The ringing's gone, replaced with a headache almost the equal of my worst hangover.

I can only hear one heartbeat. Nothing else. A single steady beating that races again for a moment, then slows. Something just happened. I'm not sure what. There is a metallic clunk. The air smells of dust, with a background hint of industrial cleaning products. Where the hell am I?

A match is struck. Some sort of fragrant candle must be burning because I can smell oranges, or the candle-chemical equivalent of them. Or I am having a stroke. My swollen eyelids admit a little of that flickering light: it's as red as the blood that I can taste in my mouth.

I open my eyes, and recognize the room, even with the candlelight. It's the broom cupboard on the third floor of Number Four, the same broom cupboard that Morrigan used to imprison Mr. D when he began his Schism. The door in front of me is solid wood and is bound in some sort of alloy. You can pretty much guarantee that no other cupboard in the world has that sort of door.

And no one is likely to visit this space anytime soon.

This is not good. Morrigan had the whole place soundproofed before he threw Mr. D into it. I should have had the door knocked out, and a regular one installed. But I never expected to end up here myself. I try to move. My hands are free but rough cord digs into the flesh of my arms: the movement only tightens my bonds. This is serious malevolent-scout knot-work.

"I wouldn't do that if I was you." The voice is unfamiliar, clipped and rasping, certainly not Jacob's. Cold metal brushes my cheek. "Don't move if you want to keep your eyes."

I freeze. The knife travels down my face, drawing blood here and there. I try and shift. Nothing. Something's damping my abilities here. I guess that's how Mr. D was contained here. Yes, this room has to go.

Time for some bluster. "You're going to have to work harder than that if you want to frighten me with a knife."

"I will, really I will." He sounds amused.

I turn my head as far around to the right as I am able and nod at the candles behind me. "You've certainly picked an intimate setting for a . . . Well, what is this? A torture session?"

There's a wry exhalation, almost a laugh, and a hand passes in front of my face. It's lined with scars all across the palm. "You RMs. You really think you know it all."

"I tend to find it's the Ankous with the problem, Mr. Rillman."

There is a definite intake of breath. I don't know whether it's an act or not, but he sounds genuinely surprised. "Where did you hear that name? I thought they had forgotten me."

"Oh, around the traps. You're quite a popular bloke here. Mr. D talks of you with a great deal of fondness."

"That shit ground my name out of the company's history. You will not speak of him again." He strikes the back of my head, hard enough that I bite my tongue, and see stars.

"OK, I won't. Just tell me: why are you trying to kill me?"

"Oh, you're something of an experiment, Mr. de Selby. A new RM, first in living memory. Who would have believed it?" Rillman says. "We both know there are deaths, and then there are deaths."

"How did you do it?" I ask, my tongue swollen and bloody in my mouth. "How did you die and come back?"

Rillman snorts. "Does it offend you? After all, you've done it. All you RMs must, death is the only way to win at the Negotiation. It is the single requisite, wouldn't you say?"

Rillman walks around to face me. There's something not quite right about his features. He's hiding them from me. They're waxy, and his hair doesn't look quite real. Now I think of it, Jacob had something of that look about him, too. Rillman smiles tightly and slips back behind me, where I can't turn my head to follow. He's just a blur back there, a blur holding sharp things.

"Look, I know you failed an Orpheus Maneuver. But that—"

Something strikes me hard in the back of the head again. Next, I realize I've come to, I can't tell how much time has passed but it can't be much. Rillman walks in circles around me, agitated. He steps in close, almost enough for me to headbutt him. He slides the knife across my cheek.

"You will not talk about that. I did not fail. I was betrayed. Ask your Mr. D. Here you will not talk about anything."

"What the fuck do you want?"

"All in good time."

He lifts the knife from my cheek. Drives it into the meat just above my knee. And God help me, I scream. Not that it does any good.

"Knives don't need to terrify, they just need a good cutting edge or a point, or in this case, both."

Blood and spittle run down my chin. "Can't we just... What do you want?"

He pulls the knife out of my knee, and slams the pommel into my jaw.

"I want you to shut up."

I spit more blood, and a tooth. My mouth is a mess, I have to keep spitting or I will choke, but it doesn't stop me from straining against the ropes binding me here. It doesn't stop me from growling in his face. "This is my region. You come in here and threaten me."

I'm almost convincing.

I try to shift again, damping field be damned. I'm desperate. I need to get out of here. But there is a cold hand, a pressure sitting in the back of my mind. Not that different to the force that held me in the Tethys.

Rillman lowers his waxen face toward mine, and smiles. "Every emperor, every RM, can be destroyed. You must know that now. You must know that nowhere is safe for you and your kind."

"Then kill me." I lift my neck to him. "Just get it over and done with."

"Oh, if it was that easy, I would."

And he's right. Already my wounds are healing; there is less blood in my mouth. The flesh of my leg is drawing together.

The phone in my pocket starts ringing, I'm amazed that I can get a signal in here, but there you go. "They're going to start looking for me," I say.

Rillman nods, reaches into my pocket and pulls out the phone. After two stomps of his left boot the phone's in pieces on the floor. "Yes, and I am sure that the broom cupboard is the first place they'll look. They're not going to worry about you for several hours. I have time."

He swings a fist into my ribs. Things break. Things tear. I'm choking on my own blood again. For a while I can't see anything. Rillman is right; this could go on for a while. My nature is such that I can take a lot of pain.

"She was mine. And I lost her. Of course, you can't understand that, because you didn't. You cheated. You stumbled and pratfalled and somehow, you called your love back." Another blow to the side of my head. "Fourteen years of marriage. Do you not understand? What do you know of that kind of love?"

More teeth are loosened. Blood chokes my throat.

What do I know of love? I think of Lissa. Wonder if I'll ever see her again. I haven't spent enough time with her, not nearly enough. There is so much we haven't done together. Things we haven't experienced. Christ, I want to marry her.

I don't care if it's unwise for RMs to marry. I don't care if it's the stupidest thing in the world. She's my girl. Mine.

"Why are you grinning?" Rillman demands.

"What do I know of love? I got her back. I got her back, you prick."

There's another couple of punches. More pain. A knife is jammed into my spine and left there.

When the pain dulls, and I can breathe again, I lift my head. "What do you want, Rillman?"

"Agony, isn't it? And with the way you heal I don't need to be delicate."

He pulls out another knife, pale as moonlight, and as narrow as a regular dinner knife. He grabs my left pinkie finger. I struggle against him, but he is stronger than I am, and the ropes that bind me are tight. "This knife isn't steel," he says, "but something I picked up in the Deepest Dark. Let's see how it works."

He pushes the blade over, and then into, my pinkie finger, hard. Skin and bone part in a swift and agonizing jolt. I feel the cracking of that bone through my entire body. I scream. And I scream. And I scream until something tears in my throat.

"Oh, we have so much more fun ahead, believe me." I struggle, my bonds tighten, and Rillman lets me; so confident that I can't escape.

He brings the knife toward my cheek.

But this time I'm ready for him. I swing my head up against his skull. Bone cracks into bone. Rillman goes down hard.

He groans. I rock backward and forward in my chair, and then I'm tipping over, landing on Rillman. I crack my skull into his head, again and again. His knife is next to him on the floor. I slide over toward it, grab it with a hand sticky with blood and cut at my bindings.

The knife's damn sharp. I'm free in a moment and I stagger to my feet. Rillman groans again. And I kick him in the head. Once. Twice. I bend down and rest the knife against his face. There's a rather large part of me taking too much delight in this.

"Oh, we have so much fun ahead, believe me." I try and reach the other knife in my back, but can't.

I find my finger on the floor. The little thing's twitching. I wonder whether, if I left it alone long enough, it would grow a new me. I push it against my wound and finger and hand begin to reconnect. It's agony, but I'll be whole again soon.

I need to get out of this tiny room. The walls are closing in.

I stumble over to the door, swing it open and stagger outside. Rillman is on the floor behind me. He isn't going anywhere.

Laughter and music echo down from the floor above. I stagger to the stairs and climb up to the fourth floor. The nearer I get the more I can make out. Christmas carols? Worse than that—contemporized Christmas carols doof doof doofing.

I kick open the door. And there are my staff having their Christmas party. A big Christmas tree is in one corner, someone is giggling by the photocopying machine. Tim is talking to some bigwigs from the state government. For all this, everything seems so forced; a party going through the motions. The door slams shut behind me.

Everyone, glasses in hand, spins around, and there I am. Me with my blood staining my shirt. Me with a bloody knife in one hand. Me with the torn and gore-stained pants. Me with blood squelching in my shoes with every step.

I walk over to the bar and pour myself a Bundy—a tall glass, neat. My pinkie finger still dangles a little. I down the rum in one gulp. No one has moved, not even Tim.

"Oh, and merry fucking Christmas," I say, waving the glass in the air. If it weren't for the bar I'm leaning on I'd drop to the floor in a heap. I nearly do, and whatever shock my presence created is broken. The whole room seems to move toward me.

"What the hell happened to you?" Tim asks, rushing from where the two government guys stand: both of them looking at me curiously. What are they going to write in their reports tomorrow?

I lift up the mess that is my left hand—though it's not nearly as messy as it was—and point at the door. "Downstairs. Broom cupboard. Francis Rillman. The fucker tried—well, more than tried—to torture me."

Tim's out of there, running back the way I've come. I look around me. Where's Lissa? Then I'm swaying. The rest of my staff aren't sure what they should be doing. I don't blame them. I can hear their elevated heartbeats. And then there's one I recognize.

"Steven! Oh, Steven."

Lissa's there, she's found me, she's holding me up. I've never been so happy to be held up, to be bound up in her arms. There's stuff we need to discuss. Not here, not now, but as soon as we can.

"Where were you?" I ask.

"Your office. Jesus, Steve, I've been trying to call you. I was getting worried, but I thought... Well, you've been all over the place lately." She touches my face. "Oh, my darling."

"Francis Rillman just tortured me." I grin at her. "I've never been tortured before. I think I did all right."

She walks me to a chair. The staff are all looking on. The poor green bastards, I really should say something, but the breath is out of me.

"Could you get the knife out of my back?" I manage at last.

She pulls, then reconsiders. "Maybe we should wait for Dr. Brooker. It seems to be lodged in your spine."

"Might explain why it hurts so much."

"It's going to be OK," she says, wiping blood from my face. And while I don't seem to be bleeding, there's a lot of it.

"Yeah, absolutely."

No one else seems sure what to do. I get the feeling that I'm letting them all down. I don't want to do that. After all, Rillman's taken care of. My wounds will heal and no one else has been hurt.

I get out of the chair, with a little help from Lissa.

"Sorry," I say to my crew. "You all party on. Really, it's OK. Someone turn up the music."

As inspirational speeches go it really doesn't cut it.

Lissa wipes some more blood from my face. "Steven, most bosses just get drunk and flirt with their staff at Christmas parties."

Tim belts back up the stairs, panting. Oscar's behind him looking very pissed off. Tim passes me my phone. It's whole again. I blink at it. I can see where the glass front is finishing healing itself: the tiniest tracework of cracks. Must be a cracker of a twenty-four month plan.

"Rillman's gone," Tim says. "There's just the chair, and blood." He looks from me to Lissa and back. His eyes are frantic. I can tell he wants to hit something. "You poor bastard."

I don't have time or the energy to comfort him. "The guy was out cold when I left him."

"Well, he's not there now."

I look up at Oscar he's only just getting off his mobile. "What happened? How did he—"

"Rillman, it has to be him, he killed Jacob. Stabbed, in his own house."

"So who was it that I was talking to in my office?"

"I don't know."

"That's reassuring."

"Look, someone died today," Oscar says. "I'm going to find the bastard who did this and there will be payback. No one does this to one of my crew."

I nod, a bit woozy with lack of blood. I know how he feels. I'm mad enough about this as it is, but if Rillman had tortured anyone else I would not be able to express my rage. At least physical damage is only going to be a memory to me.

Poor Jacob is dead and gone and, for all I know, he wasn't even properly pomped. That's too high a price.

"He was working for me, too," I say. "We'll both make the bastard pay."

A thought strikes me. A dark one. "Do you have a photo of Jacob?"

Oscar nods, fiddles with his mobile and passes it to me. The face I'm staring at is the face of the man who hit me. This is not good.

"That's him, the man who attacked me."

Oscar shakes his head. "Couldn't be. He's been dead for twelve hours."

Great, Rillman can change his appearance. The question is, can he change his appearance only to those who are dead? Or are all the living open to him as well?

Just where might Rillman be now?

My gaze shifts from Oscar to Tim and Lissa, then to the crowd of Pomps around me.

Paranoia plus.

16

"Didn't I tell you to keep out of trouble?" Dr. Brooker grunts, looking at my hand. The finger has melded nicely. Not bad for a couple of hours. The wound in my leg is scabbed up too. He looks from me to Lissa and Tim. "I did tell him to keep out of trouble."

I'm on a drip, blood filling my veins. I'm on my second bag, and I'm starting to feel great. Brooker had nearly fainted at the sight of me. Anyone else and I would have been dead, or at the very least in a coma, he reckons.

"This is getting irritating," I say.

"It'd be rather more fatal than irritating if you weren't who you are. So it's definitely Rillman?" Tim says.

"Yeah, but I still can't understand why he did it. I mean, I can't have pissed him off. The bastard doesn't know me." Rillman may not be the first person who has wanted to torture me, but he's certainly been the first to try.

"I think Rillman's testing the limits of your abilities. Trying to find out what can kill you."

"Neill said that Rillman's been a thorn in Mortmax's side for a while."

"Not here," Tim says. "There's no record of a Rillman for years in our system." He sighs. "Do you think that perhaps the Orcus are using you to draw Rillman out? I mean, there are links, plenty of them. If Rillman's seeking an end to the status quo you would be attractive to him."

I chew on that for a while. "Yeah, I'm new to my powers. I don't have any allies as such."

"And you managed what he failed to do," Lissa says. "You brought someone back from Hell."

"You pomped him. You said he seemed calm."

Lissa nods. "Maybe resigned is the better term. Most dead people are that. Perhaps he had decided on his plan of action. Maybe he was seeking me out. Death would be an easy way of doing that. He knows how we work, and it seems no real obstacle to him."

"Think about that," I say. "Think about how reckless you might be if death holds no fear, no real consequence, and you want revenge."

"It might make you willing to experiment more. Particularly in unconventional ways of killing an RM," Tim says.

"You're telling me that no one has ever tried to kill an RM before?"

Tim rolled his eyes. "Well, obviously they have, but without success, unless it's part of a Schism, killing off an RM's Pomps, weakening them until they're able to be killed. It's messy, convoluted and can really only happen inhouse. Remember, as you've probably read in my briefing notes," Tim says, giving me a stern look, "RMs give Pomps the ability to pomp. You turn them into the doorway that gives access to the Underworld and closes out Stirrers, but they also give you something in return. Through them you are able to shift, to heal. One of the reasons the party was so subdued had to do with the amount of energy all of us were expending to keep you alive."

"That, and the music, I mean those Christmas carols were tragic!" I say. Lissa glares at me, reminds me to stay on track. Tim shakes his head, but continues.

"Rillman is obviously aiming at non-traditional methods."

I remember Mr. D's words about a paradigm shift back when Morrigan was around. "He's trying to effect a change. A real change to the system."

Tim nods. "You'd have to admit that killing an RM without destroying their Pomps is a much less bloody transition." He grins. "I hate to say it, Steve, but if it's going to come down to me getting it and you getting it, or just you getting it, I know what I'd rather—"

"Hey!"

He raises his hands in the air. "With the proviso that I can get my revenge. I'm in no hurry to lose any more of my family."

"So why would Rillman want to get rid of me? I can't believe it's just because I succeeded in my Orpheus Maneuver and he didn't." But I can believe that, part of me at least. If I had failed, and for a while I thought I had, bitterness would poison me.

"Did Morrigan have any allies? Maybe Rillman was one of them," Tim says

"No, I don't think so. Morrigan ended all his allegiances brutally. By the Negotiation I think his allies and enemies were indistinguishable."

Tim nods. "Even the Stirrers were working against him."

"What we need to do is find Rillman before he actually succeeds in killing me. As well as organize a Death Moot, run Mortmax efficiently and—"

"Don't forget about the Christmas party." Tim smiles, nodding to the door outside. "Well, you've already ruined that."

Dr. Brooker grunts, looks at us both quizzically. "Christmas party?"

Oh, shit.

"Didn't you get your invitation?" Tim and I say at the same time.

"Maybe we need to cancel the Death Moot," I continue, changing the subject.

Lissa and Tim shake their heads. "No. That's one thing you cannot do. A Death Moot must never be canceled. It's a sign of weakness, and you don't want to present any weakness to the Orcus."

"But people are trying to kill us."

"Death may well be preferable," Tim says.

Speak for yourself. "How do I look?" I say, getting up, straightening my hair as best I can. My fingers catch on what I suspect are large clumps of dried blood.

Lissa smiles at me. "Like Death warmed up."

At least someone's kept their sense of humor.

I don't feel safe at home.

The rest of the Christmas party was, well, in a word, awkward. Death is something of a party killer at the best of times. Particularly when I spent a good deal of it staring intently at every staff member, or asking difficult questions that in theory only my people should be able to answer. Yes, there's going to be a staff meeting about *that.* Some of the basic pomping facts that these people didn't know shocked me. I was almost relieved when a truck collision called a good half-dozen of them away. Call me mean-spirited, but I am Australia's RM and death is my business.

Lissa had stayed by my side the whole evening, even submitted to my paranoid questions—with curt, often embarrassing, answers. Of course I knew it was her, I'm intimately familiar with her heartbeat. I have to believe that Rillman's mimicry doesn't extend that far.

Lissa's asleep almost the moment her head hits the pillow. I text Suzanne: *Need to talk.*

A few seconds later I have a response: *Yes, you do. Usual place. Let's make it another lesson.*

Yeah, but this time I'll be directing the questions.

I shift there. The Deepest Dark whispers around me. I wince, expecting more pain than I actually get.

Suzanne smiles at me, and she's in my coat. I'd ask for it back but she seems wounded in some way, a little less confident. It was less than twenty-four hours since we were here last, and I had left her to witness to the fate of one of her agents.

For the first time I see something—I hesitate to call it human—inside her. A vulnerability that I had never expected to encounter in an RM. It actually stops me for a moment. Reminds me that I'm not the only one capable of feeling pain.

"Your agent?"

Suzanne shakes her head. "It wasn't good. I don't want to talk about it. He is no longer in any pain."

Above us the great inky mass of the Stirrer god swallows an ever-increasing portion of the sky like some gargantuan and evil lava lamp.

"I was tortured today."

"I am aware of that," Suzanne says. "Don't forget I have ten Pomps on your payroll. They're switched on enough to pick up a phone. I knew you would be in touch soon enough. Your Lissa, she's sleeping?"

"Yeah, what's that got to do with anything?"

"Everything. This is your Lissa. This is all of them." Suzanne crouches down, picks up a handful of dust and does whatever it is that she does. It dances around her hand, shining ever brighter. I can see Lissa's face there, her eyes closed, whispering in her sleep. Then, with a single chopping gesture, the dust drops to the ground. "They all need sleep. Not that it is enough in the end. Gravity changes them all. They shift down, they grow heavy in their bones. They lose swift thought and swift action. They decay. That is all they have, a trudging forward into decrepitude and dust. And yet it is so beautiful. So tragic. And far better than it was before. She sleeps, your girl, but it is not enough to hold back the final sleep."

I don't want a lesson in the obvious. I want answers. "I know this. I've grown up around death," I say. "I was a Pomp, just as the rest of you were Pomps."

Suzanne gives me a patronizing pat on the shoulder. "You only think you do. You don't know death the way we *know* death. That knowledge is coming, but you don't have it yet. You're never going to feel gravity again, Steven. It doesn't apply to you, the death you will find will be fast and violent and centuries hence, if you're on your game. You will have time to see the beauty and ugliness of life for what it is: fleeting and yet, somehow, eternal.

"And how you come to that knowledge won't have anything to do with what I say, or Neill. I can guarantee that." So she's onto me, then. I try to not register any surprise. "It will come to you in its own way, as everything else has come to you, because that's how it works."

"I'm a bloody slow learner."

"There's nothing to learn. This is a bone-deep truth, whether you understand it or not. A hundred years from now you will be the same as you are now, and different in ways you can't even begin to comprehend. You've no choice in the matter."

"But there are choices to be made."

"As much as any of us can make them. We're all fighting the same fight. The enemy hasn't changed. That's a constant, too."

But I feel it has. Morrigan, in his dealings with the Stirrers, has set something in motion. Something I can't quite articulate. Suzanne watches me trying to get it out, and sees that it obviously isn't going to come.

"Rillman, what about him? He wants me dead," I say, finally.

"And yet you are most obviously not."

"Tell me how I can find him."

Suzanne looks away from me, toward the city of Devour. "If I knew a way, believe me, I would have pursued him a long time ago."

An idea strikes me then, an unpleasant one. "Are you using me as bait?"

Suzanne shakes her head. "You've drawn Rillman out. Before, he was all secrecy—back-door plans and sneaking in and out of Hell. You would make excellent bait, but I fear that the moment we used you as such Rillman would go underground again. I want you on my side," Suzanne says. "Neill's bloc is growing too powerful."

I peer over at her, surprised. "I thought he was your bloc."

"We may help each other from time to time but we are not in agreement on much. We know how to put up a unified front when we need to. But he worries me now."

"What difference does it make?"

"When you have centuries, it makes all the difference in the worlds. Believe me, you will learn that."

"What are your plans for me? The All-Death—"

Suzanne grimaces. "What did that meddlesome thing say?"

"That I will be alone. That I will fall."

Suzanne looks almost relieved, as though I've merely reaffirmed something. "We're all alone," she says. "Rillman. You. Lissa. You will learn this, Steven, if you're half as smart as I think you are. The longer you live, the more alone you are."

I turn from her, and consider the darkness of the Stirrer god above. I remember with utter clarity the immensity of its eye in that vision granted to me by Stirrer rage or my newborn power. I'd stared it down. Of course, I'd been too stupid to do anything different. Me there in that darkness, hurling its worshippers back away from the land of the living. I'd felt the strength of Orcus unity, a strength that had extended all the way down to my hundreds of Avian Pomps.

Absolutely meaningless. I knew that if it came down to it, I'd be fighting that dark alone and it scared the shit out of me.

"I don't think we have centuries anymore. Maybe my presence is what the Orcus needs, someone to add a little urgency to the proceedings to draw your attention back to that approaching hunger filling the sky."

The look that Suzanne gives me is not nearly as patronizing, though I still feel as though she considers me as little more than a dog that has just learned to fetch.

"We know it's there. Its presence is undeniable and we are doing something about it," Suzanne says. "You have to believe me."

"I really wish I could."

Suzanne nods. "This morning, I will send Faber to you. He will show you our latest work."

"Seven am," I say. "And make sure he isn't late this time."

Suzanne flashes me a vicious smile, and shifts out of there. I stand looking up at the dark. Wal drags free of my arm.

"I really hate how she does that," he sighs. "Keeping me stuck to your arm; it's very rude."

"I don't think she likes you," I say.

"What's not to like, eh? Eh?"

I don't even know where to begin.

The next morning I shift to the office, leaving Lissa to sleep under the protection of my Avian Pomps. Oscar is already there waiting outside my office. He nods at me, lets me pass through the door.

Downstairs someone is dismantling the broom cupboard's door. I can feel it coming undone even from here, and I'm pleased.

It's one place Rillman, or anyone else who might want to lock me away, can't use.

I feel Cerbo's arrival a few minutes later. Oscar knocks on the door.

"Come in," I say.

Oscar swings open the door. "He says you are expecting him."

"Yes, I am."

Cerbo nods at me. Today he's wearing a green bowler that most people could only ever get away with on St. Patrick's Day, and only a certain few of those. He carries it off with a quiet dignity.

He turns to Oscar. "It's quite all right," he says. "I have no intention of killing your boss. Couldn't if I tried."

Oscar lingers at the door a moment longer.

"This isn't Rillman," I say. "He's not going to be able to pull that one on me again."

The door shuts. Cerbo raises an eyebrow at me. "Quite the hired goon."

I let it slide. "Suzanne said you would show me what you know about the Stirrer god?"

Cerbo smiles. "And that is why I am here, Mr. de Selby." He gestures at me. "Now, if you would stand up, and come toward me."

"I was kind of expecting a PowerPoint presentation."

"What I have is much better than any computer-based simulation. Now, up, up! Get your rear out of that chair!" He seems to enjoy shouting at an RM.

I get out of my throne and walk around the desk.

"Hold my hand," Cerbo says reaching out toward me.

I hesitate, and he grimaces. "Oh, for goodness sake. You're not even my type!"

That's not why I'm hesitating, but his words push me hard enough into action.

Cerbo's hand is warm, and he grips mine hard. "This is something new. A technique Suzanne has been developing. It's based on the subset of skills required to shift."

I groan.

Cerbo squeezes my hand. "No, it is not shifting *per se*. For one, it is more... well... cinematic, Mr. de Selby. And two, it demands a little more. You'll see what I mean." He closes his eyes. "Whatever you do, don't let go. This is no pixie-dust journey we're going on, and I'm not Superman."

I'm trying to imagine Superman in a green bowler as Cerbo reaches into his jacket pocket. He pulls out his knife.

I have to fight the reflex to pull away. "What the fuck are you doing with that?"

Cerbo's eyes flick open. He regards me disdainfully. "Don't worry, it's not for you. I've been Ankou for nearly two decades to an RM who is centuries old. You pick up a few things, but I have yet to uncover a really easy way to kill an RM without first killing their Pomps. Even Morrigan couldn't do that. This knife is for me." He takes a deep breath, grits his teeth, and then runs the blade over the back of the hand holding mine. Blood flows quickly. "Remember, don't let go."

Between heartbeats, this happens: we are in the office, and then it is just a space distant beyond my imagining below us. We're vast and tiny at once, and shooting along a tunnel brighter than any glaring sun. I have to cover my eyes. Cerbo squeezes my hand even tighter. For a moment I am reminded of the All-Death's implacable grip.

Then we're in a space I've only seen once before. I remember it a little differently but at the time I was fighting to save Tim and Lissa's lives. First I am surprised by my weightlessness here. The only force binding me, giving me any sense of up or down, is Cerbo's hand. We're quite close, our hands by our hips, gripping each other as children do. Awkwardly and tight.

"Welcome to the ether. The void beyond the Deepest Dark, where the souls find flight and through which the Stirrer god approaches."

"Cool," I say.

"Indeed."

We're not flying so much as being propelled, and the source of that force is generated by Cerbo's bleeding fist. Around us souls drift, but we are moving faster than them. Occasionally I have to flick my body to one side to avoid striking one.

"Careful," Cerbo says. "You'll lose your grip."

I strike a soul then. Feel it shatter around my head. It burns, then chills on contact like ice. I swing my head back, and see it re-form behind us. After that, I don't bother avoiding them. It's like traveling on the flat bed of a ute in a snowstorm. I almost start to enjoy myself. The speed of it, the freedom. Is this how souls feel, once they are dead?

I ask Cerbo, and he shrugs.

"We cannot go far, just a few steps into the infinite. Blood is no substitute for death. But it is far enough." A great eye gazes down at us, and we race toward it, cold air roaring in my ears.

We're a long time getting close to that eye. But I can't help staring at it, as I've stared at it before, though it was much further distant then, and I was on the ground, not in this weightless place; and granted a vision, not this whistling wind-bound actuality.

"It sees us, doesn't it?" I ask, having to shout above the gale.

"I think so," Cerbo says. "But we are nothing to it. I've done this a dozen times over the past three months, and every time I am much faster getting here."

"Three months?"

"That's when we first noticed it. Well, Suzanne did. A change in the ether, a sudden rise in Stirrer activity."

"Do you think Morrigan knew about this?"

"Well, he was dealing with Stirrers. He may have known about it for some time. Or maybe it was just a coincidence that he started his Schism when he did. Do you believe in coincidence, Mr. de Selby?" Cerbo jabs his free hand toward it. "It's impressive. Very godlike, wouldn't you say?"

Darkness bunches around the mass, part storm cloud, part slug. To one side souls coruscate, and seek to flee its bulk, but even as we watch, a black tentacle extrudes from it, snaps out and drags some of those souls back into its side. A thousand, two thousand, perhaps. Screams ring through my head.

"Already it is wreaking untold damage," Cerbo says. "And the closer it gets, the harder it is for souls to escape. God knows what this is doing to the psychic balance of the universe."

We swing past the great eye. "Remember, here it is just psychic mass. When it strikes the Underworld, and through it, earth, that mass will manifest."

"How?"

"We don't know but—I'm sorry, but I think we better get out of here." Cerbo's eyes are wide. I swing my head in the direction of his gaze; feel my heart catch.

A tentacle rushes toward us. As it draws nearer I can see fringes of what look like blades. They ripple and flex. That merest filament of that limb would cut us to pieces. The ether has suddenly lost its appeal. What the hell is wrong with PowerPoint?

"Hold on," Cerbo says. "Hold on."

He pulls out his knife, brings it back down against his hand and we're suddenly reversing, flipping back, moving away, faster and faster.

And then my grip loosens. Or Cerbo releases his.

I'm left, spinning. Losing speed. Floating in that dark, Cerbo already a diminishing shape in front of me.

17

Here I am, alone in the darkness, about to be sliced into pieces or snatched into the maw of the enemy. The limb of the Stirrer god belts down toward me through the ether. It's so big I really can't comprehend it. I'm less than an ant to it, but the god will have me nonetheless. I feel Wal tear free of my arm. He scrambles out from my sleeve, takes one look at where we are, at what's coming, and shoots back under my shirt.

I try and shift. Nothing. Here I don't seem to have any purchase on reality. There's nothing to shift from. This isn't my normal state. It is neither the Underworld nor the land of the living. Desperate, I try again. I've virtually stopped moving. I'm just spinning a slow circle. *Fuck.*

Where's Cerbo? Surely he'll come back for me.

But would I, if that thing was approaching?

I imagine him telling Suzanne, "He was the one who let go, the fool. He deserved it."

Maybe this was their plan after all. If that's the case it's worked. I'm a dead man.

Ah, but I've been dead before. A calm, pricked with some sort of madness, envelops me. I grin, a wide and mocking grin. *Fuck it all.* That rage and joy which fills my dreams flares up and out. I'm not afraid of death, I *am* Death. No matter that this space beyond space is not my realm.

I reach into my jacket, my hand steady, calm as though this was any stir. My fingers close around my knife—the knife every Pomp has, to draw blood to stall a stir. The thing approaching is a Stirrer god. And I know how to deal with Stirrers. I slash my knife down hard, deeper than usual. Blood boils from my skin, arcs around me. The potent blood of an RM. And suddenly I'm bound in light, a ball of it. Purer and brighter than any star.

The tentacle flinches for a moment. Pauses. I see it illuminated in that hard blood-forged light. The blades are motionless, though each seems to pulse, and I realize that for all their sharp edges they are more like flagella than anything else. The flesh beneath is not black so much as gray, the color of ash. Beyond it the eye is watching me, and its wide pupil narrows. I can't help myself. I wink.

The universe draws a breath and then I'm racing backward. Smashing through the cold, dark air heading home. But it may not be enough.

The tentacle's pause is momentary.

Whatever I did only stunned the Stirrer god, or surprised it; less than a flea bite. I can hear the god giving chase, a great whistling roar, louder than the wind, and above that noise the scraping of its knife fringes sounds remarkably like the groaning limbs of the One Tree.

It's gaining. It's gaining.

Its shadow descends over me like a wave, but a sword-gnashing wave, all cutting edges and hunger. I cringe, fold my hands over my neck.

I drop into my office. Hit the floor hard, knocking the breath from me, and almost slamming into Cerbo, which wouldn't have been such a bad thing, I'm thinking. My breath comes quick and, with it, rage. Cerbo's on his arse pale and panting, he slides away from me, gripping his green bowler absurdly in both hands. The whole building shakes as something strikes us above. Whether it's metaphysical or not, it hits hard. I throw my arms over my head, but the ceiling holds.

"You let go," Cerbo says, looking at me eyes wide with fear or guilt, or both.

"And you couldn't come back and get me?" I'm on my feet in an instant. I grab him and shake. I'm pumped. My heart is pounding, I barely realize that I'm lifting him off the ground.

"I didn't have time," Cerbo squeaks.

"Didn't have time?" I shout.

Oscar swings open the door. Tim's with him.

"What was that?" Tim demands. They both stop, staring at me shaking Cerbo.

I put Cerbo down. I straighten my jacket and run my fingers through my hair. "Stirrer god, I think."

Cerbo nods. "That's never happened before." He looks at Tim, then Oscar. "It's all right. It nearly had us, but it can't. Not here, not yet. A finger tap is not an invasion. Now, if you would excuse us, Tim and Mr. Goon, there are some things I need to discuss with your boss."

"Yeah," I say. "Some things... Tim, I've just discovered something you should be able to do. It will be bloody, of course, and you really wouldn't want to do it. But—" I glance over at Cerbo. "Jesus, what other things should Tim be able to do? I want you to teach him. I need him to know this shit."

Cerbo dips his head. "It would be useful. You are working at a disadvantage."

"You got time to talk to this bloke?" I ask Tim. Cerbo is giving him another pained look.

"Yeah, I'll make time." I peer at Tim, he looks a bit under the weather. Maybe he didn't stop drinking after the party.

"Great, I'll send him through when we're done."

Once Oscar and Tim are gone I gesture to an office chair.

"I really am sorry," Cerbo says, sitting down. "No matter what you may think, it was not my intention to put you in danger. The Stirrer god recognized you. It certainly reacted."

"Wonderful. I've got enough enemies without a bloody god gunning for me."

"Too late for that," Cerbo says, straightening his hat.

"It's very close now, isn't it? How long do we have?"

"Best estimate? Twelve months."

"And worst?"

"Well, it just knocked on the door, didn't it?" he replies, gesturing above us.

I look up at the ceiling, at the space that I suppose I dropped through. There's a tiny black smudge there.

"So how do we stop it?"

Cerbo looks at me. "Believe me, that's what we're working on. I just don't know."

I glance at my bleeding hand. The wound is beginning to close but not as fast or as painlessly as I would like. "But it's going to involve blood, isn't it? And lots of it."

"What doesn't in our line of business, Mr. de Selby? You tell me."

"I want you out there. Teaching Tim what he needs to know. Show him what you did. Show him how to shift. But please, don't do anything that's going to kill him."

And then, with a brief dip of his head, he leaves the room. I'm alone.

I snatch up the black phone.

"We need to talk. And now!"

"The markets," Mr. D says, and is gone before I can protest. All I can do is fume into the silence of the handset.

The markets are crowded and run along the southern bank of the River Styx, its black water flowing languidly toward the rolling sea.

The crowds that gather here and buy the produce are silent in the main. It is an eerie thing, that silent shopping. There's not a hint of haggling, no spruiking, no musicians or other street performers, though a flute is playing distantly and atonally. This is a mere shadow of a living market. A memory. The tents shift, the goods within change—kangaroo hide one moment, spinning tops or fruit the next—echoing centuries of commerce. Money is exchanged, and it is various—old coins and paper; plastic, too. I can hear the click-clack of an old credit card machine.

Here, where there are so many dead, the red of the sky mingles with the blue glow of the dead's flesh. And far above us, a single branch of the One Tree reaches out across the river and the city. I can just make out the shapes of tiny figures up there, finding a place to rest, and a final passage to the Deepest Dark.

"What do you think of these oranges? Too soft?" Mr. D asks.

"You're really an extremely frustrating man." I lean in toward him, and it's all I can do to stop myself from jabbing him in the chest.

Mr. D grimaces. For a moment his face is almost as full of motion as the days when he was RM. He may have demanded we meet in the markets of the Underworld but I did not come here to look at oranges, silver jewelry, brewing ash or Troll Doll pencil erasers. Wal's not talking to me after my flight from the Stirrer god. He's fluttering around a nearby stall throwing me dirty looks and eating a dagwood dog. There's tomato sauce bearding his chin.

"How much did you know about the Stirrer god before you died?" I ask Mr. D.

"Very little, believe me. I was out of the loop."

"But you knew it was coming?"

"Only that something was coming, and then Morrigan's little Schism distracted me."

"Well, I've seen it up close, and let me tell you it terrified me."

"There was a guy called Lovecraft. Wrote horror stories."

"Yeah, I know who he was. What about him?" I say, irritated at this turn in the conversation.

"Well, with Lovecraft, sure, he was a horrible racist, but he got something right. Sometimes terror is the only response."

"Terror. OK, so what about Rillman?"

"Rillman really was a surprise to me. I thought him long gone." Mr. D squeezes an orange speculatively. "I do like a good orange. Oh! Now it's gone and changed into a pear!"

"Enough about the—"

Then I catch something out of the corner of my eye. A movement not quite right, a little too energetic, just a little too alive. There's a man, standing by a nearby stall, who isn't dead.

His arms don't glow with the blue light that every soul emits in Hell. Nothing living, not as we define it, should be here. I watch him, and try to act like I'm not watching him. His shoulders are broad, and he's wearing a beaked plague mask and a wide-brimmed black hat. Is this the same guy who cut the window-cleaning assassin's rope? He moves to another stall, beak bobbing up and down like a toy drinking bird, as he inspects with far too much interest what appears to be a collection of old *Archie* comics. I can just make out Jughead's face and crown.

"Do you see that?" I ask Mr. D.

"See what?" He shrugs, putting down the pear.

I'm getting the sort of vibe that if I make any movement toward our *Archie*-perusing beaked mate, he'll leg it. "If you can't see him, don't worry." Though how you can miss a non-glowing man in Hell wearing a plague mask is beyond me—even in the markets. The fellow really is going to look peculiar anywhere outside of Black-Death period dramas or fancy-dress parties.

"Well, you're worrying me now," Mr. D says, and looks ready to turn around. I slap a hand onto his shoulder.

"No need for that," I say. "You're not the target. Besides, how would they kill you? You're already dead."

"There are ways and means, believe me."

Hmm, maybe I need to know some of them.

"Don't you get any ideas," Mr. D snaps. "What's he doing now?"

"Anything but looking in our direction," I say.

Then he's gone. I refuse to let that stop me. There is some muddy sort of swirl where he was, a sort of crazy wake–black hole combo. I look from Mr. D then back to that murky mass. It's shrinking, and fast.

I know I'm going to regret this. I sprint at the swirling, what I guess—hope—to be a gateway and dive into it.

Silence. Icy fingers clutch my heart and squeeze—my left arm throbs. It's a real effort not to yell with the sick, deep pain of it.

Then I come out of the dark, skidding on my belly, feeling oddly refreshed. I spring to my feet, my fists clenched.

I'm still in the Underworld. Mount Coot-tha rears up beyond the river. The One Tree creaks, casting its great shadow over everything. I recognize this place! I can see the old gas stripping tower—the structure that was in part responsible for me becoming what I am. I remember the agony of the summoning ceremony I performed in its living-world clone to enter Hell and call a trapped Mr. D to me. How did I ever endure that? I just did, I guess, I had no time to react or think it through. Maybe I could again, but knowing what to expect, I doubt it. How the hell does Rillman manage it time and time again? Who's helping him?

The masked man stands by the tower, waiting for me, shifting his balance from foot to foot.

I stride toward him. "You!" My hands are balled up at my sides. I'm bigger, meaner, faster. I'm an RM. This is my territory. I loom over him. Finally, I'll get some answers! A grin goes rictal across my face. "No point in running."

"You're right," he says, in a voice I can't quite place, dancing to my left and around me.

And then I'm on my arse, blinking. My nose is bleeding, my head throbs. I have the far-too-fucking-familiar taste of my own blood in my mouth. Whirring wings flash just outside of my line of vision.

"You all right?" Wal shouts, his voice thick as treacle in my ears. I blink; he's blurry and indistinct. And still holding onto the dagwood dog.

"The prick sucker-punched me!" I say.

Wal grins. "Well, you have to be a sucker first."

Thanks. Yeah, another comment from the poster boy of my fan club. "Do you always have to be like this?"

"What are you saying? When was I any different? Grow a sense of humor."

I have to admit that he does look concerned. You don't often see an RM stunned and bleeding in their region. It's not particularly good for my ego, especially as this is the second time in two days. At least no one else has seen me this time. "He seemed to know what he was doing," I say, as Wal flies around me, searching for any other injuries.

"No shit." He lands heavily on my shoulder and I get a spatter of tomato sauce down my shirt front.

"Have you ever seen him before?"

"I don't have X-ray vision."

I sigh. "Just what help are you?"

"I'm here, aren't I? Even with a god driving down on us in the dark of the ether, something I'd rather not experience again, by the way—I'm here. And you know I always will be, you whiny bastard. We're stuck together, and I've got your back."

"Yeah, look, I'm sorry." I struggle to my feet. Wal flies from one shoulder to the other. The movement makes my head spin. "I've got work to do."

"Be careful," Wal says. "I can't look after you up there."

"I'll do my best."

"That's what I'm worried about."

18

Tim's on the phone shouting at somebody. He hangs up when I slide a chair next to his desk. I look at the dark rings under his red eyes.

"You really look like you had a big night last night," I say.

"And you look like you've just been punched in the nose again," he shoots back.

I touch my hand to my face. Yep, blood. "Just spent the morning chasing someone through the Underworld. Turns out I should have ducked when I caught up with them."

Tim passes me a box of tissues. "Who do you think it was?"

"Not Rillman, at least. It felt too different from him. An Ankou, I think, but I couldn't get a good enough fix on them. At least they didn't stab me. There's something almost honorable about a good old punch to the face." I apply tissues. "Talking of Ankous..."

"Cerbo's lesson was instructive."

"Do you think you could shift?"

"Give me three weeks, and I'll be shifting everywhere. Right now, the thought of doing it again makes me want to throw up. Steve, sorry I ever doubted you."

"This situation with Rillman is out of control, Tim. What the hell are we supposed to do?"

Tim shuffles his papers, lifts his eyes to mine. "We keep going. There's nothing else we can do. We keep going carefully and cautiously, and we do not stop. Whoever Rillman is, and whoever he's working for, they can get to us anytime they want. They've already proven it. And if Rillman can shift then there's nowhere that's safe. We just have to keep going, until either we stop him, or he stops us."

My mind turns to things that we may have some control over. "How are you going with those Closers?"

Tim frowns. "I can't find out anything. People are being very tight-lipped at the Department—and I mean *very.*" He sighs. "I can't remember the last time I came to work with a hangover. I got three of them drunk last night, after the Christmas party, and nothing. Not a bloody peep. But this is my best guess." He hands me a small sheaf of papers. "These are based on my suggestions, when I was running that portfolio."

He looks at his watch. "We've a job interview at 11:30. You'll need to be there, since we're using your office and all."

"Really? This morning's been busy enough as it is!"

"Who is it?"

"Clare Ramage. She looks good, on paper anyway. Lissa found her. I'm surprised she didn't mention anything, but, then, the week we've been having, eh? We won't know for sure until we can get her into your office, see how she handles the Underworld."

"What do you think?" The office is just a formality, both Lissa and Tim can usually tell beforehand.

"I think she'll be fine."

"OK I'll see you at 11:30. And I'll read this, right now. That's a promise."

"Make sure you keep it. None of that slipping a bookmark through it bullshit," Tim says, and maybe I shouldn't grin at him. Shit, we're so good at pushing each other's buttons we don't even need to try most of the time. Tim groans. "Now, get out of here. And be careful who you let into your room, unless you don't intend reading that, because if that's the case, buddy, I might just have to torture you myself."

He sits there, glaring at me. I stare back sheepishly.

"I'm on it," I say. "Really."

Tim just harrumphs under his breath. "Close the door on your way out."

I walk back through to my office, stopping at the kitchen to make some coffee and feeling all those eyes watching me. Maybe I *was* a little too hard on everyone last night, or maybe it's that my nose hasn't quite stopped bleeding yet. I drop Tim's notes onto the desk: they land with a satisfying and vaguely threatening thump.

After ten pages I'm glad Tim's working on my side.

The first page outlines possible threats to Australia's population should Mortmax fail. Regional Apocalypse is at the top of it. There's a half-dozen end-of-world scenarios—some of which I wasn't even aware were a possibility—and how Mortmax might be involved in them.

It's a pretty damning, but I must admit, honest appraisal. And I can see why Tim may have been pushing for closer government ties to Mortmax, and just why he might have been so resistant to the family business.

And now, since we came so close to a Regional Apocalypse, and streets were crowded with Stirrers, I know why they might just rush through an organization like the Closers.

I'm twenty pages in when the phone rings.

It's Neill. "I heard you had some trouble yesterday," he says.

"Yeah, I suppose you could call it trouble." I find it hard to keep the suspicion out of my voice.

"Death Moots create a certain . . . well . . . chaotic energy, but this is the first time this has happened. Are you sure there's no one trying to challenge you?"

"No one's killed a Pomp yet," I say. "There's just been attempts on me."

"You sure it's not that cousin of yours?" Neill asks. "It's usually the fookin' Ankous that are the problem."

"Not my cousin, I'm sure of that." I try a different tack. "Do you have a government liaison?" There's silence down the line for a moment.

"Yes, it's only something very new. I never thought we needed it before, but they were quite persuasive."

"Define persuasive. Insistent? Or coercive?"

"Well, it's certainly made stopping Stirrers much easier," Neill says. I'm putting my money on the latter.

"We've a group here called the Closers."

"What are they?"

"Police, but a unit devoted to us. You have anything like that there?"

"Not that I know of. Just a unit that keeps a closer eye on our paperwork, our visits to morgues and funerals, that sort of thing. But liaison or no, our communications with the government are a little limited. You could say that we both have secrets that the other may not like. Why do you have such a unit there?"

"The Regional Apocalypse. I think it worried them. I can't blame them, of course. It worried me."

"Times are changing," Neill says, and there's more than a hint of bitterness in his voice.

"Yeah, they're changing, all right."

I put a few more calls through, speaking as directly as I can to the various RMs. All of them seem to have something of a government presence, several when their territories cover more than one country—some have as many as twenty.

For most of them, this is something new. And for the ones that it isn't they've noticed an increased scrutiny. But that's not the only thing. Their lack of concern about the issue is disturbing. Something doesn't feel right. This is definitely going on the agenda at the Death Moot.

Talk doesn't stick to the government departments, though. Every single one of them is pitching an alliance at me, or at the very least a mutual back-scratching sort of set-up. I'm noncommittal.

I haven't hung up from the last call for more than a few heartbeats when the phone rings again.

Alex.

"Steve, I can't talk for long," he says, his voice low. "You're going to get a call soon. From Solstice. They've found the body of the man who tried to shoot you. Well, we think it is."

"Where?"

"Look, when I say they've found the body, I mean *we* did; but they've taken it away."

"Did you get much of a look? Did it fit my description?"

"No, I didn't get a look in. The Closers were already there when I arrived." Alex's voice lowers to a whisper. "I really don't like that crew. There's something... off about them."

"Tim hasn't been able to find out anything about them, either."

"Yeah, no agency is that secret. There's always someone who knows something, and is willing to talk. Usually, when there isn't, you have to wonder." There's a quiet murmuring in the background. Alex raises his voice. "Look, I've got to go. But I will talk to you soon." He hangs up abruptly.

There's another call. I don't recognize the number.

"Yes?" I say.

"Nothing to worry about, it's just Solstice."

"What can I do for you, Detective?"

"Nothing, really, it's more what I can do for you. I thought I might send some fellas over to keep an eye on your house."

"My house, or me? Am I a suspect in my own shooting, Mr. Solstice?"

Solstice clears his throat. "Of course not, but then again... stranger things, Mr. de Selby, stranger things. It wasn't your body that they picked up at Toowong Cemetery with injuries that suggest a great fall."

Toowong Cemetery sits on Mount Coot-tha, or One Tree Hill, as we know it. One of the many points close to the Underworld, it made sense that my attacker would have used it. Why hadn't I thought of that?

"Have you identified the body?"

"Well, that's just it. There's not a lot to identify, but what we have suggests that this person was a Pomp. I'd like you to take a look at him, so there—I suppose there is something you can do for me."

"Where are you?"

He tells me. It's an address, just off Milton Road, in the inner city. That's peculiar. It's not the usual morgue (or as the government likes to call it, Forensic and Scientific Services) out on Kessels Road to the south of Brisbane. This has gone wide of the usual coronial pathways. I didn't even know there was a morgue there. I'll have to check this with Tim. I don't like the idea of dead bodies being stored where we can't get at them. It throws me, to be honest.

But I want to see that body. I shift.

It's like any morgue I've ever seen, though it smells of new paint and disinfectants. It's cold, tiled halfway up the walls. A body obscured in black plastic lies on a stainless steel table, and there's the familiar, thin smell of death that can't quite be removed, no matter how many cleaning agents you use. Could be worse, Dad had some absolute horror stories about morgues in the fifties, little more than corrugated iron sheds—things started smelling pretty high in there come late spring. And the flies... No flies here, at least.

Traffic rumbles somewhere in the distance—Milton Road, I guess—though here it's quiet but for the murmur of refrigeration units, and the chirruping of a computer with what I imagine is some sort of email notification. Someone's getting a lot of emails.

Solstice looks pale beneath his tan. Even the dragon tattoo on his forearm has lost its luster. I won't go so far as to say that he looks sick, but it's close. I sometimes forget that not everybody deals with death as often as me.

"When did you start using this place?"

Solstice smiles. "That's classified. But it's new. Not even the coroner knows about this one."

"Do any of my people?"

"No, but we only keep 'persons of interest' here. And you know about it, now."

I don't like it. How could we stop a Stirrer from stirring here? "So where is he?"

Solstice walks to the nearby slab, pulls back the plastic sheeting.

There really isn't much to identify. Everything's there, but it's pulped. Features are warped and flat, and insects, or some other sort of creature, have had a go at digesting bits of what's left. The skin is chewed and tunneled, mined as though it was some sort of resource, and I guess it is. All flesh and bone is.

"Someone had gone to a bit of effort to hide the body. If a maintenance fella hadn't decided to work on the northwest corner of the cemetery he might have sat there for even longer."

I know I'm not getting the full story. I know they snatched this away from the cops, but I try to not let that show on my face.

"There's no license or wallet, obviously, and his fingerprints have come up blank. We're waiting on dental, but I'm not feeling that hopeful. But then there's this." He pulls the plastic sheeting down to the waist.

Interesting.

Along both of his arms and his chest are a series of interlinking brace tattoos, and a couple of other symbols that may have some esoteric potency, or be a load of bullshit. It's always hard to tell but they're certainly the sort of tattoos that a Pomp might have. He even possessed a bit of death iconography on a shoulder blade, a cherub like mine, though his is bigger.

"If he was a Pomp, he certainly didn't belong to me. I can feel it when my Pomps die." It was something I haven't had to experience yet, but no doubt will, soon enough. Every RM does. "He's been too long gone for me to tell if he belongs to anyone else." Could he belong to Suzanne? No, that doesn't make sense.

"Do you trust the other RMs?" Solstice asks.

I snort, can't help myself. "Do you know how RMs actually become RMs, Mr. Solstice?"

Solstice shakes his head. "A certain negotiation," he says. "Something about a tree?"

Which is pretty good. He certainly knows more than I did when I was just a Pomp. I think back to the Negotiation, wondering why something so bloody had such a civil name. After all, two mumbling death-lusting stone blades were involved. "Let me just say the process doesn't even begin to encourage trust. I wouldn't trust those bastards as far as I could throw them. Backstabbers, every one of them. After all, it's the only way you become RM. Back, front and side-stabbing, with a little slashing thrown in as well."

"And what about you?"

"I never wanted this job. And you know, I hold that as a badge of pride."

"Can't make it easy for you . . . lacking that ruthlessness. And yet, here you are, RM."

"I did what I had to."

"I suppose they'd all say that, wouldn't they? Doesn't everyone, who rises to a position of power?"

I glance at my watch. "Are we done? I've got an appointment."

"Yeah, we're done."

"And about those fellas you want to send over. Don't bother, we've got our own people."

"You trust them?"

"Absolutely."

Solstice smiles. "Just turn a blind eye to any cars parked across from your place."

"This is inhouse," I say between gritted teeth.

Solstice shakes his head. "Not when people die, it isn't."

I grin nastily at him. "That's how death works."

19

"Well, would you look at that?" Tim says. "You're early."

Tim's sitting in his office and that's where I've shifted again. "Right place, wrong time. At least your pants are on," I say.

"You don't have a clue what's going on behind this desk." Tim lights a cigarette. "I thought you were reading those briefing notes."

"Funny you should say that. I was interrupted by a call from Solstice." I open Tim's door, and wave across the room at Oscar. He grimaces at me. "Tim, I don't like how the Feds keep poking their noses into our business."

Tim sighs. "Steve, it's all about accountability."

"It sounds like you agree with their approach."

"No. But I understand it." He ashes into a Coke can. "You read my notes?"

"Most of them. But this group doesn't feel like that. I spoke to Alex, too. He says he can't get anything on them. This is Australia. We don't have any covert groups."

"What about us?"

"That's different. We're not so much covert as unacknowledged. We've been around since life began."

Tim walks with me to my office then heads to reception to wait for our possible new recruit.

Oscar's waiting outside my door. There's a certain percentage of rage beneath his professional demeanor.

"Sorry," I say. "Had an interview with the police."

Oscar grimaces, though I think he's coming to terms with me a little. "How hard is it to phone, eh?"

He opens the door to my office. Lissa's sitting in one of the chairs.

I turn to Oscar. "What's this with the security breaches today?" I ask. He grimaces again and shuts the door in my face.

"And don't you have your own office, Ms. Jones?"

"This was the only time I knew I would be able to see you," Lissa says. "There's not much window in either of our schedules... You look a little pale."

"I've been chasing shadows all day, not much chance to get a tan." I drop into the throne. "How is it that everybody knows about Rillman except me? Did you know he's regularly been crossing into the Underworld? Suzanne—"

"What about Suzanne?" Lissa says sharply.

I try not to look guilty. "Mr. D says she's told him that Rillman has been making trouble for years. Just not here. Seems it took my promotion to bring him back to Australia." It's another thing Morrigan has to answer for.

I sense another heartbeat in the building. "We have a visitor," I say. "Clare Ramage?"

"She's good," Lissa says. "One of the best I've found. Even has a bit of family history in the trade."

Oscar knocks on the door, then swings it open, giving me the thumbs-up, and a woman (Clare, I'm guessing) in her early twenties walks into the room. Tim follows her.

I scan her face to see how she copes with this space. She tilts her head. Good, she can already hear the creaking of the One Tree. My mind's not on the interview, though. I'm back at that odd morgue, trying to piece things together. Who was the assassin working for? And when did bodies stop being processed through the usual channels?

I sit through the interview trying to look interested, but it's Lissa who asks most of the questions. I hope I appear affable and bossish enough, and not that distracted. It's over in under an hour. Once Clare's gone, Tim and Lissa talk it through.

"What do you think?" Lissa asks me. I blink at her.

"About what?"

Lissa snorts. "Clare?"

I wave my hand absently at the door. "Miss Ramage was fine. Eminently employable."

Tim's phone beeps. He grimaces. "I've got to take this one."

"Ankou?"

"Nah, the Caterers. Since the ceremony they've been calling me every bloody second hour, because somebody went and left this to the last minute."

I don't know whether to be offended that they're dealing with Tim instead of me. "Yeah, you better." Tim gives Lissa a look that I can't read, and she nods. Oh no, this better not mean another lecture for me.

When Tim's out of the room, Lissa frowns. "You're losing focus again."

"No, I'm not," I mumble. How can I explain that, if anything, I'm more focused than ever before, it's just the picture that's changed. "Take my word for it, I'm not. Clare's got the job, I can make her a Pomp tomorrow. Give her one more day to think about it, and to be normal, eh?"

Lissa nods, tries to pull a smile, fails. I can understand why she's worried about me, but she doesn't need to be. Not about this. "You don't want to give her too long."

"Worried she'll change her mind?"

Lissa gets up, pecks me on the cheek, walks to the door. "Who wouldn't?"

"You, me, Tim."

Lissa laughs. Bad examples, every one of them.

I'm left alone. Lissa was the first person I turned into a Pomp: Lissa. She'd been one before, of course, but when she was resurrected back into her body, I'd had to return her powers. In those dark moments, as the Stirrers surrounded us, there had been an intimacy that was terrifying. We'd looked into each other's soul and found an echo and a challenge of, and to, our own.

I lean back in my throne and my eyes close, just for a moment.

Knives. A swinging scythe. Mist the color of blood.

I jolt awake. Fucking hell! A bloke could cut out his eyelids just to stop these visions.

Something catches my attention. A differently beating heart, a slight change in electricity. Someone has shifted into my city unannounced. And not just anywhere...

Now, that, I can't allow.

I squeeze my eyes tight, take a deep breath to prepare for the unpreparable, and shift myself to Mount Coot-tha. Old One Tree Hill.

Someone's on my turf and they shouldn't be.

20

Mount Coot-tha. Heart of the city of Brisbane, and its Underworld twin. I arrive in the middle of a bunch of tourists. None of them seem that impressed with my swearing, or the way I hop around on one foot. This shift felt like a spear being driven into my thigh. That's something new. I thought I was getting better at it. But it passes quickly, even if I'm red-faced with embarrassment.

"If you've finished your little dance," Suzanne says. "We can start today's lesson. Though take your time, I'm finding this all very amusing."

"What are you doing up here?"

"Testing your abilities, and I must say that you surprised me. I didn't really expect that you would sense me. If I had I would have showed up in, say, Tasmania. You get a gold star."

"I don't like this shifting around, unannounced—it sends a bad message," I say.

Suzanne's good humor slips a little. "It does nothing of the sort. If you can detect me, or any other RM, then they can detect you. They will know that you know they are here."

"No one can sneak up on me?"

"Not quite," Suzanne says. "An electrical storm can shield their presence, but an electrical storm is hard to shift into, and an RM who is in the middle of one tends to be wary."

"And why should an RM be wary of another RM? Aren't we supposed to be all unified?"

Suzanne raises an eyebrow. "Don't be naive. RMs can hurt you more than anyone else, except, perhaps, for this Mr. Rillman. When an RM comes unannounced you be ready. And try and remember if you have crossed anyone."

The Kuta Cafe at the top of Mount Coot-tha is open, and up here, there's a bit of wind, enough to take the edge off the summer heat. The last time I was here I spoke to Morrigan still thinking he was a friend. I know that Suzanne isn't; even "ally" would be too generous a term.

Brisbane stretches itself out around us, a vast carpet of tree-smeared suburbia. The CBD rises up in the east, a tight bunching of skyscrapers around which the Brisbane River wends, leading to Moreton Bay. A series of low, flat mountains marks the western horizon. The air is clear, a typical Brisbane summer's day.

But sometimes I'm seeing and hearing the Underworld simultaneously, a superimposed view of the land of the dead. The ruddy river. The massive root buttresses of the One Tree. The creaking, creaking, creaking as its mighty limbs are moved by the restless winds of Hell. Wal's face shifts on my tattoo. He can almost take form here, and I know he wants to.

"Do you want a coffee?"

Suzanne shakes her head. "Just a quieter place, away from all these tourists." She winces as though she has a headache. "It's too bright here."

"Just about anywhere is quieter in Brisbane than this," I say.

I lead her up to the observation platform. It's just us, now. Maybe our presence has something to do with that. Put two RMs together and there's always a bit of electricity. Though there are some kids running on the lookout below. The air crackles with the buzzing of cicadas, the kids' shouts and the ubiquitous creaking of the One Tree. This is my home.

"Lovely," Suzanne says. "Looking down at it from here I must say what a beautiful and intimate little city you have. But it's not quite the right venue for what I have planned. Are you all right to shift again?"

"Of course I am," I say.

"You're getting better at it at last." There's a glint in Suzanne's eye. "Deepest Dark then," she says.

I follow her there. And I don't throw up.

"So, Faber introduced you to the Stirrer god?"

"Up close and far too personal. It nearly killed me, thank you very much."

"Ours is a dangerous business. And none more so than when facing that god."

"Yeah, particularly when your guide lets go of your hand."

"I assure you that Faber was utterly mortified by what happened. At least you were quick-witted enough to do what had to be done."

"Yes, I was, wasn't I?"

Suzanne laughs. "There's hope for you yet. You needed to see it up close. You needed to feel just what sort of a menace it has become. To understand why this thing terrifies us—all of us—in a way that defies the usual squabbles of the Orcus."

"I had an idea already." When did Suzanne start taking this seriously? Is she playing me? But she's always playing me!

"No, you had no idea. This thing will be beaten, or it will destroy us. Life, and the Orcus. We thirteen have not faced such a threat in lifetimes beyond counting. There is nothing written about such a thing. But there are murmurings. It, or something very much like it, was defeated before. There are things you need to know. You've a rich heritage of which you are barely aware. Starting with the basics. Do you know why pomping hurts?"

"Because it does. It makes sense, there's that whole exchange of energy thing. If we're going to take something out of our universe and put it into another, of course it'll hurt."

Suzanne looks at me, and laughs. "Physics has nothing to do with what we are about, Steven." Suzanne shakes her head. "No. The pain is an additive, something the Orcus constructed through ceremony and hard work, and then entered into the process. Pomping used to be pleasurable, addictive."

"That would have been dangerous."

"You have no idea. Before there were thirteen, pomping was a nightmare. One you perhaps know too well."

My ears prick up at that. Nightmares. She sees it and smiles.

"Yes, we all have them. You've heard of the Hungry Death?"

"Just a few stories, stuff Dad would tell me when I was a kid." But the way Dad had told them, I'd never taken them seriously.

"They're just stories now, but there was a time when they weren't." Her voice slows and grows sonorous and rhythmical. "Long ago, before you and me. Before the world is the shape it is now, or shape it was before, there was only one Death. And it was called the Hungry Death because it was always hungry." She crouches down and trails a finger in the dust of the Deepest Dark. Following her is a dusty wake, now thirteen trails, which then rise and race around her fingers. They coalesce into a form—vaguely human, vaguely Stirrer. She seems to shake her head at the whimsy of it, flicks her hand and the Hungry Death is just falling dust again, but it's broken a little of her rhythm, for a moment she is just the cynical RM again. "If only it was that easy to dismiss. That painting of Mr. D's, the lurid one by the peasant."

" 'The Triumph of Death'?"

"That's the one. Picture that. You got it?" I nod my head. "Now imagine that painting, but there is only Death. And it is everywhere. The Hungry Death was a walking, shifting apocalypse. Random and violent in a...I suppose...more focused way than our world actually is, and I would suggest that you'd agree that ours is a pretty random and violent one."

"What happened to the Hungry Death?"

"You know. Close your eyes, and you know." I do nothing of the sort, just stare at her. She blinks.

"I don't blame you," Suzanne says. "When I tell you there were thirteen warriors who went to battle with it, do you start to get the idea?"

I stare at her, dumbfounded.

She sighs. "OK. Thirteen warriors. They fought the Hungry Death, and what a battle it was, fire and brimstone, storm and earthquake. All of that, real 'Book of Revelations' stuff. They fought it. And they defeated it. Six times. And each time it came back. They cut it into pieces. And it came back. They ground its marrow to dust and it came back. They even ground its marrow to dust and turned it into some sort of paste, and yet it did no good.

"Finally a seventh, desperate battle. And this time, the earth a wasteland about them, the world a wound and the dying everywhere, they had begun to question why they had even tried fighting it in the first place. They held that Hungry Death down and this time they devoured it. Thirteen warriors, and each of them absorbed one-thirteenth of the Hungry Death's essence. And it has stayed that way through time.

"You see, it was never truly vanquished. Death cannot be. The Hungry Death lives on in each of the Orcus. It is our power, and the thing which each of us fear. That is what you dream about, Steven. Death untrammeled, blood and knives and the scythe. We all dream these dreams. It is why we don't need to sleep—its power sustains us—and why we don't want to."

I blink. "So I somehow ingested a thirteenth of the Hungry Death?"

"Absorbed is perhaps the better term. The Negotiation, why do you think it is so brutal? To become an RM you must appease the Hungry Death, blood must flow, and it is the only way to draw it out of a previous RM. And once it's within you . . . Surely you have felt it there? Not just in the dreams. Don't you sometimes feel its delight in death and destruction? It's the Hungry Death that makes it easier for you to deal with the things that you must see and do. And through you, it makes it easier on your Pomps."

"So what's the All-Death? It spoke to me, and not just in a dream."

"It's an aspect of the Hungry Death, too. We use it, of course, to generate the schedule, because it exists outside of time. Through it we know who is to die and when. It knows so much, and bereft of the Hungry Death, it is relatively benign."

"It didn't feel benign when it grabbed me."

"I said relatively. It remains a part of the Hungry Death."

"So what was it, this thing in me before it became the Hungry Death?"

"Something like the Stirrer god, perhaps. We don't know. This all happened a very long time ago. Generations before even the oldest RM, before even the invention of writing."

"And all it wants is death?"

"Yes, but not in the way that the Stirrers do. Which makes me believe it really isn't like them. You must be able to feel it, the pure joy it takes in death. Stirrers wish an end to life, this needs life to sustain it. I know you feel it."

Yes, I do. Why wasn't I told about this earlier? Mr. D with his all-in-good-time. My dreams have been such a horrible space, not least because of the pleasure I find in them.

"To think of such a cruel thing in here," I tap my chest.

Suzanne pulls my hand away. "You mustn't think that. It isn't cruel, merely inventive. Couple that with a clever and cruel creature like *Homo sapiens* and you have all sorts of madness, all sorts of ways of killing." Suzanne's eyes gleam. "It is better that it exists inside us, spread across the world, and that it is only fed every few generations in a Schism and a Negotiation. Think of the ruthlessness that we forestall with our existence. Our world, our myriad of societies, exist merely because we have given people time. We have given them the space to live longer, to develop culture and technology. Death remains, as does genocide and madness, but it is not all encompassing."

I remember my Negotiation. The Orcus gathered around Morrigan and me in a circle, the hunger in their eyes. I now know where most of that came from. Come the next Negotiation will I look that way, too?

"So I rule the land and the sea around Australia as Death, because once there were warriors and they killed Death itself."

"No, you cannot kill Death, only shape its form. And no, you do not rule the sea."

"*Why* hasn't Mr. D explained this? Gaps, gaps! I've got so many bloody gaps in my knowledge. What does, then?"

"Water, and the force within it. We've made our agreements with that force to cross the seas. But we have no power there. It does with those souls who die within its substance what it will. I hope that you'll never have to deal with it. Water is a cruel negotiator." Suzanne shivers. "And that is your lesson for today. The Stirrer god is powerful. But there is a power within us, too. The secret is to use that power without destroying everything those first warriors fought for."

"And how do we do that?"

"I have a plan." Suzanne puts a finger against my lips. "But that is for another time."

I'm still thinking about plans, and Deaths of the sea, when I shift back to my office. Right on target. Tim obviously senses my return because he gives a ragged cheer from his office.

There's a message on my phone. Lissa.

"Call me, babe, when you get the chance."

I dial her number. She answers before the first ring.

"That was quick," I say.

"I was just about to call you again. Where have you been?"

I mumble something about Death Moot prep, feel a pang of guilt. If only she knew. Maybe I should just tell her about the deal with Suzanne now.

"Steven, we may have a problem. Actually there's no may about it."

"What is it?"

"Stirrers. Something new. I suppose you could call it a nest of them. I need you to come here."

"A nest? Why the hell can't we feel them?"

She gives me an address in Woolloongabba. It's a couple of suburbs south of the city. About ten minutes' drive away if the traffic isn't too bad.

I look at the schedule. There's no one spare. Besides Lissa and I should be able to handle them. I hesitate to shift there. If I can sense a shift they may be able to as well.

Oscar's standing outside my office door. I open it and he looks at me. "Going to need your help—and Travis's."

"Not a problem."

"How fast can you drive that Hummer of yours?"

Oscar gives me one of the biggest, maddest grins I have ever seen.

21

I don't expect to see Alex, but he's there with Lissa. Both of them look pretty grim.

There's no small talk. Lissa leads us up onto a flat rooftop above Vulture Street, a major tributary to the M1, the motorway that feeds into and out of the city. The traffic is building rapidly.

The Stirrers below us move with a confidence that only comes from inhabiting a body for weeks. They're sitting on the front verandah of the house, drinking what look like stubbies of beer. The house could be like any other in the suburb, or Brisbane, for that matter. It's a classic Queenslander, verandahs all around, tin roof. Very much like my parents' place. But this one has known better days; the paint's peeling so badly that we can see it from here. There's a pile of rubbish in the backyard, but that's common enough. The only odd thing about it is the roof—it's crammed with aerials, peculiar prickly bunches of them. What the hell do they need those for?

We're across the river from the city center. I can feel Number Four, and just down the road is the Gabba cricket stadium. It offends me that this is happening so close to where we are based, and even more that it's almost next door to one of the greatest cricket pitches in the world. How could Stirrers have grown so brazen? But I guess if I had a god hurtling through the ether toward earth, I'd be brazen, too, and perhaps pressured to perform. To make good, and ensure that my god was pleased.

What worries me more is that I can't taste them in the air. There's nothing. If anything, the space they occupy is too neutral. It's neither living nor dead. Are those aerials responsible for that?

The air is still and humid. Sweat sheens Lissa's forehead. Oscar and Travis are feeling it, too.

"What is this?" I ask. "The aerials. The house being so near the heart of the city. Why?"

"Yeah, I've never seen anything like it," Lissa says. "And we still wouldn't have, except for Alex."

"Alex?" I look over at him. "You found this?"

"Yeah," he says. "I tried to get in touch with you. When I couldn't, I called Lissa. Should have known she'd be able to get onto you."

"I've been a little busy today. Sorry," I say, guilt pangy and all.

Alex nods; looks like we've all been busy. "I've been looking into the Closers and this address came up several times. Something about a safe house, or being locked into the grid. I came and had a look, didn't get too close. You can tell why."

"How'd you come by the information?"

"Slightly illegally," Alex mumbles, not quite able to meet my eye. It's not the way he likes to work at all. "Been digging around emails in the Closers' server."

"Seems he has quite a knack for the cyber-espionage," Lissa says approvingly.

"Yes, well." He blushes. "That's just between you and me. I really shouldn't be here, but I want to see this done properly." Alex is about as straitlaced as they come. For him to do any digging would have been painful indeed.

"You did good." I paint a brace symbol on Oscar's wrist, Travis is already done: the paint is simply red acrylic mixed with my blood. The brace symbol is a potent guard against our "problem." It used to be, at any rate. "You have to wonder how long this has been going on." I nod at Stirrer House down below. The implications are somewhat frightening to consider. How many other Stirrer houses are there out in the 'burbs and country towns? Places where we don't keep as much of a presence?

Lissa grimaces. "A while, at best guess. I'd say three weeks, maybe four."

Solstice knew about this and he didn't tell us. Just what game is he playing? I'm going to have to give that bastard a call. Looks like the war may be building up again.

"That Stirrer god of yours is getting closer, isn't it?" Alex says.

"It's always drawing closer, but distance is a weird thing, in the Deepest Dark." If only he could see it as up close as I have.

I look around at the assembled group. "Oscar, Travis: you two call this through if we have a problem. I don't expect one, but then again, I didn't expect to come across a Stirrer safe house in the middle of Brisbane. Alex—do you want to come down with us?" I tap the brace paint. Alex nods grimly and submits to being painted.

Oscar and Travis don't look happy, but they're not going to be any good to us down there. In fact they could be a liability, even with the brace paint.

"So, how are we going to do this?" Lissa asks.

"Frontal assault will work best," I say.

"Do you want to wait for some backup?"

"Don't be silly, we've handled worse. And besides, this needs a subtle touch, I think."

"You think you can manage that?" Alex snorts, trying to tough it out. He's seen me battle hundreds of Stirrers on George Street, even saved my life with a few well-placed shots himself. But this is different.

"Do you think *you* can? We were having this sort of fun when we were five," I say, giving Lissa a bit of a hug.

Alex grimaces. "You weren't the only ones with Pomp parents. I know what I'm doing."

There are two dozen sparrows gathered around me, pecking and hopping, looking innocent as all hell. You wouldn't know that they've all pecked my hand and supped a bit on my blood. Two blocks away wait eight crows. The heavy guns don't require my blood; they're less traditional than the sparrows on that front.

When I'd first become RM I'd managed to stall several hundred Stirrers in one go, but that had just been a flare-up of my new powers—apparently that's the way it works. Since then, in the few times I'd done this, I'd returned to the original method, blood and touch. Keeps me honest, I suppose.

A sparrow jumps on my finger and chirps at me impatiently. I feel like I should be singing some sort of Disneyesque musical number.

Lissa runs her blade down her hand. It's a swift, sharp movement, and then she kisses me on the cheek.

"Be careful," I say.

"You too."

"Let's go."

We split up: approach the house from opposite sides. Half my sparrows shoot around the back, the rest follow me, a mad battering of tiny wings. Alex isn't far behind them, his gun out. I signal for him to approach the back door. He nods. He'll be safer out there, I hope.

I'm almost at the house when the first Stirrer sees me. He drops his beer. I leap over the fence, catch my foot, nearly fall flat on my face. Lissa is already past me. She swings a hand at the Stirrer. He catches it. The bastard's wearing gloves. Lissa swings around with her other hand, slaps a bloody handprint against his head.

I'm on top of the other one now. Its being scrambles and scrapes through me, and into the Deepest Dark. The body's just a body again.

The front door's unlocked. I go in first, cautious but quick.

Lissa's behind me. Every time I blink, I catch a glimpse of what my sparrows can see. Nothing has tried to use the back door yet. Alex is waiting there, gun at the ready, not that it would do much good. My crows are tearing through the air toward the building, their cries and caws growing louder with every wing beat.

I'm through to the living room, and gagging with the stench of rotten flesh. It's the first time in a while that it isn't alcohol or shift induced. And I can't quite believe what I see: two twitching bodies, tied to the ceiling, flies coating their flesh. Maggots carpet the floor beneath, a squelching, writhing mass. The spaces of the Stirrers' skin not fly-coated or maggot-bubbling are marked with symbols I don't recognize, but which none the less drive icy nails of dread through me. It doesn't stop there, though, there's something not right with the geometry of these ceilings, the way their corners meet—or don't—something that baffles my vision like the seeds of a migraine. I can smell stale smoke, too. The ceiling above, near the edges of its warped geometry, is black with scorch marks.

The bodies jerk and spasm. Eyes flick open. Lips curl with the most cunning of smiles. "You'll all be screaming by the end," their mouths, bearded with flies, whisper simultaneously. "It's coming."

The air is charged with a wild electricity. All over my body, hairs lift. My mobile phone crackles in my pocket. In the far corner of the room, a webwork of electricity sighs and hisses in the air. A living, shivering net. It slides toward me; maggots pop and bubble on the floor beneath it. My first instinct is to run. Instead, I slap the nearest body hard. The Stirrer's soul passes through me like a ball of barbed wire. And the electricity fizzles out, as though I've broken the circuit.

The second Stirrer snaps at my hand, ducks my strike, and somehow manages to scuttle across the ceiling. The length of the ropes that bind it limits the creature's movement. It blows me a kiss. "She'll be dead, they all will, and you'll know what's coming. And you won't care," it hisses. It starts to chew on the ropes. But we both know it doesn't stand a chance.

I swing a bloody fist at its face, and it's just a body again. It's another rough stall, though. I drop to a crouch with the pain of it. They have been in these bodies for weeks. Their souls have grown thorns and tangles. My sparrows are hard at work, too. Their pomps are quick on the tail of mine.

Lissa stumbles into the living room. She looks exhausted. "Now, I stayed in some dives back in my uni days, but none as bad as this. Even when I ignored the cleaning roster." She nods at the bodies. "There's a Stirrer in every room."

"You got them all?"

"The ones that your sparrows didn't get to before me."

"What the fuck is going on here?" I do my best to ignore the flashes of my Avian Pomps devouring the corpses, tugging out beakfuls of flesh.

"Something ceremonial," Lissa says, distracting me from their feast. "Maybe the Stirrers were trying to create a life-unlife interface."

"Ah, one of those." I can almost hide the sarcasm in my voice and the annoyance at another gap in my knowledge.

Lissa shakes her head, as she binds her palm. "You haven't got a clue what I'm talking about."

I kiss her forehead. I'm just happy that she's all right. "Not really. Hey, at least I'm being honest."

She submits to the kiss. There's a line of blood across her cheek. I brush it away as best as I can, but really just turn it into a smudge.

"I know. Look, Steve," she says, "I've been doing some research. If we weren't so distracted, so damn busy, I'd have told you by now. A life-unlife interface would draw the living to Hell, and the unliving here. Sort of like a door, more like a carousel, and the more Stirrers there are the faster it'd spin."

"So this would let someone enter Hell?"

"Yeah, if they were crazy, and protected somehow." I think of those arcane tattoos on my failed assassin's chest and arms. "They'd have to be a Pomp though. It's a neat way of avoiding the use of one of the Recognized Entities. I mean, you couldn't imagine Aunt Neti or Charon allowing this sort of thing."

Maybe this explains just how Rillman came back from the dead. It would certainly explain how my shooter managed to be hanging outside my office with a squeegee and a pistol.

"Well, that's one interface destroyed at least," says Lissa.

"Yeah, but they're great at hiding them. Could you feel it before you walked inside?"

"Not at all."

"What's Solstice playing at keeping this secret?"

"Maybe he doesn't trust us. Maybe he was curious to see what we'd do about it," Lissa says.

"We're going to have to be particularly rigorous then."

We walk through the house, checking that each Stirrer is still. Then I start opening cupboards, Lissa behind me. There's nothing in the kitchen, just ancient pizza boxes, and more maggots. I'll have to hose down my boots. The bedrooms are empty too, but for the corpses above us.

"Do we call and have this cleared?" Lissa asks. Each city has a team set up for removing Stirrers caught out of morgues.

"No," I say. "Solstice and his team were aware of the house. Let them clean up the mess."

In the hallway ceiling there's a trapdoor to the roof. I drag a chair over to it, push it open and peer into the ceiling recess. Something crashes at my head. I throw up my hands. And then it is gone, whatever it is, and the ceiling's all wooden beams, dust and heat.

"Are you all right?" Lissa asks.

"Yeah, just jumpy. Must have been a trapped bird." I look into the ceiling recess again. Here I can see the rough welds that hold the aerials to the roof. There's no wiring. They're attached to nothing but corrugated iron. And yet, I'd seen lightning dance toward me across the living room floor. I climb back down, scratch my head.

"What I want to know is how they managed to get into the living world without us feeling them," Lissa says.

"Thunderstorms," I say. "We've been having a lot of thunderstorms. The electrical activity can shield almost anything. And look where they set up house." I point out a window at the transformer station nearby. "That and the aerials have gotta pump out a lot of distortion. What did Alex say they called it? A grid? Suggests to me there are more of them."

Lissa leans over and pecks my cheek.

"What's that for?"

"You seem to be learning things at last." Then Lissa's eyes widen. "Where is Alex?"

A dog's barking somewhere, and then it stops. A shot rings out from the backyard.

We both spring to the back door. It's bolted shut.

I try and fix on my Avian Pomps, but they're gone. The three crows and dozen sparrows I had out there aren't watching Alex anymore. I realize, then, that they're dead. I try and catch their memories, but there's nothing. In the confusion of battle I'd not noticed I'd lost track of them.

The door might be dead bolted but it doesn't look too sturdy. I kick it hard. On the third leg-jarring belt with my boot the door bangs open.

Two Stirrers have cornered Alex in the backyard. My Avian Pomps are bloody lumps of feathers around him. A Stirrer has Alex by the wrist with one hand and it's swinging out at him with a knife. Alex is doing his best to keep his distance, but the Stirrer's pulling him in. The other Stirrer reaches out a hand to grab him. This one must be newer; its movements are clumsy, its hair and neck draped in spiderwebs.

Lissa and I race down the stairs from the back door toward Alex. I take the one with the knife, slap a bloody hand around its neck, another around its waist, and jerk it backward in some mad parody of a dance.

The other Stirrer gets a moment's notice and it swings its head toward Lissa. Alex punches out with his now free hand, and as it stumbles, Lissa stalls it. The Stirrer falls.

Mine shudders in my grip. I hold on as its rough soul scrapes through me. It's a dreadful sensation; this Stirrer's been around for a long time. Once it's hurled back to the Deepest Dark, I drop to my knees.

"You OK?" I demand, looking at Alex.

"You took your bloody time." Alex is shaking, but he manages an unsteady smile.

"I'm sorry," I say. "I didn't expect the strongest Stirrer to be out here. There's been more than a few surprises today."

"The bastard just dropped from the roof and took out your birds. They tried to protect me, but it was too fast. And then the other one appeared, stumbling out from under the house. Shit, I thought I was dead."

There's no point in brooding, in being too scared. Alex is a mate, I have to kill this fear right away. I wish I was better at this.

"So, Alex. You doing anything on Christmas Day?"

"No." Well, that's surprised him. "Mom's whooping it up on a cruise ship in the Pacific, and—"

Yeah, his dad's dead, I don't want him going there. "Well, you are now. Our place. Ten-thirty."

Alex's grin broadens. "You bloody Pomps. Just like my dad. Nothing unsettles you."

I only wish that was true.

22

If someone is opening and closing the doorway to Hell then I need to know just how that might be done. I'm sick and tired of being in the dark about this stuff. I try calling Charon, but he's out of the office. So instead I decided to visit Aunt Neti.

Tim stops me at the opening to her hallway. "I heard you had some trouble in the field today."

"If you call Stirrers generating lightning, and nearly stabbing Alex to death, then yes." I give him a rundown on the house, and what we found there. "Lissa thinks they were building a gateway between the lands of the living and the dead, and I figure that gateway may have been open for a while. And who has been using one lately? Rillman, and whoever the hell it is who's been tailing me."

"You think they're connected?"

"They have to be, don't they?"

Tim shuffles me a little deeper into the hallway and lights up. There are no smoke detectors here.

"If Alex hadn't found out about the house it would still be there. And it would still be doing whatever the hell it was doing." I jerk a thumb down the hallway. "If anyone can tell me about that it will be her."

Tim takes it in. "You want me to come with you?"

"Only if you don't have a Death Moot to help me plan."

He nods, relieved. "The Caterers are coming tomorrow. That should be interesting."

Tim walks back the way he came, and I take a deep breath and head toward Aunt Neti's residence. Wal starts to stir on my biceps. Wings flutter. With every step he takes a more 3D form.

Even down this end of the hall I can smell the cooking. It's a delightful and homely sort of smell—scones again, at a guess.

I close a fist to knock on the door, and the door swings open. I don't know why I bother.

"Is that you smoking, Mr. de Selby?" Aunt Neti's broad, many-eyed face peers down. She squints past my shoulder, checks up the hallway.

"No, I quit smoking a while back. It never stuck with me."

"Well, it stinks on you." She jabs a thumb at Wal. "Smoking cherubs, you're all class."

Wal shakes his head furiously. "Whoa, it wasn't me. I don't even smoke cigars, well, hardly..."

"I'm sorry," I say. "My cousin Tim—my Ankou—gets a bit nervous in this hallway. You know how it is."

"Well, he should be if he keeps up with the cigarettes. I was waiting for you," Aunt Neti says, and smiles, revealing teeth as dark as the space between the stars, and gums far too bright a red. There's a flash of an even redder tongue behind them.

I clear my throat. "I expected as much."

Aunt Neti titters. "Now, you come inside, young man. And we'll have ourselves a little chat."

I close the door behind me and enter the cloying warmth of her small parlor, hoping to avoid her embrace. No luck, though.

Aunt Neti's eight arms enfold me. She all but pulls me off my feet. I peck her on the cheek. Mr. D had insisted I do that, and she beams at me again. I get another glimpse of all those teeth.

I've heard rumors that she eats human fingers. Her room leads onto a garden of immense proportions and I peer through the door that leads out to it. Part of it must be connected to the living world because it is so verdant. "Fed on blood and bone," she says, watching me, clapping her eight hands together. "Plenty of it around here." She says that far too enthusiastically.

There are other doors—leading to the other regional headquarters—but all of them are shut. Shadows move behind one of them. There is a scraping and a scratching behind another. How many people have come into this drawing room and not come out? How many live between the walls, between the realms of life and death?

Well, I'm not a person in that sense. So I'm safe here. At least I tell myself that I'm safe here. And I can sort of believe that.

The tiny spider in the corner has grown considerably. It casts a large black shadow onto the wall, and it watches me with the same intensity it did last time.

Neti passes me a plate of scones after cutting them into halves and slathering first butter, then jam, then cream all over them. "Just out of the oven," she says. "And I've just opened a new jar of blackberry jam."

Mom used to make blackberry jam. Dad would make the scones. And as Mom used to say, "Steven would make a mess."

Wal pokes me in the ribs.

"Thank you," I say quickly. I pick up a scone; take a nibble at its edges. Then a decent bite. "It's delicious."

Aunt Neti beams. "Of course it is, dear. I always make scones when people come with questions. I find it loosens the tongue."

"I need to know who has been crossing over lately," I say.

Neti frowns. "There's been nothing peculiar, as far as I can tell. The last really odd crossing, well, it was you, dear. Since then, we've had nothing but the occasional blip, you know, of a soul not that happy about moving on. And when I say not happy, I mean raving, barking, madly unhappy. Has to be, to make a blip. But that's all.

Now, eat up. I spent a considerable time on those scones. Do you know how hard it is to make the flour of Hell palatable?"

I don't ask how, just nod my head. "This really is delicious."

Aunt Neti beams at me. Eyes as predatory as a hawk, waiting, waiting for the right moment. The right moment for what, I'm not sure, but it's making my skin crawl, at least as much as when she put her arms around me.

I clear my throat. "What do you know of Francis Rillman?"

"*The* Francis Rillman?"

"I suppose so."

"He was highly ambitious. He came to see me once. About something... Oh, it was a long while ago. Let me think..."

"It's really quite important."

"Oh, I know that, dear."

"He died recently."

Aunt Neti raises an eyebrow. "Really, I don't think so." She stands up and walks over to one of the closed doors. She's in and out in a heartbeat. I don't get much of a chance to see what lies beyond, but think of a scream made manifest, and you'd be partway there. She drops a book on the tiny table before her, and flips through the pages.

I try to get a look inside it.

"No, no. There is nothing as far as I can see." She passes it to me, and I can see my name there, the last entry, written in neat printing, the letters OM next to it. "This is my list of those who crossed over and back. It's a tiny book because it doesn't need to be that long. He's only here once, like you."

And there he is, a line before me, *Francis Rillman OM(F)*. Orpheus Maneuver Failed, I guess.

"Really? Lissa says she pomped him."

"She must be mistaken, dear. He's been to Hell and back but once. Have another scone, you're far too thin."

Wal reaches down to grab a scone, and she slaps him away. "You, on the other hand, could stand to lose a few pounds."

"Hey, I resent the implication. I'm a bloody cherub."

"Resent away, you look like a cherub who's eaten a smaller cherub, after frying them in batter—and not just one." She winks at me. "Now, let's just say that, hypothetically, Lissa *did* pomp Rillman and that he has come back somehow. Well, I'd not be surprised. You did something similar, after all."

I shrug. "Similar, I guess, though I never really died. But Lissa did, and I brought her back."

"Not without help you didn't." Aunt Neti's laughter peals from her like a bell ringing. She slaps both my knees. "You're an RM. You've died a dozen deaths, a hundred, a thousand, it's all you ever do."

I hate that line of reasoning. I'm really not all that different from my previous life as a Pomp. I certainly feel as confused as I ever have.

"How would Rillman have made it back?"

"Let's see... Rage and lack of compromise. You should know they are potent enough. You had your share of those, I've heard. Don't underestimate the efficacy of either."

23

When Lissa gets back into Number Four, looking exhausted, I drag her into my office. She vents, and I listen. Her day was long, another two stirs, and that after our assault on the Stirrers' house. And surely it couldn't get any hotter than this? Sure, her home city of Melbourne was hot, but it was a dry heat. People are dying, cooking and expiring, then cooking some more in the heat and the storms. And that's not even mentioning the Stirrers crowding around them. I feel guilty, that as I'm her boss and her partner I'm responsible for most of her problems.

Then it's my turn to vent. I talk about Aunt Neti. "She couldn't give me much. None of them seem capable of that."

"It's the way of upper management, and Recognized Entities," Lissa says. "They'll never give you much. It's not in their interest. I swear they love watching us feeling blindly about. They get off on it."

"I don't."

"Give it time," Lissa says, her words remind me of Suzanne's.

"Neti's certain Rillman is alive. She even showed me her book, the diary she keeps. If Rillman has died and come back, then he's doing something new."

"Well, they say he was an innovator."

"Don't sound so impressed when you say that."

"Believe me, you impress me more." She grabs her black bag. "Steve, I've had enough of work today. Can we . . . ?"

"I don't want to go home yet," I say. It's been a long day, but I'm not ready to face a sleepless night in my parents' place.

Lissa arches an eyebrow. "Well, where do you want to go?"

"I think you'll like it."

The Corolla's down in the car park. We pass people working the night shift. They smile at Lissa as we head toward the lift, and avoid eye contact with me. I don't mind, as long as they're working.

"You've done well with this lot," I say as we wait for the lift.

Lissa sighs. "It sometimes makes me wonder if this isn't the way we should have been working at Mortmax all the time. When it was just families you get people working the job who don't really want to."

That could have summed up both Lissa and me at one point. I'd like to think that we've come to some acceptance of our respective career arcs by now.

"You're happy being a Pomp aren't you?" I ask.

Lissa rubs her chin, an unconscious gesture that I always find charming. "I don't know if happy is the word. For one I have a lousy boss… But, seriously, I've had to grow up a lot these last couple of months. I've realized that sometimes you don't get what you want or, as the case may be, what you want isn't really what you want. What about you?"

The lift pings. We get in, and I don't answer. Just squeeze her hand, and when the lift stops at the basement car park I lead her to the Corolla.

I drive, Lissa lounges in the passenger seat, not bothering to hide her yawns. "Is this going to take long?"

"No, you rest. I'll wake you when we get there."

She's already out when we pull onto George Street. What an amazing ability to sleep she has. The city is bright around us. We pass the great green Christmas tree in the square and navigate our way through people staggering home from Christmas parties, dressed for air-conditioning and dining, not the soup that is a December evening in Brisbane.

There's a red light at George and Ann. I remember standing on the corner there, with the ghosts of my parents, wondering just how long I was going to live, and how the hell I was going to do it without them. Everyone faces that point in their life. Maybe you spend the rest of your days trying to answer it.

I don't know if my parents would be proud. They certainly wouldn't have approved of all the drinking. But I've done the best by them I could.

The lights change and someone beeps at me from behind. I put the car into gear, and head out of the city...or toward the city's heart. Depends on how you look at it.

Ten minutes later, the Corolla lurches up the last section of winding road that leads to Mount Coot-tha's summit. Lissa's curled in the seat beside me. I brush the hair from her face and she smiles. It's a beautiful smile, but every time I see someone sleeping a slither of jealousy burns within me. I shove it down. This isn't Lissa's fault, I have to get used to it. Besides, the guilt concerning just who I last spent time with up here takes the edge off.

I pull into a park at the top of the mountain, let the car idle. The lights of the lookout are burning. The air is cooler up here, but it's still warm. There's a storm building in the west, following a pattern that has extended over these last few weeks. Heavy clouds trail fingers of electricity across the horizon. Even with that nearing disturbance I can still feel the One Tree, though its presence is somewhat muted.

In the Underworld it would rise above me at this point, clambered over by the dead, those ready or those forced to take the next step into the Deepest Dark. Here, of course, there are just the living forests, scrubby eucalypts that sing and sigh with the approaching storm.

I've been working so hard and getting nowhere. Everything, despite my best efforts, seems to be slipping out of control. Can you really learn to be an RM on the job? Maybe this is just what being an RM is really like, and Suzanne and Co. merely put on a mask of calm efficiency as they scramble about trying to keep Mortmax running smoothly. That worries me far more than any lack that I might possess. A lot more.

The city below is luminous. Airplanes, their lights blinking, race toward the airport in the east, or rise from it, all of them veering away from the cloud front. Lissa wakes as I turn off the engine.

"Are we there yet?"

"Yeah."

She smiles at me. Her face is too pale. And though I never think of her this way, in that moment she seems so frail. And I have to kiss her. I just have to.

I hold her head in my hands, feeling like a teenager again. The car park's a popular make-out point, the city a carpet gridded with light beneath us. I kiss her and she's kissing me. My hands trace the outline of her body. As the storm nears us, the ever-present veil of heartbeats falls away, and all I can feel is her racing heart beneath my palm. I stroke her breasts, awkwardly at first. It's too open here, but then again, our first sexual experience was an embarrassing masturbation-based binding ritual in a car park.

Lissa pushes against me. Clothes can't come off fast enough. Lightning streaks the sky as if in sympathy.

"Now," she moans.

And it's fast and difficult, in that tiny car, the gearstick getting in the way, not to mention the steering wheel and a seat that almost collapses beneath our weight. But we manage it. There are moments of clumsiness, moments of rhythm. We laugh at each other, forget where we are.

The storm is already heading out to sea. The darkness seems washed of impurities, the city's lights burn brighter. I breathe in the smell of her.

"That was different," she says.

"But good?"

"Insecurity isn't very attractive, you know."

With the storm gone, Lissa's heartbeat is just one of the millions I can feel again, racing, slowing, stalling, failing. But hers is right here, by my heart; her lips so close to mine that I kiss her again.

Oscar's Hummer pulls up next to us, followed by Travis in a little red convertible.

"We might be in trouble," I say.

Lissa smirks. "We're always in trouble."

Oscar gets out of the car, taps on my window. I wind it down and look up at him as apologetically as anyone feeling as smug as I am can.

"Look," Oscar says, "if you want to die, then that's your prerogative, Steven. But if you are killed, who is going to pay me? And this business is very much word of mouth. Are you trying to ruin my business?"

"I'm sorry."

"It's my fault," Lissa says. "I wanted to come up here and watch the storm."

"Did you enjoy it?"

Lissa and I exchange a look that lasts a little too long, and then a little longer.

Oscar is blushing when I look back at him. "Yes, we did."

"You're coming home, now," he says. "Please."

Oscar's driving behind us. I have Okkervil River on the MP3, Will Sheff's voice, shouting out the lyrics to "For Real," filling the Corolla. It's all menace and yearning but right now it sounds as romantic a thing as you could ever imagine. Another storm is building. It's going to pour again soon. The Brisbane River is beside us, shining with the reflected glow of the city. The skyscrapers rise up to our left. Southbank's massive ferris wheel is a circle of fire to our right across the river. The water calls to me a little. I've been an RM for such a short time, but I'm already aware of just how many things are connected to death, how many places act as interfaces or linkages between the Underworld and the living world.

The rearview mirror shows me Oscar hunched over the wheel of his Hummer. His face is hard; then a lightning burst in the sky above conceals it. Travis is driving a little way ahead. I don't know what they think they're going to achieve if something actually happens on the freeway.

I take our exit from the M3.

And then I sense it. Something wrong. A force or a presence that didn't exist a heartbeat ago. And it's coming from beneath us. I rest my left hand on the dashboard. There's an odd beat, a rhythm, running counterbalance to the song.

"Bomb! Out!" I'm already slowing the car. I can feel it building, racing toward a crescendo of shrapnel. There's a little piece of me, the Hungry Death, I guess, that's loving it.

Lissa looks at me. She opens her door: the road is streaking by. There's no time. Up ahead, there's nothing coming, the road is clear. I yank my seatbelt free. The car's slowing, but not enough. The vibration shifts, increasing in pitch. The explosion, all that potential energy, is about to be exhaled in fire.

Lissa leaps and I do something I didn't believe was possible. I visualize it, as Suzanne must have with me, capture the movement in my skull, and then I shift beneath her. Fold her in my arms. She doesn't struggle against me, merely accepts that I can take this punishment. I hold her, bind her in me. She's warm and still against my cold flesh.

We're out, and rolling. The ground is hard and toothed. My clothes tear. The road bites, it digs its dirty teeth in deep. And ahead of us, the Corolla, slowed almost to a halt, explodes in a series of sharp detonations. Bits of our little car are tumbling from the sky.

I lie on the road, panting. Lissa gets to her feet; there are cuts all over her arms but I've taken the worst of it, thank Christ. She grabs me by the wrist and drags me from the oncoming traffic. When we're at the edge of the road she drops next to me. And then the storm unleashes all that rain, that blinding rushing rain.

Oscar's already pulling in behind us, windscreen wipers racing, hazard lights flashing. Cars are slowing, but Travis is out directing traffic. I've never seen anyone do it with such panache. When a man's that big, people pay attention.

"You all right?" I shout at Lissa. Things are leaking within me, even as I feel flesh and bone knitting. The rain's soaking me. Lissa crouches down, kisses me hard and squints; our communication is more lip-reading than anything else.

"Did you leave the fuel cap off or something?" she mouths at me.

Bones shift. Ribs slide back into place, organs repair themselves: I'm getting better at this. It itches like hell, though.

"Yeah, and I also left a bomb in the glove box. Sorry."

We look over at the Corolla. It's a flaming wreck billowing black smoke. I feel that it saved our lives.

"Jesus!" Oscar says. "Are you all right?"

"Fine. We're both fine," Lissa says. As though none of this is new to us. And it goddamn isn't.

Solstice is down among the wreckage almost before the ambulances and fire engines get there, his face set in a grimace. The storm has come and gone; the air's so thick you could serve it with a ladle.

Traffic creeps past. Gawkers mostly, peering at the wreck, and the various hues of flashing lights.

"Jesus, de Selby. It just goes from bad to worse with you, doesn't it?" He kicks at the wreckage with one steel-capped boot. "I'd understand it if you had a car worth blowing up, but this piece of shit..."

That offends me more than it ought. But at least with Solstice on the scene, I don't have to answer too many stupid questions: just put up with his gibes. Alex is here, too, keeping in the background, looking worried. He's talking to Lissa. Taking notes, and studiously avoiding Solstice.

"Are you getting anywhere with Rillman? Isn't that your fucking job?" I demand.

"The guy's a ghost. The records just stop. No surprises, I suppose. But you know all about ghosts. Do you think this Rillman could be a Stirrer?"

"No. Stirrers don't operate this way. They're not nearly as subtle."

Solstice taps a blackened hub cap with one foot. "Do you call this subtle?" He sighs. "Look, you've had a long night. Maybe you should go home. Rest up, get ready for all the questions I'm going to be asking you when I get my head around this."

He thumps my back, and stares over at Alex. "And tell that hack cop we don't need him here."

"He's here as a friend."

"He's a fucking nuisance, that's what he is."

I walk over to Alex. He's glaring at Solstice.

"What did the prick say?"

"He'd like you to leave his crime scene."

"*His* crime scene?"

"Alex, he has a point. Besides, the less he's thinking about you the better. Have you found out anything new?"

"Just how much I hate bureaucracies. Getting anything on these Closers is next to impossible. Look, the less I find the more worried it makes me," Alex says. "And then the harder I look. I'll find something."

"Good," I say. "That's what I like to hear."

Oscar gets us home quickly. I can't help thinking that, in a way, we're lucky. If that bomb had gone off in the garage, Oscar, Travis and Lissa would all be dead. If it had gone off at the lookout there's no telling how many casualties there would have been. And all because some ex-employee who predates my time with the company has a vendetta against me. Because I succeeded where he failed.

When we pull into the driveway, something else grabs my attention. This day just isn't going to end!

"Are you feeling that?" I ask Lissa.

"Yes, it's not what it should be, but after today, I recognize it."

We both look at the brace symbol above the front door. It should be glowing. It's not.

"What are you two talking about?" Oscar says.

"You're going to have to stay in the car," I say to him. "This is something you can't handle."

Lissa and I slide out of the Hummer and hurry up the front steps and onto the verandah. I have the door open in a moment, and we slip inside my parents' house. Now, I used to sneak in here a lot, when I was dating. I know every single creaking floorboard, every single shadowed alcove. Lissa follows my steps. We reach the living room with barely a sound above Lissa's racing heart and the whisper of our breathing.

Here the sensation, the taste, is stronger. But not as strong as I'd expect.

I signal to Lissa and she nods, pulling out her knife.

I creep through the living room, then into the kitchen. Lissa is behind me, the only person I would ever trust with a knife in that position.

It's sitting there, in one of the kitchen chairs.

"Get out of here," I snarl.

The Stirrer smiles. Blood has settled along its cheekbones. Its eyes are dead: blank. It turns toward us clumsily. Every movement must be difficult for this creature. It can't have inhabited the body for very long, no more than a couple of hours, maybe much less. "You don't recognize me, do you?"

"Am I supposed to?"

The Stirrer nods toward Lissa. "I took over her... remains."

How could I forget? When Morrigan murdered Lissa, this Stirrer used her body. It had even come to me and tried to make a deal.

"You bitch!" Lissa almost leaps over the table. I'm normally the one doing something stupid. I grab her arm, and it's a strain to keep her here with me.

"Not yet," I say.

The Stirrer's grin is a challenge to us both. "You need to listen to me," it says. "Things are accelerating, but we are not as unified as you might think."

"Is that what you told Morrigan?" Lissa demands.

I can feel the Stirrer now. Its absence. I can feel the things it is drawing away from the world; it's like a cloud that has passed over the sun.

"Morrigan was a mistake. It got out of our control."

I notice the brace symbol tattooed on its thumb. This Stirrer shouldn't exist. And it shouldn't have passed through all the safeguards that I have set up throughout the house.

But here it is staring at me, in a body I do not recognize, for all its Pomp tattoos. Who did he work for? The relief I feel that it's not one of my Pomps is followed quickly by guilt.

"I found him outside your home." It lifts its head and I see the red line slashed across its throat. "I just took what was convenient. You really should clean up more frequently. My host has been dead for some time."

"What do you have to say?" I ask, still holding Lissa back. She's shaking with rage.

"Not all of us are happy to see our god approaching. Some of us are scared. Some of us may be willing to change sides."

"What for?"

"To see the sun again. To live among you, godless. After all, this place was ours long before it was yours. You who live owe us that much—"

"That's it!" Lissa snarls, and shakes free of my hand. "We don't trust Stirrers around here."

She slides her knife over her palm and slams it against the Stirrer's face. There's a soft detonation, the air gathers something about itself, and takes the motion from the corpse. The body drops, all smug smiles and jerky movement taken from its limbs. I look down at it. There's no hint that a Stirrer ever inhabited the body.

Then it smashes into me. The Stirrer's soul. It's as though I've curled myself around a ball of razor wire. I drop, and howl.

I close my hands around the scythe.

It feels so good, doesn't it?

And it does.

Now let us kill.

Something shakes my shoulder, jolts me awake. My head rests on a cushion and Lissa is holding my hand, whispering soothing nonsense.

"You had me worried there."

"It'll take more than a stall to kill me, no matter how rough. Why'd you wake me from the first decent rest I've had in ages?" I murmur.

"You were screaming. And then you started to chuckle." Lissa doesn't laugh. I blink at her. "When did that start happening?"

"Just then. A stall has never hurt like that before."

Lissa smiles grimly. "I'm glad you spared me from it."

"You're welcome. The Stirrers are definitely getting stronger. And I don't like what that suggests. But next time, maybe we should let the Stirrer speak."

"I don't trust 'em," Lissa says. "Especially ones that take over my body and talk about what we owe it."

"I understand, but—"

"No buts. That Stirrer was in our house. It should never have been here."

Christ, I wish I could see things in such black and white ways. It can only mean that the Stirrer god is nearing. I have to sort this mess out with Rillman and fast; the sideshow is obscuring the main event.

Lissa frowns and crouches down by the corpse. One of its palms is marked in black ink with a bisected half circle.

"Do you recognize that?" I ask.

"Yeah, it's the same symbol our electrical friends in their safe house had on them."

"I think the Stirrers have found themselves something that counteracts the brace symbol."

"Something *that* simple? It's hard to believe it has any efficacy," Lissa says.

"The brace symbol is simple too. It has to be. Mr. D told me that the universe rails against complexity, it likes to break the curlicues and the squiggles down."

"He's a poet," Lissa says, with a wry grin. "Maybe he has something to say about all of this. Maybe you should go and find out."

"Are you going to be all right here?"

Lissa raises her bloody palm. "As long as this works I will."

If you lose your trust in blood, what do you have left? Up until the last couple of days I would have found it impossible to believe anything could trip up the old ways of stalling. Yet here we are.

"Be safe," we say simultaneously.

"I was expecting you. I could feel it, don't ask me how. Maybe we're developing some sort of link. After all, you are the closest thing I have to a living relative," Mr. D says, with two cups of steaming tea on a table by his chair. I don't bother asking where the new furniture came from. The One Tree creaks around us. He's just put down a copy of Fritz Leiber's novel *Our Lady of Darkness.* He's halfway through the book, I see. I slide a chair over to the table. There's no point rushing Mr. D. Even if I'm in a hurry, he isn't.

On the uppermost branch above us is where my Negotiation took place. A Negotiation involving more pain than I'd ever thought possible. I keep finding new limits to that. My capacity to contain it has increased and the universe seems intent on filling it.

On the branches beneath us people clamber and climb, finding places where the tree is happy to absorb them and pass them on to the Deepest Dark. Every soul has a different spot, a different length of time to be spent in the Underworld. But Pomps, once they pass, don't spend much time here. Maybe the One Tree is frightened that we'll mess it up.

"Sometimes I can feel the tree calling me," Mr. D says. "It would dearly love to have my soul. I've been here for so long and the tree is something of a stickler for the natural order of things."

"You're not tempted to go?"

He nods toward the Leiber novel, and the pile of paperbacks behind it replenished by visits to the markets below. "I've a lot of reading to catch up on. Besides, you need my help."

It's as good a reason as any I suppose. If only he was giving me more than the barest slivers of help. I bite my tongue, though.

"What do you think of your little world?" Mr. D asks gesturing out at the Underworld.

"It doesn't feel like mine."

"I was surprised by that myself. You went into this with no expectations. I envied you that."

"What do you mean?"

"There were no expectations to be disappointed. You're the regional Death. This land bows to you, but it also has a very strong sense of what it wants to be. You can either fight it, and it will struggle, even as it bends to your will, or reach some sort of agreement.

During my, er, tenure, I preferred the latter. I'd already had my fill of fighting. Nature will win out. I will, one day, let the tree take me."

"But nature doesn't always win out. A Stirrer visited me today. Walked through my braces, and it had this on its wrist." I draw the symbol in the air.

Mr. D slaps my hand. "You don't want to be drawing that symbol here!"

"What is it?"

"Nothing good, that's for sure."

"I thought this was my region."

"It is, but regions are always imperiled, and that symbol's a siege engine of a most terrible sort. I haven't seen it since—"

"Would the name Francis Rillman be tied up with it by any chance?" I get out of my chair and round on Mr. D. "What the fuck is it that you're hiding from me?"

Mr. D smiles. It's an expression that I suspect he thinks is calming but it's actually the most irritating thing I've seen all day, particularly as it is wrapped in his various faces. "I assure you, Steven, that I'm not trying to hide anything from you. I don't work that way, and if anyone should know that it's you." He sees his approach isn't exactly working and sighs. "Yes, Rillman is involved. He was one of the best Ankous I ever had. Better than Morrigan, and more trustworthy—or so I thought. Francis failed the Orpheus Maneuver, but before that he had started a Schism. And like Morrigan he made deals with the Stirrers, but unlike Morrigan he'd designed a new symbol. I can't tell you what sort of genius that must take, but there hadn't been a new symbol in pomping since the Renaissance.

"He used his in a most peculiar way. He stole my powers—well, learned to mimic them. But he wasn't smart enough—or was perhaps too smart. He killed his beloved, Maddie. You see, she was a Pomp. I liked her, too. Steven, always know your staff. Know them as deeply as you can, watch their careers, and watch your back. She was against his Schism, she refused to become a Black Sheep, even tried to stop him. And when that happened everything fell apart for him. He tried to get her back and when I stopped him, well, he wasn't happy. His Schism gambit had failed and he had lost his love. And theirs was a grand love, in spite of his ambitions. It sometimes works out that way. You know, I think he would have succeeded but for me. He certainly had Neti's support."

"Aunt Neti?"

"Yes, she could see the romance in it. But I think, too, she was pleased that he came to her, that he followed the traditions."

"She certainly thinks poorly of me."

"You're an RM. It doesn't matter what she thinks." He sips on his tea. "I really believe, now, that he may have been the inspiration for Morrigan's Schism—only Morrigan was more thorough, and heartless. But that old bastard never got his hands on the new symbol. That, I kept hidden."

"You could have told me about it."

Mr. D nods. "Yes, I could have, de Selby, but I never expected to see it again."

"So after Rillman lost the love of his life?"

"Not just once," Mr. D says, "twice. He found her in Hell, as you found Lissa. Only I was waiting on the border. She returned to the One Tree."

"What did that do to him?" I don't really need to ask the question, and Mr. D sees that, but he plays along.

"He turned to the Stirrers, got in with them even more deeply. I guess he figured that they would know what he didn't. How to get his wife back."

"Did they?"

"No, their skills don't work that way. The bastard has no sympathy from me—you don't deal with the enemy. I actually banished him from my region, would you believe? Thought that would be enough, but then I didn't expect another Schism so close to his. If he's back in the region it's only because I'm dead."

"Could I banish him?"

"I don't think so. You're too new to your powers. It'd probably kill you. No, you're going to have to face him the old way."

"With knives and death?"

"I was going to say with lawyers, law men, the full force of jurisprudence. But sure, knives and death... That could work, too." Mr. D looks mildly annoyed now, which is a fair sign that he is mightily pissed off. He's not even drinking his tea, but continues on.

"Rillman opened the door for Morrigan, gave him ideas. And more, like I said, the little bastard stole some of my powers." He indicates his face. "This. Showy as it is, was mine. He stole that from me, made it somewhat less unique, less artistic." Mr. D squints into his tea, then pushes it aside as though disgusted by what the tea leaves have told him. "I've got some beer up here if you would like."

I shake my head, remembering the ashy rubbish we'd consumed on his boat.

"He stole your ability to change your face?"

Mr. D twists the top of his beer. "Yes, only his approach is a little more utilitarian."

"He can change his form!"

"Only into the dead. Which is very useful if you don't mind murdering people. Also, it makes it extremely difficult to be found." Mr. D sighs. "I'm sorry I have left you such a mess."

"I'll deal with it," I say grimly.

"I hope so, but this may well be beyond you. Rillman's tenacity is more than a match for yours, and he is one of the smartest people I have ever met. And you, dare I say it..."

"Thank you very much," I say. "Now get me one of those beers after all. And tell me every fucking thing you know."

24

By the time I shift home, Lissa is asleep. I check her schedule. She's not starting until late. It's nearly 5:00 a.m. Christmas Eve, though it doesn't feel like it. My eyelids are heavy, but I fear what sleep offers more than anything Rillman can throw at me personally. I pull down the blinds and scrawl Lissa a note.

Oscar arranges for another crew to look after her. The body the Stirrer inhabited has already been collected. I can almost pretend that it was never here, but it's opened wounds again. Looking at the kitchen, where it had sat, and where my parents had been killed, and their bodies stolen. Too many Stirrers have been here. They've poisoned my memories of this place.

I think about its offer. No, Lissa and Mr. D are right. You don't deal with Stirrers. No matter what.

I shift to my office, and work on my presentation for the Death Moot. I check on Lissa from time to time, but she doesn't wake, poor darling.

Tim comes for me around ten. It's meet-the-Caterers day. He's already been briefed on last night's problem with an exploding car and he's employed more staff to investigate, and to search all the other vehicles for bombs. Nothing's come up yet.

My eyes feel square from staring at my computer for so long. I read Tim my Moot preamble, feeling very good about it, even statesmanlike. There's all manner of stirring stuff, demanding unity, and that the Orcus must act as one to fight this threat. And that it is not impossible. He nods his head at the end.

"I'll rewrite it for you," he says.

"Really?"

"Trust me. You'll even believe you've written it when I'm done."

He's nervous, twitchy. "Is it time?" I ask.

"Yeah, they'll be there soon," he says. "Oscar will walk us over."

Kurilpa Bridge is like a huge game of cat's cradle drawn out in steel and wire. There's a metal canopy above us, providing a little shade. I look back at the way we came, down the walkway that leads to Tank Street with its lawyer-crowded coffee shops and glass-fronted restaurants.

"Maybe we should have gotten a coffee first," I say.

Tim crushes a cigarette beneath the toe of his boot. "No time."

"Why did you choose the bridge?" Oscar asks. He studies first one bank of the river then the other, then pushes his face into his broad hands. There's clearly not enough escape routes—unless you want to dive into the river. There's plenty that way.

"Technically it won't really be the bridge, not as Brisbanites see it," Tim says. "The marquees will be set up in the space between the Underworld and the living. You'll have quite a view of the city, and the Underworld equivalent, without really touching on either."

"There'll be two marquees?" Oscar asks, and I can tell he's even less happy.

"One for the Ankous, to bitch about the RMs, and the other, the big top if you will, for the main show. Both will be air-conditioned, of course." Tim mops at his brow with a handkerchief. "Maybe the next Death Moot could be in Antarctica."

I grin. "No, they did that in 1963. It wasn't a hit. Too many bloody penguins." I remember Mr. D's stories about that one. Said it was so cold his knees ached for the whole Moot and then a week afterward.

Oscar shakes his head. We're not much help.

"Water beneath bridges is a traditional interface between the lands of the living and the dead. And Mortmax Industries is all about tradition, but I didn't make the decision," I say. "I just bled over it." I pat Tim on the back. "Both of us did, didn't we, buddy?"

Tim shudders. "Don't remind me."

"And there's still a little more blood needed," I say. "We're going to disappear for a while Oscar, but don't worry. We will be back."

Oscar shrugs. "We do what we can, boss. I'm aware there are some places that we can't follow you."

After a couple of joggers have passed us by, Tim and I pull our knives from beneath our jackets. Tim counts down silently to three and we cut our palms, heart line to thumb. I walk to the western rail of the bridge, Tim to the eastern and as one we plant our bloody palms on the bare steel.

Metal thrums. And there is a sound like someone scratching a record, a painful scritch! that runs across the heavens.

Oscar throws up his hands, and then he's gone. But it's really us who have gone.

The sky darkens, then brightens. The whole city contracts, expands and contracts again, as though reality has grown rubbery. And suddenly it is only Tim and I on the bridge. There is no traffic on the expressway, and no people here or on the streets below. The city is quiet. Oddly enough there are birds in the air and the river is teeming with fish. Its surface bubbles, the water itself a murky reddish brown, the same color as my palm print on the rail. The bridge itself is luminous, silver and white, and a bright sun burns in the sky.

"Well, I never," Tim says. "How's that for magic and stuff?"

"Now, where are these Caterers?"

A bell tolls, loud and clear. It echoes and vibrates through the bridge so that it's almost a bell itself.

"There, I think," Tim says.

A right hand, pale, long-fingered and neatly manicured, materializes in the air between Tim and me. Then another. And another until a dozen hands are present. Then left hands being to appear. And twelve men, or women—they're as androgynous as Ziggy Stardust—stand before us, all slightly shorter than me, all carefully dressed in white suits. A pair of them scurry to the center of the bridge and start taking measurements, pulling tape between them, scrawling notes down onto clipboards.

The Caterer nearest to me dips its head. He seems to be the boss.

"Mr. de Selby. A pleasure." He claps his hands. "And what a glorious venue. Shiny, new. Nothing of the gothic about it, and you would simply *not* believe how tiresome all the gothic is." He spits out the word as though it were a bitter poison, revealing neat but very sharp teeth.

The rest of the day is spent walking over nearly every inch of the bridge, marking sections with our blood, anchoring, as the Head Caterer calls it, this reality with our own. With too much blood, the bridge may sink into the living world and the Death Moot will become a crowded affair, and Mortmax will not only be paying the Caterers but also Brisbane City Council for illegally building marquees on this public thoroughfare. With too little, this reality might just drift away and the Moot with it.

Oscar calls me a couple of times, but there is no hurry in the Head Caterer, just a methodical preparation of the bridge. I can respect that, but there are several more pressing situations I should be applying myself to.

By early evening, Tim and I are feeling a little anemic. And Tim is sick of Caterers bumming cigarettes off him. But the Head Caterer is clapping his hands with joy, and already one marquee is constructed.

"This will be the best Moot in our ten thousand years of catering," he says. "The location!" He points to Mount Coot-tha in the northwest, the shadowy hint of the One Tree. "The air, so vibrant, and yet so suggestive of death. You have done well with this city. I promise you, people will not forget this Moot."

"Ten thousand years?" I say. "You've been doing this for ten thousand years?"

"Yes, and thank goodness for climate control these days. You would not believe just how feral it used to be. Cold in winter, boiling in summer. Terrible, terrible."

We shake hands, sealing the deal with a little more blood. Then the Head Caterer goes off to direct the positioning of a freezer in the kitchen set-up.

There's a door made of pine, in the middle of the bridge, nothing more really than a frame. One of the Caterers leads us to it.

"Access point," the Caterer says. "You come and go through here. Got pizza and beer coming if you boys would like to stay."

We beg off, it's Christmas Eve after all, and walk through the door. We're back into our reality. There's no Narnia-esque time transition, it's night in the real world as well, just an ear-popping step into a jogger-crowded bridge. We both leap out of the way of an oncoming cyclist. The door that we walked through is gone. Oscar's waiting patiently with Travis and Tim's burly bodyguards.

Lissa's not due home for another couple of hours. Oscar insists that we walk back to Number Four. Tim has a hair appointment in the Valley so we part company on the bridge, Tim heading to the nearest taxi rank with his security.

There's a shortcut from the bridge to George Street via a tunnel. It's well lit, though empty at this time of night. We head through it, Travis walking ahead, Oscar behind me.

Halfway in, the lights flicker and dim, and I realize that this was a mistake. Each end of the tunnel is gated, and both gates slam shut in unison.

I slap my head with my palm. Not again. When am I going to learn?

25

The lights that have dimmed suddenly flare and shatter. A ripple of glass fragments rains down and darkness engulfs us. Oscar is shielding me with his body. I hear Travis run toward us, can picture the gun already in his hand. "Down!" he hisses. "Stay down."

And I'm on the concrete still under Oscar, then he rolls to one side, ending up in a crouch.

I try desperately to make sense of things in the dark. I can hear Rillman's heartbeat. Steady and familiar. My eyes are adjusting now. There, a slight movement down the other end of the walkway. And as if on cue, a light flickers on. Rillman glares at it in irritation.

He walks toward us. He hasn't changed since the photo that Lissa showed me was taken, though that must be several decades old. He's unprepossessing, even in the suit he's wearing, and about a head shorter than me. He could be a bad parody of a chartered accountant, if only he were wearing a bowler hat.

Here he is, I'm seeing him clearly for the first time (no waxen obscuring of his features, and my eyes not swollen with blood) and he's not so bad. Not so scary. Except his eyes. They gleam with a force, a rage utterly at odds with his demeanor.

"I'd call off your goons," Rillman says. "I really don't want to hurt anyone, except you."

Travis is at my side. "Just keep out of the way," he says to me. He has his pistol aimed at Rillman's head.

"Guns don't frighten me," Rillman says. That makes one of us.

"It's not the gun you need to worry about, mate." Oscar runs at him. It's like watching a steam engine hurtle at a minnow.

Rillman moves out of the way, smooth as oil, but Oscar is turning, too. He swings a punch at Rillman's head, only it isn't there anymore, he's down, hunched at an insane angle. Then he's slipping around and punching Oscar twice in the sternum. The fight's confusing. Darkness and light. Shadows melding. Rillman is in several places at once. I can sense what he is doing, the bastard's shifting in tiny bursts. How the fuck's he doing that? Oscar doesn't stand a chance.

Travis is trying to get a clear shot, cursing under his breath.

Bone cracks and Rillman pushes Oscar away from him as though he's nothing but an irritation. The big man teeters, his arms flailing, then falls flat on his back, coughing up ropes of blood.

I turn from Oscar to Travis. His face has tightened with dismay or anger, I'm not sure. He's stopped swearing. "Stay where you are," he growls at Rillman.

Rillman laughs. He hasn't even got a sweat up and one of my guards is already down. "Stay where I am, or what?"

Travis shoots just above his head. The bullet ricochets down the tunnel. We both cringe. Oscar is on the ground, moaning.

Rillman takes a step forward. And then with no transition he's in Travis's face. A perfect shift. There's a flash of silver. "Oh, dear," Rillman exclaims.

I get to my feet, my arms reaching out toward Travis. But it's too late.

Travis takes a few steps forward, one hand clamped over his neck. Blood bubbles from between his fingers, and he falls hard on his knees. Then he gestures once, weakly—with whatever strength he has left—with his free hand, for me to run. That's all he has in him. He topples forward. One less heartbeat, one less guard.

His ghost looks at me. Blinks and shakes his head. "I'm so sorry," he says.

"You have nothing to be sorry about, Travis. Nothing," I say.

A moment later his soul flashes through me.

Rillman laughs. "Always the professional, eh? Even when it comes to pomping your own staff. You better get used to that."

I peer at Rillman. His hands are empty. What is he cutting with? His nails are short, neat. But I guess a man capable of changing his form, of shifting from space to space, is capable of just about anything in a fight.

My legs are like jelly, but I'm an RM, damn it! "I've been looking for you," I say, and my voice isn't as stern or as strong as I would like it to be.

"Yes, but not nearly hard enough," he says. "You're really rather awful at all this aren't you?"

I shrug.

Rillman pauses, takes a step back. "I thought you would be more impressive. All these weeks of watching you, watching those around you...For someone with such loyal friends, you're rather disappointing."

"You couldn't kill me with your bomb. And these insults are nothing to me"

Rillman smiles. "That bomb wasn't meant for you."

"You keep away from her."

"She'll be mine when I have time for her. And you know there is nothing you can do." He flicks his wrists in the manner of a magician. There is a thin line of gray light in his hands. It takes me a moment to realize what it is.

"Surely you're kidding."

He's holding an old-fashioned barber's razor. But the blade is unlike any razor I've ever seen: it's made of stone and it's mumbling. This isn't good; all my encounters with mumbling blades have not been good.

"I'm afraid not, Mr. de Selby." He waves the razor around his head. "This took me some time to fashion. You won't believe the lengths I went to to source the materials. Indeed, I only finished it this evening. I don't really expect it to do the job, but I need to try it on someone, need it blooded with good corporate blood. And why not yours? I rather expect it to hurt."

He comes at me fast.

I try to shift, but can't. Somehow Rillman is holding me to this place, and the time I've wasted in trying to get out of here, means he's almost upon me. I duck backward, but not nearly swiftly enough. He's come in close and he swings up and under. Then down. Almost so fast that I don't see it. Oh, but how I feel it!

The first stroke slides under my ribs, the second opens up my wrist. Both wounds blaze with agony. I kick out, and my boot makes contact, but he hops away. A dozen contradictory emotions wash across his face: hate, humor, compassion and rage among them. I can't believe I ever tried to hunt this guy. I should have been running.

"Why are you doing this?"

"It must be done. You need to learn, and I need to cut."

Blood flowers around the incision in my shirt. I slide my fingers over the wound, quick. This shouldn't be happening. But I have survived worse injuries. He jabs toward me, and this time I am ready. I swing up with my knee. Ten years of soccer as a kid taught me something about playing nasty. There's a meaty thud on contact, a winded gasp. The bastard stumbles back and I swing a fist toward his face. My knuckles strike his nose. That's gotta hurt; it certainly hurts my fist.

Rillman blinks, steps back. His eyes narrow.

"I'm not the only one who bleeds," I say.

Rillman takes a step toward me but then my winged Pomps arrive—shooting through the gates. Crows. The first one strikes him hard, just beneath the eye. Another takes a nip at his ear. Rillman slashes at the bird and the poor thing is sliced in two. But there's another one, and another.

In the distance comes the thwack, thwack, thwack of crows' wings beating. There are a lot of crows in Brisbane. And they are filled with my anger, cruel with my pain.

"C'mon, mate!" I growl, sweat dripping from my face, blood pouring from my wounds. I take an unsteady step toward him, pulling my hands from my belly and clenching them into fists, bloodier than they have ever been before. It's hardly threatening to an ex-Ankou, but it's all I have. I even manage a grin. "You better finish it now or I will find you."

"I invite you to try, Mr. de Selby. You'll only be making my job easier. I think the lesson's done for today," Rillman says, batting at the stabbing birds around him.

Suddenly, there's the sound of flesh slamming into bone. Rillman lets out a great whoomph of breath, stands there blinking.

"That's for my fucking ribs," a newly conscious Oscar growls. "And this is for what you did to Travis."

He swings again and Rillman scrambles backward, his arms flailing.

The world shivers a little, and Oscar's fist strikes air. Unbalanced, he falls. It's painful watching him get to his feet. I'd help, but I'm worried my bowels are likely to spill out the moment I move my hand.

Rillman's gone. There's just the two of us and about a hundred crows looping around in that confined space, cawing and clawing at the air where Rillman had been just a moment ago, a cacophonous cloud of wings and claws and beaks. I'm getting their view, as well as my glued-to-ground vision. I have to struggle to stop them pecking at Travis.

The gates swing open.

Oscar looks at me. "We've got to get you out of here..." Every word comes at a cost. The big man's tan has faded to a ghostly white.

Neither of us look good, and both of us are bleeding heavily. He glances over at Travis, starts toward him.

"Too late," I say, "Travis is dead. Believe me, I pomped him, there's nothing we can do."

"Ah, Jesus." It's the first time I see anything that looks like real emotion pass across his face.

The amount of blood flowing through my fingers suggests that Rillman may not need to come back to finish the job. As a Pomp I would be dead—there's no way I could have handled this sort of injury—but my body burns with energies, long tendrils of power slowly repairing flesh and bone. Every Pomp in my employ will be feeling this as I draw strength from them. I might have a couple of resignations tomorrow. Wouldn't blame anyone.

All that crackle and pop is making me dizzy. I laugh with the head rush of it all—and it hurts. Rillman wasn't joking. I hunch into my wounds, look around me.

"Can you walk?" Oscar asks me, looking almost ready to fall on his arse himself.

"Can you?"

Oscar grins the pained grimace of a wounded bear. Not dead yet. "See if you can shift out of here. Go and get some help," he says.

The wounds are already knitting. I try to shift and all I get for my trouble is a bad headache. I gulp a few deep breaths and straighten my suit, then we stumble out of the tunnel and onto the street. I call Tim; it goes to voicemail.

Then I call Lissa. She doesn't answer her phone, and I realize why.

I feel the stall that is distracting her. She's forty kilometers south of the city, too far away.

I key in Suzanne's number. "I need your help. Now."

And she's there in an instant. "Oh, dear," she says. "What has Rillman done to you?"

She looks up and down the street. "Where—? Never mind. This shouldn't have happened."

"Brooker," I say.

She nods. "This is going to hurt," she says, and holds both Oscar's and my hand.

In his surgery, Dr. Brooker almost falls out of his chair, when he sees us. "What the hell happened here?"

"I've been cut up by a bloody barber's razor made out of stone, is what," I hiss. "Oscar's the one you have to see to."

"I know my job." Dr. Brooker looks at me, then Suzanne. "Take him to his throne. I'll take care of Oscar."

"One more time," Suzanne says, and we shift again.

She leads me gently to my throne. And the moment I sit down I can feel things healing faster. It hurts though, and she wipes my brow with a handkerchief that she's pulled from a pocket.

"You'll be OK," she says.

"How can I be? No one's safe. He said he wanted to hurt me."

"He can't, not really."

"Lissa—"

"She's safe. I have her watched. Now, tell me what happened."

I run through the ambush, the fight. The injuries that Rillman sustained.

Suzanne considers this. "He'll go and lick his wounds. Rillman isn't an RM. He will need some rest after doing the things that he did in that fight, to heal his injuries. Throw in the couple of savage punches to the head that Oscar delivered and Rillman will be quiet, he has to be. He may have wanted to hurt you, but it has cost him, too."

"What do you mean you have Lissa watched?"

Suzanne laughs. "She's too important a person in your life not to be watched. You have your Avian Pomps. Well, I have my own means. She is safe." She tilts her head. "As a matter of fact she's almost here." She jabs a finger in my chest. "Don't think that this gets you out of a lesson. I'll see you in the Deepest Dark later tonight."

She shifts just as Lissa opens the door.

Lissa looks at me. "Was somebody in here?"

"Suzanne. I needed her to shift me here," I say. "I'd get up, but—"

"Jesus, if she—"

"No, Rillman. He killed Travis."

"What?"

"The bastard was fast. He got us just after we walked off the bridge. We hurt him, but Travis died. Oscar looked pretty bad when I left him with Brooker."

Lissa rushes toward me and grabs my face. "And you?"

"I'm fine. I'm fine. Though I've got my twinges. How was your day, my love?"

"Far, far better than yours. Why Suzanne?"

"Tim can't shift yet, certainly not well enough to get me back here. What would you have me do, catch a bus?"

Lissa scrunches up her face. "You know how I feel about her."

"Yes, but she saved Oscar's life. I did call you first."

"OK, enough. Now tell me everything."

I sit in the throne, the heartbeats of my country playing around me. Thirty more people die in the space of my healing, though I'm angry over only one of them. Travis shouldn't have died for me. I've already looked into the schedule; his name is flagged as too early. He had another thirty-eight years.

My wounds have knitted well, though they're quite red and inflamed. Not bad for a couple of hours. I stretch in my chair, look over at Lissa. She's let me grump for a while now. She's rubbing at her brow like she has a headache and looks ready to collapse.

"Are you all right?" I ask.

"Yeah, the new staff are great. So that's one thing. And the other states, especially Sydney and Perth, are doing well, oddly enough." She sighs. "I know accepting Suzanne's Pomps would reduce the stress on us, but I don't want you to do it."

Guilt buzzes inside me. I should feel better about it, somehow justified that me taking up Suzanne's offer was really necessary. How much longer can I keep up this lying? "Well, looks like we're going this alone. Travis is gone and Oscar isn't getting out of a hospital bed for a while," I say.

"Yeah. But we're used to that. Weren't you kind of expecting it?"

"No, I wasn't. Call me optimistic, but I really wasn't."

It's so easy to have these things taken from me, RM or not, no matter how hard I work—or don't. Ah, fatalist much, Mr. de Selby?

Lissa strokes my face. There's an ache deep in the back of my throat and it becomes a burning when I look into her eyes.

I rise from the throne, slowly; every movement has its quotient of pain. I kiss her briefly, pull back and stare at her. Lissa's lips tremble and her face is lit with something that I can only hope I am the cause of.

"It always comes down to us," I say, trying to inject more hope into my words than I feel. Then I kiss her again, a longer lingering contact this time. "What the hell are we going to do?"

Lissa sighs. "What we always do. Keep going. We can't hide from Rillman. He can chase us anywhere. Besides, neither of us is the hiding type—it didn't work with Morrigan and it won't work with

Rillman. Tomorrow's Christmas, then it's three days until the Moot. We live our lives and we fight," she says.

Hiding certainly didn't work with Morrigan. But he never wanted me to die—until the end, when he was ready and my running was done. Rillman's motives are so much darker and murkier.

There's loss on the horizon, and we're bolting toward it, faster and faster. Rillman, the Stirrer god, the Hungry Death, the bloody Death Moot. All of it's terrifying me. Lissa must see it there in my face, because she rests a hand against my cheek, bears a little of the weight of my head for a moment.

"It's Christmas tomorrow," I say. "I can't believe it. To be honest, I'd forgotten."

"What? You're telling me you haven't got me a present?"

"Of course I have!"

She smiles, eyes flaring. Gorgeous, utterly gorgeous.

"Just kiss me again," she says.

And I do.

26

The Deepest Dark is a soothing chill against my newly healed flesh. I've showered and pulled a T-shirt and jeans over my scars. It feels odd to be here, out of a suit. Sure, I'd worn a tracksuit down here once, but that feels like it was an age ago.

"You're looking good for a man who nearly died tonight."

"Thank you again for your quick assistance."

"I have a lot riding on you, Mr. de Selby."

"Things are coming to a head," I say. "I can feel it. I need to know how you know so much. And I need to know just what is important."

"These sessions aren't about how I know things, but what I know. I assure you that you will have access to an incredible network of information. Not just Twitter, not just Facebook, or Mortepedia. Give yourself time."

"What network? And what the hell is Mortepedia?"

But Suzanne puts a finger to my lips. "You know about the Hungry Death now." I push her hand away.

"Yeah, let's call it HD, for short."

Suzanne sighs. "And you know that, once, pomping was a pleasurable thing. But do you understand why we use blood?"

"It has to be blood, and your own, and it has to hurt," I say. These are things I learned from my parents, as every Pomp does. And it feels good to say them. "The drawing of lines in the sand must always have consequences. It costs to fight battles. It's not just HD that drives this. You told me as much, when you told me how it was defeated. It's the will to make a difference despite the cost, and the realization that you might fail. If failure costs nothing, perhaps we would be too reckless. If it didn't hurt to stall a Stirrer, perhaps we would just rush in with no plan, our guns blazing and find ourselves surrounded, cut off, defeated."

The grin Suzanne gives me is huge. "Blood isn't just life, it represents how delicate life is. Now, symbols are very important in this business, as you already know. The brace symbol, for one. But something as simple as a gesture can be powerful. If you give yourself to it." She raises her hand, and dust lifts from the ground and follows her, fanning out, then condensing into a tight tube that spirals around her arm. "Try it."

I do, and nothing happens. No surprise there.

Suzanne touches my head. "You were thinking about it far too much. Just lift your arm."

"Right, right, just lift my arm!" I say, flapping my arms like I'm doing some crazy impersonation of a chicken. "Nothing, see—"

Dust swings around me, up and down.

But the moment I realize what I'm doing, the dust drifts away. A good bit of it gets sucked into my lungs. Suzanne watches me cough, her eyes crinkle.

"Good work," she says. "So much of what you need to do must be done without thought. Without reflection. That's the power and the danger of this job. It must be effortless. If it's too much one way, everything becomes mechanical, without soul, without rhythm. Too much the other, and it is all chaos. Even too much balance is wrong."

"Why?"

"Death isn't effort. It's consequence. It's as natural as breathing, and all the skills that we possess—to shift, to hear the heartbeats of our region, all of them—come from that. Give yourself over to it, and in the giving you will find that there is so much more time to explore the consequences of your actions. If you are always struggling, you can never ask yourself why, or what might be. Now, lift your arm again."

I lift, extending a finger. The dust lifts too. I draw my fingers into the bed of my palm then flick them out. Dust shoots away from me, five trails of it. I lower my hand and it drops. I can feel it around me, waiting for my motion, my guidance.

Suzanne winks at me. "Well done, Steven. I expect to see you tomorrow. But not here. Tomorrow we can meet in my office."

And she is gone.

Wal pulls from my arm. The last thing I expect to see him in is a little Santa hat.

"What the hell's Mortepedia?" I ask, lifting a finger, and watching a slender thread of dust rise up to touch it.

Wal spirals around it. "Some sort of treatment for dead feet? No, that's Mortepodiatry."

I glare at him. "Rillman nearly killed me tonight."

"But he didn't," Wal says.

"He managed to kill one of my bodyguards, though."

"Well, that's the problem. You don't need bodyguards. You're an RM, you should be able to look after yourself. You don't sleep, you can shift through space, and even make dust do... things. What do you need bodyguards for?"

"Lissa—"

"Lissa's stronger than you give her credit for. Think about what you two had to go through just to be together. You think Lissa was being all helpless in that? Lissa's only a weakness if you let her be one. If you let her be a strength..."

"When did you get so wise?"

Wal beams at me. "Always have been, mate, you just never listened."

PART TWO

THE MOOT

27

The barbecue's sizzling, and I'm there behind it, nursing a beer. Dad used to do this. No turkey, no ham on Christmas Day. Just meat cooked to within millimeters of inedibility and salad. Beer, too, of course. We have a couple of dozen stubbies of Fourex and Tooheys Old swimming in ice in the laundry sink.

It's a pretty grim Christmas. Last year there were so many more people. There doesn't seem to be much of a chance of backyard cricket. I look down at the lawn, which is in need of a mow—I'm not going to have time to do it in the next few days. But the kids don't seem to mind. Alex is down there with Tim and Sally. I'm glad I invited him. Christmas is a busy time for us, but for a moment we can pretend it isn't.

A hand slides around my waist. "Look at him down there, bailed up by your cousin. Do you think they're bitching about you?"

Alex is listening intently to something Tim is saying.

"Of course not, they respect me too much," I say, kissing Lissa on the cheek. I like the feel of her next to me, though she's a bit too bony at the moment, her cheeks too wan. After the Moot in two days I expect our stress levels to improve. Our staff intake is rising, not to mention my own involvement in the business. It's amazing what more than twelve hours without someone trying to kill you can do. But it doesn't feel like it's enough.

Lissa and Tim were right. I was letting things slip out of control.

Well, I'm back now. And I know I'm getting better at the job. I've learned so much in the past week.

The more people in this house, the less space there is for ghosts to fill it. And I'm doing my best to ensure that there are no more ghosts in the near future. I miss Oscar's and Travis's presence. But Wal is right, I can handle this. I have my own eyes and ears around the house, some of which are eating beetles. I wince and take a deep swallow of my beer. They're not the greatest taste, even second hand.

"Christmas always makes me feel a little sad," Lissa says.

"You missing your parents?"

Lissa nods her head. "It's been more than a year for me. I've already had a Christmas without them." She squeezes my hand. "I know how hard it must be for you."

"Yeah, but having you here makes it easier."

"Is that smoke I smell coming from the barbie?" Tim yells, and I realize that everyone is looking at us. The barbecue is definitely smoking.

"Must mean the sausages are ready," I say, stacking them onto a plate. Sure they're a little charred, but you've got to keep up tradition.

We sit around a dinner table laden with beer, soft drink, blackened sausages and bowls of salad. The kids groan when Tim kisses Sally. And everyone ignores my quick pash with Lissa.

Here is what I'm fighting for. This family. These connections old and new. We eat together, we laugh together. And seventy people around the country die. It's not too bad. And there are Pomps for every single one of them.

Perhaps, despite my doubts, the system's working.

Our guests are gone by early evening. The sky is smudged with the last tints of sunset. The city's quiet, the suburbs marked by the distant rumble of an engine, or the bark of a dog. Crows caw in nearby trees and noisy mynas live up to their name, chirping, chirping, chirping, as they hunt cicadas or try and push another bird out of their territory. They avoid my Avians, though, and shoot from the yard every time they hear the whoosh of black wings, the thrashing beat of a crow taking flight.

I sit on the back porch thinking, Lissa curled up next to me. Finally, some time to talk.

"So you're telling me the Hungry Death is real," Lissa says.

"Yes, very much so." I smile at her. "I call it HD."

Lissa groans. "But I thought the Hungry...I mean, HD was destroyed," she says.

"No. More like redistributed." I tap my chest. "The Orcus, we're all the Hungry Death now. And the other thing—Christ, I really couldn't believe it. Did you know pomping was once addictive?"

Lissa lifts to one elbow. "Where are you getting all this information?"

"Mr. D. He's been quite forthcoming of late."

Lissa smiles. "I'm glad you two are finally connecting."

"All it took was a fishing trip and a run-in with a giant shark, among other things."

"They say giant sharks are very much part of the male bonding process," Lissa says. She yawns, lays her head down on my lap. "Let's continue this conversation later. Say, once I've had a nap."

I watch her fall asleep, stroking her face, pulling her hair away from her eyes. Having Lissa here this Christmas has made it just about bearable, but my parents' absence is palpable and agonizing. I finish my beer. My head dips, my eyes close and I'm in a dream at once.

The Hungry Death laughs, and dances around the corpses of Lissa and my family. This new family. The one I haven't lost yet.

But you will. *The shadow that is the Hungry Death dips into a bow.* Merry Christmas, Mr. de Selby.

In one swift movement it wrenches Lissa's head from her shoulders, and hurls it at my face. Her dead eyes open, unseeing, never to behold me again.

I wake with a jolt. Only a moment's passed since my eyes closed, scarcely more than an eye blink. Lissa's still next to me, her heartbeat is strong. She's a thousand times more alive than when I first saw her, and I will not see her dead again. Never. I refuse to.

And it's so lovely to know that *that* is inside me, and is part of me in such a fundamental way. So very lovely indeed.

"You know," I whisper to it. "All I really wanted for Christmas was a pair of socks."

I slide away from Lissa. There's an ibis on a nearby roof, looking like a weathervane. It turns its long beaked face toward me.

"Lissa's sleeping," I say. "Keep an eye on her."

It dips its head, and scrambles across the roof for a better view. A crow shoots above me, landing on our roof with a scrape of claws. I get a confusion of perspectives looking in toward Lissa and away. The suburb is quiet, but for kids riding their new bikes, or people getting ready for a late Christmas dinner. Aircons are sighing, beetles are whirring. There's a clatter and a snap from up on the roof, and for a moment I can taste the crow's gecko dinner. *Ugh.*

I walk back to Lissa, kiss her on the brow. She startles me by actually opening her eyes.

"Where are you going?"

"Somewhere you can't come. Don't worry, I'll be safe—well, safeish. I've got work to do."

"It doesn't stop for you, does it?"

I smile. "You know, there was a while there when I thought it did. That I deserved a break. But when I stop, people die, people who I care about. And when they die, I die a bit, too."

Lissa touches my face, with a hand so perfect, so clear in my mind that I could hold it forever. “Merry Christmas,” she says.

And I think about HD, and its last words to me. I can’t let it spoil this. I’ll be damned if I’m going to give it even a minor victory.

“Yeah, merry Christmas.”

Then I shift, leaving her and my Avian Pomps behind.

28

Even this early in the morning Suzanne's Boston offices are a picture of efficiency. People work behind terminals, tapping away furiously, calculating the best routes to a pomp or a stir. A stocking taped beside a noticeboard is the only concession I can see to Christmas here.

Suzanne used to base herself in New York, but found it too noisy; "too clamorous," as she put it. I can understand that—such a big city, so many beating hearts hard up against each other. Washington, she'd never cared for, just as I could never imagine basing myself in Canberra. Capital cities are modern constructs. Our regions were built on different models.

The blinds are up, and it's snowing outside. Suzanne and Cerbo are both waiting for me.

"Merry Christmas, Mr. de Selby," Suzanne says, and pecks me on the cheek before I even realize what she's doing.

"You, too, Ms. Whitman."

Suzanne leads Cerbo and me into her office. "I can't tell you how much I am looking forward to spending a few days in Australia," she says, once she's shut her door and sat in her throne. "I've actually booked a room at the Marriott, a couple of blocks away from the bridge. Beautiful view."

I'm not here for small talk. "Things are getting worse," I say. "Stirrers are growing in numbers and I can't detect them."

"We've had problems here, too," Suzanne says. "The god's presence is making them almost reckless. You've seen it, you can understand why."

"Rillman isn't helping, either." I describe the symbol Rillman designed, and its powers. I'd emailed the details out to every RM, but it doesn't hurt to go over it again.

"No, he is proving to be something of a trial," Suzanne says.

"That may be the biggest understatement I have heard in my life. Are you practicing for a political career? A trial? Christ! And I need to know as much as I can about this god. Is there even any hope of stopping it?"

Suzanne nods at Cerbo.

"All I can tell you is this, and it goes back a ways," Cerbo says, pouring me a coffee, which I didn't ask for but accept nonetheless. "Six hundred million years ago something happened. Call it Snowball Earth, call it whatever you want, but after that, life grew more complicated, and the Stirrers' grip on this world ended." His voice speeds up: words tumble into each other with his excitement. I've never seen Cerbo so wound up. He's a nerd of the apocalypse. "You can see it more clearly in the Underworld. Look at the base of the One Tree; you'll see stromatolites crowding in like slimy green warts. We even have intelligence—" Cerbo looks at Suzanne, and she nods. "—we've even had intelligence that the Stirrers keep some in the heart of their city. Get out on the Tethys, go more than a few miles out, and what do you find? Nothing, no echoes of anything. Life hugs the shore. There's probably patches or places that correspond roughly to life and death on the earth but the sea of Hell is vast and I haven't found them. Believe me, I've looked."

"So what are you telling me?"

"What you probably already know, and what you will know as time goes by, ever quicker for you—that life is precarious. I think the Stirrer god existed before the Stirrers; a long time before. Maybe it's as old as the birth of the universe and Underverse itself."

"Old doesn't mean smart," I say.

"But it does mean tenacious and robust. That Stirrer god may be the most ancient consciousness in existence."

"So that's what we're up against?"

Cerbo nods.

I think about it for a moment. Try and find the most positive outcome. "Well, life won before, obviously. We're all still here. Things are alive. Life can win again."

Cerbo shakes his head. "But you see, I think that was an accidental victory, a consequence of forces that just slipped in life's favor. That is, if you can even call it a victory. Life exploded after those events, but the desolation beforehand... And this time..."

"And if the world shifted that way again?"

"It may well be worse than the Stirrer god itself. You don't know how bad the earth would be if we returned to those minus-fifty-degree Celsius temperatures."

I shrug. "I've seen *The Empire Strikes Back*."

Cerbo's smile is thinner than his mustache. "Humor is an inadequate defense. And it would be nothing like that. The planet Hoth would be a walk in the park on a summer's day compared to that."

"What do we do?"

"I don't know if there's anything we can do."

Suzanne grabs my hand. "See? See how difficult this is? This is what we are up against. I ask that you not judge any of us for the choices we may have to make in the days ahead. You, least of all."

I open my mouth to speak. Suzanne's phone rings, and mine follows a few moments later. We look at each other. When an RM's phone rings it's never a good thing.

It's Tim on mine. I answer it, trying to work out just who is calling Suzanne.

"Steve?" Tim asks. He sounds a little frightened. He'd been laughing at my table only a few hours ago. I immediately think the worst.

"Yeah." *Just give me the bad news.*

"Neill's dead."

I look at Suzanne and Cerbo. They're both pale as sheets, both getting the same message.

"Dead?"

"Yeah, it seems that Rillman has had better luck in South Africa."

An RM? Someone has managed to do what I thought impossible. "Is it a Schism?"

"No. David, Neill's Ankou, called me. Let me tell you, the guy was in a state. Someone came at Neill with knives, cut him up badly. Cut him into little pieces, is how David put it."

Then Tim's voice falls away. He's still talking, but I can't hear him. Something is clawing its way into my chest. A force, a strength that's part dark chuckle, part dread fear, part chest imploder. I recognize it at once. With Neill dead, a twelfth of his share of the Hungry Death is drawn into me.

I drop to the floor, maybe black out, because the next thing I see is Cerbo hesitating between Suzanne and me. We're *both* on the carpet.

"Well, can you help me get up?" Suzanne says, the first to recover. Her eyes are bright.

And yet, Cerbo hesitates. "That hasn't happened yet," Suzanne growls. "Here, now. Focus on me."

Cerbo runs to Suzanne's side, pulling her to her feet.

What the hell was that about? I wonder. I'm shaky, but standing now. Suzanne glances at me.

"This is not good," she says.

"But Neill has been dead for a while."

"The transfer isn't instantaneous. The Hungry Death has to find us. It's drawn to our flesh, but it takes time." Suzanne shakes her head. "Poor Neill."

"I thought you said the transition needed blood," I say.

"Well, there was plenty of it—Neill's blood," Suzanne says grimly.

"This changes things," Cerbo says. "Surely you can—"

"It changes nothing." Suzanne smiles so viciously at Cerbo that he quails.

She looks at me. "Tend to your region, Steven. I must tend to mine."

"What about Neill's region? Who's tending to it?"

"Charlie Top. At least, until we can organize some sort of transition. A Schism and Negotiation is messy, but this is far worse. It will have to do. We've two days until the Moot. We can organize something then."

I try and imagine something messier than a Schism. I can't, but then I'm not really the most knowledgeable RM. What I really don't like is the stronger HD inside me. The mere thought of all that carnage pulls at my lips. *He* pulls at my lips, from the inside. It's an effort not to smile, but I won't give HD that satisfaction. This is my body.

Suzanne waves me away with one hand. And I go.

I shift to my office, my head pounding with this new fragment of the Hungry Death. I tumble into my throne and the comfort it provides. The throne is slightly bigger, its edges harder, and yet I find it more comfortable to sit in. I decide I don't like that and I get to my feet, walk about my office, pull open the door.

The office is busy, but that's what you expect at this time of year, and in this trade. Holidays mean nothing—other than a serious inflation of the payroll, according to Tim.

Word has spread fast about Neill. Lissa's left a message on my phone, she's coming in straightaway. I look at my watch. It's getting late. People glance hurriedly away as I catch their eye. This is an office that is spooked. I don't blame them.

I make a show of going to the photocopier, try to look like everything is normal. It seems to have the opposite effect, particularly when I jam the bloody machine. Right, then, a more direct approach is needed. These people haven't deserted me, and I damn well won't desert them. I walk to the center of the office, and clear my throat. I've heard my share of inspirational speeches.

"As you have probably heard, the South African RM has died." The office is silent, listening. "Well, we have a Death Moot to run. In just three days, the remaining RMs will be here. Things are going to get hectic, but I am not going anywhere. Rillman has tried to kill me numerous times, and failed. I will not desert you."

I don't notice Tim until he's standing beside me. Lissa's here, too, now. She smiles hesitantly at me.

"We'll see this out," Tim says.

"We've faced worse." Lissa's voice is hard and strong. She holds my hand. "But it won't mean anything if we don't keep pomping or if we stop stalling Stirrers. We can't let Neill's death distract us. Everything dies, we all know that."

"And we have to make sure that that keeps happening. We have to be strong. I won't let you down." I don't know if that's enough, but it's all I have.

"Where were you?" Lissa asks me, once everyone returns to work—inspired, or terrified, or hunting for the job pages.

"Checking out the bridge," I lie.

Tim looks like he's about to say something, and then seems to think the better of it.

I guide them both into my office, and then the black phone, Mr. D's phone, rings.

29

There's a first time for everything.

I snatch it up.

"Neti's rooms," Mr. D says in a tone I've never heard before. "Now."

Mr. D can be direct when he needs to be.

"What the hell is going on?" Lissa demands.

"I need you to stay here," I say. "Both of you. It's something to do with Neti. Mr. D sounds frightened."

I head out the door, then across the office floor. I'm running by the time I hit the hall. Wal shudders on my arm and begins to slide free, his ink turning to muscle and bone. He tears from my flesh with the hummingbird whirr of a cherub's flight.

"Where are we going in such a hurry?"

"Neti's rooms. Mr. D—"

"Bugger."

I don't bother knocking this time. I open Neti's door, almost hitting Mr. D in the head in the process.

"Watch yourself," Mr. D says.

"Neti?"

"Oh, she's dead. Well and truly, more than I could have ever believed."

But that much is obvious already. There's not much of her left. Her little parlor is splattered with blood. It's everywhere. Strings of it dangle from light fittings, puddles gleam red and slick all across the floor. Is this what Rillman had wanted to do to me?

"I've never seen anything like this," Mr. D says. But I have. HD is having a grand old time, I can feel him tugging at the corner of my lips.

I try and imagine the fight. There are burn marks everywhere, just like the Stirrer safe house. And the smell of cooking flesh, not the usual wholesome odors of scones or cake—though there is some of that in the background. The spider in the corner hangs limp and dead.

Wal flits around us, looking slightly green. "What does this mean?" he says.

"Rillman took a great deal of pleasure in doing this," I say.

"Obviously," Mr. D says.

"Who's going to replace her?" Wal asks, puffing out his chest, and riffling through her collection of china plates. I wave him away from there.

"Something will replace her, but it will be different. And it will come in its own time. That's the way these things work," says Mr. D.

Neti looks so small, but that's because she is in so many different pieces. I'm Death, so it's beneath me to gag, but it's hard not to. Her limbs are spread around the room. Her eyes are sightless. The television chatters; an inane game show. And it looks like she is watching it. Her strength and her menace are gone. Aunt Neti is dead, and murdered with such cruel joy. HD cheers a little.

"Where are the Knives of Negotiation?" I say suddenly remembering them. "Please tell me they're safe."

Mr. D pales. He rushes to the black cabinet, does something intricate with its scrollwork and one of its doors slides to one side. The knives' usual resting place. "Nothing," he says.

My brain ticks over. Rillman must have started with his stony razor, covered with my blood, perhaps to give it greater efficacy. And then, when he had incapacitated Neti, he snatched the knives and put them to quick snicker-snack use, finishing off the job. Then he probably shifted directly to Neill's office. Aunt Neti's been dead a while. Rillman had been anxious to leave in the tunnel, and not just because my Avian Pomps had arrived. He'd never expected to take so long with me.

There is a plate of scones on the table, untouched. Neti was expecting Rillman, or someone. Like she said, she only makes scones when people are coming to her with questions. Her prescience had failed as to Rillman's real intentions.

I wonder if she wasn't working with him in some way. Maybe the Stirrer safe houses, their grid, is being used for something else. Maybe Rillman was using both sides.

I have never seen Mr. D look so rattled. "So what do we do from here?" I ask.

"We talk strategy. Rillman is killing RMs, and suddenly the focus has turned away from the real threat, the coming Stirrer god."

"Well, that's got them scared as well." I sigh. I really don't know whom I can trust at all. But one thing is certain; Mr. D doesn't have the answers.

But there's someone who does, and I might just catch her.

"I'm going to have to leave you here to clean up," I say to Mr. D.

"Of course," Mr. D says, though he is obviously affronted. "I of all people know how busy you are."

I give him a quick salute and shift.

Eight long arms snap out at me, but only one connects. It's enough to put me on my arse. The One Tree creaks around us in sympathy with her or me, I'm not sure.

"Oh, it's you." Several hands help me up.

"I didn't expect Rillman would visit you here."

"How did you know, dear?" Aunt Neti asks. She doesn't look happy, but I wouldn't be either if someone I'd considered an ally had just chopped me into little pieces.

"You made him scones. You were expecting his visit." I grimace. "I kind of guessed it."

Aunt Neti scowls. "When you broke the rules, and didn't even choose me to allow your Orpheus Maneuver, well, that was too much."

"Charon was just there," I say. "I didn't realize that there was any other way."

"Exactly. At least Rillman understood how it was meant to be done. I was the one who helped his Orpheus Maneuver. I felt so guilty that it failed, not because of anything I did, but that blasted Mr. D."

"I thought Mr. D was your friend."

Aunt Neti nods. "Keep your friends close, and your enemies closer. You would do well to remember that, Mr. de Selby, when it all comes falling down around you. Rillman failed, and I felt that I owed him. Besides, once you had clearly disdained me, well, what allegiance did I owe to you?

"I was happy to cover for him, to let him return to the land of the living. We REs perform Orpheus Maneuvers all the time; we let the curtains slip between life and death. It's not such a big deal for us, because we're not really alive. But I never meant to create a monster, and certainly not one so dangerous. My indulgence never went as far as the stone knives."

I glare at her. "It should never have gone as far as your lies. You owed your loyalty to me."

Aunt Neti snorts. Her eight arms wave around her, a halo of limbs, and then she's jabbing them in my face. "And what do you owe yours to? Not much, as far as I can see. With your rule-breaking, your moaning. And when did you ever really come to me for advice? There are things you could have learned if you trusted me. But no, you avoided your Aunt Neti, unless it was absolutely necessary. My Francis never did that. And you skimped on your duties, drinking, not showing up for work. People talk, Mr. de Selby, and your Aunt Neti listens."

"And look where that's gotten you," I snap. "A place on the One Tree, and no power at all."

The air seems knocked out of her. She folds her hands neatly around her waist, and dips her head.

"Yes... Well, it's a fabulous view," Aunt Neti sighs. I can see she's already growing listless with death. Soon the One Tree will have her and all that will remain will be a fading memory. "You're right, of course, but it's too late for me now. There are some lessons that you take to the grave."

30

Evening after a long and confusing day. HD is making me jittery. The Moot's looming and I'm home. I want to be with Lissa, but that's not whom I've got. The kitchen buzzes with the energy of two RMs. I wonder what Dad would think. I wonder if he would be proud. I doubt it. Maybe, if I'd let Lissa in on my secret. It's been a long day.

I don't like having the meeting here, at home. But Suzanne insisted. Lissa isn't due back for another couple of hours. There is a stir expected at the Princess Alexandra Hospital.

"I never thought I'd see the day," Suzanne said. "But here we are, a Recognized Entity is dead. Killed not by one of us, nor by our enemy, but by that stupid, vengeance-craving man."

"And with those knives. He can wreak bloody havoc with them," I say. "Maybe we should consider canceling the Death Moot."

"No," Suzanne growls. "The Death Moot goes ahead. To cancel it would set an alarming precedent. We're better off together, stronger. Unless, that is, if he manages to kill us all... Well, that thing that we contain, it won't be contained anymore."

"Where would it go?"

Suzanne's smile is wide. "Imagine your dreams, imagine that made reality. That shadowy, lurching Hungry Death; that relentless slaughter. De Selby, it's in us all, it's in everything living. But in us... us twelve, now... it's magnified, personified. Death is part of life, but without anyone to control it... all that power is not a legacy I want to leave for the world. Still—"

"Still, if it's going to happen, it's better to be dead than deal with it," I say.

Suzanne shakes her head. "If that sort of thing occurs then we've a major biblical sort of problem—actually, nastier than anything in the Bible. Death won't save you. Maybe I'm wrong, Steven, but it terrifies me, and it should terrify you, too."

"I don't think I know enough to be terrified."

Suzanne frowns. "Ultimately that's what it's all about, our business. Managing Death, keeping the Hungry Death under control and following laws more conducive to life. Whenever we fail, whenever we let it slip out of control, bad things happen. That's just the way it works. Our governments may want to impose their own system of management on this, no matter that they don't have nearly the unified approach that we possess. We're older than any system of legislature or governance. If we fail at our business, they have no chance of filling the void.

"You may not trust the Orcus, but believe me when I say that there is a certain purity in what we do, in what we had to give up to become this. You just lost your innocence in a different way. It was torn from you. For the rest of us, we tore it from ourselves.

"We chose this path with our eyes open. We knew the cost of what we did, of those that we killed. I loved my family, I loved my friends, but I knew I could be a better RM than my predecessor. Did I ever tell you that he was my lover?

"I killed him to become this, because he was weak, because I could see battles far ahead that I knew he wouldn't be able to fight. He confided in me, bared his shortcomings, and the only way I could see to deal with his weakness was to take the job from him, and the only way that I could do that was via a Schism and the Negotiation. Do you know what it is like to not just lose the ones that you love, but to deliberately take them away? It eats you out like a cancer. But what choice did I have?

"Ask yourself what Morrigan might have seen coming, what fears drove his decisions. I dare say it was more complicated than just a lust for power. You know us, we're not all bad, we went into this knowingly and passionately and with a desire to change the world." Suzanne lowers her gaze. "You know history, the violence that made each of us Death. But don't you ever fool yourself into thinking you can understand us."

"You're murderers, one and all," I say.

Suzanne nods. "Oh, yes, we are. And all of us suffer for it. This job is our punishment as much as it is our prize. This business and the Hungry Death inside us, it's horrible isn't it? I pity you, sometimes, Steven, that you don't even have the comfort of your passion to protect you. Oh, how that must hurt, and there is no one to share it with. This job isn't about giving up everything for your love, it's about giving up your love, for everything."

"And where does that leave you?"

"I didn't say it was the right choice, but it was the choice we made. I'm not expecting sympathy, or even understanding. Just acceptance. This is what we have done. All of us suffer, that is the only thing that truly links humanity. We exist, and I truly believe this, to reduce the quantity of suffering in the world even if it means we must bleed ourselves."

I can't look at her. Love and family, even in the face of suffering, are the most important things to me. The only things I have left to believe in. And maybe that is being selfish. I know it's selfish. How can I be an RM if I can't give them up?

She grips my hand. "Oh, Steven. There's so much you still don't understand. I pity you. The lessons of your time are far crueler than anyone could expect."

"Don't pity me," I say, and I've never seen her look so amused.

She grabs my face, jerks my head toward hers, and kisses me hungrily. Her lips are as cold as mine, her heart as silent and stealthy as the one in my chest. For a moment I am intoxicated.

Yes, it would be easier. She would understand me in ways that Lissa can't hope to. We could have this forever.

But the thought lasts only for a moment. I pull away, wipe my mouth with my sleeve. *Bloody hell, what was I thinking?*

"No," I say.

Then I hear the intake of breath. Recognize the new heartbeat in the room.

"What are you doing here?" Lissa's eyes are wide with hurt, but they're ready to ignite into anger. All it needs is someone as unsubtle—or cruel—as Suzanne to set it off. Or someone as stupid as me.

My cheeks are burning. It's not as if I did anything wrong... Other than lie to her. Just how did that happen again?

"I'm surprised he didn't tell you," Suzanne says. "I made him an offer he couldn't refuse, and well..." She looks at me slyly, "He didn't refuse it."

"You bitch!" Lissa snarls. "You can't keep out of my family's business, can you?"

"Business is business, Lissa. Nothing more. What happened between your father and me... I understand why you might blame me. But—"

"I don't blame you." Lissa's right hand clenches into a fist. "Oh, hang on a minute, yes, I do."

"That's enough." I raise my hands in the air, step between the two of them. "It's all just a—" And Lissa's fist connects with my jaw. She looks from me to Suzanne and back again. I'm not sure whom she meant to hit. I don't think she is, either.

"You bastard," she says—that's definitely aimed at me. "You had to go and do this."

And she's out of that room before I can open my mouth.

I rub my jaw, spin on Suzanne. "You set me up! You arranged for her to come home!"

Suzanne's face hardens. "You didn't see this coming?"

"No, I didn't."

"Why the hell did you flirt with me?"

My face is burning. "I never—"

"You did. The coat, the lingering looks."

"I thought I was just playing your game." And then rage explodes inside me. "Piss off, now. *GO!*"

"I'll let you get away with that, but only because I feel a certain element of sympathy. Particularly with what lies ahead. But you will never talk to me like that again." Suzanne shifts away.

I'm left in the empty room. I run to the hallway. Lissa's nowhere to be seen. Out onto the verandah, and then onto the street. Heat slaps me in the face nearly as hard as Lissa's right hook.

I don't mind the pain. I deserve it.

Where the hell is Lissa? I close my eyes, feel her heartbeat. She's back in the kitchen. I run to her.

"You lie to me about not meeting her, about not accepting her offer, and then you're kissing." She wipes at her eyes. "If you want to be with one of them, I can understand that. They're your people now. But to try and keep us going, while—oh, Jesus, Steven. I never thought you'd be such a prick."

"Yeah, I'm a prick. I won't argue with you. I'm an absolute arsehole."

"Agreeing with me isn't helping your case."

"But I love you."

"Did you take up her offer?"

"Yes, but I had no choice."

"You could have chosen to tell me about it," Lissa says. "You could have told me everything. I'm a grown-up. You could have trusted me with this."

"There's no lies between us," I say, which is technically a lie. Why do I keep digging myself deeper and deeper holes?

"Just half-truths." Lissa shakes her head. "So, Steven, you got your ten extra Pomps. But you lost one as well. I'm not going to take this. Not now. I'm leaving."

"OK," I say, because I don't know what else to say. I'm sick with shock. "But I love you."

"Maybe you think you do. But this isn't love. These lies aren't love." She steps toward me. Her heart is racing at 130 bpm, and then it slows, shifts down to eighty. "Now, you know what you need to do?"

"No."

"Do I have to spell it out for you? I'm resigning."

"But—"

"If you don't do this I'll hate you forever."

"We need you. Mortmax needs you."

"Don't you dare play that card. You'll do all right. You have her help, after all."

"I don't want her help."

"It didn't look like it when I walked in."

"Lissa—"

"Just do it!"

I look into her eyes, and she holds my gaze. I reach over and she grabs my hands. It was such an easy gesture once, but now so awkward. My hands shake. She's closed to me, but then she opens up, and I can feel her anger as a visceral thing, a burning agony. It shocks me, even though I was expecting it.

I don't want to do this. It's too painful. I'd let go but she's holding my hands so tightly that my fingers hurt.

I draw the energy back from her, the bit of me that makes pomping possible. I unpick it from her essence. I've never had to do this before, and maybe I couldn't if Suzanne hadn't taught me. It's as easy as opening a door. But what it reveals... Here, I can see how I have wounded her. How stupid I was. We're both crying by the time it's done. My lip quivers. "I'm so sorry."

"So am I," Lissa says. She pushes past me, heading into the bedroom. "Don't follow me!"

A few minutes later, she's back in the kitchen with a bag bulging with her clothes. She drops it, and a black skirt and blouse tumble free. She glowers, kicks her bag away in frustration. She's no longer a Pomp. She's no longer my girl.

I crouch down to help her pick up her things. She pushes my hands away.

"I can manage," she says.

"You don't need to leave, I'll—you can stay here."

"You'll leave me in your parents' house? Where everything will just remind me of you?" She bends down, grabs the clothes and shoves them back into her bag.

"We can work this out. I can do better. No more lies."

Lissa scowls, her lips move as though to frame some sarcastic response and then she seems to think better of it. "I need time to think."

"But I—"

"And you have a Death Moot to run. Don't let me get in the way of that."

Why didn't I tell her about Suzanne? What stopped me from mentioning it? I have no excuse, or I have far too many.

"Lissa, I was set up. I'm sure of it. She wanted you to walk in." Even to my ears that sounds far too desperate.

"So I could see you kissing her?"

"Yes! This won't happen again... Christ, it didn't happen the first time."

"Really?" Lissa throws up her hands. "Yeah, I've seen how it didn't happen. Don't you see? I've watched all this play out before." Lissa picks up her bag. "I can't be this person. Not with you. Mom and Dad, they had their problems, and I swore I would never be like that. And I won't."

"But—" I reach out toward her.

She steps away from me, throws her bag over her shoulder. "I'll come back for the rest later."

"Where are you going?"

"Somewhere. Anywhere but here. And don't send any of your bloody Avians after me." She walks back down the hall, and I follow her to the front door.

"This could have been so good," she says.

"It still—" Lissa shuts the door in my face. I flinch backward, then grab the handle, fling the door open. Lissa is hunched down on the stairs, sobbing.

"I thought you were going away."

She clambers to her feet. "Oh, fuck you."

"Stay with me, I can protect you."

Lissa's eyes flare. "You can't even protect yourself! The prick blew up our car, Steven. If he hadn't, I wouldn't be waiting for a fucking taxi right now! He killed Travis and Jacob, he nearly killed Oscar."

"But he'll track you down."

"I'm not a Pomp now. You know that's going to make it harder. I've pulled out of the game. If he comes after me, and if you do, too, you better be prepared for the consequences."

"You can't—"

"Don't tell me what I can and can't do. You stay away until I'm ready. To forgive you, or not to forgive you. You lied to me. And you lied to me about her."

"I wanted to spare your feelings."

"No, you didn't want it to be *difficult*. And that worked out so well. Love isn't easy, Steven. It's hard."

I want to ask her why she's leaving, then. Why she's taking the easy option. But I'm the one who has wounded her. I have no right.

She slams her bag onto her shoulder again, and swings around toward the road. "Don't come near me."

I stand there, my mouth hanging open. I deserve it. I'm a fool. I can no more touch her now than when she was a ghost.

A taxi pulls into the street. Lissa looks back at me as it stops beside her. Her eyes are hard. Then she jumps into the cab. I watch it go.

There'll be time to make it right. But not now. Now she's safer away from me. I have to believe that. The day after tomorrow, the Death Moot begins.

A sparrow looks at me. I nod at it. And send the little Avian Pomp after the taxi.

31

I'm still in shock on the morning of the Moot. A day of prep has done little to dull the pain. Lissa's taken up residence in a hotel. The blinds are shut, and my Avians have no view of what is going on beyond them. Only her heartbeat reassures me that she is alive.

It took me three years to get over Robyn. I'm not going to lose Lissa.

Tim was more sympathetic than I thought I deserved. Maybe he's terrified I'm going to lose it. By 8:00 a.m. he has rewritten my opening address, and left me to link my speech with some animations I've sourced from Cerbo. I've never used PowerPoint before, but have found some amazing transitions. I'm feeling almost professional.

It must be the calm before the storm. Rillman's been quiet, there have been no attacks, which worries me. What is he planning? Not a single RM has called me. Perhaps they are steeling themselves for the two days ahead, perhaps they are too busy hiding from Rillman. I'd have at least expected Suzanne to ring to gloat, or to apologize.

Only Solstice gets in contact. Reckons he might have something on Rillman, but he wants to follow it up first. I talk to him about Lissa. He offers me some security, two guards. I think about it. Suzanne said she had someone watching Lissa. But do I trust her? Not really. Not after what she pulled in my kitchen. I give him Lissa's address. The Death Moot is going to keep me busy for the next forty-eight hours, and my Avians certainly aren't going to be able to get inside the hotel she's staying in.

Then I check on Oscar. He's doing OK, but Brooker doesn't expect him to be out of bed for another week. I talk to Oscar about Lissa, and he listens, but offers no comment. I tell him I think I'm ready to look after myself, and he smiles. "Yeah, I think you are, too."

I receive one call from the Caterers, everything is prepared, that the bridge is waiting.

I walk over to Tim's office, knock on the door.

He opens it, and smiles at me nervously. "Ready?"

"Yeah."

He comes over to me, straightens my tie. "You are now. How'd you go with that PowerPoint presentation? Hope you didn't put in too many fancy transitions."

"Of course not."

I grasp his hand and we shift onto the Kurilpa Bridge.

And here it is. Everything has been set up for this moment. This Moot. The bridge is just wide enough for our marquees. It certainly wouldn't be in the mortal realm, not if you needed to accommodate all the pedestrian traffic as well. The marquees are worth the rather large amount of money we paid for them. As is the lighting, and the aircon, which is keeping the space to a comfortable twenty-five degrees.

The Orcus sits around the table, each in their throne. Li An smiles at me. Kiri nods. Anna Kranski gives me a little salute. Devesh Singh is mumbling into his coffee. Charlie Top, now Middle and South Africa's RM, is tweeting like mad on his phone. Suzanne is sitting at the other end of the long table, a coffee by her side.

Here we talk as equals. And we're all looking a bit ridiculous. I've bought them all Akubras to wear—it seems the thing at these international conferences. I want to laugh but the Hungry Death bubbles beneath my skin, whispering to its eleven selves, calling them, and they call back. Its presence has never manifested itself so strongly before. I find it quite terrifying, and a relief that it's not just focused in one person.

How could you handle all that hunger and not go insane?

En masse there is a density and a gravity about the RMs that is impressive. I can't quite believe that I share it. Neill's absence is a void that can't be ignored, though no one is talking about it. That will come later, I guess.

I begin my speech welcoming them all here. They laugh in the right places, though I can't say my delivery is that good. Lissa helped me come up with most of the jokes. I'm still not sure what happened. How could I break her heart so easily? Maybe I thought I'd earned it.

The Moot progresses. The first topic on the agenda is something small, a matter of profits in the last quarter. Suzanne brings that one to the table. I'm actually surprised that she uses a PowerPoint presentation; I was kind of expecting something with animated dust or lightning. The topic is dry, but people seem interested. Maybe it's a break from all the events of the last week. The morning session moves surprisingly swiftly, though I don't hear too much of it.

I'm thinking about my core presentation this afternoon. I have so much to discuss, and, even with Tim's rewrites, I'm not sure that I can pull it off.

Lunch is called at around twelve-thirty.

With all of us together the air is charged with the sort of electricity you'd expect just before a massive storm. In fact, there's one forming in the western suburbs. Thick, rain-heavy cloud is growing darker and darker, and it's heading our way. I'm outside, taking a breather from all the food and the talk. Li An has joined me on the bridge. I don't know why, though. He hasn't said anything yet, and we've been out here for ten minutes.

From the bridge we can see both the Underworld and the living one. On one side is the cultural precinct starting with the sharp lines and angles of the Gallery of Modern Art, and on the other rise the skyscrapers that make up the CBD. The storm is building on Mount Coot-tha. I watch as the Caterers run from line to line on the marquees, double-checking that everything is as it should be, and will stand up to the tempest.

Li An nods at the Caterers and finally speaks. "Happens all the time, these storms," he says. "You get used to it." He spits out an olive pit and frowns. "Never get used to the miserable catering, though. After ten thousand years you'd think they'd know how to use a bain-marie."

My face burns. He doesn't stop eating the nibblies, nor swigging down on a glass of white, though, all of which cost me more money than I want to think about right now.

He pats my shoulder gently. "Of course, you won't need to worry about that, soon." He sighs. "Got any of those little sandwiches? I do like those little sandwiches."

What the hell is he talking about? I open my mouth to thank him for the vote of support when the air is split with a tremendous thunderclap.

Two black flags, marked with the brace symbol, snap in the wind above the Ankous' marquee. The RMs call it the whinge tent. As far as I can see it's justified, the title and the whingeing. We make them work hard and then some. Tim knows he doesn't have to put up with my shit, but the rest of them don't have the advantage of a family connection. This must be their only chance to vent.

Tim stands by their marquee with the other Ankous, apparently holding court. He looks far more comfortable than me, though I've noticed that he's drawing on a cigarette faster than I thought was humanly possible.

He nods at me. Yeah, something's going on there, and he's not happy. He gestures at his phone; I yank mine out of my pocket a moment before it signals that I've received a text.

Be careful, Tim's written. *They're up to something.*

A few more specifics would be helpful.

A hand, a big hand, slaps down on my shoulder and I somehow manage not to yelp.

"Good spot, this," Kiri Baker says. He's about as broad across as I am tall. He smiles a wide, bright smile. "Nice."

I nod my head. "Yeah."

"So, you still seeing Mr. D for advice?"

"Yeah."

"He still doing that face thing?"

I nod, and Kiri shivers. "Fuck, that used to scare the bejesus out of me. Dramatic bloke, isn't he? Gotta have a hobby, I suppose." He slaps me on the shoulder again and squeezes. "We southerners have to stick together, eh?"

Hm, that didn't count for much when we had a Schism a couple of months ago.

Kiri sighs. "It's a shame we'll never have a chance to know what might have come of that." I turn sharply and look at him. He's grinning. "Desperate times. Now, I've got to get some of those little sandwiches." He walks back into the marquee.

What do these people know that I don't?

It's my turn at the podium again. I pull out my PowerPoint; relate all that I know about the Stirrer god. The things that Cerbo has told me, my own experiences. I even mention the visit from the Stirrer that inhabited Lissa, suggesting that Stirrers may not be as unified as we once thought.

I cannot feel any heartbeats, which is a blessed relief. Must be the storm. I look at the eleven RMs before me. They may be my people now, but I can't show any weakness. My only strength, Mr. D reckons, is that none of them is likely to remember what it was like to be new to the job. They expect a higher level of knowledge than I have.

Huff and bluff, I think to myself. If there's anything I'm good at it's bullshit.

"We have to do something," I say.

"But what?" Charlie Top asks. "My resources are stretched as they are, particularly now that I'm shackled to South Africa, too. Do you not know how many wars my poor Pomps are working? Will you give me more crew to work them?" He looks over at Suzanne. "Not that it matters," he says under his breath, and makes a show of looking at his watch.

"I don't have any to give," I say. Everyone laughs at that, and I fail to see the joke.

"Exactly," Charlie says. "You developed world RMs never have anything to give. We're all part of Mortmax and yet what do you all do? Cut back our supplies or provide them with so many conditions that—"

"It's not the time to discuss this," Kiri breaks in. "We have deeper issues at stake. Rillman has killed an RM. Mortmax's thorn has grown thornier. We all felt it, we've all borne that new burden."

"Which is why de Selby must know these things," Charlie says. "Why he must understand the issues of our regions before it's too late."

"It's what I'm after," I say. "A unified approach to dealing with this problem."

"Yes, but what you don't understand, Mr. de Selby, is that the threat Rillman offers is more immediate," Anna Kranski says.

"How can it be more immediate than *this*?" I slam my hand on the projector and the inky black illustration of the Stirrer god that covers the far wall shakes. "It's coming. And it's getting faster and hungrier and more powerful."

"We have months, if not years, to resolve that issue. Well, you will," Charlie says. "Perhaps you might want to work out how to use PowerPoint, too. All those transitions!"

My jaw drops. "I thought the transitions worked very well."

Charlie Top snorts. "In my experience things aren't ever as neat."

"And what exactly is your experience?" I demand.

"I was old before you were born."

"Ha! What's a few centuries?" I say.

"Actually, Mr. de Selby, a few millennia."

"Well, I've yet to see the wisdom of them." I close the PowerPoint presentation. "We know so little, because we share so little. We have to be united. We have to be because there is no one else but us."

Charlie looks over at Suzanne, and smiles somberly. "He may just be ready."

What the fuck is he talking about? And what the fuck have all those veiled comments been about? I get the feeling I'm about to find out.

Kiri whistles and jabs a thumb toward the doorway. "There's one motherfucker of a storm coming."

Wind shakes the marquee like some curious, angry giant. Then the tent is gone, hurled into the air, and I'm having some sort of Dorothy Gale moment. Lightning dances across the river, spanning the water at some points so that it looks like a bridge of flame. And at its heart is a figure, grinding two knives together. Around him stand half a dozen Stirrers, their arms tattooed with a familiar pattern, their hair writhing with esoteric energies.

Sensing the threat, my sparrows and crows swarm, but they can't draw close. The moment they do, lightning blasts them out of existence.

Suzanne grabs my hand. "This is it, Steven. I'm sorry it's all going to rest on your shoulders."

"What the hell are you talking about?"

"You never were the brightest one, were you? Just look after Faber for me. He has always been such a loyal Ankou." She grabs my face, kisses me once on the cheek, and then the lips, the latter a lingering thing that possesses a surprising tenderness. "Pity, I think I would have enjoyed getting to know you better."

They can't be serious. They can't leave all this to me! I didn't even want to be RM, and I certainly don't want to run all of Mortmax Industries. I can't.

The other RMs surround us. I remember them circling me while I fought Morrigan in the Negotiation, with all that hunger in their eyes. There's none of that rapacity now, just a grim fear. These Deaths are going to face their own mortality. They've forgotten what that is like, and now it's time to die. But for me, it's all too familiar.

It's one thing to serve it out, to be the creeping replication of cancer cells, the rupturing or blockages that halt a heart, or the shriek of metal against metal and the burn of petrol waiting to ignite on a highway. But it's an altogether different thing to be on the receiving end.

"We've been working hard to bring Rillman out into the open. The man has been actively lobbying against us in various parliaments for a long time. And he can be extremely persuasive, as you would expect from a man who came back from the dead. We never thought he'd get his hands on the knives so swiftly. Steven, you have proven a remarkable accelerant."

"Yeah, people say that about me."

Suzanne ignores me. "You were the perfect bait though; imagine, an RM who had also completed a successful Orpheus Maneuver. How could Rillman ever resist that? I'm sorry about what he did to you."

"And Lissa? Walking in on you—me...?"

"We needed Lissa out of the way. She was in too much danger, and if anything happened to her, we know how that might affect someone at the stage you are in of your career. The last thing we wanted was a rogue RM. I must apologize for that. It was my idea. I sent one of my own Pomps to the Princess Alexandra so that she'd come home. You were set up again."

"Again?"

"Well, Morrigan did it so successfully. We thought we could as well."

"Successfully? Look how that ended up."

"Hm, well, there's a theory that bait is best when it doesn't realize just what it is. Even Mr. D agreed on this. Why do you think we allowed you to have him as a mentor? You are the first RM in the history of the Orcus to have such a guide!"

Mr. D was in on this, too? I thought we'd reached a nice balance of trust and untrust, and now...

"Who else knew about it? Tim?"

"Tim's canny, but no. He does now. All the Ankous do. He loves you too much to keep something like that quiet. Steven, people love you, despite you making it so hard for them. They really do."

"So you baited the hook with me? Thank you very much."

"You were being watched. We wouldn't have let Rillman hurt you very much. And as for your relationship with Lissa, you did a good enough job of messing that up yourself, despite my help."

"But did your spies have to punch me in the face?"

"Let me tell you, he was disciplined for that."

"For punching me?"

"No, for being caught and needing to."

The lightning cages and crackles around us, a net of fire that sets the hair on my flesh on end. The other RMs look at each other, and then at Suzanne.

The Ankous' marquee follows its twin into the air. Twelve Caterers rush toward the kitchen, place their hands on it and are gone. Can't guess how much this is going to cost.

I can hardly hear Suzanne's voice. "You have to get away from here," she's saying. "The Ankous are already gone, including Tim. They're safe for the moment. And find your Lissa. Things may not end as badly as we fear, and if that's the case we'll find you. If they do end badly, well... you'll know."

But I know it will end badly. I know they're all preparing to die. This is the path they have chosen, the plan they laid out when I became RM.

Suzanne is shaking her head. "Steven, you may be a bit slow on the uptake, but really, your heart is in the right place. You're the only one of us who might stand a chance with the Hungry Death inside of them. You're the only one who might hold out against the coming darkness."

I want to hit something, anything. "So all that shit about you having a plan, about doing something. The plan was to leave it all up to me."

"Not just you. You will have our Pomps, our Ankous, and your precious Mr. D. Let me tell you, he won't give in to the One Tree for anything now with the kind of influence he'll have."

Like I'm ever going to talk to Mr. D again. Fuck him. Fuck all of them.

"You have to realize that the Hungry Death has been manipulating us all these years, driving our Negotiations to greater and greater violence. We started playing its game, and that's not how you control something like the Hungry Death. You made me realize that. So, Steven, you're not as stupid as you think.

"You'll succeed at this in a way that none of us can. Surely you can perceive what an important moment this is? Just what we're giving up? This is *you*. This is all *your* doing. You've made us all a little bit human again with your presence, your... flaws. Don't forget that."

She leans toward me, fast, and kisses my lips hard, one more time. My face burns. "There has to be another way. It's not too late. Please—"

"No. You're going to need all of the Hungry Death inside you to defeat what's coming. We're giving up our disunity in favor of your sense of purpose. Madness, isn't it?"

"Neill didn't want this, did he?"

Suzanne winks at me. "Why do you think he's dead?"

"You organized that somehow. Made it easy for Rillman to get to him!"

"I'm a ruthless RM when I have to be. Don't hold it against me, de Selby. It's all I know, it's the reason I can't do what you have to."

Lightning sparks against the bridge, a flashing beat of fire that webs its steel masts. Everything seems caught in the flame. I feel like I'm in an out-take of *Highlander.*

"There can be only one," I mumble. My legs are weak. This is too much. Here I am, sick with fear in the eye of the storm.

Suzanne smiles. "Now you're getting it. But there will actually be two. You, and the Hungry Death inside you. It will test you, oh, how it will test you. But then what doesn't? You'll be Death, Mr. de Selby. Death of a whole world. What a glorious thing."

The bridge shudders, jolts. And then Rillman shifts onto Kurilpa, followed by his Stirrers. Lightning flashes everywhere, arcing around us. Suzanne and I look at each other, almost embarrassed by the melodrama of the moment.

"He's nearly tiresome enough to make death pleasurable," Suzanne says.

Rillman shifts to the rail of the bridge. He smacks the knives together. Lightning shivers from the blades, dancing between him and his Stirrers. They're generating it between themselves somehow, just as they've been generating the storms in Brisbane, I realize. The lightning curls around Rillman in a way that no lightning should.

I can feel something building. Electricity crackles in my ears. There's a moment of silence, an indrawn breath.

"Death is coming!" Rillman roars, and lightning drives into the assembled Orcus. They don't even flinch, though behind them I'm throwing my hands up over my face.

"Just get on with it!" Li An yells, ripping off his Akubra, and batting out the flames.

More sparks. Rillman has really invested in the show. With each burst the Orcus loses more of its civility. Clothes sear and burn, but flesh remains unharmed.

This isn't going to hurt them. It's what will come next: the edge of stony knives.

Kiri turns to me. He pats my back, reaches out a hand. "No hard feelings, eh?"

"None," I say, biting down a harsher response. This is not the time or the place.

Kiri grins, then bows. "Let's get started, eh?"

He's surprisingly light-footed as he sprints toward Rillman. The knives flash out. Kiri drops beneath the first blade, swings a fist toward Rillman's face. He connects, but barely. The second knife juts from his chest, eight inches of blade. Kiri looks at me, and then at the rest of the Orcus.

"Well, c'mon!" he roars, spittles of blood trailing his exclamation.

Whatever seal of indecision there was, breaks. The rest of the Orcus run toward Rillman, Suzanne pulling back. "You really can't stay here," she says.

"I want to stay."

"There's nothing you can do here. Just be ready for what comes. Promise me you will go."

"Why do I get the feeling I'm still being played?"

Suzanne shrugs. "Steven, I think it will always seem like that. But the truth is that you're always bigger than the game. That's one of the main reasons why we chose you."

Rillman pulls the blade from Kiri's chest and blood fountains from the wound. Kiri stumbles back. But he doesn't fall. He swings another fist at Rillman's head, but there's a gray blade arcing, dancing in front of him. Kiri's fist goes one way, and his arm the other in a spout of blood.

Now Kiri falls.

Suzanne shoves my shoulder, pushes me back. "Just go!"

"And what if I don't?"

"Then we've made the biggest mistake of our lives. Christ, Steven, man up. Don't fail us."

I try to shift. Nothing. "I can't," I say.

"Of course, there's too much electrical disturbance, far beyond any normal storm. You're going to have to jump off the bridge."

"Really? But that's water beneath. What if—"

"He will not interfere. We have treaties, it's not like you're snatching souls from him. Go, or I'll throw you over the fucking edge myself."

"I could—"

Suzanne grimaces. "Get the hell out of here."

I run to the nearest rail, clamber to the top. Electricity races up my arms and I smell hair burning. It's a long way down. I glance back at Suzanne, but she's already striding toward the melee with a sense of purpose that I can only envy.

Right then. I take a deep breath and step off into the air.

When I hit, the water's warm and murky, the current strong. I'm down deep, and thrashing in the dark. Something brushes my arm. I kick out and up, no breath in me, my clothes heavy.

When I break the surface, coughing and spluttering, my lungs burning, snot running down my cheeks, the bridge is already forty meters away, the air still crackling. Someone's screaming, but I can't tell if it's Rillman or an RM.

There's a gentle tugging on my foot. A dim, streamlined shape beneath me.

Please, no more sharks. I've had enough of sharks.

I close my eyes. And shift.

32

My head throbs, feels like it's about to pop. What the hell have they asked me to do? What were they thinking? All Suzanne's talk of disunity, but then to be so unified in marching toward their destruction. Surely that belies their argument!

I can't do this.

But I have no choice.

They've chosen me. Does it make them brave or cowards? After all, they're leaving me with one god-awful mess.

I can't do this alone. But then I realize that I'm not. That I've never truly been alone. Lissa, Tim, Alex—they've got my back. They've never failed me.

Lissa! I need to find Lissa.

Suzanne's logic seems right on this one. Rillman will hunt her down if he can't find me, and I doubt Solstice's protection will be up to the job. But they're the least of my reasons. I would die for Lissa.

I shift to a point in the center of the city. To the immediate west, the lightning storm is a webbed incandescence. My senses have expanded, but they are still dulled by Rillman's electrical web. I search her out. There is nothing. She is not in the city. I try her hotel room. It's empty. No, not quite. I can sense something, a recent death nearby. I shift to the room next door. There's a body there. A Pomp, one of Suzanne's. The poor guy's throat is slashed. This is not good.

I grab my phone. It's dripping wet, but it seems to be working. A no-signal message flashes at me. Maybe that's from the dunking. Maybe it's Rillman's electrical attack. I shift to Number Four.

Chaos! All the Ankous are here, their heartbeats clamoring. I stand in the middle of them, saturated with river water. I can't help scowling at them all.

"How many of you knew about this?" I demand. None of them look me in the eye. They're all frightened.

"Tim?"

He shrugs. "I didn't know anything. You think I could keep this a secret?"

"Is there anything I can do?"

"Not unless you can shift back onto that bridge," Li An's Ankou says. I don't know her name. I'm going to have to learn all their names. No time for that now.

"No, not with the amount of electricity being generated," I say. "There's no way."

"And while we quake, our masters die on that bridge," she says.

I grimace. "Well, if there's nothing we can do about Rillman, I need you to return to your offices. Keep everything running. We can't let the Stirrers take advantage. The Death Moot is a bust, but we have work to do. Your people need you. *I* need you, all of you, to keep doing what you do best. They're not dead yet." Though I can't help thinking of Kiri, the blade jutting from his chest; the ease with which Rillman took out Travis. "Go! See to your schedules."

One by one the Ankous leave.

Now it's just Tim and my staff. They're all looking at me. "And that goes for you, too. We have souls to pomp. Stirrers to hunt down."

They scatter quickly to their workstations. I motion to Tim. "Meeting, now."

"I swear," Tim says. "I knew nothing about this. Not until they shifted us here, together."

"That's OK," I say. "I've got to find Lissa. I can't feel her, she's not in the country anymore. Rillman's likely to go after her."

"And just how are you going to find her? She's not a Pomp anymore."

"I have my means."

Tim raises his eyebrows. "And I have her email password. It was an accident," he says quickly. "I didn't mean to uncover it, but—"

There's a commotion at the lift. Alex. He's paler than I've ever seen him. Someone tries to stop him but he just pushes past them, and stalks over to us.

"I've been trying to call," Alex says. "But the phones are out, all over the city. Did you have anything to do with that?"

"Rillman," I say. "He's killing the RMs, and I'm stuck here. Maybe Solstice—"

"That's just it. That's why I've been trying to call. There is no Solstice," Alex says. "There are no Closers. It's a front. I don't know how he managed it, who he bribed, but Internal Affairs are raiding his offices now. The staff—half of them are Stirrers. We're going to need your help, or more people are going to die."

Lissa! Solstice had people following Lissa! If they're Stirrers...

Tim's already running through the office, directing staff to call every Pomp they can. I look at Alex.

"You and Tim are going to have to deal with this. I need to find Lissa, she's in danger."

He nods. "We can handle it."

I shift home and rifle through what is left of Lissa's things there as I boot up my Notebook. No clues. My phone chirps; a text from Tim: Lissa's email password.

I get online, open her email and there it is. A ticket booked to Wellington. She has an aunt living on the North Island. Flights to New Zealand are so cheap these days it makes sense she'd visit her. By my laptop is the photo album of Lissa's. She must have been flicking through it before our fight. There's an old Polaroid from a Death Moot marked "1974." Lissa's parents are pressed into a small group with Suzanne—she's looking as fresh as ever. I recognize that forced grin.

Lissa's mom's face is fixed. She must have known by then. Christ, any business is a small world. I know how I would feel if I thought Lissa was seeing someone behind my back. How did I ever let this happen? I should have been up front about the deal from the beginning.

Then I see Rillman, his tight smile, his arm around Don, Alex's dad, at the side of the group.

It's him all right. But that's not what catches my eye, makes me suck in a sharp breath. There's a tattoo running down his forearm. A tattoo I've seen before.

Smauget. The dragon.

Solstice is Rillman.

Or Rillman became Solstice.

What might Stirrers do on a plane?

I focus my mind on Lissa, reaching out across the distance, reaching out beyond the edge of the shore. And *there*. I sense her! I've never shifted into a moving vehicle before, let alone a plane, but she is my center, my heart. I could shift to her anywhere.

A moment later I am thirty thousand feet in the air, standing next to Lissa.

I exhale, a sigh that really wants to become a scream, but I stop it before that. Shit, how did things get so bad, so quickly? Lissa looks at me and scowls, but that doesn't disguise how tightly she is holding onto her seat. It seems the plane's hit some nasty turbulence.

The flight's crowded. If anyone is surprised by my sudden appearance they don't show it. I look down the aisle. No one seems to have noticed me, but that may well be because of the bad weather.

The seat next to Lissa is empty, and I drop into it.

"That seat's taken," Lissa says. She looks tired, but resolute.

There's maybe one too many Disney pins on her blouse, as though she's overcompensating.

"We need to talk," I say.

"I told you not to follow me." She doesn't let go of her seat. The seatbelt sign is flashing. She sniffs the air. "I can smell smoke. You've been smoking?"

I shake my head. "Of course not. I only smoke when I'm drunk."

"And when aren't you drunk these days?"

I brush the insult aside. "There's something you need to know."

"You've left it a bit late, wouldn't you say?"

"I don't think it's ever too late for us. I have to believe that." I lower my voice to a whisper. "It's Solstice. He's Rillman."

"What?"

"I don't have time to explain, but he's got two guys tailing you. Don't ask me how I know. I think they're Stirrers."

Lissa's face hardens. "The prick!" Then her eyes narrow. "You got him to tail me. You're the reason they're here in the first place."

"Look, no matter how much it might look like that, he wants you dead. He knows I'm hopeless without you." I don't mention Suzanne's guard or the fact that he's dead.

Lissa doesn't look too satisfied with the answer I've given her, but she's already thinking the problem through. "Right. If they're Stirrers you're going to need a Pomp by your side."

"You'd do that?"

"Bloody hell, de Selby, I love you."

Yeah, she does. No matter how things turn out, no matter how stupid I've been, she loves me!

"Then you have to know I would never cheat on you. That I couldn't."

"But why did you lie to me?"

"Because you were so against the whole idea of Suzanne's offer. Lissa, I didn't want to hurt you."

"How about a little trust?" she says.

"Exactly!"

And now we're glaring at each other again.

"This isn't over," Lissa sighs. "Just do what you have to do."

She reaches up and touches my lips with her fingers. There's serious voltage in that gesture, more electricity than anything Rillman generated on the bridge. It silences me and, oddly enough, focuses me on the job at hand.

I hold her head and transfer my power into her: feel that familiar link. It's such an intense intimacy. For a moment, we are closer than ever. Bound in each other. Feeling what the other is feeling. It's like gazing in a mirror with another's eyes. The familiar becomes unfamiliar. Our eyes widen. Our breaths quicken. What wounds me most of all is the hurt I sense within her. This is my fault. I caused this pain, and anger.

I shudder with the strength of it, and then my fingers drop from her brow. Lissa is a Pomp again. She blinks at me, and I catch myself blinking, too.

"I should never have hurt you," I whisper.

"Steven, this is about us. Not just you. We got into this quickly; it was always going to be difficult. I—I'm not used to long-term relationships. I thought it would be easy, and—but I wouldn't have it any other way. Trust me next time. Trust me to be strong enough, because I am."

Yeah, she's stronger than me.

"And what about you? Why don't you trust me to do the right thing? I made a mistake, but I would never cheat on you. I'm not your father, and—"

The plane shudders. The storm outside is building. We have to find those Stirrers.

I look around. There's no one I'd consider suspicious. Then I glance at the front of the plane. The toilet light is on, and it's flickering, flaring from dim to bright. And always just before the lightning bursts outside.

"In there," I say, slipping Lissa my knife once I've surreptitiously slit my own palm.

I walk down the aisle to the toilet door. One of the attendants shuffles toward me, gripping the seats tightly, but my glare is enough to stop them.

At the front of the plane I can hear the pilots' muted talk in the cabin. They don't sound too happy. Having a Stirrer so close wouldn't be helping either. Reflex times would be slowing. Everybody on the plane including the pilots probably has a headache. Not good when you're trying to fly through a storm. And looking through the nearest window I can tell this is a whopper.

I knock on the toilet door, and the moment I touch it, I recognize the presence of the Stirrer. Right then. I lean back, put my shoulders against the door behind me, and kick as hard as I can.

The door crumples. The Stirrer's sitting on the toilet lid. Its eyes widen, almost comically so.

"You."

"Yeah, me."

Someone crashes down the aisle toward me. Another Stirrer. I turn my head in time to see Lissa leap out of her chair and stall it. And then my Stirrer is swinging a fist at my skull. I duck back, and it grabs me by the lapels and swings its head against mine.

Hey, that's my move.

I almost drop to the floor with the force of it. I slam my bloody palm in its face and it staggers back, its eyes flickering. Outside, lightning crashes and crackles. The plane swings violently to the left, a drunken sort of lurch.

I slap my palm against its face again, and this time it collapses on the floor. Then both souls lance rough-edged and furious through me. I drop to my knees as shocked attendants rush in my direction.

I look over at Lissa, and she's OK.

Then it hits me, a psychic fist clenched around my heart. Hard nails of pain rip through my flesh. It's another fragment of the Hungry Death. I'm floored by it. My back bends, my limbs stiffen. It lasts only a moment, then I can move again.

I get to my feet; giddy with power.

I push the attendants out of the way, which is easy. They scramble toward their seats. The seatbelt lights are still flashing and there's a rough noise coming from one of the engines. The plane drops, people scream. All the lights above Lissa's head go off, then flare back on in a way that no lights should.

I realize I shouldn't be here. How could I have been so stupid? I'm barely containing all this death pouring into me. My flesh creaks, my eyes feel like they might burst with the strain of this. Another fragment. I grit my teeth and stagger down the aisle. I can taste blood. It's filling my lungs, lubricating or facilitating the arrival of the Hungry Death.

Maybe that will be the last one. Maybe Rillman has been stopped. I think of the battle raging on the bridge, all those RMs dying, cramming me with this manic, lustful energy.

I try and shift. I can't. It's like the Sea of Hell again. Something is holding me to this place—or someone.

"You need to be in your seat." A flight attendant, perhaps a little braver than the rest, is at my side. Every passenger on the plane is staring at me. A couple of the bigger ones are considering doing something. What? What could they do against me?

I swear that, for a moment, the attendant recognizes me on some deeper level: what it is that I am. Or maybe she just sees a crazy person. She nods her head, swallows a deep breath. "OK, sir."

She scrambles away, moving like a crab; I've never seen a flight attendant so spooked before. Someone else is already asking for assistance. I can tell she really wants to go to her own seat, that she's as scared as the others, but it doesn't stop her. She helps them with their seatbelt.

A dreadful hush descends upon the plane. HD is rapturous, positively bloody gleeful. I push it down.

I'm back with Lissa; stepping over the Stirrer corpse. "I have to get out of here," I say.

"What's wrong?"

"Rillman. He's killing RMs. I'm absorbing more of the Hungry Death. I could destroy this plane."

"Shift then. The Stirrers are dealt with," Lissa says.

"I'm trying." I close my eyes, concentrate. It's no good.

Another wave of the Hungry Death strikes me. The lights around me explode. The plane can't handle what's going to happen. HD swells. I try to shift again. Still nothing. I look around wildly for an exit hatch.

There, not too far away. I take a step toward it.

Lightning strikes the plane, a dozen incendiary bursts. And some of them are coming from me. Outside, the storm is raging, with a darkness deeper than anything the Stirrers are capable of. The plane judders, swings, drops. I slam into the ceiling. The attendant has hit her head. Blood flows. A trolley hurtles past me, crashes into the attendant. Her death pulses through my flesh. People scream. HD howls out its pleasure.

I try to shift again. Still no good. I'm fixed here by the transformation occurring within me, the new and horrible thing I'm becoming.

Lissa looks at me. She has her seatbelt on tight.

Shift, damn it! Shift! They're all going to die if I don't. But I can't. It *wants* them to die.

And all I have is the thin fabric of you, the Hungry Death whispers with more force than I've ever experienced. *I can pull myself through that whenever I want to. And I will. You were one of thirteen warriors, but twelve have deserted you.*

Shut up. Shut up. Shut up.

The plane jolts like a creature kicked and whipped and gripped by a deathly god. The sky is a dark fist around it. *Fuck. Oh fuck. This is all my stupid fault.*

There's a moment of calm. And my phone chirps. I look at the LCD: the schedule. Oh, no. Two hundred names. Lissa's is at the top.

It's too late.

"Steven—" Lissa's hand folds over mine.

The plane bucks, up and down, faster than I can adjust to. I feel the plane flash in and out of this world and Hell. My presence is causing this. The transition alone is killing some people. I'm weightless, then heavy. I smack my head against the nearest headrest. Lissa's hand slips from mine.

Time runs down here, bleeds away. Death is coming. I'm coming. This is all my fault. The air stinks of blood and piss and smoke.

"Hold my hand," I say to Lissa, snatching it anyway, just as the plane starts to tumble. There's a noise like the grinding of giant teeth, a dreadful rending. The plane is lit with a blue light. The pre-death light. Lissa's as bright with it as the others. I have seen her that way before, and I will not see it again.

The last fragment of the Hungry Death enters me. I feel it pushing against my flesh. The Orcus are dead, all but me. I am the last. And it terrifies me. HD loves it.

Lissa's not looking at me: her eyes are wide. The noise must be terrible but I can barely hear it. I snap my head around in time to see the back end of the plane split from the front, as though something has torn it off.

This plane falls tonight. Two hundred shattered lives. And it's but the beginning. All that ending ahead, and me/we at the fore.

I wish HD would shut the fuck up.

There are screams, guttural, terrified. Someone laughs. It's a peculiar sound; it cuts through me. And HD is joining in.

"I picked the wrong bloody flight, didn't I?" Lissa says.

"Jesus," I breathe. Every time I blink I can see the One Tree. I can hear it creaking. I force my eyes open. "Oh, Jesus."

Lissa holds my gaze.

"Don't be scared," she says, above all that noise.

Mr. D's words come to me: Sometimes terror is the only response. I'm not scared. I'm terrified.

She touches my face. "It's OK, Steven." Her hands do not shake, there is more strength in that touch than in all of me. We have been here before. I just never expected to be here again so soon.

"I love you," I say.

I grab Lissa's hand and try and shift. It hurts. HD pushes against me. It's hard and toothed. The meat of me is screaming with it. I haven't felt this human since...since Morrigan cut me with the stony blade. The universe pushes. But I push back. I push back hard and it shrinks away. And this time I shift.

But Lissa doesn't come with me. I'm standing in my office. Alone. HD screams.

I shift back. Back to her.

This shift is not resisted. I see now that this is where I am meant to be, what I am meant to witness.

The plane crumbles and tumbles around me. People scream, and die. Their souls lash through me: bullet-quick and burning. It hurts, but I ignore it. I reach out for Lissa.

"No!" she says. I can't hear her, of course. The roar of a plane breaking, tumbling, dying, drowns her out. But I can read her lips.

I clutch at her. Wrap my arms around her, and shift again. Pain. A nest of needles jutting through every cell of me, and twisting. I'm shrieking in my office, blood running from my lips, my eyes, my ears, my arse. Every orifice bleeds.

No Lissa. She is not here.

I shift again.

The plane. The plummeting cage. Outside I see the One Tree looming and then a wing clips a branch. Metal grinds, windows crack and blow out.

"Sorry," she says, and squeezes my hand.

She shouldn't say that. This is my fault. All of it.

She touches my face. "It's all right."

"I'll follow you. I'll follow you to the end of fucking time if I have to." And then there is an explosion. The whole sky seems on fire.

I wrap my arms around her, shield her from the worst of it. I'm hit, but heal almost as fast as the wounds make their mark. There is so much strength in me. But not enough for her.

And there isn't a plane anymore. Just fragments dropping toward a black and perilous sea. The air roars and all around us, people fall. All around us is the death that I made.

She falls. And falls.

And I can't lift her up, so I hold her close. I whisper my love. I press my lips against her, and I fall with her.

We plummet toward water dark as slate in the storm. She holds my gaze with a strength that amazes me. An implacable acceptance. I can feel her heartbeat, like I can feel all their heartbeats, and it is racing. But she doesn't look away.

I am going to lose her.

Let me, the Hungry Death whispers, *Let me.*

And I do. I let it fill me. I make a void for it within my soul, and for the first time in my life I have an inkling of what real power is. I shift.

And this time she comes with me. We're here, in my office.

She belts her hands against my chest. "No! You shouldn't have, you shouldn't have!"

"Stay here. I'll be back. I promise."

"Where are you going?" Lissa asks, weeping.

"To bear witness. To pomp the souls of those lost."

There are bodies in the water, lifeless. Only their souls know motion among the flotsam, bits of plane, and pieces of people's lives. I hover cross-legged, shifting above them, and it is effortless. But the wonder has been sucked from it, by these dead: one hundred and fifty in total. Their souls thrash in the water, bound there, unable to do more than keep their essences afloat. Out here, if I don't do anything...

Long gray limbs slither from the sea. Water spills from narrow bald heads, beneath which beam mouths long and beakish. The ocean wants these souls for itself. It wants them restless and heaving in the depths. The gray shapes flash toward the souls of the dead. I glare at them. HD howls. And they hesitate.

"These are mine," the Water whispers. "Not yours. You have no dominion in my seas."

"This time I do."

"You would challenge me, Orcus?"

Orcus. I blink at the title, at the stupid formality of it. But it is true. It is what I am. I am Orcus, my region is the earth. I am the only one capable of pomping these souls to Hell away from the shore. Children! There are children here. Dozens of them. And, God help me, HD guffaws with pleasure.

"Yes," I say, "and you cannot stop me."

I close my eyes, and draw the souls within me. It's hard work pulling them from the suck and cold of the sea. I'm sweating and shaking by the end, with the effort of it. The Water was right. I have no dominion here, but I do have my power. Finally they are gone, sent to the Underworld, which is their right, no matter that it has come too soon for all of them.

The gray forms drop beneath the water. "Orcus, you do yourself no good in making an enemy of me."

"One more enemy. What does it matter?"

Then the Water beneath me is just water again, and the dead are soulless and drifting among the wreckage. I've done what I can here.

It's time to find Rillman. The bastard has to pay.

33

I can sense his heartbeat. It can't hide its secrets from me. I close my eyes and shift.

The Deepest Dark. Why here? Which is precisely the question Wal asks when he crawls out from under my shirt. I can sense Rillman circling around, shifting from space to space. I catch glimpses of him. A leg. A foot. A hand tight around a knife hilt. His feet send up clouds of dust. Closer and closer. I wait.

And then, through the dark to my left, two stony blades jab out at me.

I jerk to the right, though one of the blade points cuts through my suit, bites shallowly into my stomach. It burns. I resist the urge to crouch over it, as though to stop my guts spilling. But the wound is already healed.

"Out you come," I snarl.

A body takes form in the dark, arms and shoulders, then head, torso and legs knitted from all that cold shadow.

Solstice smiles. Who else would it be?

"So what do I call you? Rillman or Solstice?"

His limbs move with a jerky energy that Solstice never had. I wonder at the strength of will it must have taken Rillman to contain all that madness. He doesn't need to now, and it bursts from him as wild as any storm.

"I never really liked the name Solstice, but you take what the mask gives you. And he was such a good mask." Then he changes, becomes the Rillman I know. The Rillman in the tunnel. The dull, smiling bloke in Lissa's photo album. He shrugs. "You know, after I failed, I killed myself. Not once, but twice. And every time I came back. She helped me come back."

"Aunt Neti?"

"Yes, even when I didn't want to. And then RMs noticed. They tried to kill me, too, and each time I died, I came back, different, stronger."

Around him swings the tiny dragon, Smauget, its red eyes aflame. It darts toward my face. There's a blur of movement, a shrill yowl, and Wal has snatched it from the air. The dragon hisses and snaps, its tiny mouth going for Wal's jugular, but the little fella is ready for it. He catches it by the throat, and they tumble to the ground.

"Leave this to me," he says, from between clenched teeth. "You deal with him."

Rillman holds the knives at a distance from his chest, as though even he's afraid of what they are. I don't blame him. I understand their will intimately. The knives blur the air like light sticks waving in the depths of a cave.

They whisper and snort, *Hello, hello.*

"I am better armed now. These things kill RMs like you wouldn't believe. They're simplicity itself. And here, you don't have any Avian Pomps to protect you," Rillman says.

"Why did you kill them?" I ask.

"Who? The RMs, well, you know that they deserved it."

"Not them. This isn't about them."

I lift my hand. Dust shapes itself into a plane. Dust people tumble from it.

Rillman almost drops the knives. They shudder in his hands. "What?" The emotions that play across his face shock me. It's almost as variable as Mr. D's. Joy, sadness and a mad hunger mix and meld across his features, and it would almost be comedic if he wasn't waving knives in my face. Then I realize that Rillman isn't well at all.

I could almost pity him.

"Your Stirrer drones," I spit. "The ones with Lissa. I took them out, and then the Hungry Death came. I wouldn't have been there but for you. Its presence within me wouldn't have destroyed that plane."

Rillman snorts. "You RMs, always ready to blame anyone but yourselves. Lissa was meant to die. To make you understand. To teach you the mechanics of pain. And my attacks on you? That was their purpose, too. To hurt, to blind, to scare. I take it that you managed to save her. Too bad about the others, eh? They were your doing."

"I understand pain." HD snickers. It's intimate with pain as well.

"Ah, you only think you do. Maddie, I killed her. But I could have brought her back. And there he was, your Mr. D. Smug and useless. There he waited, in the dark that slides along the borders of the Underworld. And with a fucking grin on his face, he hurled her back. I was done, then. I was spent; no chance of another Schism. He had nothing to fear from me, but he hurled her back. And even now, dead, he is not dead. And you have made it so. The favored one, the fucking coddled one. The man who didn't want to be Death. How can you expect to do anything? How can you expect to hold back anything?"

"That's it," I say. "It starts and ends here. And the rest? The rest we will have to see."

A little calm returns to Rillman, a crooked smile. "That's what the Orcus said, and there's very little left of any of them."

"I'm something altogether different now," I say.

The knives flash toward me, but I'm ducking and weaving. It's motion absent of thought, fed on instinct. I've fought with these knives before. My movement is fast and sinuous. Something is hardening within me. A dreadful resolve, a chuckling vastness. The knives slice the air millimeters above my face, then to my left and right, never quite touching.

Rillman growls.

I gesture at the dust around my boots. It flashes up in a tight spiral between us—Suzanne would have been pleased—and into his eyes. My fist follows it. Rillman stumbles back. Wipes at his nose with his wrist. A knot of blood and snot stretches from his nostrils to his arm, then breaks.

His heart beats loud in my ears, and it's no longer that familiar steady rhythm. It's pounding, racing—160 bpms at least. His pupils are dilated. I know he's on something and it's raging through his body like fire. He comes back at me, fast. But something is burning through my body, too.

The knives dance figure eights before him. It would almost be beautiful, but I've no eye for beauty now. HD argues the point, but I ignore it.

More dust, a blinding burst. He staggers, his eyes stung. I kick him in the chest. He crashes backward, lands hard.

"Dust? Is that all you have?" he pants, getting to his feet, wiping at his eyes with his wrists. He's half blind, but it doesn't stop him. I'd almost respect that, but I am hatred now. I am blazing anger.

"It's all I need." I launch more dust at him. Rillman slices through it with the knives, but it's only dust, it doesn't bleed. Not like him. He doesn't even know that he's beaten.

He charges at me. And this time I don't care to obscure his run. No dust. Just him and me.

"I want you to know that you made this," I say. The blades whirr around me, jabbing toward me and away, and I weave in time with them in perfect synchrony. The poor bastard doesn't understand that they are dancing for me. "Your desire for revenge. To cause me pain. To bring down the Orcus. To hurt me and mine. All of it. The whole fucking concatenation of hate and fear. You made it all, and now..." I snatch the blades from his hands, one, two... "These are mine."

I kick him to the ground, easily. Rillman lies there, bleeding. "What are you?"

"You don't get it at all, do you? I'm Steven de Selby," I say, picking him up with one hand, as though he weighs nothing. And he doesn't. No one does now. "I am Death."

I backhand him casually in the face. Bone cracks. He drops to the ground, and I stand over him. I grit my teeth, and feel my face shift. It's agony and it's glorious. For a moment all I am is pain. All I am is Death.

The knives in my hand slide toward each other, bind each other in their stony gravity, and then I am holding a scythe. It shivers with the deepest of hungers in my grip.

Mayhem. Murder. Death, it breathes.

And God help me, I swing the scythe above my head.

Wal rushes in between us. "Whoa, whoa!" He hovers there, his wings beating so fast that they lift up dust. His eyes are wide with a kind of terror that I'm unacquainted with, and they're directed at me.

"Go away," I say.

"If you kill him, you won't get answers."

I jab my finger at his face. "But that's just it. I am the answer, am I not?"

All I want is death. His death. The world's death. HD cackles, like a drunk crashing toward damnation.

Then a squeak of brakes alerts me to his presence. My old boss.

"Stop this now," Mr. D says, sliding off his bike. His face is pale; he's out of breath. Must have been riding since I entered the Underworld.

"You," I growl. "This is as much your fault as his. Letting them—letting *all* of them—do this to me."

But it is glorious!

Mr. D holds my gaze. "Yes... They were convincing, Steven."

"Convincing!" I swing the scythe above his head. It would be nothing to lop it off. Mr. D doesn't move. "Is that all you can say?"

"You didn't prepare him for any of this," Rillman says.

Mr. D glances over at him. "Good evening, Francis."

Rillman spits toward him. "Hell must be so hungry for you."

"It's hungry for all of us," Mr. D says. "It will have me in its own good time, believe me."

"I'd kill you if I could," Rillman breathes.

"You're not the only one." Mr. D places a hand on my shoulder. "Steven, I am so sorry."

I brush his hand away. "You should go now. You have no power here."

"None of us do, Steven. The rules that bind us do so tightly. You have choices, but what horrible, horrible choices. Leave this idiot. The other RMs are still on the tree; they won't be for much longer. Go to them, find out anything more you can."

"I don't need them anymore. I want you gone." My voice is barely a whisper, but there is a dreadful force behind it. Mr. D diminishes, nods.

"As you wish." He throws a glance askew at Wal, as if to say sorry. Then he picks up his bike and rides away into the dark. I watch him until the gloom swallows the flickering red of his tail-light.

Rillman coughs. Wal flits in front of him again.

"You want me to go, too? I swear I won't go so easily," Wal says. Nonetheless I tap my arm and he is nothing more than a tattoo, his face twisted with a bunched zippering of cherubic teeth.

I fashion a chair out of dust, and drop Rillman in it.

He coughs, spits blood. He's not bound. I don't need to do that.

"You can run," I say. "But I will find you. Have no doubt of that."

He eyes the knives I've left resting on a nearby root tip of the One

Tree. They're no longer the scythe. I raise one hand and that's what they become. I'm intuiting a lot, but I know I can call that scythe to me in a second, just as I know its name is Mog. In a breath, a single breath of that name, it will find me.

He looks shiftily from the scythe to me, and back again. I dare him with my eyes. But Rillman has had enough.

"Why did you do this?" I ask. "Tell me and I might be gentle with you."

"I hate you," Rillman growls. "You got what I wanted. While Mr. D was alive he locked me out. But you, you were so interesting. So naive. You were the only RM not like them. You were the one who I wanted to suffer, not just kill, because you didn't deserve what you had been given. I've been a long time in planning this, and when you won your Negotiation and changed the rules... Well, you have to realize that I had to make you pay." He sneers at me. "Is it any wonder that governments agreed to my requests, when I showed them what I was capable of, with but the merest sliver of an RM's powers? They've been frightened of Mortmax for a long time, the consequences of it. And they're terrified of you."

Yeah, they have a bloody good reason to be now. HD's pleasure radiates through me.

"I knew it would only be a matter of time until it fell apart, and the world's governments would be left picking up the pieces anyway. The Thirteen have lurched along for an age. But everything ends." He fiddles with his tie with his restless jerky fingers.

"Yeah, when you murder them."

Rillman's face darkens. "All of them were murderers. Every single one, and I know you're not stupid enough to believe otherwise. You want to become a murderer, Steven?"

"I'm Death. It's what I do." Mog quivers in its resting place. And the new and ancient part of me remembers its endless predation, its racing hunger. It would be easy to give in to that. After all, it's what nature intended. It's so like humanity to shape things into much more convoluted patterns. I've a chance to break them all, starting with the death of Rillman. One enemy removed. "And maybe it's your time," I say.

Rillman shakes his head. "I've read your files, Steven, it's not in you." He's waiting. There's a pulsing vein in his forehead and a slight smile breaks the line of his lips. Then he scowls and maybe, for the first time, I have the real measure of the man, and what I see is shocking. There is too much of my rage in there. "You're just not that kind of guy."

I grab him by his lapels and lift. "I am now."

This close, I can feel what it is that gives him power: the thing that Neti gave him that allows him to slip from the land of the living to the land of the dead, and back again. It shivers inside him like a second beating heart. This is a free pass between the gates of the two worlds, and it belongs to me! I don't know how Aunt Neti stole it, but I want it back. I yank him to his feet, touch his face with my hands, grip his skull hard, and draw that power from him.

It hurts. Because what he has is fed by pain and anger. I drag it into me; more power, more of the essence that is now so much of what I am. I understand the truth that is the Hungry Death, its persuasive presence, and the tiny thing that is the man before me. I close one hand around his neck, curious how that might feel, and then the other hand.

And I squeeze.

He grabs my wrists. He struggles. He kicks out at me, and thrashes. But I do not relax my grip. If anything I tighten it. HD laughs, and I laugh too, until I feel Rillman's spirit pomp through me. It bursts free, not toward the One Tree, but straight into the Deepest Dark. I watch it there, and then, something bright and eight-armed snatches out and grinds out the light within it.

I'm left staring up into the dark.

I drop Rillman's body.

Mog drifts toward me. I close a fist around its curving snath and back away from the corpse. Let the dust engulf the body.

I'm empty, weak. I can barely stand. My hands grip Mog so tightly that my knuckles ache. It's the only thing that is keeping me upright.

Wal pulls himself from my arm. "What have you done?"

The body is there, between the two of us. It's answer enough.

34

I shift to my office. It's late. Ten. I can hear someone using the photocopier. Such an everyday sound.

I'm sick, but it's not from the shifting. Mr. D was right, all I needed was practice. I smile, and spew into the bin, but it's not cathartic. There's no release in it. Just pain.

I slump into my throne. It's bigger now, far bigger, all encompassing. It dominates the room like the dark seat of some dark empire, and yet I hardly notice it. I settle in, and my pain ebbs, a little. But I have worse hurts. I put my head in my hands.

All the world's heartbeats rain down on me, all those clocks winding down, all that strength pulsing toward its undoing.

And that's the least of it. Every time I close my eyes they're there—those innocent deaths of which I was the cause, that final pomping of Rillman's soul.

I sit in my throne, sobbing, drowning in the world's pulse. Tim's is there. So is Lissa's. I can pick them out like threads. Mr. D once said that the sound becomes soothing—the cacophony a lullaby. Here I am, struck by those billions of heartbeats, and then I feel Lissa nearby. I drag myself from the comfort of the throne and Mog blurs, becomes the knives again. They rest, bound by sheaths knitted from evening, on my belt. I shift through the wall, and there she is.

"Steven, are you all right?" She's been crying, too. I should have sought her out straightaway, but I couldn't face her. I can barely face her now.

"Yes," I say. "Are you?"

"I think so."

Then I'm holding her and I can almost forget the pain and guilt I'm feeling. Finally she pulls from me.

"You shouldn't have done that," she says. A vein pulses in my head. Does she know? "You shouldn't have come after me like that."

"You know I had no choice. I've nothing left but you."

"I know you were trying to do the right thing. But Christ, you—"

"I should have told you about Suzanne. No more secrets, right? I promise."

She touches the knives at my belt, curiously.

"They're mine," I say, "and, to be honest, I don't want them out of my sight. I'm the only RM left standing. Mortmax International is my responsibility now."

"And HD?"

"It's under control, I think... I don't know. Rillman—Solstice is gone. He won't be a problem anymore."

In my office I can hear the unmistakable ring of the black phone. I ignore it. Lissa looks at me questioningly. "It can wait," I say. "We need to get out of here."

Lissa holds me tight, and it's all I can do not to crush her in my grip, so desperately do I need that contact. "Where do you want to go?" she asks.

"Home," I say.

I shift with her in my arms. And we are back in my parents' place, in the hallway, Mom's perfume as strong as ever.

"We're going to move out of here. It was always a mistake to live here," I say.

I can't bear my parents looking down at me from those photos. I know how they would judge me for what I've done, what I am.

"Are you sure?" Lissa asks, though I can tell she's pleased. This was never our home. I nod. "Then we need to find a place that Stirrers can't just stroll into," she says.

I can tell Lissa wants to talk this through, all of it. And I want to as well. But there's a weight of exhaustion pulling on her. She's worn out with worry, with the hell that has been this last week. And we have time. There's no Death Moot or Rillman to concern us now, and the Stirrer god isn't here yet.

"Try and rest," I say. "We have so much to do, but not now."

I walk with her to the bed. Lissa's fast beneath the sheets and even quicker to fall asleep. I stand there looking at the person I have risked all for, and for a moment I feel better.

I call Tim.

"Jesus, what happened to you?" he asks. "I came to the office, and you'd both just left."

I don't want to talk about it. Tim's going to have to trust me. "How are the Ankous?"

He's a while in answering. I can't tell if I've offended him, which probably means I have. "They're all right. In shock, but that's understandable. Mortmax has suffered its biggest, loss . . . gain . . . Shit, I don't know, what's happened? What the hell do we even call you?"

"Steve," I say. "I'm your cousin, remember?"

"Steve. Solstice's offices, they were worse than anything Morrigan ever did. The rotting dead. Their rage and, God, their laughter. That's what's going to stick with me the most. They laughed as we stalled them, every single one, as though it didn't matter. I'm fucking terrified."

I'm more than familiar with that laughter. "Sometimes it's a reasonable response. Listen, Tim, we're going to have to start mobilizing," I say. "The Stirrer god is coming. But we will be ready."

"Are you OK? You sound—"

"I'm exhausted," I say. "Bloody knackered. I'll call you tomorrow. We both need to think, and to rest—that most of all. You can't do anything if you're tired."

"I thought you couldn't sleep."

"I can now," I say. "You should, too."

"One more thing," he says. "The black phone in your office keeps ringing."

"Don't answer it," I say. "I can deal with that tomorrow, too."

I hang up, and take a shower. But I can't wash HD or the thing I've done from me. Wal is on my biceps, and he looks frightened. When I'm done, I walk to the back balcony, the towel wrapped around my waist.

Another storm rolls in from the south, but this one's soft and earthy, and while it may hide a stir or two, it's just a storm. I watch it build for a while. Rain falls, light spatters at first, and then it's a real downpour.

Lightning bursts in the distance. I wait for the thunder to come rumbling through the suburbs, and when it does I turn to go inside.

Something catches my eye.

They must have been there for a while, silently waiting for my scrutiny: a shivering darkness spread across the lawn. Sharp beaks. Slick black feathers, glossy with the rain. A thousand crows, at least. And they have bowed down low, their wings extended.

"Awcus, awcus," they caw.

I dip my head.

HD seems pleased, all this laid out for it and me. I raise a hand, gesture toward the sky. As one they beat their wings into the angry air, and batter hard against the rain. The vast murder of crows breaks from the ground, finds the night sky and is gone. I could have dreamed the whole thing, but for the dark feathers fluttering down.

Awcus.

I walk into the living room and pour myself a drink, a big one.

Lissa's asleep when I stumble back into the bedroom. The rain hammers on the iron roof but it's ebbing. HD roils within me, grinning its ceaseless grin. But I force it down. I'm tired and on my way to being drunk. I can't stifle a yawn. I settle next to Lissa, slide my arm around her. So tired. She moans something in her sleep, then calms.

The dying rain and Lissa's breathing are the most perfect sounds in the world. I'm not sure when sleep claims me.

Death. Mayhem. Madness and blood. The metronomic sweeping of the scythe.

But I sleep soundly.

ACKNOWLEDGMENTS

So Book Two. Who'd have thought?

Once again, for the last stages (after the big grub of a first draft), a huge thank you to my publisher Bernadette Foley, my structural editor Nicola O'Shea and my copy editor Roberta Ivers. This was foreign ground to me, and you've made the whole process a lot less scary than it could have been. If the book's a butterfly it's because of the chrysalis you lot wove... maybe I'm taking that metaphor too far.

Thanks again to everyone at Avid Reader Bookstore (and the cafe) for being amazing, and for still putting up with the least available casual staff member in the universe, and to Paul Landymore, my SF Sunday compadre who never lets me get away with much. Thanks also to the city of Brisbane, with whom I have taken even more liberties—particularly concerning her bridges—and to my Aunty Liz, who isn't going to like the swearing but switched me onto fantasy when I was a very young lad. All those Greek myths and tragedies: you can't get a better gift than that.

Thanks to Diana, who has to put up with everything, and still loves me.

And thanks to you, who have followed me onto Book Two. I hope you liked it.

BOOK THREE

THE BUSINESS OF DEATH

PART ONE

THE OTHER EMPIRE

All earth was but one thought—and that was death.

"DARKNESS"—LORD BYRON

1

I know he's pissed off even before I see him on the shoreline. The text he'd sent me was something of a giveaway.

Steve. Here. NOW!

As if I'm some sort of dog to be called to heel. The Hungry Death rails inside me and suggests we cut him off at the legs about an inch beneath the knees. Me, I know my cousin—it really wouldn't stop him.

Of course, it wasn't his first text of the day. Or his last, which read: *NOW MEANS NOW!*

Anyone but Tim (OK, and Lissa too) and I'd ignore a message like that. It really is the most passive aggressive form of communcation. He only does it when he's having a tantrum.

A few minutes before I'd stalled a Stirrer in Chermside, outside David Jones of all places, took it down so swift and so casually, that no one noticed. Just me and the body left leaning, eyes closed, on a bench. A perfect stall—I'd considered buying a couple of new shirts to celebrate, but those texts just kept coming. They were worse than Stirrers really—blood and touch can't banish them.

I'm Steven de Selby.

I'm the Orcus. The Thirteen who became one. CEO of Mortmax Industries. A guy with enough titles that even my eyes glaze over reciting them all. What it boils down to is this: I'm Death.

And I'm still learning on the job. I have to. There's no one to replace me or share the load. Maybe down the line, but not yet. Doesn't help that I'm not on talking terms with my mentor Mr. D, and, sure, we might both be to blame for that. But it's left me alone and I feel it.

Things I know about Death:

I've no great power, but there's a fairytale madness lodged in me like a splinter around which the flesh has grown swollen and obdurate. I call it HD, short for Hungry Death, in the hope such familiarity gives me a little control. I've a scythe called Mog, which could cut out the heart of the world—a heart built of billions of beats, each of which I can hear whether I want to or not. The World Pulse.

I watch the world through my eyes, and the eyes of my Avian Pomps. Birds, but only certain ones—crows, lots of them; sparrows, not so many, their loyalties are a bit prickly; and the odd ibis, and what ibis isn't odd? It's something about the ridiculous beak, I think, or the honking.

I can shift through space. Shift between here and the Underworld, and the Deepest Dark—that basement of Hell where life's cruellest troubles are bred predatory and long-toothed. But I can't shift through time. I am as intimately bound in its threads as anyone. I'm the sand in an hourglass that can never be tipped over. I can only go one way.

I can be hurt, but not killed. At least I don't think so. But to say this has been thoroughly tested is... well, it hasn't been. As for the hurt—it hurts!

And I preside over a multi-national business and a world on the edge.

How completely on the edge it really is I've only understood these last few months. To think that once I considered Stirrers to be little more than a nuisance. But that was before I became familiar with their god. The one racing towards our world, through the Deepest Dark, its sole purpose to grind us off the face of the planet, scrub it clean of every hint of life, and return its unliving worshippers as the sole form of earthly existence.

Every day I feel it getting closer. It's a weight in my bones, a certainty of death coming on a grand and almost unthinkable scale.

Every death is a story and every death is mine.

Yeah, I'm a busy man.

And that's not even counting the constant battle I have containing the madness of the Hungry Death. No one wants that thing taking control of my body, least of all me. I like autonomy. I like not slicing the world into little pieces... most of the time.

You can't say the same thing about old HD: it twitches just beneath my skin like five cups of double-shot espresso mixed with bloodlust. Sometimes I wake in the dark, not even knowing I've slept, right hand clutching the scythe, looking to do (or having done) what, I don't know. Or at least I tell myself I don't know.

Crows sing on the powerlines behind us, vocal and squabbling, their caws of discontent sound like ducks on helium. If I let them they'd be swooping on a cloud of midges blown in from across the water. Their hunger's an ache in the back of my throat. They're watching me watch Tim.

My cousin waits for me on the edge of a stony wall that drops away to slimy rocks, tiny waves slapping and sucking against it. He grinds out a cigarette with the toe of his polished boot and lights up another, all this as he stares out across the bay to Stradbroke Island. He's dressed in a suit, standard gear for a Pomp, though he could be any senior partner of any company.

The set of his shoulders says everything I need to know, backs up those texts. I walk up beside him, and he doesn't turn or even acknowledge my presence, but I know he knows I'm here. There's an electricity when you get Pomps in a space together, a dull toothachey buzzing. He's my Ankou, my second-in-command, and I'm his boss. Not that there's even a hint of deference.

Ah, the liberties family take.

"What's up?" I say after a while, but not nearly long enough, I don't have time to keep playing games and draw this out. As much as I'd like to.

Tim regards me bleakly; his lips thin. I know what's up. But he damn well got me out here.

"You should have never snatched those souls from it," he says.

One hundred and fifty souls. A crowded plane, and me responsible for its crashing into the sea. Those souls were mine, even if it was the Death of the Water's territory.

I scowl at Tim. *Arrogant pup! How dare he tell me what to do?*

But the bastard's scowl-proof. He returns my glare with a look of cold disregard. "They're out there." He points, seawards, and offers me a pair of binoculars, but there's not really any need.

There are eight waterspouts, easily visible between here and North Straddie. They dance and shift around each other with unnatural grace. It would be beautiful if it weren't so eerie. The air is silent over the water, not a bird in the sky, not a boat nearby. There's a dark mass to the west of the spouts.

"What's that?" I ask gesturing towards it.

"Fish," Tim says. "They're terrified."

"I don't blame them."

"You should be too."

I snort, waving my hands at the immensity of the water as though it's nothing but a pond and those spouts are little more than irritating and particularly well-coordinated geese. "We're equals. This is merely a Death having a huge hissy fit." I look at him significantly. "A bit like a man who insists on only voicing his displeasure via texts."

"Equals!" Tim laughs. "You, and an entity, which has been the Death of the Water for eons? Sure, I've had some ministers who thought they were the shit, but this is a new level of ridiculous. This is a being intimate with the depth and breadth of its powers, a creature as vast as the sky; its territory covers seven tenths of the earth's surface... seven fucking tenths. Do I need to go on?"

I shrug. "You were getting a bit of a rhythm going there."

Tim taps the ash off the end of his cigarette, a gesture far more aggressive than it should be. "This isn't a joke."

A news chopper angles in low towards the twisters. Another follows on its tail. The damn things run in packs. The silence out to sea is broken by their approach. Idiots. I hope the pilots don't get too close. These spouts strike me as pretty vindictive, and I know I'm not up to stealing more souls from the sea. I wouldn't dare. Tim's right, we're hardly equals.

It's one reason I've put off doing anything. The Death of the Water is unpredictable, I don't know how it might respond. And my guesses aren't particularly pretty. HD's are even worse.

"Slow news day," I say.

"Steve, something like these spouts trashed Tweed Heads the other day. And that's the least of it. People are drowning. Murdered." He pauses, thinks about it. "Is it murder when Death takes you? No, let's stick with drowned."

"People drown all the time."

"Not this far into autumn. And not in these numbers. We've had nearly a hundred percent rise in the number of drowning-related deaths on Australian beaches. We're not the only ones who have noticed either. Do you ever watch the news, or read the papers?"

"I try not to. Far too depressing. I do have a stab at the crosswords though."

"What? Well... you really should." Tim takes a long drag on his cigarette, flicks the stub at his feet. "Steve, when you want to piss someone off, I can't fault you. You aim high."

"It could be totally unrelated," I say, hopefully.

"Yeah... unrelated." Tim taps his phone. Mine shudders in sympathy a moment later.

I squint at the screen. There's a whole bunch of coordinates—at least that's what I think they are.

"In case you don't get it, they're all coastal." Ah-ha, I'm right—coordinates. "And they're only the ones we know about. Oh, and some smart guy at the office even worked out what you get if you substitute letters for the coordinates." He looks at me expectantly.

"Don't leave me hanging, mate."

Tim shakes his head. "It spells your name."

"Really?" I peer at the numbers. "I can't see it. How do you get a name out of coordinates?"

Tim waves his hands vaguely in the air. "It's there, believe me. And if Owen in the office can work this out, on his lunch break no less, there are all sorts of agencies across the world that can too, none of which we want to make any more nervous than they already are." Tim's voice cracks a little. "Steve, we're Pomps, we send souls to the Underworld, and we fight Stirrers—and God knows there have been enough of those lately. We're not equipped to deal with the Death of the Water. Christ, it should be an ally. We *need* allies, Steve. There's the whole End of Days thing looming."

"I know," I say, and I do. "I know, but that bastard wasn't going to get those souls. They were mine." I growl those last words, the knives in their sheaths beneath my jacket stir. Tim steps back, and I don't like the way his heartbeat shifts up a notch. Tim shouldn't be frightened of me.

Yes, he should.

I take a deep breath, and push HD down. Tim relaxes, but he doesn't move any closer. My hands shake.

"Mate," he says, "the Death of the Water's taking them whether you want it to or not. These are unscheduled deaths."

Death runs to a schedule. Mine. Cerbo tried to explain it to me once. If the schedule starts breaking down...it's not good. And already unscheduled things are happening. Stirrers stirring when they shouldn't be, people dying with years left in them. A vast weight of death is coming, and the schedule isn't reflecting it at all.

"I'm going to have to sort that out," I say, not really that confident which issue I'm talking about, or if I'm up to the job of sorting either. "And I will."

Tim walks from the shore to a nearby picnic table, jumps up and sits lightly on top. For a moment, I'm remembering him as kid. There's something unconsidered and natural in the movement, despite the frown on his face, and I realize it's because he's totally engaged with the problem, and that he's come up with some new solution, finally we're past the acrimony and onto the action. "I'm thinking maybe we need someone else to negotiate this," he says.

"Your reasoning being?"

"We can't afford to lose you. You're the Orcus; you're our most potent force in the battle that's coming. Use someone else to... um, to test the waters."

"Too risky. I made this mess. I don't want anyone else to get hurt as result." Besides, if I can't deal with something as simple as an aggrieved Death, how am I going to deal with a god? Though when you work in a business where the term "negotiation" also describes a knife fight to the death... "Who were you thinking of?"

"Not really a who, but a what... Charon."

"I don't think the ferryman's going to be happy with that." Except, boats, water, there's an affinity there. They may even get along. Water has to have some friends, surely. "And that's if I can even find him. He's been keeping a low profile lately."

"Maybe he feels threatened after what happened to Neti."

"Could be, though I doubt it." I find it hard to imagine Charon's threatened by anything. Neti wasn't either, until Francis Rillman, one time Mortmax Ankou, sliced and diced her—but we dealt with him.

Yes we did.

"You find him, and you get this mess sorted." Tim says, not looking at me, facing the sea and those churning shafts of water. His phone's rung three times in the course of this conversation. All, I've gotten is a text from Lissa asking when I'm going to be putting in an appearance for lunch.

Is it wrong I'm more worried about that than this?

"I'll consider it. But until I do, don't you tell Lissa," I say.

"Is that wise? Secrets haven't been that good for you two, remember?"

"No, a scheming RM who just happened to have also slept with Lissa's father wasn't good for us." I look at Tim, and he's clamping down hard on a chuckle. Yeah, that's the soap opera that was my life last Christmas. Five months on and I'm not even close to ready to laugh about it, and I'm more than a bit annoyed that he is. "You haven't seen the Death of the Water. No one's going to be getting jealous over that."

"It's not jealousy. It's disgust at duplicity, mate. You need to be more honest."

"I am." Not always, not nearly enough. For one, there's how I dealt with Rillman. His body is buried in dust in the deepest part of the Underworld. That's a secret I'm never sharing. Not with Tim, not with Lissa. I can almost convince myself it never happened, or, at the very least, that the bastard deserved it. "She knows I took those souls, she just doesn't know it made me an enemy."

This is much harder to hide, can't kick a pile of dust over the sea. All you're going to end up with is mud and that sticks. On the plus side, this snatching of one hundred and fifty souls from the Death of the Water can't be anything but justifiable. Hell's never going to be confused with a great time, but all the rumors I've heard suggest the Death of the Water's equivalent is much, much worse.

"Have you asked her yet?" Tim's voice softens. "Well, have you?"

"As if you'd not know by now."

"You ask her, and then you sort this out."

Tim's gotten me into and out of a lot of trouble. But this is something I'm going to have to resolve myself.

"Absolutely, I'll ask her, and I'll make peace with the Death of the Water straight after."

Yeah, easy, right.

"One thing though," I say.

Tim's sunglasses hide his eyes but I know they're narrowing. "Yes."

"You haven't said anything about my hair."

He flicks his cigarette butt in the air, gets to his feet, and grinds it to a black smear, all without looking at me.

"Look, I only got it cut yesterday."

But he's already gone. Shifted back to the office. I'm left staring at the angry dancing water, my crows squabbling like a bunch of naughty school kids behind me.

"Soon," I say. "Soon."

And maybe it hears me, because all at once the waterspouts are gone, and there's nothing but vapor and a rainbow.

Spooky.

Why do I always put these things off?

2

So, I have two major issues, not counting the nearing End of Days: how do you make peace with the Death of the Water, and how do you ask a girl to marry you?

The first, well, I've got something of an idea. The second . . . not so much.

I sit at a table outside a cafe in West End waiting for Lissa to pay the bill because I forgot my wallet—perfect illustration of how distracted I am. I should be too busy to worry about this, but I can't help it. I keep waiting for the moment to present itself, but it never does.

See, here's the thing—is she going to think I'm asking because the world's end is nigh and it isn't much of a commitment?

Ask, then save world?

Save world, then ask?

Problem is, what if I don't save the world? What if I ask and she says no, and I don't feel like doing the whole saviour thing after that? I mean, it's the kind of work you have to put your heart into.

Bugger, it would be easy (I guess) if I had another job. But I'm the guy who got to be Death.

Trust me, you don't want to be following my career path. For one, there was a lot of blood and slaughter involved. Before I came along, those who wanted what I have sacrificed their friends and family willingly—even excitedly—in what is known as a Schism.

Not me. Not at all. In less than a week I had everything blown out of my life in a burst of gunshots and explosions. Most of my family and friends died, killed by Morrigan—a man closer to me than any uncle. My home- and work-life were irrevocably altered. And Australia nearly passed the tipping point into a Regional Apocalypse.

To say it sucked is somewhat understating the case.

And that was before I became one of the Orcus.

And, just when I was getting used to it, as much as you ever can—the constant cumulative pulse of a nation's hearts; the nightmares, natural and supernatural alike; the lack of sleep; the rising death lust—just as I learned to cope, it got a hell of a lot worse. The only people who really understood me, my fellow Orcus, all went and sacrificed themselves because they thought I had the best chance of defeating a god intent on the end of the world.

I certainly wasn't consulted in that sudden promotion from Regional to Global.

But I managed, partly because I'm not completely me anymore. I've indulged HD only once. And I regret that indulgence . . . sometimes. I should never have strangled Francis Rillman. I should never have let HD take such control, nor should I have enjoyed it so: squeezing the life out of him. I'd laughed in his face.

That's not the man my parents loved. That's not the man I'd believed myself to be.

Should I tell her? Should I divulge, repent, whatever it is I need to do? And how does that factor into her response to my proposal? Gotta be a tick in the negative column certainly. HD is rather keen to see me come clean. It would, HD loves it when the shit hits the fan.

I glance at my watch. Two-thirty. I need to be back in the office soon, so much to do, and Lissa has a soul to pomp on the Southside around three-thirty. We hold off too long and she'll be stuck in traffic. Death waits for no one—the M3 motorway leading south out of the city on the other hand . . .

The world's pulse thump-thumps away within me. HD rattles

the bars of his cage, not a pleasant feeling when you're the cage itself. It's a typical situation, and sensation, these days, as is my circling of that question.

There's an engagement ring in my pocket. I've slipped it, and its little red box, from jacket pocket to jacket pocket for three weeks. Can't forget that, but I can forget my wallet.

I peer into the cafe. How long does it take to pay a bill?

Lissa's chatting away with the barista. I've never known a person who makes friends so easily. She says something and the guy laughs—a little too heartily. Would he take as long to ask her to marry him? HD suggests we kill him.

No. No. We do not kill cute guys who flirt with my girl.

The barista laughs again, even reaches out a hand to touch her arm.

Never too late to make an exception. HD's quick to agree. A single breath and I could call the scythe of Death into being.

Lissa turns from the laughter, and looks in my direction, for a moment I think she's read my mind, but her grin is too warm and the smile is directed at me.

Who wouldn't want to laugh with a girl like that? She's everything I find gorgeous and challenging and wonderful. She made my heart beat faster from the first time I saw her. Quite remarkable considering she was dead, a soul come to warn me, to tell me to run. I'd fallen in love with her before she opened her mouth, and I haven't stopped.

She's in her standard get up. Black and black. Black skirt ending a little above the knees, black long-sleeved blouse, dark hair, cut messy and short, framing a pale face quick to smile or frown. None of which comes close to describing how impossibly radiant she is.

Pinned to her blouse is one of her favorite Mickey Mouse brooches, classic mid-fifties Mickey stomping along merrily. For a touch of variety Lissa's wearing purple Doc Marten boots—she has a green pair at home, but she favors the purple. There's a knife hidden up her left sleeve, strapped to her wrist, another in her left boot. She blinks as she leaves the dark of the cafe for the street. Her eyes, green flecked with gray, focus on me. There's something reckless and measured in the gaze. I feel at once mocked and loved, and I want it all. How does she do that?

Lissa grabs her handbag (black) from the chair beside me, and slips her purse into the bag's cavernous interior.

"You were laughing a lot in there."

"I know, he's cute, huh?"

I can't help but pout. What about me? I'm wearing my best suit here. And I know my hair looks fine. If anything I'm overdressed for West End.

I take her hand and she squeezes mine. The contact shocks me as it always does, even now. A bit over six months ago, touching Lissa would have sent her to Hell, literally. It's what Pomps do. It's what pomping is all about. And me, back then, so unprofessional, so immediately in love, I couldn't do it.

It saved my life.

And it saved hers, too. I pulled an Orpheus Maneuver and brought her back from the Underworld. It was a complicated beginning to our relationship but better than no beginning at all.

We walk out from under the cafe's awning and into the most perfect sort of autumn day. The sky is an utterly stunning blue. It should take the breath from me, put everything in context, except I can feel the weight of the ring in my pocket like it's a bowling ball, and my context involves enemies avid for the world's ending.

I've a lump in my throat.

I shouldn't want this over with but I do. Christ!

Lissa stops, considers me and frowns.

"What?" I ask.

"You look a bit off-color."

"I'm fine."

"Are you sure?"

"Really, I'm fine." Though I want to say, see what this is doing to me! "I'm fine."

Lissa has parked the car around the corner on Vulture Street.

We're standing on a crossroads. Now that's gotta be symbolic. I scan the road. Nothing peculiar. There are plenty of people about. Someone's playing a harmonica very much out of tune down the street, they're getting a good rhythm though. I swallow, and take a deep breath. It's time.

"Well there is something. I've, that is to say... Will you—"

Lissa's hand clenches around mine.

"Run," she says. "Now."

3

Lissa yanks me ahead of her, though she's quick to pass.

I hear the car just before I see it.

An old Holden, V8 by the deep rumble of its engine, thing's twice the size of most modern cars. It cuts through the traffic as though there isn't any. Brakes shriek, a car swerves out of the way and into oncoming vehicles. The collision reverberates down the street followed by even more bangs, glass shatters. People are hurt, someone's screaming, someone's dying. I'm running, Lissa a little ahead, looking for somewhere to take cover. About a hundred meters up the road there's a car park, bordered by a low red-brick fence. I'm never going to make it, and if I shift out of here now, I'm going to leave Lissa defenseless.

I glance back.

The Holden's wheels thump out a beat as it bangs up over the gutter. The chassis of the car grinds and sparks against the concrete. The vehicle takes out a bench, knocks it aside, but not without doing more damage. Black smoke roils along the street and with it the stench of burning rubber and oil. I watch the driver hunched over the wheel, his eyes flicking between Lissa and me.

Crows and sparrows descend on the scene. My Avian Pomps. I get a multiplicity of views. Including, oh dear—

I hit the telephone pole hard, knocks the breath from me. Should've been watching where I was going instead of what was following me. I'm on the ground between the pole and the car, which is rapidly closing in, head ringing.

Crows descend, striking the windshield, with bone-cracking, crow-killing force.

"Up you get." Lissa grabs my hand, heaves me back to my feet, and we run as the car slams into the pole not quite front-on. Metal roars. Its fuel tank explodes. We both hit the ground again, showered in debris. I cover Lissa with my body, wrap myself around her, as something, maybe a tire, dislocates my shoulder, and bounces down the footpath (yep, definitely a tire) and into a shop window.

Lissa's panting as I get to my feet. I help her up, carefully studying her for injuries. Other than an elevated heartbeat and a skinned knee, I can't sense any hurt in her. I start to breathe again.

I realize I'm leaning on Mog with my good arm. Where the hell did my scythe come from? More than a touch embarrassing, like discovering your fly is undone, you're not wearing underpants, and you have an erection.

"Put it away," Lissa says, trying to obscure it from the oncoming crowd with her body.

The scythe's stony snath grows slick with condensation. In humid Brisbane, Mog's always so much colder than the air around it.

Right now though, I don't care about the scythe. I round on her. "Don't you ever come back for me. Putting your life at risk like that," I say. "I can look after myself."

"Look after yourself." Lissa snorts. She's about to say something else but she doesn't, there's a dead man standing next to us.

He scratches his balding head and blinks the newly deceased blink, shocked at what has happened, seeing the world as a dead person sees it. The shock will quickly fade, that's a living thing. Vengeful spirits, well they're rare, apathy is the rule of thumb for the dead.

What are often considered angry spirits are usually only the dead that haven't been pomped—confusion mistaken for rage. The dead's concerns are suddenly and drastically different to those of the living, the most pressing being how to get to the Underworld.

The answer is standing beside him. Right now this guy doesn't know what the hell is going on, but I can tell it is dawning on him.

"What..." his voice fades away. "Am I?"

"Yeah," I say. "Can't talk now."

I feel bad, I feel positively awful, but I don't have time for this. I reach over and touch him, if a sensation like pushing your hand through slightly stinging smoke can be described as touching. The pomp is quick, barely an ache. But it doesn't mean I don't suffer in other ways. This man shouldn't have died. Stirrers are messing with the schedule—if it really was a Stirrer in the V8 and not just some guy who didn't like the way I looked. Once again they're ending lives before they're due, adding confusion to an already confusing prescience.

"Efficient," Lissa says. "But hardly compassionate."

"Don't try and change the subject by critiquing my pomping skills."

Vulture Street is dense with smoke. People are already running to help, stopping a few meters from Lissa and me. Hesitating, because here, the smoke is thicker. Though it's not only that. I'm Death, and now, having seconds ago pomped someone, I'm projecting all sorts of feelings that those unused to death find threatening. We're a deathless society in the main. A reminder that this is merely an illusion is always shocking to punters. Of course, it could just be that I'm holding a bloody big scythe made of stone in one hand.

"Sorry, it's my job, remember," Lissa says. "One of them anyway."

"What to critique me?"

"No, finding and teaching Pomps. I'll admit there's a critiquing element. But I'm not changing the subject, I never change the subject."

"Yes, you are." I glower at her. I'm good at the glower. Practiced at it. HD is even better. You can't face down that combined glowering. Well maybe Lissa could, but not this time.

She shakes her head. "When I see you in trouble, I just—"

"I know. I feel the same. But try not to get yourself killed." *What the hell are we arguing about?* "Are you OK?"

"I'm fine," she says.

"Then could you help me pop my shoulder back in?"

Lissa goggles at me. "Your shoulder?"

"Yeah, it's dislocated. It's starting to hurt a bit."

"Steven! You should have told me sooner." She grabs my arm, and wrenches with sick-making force, there's a satisfying pop. Certainly feels better, but I heal quickly.

"You did that well," I say. Lissa never ceases to surprise me.

"Of course I did," she says.

I will Mog to become the two Knives of Negotiation. The scythe shrinks, breaks in two. Both knives mumble a quick hello. I slide the first blade back into its sheath beneath my jacket, the second I keep out. It mumbles at me in the baby talk of death. For some reason civilians never notice the knives—just like they never see the dead—the scythe on the other hand...

We approach the wreck of the car. Within it, what's left of the driver is tugging at the seatbelt. It's definitely a Stirrer. I can see the sharp edge of a fractured humerus jutting through a tear in its shirt-sleeve. Even now the Stirrer draws life through itself, an uncontrolled and continuous pomping that sucks the souls of not just the dead, but the living, too. If you're not braced or a Pomp, hang around a Stirrer long enough and you're gone, soul drained away, and there's another Stirrer shambling about, or driving cars at me and mine.

I turn towards Lissa. She already has her blade in one hand. I fling my arm out to stop her racing past me. "Let me deal with this," I say. "I don't want you getting too close to that car."

She doesn't move. "I can handle myself," she says.

"And I know that." I glower at her again. She glowers back. "You don't know what kind of carcinogens you're breathing in here."

Lissa stomps away and I slide the mumbling blade down my palm, wincing with the pain—no matter how many times you do it the cutting hurts. My hand is dripping, slick with my warmth, the knife cut deep. You need blood to stall a Stirrer, not just any blood, only a Pomp's will do.

I reach in to stall the Stirrer and send it back to the Deepest Dark. It clenches a hand around my wrist, careful not to touch my blood. I've made a rookie mistake. I pull, but it doesn't let go. The thing's got forearms the size of my thighs.

"He's coming," it says, through the torn ruin of a face. Muscles, revealed behind a hanging flap of skin, move like gore-slicked worms. "And she will die first."

Nothing too odd there, they've all been like this lately. So damn chatty. What ever happened to a groan, or a sigh, or a moan and a hiss of hatred? But this . . . I'm so over this. "You try and kill her, and I will cut that god of yours from existence itself. Hang on, I've every intention of doing that anyway."

"Words, nothing but words. You couldn't stop him before and you can't now." The Stirrer chuckles. What the fuck is it on about, and when did Stirrers start referring to themselves as he or she? "He's coming. And your words will scatter in the winds of the void."

Yeah.

Yeah.

Yeah.

I swing my knife hand into its face, break a couple of teeth. The Stirrer grunts (that's more like it) and I wrench my blood-slicked fist free, wriggling my fingers.

"Talk to the hand, eh," I slap my palm against its face, and the Stirrer, that alien soul animating a human body, is sent back to the Deepest Dark. I've shut the door on this corpse. I check its wrists. Yes, the bastard has a mask symbol—a bisected half circle—tattooed about three centimeters behind his thumb.

Pushed on by the nearing god, or just driven to brazenness, Stirrers are inhabiting the bodies of the dead in growing numbers. We've managed to contain that growth a little with our blood (literally) and the brace symbol: a triangle with its point facing down and a not-quite-straight line bisecting it. But just as we have a symbol to halt them, they have their own: something designed by Francis Rillman. I've started calling it the mask, because that is what it does. Hides their presence from us. More worryingly, it reduces the efficacy of our brace.

A Stirrer marked with the mask can go anywhere it wants, safe from detection, and is pretty much indistinguishable from your regular punter, unless you touch it. Sure, there are other signs; Stirrers are a long while getting used to their stolen body's muscles, and they tend to lurch a little. But once we could tell a Stirrer a block away just by feeling their presence, tasting their rottenness on the air. Not anymore. Now, if we don't see them first... well, you don't want a Stirrer to see you first.

Work as a Pomp always had an element of danger, but I'm starting to look back on those dangers of old with fondness.

I slide my knife into its sheath and back away from the smoking wreck. Vulture Street is a chaotic tangle of cars. More like a war zone than an inner-city-suburban street. The screamer's still screaming. Sirens build in the distance, overture to a different kind of conflict. State officials are rarely happy to see me; I'm too difficult to explain. The guy playing the harmonica starts up again. Where else is he ever going to get such a good audience?

"He's dead," I say to the gathered crowd, trying to sound at once authoritative and shocked and saddened. Lissa's already got people standing as far away as possible—the telephone pole might topple, the car could explode... again. Neither is likely. I'd sense the possibility of so many deaths. But there's always the chance.

That no one wants to question our presence or why I was holding a scythe a few minutes ago doesn't surprise me. Project enough authority and people are generally willing to accept it. I know I was. Morrigan called it the sheep factor.

Lissa looks in my direction, and I nod towards the pile-up, something's stirring there. My work isn't done yet.

"Did you actually say, 'Talk to the hand'?" Lissa asks coming over to me.

"I might have. Look, I need to stall the other Stirrer."

She grabs my wrist. "Wait. What did you want to ask me, at the lights, before all this happened?"

"Nothing." I pull free of her. "I've forgotten."

Nothing? I've forgotten? What the hell sort of answer is that?!

"Couldn't have been too important then."

"No. Not too important."

"You got another quip worked out?"

"I don't quip. I—Hey! I thought that was pretty funny."

"Go, before it gets away. Talk to the hand... Jesus, de Selby."

I wish I could convince harmonica guy to shut up. HD reminds me there is a way. I tell it to be quiet. I pick through the wreckage, hunting the body. The Stirrer's presence grows in my mind; I follow it, the back of my throat scratchy with the rough scent of the Stirrer. A woman's already with the screamer, holding their hand, calming them down. The bravery of some people amazes me.

The Stirrer has crawled about twenty meters away from the road, and is crouched behind a fence in a garden bed—already the flowers are dying. A crow caws surreptitiously from the telephone wires above, jabs its beak down, staring at me with dark eyes.

The Stirrer's revealed to me slowly. First a shiny scalp, followed by the shirt—torn and spattered with blood. If you didn't know any better you'd think it was a man sick and in shock. However, the Stirrer's anything but. Each second sees it grow stronger even as the world around it weakens and dies: its essence drawn away into the Underworld. As I approach the fence the Stirrer searches frantically through its pockets. Its lip curls in triumph, fingers clutching a pen, I watch it mark its wrist with the mask symbol, clumsily, but it's enough. Suddenly I can't feel it anymore.

Not that I need to.

With a groan it lifts itself shakily to its feet. The new stirred thing registers me. Its eyes widen, lips draw back in a grimace of hatred, and it holds the pen before itself like a knife.

But it can barely hold it steady. I knock the pen from its fingers.

"No you don't," I say, slapping the Stirrer gently on the neck with my hand. There's enough blood on my fingers to do the job.

Another stall. I lay the body down, walk away from it. The whole street is backed up with traffic, gawkers and people trying to help. The sirens are almost upon us, firies, ambos and cops. All of them racing to this mess. The blue sky is obscured by smoke.

I call Alex, my contact in the police force, and a good friend—his father, Don, was a Pomp, one of many killed by Morrigan in the Schism.

"I heard," he says the moment he picks up. "I'm en route, stay there."

"I had no intention of doing otherwise."

"You asked her yet?"

"What?" I don't really want to talk about this now.

"You know what I'm saying—had a beer with Tim the other day. You haven't have you?"

"It's not that easy, you know."

"Gutless," Alex harrumphs. "If it was me..."

"It's not you though is it?"

"I'll be there soon."

I call work, get them to cancel my afternoon meeting with Cerbo, I'm going to be a little late.

The first police car is already pulling in.

I wave over at Lissa, signal that I got the second Stirrer and she nods. If she doesn't get on the road to the Princess Alexandra Hospital soon she's going to be late. You don't want to leave a soul wandering, it's poor form, unprofessional. I watch Lissa stomp off to the car, admiring her from behind, wishing I was walking beside her. Regretting the stupid timing of it all. Angry at what's happened here.

And if I sound cold, well, life's full of tragedies—little, big, slow and fast—my people attend them all at the end.

But what I can't stand is when they come from me.

My presence alone shouldn't lead to death. HD is angry that there wasn't more slaughter. I'm circling a dozen conflicting emotions at once.

When is Alex getting here? I have work to do, but it seems Death must wait for someone after all.

And HD whispers that one day, soon perhaps, his time will come and all the stars, planets and moons will be snipped, snipped, snipped from their threads, and the world run awash with blood. No waiting, just destruction.

Death. And Death. And Death.

Shut up.

I could do with a drink. That thirst provides a counter beat to HD, though one alarmingly similar. We share more in common than I would like.

I check on the first Stirrer, just in case. Smoke keeps billowing. The crowd keeps its distance. But the corpse in the car doesn't move again.

It just burns.

4

It takes me even longer than I had expected to extricate myself from that mess and return to Number Four, Mortmax's office space on George Street in the city. But it can't be helped. Alex had done his best to get me out of there quickly, but an exploding car, five vehicle pile-up, multiple deaths, and a guy seen holding a scythe right next to it all means he can't fast talk it away.

Though I'm certain I'm not the first person to stand around West End with a scythe. Should be more of it, if you ask me, and fewer buskers. Alex doesn't mention my haircut. So, Tim isn't on the phone to him at all hours with updates then.

I shift into the office, no time to walk across the slow curve of Victoria Street Bridge, instead I step from one bit of earthly reality to another in an instant.

Smoke, sirens and that awful harmonica—I'm beginning to think the "harm" in harmonica has nothing to do with harmonics—are traded for the gentle hum of my computer, the distant murmur of a busy office and the constant background creaking of the One Tree that overarches the Underworld. Pieter Brueghel's "The Triumph of Death" hangs in my office. I'm not feeling that triumphant today, and even the painting's gaudy cheerfulness can't compensate. I walk to the curtains behind my desk and throw them open.

Windows to Hell and earth meet at the corner of my office, a trick of supernatural architectural genius that continues to astound me.

The Underworld looks pretty dark and dismal today, a complete contrast to the brilliant blue of Brisbane's sky, the traffic down below moves sluggishly, but so do the cars on George Street. Nothing much going on in either world but the day-to-day life-unlife activities.

The light of Hell has been worrying me lately. I've been watching it run down. Not sure what it is I am doing wrong. I've had to move the pot of daisies given to me by Madeleine Danning, East European RM, (RIP) over to the earthly side, there just wasn't enough light for them streaming in from Hell.

I close my eyes and lean my head against the cold glass. It throbs in time with the creaking of the One Tree. The deaths of thousands pass through me via those in my employ. Pomps successfully made all over the world. The World Pulse shifts subtly with each death, while remaining pretty much the same. Births keep coming into and falling away from that gestalt beat. And part of me follows each death closely, taking a quiet delight in it all. Another part shudders, wounded.

I'm not sure which part I am—if there's a real me, or if there's nothing more than these two poles of perception. I know it's an important question, but I dare not think about it too much. There's madness in those kinds of thoughts—and I have enough in me already.

Lissa was right, I could have been a bit more compassionate with the poor bastard I pomped today. I wonder how he's faring in the Underworld, if he's already started his slow march to the One Tree, or if he's elected to stay a while and play at the shadow life of Hell—there are always plenty of souls that do, though the Tree has them in the end.

Punters, they live and die oblivious. Maybe it's better that way. When you're born into a Pomp family you don't get the choice. You're raised on death, and even if you decide to become a Black Sheep, and work at something other than pomping, you're always going to be aware of the battle going on, and you're never going to shake the memories of the hundreds of funerals you attended as a child.

I knew there was an afterlife from the age of three. I knew my parents sent people there. I thought it must be OK. After all, it was where everyone ended up.

But when I asked my dad just what it was like, he'd said it wasn't very nice. I'd pressed him to explain, and eventually he had.

Dad wasn't into sugar coating.

I liked my bedroom didn't I? Yes. But did I like it when I was told to go there because I'd been naughty, or I didn't want to go to bed? That was what the Underworld was like. Any place where you were sent whether or not you wanted to go wasn't very nice.

Like an office. Like a career where you attend thousands upon thousands of downfalls every day, and where underlings call you, not out of respect or desire, but habit.

Of course, I've learned it isn't as simple as that. Nothing ever is.

I have an intimate relationship with the Underworld now, and Dad was sort of right. We don't have a choice over our birth or our death—not really—but we have a choice over what we do in between. It's fundamental, and obvious, but after my parents and most of my friends were murdered, I'd moped around as though the world owed me something. Fair enough, a natural response, except most people aren't Death. I'd had to snap out of it quick smart.

And I don't think I would have if it hadn't been for Lissa and Tim.

My phone shudders out a text in my pocket to the tune of Weezer's "Buddy Holly"—I've got my nineties nostalgia on today.

It's Lissa.

Made it! Time to spare.

But I knew that. I have an Avian Pomp, a crow, checking up on her as she walks through the big glass door of the main entrance—at a distance of course, I know how she feels about me spying on her. Yeah, it's creepy, but she's my girl and I like to know she's safe.

She doesn't look like someone tried to kill her less than an hour ago. She's everything a professional Pomp should be. Admirable posture, neatly dressed, face the very picture of compassion. You'd have to notice the scars on her hands to know there is a war going on. We all have those, but she has more than most. She's so damn good at her job.

I could watch her talk the soul down to the Underworld, listen to the calming rhythm of her voice, but I leave her there, walking deep into the guts of the hospital. Some places my birds can't follow. Besides, the Avian chooses that moment to snatch a bug out of the air.

I get out of there as it starts cracking the struggling insect open on the concrete footpath. Not nearly fast enough; I get a bitter mashed-beetle taste in my mouth.

Back in my own skull as much as I am able, I enjoy a moment or two of calm. No phone ringing. The door to my office closed.

I drop into the throne of Death and power surges through me, a sense of absolute interconnectedness with my employees. I feel Pomps struggling with Stirrers. I feel Pomps pomping souls. My face twists with a savage grin that is more HD than me. I feel the heartbeats of the world amplified tenfold. Some are ending, some beginning. All that life and death stuff. And there I am at its center.

For a moment the bit that's me isn't. I become a flood of sensation, death and hunger. It's the tragicomic sputtering of a multitude of final moments grown suddenly vivid and intense. A series of lightning bursts, none that linger, each crowded out by the next. Death after death after death.

I drown in it and break free. And it's like I'm gasping for air, only the air is me. Steven de Selby pushing back, taking shape.

Floods, famines, disease. All these deaths have me salivating, and I know HD yearns for more.

I ram HD and that endless stream of information down, down, down, packing it away until it becomes a kind of psychic tinnitus that I can, almost, ignore.

It's never easy, but I've been getting better at it. If I wasn't, I think I would have gone mad by now.

I pour myself some Black Label Bundy Rum, just to wash the taste of bug out of my mouth, and consider "The Triumph of Death." Skeletons rushing around having all sorts of fun with Hell on earth. I'm so used to it now that I find it comforting.

Finally I get out of my throne, my hands shaking a little, finish the rum in a couple of gulps (I've earned it, haven't I?) and swing open my door.

Number Four is busy as usual. I catch the familiar odors of aftershave, perfume and slightly burnt coffee, the consequence of staff that have no idea how to operate an espresso machine. Pomps sit at desks, before computers, sorting through the increasingly problematic Schedule of Deaths, trying to calculate which bodies might stir, and which will only require a pomp—it's getting harder and harder to tell.

Everyone's tired. These last few days, souls have not wanted to go. Pomps have been rough. It always hurts a little, but the raw pain of sending the dead to Hell has been even rawer of late.

Here is the heartland of our campaign. Number Four may look like any other office, but we're not only interested in good returns for our shareholders—most of that's done in the floors below through everyday brokerage and investments, enhanced by a little Deathly foresight. On this floor there are battles being planned. We're here to open and close the way to Hell. My Pomps and I are the doors and the locks. Souls are pomped. Stirrers are stalled.

There are around 140,000 deaths a year in Australia. Fifty-seven million or so deaths per year in the world. At Mortmax we're responsible for ensuring all souls go one way, and that nothing comes back. We're very good at it. We've had a lot of practice. Mortmax has existed in one form or another for over seventy thousand years. Death followed humanity out of Africa. Its Pomps have spread around the world. Unfortunately, the Stirrers spread with us, an inescapable and angry echo of the past.

But mixed with that sense of purpose, that industry, is something else I've been noticing lately. Fear, a quiet dread. The Stirrer god is coming, and every Stirrer seems intent on reminding us of that. I've come across people whispering in the kitchen, stopping the instant they see me. I've heard crying coming from the toilets. The End of Days is almost upon us, and we're not quite sure what we can do about it.

Tim's door opens at the opposite side of Number Four, like he's been waiting for me to exit my office. He waves at me—the kind of "we need to talk now" gesture I'm all too familiar with.

You could slash his throat. Make an example of him.

I try not to smile at that, as Tim stalks toward my room. He's grimacing, and my Pomps keep a wide berth. Watching his passage through the office is fascinating; I think my staff just might be more scared of Tim than of me. Brooding about our morning meeting, I guess. I step back from the door, let him through, shutting it quickly behind him.

He winces as he catches my breath. "You know if you're going to drink on the job—"

I wave him away. "Oh, the day I've had."

"Just saying."

"You give up cigarettes. I'll give up drinking."

He almost looks hurt. Can I hurt my cousin that easily? Surely not after all we've been through. If he's that sensitive—

"Why is there a tire mark on the shoulder of your jacket?" He squints, walking around me.

"What?" I shrug myself out of my jacket and groan at the filthy pattern scarring what was once pristine wool. The material's torn around the sleeve. I give it a shake and we both cough at the dust it throws up. I'm also missing a cufflink, a little Death's Head one Lissa had bought me as a present. Bugger.

"I knew you were attacked today, but I didn't know that the car drove over you," Tim says offering me a cigarette, which is really only his excuse to light one up himself.

I shake my head. "Only the tire, the rest of the car was in pieces."

"And did you ask her?"

I fiddle with my French cuffs, holding them neat with a paperclip.

"I—um, I was going to, and then...look at that tire mark, eh." I frown. "And thank you very much for sharing my problems with Alex."

"A man's gotta vent," Tim says. "And how is it a problem? You love her, she loves you, just get on with it."

"You can't tell me it was easy with you and Sally."

He clears a space on my desk, and sits down. "Easy? No, but I didn't have the end of the world to contend with, that puts a slight urgency on the matter. I was only just out of uni. I thought I knew everything."

I bite my tongue, hold back asking him what's changed, and why he can't use a bloody chair once in a while.

"Cerbo's rather anxious to see you."

Faber Cerbo was the Ankou to Suzanne Whitman—North America's RM. He and Tim are my two most senior members of staff.

Cerbo is also my authority on the Stirrer god. He's pored over almost every ancient volume we can get our hands on. Problem is, last time something like this approached the earth humans weren't even a glimmer in the eye of an early mammalian ancestor. To say that there are slim historical pickings is like saying the pyramids were a bit of an effort to construct.

What we had was based on guesswork and fossil evidence. And it's flimsy—wind whistling through the holes in it—evidence at that. Far better minds than mine were debating about it in the Pomp community. But we were running out of time.

"You did explain to him why I cancelled?"

"I did, but he'd like to see you as soon as possible. He says something else has turned up."

"That's all he said? What 'something else'?"

Tim smiles thinly, "I don't think he trusts me."

I don't think he does either. It's the government connection. Tim was a major player in the department of Pomp/government relations before he became Ankou. And there's evidence to suggest that that department, manipulated by Rillman disguised as one Magritte Solstice (yes, he was a "fingers in all sorts of pies" kind of guy), allowed a fraudulent and Anti-Pomp arm of the Federal Police to exist unnoticed until it became a major threat.

Tim says he knew nothing about it, and neither did his replacement Doug Anderson, but I can understand why Cerbo doesn't believe him. We don't exactly have a healthy, trusting workplace. And Cerbo is steeped in that corporate culture, but enough is enough.

"It doesn't matter whether he trusts you. We're all Pomps. And our enemy is coming. We need to stick together."

"I tried that on, and all it did was make him even more evasive."

Cerbo doesn't worry easily. I've got a feeling I better visit him now. "Anything else more pressing?"

"What isn't pressing these days?"

HD gives him a look, and I let it. The knives shudder in their hilts. I have to strain to stop it going any further. I'm not even sure Tim notices.

"Nothing I can't handle," Tim continues, and he says it so confidently, that I stop him before he opens the door.

"One more thing," I say. "Just between you and me."

"Yes?"

"Do you ever get the feeling that we're all playing at this... work. That we're blithely ignoring the elephant in the room."

"Elephant?"

"The Stirrer god, idiot! All this bullshit, this distrust, trying to carry on as though nothing is going on."

"Oh, it's going on." Tim glares at me, maybe I've overstepped the boundaries, but, hey, he was the one who sent me those texts this morning. "You look at that 'elephant' too long and it'll drive you insane." I'd taken Tim to observe the approaching Stirrer god a few months back. He hadn't liked it, neither had I. It had grown bigger in the sky of the Deepest Dark since I'd last seen it. Its devouring flesh swallowing souls at an alarming rate. "Hang on," Tim says, "isn't that what Cerbo does?"

"Never you mind about that, Cerbo's the most dangerously sane person I know," I say. "But aren't you worried?"

Tim shakes his head. "Nah, not while we have Steven de Selby on our side, the luckiest fucking bastard on the planet."

I just wish the rest of the office felt that way. I shift to the Boston offices.

An eye blink and I'm there, beats the shit out of transpacific flights, and waiting in line at customs.

Doesn't mean there isn't the occasional problem. Cerbo's knife is out, and it's pointed at my chest.

5

"Oh, it's you," he says.

It's extremely provocative, and not a little dangerous to shift directly into an Ankou's office. But you could say much the same for pointing a knife at your boss. And while I don't want to be an arsehole about it, every office of Mortmax Industries is my office. They're all my Number Fours.

If Cerbo can't quite hide a flicker of annoyance at my sudden appearance, he's very good at pushing it down almost at once. Almost as good as he is at slipping the knife from his hand back into its sheath. Even sitting in his office in Boston he's appropriately paranoid. He makes a show of straightening his cap: a finger brushes his narrow mustache. Neat, lean, serious, Cerbo is always on, always focused on the job. But today there are bags under his eyes, and it looks like he's wearing yesterday's suit.

There are leather-bound volumes piled precisely on one corner of his desk, an e-reader next to them. Most of what he needs to read is electronic, but there are a few volumes from the older regions that have yet to be scanned. Including what looks like a scroll. His office smells a little like a second-hand bookstore—rotting paper, coffee and just a hint of sweat.

He's sitting in the plain leather, but no doubt excessively expensive, chair that replaced Suzanne's throne of Death after it faded away with her soul, all the throne's power passing into mine. His other hand, the one that hadn't just been holding a knife, lowers a thick book onto a notepad. There's something scribbled there, but I can't quite make it out.

"I know I cancelled a meeting but you're not planning a Schism are you?" I ask, framing it with as unthreatening a smile as possible.

Cerbo's boss Suzanne Whitman was one of the eleven RMs who sacrificed their lives so I could become Orcus. The logic being that a single Death, rather than Death diffused through thirteen souls, would have a better chance at defeating the Stirrer god. I don't know whether or not I agree with that logic. And I'm positive most of the Ankous the RMs left behind don't, they've certainly proven themselves resistant to my admittedly limited charms. But what's done is done, and the RMs are gone beyond even the root tips of the One Tree. I'm the Orcus now. And we all have to deal with that.

But dealing can mean a multitude of interesting unfriendly-to-Steve things in a business founded in bloody coups. Actually, as far as Mortmax is concerned, the term "bloody coup" is an exercise in clinical understatement.

"Mr. de Selby, I wouldn't want your position even if they paid me your salary."

Yeah, but once the Stirrer god is dealt with I reckon things might change. Cerbo strikes me as a man who makes plans—careful long-term plans—and why sit on a plain leather chair when you can sit on the throne of Death?

He pushes the notepad toward me. Even though the writing is neatly laid out I can't make much sense of it—one of the symbols that mark it may be a Feynman diagram if I remember my old physics lessons properly, or it could just be a squiggle.

"I'm not making much progress."

"What's it say?"

"A god is coming. And I don't think it's going to be late," he says pointedly.

"I tried to get here earlier, but had a few distractions."

"Have you asked her yet?"

What? Does everybody know? I clench my teeth a little. "Not that sort of distraction," I say. "More of a car trying to squash me into the footpath."

"I don't know why they bother, it's not as if they can kill you."

"Maybe they don't want to kill me, but it might hurt me enough to keep me off the job for a couple of days. They're trying to get me out of the way," I say. "You've been following things. Stirrers are building again around Brisbane. I've needed to pull people in from all over the place to keep on top of it. Even I've had to start hunting them when I have a spare moment."

"It's good to keep your hand in."

"Yes, but I'd prefer to have more of a say in it."

"Draw in even more staff if you need to. As your number of stirs has increased, ours have declined. And that's been happening across the board. You're Orcus, your decisions drive and define our company, and this war. It is OK for you to direct Pomps where you want."

"Yes, but what if that's exactly what the Stirrer god wants?"

"I don't think so," Cerbo says. "What I think is happening is that, for whatever reason, perhaps only because you have chosen to base yourself there, the Stirrer god has in turn chosen Australia as some sort of focal point."

"You think I'm in some way responsible for the End of Days?"

"I've considered it. Not responsible as such, merely a target for the god to aim at. Suzanne certainly believed it. Though in my darkest moments I wonder. What if it's your very presence as Orcus that ignites the final flame, so to speak? Or perhaps it sees a weakness, a flaw in you that it can use. Both disturbing propositions wouldn't you say?"

"Or maybe it just knows that it can't lose and wants a big old fight before it devours all life from the world." HD lets out an anticipatory growl, and tugs at my face. Cerbo must see a little of it, because he pales.

"It could be any one of those things," Cerbo says. "Which is why I just wish you'd let me send spies back into the Stirrer city."

Suzanne had sent spies transformed into Stirrers deep into the city of Devour. They never lasted long, and while their information had at times proven invaluable, or so Cerbo told me, the mortality rate had been almost total. To say that the few who had come back were damaged is something of an understatement.

"No," I say. "I refuse to send people to die."

"Sometimes that's what running the business requires."

"Maybe before me, but not now." We hold each other's gaze, Cerbo is the first to look away.

"I would prefer it if you visited me a bit more often."

I try and soothe him with a smile. "I think it's only fair that I visit my other offices. Ari likes visits too. So do Mill, David and Ishi, they all do."

"I wouldn't trust Ariana. She lacks subtlety."

Like I would trust any Ankou other than Tim. "Wouldn't that be a reason to trust her? Besides she's an Ankou—you're all about subtlety." And knives, and dreaming of the top job, because they all think they could do it so much better. Personally I trust Ari more than I ever will Cerbo, she's ballsy and proud, and she reminds me of Lissa. "And people start to panic if they see me with you too much."

Cerbo tilts his head, I'm sure he'd like it known that I visit him more frequently. I can see the cogs of his mind working overtime on this one. At last he smiles. "They think the god's here, or nearly here."

"Yeah, the End of Days is easier to deal with in the abstract, or at least with the thought that there are days in front of the 'end of' bit."

"Yes, and I'd like to know just when, but... there's not enough to tell me one way or another," he says significantly. And we're back to those damn spies, or lack thereof.

"What do you think?"

We've both seen the vast thing staining the heavens of the Deepest Dark, devouring souls like they were sweetmeats.

Cerbo gets out of his chair. "Come with me."

There's a door in one side of the office, an old wooden thing. He pulls a key from his pocket, inserts it in the lock, and with some effort, as though the lock is stuck, or rusted, turns the key. He smiles at the click, and pushes the door open.

I don't know what I was expecting but it wasn't this.

The room beyond is tiny: more a chamber, ascetic in the extreme. A single bed and a small table on which an old book sits—its cover cracked, its pages well thumbed. In one corner of the room is a small dressing table, topped with a tiny mirror and two lipsticks. Next to the table is a narrow wardrobe, the sort you'd have to really squeeze into to find Narnia, and at the risk of getting stuck halfway.

"This is her room," Cerbo says. "And all she owned."

"Suzanne lived here?" Even more surprising, I could almost have imagined Suzanne Whitman using this as a quiet room, but...

"Yes. I believe you would find the same situation with the other RMs, a few centuries and the gathering of possessions seems to lose its appeal. The job itself is its own reward."

Mr. D obviously hadn't reached that kind of corporate Zen state, what with his boat and his houses along the coast. I'd always expected Suzanne to live in a Brownstone in some exclusive neighbourhood in Boston, with a library taking up several rooms. The smell of dust and books. Not this tiny room, smelling just so faintly of must and time passing slowly, inching into eons.

The bed is made up, a single pillow, a single thin blanket. For a moment I feel a twinge of sadness. A made bed and this tiny room. All that's left of her.

"It was here that she would stay, if she needed rest, in those few times that she needed rest. Suzanne gave the End of Days far more thought and time than any mortal could. And she believed that it would start in your region."

"Another reason why she manipulated me into becoming Orcus?" I hadn't heard this one before, though it makes sense. Why else would the Stirrers have been so anxious to deal with the last two Australian

Ankous? I wonder if the threat had been expected to start in another region if I'd still be alive or if someone else would be Orcus. I open my mouth to speak, but Cerbo seems to have anticipated the thought.

"The least of reasons, believe me, Steven, but no doubt a factor."

I look down at the book, *Huckleberry Finn.* Who'd have thought! Each to their own. I want to pick it up, have a look (see if it's signed) but to do so seems somehow disrespectful.

"I don't like coming into this room," Cerbo says. "But here, under the book..." He pushes it gently to one side.

There, carved in the table is a date and the letter M. The wound is relatively fresh. I run my hands over it, cut so smooth you'd have thought she used a really tiny router. This meant something, it was important.

May 24. M

It's only a week away. So close. Surely not, and yet, it feels... right. Shit. I don't know whether or not to feel frightened or relieved. My skin prickles. HD slides around inside me with a new urgency. There's something else, too. Something familiar about that date. I can't quite put my finger on it. The only M-word I can think of right now is "marriage." No, this is much more ominous. But then again... marriage. Did they know something that I didn't?

I look over at Cerbo. "What does it mean?"

Cerbo shrugs. "I was hoping Suzanne would have told you. She didn't tell me. If I hadn't been cleaning up in here, dusting, I wouldn't have found it."

"You do your own dusting?"

Cerbo puffs up to full height: it's almost threatening. "Of course I do, as if I would trust the job to anyone else. Dust holds too many secrets."

I smile at him. "But, hang on, Suzanne died over four months ago..."

Cerbo blushes, I don't know if I've ever seen him blush before.

"I—I haven't been able to bring myself to come in here. Today was the first day I've managed to walk through that door."

"It's all right," I say, wishing that he had, and that we had more than a handful of days to work out the significance of the date, if there is any significance at all. "She must have wanted you to find it."

"Yes. One doesn't carve into a fifteenth-century side table for no reason."

But that doesn't make complete sense. Suzanne was a woman who planned everything. To leave such a clue and not to provide any context seems very unlike her.

Perhaps she really hadn't expected to die.

"Did Suzanne ever write a diary?"

Cerbo laughs. "Not that I am aware."

"Have you ever looked?" He blushes again. OK, so he has. "And you never found anything?"

"Not a thing," he says. I leave it at that. I can imagine why this may not have come up in conversation at the Death Moot, the last day Suzanne was alive. Things had been crazy then, all she had planned was coming to fruition, including her own death. There's no way she couldn't have been anything but distracted. And in my experience, nothing ever goes as smoothly as planned. And yet she left this final mark.

May 24. Why is that date niggling me? "See if you can find anything. Any reference at all to do with the twenty-fourth. Get in touch with the other Ankous, just be subtle about it." I say.

"I am the very definition of subtlety."

Unlike, Ari, apparently, I want to say, but I hold my tongue.

I look back to his office door. "How are things here?"

"Running smoothly," Cerbo says guardedly.

"Yeah, but what's the mood?"

Cerbo's silence is answer enough.

"We can all feel it coming now," I say.

"Yes. It's not far away. The twenty-fourth or not."

"Are we ready?"

"Do you want me to lie to you? It'd help if we knew what we needed to be ready for. But we don't."

"We can bleed. We can stall. Maybe that will be enough."

Cerbo smiles as bright and false a smile as I have ever seen, and I shift from Suzanne's chamber back to my office.

May 24. That doesn't leave much time, this could be nothing more than a coincidence, but that cold hard certainty is growing inside me. My hands are shaking. I peer at the calendar under the mess on my desk. Seven days, an interminable length of time, and not nearly enough. Not if it's true, and truth is what I require. I need more than a sense of anxiety inside me to believe that this is actually going to happen. Much more.

I've been tossed around by other people's truths these past few months, just taken them as *fait accompli,* including this job. It's time I made a few of my own. Or at least found them myself.

I've a hunch that if this date is important it might show up somewhere else.

A place I've been avoiding because of the memory it evokes, and the brutal mess that I last saw there. A bloody, almost offhand scattering of limbs and flesh, and that was only the beginning.

Aunt Neti had kept meticulous records of the goings-in and goings-out of the Underworld. If anyone is likely to have left information corresponding with Suzanne's date, it would be Neti. A second reference to that date will certainly suggest that my worry is well founded.

But that means going to her rooms.

I wasn't fond of them when she was alive. Sometimes things get worse after people die, and not just because of the hole they leave. I don't think Neti's rooms are going to have gotten any better.

6

When you decide to do something. You're better off just doing it.

That was my mum's philosophy.

Mine was, and still is: think about it, procrastinate, check email, post a couple of witty tweets, check email, check hair in the mirror by my filing cabinet, consider filing, consider employing someone to do my filing, see if anyone's relationship status has changed on Facebook. Normally I was a star at the whole thing, but not today. I only got as far as opening the Twitter app on my phone.

I need to sort this out, see if there is anything connecting Suzanne's scribbling with Aunt Neti. Maybe their nearness to death had made them both somewhat prescient. Not that I've ever come across anything like that before, other than the insane or extremely senile All-Death, but there is always a first time. What worries me more is if they both had, if all the RMs had seen this date as a probable starting point, all the RMs except me. I mean, why hadn't I?

Ah, fuck it!

I get out of my throne and walk to the door.

The moment I open it, heart rates in the space beyond quicken, and not in a "happy to see me" kind of way. Tim scares them, but my presence can invoke a deeper back-brain sort of terror. And today I can really feel it.

I don't like this reaction in my staff at all. Maybe it is partly exacerbated by my own anxiety. It's hardly as if I'm a punitive sort of boss—even if HD would like to get swinging with the scythe. People cast furtive glances in my direction, and I try and smile harmlessly. Doesn't seem to do much good though.

To everyone outside the offices of Mortmax International, I'm just a guy in a suit with great hair. Here, people know I'm Death, and some of them even understand what that means. I want people to treat me normally, but I suppose, when I think about it, this is how people would treat me normally.

I remember how I'd try and avoid my old boss, Mr. D—hey, the one that I am avoiding now—he made me very... uncomfortable. Sure, he liked to change his face a lot, shifting from skull, to splatter, to smiling middle-aged man in the space of seconds, and that was kind of threatening—Dad said the trick was to talk to his hairline, because it rarely changed—but Mr. D was never as powerful as I have become.

I stroll through the room.

HD feeds on the discomfort, like it's a pack of pork rinds—light, tasty, and ultimately unsatisfying. It suggests we take out the particularly timorous ones now, like right now, they're going to be no use in the coming war—and it's ravenous—can't it just kill a few?

I smile. Avoid eye contact. Let people get on with their work, and focus on my own.

There are things I'm frightened of too.

There's a hallway that I don't like to look down. That I like to imagine doesn't even exist.

It leads to what used to be Aunt Neti's rooms, and those rooms lead, via corridors, to all of Mortmax's offices. My Ankous can all shift, so the corridors haven't been used in a while, and Neti's rooms are empty. Aunt Neti, guardian of the gates of Hell, was murdered. And nothing has come to replace her. That worries me. Maybe her replacement's waiting to see how everything pans out with the Stirrer god. Or it could just think that there's no point.

When the entire population is thrown into the Underworld, and the living world itself becomes almost indistinguishable from the dead, who's going to require someone to open the gate?

It could just be that whatever will replace her doesn't like me: I wasn't Aunt Neti's biggest fan. And she certainly wasn't mine. We had our differences of opinion. Ha, she hated me!

And all because I'd performed an Orpheus Maneuver without her. I'd used the agency of Charon instead. Like a lot of things, I really hadn't known any better—and when you're in Hell you take what you can get. Not that it would have mattered, she was really angry with Mr. D and since he was no longer part of the living world she had used me as a whipping boy. After all it was the second time that he had crossed her. The first time, he'd denied Rillman his own chance at an Orpheus Maneuver, and sent Rillman's wife back to the Underworld.

Though I'd been shocked at Neti's betrayal, I probably should have seen it coming. Everyone else must have, because through that betrayal Suzanne's plans had been affected. Without it, I wouldn't be the only member of the Orcus. I wouldn't have crows bowing at me every time I go for a jog in the park.

And she really did terrify me. Her eyes (and she had dozens of them) were too hungry as they scanned my face. Her many hands too touchy-feely and pinchy, as though she were the witch in Hansel and Gretel—just waiting for me to be plump enough.

The door projects menace, and it's far too silent. Though I didn't like it at the time, I miss the occasional echoing cackle coming from Aunt Neti's rooms—as she yelled at one of her game shows. That doorway is an eye, staring blankly out.

I'm safe. I have HD. I have Mog. I am Death. But regardless of that, I'm not comfortable doing this. It's not like I've been Orcus for centuries. I haven't forgotten what it is to fear: can't even pretend that I have.

Last time I visited Neti I had my inkling, Wal, for company. But we're not talking, or I'm not ready to talk to him, so he remains a tattoo stuck silently to my arm—keeping him there is a trick I picked up from Suzanne. Sure, I could release him—his irritation alone might be enough of a distraction—but I'm a big boy, some things you have to do by yourself. It's time I engaged with that concept properly.

The door isn't locked. I open it and peer into Aunt Neti's parlor. The whole room used to smell of scones. Now it's fusty and stale, with just a hint of the charnel house behind it all

The light is off.

I reach for the switch and something runs across the back of my hand.

I pull my arm away from the wall fast enough that my elbow clips my ribs. Winded, I check my fingers. Nothing, I reach around again. There's a loud hissing. I hesitate. Did Neti have gas in here? Surely not. But I can't just hover outside the room forever, and there's no way I'm walking back into the office without finding what I need.

Either this light comes on, or I'm going to have to stumble through a dark and hissing room, feeling blindly around before me. Who knows what I'll find, or what will find me.

You'd think Death could see in the dark. Nope. Not this sort of darkness anyway. This is cave dark. A bottom of the ocean, never touched by sunlight, blacker than coal sort of dark.

I take a deep breath. *One. Two. Three.*

I reach around and flick the switch.

Right, then.

The walls and ceilings are carpeted thick with spiders.

A scurrying, writhing, hissing mass. Spiders and spiders and spiders. Could be worse, could be cockroaches. At least spiders can't fly. I step into the room, my boot crunches on the carpet. The hissing lifts a notch. I step very quickly back out the door, looking down at the floor. The carpet isn't carpeted with spiders, just their leavings. That's something at least.

Now, I'm a Brisbane boy, I've got no issue with insects. We've a hot and humid environment, and some of the shit I've seen flit and scurry through my bedroom window, well...if it doesn't bite me, I don't go crazy with my cricket bat. But spiders and cockroaches, both of them...yeah, not that fond. At least these ones aren't the palm-sized wolf spiders that like to creep about the house, or the gigantic golden-orb spiders with webs that look strong enough to catch the occasional early-morning or late-night jogger.

No. These are tiny, thumbnail-sized and dark.

As Neti's creatures, they obviously continue to bear me some ill will. Maybe I don't need to do this. But Neti's calendar is there, just a few steps away. I know it's several magnitudes of overkill, but I summon Mog (HD argues that there's nothing at all overkill about it).

"Hello. Hello."

The Knives of Negotiation interlock, and become my scythe. There's a familiar cold that runs through my fingers and into my arms.

I take a deep breath, as though I'm about to dive down and deep into something unpleasant, and walk towards the calendar. Strands of web brush my neck. Every step I take is attended to with a hiss.

"I'm not staying long," I breathe.

The calendar is only partially covered with spiders. I'm as gentle as I can be in brushing them off. It's a cute calendar: LOLcats—never really got them, can't say that they make me LOL. And this is a death-themed one—where do people find this stuff?

I flip open the calendar to May (a kitten wearing pink sunglasses curled up inside a skull) and there it is. That date again, circled, with an "M?" written beside it.

The roof is getting lower. What does Neti have going on here? Then I realize what it is. The spiders, en masse, are sliding down on strands of web.

I drop to a crouch, knees cracking, and run, as quickly as possible in that position, towards the door. The spiders hurry their descent. I can hear their spidery little limbs extruding more web. I swear their little mandibles are opening and snapping shut in unison. I'm almost there when the door closes.

7

The first of the spiders crawl in my hair and down my neck as I yank at the door handle. Nothing, its edges are bound up in web. Another hard pull, one foot up against the frame, and the door doesn't budge.

The biting begins about five seconds later.

Oh! This is enough!

I bat at dozens of the things as they scramble over me, scurrying under my shirt, and skittering down my front and back. There are so many of them that I can't tell where one begins and the others end. It's just a scrambling, furry, biting mass.

I swing my scythe about my head, the blade sings through the air. Around and around. All this seems to do is drop more spiders onto me.

The long snath of the scythe tangles in web.

I'd have been much better off with my Avian Pomps—they'd have had a feast, even if I'd have had to endure the sensation of spiders slithering down beaks and the taste of spidery guts.

The hissing intensifies. I've managed to piss off more arachnids driving them to attack. But HD is taking a great delight in all of this. The scythe describes arcs left and right. I make contact with a china vase. It explodes against the wall. Packed with spiders they drop in a black and shuddery ball at my boots. They don't stay there, but scurry up over my shoes and into my pants.

Then I remember that I don't need doors.

Dolt!

I shift into the hallway. I'm covered in web and spiders. I'm slapping at my hands and face. I roll onto my back. Spiders pop beneath me.

The biting grows even more vicious. I struggle to my feet.

Mog separates and becomes the Knives of Negotiation again. I stumble-rush down the hall. The spiders are crawling under my shirt, up and down under my pants. Boxers, why did I wear boxers? Something brushes against a testicle, that something quickly becomes many somethings. I try to shift, but this last sensation is too much: my concentration is shot.

It's quite the exit from the hallway.

I nearly knock over Lundwall, my assistant, as I race across the floor for my office. He steps back, narrowly avoiding one of my blades. He's holding a sheet of paper and flings it before him, shieldlike. The nearest blade neatly cuts it in two; wide eyes reveal themselves behind the cut.

"Mr. de Selby—"

I spin on my heel and glare at him, not that it's his fault. Lundwall quails, and I feel terrible, but I've spiders in with my privates.

"Not now. Later, but not now!" I say, and slam the door behind me.

Right.

Sure, I don't usually project much in the way of gravitas, never did, but that... that was ridiculous.

I strip in my office. If you can call the way I rip those clothes off stripping. More of a shredding really. Red welts are forming on my flesh, and the spiders haven't stopped with their biting.

I'm mostly naked, slapping and scratching spiders from my flesh (and there are always more of them, every time I think I'm done, my hands encounter another one or another dozen), when the door opens.

Lissa, back safe from PA Hospital. Thank Christ!

And half of Number Four can see me dancing with my underpants around my ankles. "Shut the door! Shut the bloody door!" I yell, yanking my boxers back up to my waist.

Lissa takes her time. If anyone has shot footage of this with their phones, and I end up seeing it on bloody YouTube... nope, no gravitas, anti-gravitas if anything.

At least I may have reduced the level of fear they feel around me now.

"Aunt Neti. Spiders," I say. "Spiders everywhere."

She's smirking as I get my boxers off again, searching furiously for any hangers-on. "You know, traditionally it's ants in the pants."

"Really, that's the best you can do?"

"I think I'm being very reserved. You're always so entertaining."

"Great, I'm glad."

One of the little fellas scurries towards her. Lissa neatly stomps her boot down. "I never liked Aunt Neti, and the stuff she put you through—all because you offended her delicate sensibilities." She stomps another couple of spiders into the carpet. "What the hell were you doing going into her rooms anyway?"

"Following a hunch," I say, double-checking around the jewels. "Don't you dare open that door."

"Never. A hunch about what?"

I'm spider-free. I think. And I pull up my pants, slip on my shirt. Lissa watching me all the while. "Had a meeting with Cerbo. And he showed me something interesting. There was a date scratched on a table in Suzanne's bedroom."

Lissa's eyes narrow. She and Suzanne had history—Suzanne once slept with her father, a brief fling that nearly ended her parents' marriage, and then, well, I'd lied to Lissa about a deal I'd made with Suzanne—it hadn't ended well.

"No, nothing untoward," I say. "Cerbo was showing me her chambers." Why does that suddenly sound like a double entendre? "Suzanne had scratched this date just before the Death Moot. Aunt Neti had had the same date marked on her calendar. Her calendar covered with spiders." I shudder.

"And what date is that?"

"May 24. It rings a bell for some reason," I say.

Lissa reacts the same way I did, though she hides it well. The twenty-fourth is so close. It's a shock. But then again, is it really? Things have been building, a gloom descending as surely as Neti's little friends.

"Hmm, the twenty-fourth, nothing, no public holidays, nothing," Lissa says. If only it was that simple, that end of the world events followed public holidays. It would certainly make scheduling in conflicts a lot easier, even if it would make it more expensive in wages—there's an up and down side to everything.

"Yeah," I murmur, "but there was more. She'd written the letter 'M' by the date."

Lissa frowns."Could be anything. Is there are a full moon that day?"

"No, I checked. It's not a full moon until the twenty-eighth." I straighten my tie. Shake out my torn jacket. Another couple of spiders tumble to the ground, emitting little pissed-off arachnid hisses. I check the lining carefully—spider free—then glance at the mirror. You'd think I was going gray, I have that much web in my hair. It takes a moment to get the stuff out with my fingers. I'm using a good gel so my hair's looking fine, you wouldn't know that I ran down a hall yowling and covered with spiders less than five minutes ago.

All that venom must be making me feel woozy. Blood rushes from my head; next thing I know Lissa's leading me to the throne.

"Take it easy," she says.

"Don't know how many times I was bitten. Normally I could handle this, I've recovered from much worse."

"These toxins aren't mortal toxins, Steve. It's all right, this'll do the trick." I drop into the throne.

At once its energy fills me, accelerates my powers. The venom boils from my flesh. Toxins steam from my shirt, staining the material.

I blink. Lissa's staring at me in wonder or dismay, I can't really tell which.

"That was new," I say. "Stab wounds, I've dealt with plenty of those, but spider bites..."

"First time for everything," Lissa says.

It's certainly not the first time that she has saved me. I want to kiss her, but she's got her serious face on. The date's picking at her thoughts as much as mine, there's something prickly and familiar about it. But it's not coming to me.

"I think you're going to have to take this to Mr. D." She looks at the black phone on my desk. It is a direct link to Mr. D. I don't want to use it.

"Yeah, I suppose." Mr. D and I have had something of a falling out. He kept too much information from me when I was trying to organize the Death Moot—not least of all was what the other RMs were planning. That I was at once bait in a complicated trap, and heir apparent. "How was your pomp?"

"Terrible, turned into a stall, Stirrer started walking down the corridor, almost made it to the lift and—don't you be changing the bloody subject. You're going to have to sort out this issue of yours with Mr. D."

I admit that our mentor-mentee relationship had been somewhat compromised, but he started it. "He nearly killed us all."

"Yeah, and he's tried to apologize several times and you keep cutting him out."

There's more to it than that. Mr. D and Wal are the only beings aware of what I did to Rillman. When I think of Mr. D my guilt is drawn in the starkest of stark relief, and it hurts.

I'm not a murderer.

Except I am. And part of me, not just the murderous HD, enjoyed it.

I'm Death but I don't want to be a monster.

After I killed Rillman, the black phone rang for three days straight. And I didn't answer it. At first I told myself that it was just because I was too busy. There was so much to sort out, Ankous to placate and new regions to discover and get a grip on. Not to mention funeral services for all the RMs who had been killed.

I was Orcus.

My responsibilities had increased twelve-fold. So, I just let it ring, no matter how uncomfortable it made everyone in the office. And you could see it, the mood shifting from muted jubilation at the destruction of Rillman's Stirrer stronghold, even at the sudden elevation of their employer (though no one, including me, was sure what that meant), to shocked efficiency (Stirrers kept on stirring, and that damn phone kept on ringing), to grim trudging on. The phone would stop, people would just about start breathing again, and then it would begin ringing once more. Mr. D's determination impressed even me.

On the second day, I'd thrown it against the wall. Didn't halt the ringing, just left a great scar in the handset. I could have answered it instead. I almost broke, but I didn't. If Mr. D could be stubborn, then so could I, damn it.

Three days of ringing. Then nothing.

I'd not bothered calling him again. I really hadn't needed to, what with the combined experience of thirteen Ankous to draw on. I'd learned more in a single conversation with any of them than in the many, convoluted attempts at teaching that Mr. D had made. But that didn't mean they had a complete understanding of what I was. Only Mr. D knew, at least in part, how it felt to be me. He'd grappled with HD, and dreamt my bloody dreams. And he'd functioned for over a century.

But I couldn't talk to him. He would look at me, and his eyes might judge or they might not, but regardless they were the eyes of someone who knew I'd killed Rillman.

He is, after all, one of my few connections with the past. All through my life he was there, a constant background figure, a little scary, yes—he was the Big Boss after all—but reliable.

Mr. D was the RM of my parents, and their parents too. They'd deferred to him. He was the ultimate source of wisdom in the company, and the Australian figurehead.

I may have found him lacking. I may have issues, built up over the systemic failure of his business, and the way he had let two Schisms occur and not told me about either of them. Mr. D was flawed. Seriously flawed, but I couldn't talk, could I. Not really.

I pick up the black handset. Silence. The scratch is rough against my palm.

Francis had struggled as I choked him.

But I hadn't let go.

There's nothing down the end of the line.

"We need to talk," I say. "Do you think we can do that?"

Not a sound. Not a breath.

I put the phone back in its cradle, Lissa looks at me curiously. "I'm going to have to visit him myself. He's not answering."

Lissa shakes her head. "You two! Make this right. Now. We need him."

I don't know about that, but part of me misses him.

"Do it," Lissa says. She kisses me hard, I'm not too enthusiastic in my response, would she kiss me so wildly if she knew what I'd done to Rillman?

Lissa pulls away with a grimace, eyes searching mine. "All right. All right," I grumble.

She grabs my hand, then inspects my shirtsleeve, unable to hide her disappointment. "Don't tell me you lost one of the cufflinks I gave you."

"I'm sorry," I say.

"Out of here. We'll talk about it later."

I kiss her once, noncommittally on the forehead, then shift to the topmost branch of the One Tree, and Mr. D.

He's not there. A cold wind's blowing in from the coast. And it's dark, darker even than Hell had appeared from my window. Something's not right. And my best shot at getting an answer is gone.

Maybe my mentor has finally succumbed to the pressure of the One Tree's call.

Maybe Mr. D has given in to death.

If that's the case it's all my fault.

8

Why is it so bloody dark here? I don't ever remember it being so dark. I shiver as I walk over to Mr. D's rocking chair, nudge it gently with a thumb and watch it rock backward and forward.

Lissa's not going to be happy.

I slump into the rocker, push myself up and down, knees almost touching my chest. My knives slide stealthily from their sheaths, and in a moment I'm gripping Mog, resting the snath across my lap.

The Underworld is the only place that I really feel comfortable holding the scythe. Here it becomes a natural extension of myself. And here I don't have Tim and Lissa looking at me, judging me. Yeah, maybe in Hell the Orcus with a scythe looks less like a poseur. I don't know.

Of course there are worse accessories than a scythe. A beret for instance. I remember the summer that Tim wore a beret. Ha! I reckon you either have to be a French poet or Sylvester Stallone to pull that look off, not a fresh-out-of-uni business graduate. I have no idea what possessed him to wear it. He looked like an even spottier Rick from *The Young Ones*. Yeah, I gave him a lot of shit for that one.

Maybe I just paid out on him the whole summer because he'd managed to finish a degree, and I hadn't. Ah, the things I put my friends through.

So where do I go now Mr. D is gone? Charon, I guess. I need to talk to him anyway. Like Neti was, he's a Recognized Entity, and I guess he'll be aware of that date. I can't tell if I'm feeling sad or relieved, I grip the scythe tightly and swing it upright.

"So you've gotten over the whole drama of being Orcus, eh?" comes a voice from behind me.

I'm on my feet and slicing the scythe in a broad circle around me without even thinking. The air crackles, a streak of light follows the movement.

Mr. D shuffles backwards, he's holding a candle in one hand. The flame flickers in sync with his steps, but it doesn't go out. Not even when the scythe blade passes right through it.

"Settle down," he says, waving a finger at me. "You could take out an eye with that thing."

"Only if I wanted to."

"Well, if that's the case, why don't you? Your silence has been almost as blinding," Mr. D mumbles, he hobbles past me, and drops heavily into his rocker.

He doesn't look all that great. Looks like he's been sleeping rough, to be honest, he doesn't smell that great either.

"As a matter of fact," he continues, "your avoidance of the Underworld has set an alarming precedent, a chain of events... you know how these things go."

"Dark here," I say.

"It's dark here precisely because you have been avoiding your duties. The sun doesn't shine out of your rear end, as much as you'd like to think it does, but it may as well. You are Death; the Underworld requires your presence. Three months of this darkness building... you wouldn't believe how hard it is to read when all you have, other than the odd candle is the illumination of the dead. I'm not saying that you have to live in the Underworld. But just a bit of time would make a lot of difference." Mr. D gestures skywards. "See, it's already starting to lighten up."

I thought it was my eyes adjusting, but he's right. It's as though someone is slowly, slowly dialling up a dimmer. The sky above us grows ruddy and luminescent.

"This is all because of me?" I ask.

"Who else? You are Death. And this is your Underworld." I walk to the edge of the branch. Down below me the city packs away the dark and reveals itself. Skyscrapers, apartment buildings, forests and suburbs stretching on to the limits of my sight. And through it all, the thick dark thread of the river. Was it really running down without me? All I thought I had to do was send souls here. Once again, it's rather more complicated than I believed.

"I thought you'd succumbed to the One Tree's call."

"Not yet, though I've had to struggle. Not easy to justify your existence when your function is denied. Steve, how did we end up like this, again?"

"You, it was..."

Mr. D is looking at me intently, calmly. Annoyingly calmly.

"What I mean..." I clear my throat, cough into my fist. "I was ashamed."

"Yes, well... I didn't provide much help. I could have been better. And, you see, Suzanne had her plan. I wanted to say something. I didn't expect it to end the way it did. What you did to Rillman—I can't condone it. But I didn't help the situation. We made you what you are, Steven. But the thing about you—and it's very much to your credit—is that you're never quite the blank canvas that people believe." Mr. D reaches out a hand. "Friends, eh?"

We shake hands, and both of us smile. And avoid looking in each other's eyes. This is about as emotional as either of us are going to get. But, it's a good moment. And you don't get too many of those.

"So... is it the end of the world yet?"

"Not yet," I say. "We need to talk."

Mr. D smiles. "Obviously." He nods at my arm. "Where's the little fella?"

"You two together, I don't know..."

"We'll be good..." He clears his throat. "And it'd be nice. You know, the old gang."

I sigh. "Very well."

I close my eyes and release Wal from my arm.

He flies around my head, looking me up and down with those unsettling Modigliani eyes of his, blank, colorless and almond shaped, yet so expressive. He glances over at Mr. D, and clenches one tiny fist. "Just mind who you're calling little fella, eh?"

Mr. D grins at him, and Wal abruptly turns his back on my old boss and regards me steadily.

"Hey," Wal says.

I nod at him. "Hey."

Both our heys say volumes. There's hurt and anger, and forgiveness there. Yeah, and a lot of "we're going to need to talk very seriously later." But I'm happy to see him, happier than I ever expected.

Mr. D claps his hands together. "Right. We can't talk here, far too dismal. And, if the world isn't over just yet how about a round of minigolf?"

What do you say to someone you haven't spoken to in months? Particularly when it ended so badly. Part of me wants to hit Mr. D for the secrets he hid from me. Part of me really can't bear to face him.

Wal flies in circles around the both of us, keeping his back to me. He hasn't spoken to me beyond that hey—which is totally killing that warm fuzzy feeling I had, and ruining my game. I haven't made par yet, not even on the easy holes. I've hit every trap, fished my ball out of every chasm, every pond of blood or fire. My armpits are stained with sweat; my shoes are slick with gore, and just a bit melty.

Mr. D is a deft hand. Making two shots, no more, on even the most difficult holes.

"I didn't know that the Underworld had minigolf."

Wal sniffs, loudly.

"It has a lot of things," Mr. D says bending over his putter on the thirteenth green—the ball's about two feet from the hole. Somehow I've ended up holding the pin, the flag blowing in a stiff hellish breeze. "The back nine on this one is particularly challenging. Now, what did you want to talk to me about?" There's a slight hurt tone to his voice. I'm doing my best to ignore it.

You'd think we'd been through enough that we could talk about our feelings. But we're men, Australian men (and an Australian cherub), of course we can't. *Cut to the bloody chase, de Selby.* I want the bad blood between us gone, but if that isn't going to happen I need to move on. Even so, Mr. D still owes me his advice.

"What does 24 May mean to you?" I ask.

Mr. D stops, mid putt. "Where did you hear that?" It's the first time that he looks at me directly. I catch a glimpse of serious in all those faces he contains. All the deaths various, each is registering confusion. HD finds the deathly mash-up amusing. Me, I like a good, solid, unchangeable face.

"The date keeps coming up. Do you know anything?"

Mr. D swings his putter, misses the hole. Nearly missed the ball. He shakes his head. "It's probably nothing."

"We both know it's not nothing. That date. It was scratched into a table in Suzanne's room. Aunt Neti had it marked on her calendar. Both had written the letter M by it."

Mr. D purses his lips. "M, eh," he says, "I don't like the sound of that. I was hoping—" He peers at me. "What were you doing in Aunt Neti's rooms?"

"Being attacked by spiders."

"Oh, they'll do that," Wal says, still without looking at me.

"Spiders can hold onto a grudge like nobody's business." Not just spiders apparently.

I ignore the snark."You said you were hoping. Hoping what?"

Mr. D waves Wal away, the little cherub's chest puffs with the indignation. "Think about that date," Mr. D says. "Think about just who is connected to it. You know them. You might be trying hard to forget, but you know him."

Him? May 24... my eyes widen. *Oh, no. That's fucking ridiculous.*

Every year, since I can remember, there were parties, great big family (when I had a great big family) gatherings. If we didn't have it at our place—he'd take us all out to dinner. I remember smoking cigars with him on the balcony at the Siana Restaurant near Eagle Pier staring at the Story Bridge out over the river. I remember when I was five and I baked him a cake. He said it was the best cake anyone had ever made him—even if I'd burnt one side of it to a crisp.

"Yes," Mr. D says, nodding.

"It's Morrigan's birthday."

"Hell of a coincidence," he says, sounding like he doesn't believe in coincidences at all. And neither do I. Morrigan is gone. Someone's trying to distract us from the truth. "And maybe it wasn't a coincidence. Maybe they were planning him a party. Maybe they all expected him to win."

That could be possible, after all I have Morrigan's birthday in my Google calendar—I'm terrible at remembering birthdays, and even worse at remembering to check my calendar.

Oddly enough, Morrigan, while stern and utilitarian about everything else, did love his birthday. Only last year we'd all gone out to Cloudland in the Valley. All of us, descending on that place, it had been a hell of a—the memory of that happier time almost knocks the wind from me.

"Morrigan's gone," I say. "He died at the Negotiation, his soul was destroyed: you told me yourself."

"Yes, no soul for him. But quite a coincidence, wouldn't you say?"

I have a terrible thought. What if Morrigan had been the one needed to defeat the Stirrer god? Surely not. The idea's ridiculous. There has to be another reason.

"If he has something to do with this…" I trail off. That's all I've got.

"Yes, he's gone. But he may have notes. May have plans somewhere. Maybe he was getting ready for the apocalypse."

"We checked his computers."

"But did you check the right ones? If he had plans he wouldn't have left them lying around. As contemptuous as he was of me, I know he wouldn't have risked discovery," Mr. D grins wickedly. "I could be quite imaginative in my punishment."

I nod my head. "I'll look again. Carefully. I thought this was all over." The idea of Morrigan holding the key to the world's salvation has a neatness to it that appeals. Finally the evil prick might actually do some good.

"It's never all over for you."

"Another distraction," I say. "Between this and my dispute with the Death of the Water…"

"Your what?!" Mr. D waves his putter in my face, I gently push it aside.

"I've pissed off the Death of the Water."

"Oh dear. You are going to have to sort that out now. Now, I mean. Right this instant."

"The Water is mad."

"The Water is Death. It could drown the earth. Do you want to lose every city on the coast? If it hasn't happened yet, then it is being incredibly restrained. Crete, they had a minor dispute with the Water once, and you know what happened to them, no more leaping bulls." Mr. D drops his putter and shakes me. "Steven, I know we've had our differences, but you should have come to me sooner."

"You lied to me." I yank myself from his grip, and Mog's back in one hand, the putter in the other. I chuck the golf club away.

Mr. D's eyes flick from the blade to my face. He raises his hands, shifts backwards a little. Even Wal is keeping his distance.

"What choice did I have?" Mr. D demands. "Suzanne's plan had merit. You were the perfect candidate. And if I had told you..."

"What? I would have been informed? I would have been able to make a decision?"

"No, she might have gone with someone else. The moment a person knows that they're being groomed for anything, their attitude changes. I like you, Steve. I didn't think you deserved to die."

"Well, I—"

"You have to speak to the Death of the Water. You can't afford to waste any more time. The Stirrer god is coming. It may even get here on 24 May. Right now its presence is building, don't tell me you can't feel it. And as it builds your own powers will be disrupted. Your ability to detect Stirrers for one, maybe even your ability to control that monster inside you. Bad things are coming, wicked things, but if you don't sort out your differences with the Death of the Water then there may not be anything left for the god to destroy."

I know all this. I take a deep breath, resist the urge to strangle Mr. D. "How do I speak to the Death of the Water? Take a bit of a dip?"

"No. No. No." Mr. D searches his pockets. "Damn, I thought I had a number. Charon should have it, they're good friends, I think. I mean it makes sense."

Totally. "Number?"

"Phone number." He gives up his hunt. "Have there been a lot of drownings lately?"

I frown. "Yes."

"I think you should check the papers. See what has been happening. If there have been more than usual it will be apparent."

I know exactly how many there have been, and I know how many are left—just one. But I don't dare tell Mr. D this.

"You have to keep up-to-date with what your other half is doing. Get the figures right so you know just what he has been taking. He will come in all aggrieved. The Death of the Water always feels unappreciated."

"So I've pissed off something that already has a chip on its shoulder?"

"Not a chip, more like a slab. Oh, and don't make any stupid deals. Certainly none you're not prepared to go through with."

"I've no intention of doing anything stupid at all."

Mr. D smiles grimly, his face shifting faster and faster. All manner of deaths passing over it. "Doesn't matter what your intentions are. You've pissed off a Death. Not a co-worker, or an underling—that's a whole other empire out there, a bigger one than yours, and it's angry."

9

Mr D has a point, and it's really only backing up what Tim said the other day. If I don't sort out my issues with Water, I'm never going to be able to deal with the god that's coming. I'm only just realizing what that's going to cost me. And if it's really going to manifest on the twenty-fourth, I better be ready and all allied up. I don't know what it is about me that finds putting things off so attractive, but it keeps leading me deeper and deeper into trouble. And it's not as if I can put off the end of the world. That's coming regardless.

Yet here I am, a man who has made enemies with his only ally, and not done anything to see a cessation of the argument. On top of which I then chose to hide from my mentor, whose advice will be pivotal in the upcoming conflict. And I've yet to ask Lissa to marry me. What the hell kind of man am I?

I close my eyes, focus on Charon, and shift. I end up in a small ferry terminal jutting into the Styx. I look out across still, dark water. It's quiet, no lapping of waves against the shore. I squint into the murk. There's no ferry and there's no Charon.

The river is silent. Motionless. It alarms me, that quiet. There's too much of the End of Days in it. *End of Days. End of Days. Everything's the End of Days!* I whistle a couple of bars of Hank Williams's "Ramblin' Man" into the dark, and the sound is swallowed up. But at least I'm grinning now.

I crouch down and stare at the river, and discover why it's so silent. The water's frozen. The ice cracks and groans in time with the One Tree.

Where the hell is Charon? All I can do is follow the memory of his presence like a scent. And in doing so I realize he permeates the Underworld almost as completely as I do. Here he has sat at a riverside cafe, or stood on the walkway of the Go Between Bridge, at the top of the gentle arch admiring the river, with which he shares such an intimate relationship, below. Everywhere there is a hint of him: a memory that strikes me. I can almost hear the flap of his rubber thongs and taste the choking smoke of his cigarettes.

I shift, and Wal with me, through the Underworld, from one ferry stop to the next, watching as the lights go on, the traffic starts its moving, the Tree creaks even louder, and the dead do the things that dead people do—shadow stuff, reflections of all the living things and their movement in the living world.

The river quickens. Liquefies. Cracks snake across the frozen face of the water. As I watch, lumps of dark ice start moving, rushing with the river out to the sea of Hell.

I'm responsible for all of this.

Little old me. Maybe the sun does shine out of my arse after all.

I pause for a while to watch my Underworld flower. The sky continues to brighten. The river flows. Somewhere, nearby, birds sing the melancholy tunes of the land of the dead.

"Impressive isn't it?" Wal says, dipping chubby fingers into the water. "I'd have never believed it if I hadn't seen it with my own eyes."

"You better get used to it. With great power comes—"

"Yeah, I know. I've grown up since you last saw me."

"Really? You could have fooled me. No offense intended, of course."

Charon's in none of his usual haunts. The docks are empty. The river is busy with baroque CityCats—the catamarans running up and down it, filled to capacity. There's never a shortage of the dead. Where is he?

Somewhere water's crashing, somewhere bleak creatures howl and whales are singing. Somewhere saws are sawing. There's the biting smell of wood being shaped and worked. And the even stronger scent of tar bubbling. I make my way around Mount Coot-tha. Shifting then walking, clambering over the humps of great root buttresses.

I find him in front of a . . . to be honest, I'm not sure what it is, but it's big.

"Mr. de Selby," he rasps. "It's a pleasure as always."

"What the hell is that?"

"It's an Ark of course."

Of course it is.

"What the hell do you want an Ark for?" I ask above the sound of hammering and sawing, the random outbursts of swearing.

Tar bubbles in two steel pots the size of buses nearby. The heat they're producing is rather pleasant, Charon almost has a rosy hue, the smell not so much.

"Just a second." Charon bends down. The fellow's tall, easily a foot or so taller than me, and skeletally thin, he picks at the tight pale skin beneath his left rubber thong, just behind his big toe. "There you are, you bastard. Always something getting stuck in there, maybe I should reconsider the old rubber pluggers, eh?" he says, tapping his thongs. He squints down at his foot and yanks hard, I can't help gagging a little at the sound of flesh tearing. There's a shriek and a tiny black bug writhes between his thumb and forefinger.

Charon rises, bones clicking all along his spine, and shows me the writhing thing. "Wood mite," he crows. "Bloody thing's been bothering me for days."

Thumb and forefinger close, pincer-like, and the little mite screams again. Far too loud and human a sound for such a tiny creature. It pops. Wal winces, and darts around behind me. I can't judge at all, I was mashing up spiders not that long ago. Yeah, and I strangled a man with my own two hands. Mite popping is a mere trifle.

Charon wipes the bloody mess all over his jeans—there's rather a lot of it—then licks his fingers clean.

"Now, oh the Ark. I'm the boatman. I'm responsible. After all, what's an Ark but a bloody big ferry? And when the going gets biblical, you know..."

"Responsible for what?"

"If the world goes to shit and I need to get everyone to the other side." He smiles up at the brightening sky. "Thanks for the light. I've never liked working in the dark, brings back memories of the old days. There was a time when everything was dark, everything. All manner of nasties could sneak up on you, including me, often enough."

I consider the Ark. It's resting on the side of the mountain, the bulky boat obscuring most of the nearest stony face, shackled in scaffolding, and lodged between two massive root buttresses. Charon's boatmen scurry like hyperactive ants all over the structure.

I'm shocked at Charon's lack of faith in me. So shocked that I'm actually shocked at how shocked I am. "I know, it's big and all," I say, "but that's not going to be able to carry every soul, surely."

"You'd be surprised how compact souls are, mate. I'm not saying that it isn't going to be a bit squashy, but..."

He's got a point.

"You close to finishing it?"

Charon winces. "You're asking about the twenty-fourth, eh? It's going to be close. I won't lie to you. And I may yet fail, but that's in the offing for everything that finds itself with enough ambition to make plans."

"You knew about the twenty-fourth?"

"You didn't?" Charon whistles. "You didn't, did you? All that maneuvering and they neglect to tell you that."

No one told me anything. But I'm not about to admit that to him. I shrug.

"It's been nice to have a distraction," Charon says. "Was a time when all I did was wait for people to give me coin at the riverbank. Tedious, tedious business."

"Good to have a hobby." Mine's stalling Stirrers, I guess.

"Mr. de Selby, this hobby may well be humanity's last hope. But surely you didn't seek me out merely to gawp at my construction, what do you want?"

"I need you to talk to the Death of the Water for me."

"Death of the Water, eh. Why would you..." Charon's eyes narrow, he breathes out as though he is bearing the weight of the world on his shoulders, and he shakes his head. "Right, it's the whole boat thing. I fiddle around with boats, and suddenly I'm best of pals with the bloody Death of the Water."

"Well, Mr. D said...I mean, it makes sense doesn't it?"

"Makes sense? Makes sense?! Not one little bit! I cross rivers. I don't do oceans. I don't even like salt water all that much, and part of that is because of him. Give me a nice broad river like the Styx, where you can see the shore on the other side—it might be shrouded in mist, it might be obscured by the whole life-death interface, but you know it's there. But oceans, that's long-haul merchant marine kind of bollocks. Do I look like a merchant marine to you?" I open my mouth to speak, but he doesn't let me answer. "No. If you have a problem with the Death of the Water, then you're going to have to sort that out yourself."

"What about that?" I say jabbing a thumb at the Ark.

"That, my dear Orcus, that is different. That's a *last* resort. And do please note the stress on the word last."

"But—"

"I can't be seen taking sides, for one—though I can see it has a point, you did take away its souls. And I'm busy. I've a bloody Ark to build."

"So you think it's hopeless?"

Charon sighs. "Just being a realist. You can't blame a bloke for that." He coughs, fumbles in his jeans for a packet of cigarettes, plucks one out with the same efficiency he'd used on the bug, then jiggles the packet under my nose.

I wave them away. "No, I guess you can't."

"Steven, you're going to have to start sorting out your own problems. You're the top of the rung. You're the one with the view. You know things that the rest of us can't, not even beings like me."

"I s'pose," I say.

"Time you act like you do, eh." His face softens then, and he reaches into one of the pockets of his voluminous jeans, pulls out a tiny notepad and pen, one of those you'd expect to buy at a slightly twee stationery shop. Actually, is that Hello Kitty?

He scribbles something on the notepad, rips out the page and pushes it into my hand. "That's the Death of the Water's number."

"I still can't believe the Death of the Water has a phone."

"Well you do, don't you, Orcus?"

Fair enough.

"Call that number when you're ready to talk. It'll be waiting. Water's always waiting for something, bitter monstrous thing." For a moment, Charon rests a bony hand on my arm. "You know, the Death of the Water could have stopped you at the outset, I think. But he didn't. He let you take those souls from him, so you would owe him. He's a devious watery prick. You be careful."

"I will."

Charon doesn't look convinced. "Now, if that's all, please leave, I've got a boat to build."

I have to ask, before I go. "So what do you think happens on the twenty-fourth?"

"I'll have my Ark finished so that it doesn't matter."

10

Despite Mr. D's advice, I decide not to call the Death of the Water straight away. I'm tired, suddenly it feels like too much, I need some time with Lissa. I need to talk to her before I set up anything else, just in case it all goes horribly wrong, as things in my life have a tendency to do.

Restless, and impatient, I wait for Lissa to come home. I walk through our rooms, which are empty in the most part, characterless but for some clutter, because we haven't had time to fill them with ourselves yet. It's hardly a soothing environment.

Lissa had chosen the new apartment. Twenty stories up and a few streets down from Number Four. Convenient and far harder to infiltrate than a Queenslander—although pretty much anything else is, no matter what you do you can never really secure a house designed to be open to the air. The door to the apartment has been replaced with one that is more reinforced than most tanks. It once opened onto a broom cupboard that was used to imprison both Mr. D and later me, so, yes, I know it works. Though it's been modified so I can shift in its presence. The unit's walls, floors and ceilings are marked with enough brace symbols to make even the toughest Stirrer quail.

It's an easy stroll to work from here. I might be able to shift, but I enjoy the walk, and the connection it offers with my city. It would be too easy to shift from the unit to Number Four, never seeing the light, and lose contact with everything that I'm fighting for in the process. Death is meaningless without life.

I like our new home, really I do. The first couple of months of our relationship had been spent at my parents' house in the burbs. But that had proven to be less than ideal. My place before that was crammed full of stuff: CDs, DVDs, but Morrigan blew all of that up and I haven't bothered collecting them again, beyond a few obvious classics. Once you've lost everything the appeal of accumulating stuff fades. Maybe Suzanne and I aren't all that different after all.

Last year I would have never understood Suzanne's single room, now I can see myself having something similar in some distant future, if I'm allowed that—too many things become memories and too many memories grow barbs.

When we'd sold Mum and Dad's house I'd sold the furniture as well. The sight of it was too painful. Here we have a bed, a few chairs around a dining table. All basic stuff, because we were too tired and busy to do anything else.

It doesn't mean you can't have a little art around you though. I've a Decemberists poster in the living room, keep meaning to frame it, currently it's in a state of gradual fall, held up with not nearly enough Blu-Tac. But even though we don't have a lot of stuff we've not avoided mess. Lissa's managed to scatter most of her clothes throughout the flat. I resist the urge to pick them up. I guess she's more comfortable here, that it's a *good* sign.

I admire our view and watch the bats trade places with the birds, feel the weariness of crows and sparrows seeking shelter. Some of them grumble, but they're obedient to my will. I need every eye open. An avian catches sight of something peculiar, and I can be there in a moment.

The river winds away below me. From this vantage point the two major bridges are visible, the iron post-industrial bulk of the Story

Bridge to my left, and a hint of the white concrete of the Captain Cook Bridge to the right. These two bridges span the brown water of the Brisbane River and feed the traffic of the southern suburbs, and beyond, into the city. Seeing them both makes me ache a little. They've led me in and out of trouble all my life, they've promised the excitement of the inner city, and the boredom of the outer suburbs. From here, it's obvious that Brisbane is a city of hills, of bends and suburbs that curl into each other like shells. It should be messy, but it isn't. And I love it.

There's been a constant pressure on me to move Mortmax's global headquarters to some more central location, or, at the very least, Sydney. But I can no more do that than tear out my heart. Brisbane has settled in me as deeply as old HD ever can.

This is my city. And it will always be my city.

I look from the lights, down to the shimmering river, this brown coil of water runs into the not-too-distant sea and the first problem that needs untangling.

I hear Lissa's beating heart before she opens the door to the unit. It's no effort to pick it from the multitude of heartbeats, just as I'd always recognize her face.

She's holding a bag of Chinese takeaway in one hand. My stomach rumbles.

"I can hear that from here," she says.

"And how was your day?"

"Besides saving my boyfriend from assassination, and stalling Stirrers." She counts them out on her free hand, "Let's see, there was one at PA, another at the Wesley, and two down in Logan. Oh and I saw you dancing around in the nude. I'd say it was pretty normal, and you?"

"We need to talk."

Lissa puts the bag down on the table, her brow furrowed. "Sounds serious."

"Well, it is." Doesn't help that my stomach chooses that moment to rumble again.

"All right. Do I need to sit down?"

"Maybe."

She doesn't, just walks towards me. And I have to reach out and touch her hand, fingers slowly stroking her knuckles. I know how sore her palms must be.

"I've done bad things that I need to set right. Tomorrow I'm going to talk to the Death of the Water, and I'm not sure that I'm going to make it back."

"Death of the Water?"

"Yes, I may have pissed him off when I pomped those souls in the plane crash."

"So that's the bad thing? Saving those souls?"

"It was impolitic. And I said bad things, not thing."

Lissa's eyes narrow. "I got the plural, Steven. You can't call that a bad thing. Do you know what the Death of the Water does with its souls?"

"I know it's not good. But I didn't think it through. It was power as much as guilt that drove me to it. Those souls were my responsibility, and I sent them there, however inadvertently, but I think I really snatched them away because I could."

"So now you need to make peace?"

"Yeah. If I don't do this... well, we need it. We need an ally."

"I understand. I'm not happy, but I understand. Oh, the enemies you make—they're of the highest caliber."

"Yeah, people keep telling me that. There's something else," I say, I clear my throat. My eyes sting, I know I'm barely holding back tears. "Rillman, I killed him."

Lissa doesn't look surprised at all. "I know."

"But—"

"It's obvious. What were you going to do? Life isn't a Batman comic, there's no Arkham Asylum in our world—though that place was hardly very effective anyway, all they ever did was escape. You didn't have any choice. Rillman was insane. He'd have kept coming after you until you were dead, probably killing Tim and me in the process."

"I strangled the bastard. I crushed his life out with my hands, and I enjoyed it."

"You enjoyed it, or was it HD doing the enjoying?"

"Both, I guess."

"Hmm, you enjoyed killing the man who had tortured you, had threatened to repeat everything that Morrigan had done to you over again. Steven, you are a monster."

"But I am a—"

"Bullshit. Have you killed anyone else lately? Are you sneaking out and slicing off heads with that scythe of yours?"

"No." Even if sometimes—more often than sometimes, if I'm honest—I feel it, roiling away inside me, desperate for blood, death, destruction. "No."

"And you never will. Steven, you contain the Hungry Death inside you. And I won't lie to you, there are moments that I can see the homicidal prick staring out, but it's never there for long, and it's never alone. I know that you're always standing behind it, or driving it back. You're stronger than it is. You've proven yourself stronger than it. Don't you see that? If after everything that had happened you had lost control, gone on a killing rampage, wiped out a continent or two, yes, then I would have a little trouble forgiving you—but you didn't. You stopped at Rillman." She touches my face. "You were given this thing, without wanting it at all. But I'm proud how you have stepped up. And keep stepping up."

"Thank you. But it still hurts. It still shocks me that I could do it. Mr. D's disappointment..."

"Mr. D was the one who hurled Rillman's wife back to Hell, and remember he once pulled off a successful Schism himself. He started all of this. He's hardly in a position of moral superiority. You did what you had to do, and you always will."

She pecks me on the cheek and walks back to the food. I follow her to get out the plates. How wonderful is my girl? So forgiving, so wise, and with an appreciation of classic comics. I know how lucky I am. Maybe it's time. I clear my throat, hands shaking as I put down the plates.

"Killed Rillman," she says with a wry chuckle, eyes burning into my soul. "Phew, for a minute there I thought you were going to ask me to marry you."

We eat dinner, barely, before Lissa drags me to the bedroom, and proves she doesn't find me monstrous—twice.

Afterward she lies on my chest. I can still taste her. The room smells of us. The warmth of her and her presence is so reassuring and so vital. Right now, with her holding me, I can almost imagine that I'm alive. Even HD is merely a shadow, ill-defined at the back of my cells.

"What do you think the end of the world will be like?" Lissa asks.

"I don't know, something between radio static and Cormac McCarthy's *The Road*?"

Lissa sighs. "But that wasn't really the end of the world though was it, just the road toward it, the road we're all on. It's so like you to imagine noise."

"What do you think it will be like?" I can feel HD uncoiling, interest growing. It's an odd tingling sensation, not that far from arousal.

"Beautiful and terrible at once. Nothing we can ever see, except maybe you. And it will be silent, so silent, not a breath of wind, nothing stirring, nothing moving, and nothing growing: silence given form forever."

"Sounds kind of nice," I say.

"You wouldn't like it," Lissa says.

"But you would?" She's right. I do like my noise. I think of the frozen Styx and how its silence had discomforted me.

She doesn't answer me. And soon she's asleep.

I listen to her breathing, that's a sound I adore, her heartbeat slowing with it, but remaining indisputedly hers. Sleep really isn't for me anymore, but sometimes, when I let them and the stars or the moon or whatever are in alignment those twin sounds can guide me there.

Slowly and steadily I follow her breath and her beating heart.

I dream.

Blood, a whole sea of it, a wave crashing down on me and mine. Lissa's motionless beside me. Her wrists are open. Her face is the blue of the dead, the recently bled. There's no life to give her any other color. I can't hear her heart beating. I can't hear anyone's. Even the waves are silent.

Then soundlessly and slowly bicycles fall. The first one smashes down beside me, sinks into the sanguine sea. The second knocks Lissa from my hands, and I'm scrambling through blood to find her. I catch a glimpse of her face. Reach out, but she is gone.

I wake with a jolt. Lissa wakes with me, her heartbeat thudding in my skull.

Thank Christ.

"It's all right," I say, quietly. "Go back to sleep."

"Another dream?"

"Yeah, another one." The clock by her bed, a ruby luminescence—5:30. The sky is lightening outside, though dawn's at least an hour away. I kiss her gently on the forehead. "I have to go," I say.

Lissa grabs my hand. "What you told me," Lissa says, not sounding nearly as sleepy as I would expect, "is that your last secret?"

"Yeah, it's my last."

Lissa grins. "Haven't had time to find some new ones yet? Steve, we're all secrets and lies and truth and love. And I know that you love me, that much isn't a lie."

"And what about you?"

"What do you think?"

I kiss her one last time. Lissa doesn't tell me to be careful. We both know where I'm going and there's nothing careful about that.

11

Five forty-five a.m. and I'm standing on top of the Story Bridge, sipping Bundy Rum out of a flask, looking down at the sporadic early-morning traffic and the river beneath.

To the left of me is Kangaroo Point, to the right Fortitude Valley—too many drunk nights spent in the pubs and clubs of the latter. Here, I am above it all, at the point where North and South Brisbane meet. There's power here, all of it balanced on this steel bridge. And here, as night begins its transition to day, it expresses itself as an ache in my bones. HD thrashes back and forth inside me like a great white shark trapped in a goldfish bowl.

The bridge thrums, the steel shifts, almost imperceptibly as the day begins to warm. The sun is a while off, but the bridge is getting ready for it.

I picked the bridge because it gives me height and sight, and it's water-bound and water-crossing without being of the sea. Seems like a neutral enough sort of location for a one-on-one with the Death of the Water.

A wind blows down the river, somehow sharpened by the skyline behind me. The chill slices through my suit. A couple more mouthfuls of my rum and it's not such a problem. Maybe I shouldn't be drinking before setting up this meeting, but I can't remember a meeting that I've attended in the last five months where I haven't had at least a little to drink.

It's not like I don't have it under control or anything.

The wind drives the early morning mist before it in billowing ripples of gray. It'll be another hour or two until the sun burns it all away. Buildings jut out of the gray like the apocalypse has already happened. Lights wink. Above me planes circle, waiting out the mist, or being redirected to the Gold Coast.

More rum, and I unlock my phone, clear my throat, and tap in the number. It doesn't ring, there's nothing but the sound of the wind blowing through my mouthpiece. Wouldn't it be nice, for once, to get a warm greeting on a phone call with a supernatural entity? I'm the one that's supposed to be grim.

"Right then," I say. "I'm ready to talk. Here, or somewhere neutral, a place of your choosing."

I hang up, and I know that it's heard me at once. There's noise before sight, the whole bridge thrums in time with it. A dim hissing that grows with each beat of the World Pulse.

Right. This is enough.

How dare the Death of the Water think it can waltz (well, twist) in here and start doing things like this? The sea, the ocean, that is its territory. This thread of river is mine, no matter how it feeds into the sea. It's mine, and my opposite should know better.

Yeah, like I should have known better when I snatched those 150 souls from the sea.

As much as Tim would like to think not, I am aware of the statistics. There have been 149 deaths by drowning around the coast in the last few months. None of them were meant to happen—all of them were unscheduled.

This has to stop. If I can save just one soul from going to the Death of the Water, I will. I'm stubborn, yes, but de Selbys always are.

I quickly text Lissa, tell her I'll be back as soon as I can. Then jump to the top of the handrail and watch the waterspout draw near. The traffic beneath me is at a standstill. The waterspout sways. It dances.

"So you want to chat here?" I say.

The waterspout is silent. It sways cobralike a few meters before the bridge, an angry storm narrowed to one slender point. A cold spray of water drenches me.

"What the hell is this passive aggressive shit anyway? We're both adults here. Surely we can . . . Ah, fuck it!" I don't know I'm going to do it, until I do.

I leap off the bridge and into the swirling water, turning my head at the last moment to catch a glimpse of my city. The buildings shine in the early-morning light, and I can't shake the feeling that I'm saying goodbye for the last time.

There's a flash, a sensation of burning and stretching similar to a shift, but I'm not doing it. Then I am somewhere else. Water, colder, deeper. I know it towers above me, that it stretches away from me, from shore to shore. A weight that would crush the life from anything of the earth. But I am not alive. Not really, I am the opposite of that. Doesn't stop the pressure. I creak in ways alarming.

My hands are wrenched back, hard enough that my arms are nearly pulled from their sockets. A hood slides over my head and what feel like plastic ties are tightened around my wrists. Hands grip my biceps firmly and easily.

My lungs are painfully, but uselessly, full, and, for a moment, I panic. Then I give in to it. Stop fighting, and, while I don't exactly breathe, something's going on within me with enough vitality that I don't black out. HD swells to replace my air. He's keeping me alive, pushing against the pressure of the sea. Sometimes the homicidal bastard comes in handy

Water all around me. Somewhere nearby whales are singing. Songs of predation, love, lust and war. In the water, at these depths, I can't see, but I can feel vast presences slide past me. Shifts in pressure, moments of deeper cold. The small hairs rise along the back of my neck, and I remember how insignificant I am.

I'm glad I sent Lissa a text. There's no way this is going to go well.

I blink sightlessly into the dark. I can't speak. I can't breathe, but my feet are touching the bottom of the ocean. Something nudges my back. I stumble forward.

"Walk or stay here forever," a voice whispers in my ear.

Handcuffed and hooded at the bottom of the sea isn't good. But this voice, that's a whole new level of not-goodness.

There's more pushing, jabbing really, rough and cruel.

I walk, lungs, nose, lips filled with the briny muck of the sea. The ground sucks at my boots, sometimes I sink so deep that I have to be pulled out. Things brush against me, and I stumble frequently, but I keep walking.

I've a meeting with the Death of the Water.

In that deep and heavy cold I move. Every step is a slow one. The water pushes down with a steely pressure, though sometimes I can feel a wind brushing against my face, a sense of strolling through open airless spaces.

I don't know how long we travel. But there are interludes, brief moments where the hood is snatched away and I'm led to examine machines the size of mountains that throb with energies that I recognize, but can't even begin to understand.

Figures move over these terrible engines, glowing softly blue, working ceaselessly upon them. And I feel like I'm in some sort of poem by William Blake mashed up with the *Matrix* and, God help me, *Sea Quest*. I may be Orcus, but I am a child of television.

I try and shift, but can't, the water itself is holding me here, resisting my will with an implacable strength. HD rumbles inside me. Mumbling. I feel it strain with the pressures of keeping me whole. I creak, my teeth ache and my feet rot. I trudge, sometimes knee-deep, through the silt and seepage. I've visions too, of blood, of ships sliding and sinking into the depths. Of boulders as big as cities, trailing forests of kelp fronds that extend for hundreds of meters, circling each other like the mechanism of some monstrous organic engine.

And souls, so many souls, shackled to these great machines, keeping them moving, working with and against the currents. Stone and fire. There's a beat to them much like the creaking of the One Tree, and now I recognize it, it's hard to miss.

Mr. D said to sort this out. But I thought it would be in a much different fashion, over a table, maybe with some lawyers or their paranormal equivalent (almost indistinguishable from the real thing). When I pulled those souls from the water. I really pissed it off. I get that now in a way that no waterspouts or threats could ever really convey.

We walk and we wade, we walk and we trudge. An endless slog. I hear whale songs again. I feel the curious nips and prods of fish. I do not come to harm, just an endless trudging. We do not halt.

When I need to, I piss into the sea, but I do not need to often—more's the pity. I've dried out on the inside, becoming something sere and empty, only capable of movement, and then only in the direction that I am pushed.

I'm not sure how much later it is, but I almost don't realize that my legs have stopped moving, until I do. And then I have no idea how long I've been standing still.

The hood is snatched off, whatever does the snatching is gone by the time my eyes adjust. I'm alone and chained to a wall.

I turn my head. I can't see or hear anything different. My ears pop.

I can't feel water anymore, I'm surrounded by air.

For a moment, I wonder if I am going to explode. All that pressure is gone. But I do not, HD works again at keeping me whole. Maybe because it cares, or because it so hates the Death of the Water? I don't know.

The air is loud with my breathing and stinks of brine and my sweat. I drop to the ground. It is hard and stony. It digs into my flesh. But it doesn't cut. I can be as unyielding as it, things weigh down my wrists, enclose me in cold.

My shoes are gone, and one of my socks. I peel the other one off, and a good bit of my skin comes with it. I throw it as far away from me as possible, which isn't very far in my present condition. I imagine Tim mocking me for such a girly throw. I imagine Lissa, picking the thing up in disgust, and showing me how it's done.

I realize that I am thirsty. Water, water everywhere and not a drop to drink. I can't help but smile at that, of course smiling cracks my lips, and it's only once the blood starts flowing that my body thinks to heal itself.

I'm alone.

In a space, dark, but for a soft luminosity so slight I can barely see my hands. It's more murk than a darkness. My clothes are wet and tight around me, the sleeves of my jacket have shrunk, half the buttons have come off my shirt. My wrists are bound in cold iron. Beneath me I can feel a tangle of chain, leading back into the wall. The smell of salt, and rot grows heavier in the air. At least there is air, I suppose. And water, fresh water, I can sense it nearby.

The smell of it, or the pulse of it.

All I want to do is drink. I've a thirst that could tear my throat out.

I scramble across the rocks, and, at the limits of my chains, I find the pool—if it can even be called that. It's more a damp space in the stone from which I can work handfuls of that glorious water into my mouth. It's salty, or maybe my lips, my flesh, are so permeated by the sea I can't help but taste salt in everything.

Regardless, the water is the sweetest thing I have ever tasted.

Until my stomach rebels, and tries to push the water back out. I pull my knees in close, and rock backward and forward. It seems to help. If I was anyone but me, I'd be throwing up right now. HD takes over. I feel it persuade my guts to function, to draw this water inside me—not a pleasant sensation.

Time passes. Or maybe it doesn't. I can't tell anymore.

I try and shift, again. And fail. Again. I didn't expect it to work. Sometimes this mode of transportation is even more piss-poor in its reliability than a cut-price airline. I'd be better off with a bloody *go* card. One of the things that neither Suzanne nor Mr. D had taught me was that shifting is so fragile, so easily disrupted. I'd learned that the hard way.

I beat my fists against the stone. Frustration a painful knot in my belly that even the torn knuckles can't release.

I sense a shift in the World Pulse, a subtle change in its rhythm. Something has happened above, and I can't tell what is.

My tears, when they come, are soft and silent, the most gentle of fluid, but I'm too dry to produce much.

Fuck it! Fuck it! Fuck it!

I whisper the lyrics to Queen's "We are the Champions." Feeling in the mood for some irony. And, you know, it helps. I'm about halfway through, my voice rising from a cracked frailty to something almost defiant, when the earth shudders.

And I stop. My singing's not that bad surely.

"To be Death, and to be brought so low. How must that feel?" A voice whispers from the water, the voice of the water itself.

"Not too bad really," I say, as my teeth start chattering. I wipe at my eyes. "I've been treated worse—believe me. I've enemies, real enemies on the surface. Oh, and I did some time in retail you know, and the customers—"

"Shut up."

"Just answering your question." I gesture, chains rattling, at the cave walls. "This is not how I usually organize a meeting. Generally you work through my assistant Lundwall... well, at least the first time. There is much chagrin, a few embarrassed phone calls, until... but not this. Not the chains not the, well, coercive nature of it all."

"You would not have come."

"Believe me. You were next on my list. And, hey, I called you, remember."

"You would not have come here of your own free will. You would not have seen."

"Yeah, well, I would have preferred this nice café in Toowong. Anywhere but here, really. But you were...it's not too late. Just check my diary—the app's on my phone."

"You earthly things, so complicated, and so ridiculous." A figure slips from the water. It is dark and shimmering at once. Opaque and translucent. And, even here, even in the depths of a sea so harsh in its hatred of me, I can't help but notice that it's slightly balding: in fact, it's got something of a comb-over going on.

HD responds to the Death of Water with a snarl, and it's all I can do to stop it wrenching at the chains.

My balding erstwhile ally sighs. "I am Water. I am the grasping of the wet. The pulling down. The deathly draw, and the gyring storm. You called me, and when you call me, it will always end up here."

"Enough of the teen poetry. Let's just get to it."

Water flashes me an angry grin. "Those souls were mine," it says. "And you owe me one more."

"I know I did wrong, but I had a sense of obligation. Those people died because of me. Haven't you taken enough?"

"There is a purpose to what I do. Your walk should have shown you that."

"The machines?"

"Yes, the machines. They are my weapons against the Stirrer god. They're the engines that my dead stoke. To steal from me is to steal from this world's defense."

"I don't doubt it, but those souls were mine. They should have never died."

"*Should* is the only way of it. All things *should* die." It looms over me. "You cannot tell me that you do not understand that."

"But it wasn't their time."

"Time has no relevance. What is a year, a decade, a century? These things are meaningless to the Deepest Depths out of which we're all sprung, and of which these depths are mere mimicry, and into which we will return. What agency we have is in the service of that journey."

"Well, it's a bit grim though isn't it?"

"Your accoutrement would agree with that assessment."

"My accoutra-what?"

Water crouches beside me. "The scythe, it's not a happy smiley puppet is it?"

I have to grin at that, and Water grins back.

"The work is cold work, dark work, but necessary for all that. I lost my souls, a price must be paid."

"And I will pay it. You have my word."

Water's smile grows wide. "You will pay it."

"Not now. Not now with the Stirrer god so close. But I will pay it."

Water frowns. "Yes, that is a priority. But you do not understand."

"What?"

"That this is not the first time. Nor will it be the last that such things threaten the earth. I will always demand my toll. When this god is defeated there will come another, and more engines will need to be built. It never stops until it does, and when that day comes you and I may be the only ones to see it."

"And how many have you defeated. How many gods?"

"One. There is only one, and its manifestation."

"Manifestation?"

"The god will walk among you all, as one of you. The god will light the sky. It always lights the sky as prelude to its shrouding of it."

"So there will be two battles?"

"Yes."

"Lucky there are two of us then," I say. "So how the hell do we deal with this?"

"We make plans. Curious and cruel, and we save this world, and when it's done–"

"I will fulfil my promise," I say, feeling the chill of it. The reckless horror. Don't make a stupid deal with Death, but sometimes you have to.

I reach out a hand. We shake. Then we talk saving the world. Here, beneath the sea, with the two of us, I can almost believe that it's possible. The one thing I don't let myself consider for long, can't let myself consider, even though I already know the answer, is how I am going to fulfil my end of the bargain.

What human soul could I ever knowingly send down here?

The Death of the Water turns its head, as though someone has banged on a door behind him. I hear it too: a swift knocking.

No, not a knocking, a pulse. The frantic beating of a heart. And, for all its pace, I recognize it.

No. What is she doing?

"Lissa." The word comes from me, almost an involuntary response.

Water dips its head, cups a hand around its right ear.

"Yes, I have kept you too long. Yes, she is right to do this." What the hell is it talking about? "You may go now. You may answer that call."

"I can't, you've shackled me."

Water raises its hand absently. The iron drops from my wrists. I rub at the red marks there. "Thank you." It's hard to muster any enthusiasm, but I can't risk offending it again. I need to get out of here, and fast. Before...

"You will not be thanking me for long."

There's a pressure in my skull. A distant rumbling. Something tugs at my flesh—countless somethings. It's like shifting only more intimate, there are all sorts of sharp to it. The skin across my chest burns.

I look down. Blood stains my shirt.

Water turns its head behind me. Squints, as though the beating is coming from there now. I can't tell. It seems to be all around me, a halo of noise.

Water's eyes widen. "You do have friends. Such remarkable friends."

My body shudders. Folds into itself, utterly ignoring anything that my muscles tell it to do. I try and straighten. But I can't.

What the fuck is happening?

"This is not over," Water says. "You have given your word."

Her heartbeat builds to a tectonic sort of rumbling. It rushes around me like a murder of crows, sound given form slaps and scratches at my face. Lissa's heart pounds; beats so fast that surely it will be the death of it.

Why? What is happening on the surface? What is the cause of her terror and pain?

Then I understand.

Summoning.

Lissa has performed a summoning.

I try and shift, but it's too late, she's already begun.

"Don't fight it, or you will kill her," Water says.

I can taste her blood, feel it jetting from her veins.

I know how that feels. I've done this before. I cut my arteries, and bled myself dry to draw Mr. D to me. I never realized that it was agony for both parties. I would take all this pain from her. Free her of suffering, but I can't.

I give myself up to it. Water's right, I can't fight this. And even if I don't struggle, there's still a chance Lissa might die.

I let Lissa summon me.

12

I'm crouched over and dropping to my knees in a point between Hell and earth. A nexus, not quite either.

I blink back tears and get to my feet. Where is she? Lissa summoned me, but now I'm here, and I can't find her. I know where I am. The old lighthouselike gas-stripping tower that exists in both versions of Brisbane is a familiar presence beside me. A comfort, if I wasn't so desperate to find Lissa. I run around it.

There's no doorway. She's inside and I'm out here.

To open the door into the tower you need to touch its metal surface, and drive a knife through your hand. Maybe she's inside, maybe she can't get out.

I've got the two sharpest knives in the world sheathed beneath my jacket. I yank one free. Slap my palm against the tower. Then stop. The tower's vibrating. The knife mumbles out its disappointment. I take a step back.

A line of light runs up the side of the tower, not far from where my hand rests. There's a click and a segment of the wall bangs back against itself.

Lissa walks through the opening, she's holding a towel in her hands.

"What the fuck are you doing?" I can't help the cracked roar that comes from my mouth, anger and relief vying for dominance.

Lissa smiles, a haunted, weary smile. "You're welcome," she says, throwing the bunched up towel at my chest. It's stained with her blood. I can smell her death on it. HD rises in me, and I catch myself grinning at her.

But I'm not happy that she would put herself at such risk.

I know how dangerous the ceremony she performed is. I've done it myself. I've slid the blade into my arteries, and stumbled forward, screaming, as my blood spattered the walls. I've scrambled in the makings of my own mortality to call Death to me.

And I never wanted anyone, least of all Lissa to experience that.

And now she has.

My lip quivers. "What if—"

She puts a finger hard against my lips. "No what-ifs. I had to."

I hold her hand to my mouth and stare into her eyes. Oh God, her eyes! I could look into those forever and see something different every time, and something wonderfully familiar.

"I'm so sorry," I say, and I mean it. Though I don't think she understands me.

"I died once and you brought me back," she whispers and her voice is breaking. "You and me, we always suffer for our love."

"You could have died." I kiss her fingers.

"But I didn't. I knew what I was doing." Yes, she does, she guided me through the process.

But none of that matters in the face of the actuality of it.

You cannot know that sort of pain until you experience it. I think about the ceremony she performed. How agonizing it is. The first cut is easy, if you do it quick, the second as arterial blood is bursting from the first, much more difficult. A few millimeters out and you can die. You nearly do as it is, if you pull it off.

"You could have died," I repeat.

"I thought you already were dead," she says. "Steve the last time I saw you was five days ago."

"Five days! I was gone five days?"

We don't have much time. Five days gone and the twenty-fourth is tomorrow.

"Five of the longest days of my life. Tim was against it, from the start, I don't want you to think he supported this. Said I was being stupid, that we had to give you time. No one calls me stupid. But, after that I held off, I'm sorry that I held off."

"No, there were things I needed to do. You were right to hold off. Oh, my darling, the pain, you—"

She shivers. "But it didn't last for long. And I didn't die. And I have you back."

"Yeah everyone's a winner."

She looks so frail, so worn, but not beaten. "Enough," she says. "I got you back."

Lissa is the strongest person I have ever met. And she loves me. I can feel that love, a rumbling in my throat. A tightness in my chest.

"Don't you ever do that to me again," she says. "Don't you leave like that."

She grabs me, almost throws me into the tower. Lissa rips at my shirt. Claws my chest. I feel the skin tear. The stinging passage of her rage and her love.

Naked, raw. I want her so badly. And she wants me.

There's a liquid friction that burns away all resistance, and we're one. Life and death fuck. They war inside us both. Teeth clash. She bites my lip, and I taste blood.

I come hard and fast, and she draws my hand down into her, drags a rough rhythm from my fingers that has her gasping.

"I brought you back," she gasps. "I brought you back." And then she is quiet.

I've never felt so clumsy, never felt so foolish, never felt so wonderful. She is warm where I have only known cold these last days. Her breath is hot against my neck.

I can't help it, I cry.

"Thank you," I say. "Thank you for bringing me back. Thank you for everything."

"You would do the same," she says.

Yeah, I would. I kiss her, breathe in the smell of her, and taste the salt on her skin like it's some transformative thing. "I'm sorry," I say. "I shouldn't have shouted at you."

"I would do the same," she says, and pulls my hand to her breast. I can feel her beating heart now, not just hear it.

Then it hits me all over again. "Five days!" What the hell was the Death of Water playing at? And what has been going on in the world above?

"I thought it might take a while to sink in," Lissa says.

"What have I missed out on?"

"Take me to Mt Coot-tha," Lissa says. "Let me show you why people agreed to me calling you back."

"Hold me tight," I say, and she does as we shift to the top of the mountain.

There's a hush in the air. Which is odd because the lookout is crowded, even this early in the morning. Five a.m., but you'd think it was midday.

No one is looking down. I follow their gaze, skyward. At first I think there's a second sun above me. But that's not what it is at all.

There's a great comet, luminous and vast, filling the sky, a tiny tail beginning to develop. I'm at once awed and angry. HD is raging too. Marvelling at this thing's obvious capacity for destruction—forget about a scythe. That's small fry to this.

Rage turns to fear. There's no doubt in my mind where this is headed. I recognize it with a grim certainty. That's the odd rhythm I feel in the world's pulse, all those hearts beating with the knowledge of this deathly immanence. Did the dinosaurs' hearts beat this way at the end as they looked up and saw the Stirrer god made manifest?

"A god will light the sky," I say.

"What?"

"It's what the Death of the Water said: a god will light the sky. And there we have it."

"That's why I needed to summon you. To see if you were alive," Lissa says without sounding at all convincing. "Tim was against the idea, until yesterday, when that showed up. You could say the End of Days is already here. Although, with that thing bright in the sky there are no *days,* just one long *day*. The whole world's scared now, Steven. Not just those of us who know. And you've been away through all of it."

"What's Cerbo have to say about it?"

"You probably want to talk to him."

"Anyone asked Bruce Willis what he's going to do?" I'm still heady with lust, with the presence of her. All I can smell is Lissa, and it's intoxicating.

"Steve, this is no joking matter. Best estimate is there're twenty-two days until it hits."

"Whose estimate?"

"Ours. The schedule. In less than a month all life on earth ends."

13

"The schedule said what?" I ask, even though I can feel it now, the deathly void we're hurtling toward.

"Yesterday," Lissa says. "Just as the comet appeared, everything changed. All the long-term projections, they shrank. At first I thought... to be honest, Steve, I thought it was you—that you had died. But then the schedule, I suppose you could say it rebooted itself. Deaths increase dramatically tomorrow, and continue to rise, but in three weeks the mortality rate of the planet is total."

"We're going to have to put on extra staff," I say. "Shirley in payroll is going to hate... God, she complains enough as it is."

"Can you please take this seriously?"

"I am, believe me I am."

"Everything suggests, and persuasively, that it's a planet-killer."

"Define planet-killer."

"Not just humans, everything but the toughest bacteria are going to have a hard time surviving when that hits. Let alone the aftermath. The air will burn, the whole world will be shrouded in dust."

"I don't know how I'm expected to stop it. In fact I don't think I can."

"Cerbo has some ideas, but I think you're better off talking to him about them."

"Yeah, but from what the Death of the Water has told me, we're going to have our own problems."

"What?"

"The comet is the least of it. We're going to have to face another threat, this one will appear human." I glance around: the coffee shop is doing a decent trade. The traffic down in the city is behaving like Brisbane traffic has always behaved. "Civilization doesn't appear to have collapsed."

"Oh, there's been riots, not in Australia yet, but there was a huge one in Paris, and a terrible one in Seattle of all places. A couple of cults have committed mass suicides...but no, not yet. Mainly because every major astronomy body has denied it's going to hit the earth. Regardless, the day it appeared share markets took a dive and chaos isn't far away. Everyone is waiting for it to happen. They're just not sure how it's going to manifest."

Just like our Stirrer god, I guess.

I kiss Lissa gently on the cheek, then shift with her to our unit.

"We've got to start mobilizing," I say, dragging her toward the bathroom. "The war's coming. I have to see Cerbo. But, first, I'm having a shower. You and me both."

Cerbo gets up from behind his desk, his hands are shaking just a little, there are dark shadows beneath his eyes, but he manages a smile. "Can't tell you how glad I am to see you," he says, reaching out to shake my hand. To hell with it, I give him a hug.

"Nearly as glad as I am to see you," I say. We pull apart, both of us grinning. "The problem with the Death of the Water has been resolved."

"We were beginning to worry."

"With reason, I don't think it meant to let me walk out of there, but I think it was worth it, and I've learnt some interesting stuff."

"You've seen the comet, of course."

"Yes, and from my little chat with the Death of the Water it's definitely the Stirrer god manifest."

"How do we fight that?"

"Far as I can tell, we don't. That's the Death of the Water's job. See, here's the thing, the god doesn't just manifest in the sky, it walks among us too."

"It takes a human form?"

"It takes a mortal form," I say. "Mortal being the key word. I'm thinking that was what the "M" was all about on Suzanne's table."

Cerbo flicks through his notes. "I always wondered how it would appear. That thing we've seen in the Deepest Dark just wasn't going to work here—different physics apply for one, and the Underworld operates to stranger rules. To meld the worlds together you'd need something showy, and something precise. A human and a comet: there's resonance there. And the fact that we are expecting it to start on Morrigan's birthday. Perhaps...

"Look, Morrigan was tenacious in life, and one who liked to plan. If anyone is capable of coming back from such utter annihilation it would be him."

"No," I say. "Morrigan may have something to do with this. Some knowledge, but that is all. First place I'm going to check though is his old house."

"What are you expecting to find?"

"I don't know, but I don't think I'll see him sitting in the parlor smoking a pipe."

Cerbo sighs. "You're probably right. But before you go chasing ghosts. Visit your Ankous. They're nervous, frightened, there's a god in the sky. See to them, before you go on your hunt. You owe them that much at least."

So, I spend the morning visiting my Ankous assuring them that I have patched up things with the Death of the Water. I'm quick, maybe too quick, but my presence is almost enough. Ari seems pleased with my appearance at her base in Cardiff, where she is all efficiency with a hint of disdain. She hands me two bottles of Bundy Rum. "That is what you like, isn't it?"

I take them from her silently, and place them on her desk.

"Not anymore," I say.

I even manage not to look at them for the rest of our conversation. I don't know whether I've impressed or insulted her. Probably both.

"We're running out of time," she says.

"We've always been running out of time. Which is why you need to be ready. I'll call you when I need you."

"I'll be waiting," she says.

I know she picks up one of those bottles of rum, opens it and has a long, hard drink the moment I'm gone. And I envy her.

David, in Jo'burg as usual, seems a bit put out by my manner, and my message. I think he still blames me for what happened to Neill, his old RM. Those responsible for his murder are gone, I'm the closest person he's going get. Why does it always turn out that way?

Jing in Shanghai is so reserved that I can't tell what she's thinking. I almost detect a hint of disappointment at my appearance. I shift from regional Number Four to regional Number Four. Cerbo's absolutely right, as much as I am itching to find out how Morrigan is involved in the End of Days, Mortmax needs to know that I am back.

Everywhere I go I can feel the fear behind the civility and the regular functioning of Mortmax. These are people desperately holding on to normalcy, because it's all they have. Time's running down, and we're all too aware of that.

I stress that I'm doing everything I can, and they all say they believe me, but I can't see too much of that in their eyes.

I even manage to get some more Pomps out of each region, though no one is that keen to give me too many, even though we're rubbing up against the twenty-fourth. I've found that while I may be

Mortmax's CEO I'm not all-powerful. Not even Mog can make me that. These are hardened Ankous, they know how to stand up to one of the Orcus, and their skills haven't slipped now that there is only The Orcus.

They are deferential but I know that they mumble behind my back. That as much as they hope otherwise, they doubt I am up to the job. And several of them are not above considering another Schism. Corporate culture doesn't change overnight. And unlike Australia—where it pretty much did, because in one night Morrigan slaughtered just about everyone in the business—they may have lost their Regional Managers, but they didn't lose anyone else.

If they could, there's not a single one of them that wouldn't slash my throat for a chance at the top job. Not a single one—from Cerbo to David and Christine. Except Tim, of course. That's the other vexing thing, though. Tim gets a much easier job of it. I feel that they respect him, much more than they've ever respected me. The same goes for Lissa. They approach my two closest friends with a warmth, a genuine warmth. Tim and Lissa are seen as deserving. Tim and Lissa have reputations. And they didn't spend the first three months on the job in various degrees of drunk.

I know I should have worked harder at changing that perception, and maybe I have a little, but they still think I'm an absolute fucking dolt. As far as they see it, a slacker has taken hold of the reins.

Morrigan's house is in the outer suburbs, near Eight Mile Plains, about twenty minutes south of Brisbane's CBD. It's my house now. I'd been surprised to discover that he'd left it to me in his will. You can't say that Morrigan didn't plan for every eventuality. I guess he never expected it to turn out this way, and it had been really hard for me to resist burning his house to the ground, just like he did mine.

His house is in one of the few streets in Brisbane that are lined with deciduous trees, and they've already dropped most of their leaves. Gives the area a mood that a lot of Brisbane doesn't have, feels a couple of degrees colder here too, though I know it's an illusion. When the wind blows it crackles. The street is almost charmingly eerie, an otherworld sort of Brisbane, here in one of the southernmost tips of the city.

And it's quiet. Far too quiet for late morning in the burbs. I realize then that I don't hear any heartbeats. That's not right. Unless something is blocking them. My skin prickles. Stirrers.

I don't know why I haven't noticed it until now, but the house next to Morrigan's possesses an awful lot of aerials. And the one behind his does too, not to mention the one on the other side. That stops me. I check the lawn beneath my feet. It's dead, dry compacted soil. Other than my Avians there are no birds moving in the sky overhead. There's a shrill dog barking a couple of blocks away. But it stops even as I listen. My skin tightens, I can taste something familiar and unpleasant in the air: faint, hidden, but no less recognizable for it. And now that I am standing very still I can feel them.

Five months ago, Alex had come across a house in the inner burbs, its roof crammed with aerials, its rooms covered with arcane symbols and filled with Stirrers—like a share house of the Undead. Lissa had suggested the place had been used to create a thinning in the earth-Hell interface, the offshoot of which was the generation of storms, storms that dulled my senses to both Stirrers and the assassin/torturer of the season, Francis Rillman. After we had, I had... dealt with Rillman, we'd scoured the city for similar hiding places, and come up with nothing.

Two months of concerted hunting and while the number of stirs had gradually increased, we'd not found a single residence. Until now.

Morrigan's place is surrounded by them. How did my Avians miss this? They've caught sight of Stirrers all up and down the coast. All

I can think is that they've been established only recently—it's been a couple of months since I last came here. Mr. D is right. The presence of the approaching Stirrer god is doing more than increasing the anxiety levels at work. It's also reducing my perceptions.

I close my eyes to get my nearest Avian's view. It's of my back from below. Funny, I didn't think I had a crow that close. I turn around and look across the lawn. I can't see anything, but the Avian is watching me. I summon it. Nothing. I walk towards it, growing taller in its sight.

There it is, or what's left of it. A crow's skull at the base of the nearest telephone pole. Charred tendrils of flesh and feathers cling to the bone. I crouch down, and pick it up. A flash of light, my fingers sting. I drop the skull and it shatters, taking its vision with it.

Not good at all.

The game has changed and I don't know the rules. Something has flipped while I wasn't looking. Perhaps the Stirrers have merely been in hiding. The thought's terrifying and oddly exhilarating. At least something is happening. While the Stirrers did nothing there was no way we could fight them. Now they are in motion, now we have a chance to hit back.

I whisper Mog into being, the knives slide from their sheaths, and wrap around each other, swift as a breath, and I'm holding the scythe. I walk across Morrigan's yard, leap over the fence to the house closest, and straight onto a dead lawn that collapses beneath me. I throw my arms out towards the edge of the pit, but it's too late. I fall and fall hard.

A wooden shaft drives through my ribcage and out my shoulder. I'd scream, but the breath is knocked from me. My weight is dragging me down the spike, leaving a dewy red stripe of bubbling blood as it goes. The damn thing's driven through a lung. I'm faced with the sick-making sensation of my skin healing around the wound, and then breaking again as I sink. Each time it does, I dry heave, which only tears my flesh even more. My boots touch the ground and start bearing my weight.

Mog's just out of reach and I whisper it to me. There's something comforting about the contact, though even moving the muscles required to close my fingers around it is agony.

Not that clever, I think. I try and breathe, manage a few shallow breaths, spots dance before my eyes. The wound's pushing against the wood trying to heal it away, as if it might somehow crush it. Give it time, days or weeks, and it probably will. But I don't have days or weeks. The shaft extends three feet above my head. I try to stand on my toes, but the merest movement upwards hurts bad enough that I almost black out. Can't pull myself free, but I can shift.

I do, just a few feet. The pain almost drops me to my knees, blood gouts from the entry and exit points. But only for a moment, my skin closes over the wound, these are regular wounds, no supernatural toxins, and my body deals with them swiftly. Muscle heals. Jesus, it hurts and I stand there unsteady on my feet, helped only by leaning on the shafts around me. They must have built this late at night, maybe coopted whoever came along to check up on it. Snap someone's neck, inhabit the body with a Stirrer, and you've got another worker. The invasion's begun. I raise my head and stare up at the comet in the sky.

Once I can breathe clearly, I notice the smell. There's a dog down here with me. No, two dogs.

They're remarkably well preserved, but that would make sense. Not much can live near a Stirrer for long, not even bacteria. They draw life through to the Underworld like vacuum cleaners. Keeps their bodies smelling fresh too. I peer down at the dogs. One looks like it may have choked to death, its collar twisted tight around its neck. I imagine the poor things' last moments. Don't need to imagine too hard. Fucking Stirrers.

One of the dog's eyes open. It growls at me, it twists it head hard, snaps the brittle leather of its collar, and jumps to its feet.

Not a zombie dog, surely. I take a step back and yelp as the other dog's teeth clamp around my ankle. I swing my scythe as best I can in the cramped confines of the pit. The snath of the scythe connects with the head of the dog that is wrapped around my leg. Dog jawbone breaks and the pressure's released.

I'm already whispering the Knives of Negotiation back into existence. Better for this sort of fighting. The first dog leaps up at my throat. But I'm ready for it, I neatly sever its head from its body. These knives are sharp. Sometimes I forget just how sharp. The look of shock on the Stirrer-dog's face is almost comical.

The other dog backs away. I throw my knife at its skull, splitting it in two.

I've never seen this before. I didn't even know that Stirrers could inhabit animals. Is it really a Stirrer inhabiting the corpse or a Stirrer-dog equivalent? Regardless, it's a worrying development heaped onto a whole series of worrying developments.

Well, two can play at this game. I shift out of the pit and do what I should have done earlier: summon my Avian Pomps. In a few moments they line the fence like something out of Hitchcock's *The Birds*. I tell them to wait there, that this may not be as bad as I think.

There's a mask painted over the door of Morrigan's neighbor's house. It's glowing softly. Do they know I'm here? Are there masks glowing inside?

I kick the door open. My skin crawls, like it's trying to slip my bones and get the hell out of there.

The room is a basic plan, one of those cookie-cutter homes, door leading into a living room, leading into a kitchen. Bedrooms and bathroom presumably tucked away down a corridor to the right. Someone put in a real effort to make something of it though. There are paintings on the walls, two broad bookcases filled with books, or what once were books. They're ash now, the bookcases burnt black. The paintings are smeared with excrement and old blood, but the real show is on the ceiling, bound there in wire. Half-a-dozen Stirrers. And they can no longer be mistaken for human. Eyeless, their fingers scarred and black from tip to palm. They scratch about overhead, like newly woken things. I wonder if my presence has somehow activated them.

The floor is covered in what I suspect is dried fecal matter and pus. Something drops to the ground from the ceiling. A twisted little white shape. A maggot of some sort. There's a loud sniffing, snuffling sound coming from above my head. The creatures no longer require breath, it's a desiccated sort of snorting.

I heft Mog in one hand and swing, cutting through wire and flesh. The first Stirrer falls, squealing like a pig. It grabs at my legs as I stall it. Its soul tears through me. There's nothing delicate or subtle about that pain. This is a Stirrer long in its host and it doesn't want to go. I take the next one as swiftly as I can. And the next. The air crackles, something builds. I look to the Stirrer in the far corner of the room. Its fingertips are consumed by blue flame. The flesh along its limbs darkens and bubbles.

A burst of electricity strikes me.

I'm hurled back through the doorway. My heart stops, only to start up again. No easy way to death for me. The stench of burning hair fills the room. My hair!

The Stirrer cackles a breathy whistling chortle that can't be described as human.

Thing is, I'm not human either.

And I'm not alone.

Crows and sparrows fill the room. Beaks drive through flesh, claws scratch. Dry blood rains down. In a furious confusion of feathers and avian screams the Stirrers are stalled.

There are more in the other rooms. But we are swift in dispatching them. We've had plenty of practice.

When the job is done. I stagger outside, run a hand over my healing scalp. There's no chance of hair for weeks.

Well, that just makes me angrier.

The next three houses are worse, though I negotiate their lawns carefully to avoid any traps and I use my Avians without hesitation. Fire and feathers and screams, though I think there's no one left to hear them. They've used families. Kids and adults. They've made an aberration of suburbia, they've cut out the heart of the world where I grew up and reinserted howling pod people.

Each stall becomes dirtier and grimmer. But I do the work, and I do it without complaint. There's a satisfaction to it.

When I'm almost done, one of the last Stirrers stalling beneath my bloody fingers, crows dispatching the rest, my phone rings.

It's Tim.

"I'm back, mate."

The silence down the other end of the line extends for painful moments. "Yeah. I had to find out from Cerbo. Cerbo, of all bloody people. Oh, then the other Ankous, talking about you, fucking tweeting about you, about how confident you seemed—statesman-like, would you believe. Couldn't you have at least called? Let me know that you were OK?"

"I was going to, but I had to follow a hunch first."

"What hunch?"

The Stirrer hangs limply from its chains, my bloody palm print across its face.

"I'll tell you about it soon, I promise. I'll be back in the office once I'm done."

"You can't tell me about it now?"

"I'm in the process of working through it. Don't need any distractions. Moment I'm done, you'll be the first to know. The problem with the Death of the Water is sorted, though. That's something isn't it? You should be pleased to know about that. You and Lissa have kept everything running smoothly."

"Yes, I s'pose she told you about the schedule."

"She did."

"Steve, I didn't want her to do the summoning. I know how you feel about it. I argued against it, repeatedly, but that schedule, the bloody thing in the sky. We needed you."

"It's all right."

"Lissa wouldn't even let me stand watch. If something went wrong—"

"Believe me, Tim. If something had gone wrong there would have been nothing you could've done."

"And we'd have been enemies for life."

"No, I would have forgiven you, on your deathbed, of course. That is if the Death of the Water even let me go. Right now, life doesn't look like it's going to be that long."

"Don't talk like that. Where are you?"

"Morrigan's place or close enough."

"What the fuck are you doing there?"

"Killing Stirrers is what. This whole fucking street is mad with them."

"What?"

"We've been duped. Not completely sure how, but we have. They used a crow skull to—look, I'll explain later."

"You need a hand?"

"No, you keep doing what you're doing." I can hear kids laughing, the sound just makes me angrier about what the Stirrers have done here. "You home?"

"Yeah."

"Hug Sally and the kids for me will you."

"OK. You sure, you don't—"

"I'm sure, mate. I'll see you tomorrow." I switch off my phone, and walk out of that last house. A home once, where kids like Tim's laughed.

The air is already clearing. but it can never clear enough.

I look back at Morrigan's house, its clean lines, its welcome mat at the front door.

Whatever I need to find will be in there. Any doubts I had about that were cleared up by the fricking Stirrer colony surrounding it.

14

I've only been here once since he died, and that was to lay brace symbols on every surface. But I've also kept the building under constant surveillance, with no less than two Avian Pomps keeping watch at any time. Or so I thought. Not that I ever suspected that Morrigan could possibly be a threat, just that he might have had allies, and that those allies might show up, come poking around. No one but the occasional hawker has come and gone.

My focus was too narrow, though, if all this Stirrer activity was going on just doors away.

I could have sold the place ten times over in the last six months, and have received increasingly frustrated letters from realtors suggesting just that. But I can't bring myself to. And, now I think of it, the requests stopped coming a couple of months ago.

The house is as Morrigan left it, nothing moved or disturbed. He wasn't really that into possessions, perhaps he'd already slipped into the mindset of an RM. The air is stale, trapped and musty. Outside there's a swimming pool covered over—but there's a hint of chlorine to the fustiness of a closed house. Dust's everywhere, a thick layer of the stuff that I trail a finger through. In the Underworld the dust does my bidding, here it's only worthy of a vacuum.

Morrigan would have hated to see it. He was always such a fastidious bloke.

But for the dust, Morrigan could still be living here. He is everywhere. There's Escher's "Eye (Reflecting Skull)" on one wall, and in his bedroom there's a full-size reproduction of Klimt's painting "Death and Life." He loved the iconography.

I walk through the house. Can't sense anything at all. No deathly presences, no objects of power beyond that of my knives.

There's a walk-in wardrobe filled with little more than suits, silk shirts, underwear and a few T-shirts of the sort that you pick up at conferences and moots, and wear when you're doing yard work. Nothing hidden in the wardrobe, no shoeboxes of secrets. Just a couple of trophies, a few photos of Morrigan with Mr. D and my parents, even one of him with me, back when I was a teen, my hair almost down to my arse. Morrigan looks happy in that photo. Me, I just look spotty and a little too metal.

Frustrated, I close my eyes, and concentrate.

There's a soft buzzing at the limits of my perception. An electrical hum. Something's running, generating a field, stymieing my senses.

I shift to the fuse box. Flick off the circuit breakers one by one. And then I can feel it.

There's a space behind the refrigerator and it's there I find the box. An old metal one giving off a peculiar flavor. The lid looks like it should just lift off.

I touch it and—

What?

I blink.

The air is cold, a good five degrees chillier at least than Brisbane. I haven't left Australia, but I am eight hundred kilometers away. Southwest of Brisbane.

I lean against a sign that says "Dubbo 20 km." I'm on the Mitchell Highway, in an entirely different state. Morrigan has a sense of humor. I know he hated the country. Dad, who was big on camping and fishing, had never been able to convince Morrigan to come out bush with us. Said the air gave him hives. Thinking back, he was probably just too busy planning everyone's death in a Schism.

A crow alerted by my presence lands on a tall rock nearby and looks at me curiously, and with not a little alarm. It squawks at me.

"I know," I say. "I know."

The crow dips into a shallow bow and there's a touch of piss-take about it. I don't get out to rural parts as much as I should, but Australia's a big country.

Morrigan's set up some sort of pushing defense—a kind of combination of a shift and a kick in the chest with a size twelve boot.

Thank goodness I hadn't sent a Pomp to dig through the house, the poor bastard would have had trouble trying to explain this to the office in Dubbo, once he got there of course. And if he wasn't just torn apart instead. I check my phone, no signal.

The crow's suddenly in the air again. Circling above me, calling out in alarm. And I can see what it sees.

Not good.

Shapes move in the nearby fields either side. They're silent and low to the ground, and they're coming toward me fast. Damn it, more Stirrer-dogs. But I'm ready for them. Mog in hand.

The first, an Alsatian, leaps at my throat, but I catch it with the sharp point of my scythe. Its weight forces Mog to the ground, just as a staffie closes its jaws around my left calf. I slap a bloody hand against its neck and the staffie grows limp, but its jaws don't loosen. I've a dead dog attached to my leg like a tick, as more of the animals close in.

I could shift out of here, but this, like the Stirrer nests, needs to be dealt with now. Wrenching the scythe out of the Alsatian is harder work than I expect, and by then I've two more dogs snapping at me.

The scythe's just too clumsy for this sort of work. They may as well be spiders. I release the knives and slash out at the silent dogs, they back away, just beyond my reach. I slide the blades over my palms and draw out some fresh blood.

I stall them all with swift pats. One tries to run from me, but I shift directly in front of it. Tackle the thing around the legs with my bleeding hands. That last one's a border collie, like my Molly Millions.

It hurts to see dogs used so, and I'm sobbing by the time I shift back to Morrigan's. Morrigan, the prick who killed my Molly.

This time I'm ready. I concentrate, lower my hands carefully, and touch the box.

As the push happens I push back. There are two shifts at work against each other, and I'm the stronger.

There's a sound like tearing paper, which may actually be reality ripping around the edges. Kind of like some had feared the Large Hadron Collider might cause, only worse. That sets me in a panic but by then it's too late. My ears pop, and I find myself on my arse. The air smells charred. But the shield is destroyed. The box is just a box again.

I lift the lid.

The wonderful odor of burning increases, but that's to be expected. The defense had pushed hard. It's just the friction of two forces at play against each other.

Inside the box is a book.

Curiouser and bloody curiouser. There's nothing special about it, your bog-standard Moleskine notebook. It has a dark cover, it's a couple of hundred pages thick. I reach down to grab the book. The ceiling creaks. Holding the book in one hand, I look up.

Then the roof collapses on me. Fire and smoke a crushing cage.

I shift, arms thrown up in the air. End up out on the front yard.

The house is ablaze. I'm ablaze. I yelp, start rolling on the ground. Whatever's left of my hair goes up in flame.

HD's having a great old time inside me.

I consider the conflagration; if I'm lucky the fire will catch the neighboring houses and remove the taint of the Stirrers. But, regardless, Morrigan's place is gone.

People are already coming out of the house on the corner. I can't be seen here. I need to get away. HD suggests that we kill all witnesses, just to be sure. The blades snicker inside my jacket. I need to get away.

I shift again. This time to the office.

Taking Morrigan's book with me.

15

"So have you read it yet?" Tim asks, the first intelligent thing he's said after rubbing my bald skull. If you ever piss off your cousin, sudden baldness is a sure way of generating instant forgiveness and ridicule. End of Days drawing near and he's still capable of paying out on me. Lissa had given me an even harder time, once she'd made sure I was OK.

"No, well, there's nothing to read."

We've spoken about the Stirrers, but it's the book that has everyone worried. I've even called Cerbo in.

The book sits on the desk; normally the throne is the most eye-catching thing in the office, followed by "The Triumph of Death." But not now, this little notebook draws the eye, draws it and holds it. Lissa, Tim, Cerbo and I crowd around the Moleskine, as though we're looking at a bomb rather than a book.

And perhaps we are.

I feel like we should be dressed in some sort of body armor observing this thing through the eyes of a remote-controlled robot.

But it hasn't blown up yet.

"What do we do with it?" I ask them.

Cerbo reaches a hand out to touch the cover, pulling his fingers away at the last minute. "Destroy it. I don't think we have any other option."

I look over at Tim. "What about you?"

"Yeah, we burn it."

"But what if it's useful to us in some way?" I pick the notebook up. "Maybe this was Morrigan's plan for saving the world. He was dealing with the Stirrers: he knew what was coming. I'm sure he would have come up with a plan. And there's definitely a vibe of power about it, you can't deny that."

Cerbo grimaces. "Yes, there is. Which is why it worries me, Morrigan's more likely to have built a weapon to destroy us than something to save us."

"Yeah, he was a vindictive prick," Lissa says.

Holding the book now, I know that they're right. There's a sense of impatience about it on par with a Brisbane bus driver waiting at a pedestrian crossing. It's burning to plow down everything in its path, flip the gears into reverse and finish off the job.

"There's almost an erotic charge to the book or something... kind of arousing." I drop the Moleskine on the desk.

"You share far too much, mate," Tim says.

"I've got some erotic stuff at home, if you need a substitute," Lissa says.

I wink at her. "Maybe later."

Cerbo pointedly looks anywhere but at Lissa or me. He clears his throat, leans over the book. "Can I touch it?"

Lissa chuckles, and I give her a look. Who's being childish now?

"Why not," I say, "it hasn't done anything other than seem ominous, and you could say that about my throne."

Cerbo glances over at my throne. There's something in his gaze that suggests he'd more than like to touch it. I find my hands reaching for the knives in my belt, a stupid and somewhat embarrassing automatic reaction. HD wants it to go further. I just straighten my jacket.

"Ahh, this is why they ban books!" Tim says.

"Books can be dangerous, but then, there's dangerous and *dangerous*."

Cerbo prods it with a finger, when nothing happens he picks it up and opens it. There is no explosion, no sudden exhalation of air, or a wind blown in from nowhere. The book remains definitively a book.

"The pages, are they all covered with this ink?" Cerbo spins, looks at me closely, squinting, then pokes me. "You don't feel possessed or anything do you?"

"What, other than having the fucking Hungry Death inside me? Mate, I think it'd be a pretty tight fit if something else decided to take up residence."

"Just asking." He glances at Lissa.

"No. It's definitely him." She smiles. "Still a royal pain in the arse."

"Certainly less hair than I'm used to," Tim says.

More jacket straightening. I manage a "Ha."

Cerbo peers closely at the book. "This, whatever it is, it's important." He pulls out a flashlight from his pocket. Tim and I exchange looks. "What?" Cerbo says. "You're telling me you don't keep a flashlight on your person at all times? What if you shift somewhere and it's dark? What if you chase a Stirrer down the sewers? What if you drop your car keys in a dimly lit car park? Amateurs." He holds the flashlight in his mouth then takes out a small jeweler's loupe from another pocket and brings it to his left eye.

"You use that to find your really tiny keys do you?" Tim asks.

Cerbo doesn't answer, just leans in closely, eye scrunched over the loupe, flashlight shining. "There are markings here, variations in the consistency and shade of the ink. Did you see?"

"No."

"It's telling us something. All books do. Morrigan hid this and guarded it, what if it's something that we need? What if it's the key to our fight against the Stirrers?" Cerbo peers even closer at the book, his nose almost touching the paper. He sniffs, I half expect him to lick the damn thing.

But he doesn't. Instead he jerks his head back, and almost drops the notebook onto the desk. "We need to destroy it. Now."

"What?"

"The markings, look at them." He hands me the book and the loupe. The page comes into focus.

It's like falling into a storm of wings. So many of them. But they're not crows. They're sparrows like the ones Morrigan used to have tattooed on his back and arms, like the ones that used to come alive as inklings. And they're moving.

For a brief instant I can feel Morrigan too. He's everywhere in this book.

This is no weapon, certainly nothing we can use. But the threat implicit in it is a force that clenches around my heart. It's like seeing Morrigan again, like having him stand directly in front of me. Anger and terror battle it out inside me. I can't suppress a shudder.

I drop the book, but Lissa catches it before it hits the ground. She reaches out her free hand and clicks at me, and I pass her the loupe.

"Just tell me what's in it," Tim says.

"Sparrows, lots and lots of sparrows," Lissa says. "And they're in motion."

"Yeah, we better destroy this," I say. "It's wrong, the book is wrong."

Cerbo nods. He feels about in his pockets then stops. "Anyone have any matches?"

Tim snorts. There's the click of his Zippo lighter.

Lissa steps back away from the flame. "Is this wise? I can understand the instinctual reaction is to get rid of it. But what if Morrigan wants you to do that? The book was hidden. Who else but you would have found it? Who else could have broken the lock that kept it hidden?"

"Morrigan never expected to die," I say. "This thing was for his eyes only. I refuse to believe that he planned beyond his own death."

Tim nods. "The guy couldn't imagine his death, only those of other people." He reaches forward with the lighter. "But just in case... We don't need any more complications. Not now."

Cerbo grabs the Moleskine and stands next to Tim.

Everyone looks at me.

Ultimately, this is my call. And Tim's right, we need complications like a hole in the head. "Do it," I say.

The finger of flame runs over the book and it catches at once. The smoke smells of Morrigan's cologne, some expensive Italian stuff he used to have imported. It's almost as if he has walked into the room.

And the book screams.

A dark shape flies from the smoke. A sparrow, broken free from the pages. Another follows it.

"Get them," Cerbo says, dropping the flaming notebook onto the desk, and smacking out the flames with his palm.

Tim and I collide chasing after the bird, a solid head bashing. I'm shaking the stars from my vision as Lissa neatly cuts one of the sparrows out of the air with her knife. It splatters to the floor as a puddle of ink. She's aiming at the other one when the door opens.

"Close it," I yell at Lundwall, but it's too late. The inkling's through the door, Lundwall scrambles out of the way and into the doorframe, throwing whatever paper he's holding up into the air. He collects himself, and turns, running after the bird. No way he's going to catch it.

The sparrow darts across the office, keeping high, wings beating fast. It pelts straight towards an open window. It's through in an eye blink, and out above George Street. But I have my own sparrows there. And they don't take to this intruder well. By the time I've reached the window they've torn it to shreds. I can taste the ink in my mouth, it's bitter and rank.

I close the window and glance back at Lissa and crew, and rub my hands. "See? All taken care of." I turn to Lundwall. "Do you think you can manage a coffee, mate?"

He nods stiffly and shuffles over to the kitchen.

"It's not Lundwall's fault," Lissa says.

"I know. I just need a coffee. All I can taste is that damn inkling."

We march back into my office, and consider the now-smoking book. If the flames set the sparrows free, I'm beginning to think the fire in Morrigan's house wasn't some sort of defense system at all. The book was meant to burn, and whatever was meant to happen was meant to happen there, possibly with me buried under the rubble of a smoldering building.

"The flames must have activated it," Cerbo says, he lifts his gaze to Lissa. "I'm sorry, you were absolutely right. We should have listened to you."

Lissa's arms are crossed, but she's leaning in towards Cerbo most aggressively. "And that's supposed to make me feel better, how?" She glares at Tim's Zippo, then Tim who's still rubbing his head, he's already got a dark lump forming just beneath his hairline. "Another glaring example of why smoking's bad for you."

Tim grimaces.

I step between them. "Look it doesn't matter. The threat was dealt with."

"Question is, what do we do with the book?" Tim says.

"It needs to be hidden, somewhere safe," Cerbo says. "Somewhere out of the way, until we have time to deal with it properly."

"I think I know exactly where," I say.

Cerbo smiles. "Good, now keep it to yourself. The more people who know, the more danger we're all in."

"You think someone's going to come after this book?"

"Some *things* more likely," Cerbo says. "The fire's in the sky. A signal and threat. Whatever is going to happen is ramping up."

"Yeah, like the Stirrer nests that I found around Morrigan's place. I've my crows searching out more, now I know what to look for, and now the Stirrers seem to not care about hiding. The last time we found something like this it was being used to generate storms and conceal Stirrer movements. Now I'm guessing it's being used to generate something else."

"I think you're right," Cerbo says. "It may be some sort of guidance system. The energy of the Stirrers drawing that thing in the sky closer, steering it. This nest phenomenon has only occurred in Brisbane, that would seem to back the idea up." He looks at me. "Everything is being pointed at you, Steven. I guess they figure if they get you out of the way as quickly as possible there's no one left to stop their god."

"Then maybe we should be focussing on destroying the nests," Tim says.

"Get the Ankous here," I say. "Three hours from now. I may have seen them all today but we need a mini-moot. We're going to need all the help we can get."

I'm getting images in my head, crows alerting me to Stirrer houses, one after the other. HD's chuckling and enraged at once. My attempts at dealing with them, hunting them down one by one have failed. I totally misunderstood their strategy.

Tim's already on the phone. I look at Cerbo and Lissa as I pick up the book. It's still warm, but nothing comes flying out.

"I'll see that this is safe, and then we need to discuss the nests. There's at least twenty of the bastards. How the fuck did I miss them?"

"That doesn't matter now," Lissa says, though she seems shocked. "I'll get some teams together, we can be ready to go tomorrow. It's cutting it fine, but we need to do this right. You get that somewhere safe."

I think about the pact I've made with the Death of the Water. It's a good deal, but only if this works. If it doesn't, we're all fucked anyway, and if it does...in my braver moments I like to believe that it doesn't worry me.

I kiss her, not caring that Cerbo is in the room. I don't know how many kisses I have left. I can't waste the opportunity for one now. "I'll be back," I say.

"You better be, or I'll summon you again."

"That's nice to know."

Lissa shakes her head. "Believe me, it isn't."

I shift.

Mr. D stands on the edge of his branch of the One Tree, a book gripped firmly in one hand. The mountains of Hell rise up in the distance, and just east of them the dark waters of the Tethys seethe. The sky glows a brilliant red. Once again Hell is lightening with my presence, that kind of reaction could really screw with your head. But I've got so many things already screwing with mine I hardly notice.

Wal pulls himself free of my arm. I've decided that I'm not going to block him anymore. I've missed him. He nods at me and laughs. "Hey, Kojak."

Then again...

"You've been gone a while." Mr. D says, not turning to look at me.

"Well, somebody suggested I go and talk with the Death of the Water, turned out it had more than talk in mind."

Mr. D turns to me, his face shifting through various aspects of death, pain, delight. I wish, sometimes, that I could just get one look from him. But then again, I'm not exactly sure what a normal facial expression would look like on Mr. D. "My God, you're bald! Trouble?"

I rub my scalp self-consciously. "The guy held me hostage for a week. I'd still be down there, I think, except Lissa performed a summoning."

Mr. D whistles, walking towards his chair and table. "She did? That girl loves you. Have you asked her to marry you yet?"

What the? "You been talking to Tim?"

"A couple of weeks ago. Only via tweets, though we do have a nice #willheorwonthe tag going on—the odds are on the won't." That stings me harder than I'm prepared to admit. Mr. D places the book carefully on the table: it's a Le Guin, *The Dispossessed.* I can't fault his taste in literature. Wal flits down, picks up the book and flicks through it. "Well, you didn't answer me, have you asked her to marry you?"

"Not yet."

"Stop wasting time." Mr. D yanks the novel from Wal's clutches, and puts it back down. "Lissa's a keeper, and to think you nearly lost her over that ridiculous affair with Suzanne Whitman."

"I did not have an affair with Suzanne. She was nothing more than a mentor."

"One that you were so proud of that you decided to keep it a secret." He turns back to gaze over the edge of the One Tree, waves his hand airily. "But that's ancient history, there are far more pressing matters than who slept with whom, or who betrayed which mentor. Far more pressing matters indeed."

Is he right or is he right! Wal hovers by his side, both are transfixed by something going on below.

"What are you looking at?"

"I'm not sure, but I think it may well be one of those more pressing matters."

Mr. D makes room for me on the edge of the branch. Wal hovers in the open space above the void. It's a vertiginous drop, tumbling down to Underworld Brisbane. I see Mr. D's "pressing matter" at once.

The dead are walking away from the One Tree. Not all of them, there are some that continue making their progress up the hill, but thousands at least are following the curve of the mountain away from the city.

"How long has this been going on?"

"A while, I think. Slowly at first, just a few. I only noticed it when I last went down to the markets on the riverbank yesterday. Hardly a soul about. Where do you think they're going?" Mr. D says.

"I have an idea. Charon's building an Ark."

"He's building an Ark? Can't that fellow have a solution that doesn't involve a bloody boat? It shows a decided lack of imagination."

"It can't be that big a problem surely. I mean, if I was a soul I don't know if I'd really like to take my chances in the Deepest Dark right now, the Stirrer god is devouring more souls every day."

"Oh, it can create a problem all right. What do you think sustains the One Tree?"

I shrug.

"The souls of the dead. They are drawn to the One Tree, and through it to the Deepest Dark. They are nutrient and water to it. They are everything that the One Tree requires, without it this tree will die."

"The Tree hasn't been here forever though. Everything passes, everything leads to a new way eventually, a paradigm shift."

Mr. D shakes his head. "Steven, you bandy that phrase about far too much."

"It's your phrase!"

"Yes, but I use it properly. Sure, there was a time before the One Tree, just as there was a time before toilet paper—and let me tell you which time I prefer."

I put the burnt notebook next to *The Dispossessed* on his table. Mr. D looks at it curiously.

"What's that?"

"Something I found in Morrigan's house."

Mr. D sniffs. "Let me guess, you burnt it, and activated it somehow."

"It was burnt, yes, but what it activated was dealt with. I need you to keep what's left of it safe."

"The question is, will I be safe from it?"

Mr. D has managed to survive even death. He's hung around when every other RM has gone, devoured and deposited by the One Tree. I can't imagine anything threatening him.

"You'll be fine," I say. It doesn't come across as confidently as I intend it to.

So many people in my life have died in this last year. Better people, stronger people, more caring people. People who I loved. I can't promise Mr. D anything.

16

When I shift back to my office, Faber Cerbo's sitting there alone. He jumps, startled by my sudden arrival. No knife this time. Even he is not that stupid.

"It's done," I say.

Cerbo's smile is about as wan as you can get.

"You got something on your mind?" I ask.

"Yes. You see, I have an idea."

"It certainly doesn't look like a good idea."

"It may not be a good idea, it may be a horrible one, but it might work." He takes a deep breath. "While you were away, trapped beneath the sea, it came to me. Something that you said about blood being enough. Well, I think you're right. To stop this god maybe all you need is a lot of it. I've done the math. If you used the blood of every Pomp, there might just be enough—"

"No. It's—no."

The only one smiling now is HD.

"I know you don't want to do it, but this plan, it may be our best chance."

I shake my head. "Kill every Pomp and use their blood to stall a Stirrer god? No, I'm not going to do that."

"They're all going to die anyway, if we don't stop it. Them and everything else. It's ridiculous, I know, here I am arguing for my own death, but I'd rather that than be responsible for the end of all life, not that I'd have long to dwell on it all, being dead. Wouldn't you?"

"No, and you aren't responsible, Faber. I'm responsible." I realize I'm shouting. I lower my voice. "There has to be another option."

"The only other option is to let the Stirrer god set the time and place for the confrontation, fight it entirely on its own terms—terms which, despite my best efforts, we don't have more than the merest inkling of, I might add—and be defeated. Same outcome, wouldn't you say, Mr. de Selby?"

"You only call me that when you're pissed off with me."

"I do not."

"I am not killing my employees. I refuse to do that, it's what made me different from the other RMs, it's why Suzanne chose me for this role, and it's who I am." I glare at Cerbo. "Faber, you find me a way of beating this thing, a way that doesn't involve killing everyone I care about, and we'll talk."

I can't tell if he's relieved or disappointed with my response. "What if that's the only way?"

"It can't be, I refuse to believe it." I remember my dream, the ocean of blood. Was this what my subconscious mind was throwing at me? "And how would it even work anyway?"

"You'd call it to you. Just as you can call your Avians, or your scythe."

"Call the fucking blood to me?" *I can do that?*

"Steven, think of the potency of that blood. Maybe that's what the scythe is for. The end game in a battle with Stirrers. You drain the blood of all the Pomps in the world, and no Stirrer will be able to face that."

"No, it isn't going to happen," I say. "Not that way. A new world can't be built on that sort of bloodshed."

"It's not murder. It's not madness. It's sacrifice. It's what being a Pomp is about—isn't it? Just on a larger scale. Think about it. When all the Stirrers and their god are defeated, you're not going to need

Pomps. Not in the way you need them now. The workload's going to be lighter."

"No."

Cerbo sighs. "I understand. I can even say that I'm slightly relieved. But remember, as long as you have your scythe that's an option."

"Would you do it?"

I can see the answer in his eyes. "You do whatever it takes. Of course I would do it."

"The world burns before I kill all of you to save it. The whole fucking universe."

"Now look who's being extreme. I'll be back for the meeting," Cerbo says. "I need to make peace with some things."

"It's all crashing to an end isn't it?" I say.

"Yes," Cerbo says. "One way or another, one sacrifice or another, yes."

I need to talk to someone in the government. I need to know what strategies they have, and how we might be able to use them if worse comes to worse. Thing is, I call my usual contacts and no one answers. I try Tim, but he's busy wrangling Ankous. Worse than cats, as he puts it.

So I call Alex.

"Where have you been?" he says.

"I'll tell you about it over a drink one day," I say. "But we need to talk. Face to face, if possible."

"As it happens I'm having a coffee right now. Springwood, got the afternoon off. Luv-a-Coffee in Centro."

I shift there, and glance around; I'm in the right cafe in Springwood, standing right next to my target. My appearance startles a guy pushing a shopping trolley. I wink at him, he frowns, moves on, because no one appears out of thin air—not even in the southern suburbs.

"Well, you've moved out into the sticks haven't you?"

Alex looks up from his chai latte, sliding his hand over a card. "Christ, Steve, you surprised me. And what's with the hair?"

"Has to be a first for everything, I suppose. And I don't want to talk about it." My jaw drops. "Are you wearing a skivvy?"

"It's cold."

"But come on. A skivvy . . . you look like a Wiggle."

I pull the chair out from beside him.

"What you got there?" I ask, trying to get a view of the card he's obscuring not particularly well. Alex and sleight of hand don't really gel.

"Season pass to the Lions' games." He shakes his head. "I forgot, I got these when Dad was . . . It's stupid. I haven't been to a game all year."

"I'll come with you," I offer.

Alex squints at me. "Didn't know you followed AFL."

"Nah, I'm Bronco's boy," I say, "but I can tolerate Aussie Rules."

"Tolerate?" He slides the card back into his wallet.

I grin at him. "Just saying, that's all. Putting the offer out there."

Alex nods. "Appreciated. Might be fun."

"Yeah. When this is all done with, it would be good to, well, to think of something other than bloody Stirrers."

"You think it's that close?"

"Tomorrow, maybe today. Brisbane, as far as we can tell."

"That what this is all about?" He looks from me to the comet.

I nod. "I need to know what we can expect from your lot if everything goes down as badly as I suspect it will."

"Doug Anderson's the one you need to talk to." Alex sighs. "Steve, you know all this shit. He's been your liaison since Tim left the department."

"Can you talk to him for me? Tee up a meeting. He's not been taking my calls, and I've got Tim off chasing other things."

Alex shakes his head. "Hardly in his good books at the moment."

"Why?"

"I don't think he likes my association with you. Undermines his authority somewhat."

"Christ, after the stuff we've been through! You're my unofficial liaison, but I need my official one now."

"Yeah. Office politics, though, you know how it is."

It was office politics that started all this. "Of course, I do. But I still need to know where we stand; things are coming to a head. And, you're a cop, you don't even work in his office."

Alex sips his latte. "We Black Sheep really like to put that stuff behind us. Him, on the other hand, I've never seen anyone work as hard. He resents what I gave up."

"So when did you decide that you didn't want to be a Pomp?"

"Very early on. It never felt right to me, *for* me. Dad pushed it for a while, but I know he was proud of the choice I made."

I nod. "Saved my life."

Alex smirks. "On numerous occasions." He sips his coffee. "What about you? Why did you decide to become a Pomp?"

"I couldn't think of anything else."

Alex laughs. "Well, you've done all right for yourself."

"Yeah, I'm a star."

"Fucking glass-half-empty de Selby, eh," he says dismissively, pulling out his mobile.

I order myself a takeaway coffee, leaving Alex to deal with Doug by himself—he hates an audience. By the time the coffee's ready Alex is hanging up, there's a thin line of tension between his eyes that I don't think he had before.

"Doug didn't sound happy," he says, letting the phone skitter across the table.

"Right now he has reason not to be."

"He said to meet him in the usual place in twenty minutes. I impressed upon him the urgency of the matter. What's the usual place?"

"It's a secret."

"You be careful."

"It's all I ever am." I give him a little salute and shift out of there.

Tim's still busy when I get back, so I grab Lissa.

"I think I'm going to need your negotiating skills," I say.

"Who have you pissed off?"

"No one, not yet. I've a meeting in about fifteen minutes with Doug."

"Aw, Dougie. What a lovely guy. How can you piss off Doug? The usual place?"

"How do you know about that?" I thought my meeting place with Doug was secret. Sure we've met a half-dozen times there, usually had a beer afterwards, when the talk became less formal. But as far as I know no one had ever seen us there.

"I have my ways," Lissa says.

I raise an eyebrow.

"Well, you follow me with those Avians of yours. Sometimes I just follow you."

"He's late," I say, needlessly and for about the fifth time.

"It's too bloody cloak and dagger for me," Lissa says lifting her voice above the whale song. I admire her profile, and she catches me looking. Her lip curls, the slightest movement, but I see it, and she knows I do. Her green eyes widen—there's mockery and love in there, and something deeper, and darker. A shared hurt, a history more convoluted than our six months together deserves. For a moment, all I want to do is kiss her.

I'm glad she's with me. Since my little underwater expedition I really don't like being all that far from her.

I'm holding her hand, which makes it less cloak and dagger more pseudo date in odd location, with a dash of peril; about all we have time for these days.

We're standing in the long, dark hallway that runs outside the Queensland Museum and works a little like a wind tunnel, three life-size model humpback whales floating above us. A little down the way, an ultralight plane is suspended from the ceiling, but it's the humpbacks that are making all the noise, well, the speakers bolted into the walls beneath them.

Lissa groans. "If I hear any more bloody clicking."

Whale song is haunting and powerful, but half an hour of it can be a bit much, I guess. And, a lot of it sounds like someone letting air out of a balloon. HD is raging. It can't stand the singing, and it's keeping me on edge. That and the memories it evokes. Just this morning I was a prisoner of the Death of the Water

I grind my teeth, squeeze Lissa's hand a little tighter, and drive HD down. It'll rise back up, it always does, I don't have much space within me to push it into: something that alarms me every time I wake up in the morning and see HD staring back at me out of the mirror. Its madness and horror, the source of all my strength.

The stone blades are mumbling too, in sympathy with HD.

Lissa frowns. "It's troubling you again?"

"It's always troubling me," I say.

Footsteps echo down the hallway. Lissa and I glance at each other.

"Just me," Doug says. "Sorry I'm late."

"Couldn't we have met at a cafe?" Lissa says.

Doug shakes his head and gestures at a nearby bench. Lissa and I sit down, Doug paces in front of us. "No, I know the CCTV doesn't work here. There's no one to see us meet, and no way that anyone can sneak up on us." His voice is low, I recognize the mildly panicked expression on his face.

Doug's sympathetic, but he's hardly influential. Not after the events of the last few months. Mortmax has grown increasingly threatening in the government's eyes. Not only State or Federal.

Every government agency in the world that has something to do with us has been keeping a very close eye on me and my Pomps' activities. They need us, but they're not sure how much they can trust us, or what happens if we fail.

Frightened governments aren't a good thing. They never function well. Even if they have a reason to be frightened. But he's all I have.

The wind skitters paper down the long hall. Doug jumps.

"What's up?" I say. "This isn't like you at all."

"Alex's call reminded me of something you need to know," Doug says then slashes out at me with a knife. The knife point buries itself in my chest.

Can't say I expected that.

But HD is always ready. I catch Doug's wrist, pull his hand back, and with it the blade. It slides free from my lung with a wet sound. HD rises inside me. It wants to kill again. Not now. Doug struggles but I don't let him go.

"Stop this!" I can't feel a pulse. I look into Doug's eyes, there's no one home. At least no one known as Doug.

A Stirrer exists in there now. Doug's been dead for some time: the Stirrer's working his body too smoothly for it to be just a day or so. Bleak eyes stare out at me, even as the lips curl into a smile.

"It is coming. And your world will end, starting with her." The Stirrer snaps its free hand up and jabs a finger at Lissa.

"Bullshit, what bullshit," Lissa says, already sliding her knife down her palm.

Lissa strikes Doug's head with her bloody palm, grimacing as the Stirrer's soul slides through her and back to the Deepest Dark where it belongs.

Doug's a dead-weight in my arms. I let him drop, poor bastard.

I check his hand, and there it is below his thumb. The mask tattooed in the finest detail. I lower his arm gently onto his chest, something feels wrong. Doug's face is calm, but for where Lissa's blood has marked him. You'd think it was a peaceful death. I peer under his shirt. There's a hole in his chest about the size of my fist.

Nothing peaceful about it.

Lissa's already on the phone, calling through a pick-up for the corpse. An ambulance will arrive shortly. The body will be taken away and burnt. Once burial would have been enough, but now we're not taking any chances.

"The one guy in the government sympathetic to us and he's dead," I say once she's off the phone.

"When the hell did this happen?"

"A while back, obviously, the way he was walking and talking. No one pomped Doug's soul. Or, at the very least, I didn't sense it."

I let that hang between us. An ambulance is drawing near. Sirens competing with the whale song.

"Disturbing," Lissa says, she's already looking away from the body. A body's a body, it's not the interesting part for Pomps, and it's certainly the least interesting part today. Mr. D was right, the Stirrer god's presence is causing major disruptions. Things I'm only beginning to understand.

Death not aware of a death: disturbing is an understatement.

Tim sits down and shakes his head. "I can't believe it. Doug... poor, poor bastard."

"I liked him," I say.

"Any idea how long he's been dead?"

"At least a week."

"A week!" Tim pales, and reaches for his cigarettes. "I had drinks with him three days ago, they were starting to panic about your disappearance."

Tim had quite a bit to drink if he hadn't noticed. I must be giving him a bit of a look because he puffs up his chest.

"Used to be I had drinks with you, mate," he says with a hint of bitterness. "Then you started drinking alone."

I shake my head at that. I want to tell him I haven't had a drop since Lissa summoned me, no matter how much I've needed it, but I can't. A day's not long enough. Trumpeting about a day without alcohol makes it sound like I have more of a problem than I'm willing to admit.

"So, we're without allies again," Tim says. "The government itself has been compromised. Even the bit that should have known better than to get into such trouble."

"Well, there was always a chance it would happen," I say. "I mean, Stirrers had already started infiltrating the suburbs, and dogs, bureaucrats had to be next."

Tim gives me such a nasty look.

"I've spoken to Alex," I say, "and we've shipped extra brace paint to his District, and he's even passed some of it on to State Intelligence and Security Operations. And, no one in a ministerial position seems to be affected."

"How do you know?"

"I can sense their heartbeats." Tim looks impressed. "I'm not just a pretty face you know," I say.

"Yeah, you've got great hearing. Talking of which," he lifts a sheath of papers from his lap, "I've got a speech written up for you, for this afternoon. The Ankous are going to need something impressive."

"You saying I can't come up with the goods?"

"One day out from the end of world, and we're chasing our tails. Do I need to say more?"

"I don't like speeches," I say, rubbing my head. It's itching, I can't stand this not having hair, maybe I need to rub oil in it or something.

"Exactly and not a problem," Tim says. "I've Steveified it, it's more a series of dot points."

"I know what I'm going to say."

"Yes, and it's written down here—in convenient dot-point form. These are Ankous you're talking to, you need to be pretty slick."

I take the notes from him. Glance through them. Yeah, it's pretty much what I was going to say, only better. Tim's been writing speeches for nearly a decade, he's got it down to a fine art. I get to the bottom and there's a little squiggle and the letters SSR.

"What's SSR?" I ask.

"Oh, Something Stirring Required."

"You know I'm going to get to that bit and laugh. I'm not Winston Churchill."

"No, he never had to fight against a god. You're going to need something stirring, really stirring."

I hand it back to him. "How about you have a go, eh?"

Tim tears up a little. My offer's really touched him. "I suppose I could."

I lean back in my throne, lifting the front legs an inch from the ground, and reconsider Cerbo's suggestion. The sheer audacity and bravery of it is shocking. It's the sort of thing that the Stirrers wouldn't expect. Our job is based on sacrifice and blood, but never to that extent. Whose is?

Maybe Cerbo's right. But the sacrifices I'm prepared to make are personal. I demand that my staff fight, but I could never demand that they die. I can only expect that of me.

"You ever think it might just be their time?" I ask Tim.

"Their?"

"Stirrers."

"If it is, well they're going to have to earn it. This was once their world, but they lost it, those days passed over a billion years ago. You don't get that back, we're here now."

"I like my evil black and white."

"You're Death, you're already morally ambiguous."

"Yeah, but what isn't?"

"All I know is that if they win that's it for all life, from bacteria up. All of it's gone, and it might as well have never happened."

"But everything ends, maybe our time's up."

Tim nods his head. "Yeah, everything ends and it's our job to know when time's up. It ain't up." He hands me back the notes. "Put that in your speech."

Thirteen Ankous sit around my desk. Hell and earth behind us. The different light of each zone provides a peculiar and varied illumination. Some faces are partly shadowed, others clearly lit, but all possess a look of expectation, dread and utter weariness. And not a few of them keep glancing at my bald scalp.

I wait for the coffees to be brought in.

"Is there a reason for this meeting?" asks Ari Jacobstein, not even looking at her coffee. She's been running the UK since Anna died, and I know that she has been watching everything that Cerbo has been doing closely. These Ankous know more about the business than I do. Having me as their boss may have provided them with some much needed humility, but I can't help feeling it would be better if I could just upgrade them all to Regional Managers. The Hungry Death inside me doesn't agree at all. It wouldn't.

I lean forward in my throne and nod. "There's a reason, Ms. Jacobstein," I say. "Everything suggests that whatever is going to happen will happen tomorrow, and that it will most likely occur here. Don't tell me you can't feel it. You all look like you've aged years in the past few days. You need to be ready to mobilize."

There's an intake of breath.

"The rumors are true then?" David, South Africa's Ankou, says.

"Yes. I never meant to keep this hidden, but then I never meant to be snatched away by the Death of the Water. And neither Cerbo nor Tim are big on sharing information. The Stirrer god is almost here."

Ari's lips tighten. "So we can't stop it?"

"No, I wanted to take the fight to it, but Cerbo has been unable to find a way to do that which didn't involve considerable casualties," I grimace. "And by considerable I mean a hundred per cent. Killing every Pomp to defeat this threat is not an option."

"You contemplated this?" asks David. He glances at Ari and rolls his eyes, she grins at him, and I don't know whether he thinks I should or I shouldn't have.

"I considered every suggestion brought to me," I say. What I don't say is how Cerbo had pushed for it. "Do you have any that you would like to offer, David?"

"I—"

"Very well, then. Now, while Cerbo's idea is not an option, mobilizing every single Pomp we can spare and getting them here, that can be done. I know you lot haven't been as busy as the Australian branch, and that Stirrer numbers have fallen away to almost nothing in your regions. I want you to be ready to use the various corridors of your respective Number Fours to feed Pomps into Brisbane. We're going to have to bulk up our numbers, a lot."

"We will consider your suggestion," David says. I almost reach over the desk grab him by his lapels and shake. Damn it, I almost drag out my knives and cut his throat. The intention must be pretty plain because he leans back slightly.

"You'll consider nothing," I say. "Other than the quickest way to get your Pomps here when we call. This isn't a suggestion."

"Then what is it?"

"It's a fucking command. I've sat around, conferred, chatted, and talked things through. I've been everything that's expected of me. But truth is, I'm growing impatient."

"Are you threatening us?" Ari says, and she looks rather like she hopes I am.

"Threatening doesn't even begin to describe what I am doing."

I lean forward in my chair. HD pulls the broadest, scariest smile across my face.

Tim raises his hand. "What Steve is trying to say is—"

"What I'm trying to say is quite simple. The fight begins and ends here. For whatever reason, the End of Days is going to be decided in Brisbane. And this is where we will fight it. And I need your help, but if you aren't willing to help me... I'm sure your subordinates are."

Ari actually smiles at me genuinely. At last, something they understand.

Good lord, I'd been going about it all the wrong way. My visits, my polite requests. All I'd done was confuse them. They'd just expected me to come out and tell them what to do!

"We fight, and we fight until we win. And we do it the old-fashioned way, with knives and blood."

I stand up and call the Knives of Negotiation from their dark sheaths. In a moment they have become the scythe. The Ankous cringe, but there's a touch of supplication there. They may not respect me all that much, but they're a fan of what the Death of the Water called the accoutrement. "Don't forget we have this weapon at our disposal. Don't forget what I contain within me." Madness. Death. Destruction. "We are not powerless, and we will not lose. Comet or no comet."

The scythe becomes the knives once more, hidden within my jacket. My eyes catch Lissa's. Her lips curve a little smilewise, and I know I've won my audience. They may not realize, but she's the one who really counts. Endlessly skeptical. Endlessly forgiving. I only hope I am as good. We're saint and sinner bound up in each other, not sure when we're which.

We'd sacrifice everything for the other. That has to count for something.

"Go home," I say. "Put your house in order. Hold your loved ones, though you will not be able to for long. Soon we are going to fight.

And some of us will fall. But we will win, because we have to. Because it isn't our time to lose."

"That went well, I think," I say once they've all gone.

"Really," Tim leans against the door to my office. "What about the speech I gave you?"

Oh, I'd forgotten about Tim's speech. "Sorry, mate. Just the adrenaline. Public speaking, you know how it is. They reckon more people dread public speaking than death. Well, with me, it's certainly true."

"Yeah, you did OK," Tim concedes. "They seemed to respond well. But did you have to pull out the damn scythe?"

Lissa snorts. "It's a bad habit he has."

"Shock," says Cerbo. "They were in shock. I know I am."

What? You were the one who wanted to sacrifice them all! "Why?" I demand.

"Because for the first time you sound like Suzanne. You sound like a leader."

I feel my face burn. I don't know if I'm pleased or insulted.

"I suppose I better put my house in order, too," Cerbo says and with a nod he shifts back to the States.

I send Tim off to be with his family. A new shift of Pomps come on, they're rowdy for ten minutes or so then quiet as they settle into work, and it's Lissa and me, alone in my office.

"So," I say. "What are we going to do with ourselves?"

"Let's go home, make some dinner. See what happens."

"Sounds like a good idea," I say. The day has been crazy hectic, but tonight doesn't have to be.

I pull her to me to shift us to our unit but Lissa shakes her head. "No, let's just walk. OK?"

And we do.

17

Lissa and I leave Number Four by the front door, hand in hand. Today may have been the busiest day of my life, but tomorrow could be the last. We stroll down George Street and into Alice Street, the Botanical Gardens to our right. The moon's yet to rise. Our shadows join, then part, join, then part, as we pass beneath the street lights. Even this late, a steady flow of traffic rumbles by heading towards the Expressway's on-ramp and the Captain Cook Bridge. A couple of drunks are doing something loud and stupid in the gardens and not seeing the cop walking toward them from the road. Ah, now that brings back memories.

You could almost believe that nothing has changed and that the end of the world isn't nigh.

Almost.

I stop at the doors to our building and take a deep breath.

"Isn't it something," I say, "coming home together."

Lissa slides her arm around my waist and squeezes. "Yeah, it is."

A car honks its horn at us or the drunks in the gardens, I don't know which, but the moment is broken. And I catch a glimpse of the comet and can't pretend the world isn't slouching towards something dark and deadly.

We go inside and take the lift up to our floor.

Dinner is simple, bread and cheese. Lissa drinks a couple of glasses of wine, I stick to the water. It's at once harder and easier than I had thought it would be. Is this the start of something new? I can't say, there's a bottle of rum under the bed in the spare room. There are another two in the kitchen. I could... but I don't.

I can't remember when we last just chatted like this. Maybe it was on the road heading up north through Central Queensland, she a dead girl, bound to me by an embarrassing ceremony involving masturbation and magic, and me fleeing for my life. How can we talk so easily when the end of the world is glowing in the sky? Maybe because it's a relief.

For the first time since I saw Lissa in the Wintergarden those many months ago, and Jim McKean's Stirrer-inhabited body started shooting at me, I don't feel afraid. I don't need to drink.

For a moment I think of the gift that the Death of the Water gave me—even if it's come at a cost.

Lissa kisses me. "I like you much better when you're sober."

What? Do my lips move when I'm thinking? "When am I not sober?"

Lissa laughs. "The question is, when have you been sober?"

"I resent the implication."

"I'm not implying anything, Steven. You've been drinking like there's no tomorrow for nearly five months."

"Maybe there isn't any tomorrow."

"I know that you don't really believe that."

I sit up. "You're right, I don't. There's going to be a tomorrow, and a tomorrow after that." I look out at the comet. "Even with that thing in the sky, I'm certain of the tomorrows."

"That's my boy," Lissa says.

Problem is, I'm not certain of our tomorrows being together.

"Maybe that's why the Death of the Water held me so long. He was letting me dry out. I'm the Orcus, nothing can really harm me, but all that drinking was starting to screw with my head."

"What, the Death of the Water as rehab? I prefer to think of it as a malicious sociopath."

"How did you put up with me?"

Lissa kisses me again, softly on the forehead. "Steve, I lost my parents two years ago. What followed after . . . I did some crazy things, self-destructive things. I dated Eric Tremaine for one."

"That explains it. I always wondered how you ended up with that jerk."

"Eric was a charming jerk, and older than me, but I knew he was trouble. I just wanted to hurt myself. I couldn't . . . I couldn't understand why I was alive and my parents weren't. I didn't believe I deserved it."

"What? Deserved all that pain, all that loss?"

"But I was still breathing, and they weren't. We see death every day, but we never really deal with it. You've been through so many changes, was it any wonder that you would have some teething problems?" Lissa says.

Teething problems is putting it mildly, and we both know it. Nearly destroying our relationship. Putting everyone in the business offside. Hardly teething, more like desperate failure. But here I was, still moving.

"They would have been much worse without you," she says. "And it's not just the loss you've experienced and the awful things you've gained. I know what you do every night. I know how you go out and hunt them, they're cunning and cruel the ones that you chase. Is it any wonder that you drink?"

"Why do you stay with me?"

"Because for all that, you're pretty fabulous, Mr. de Selby. I'm proud of you. You've done well, you've done better than well."

"We all have."

I open the balcony door. "You know, I always wanted to see a decent comet. When I was kid . . . do you remember Halley's Comet?"

"Yeah," Lissa says. "Totally disappointing. Nothing like this."

"See? There's an upside to everything." I put my hands on the balcony rail. Something catches my eye, down on the ground. It's a fraction of a glimpse, but I have a crow that gives me more.

A white figure below, wearing a bright orange wig, stumbles clumsily from the footpath into the building.

"A Stirrer's walked through the front," I say.

Lissa leans over the balcony, but it's too late to catch sight of it. "Really?" She sighs, crinkles her face with concentration. "Yeah, I can feel it."

The sensation is at once familiar and shocking, because we haven't felt it in a while. "It's unmasked," I say.

"Why would it be unmasked?"

"Maybe it wants us to know it's here." And we certainly do. Its presence builds. A sick bitterness in my throat. A dark anticipation that lifts the hairs on the back of my neck.

There's a knock on the door. Nothing ominous. Nothing threatening or sly. Just a quick rap of knuckles against enchanted wood.

I walk towards the door, but Lissa pushes past me.

"Before you open that there's something you need to know," I say.

"What?" Lissa demands. "It's a Stirrer, there's nothing I need to know."

"OK then."

Lissa flings back the door. "It's a clown! It's a fucking clown."

"Yeah, a clown."

"I hate clowns."

"I know." And she does. Lissa may be able to fight Stirrers without blinking, she's faced off some pretty terrifying shit, but give her a clown and she falls apart. It's what happens when you read Stephen King's *It* as a child. She's not all that fond of Tim Curry either.

"You prick!"

The Stirrer takes a step forward, hands stretched out before it, and winces as the collective power of all the brace symbols in the unit strikes it.

I've got to say, I'm impressed. Lissa, well, she's less so.

"I'm unarmed," the Stirrer says softly.

"You don't need to be," Lissa snaps. A Stirrer's presence is deadly enough. "Get the fuck out of here, before you kill my goldfish."

"I only want to talk." The Stirrer raises its hands.

"You trying to make my skin crawl?"

The Stirrer looks down at its painted palms. "I was trying not to draw attention to myself."

"Really," Lissa says. "When does dressing up as a clown not draw attention?"

"This body is quite . . . old. The paint, it hides the decay."

"Can you juggle?" I say.

The Stirrer frowns. "He could. He could juggle before he died. He lived alone. He died alone, no one found the body."

"You're telling me his soul's still out there?" I ask.

"No. No, I let it pass through me. A fair exchange. But such a sad death."

"A death which you are mocking dressed like a clown," Lissa says.

"No, he was good clown."

"There's no such thing as a good clown!" Lissa leans against the door, her knife out, pointed at its face.

"Please, before you try that," the Stirrer says, glancing at Lissa's dagger. "I want you to listen."

"What, another threat? Another ominous pronouncement? I'm tired of all that. I know what's coming," I say.

The Stirrer shakes its head vigorously. "I promise you that you won't get any of that from me."

"You've twenty seconds, and come inside," I say, ignoring Lissa's black stare. I chuck it a pen. The clown quickly draws the mask, and comes inside. "Twenty seconds," I say, looking at my watch.

The Stirrer takes a deep breath or the imitation of one. "I understand why you wouldn't trust us, Mr. de Selby. We've had our . . . problems. But I really would prefer it if you don't stall me immediately."

"Its words are poison," Lissa spits.

The Stirrer has gone to a considerable amount of trouble to prevent being stalled. The body it inhabits may have dressed as a clown, but it's also an excellent defense against stalling: the gloves, the layers of clothes, and the greasepaint itself.

"My name is Lon, and like some of my kind I have grown weary of this war. You would not believe how infrequently someone with my beliefs achieves a stir. The process is rigorously controlled. The last time you stalled one of my compatriots who tried talking to you we were extremely disheartened."

I can imagine that to be true. A Stirrer had waited for us in my parents' kitchen—not too wise a choice since Stirrers had killed my parents there. Not only that, but it had been the same Stirrer that had once inhabited Lissa's body while she was dead. Maybe we should have given it time to talk. But the wounds were too fresh, and we'd been distracted by Rillman's attempts on my life.

Lissa seems pleased at the Stirrer's words—the wounds may still be too fresh for this conversation to occur. She looks about ready to slide the knife down her palm. I'm signaling at her to stop, and it's hard for me to muster the will to do that. This hatred and mistrust is so ingrained.

HD flares up inside me, and I'm almost dragging a stony knife down my own palm.

Lon takes a step back, pulling its arms in closer to its stomach. "Yes, there is enmity between our races. But there need not be."

"Enmity," Lissa growls. "I'll give him bloody enmity."

"We are enemies as ancient as life itself," the Stirrer says hurriedly. "But even we, my people, my clan, if you will, think this is taking it too far. We have our city, and our excursions into your world. Is there any need for more? I am not here to threaten or to harm."

"Then why are you here?"

"Once you would have had human spies in our city, but the last of those was caught and killed months ago."

I nod my head.

"You have no one to tell you that our god can be defeated, but the window is a narrow one."

"How narrow?"

"It has marked the sky with its coming. And soon, it will also walk the earth and the Underworld as one of you to prepare the way. It is at that time that it will be weak, and can be stopped."

"And how do I stop it?"

Its gaze drops to the blades at my belt. "With the scythe."

"Where will this person appear? When?"

The Stirrer shakes its head. "I don't know that. Only that it will be in a place familiar to you. And that it is soon. You must be ready to strike, and strike hard, or the days of your world are at an end."

The Stirrer looks at Lissa. "You have my word that I did not kill this body. A blockage in his heart took him. Nothing more. I can do no more good in this world, send me home."

"Why are you doing this?" Lissa demands. "Really."

"To some of us our home is beautiful, and our home." Lon sounds almost snarky. "This desire to regain what was lost so long ago—it is an empty thing." The Stirrer stares at me. "You have seen our city, and our lands."

I think of the cold and the dark. The soft sounds of the roots of the One Tree, and the sky luminous and shifting. The way dust will dance if you know how to guide it, and the things that it shapes, the color that it reveals. "Yes there is beauty there."

"Christ," Lissa says. "We've got ourselves a Stirrer equivalent of an atheist."

Lon shakes its head. "No, our god is undeniably extant. The truth is I don't like being told what to do. This has nothing to do with belief. I believe that the start of days is upon us, but I would rather they were stalled." It shudders. Its red clown-lips flap. "Now, let me go home," it manages a truly horrible grin, "before I kill your goldfish."

Lissa cuts her hand, touches the Stirrer's face, and when he is gone she frowns.

"That's the first time that's ever happened."

"A Stirrer wanting to go home?"

"Yes, but no, not that exactly. It's the first time it hasn't hurt to send one there."

She shivers, and I pull her to me.

"Fucking clowns," she says.

I've my crows hunting Stirrers throughout the city, seeking out nests. They darken the sky with their scrutiny, streaking from the edges of the Sunshine Coast to the Gold Coast, the great suburban swathes that make up not only Brisbane but the whole of South East Queensland.

People love it here. They come in their thousands, two thousand every week. The population is swelling, and not just the human population, but those things that use the dead as hosts. I've hunted in the darkest alleyways of the Valley, and in the sprawling houses of Hamilton. They're everywhere. And without my ability to shift, and my eyes in the sky, I wouldn't be able to cope with the increase.

Imagine a net, dark and spreading across a city. Every strand is an eye carried on wings that beat and snatch against the air. Brisbane is a big city, broad, not the most populous in Australia, by any means, that title belongs to Sydney, but it is spread out, rolling up and down the hilly plains—the Mcmansions in the outer suburbs, the units closer in, a few pockets of older places hanging on grimly. And my net covers it all.

When Lissa sleeps, I go out and I stall what I can. There's not an evening when I'm not busy, scarcely an hour passes where a Stirrer isn't found and I'm forced to drop everything and drive it back to the Deepest Dark and the city of Devour.

And I've learnt to savor the job.

Here is something that I know how to do. I don't need to negotiate my way through the corporate minefield. I don't need to ring Ankous and get their opinions. My only focus is the hunt. It's like my old pomping days—which, come to think of it, aren't really all that old.

I sit in my living room and fiddle with my iPod. Slide through my backlist of Okkervil River, or Gotye—occasionally I even indulge in some Killswitch Engage. You need a soundtrack to your life, and there has always been one to mine.

I nurse a coffee in my lap, hands cupped around its heat, as the music plays. I spread my consciousness out through my Pomps, or draw their experiences into me. The things I see, and the things I've seen. Crap I'd never even suspected might go on, not even after years of pomping, of coming up hard against the end of people's lives. I've watched pomps and stalls from Antarctica (we have two Pomps there, both part-time) to the Arctic Circle. I've heard the same conversations bound in different cultural imperatives hundreds of thousands of times. I've seen all manner of excess and stupidity, all sorts of dignity and sadness. People killed for food, wealth, status and greed. People drowning in their own hungers. And I've encountered such grinding desperate poverty that it nearly steals the breath from me.

Once this god is dealt with there are other problems that need attending to.

Death is just and impartial. But life... Christ. Life is the cruellest of rigged lotteries.

I let myself doze a little, try and disengage from the world. I dream of black ink, an ocean of it covering the earth in darkness. And there I am swimming.

Hands grab me, and pull.

I wake up. My mouth tasting of ink, as though I'd grabbed a pen and bitten it in half—which I'd done once, back in primary school, to impress a girl (it didn't). I suck and spit out nearly half a tube of toothpaste to remove the worst of the taste: and still the memory of it lingers. No more sleep for me. I sit and watch my darling dream instead.

The twenty-fourth starts slowly. Like any other day, but it isn't. We can all feel it. My Ankous are ready to act the moment something happens. I'm getting nervous phone calls from them every half-hour or so.

When my crows alert me to a Stirrer in Mount Gravatt around midday, it's a blessed relief. Maybe it thought it could escape my scrutiny in the lunchtime rush. And perhaps it would have, if it hadn't passed a tree in which some of my Avians roost. I think the crow that saw it was almost as shocked as me.

I shift, and follow it quietly at a distance, but it must sense me because it stops and waits at a street corner. I get a little closer and it turns its head in my direction. Dark eyes stare.

The Garden City mall is to the left of us, but we're out on Logan Road, all traffic lights and trucks, cars and smoking buses shuffling for ascendancy. "Get any good bargains?" I say, above the rumble of a bus.

The Stirrer stops, swings its head all the way around toward me, bones cracking. It picks up speed, staring at me as it pushes the shopping cart away.

"You shouldn't be here," I say, shifting to its side, taking far too much pleasure from its terror.

The Stirrer bolts from me, but I shift in front of it, stopping the cart with a boot. And it stands there, realizing it has nowhere to go. It tosses the shopping cart towards me, but I have already shifted again, beside it, close enough that we could be sharing a secret. Perhaps we are.

"It doesn't matter," it mumbles. "None of this matters. Our world is coming back, soon enough we will no longer be hunted."

"Probably," I say, and slap it once on the cheek with my bloody palm. It shivers, then drops.

I look in the cart—aerials.

I look up into the beady eyes of my crow, rather than through them.

"Awcus," it mutters softly.

"There's hunting to do," I say.

18

It takes a long time to organize a raid. And the day, if it is the beginning of the end, has been alarmingly free of portends. Sure the sky is lit with the great glowing orb of the comet, but there has been no increase in stirs. In fact, we've had a decrease. As though the Stirrers themselves are holding off. I don't even want to think what that might mean.

My Ankous are waiting. We're all waiting. After the last day's sprinting, time seems to have slowed. Each hour of nothing is another knot of tension in my neck. The anxiety level in the office is insane.

The twenty-fourth is here and not a thing has changed in the world at large.

Several of the blokes in the office have imitated my new haircut. Even Lundwall is sporting a shaven skull.

"You've started a trend," Lissa tells me.

I rub my stubbly head. Maybe it's not too bad after all.

Things are going to happen soon and we can all feel it. I've found what I think is the last of the houses. Forty in all, that large a number at once fills me with rage and embarrassment. This is my city, how dare they? And this is my city, how did I let it happen? They ring the Brisbane area from in as close as Toowong, west to Darra, south to Rochedale and almost as far north as Noosa.

I've had people try and make sense of their location, maybe read some sort of pattern in it, but no, other than surrounding Brisbane there's no real sense to them. Certainly no logic that we can ascertain.

Lissa has assembled thirty-nine teams of three. Three's enough, I think, to deal with a house full of Stirrers. I'll be taking a place on my own. Lissa's leading a team into Ascot. Even Lundwall is in on the act, he'll be taking a team into a place in Bardon, not far from the cemetery.

Tim's staying at Number Four. Monitoring everything from there. Knives glint in the strip lighting, people are suited up, body armor beneath their jackets. This is as professional a raid as I've ever seen, and I can't help but think of Dad in his daggy and somewhat crushed sports jacket, hunting Stirrers back in the day.

He'd have laughed at what he would have seen as overkill. But things have changed in the last six months. Different generation. Different problems. Too bloody right.

I look at my watch, it's after one. The office is quiet but for our prep. Maybe we've got it wrong, or maybe all we ever needed to do was destroy a few Stirrer strongholds. Imagine if it's that easy.

If only I could believe it.

I've run through our strategy twice, but I can see that people are still working it through in their minds. The northern teams are already on their way. This last bunch are inner suburbs, they can be ready in less than half an hour.

"Any questions?" I say.

"No," Lundwall says. "We get in there, and we stall these things, seems pretty simple to me."

"Don't get too cocky," I say. "They'll be on the ceiling, maybe in the roof. Be careful."

Lissa pats my back. "It's OK. You're not the only one who's been hunting Stirrers these last few months. We'll deal."

"Watch out for traps, pit traps and dogs. And if anyone has trouble, call it in, and call me. I will shift there as fast as I can."

It should be quick in and quick out.

The moment I arrive I can feel it, I'm alert to the sensation. The rot at the edges, where the Stirrers' influence is strong enough to kill everything but the hardiest and hungriest of bacteria. The trees around the place are dead, one looks about ready to fall over in the next strong breeze. The lawn is a sere old thing slipping away to dust.

The house is a big brick-veneer building, built in the mid-eighties in a boom time. It's in the heart of the suburb of Sinnamon Park, on the western fringe of the city. The building has a huge glass frontage, with Doric pillars leading toward the front door. It projects despair, and not just because it lacks any architectural integrity. The place is a complete mess, but it would be worse if the Stirrers' presence hadn't killed off all the weeds and creeping vines.

I kick open the door and—

Ears ringing.

On my arse. Coughing.

The house a flaming wreck, bits of brick and glass are still raining down.

The dead tree is now on the other side of the road and it's burning.

For a moment, all I can think of is Molly Millions, my dog. And my house, the one that Morrigan blew up. I shake my head to stop the ringing. Doesn't work. All along the street, car alarms start their shrieking. I can barely see through the smoke. I shake my head.

I grab my phone with numb fingers, drop it, scrabble along the ground to pick it up. I try to call Tim. The line's busy.

Lissa!

I shift to her position, the building isn't a building anymore.

Then come the deaths.

They slam into me worse than any explosion.

But I can feel Lissa's heartbeat.

She's still alive!

Not here, out the back.

I race around the ruined building, and there she is, in the backyard. Up against the fence. Stunned. She blinks, wipes at her gritty face until I hiss at her to stop. Not to move. Everyone else is dead here.

"What happened?" she says, as I search her body desperately for injuries. She's all right.

"Gone, they're all gone. It was a trap."

"Can't be. Where's Clare? I sent her around the front, thought she'd be safer."

I shake my head. I just pomped her. Clare, and so many other young Pomps.

It's happening again!

"I'll get you out of here," I say, holding her to me. I shift.

Phones are ringing off the bloody hook at Number Four. And no one is answering them. At least ten Pomp souls have found themselves here, confused and babbling. People are crying as they send them to the Underworld. I've Lissa in my arms. I stride to the sick bay. The door opens, Dr. Brooker's not here.

"What the fuck happened?" Tim demands, running in after me.

"No time," I say, and lay Lissa down on the bed in the sick bay.

"Is she OK?"

"Call Dr. Brooker."

"And what about you?"

I don't answer, just shift from the office to the first building on my list. All the Pomps I'd sent there are dead. Souls milling on the fringes of the chaos. The house is a black flower of rubble and pipes gushing water. A secondary explosion goes off somewhere. I gather their souls into me and move on.

Each house is more of the same. And at each residence I pomp more souls, not everyone made it back to Number Four. It is the least I can do, and the most. The mortality rate is nearly total. A few survive. A few I pull from the rubble. Emergency services are already on their way.

Michael. Charlize and Owen. So many. So many of my best are dead.

Lundwall's spirit finds me, or I find him. He's in his best suit, looking as stiff and awkward as ever.

He blinks at me. "I'm sorry," he says, and it tears me up inside.

Why are the dead always so sorry? It's not his fault. He should be angry. He should be trying to take this out on me. But instead, I think he's about to cry. This was his first job out of the office. And he worked so hard.

I can barely meet his gaze, but I have to.

"You've nothing to be sorry about," I say.

"Yes, but I do, I heard the click as I opened the door. Maybe if I'd yelled—"

He did better than me.

"No, it was too late by then."

"I failed you."

"No, I failed you." I touch his soul. It slides through me like a razor, and I bear the pain silently.

Poor, poor Lundwall.

He's not the first, and he's not the last, but his pomp stays with me. It haunts me more than any death I've known since the Schism. How did I let this happen again?

I shift back to Number Four. Brooker and Tim are talking softly, my heart stops for a moment until I see Lissa walk from the sick bay, white hospital blanket around her shoulders. She looks OK, more shocked than anything.

I know I should go over to them. But I have just pomped so many of my best. People I sent to die. I can't face them, not Dr. Brooker, Tim or Lissa. Instead I walk to the lift and take it down. Hoping that no one has seen me. Not really caring if they have.

19

On the ground floor, I hesitate at the door, maybe the first time I've ever hesitated going out.

I'm the only one here, there's no one at the desk. Then I remember why. Bill Kemble who worked it was one of the Pomps that died this afternoon; no one's thought to replace him. Maybe I should just get back up there. But the thought fills me with a grim panic. I have to get out, just for a little while.

This is all my fault, how can it be anything but? I was the one that spoke to my Ankous yesterday about being responsible. Sure it had seemed sexy and powerful then, and it had made Lissa smile. But right now just the thought of those words makes me want to vomit.

I never expected this to happen, but surely some part of me must have known. I search my soul, and I can find no presentiment of my Pomps' deaths. If I could I'd take some comfort in the challenge this throws to the schedule, that it's not set in stone. But I can't see a joy in uncertainty, only more fear, and more pain.

Lissa's going to be OK, but that doesn't bring back the dead.

The lift doors closing behind me makes up my mind.

Wait too long and people are going to find me here whether I want them to or not. I lean against the front door, and stumble out onto George Street. I swear I can smell smoke. The air buzzes with the distant droning of sirens. News choppers are racing through the sky. Our raid has given everyone something to talk about. Every suburb is burning.

I push my way through the late afternoon press of crowds, my clothes torn and smelling of blood and fire—everyone gets out of my way. A cool wind, blown up from the river, pushes me down the street, and I let it take me.

HD's a smiling presence mocking me endlessly, pushing me deeper into shock rather than making me more resilient.

The closer I get to Queen Street Mall, the more people I encounter. Regular oblivious folk, all of whom—if the schedule is correct, if the feeling deep within me is right—will be dead far, far sooner than they expect.

The sky is gray and cold, obscuring the pale light of the comet, though every now and then a break in the clouds lets some of the luminosity through.

Dislocated. Hungry for distraction, I stare at these poor soon-to-be-dead things.

Typically for Brisbane, the instant the temperature drops a few degrees, everyone has their jackets out, and most of them are at least a decade old. They just don't get nearly enough wear to justify buying a new one every year (or even every decade). When winter comes, Brisbanites suddenly dress like it's the nineties.

The eerie blue light of the comet reflects off everything. I find it grimly appropriate that this thing from the Deepest Dark should paint the city in such an unearthly luminescence.

The clouds close again, the wind strengthens and suddenly rain falls. That soaking, cool, Brisbane autumn rain that has more than a bit of winter in it. Water crashes down, not raindrops but rainstrands. There's a thunderclap that must echo all the way out to Logan. I don't jump, I'd seen the lightning flash, but still it startles me. Dulls my senses, like storms always do.

A hand grabs me from behind. I'm spun around and into the face of a very angry Lissa. Damn storm, it had shielded her presence from me.

"Steve, just what the fuck are you doing?"

"I can't handle this anymore," I say. "I tried and I failed. I just killed 110 of my best Pomps. I killed them. I was responsible for that."

"Did you set the bombs? Did you invite the Stirrers into our world?"

"No, I—"

"No, you listen to me, Steve. I love you, but Christ you can be a whinging prick. They died because we are trying to save the world. They knew it was a risk, we all did.

"It's a tragedy. But you, staying out here, doing nothing, running away, what does that do to their memory?"

"I let them down."

"No," she slaps my face, hard. "You did your best. And you'll keep doing your best. Because you're all we have. Because you're my Steven de Selby, and through luck, mischance, whatever the fuck it is, right here and now the whole world needs you to keep it together. And if you don't, I'll kill you myself."

She kisses me hard, in the rain and the cold, in the middle of the Queen Street Mall. It's passionate and brief, because a familiar foulness has filled my mouth. It drives Lissa back, and has me gasping.

"Are you all right?"

I cough. Spit up something dark, it swirls away in the rain.

Ink.

"Something's wrong," I say, then cough up more.

A sparrow smashes to the ground at my feet. I crouch down to look at it. It isn't one of mine. Or maybe it was but it isn't anymore. Its beady eyes are filmed in darkness. It shakes its tiny body and ink splatters everywhere. I reach to touch it, and it skips away, beats its wings and claws its way back into the air.

It flies raggedly around my head, and then the sparrow lands jerkily at my feet again. Ink spills from its feathers like an infection. Another lands next to it. And another. I call my crows, but I can feel their hesitation. They like this about as much as I do. They want to be anywhere but here.

I cough more ink.

"Out of here, now," I say to Lissa. She doesn't move, just holds my hand.

The first sparrow looks at me through its filmy eyes. It coughs once, loudly, then after hopping in the direction of my feet, it springs up into the air straight at my head. I fling up my hands. I'm barely moving before it's pecked at the soft flesh between my forefinger and thumb.

The crows above me caw, but they don't come any closer.

Sparrows, it's always the fucking sparrows.

The first sparrow, the one that drew blood, flutters clumsily in the air a few feet from me. It gives out a peculiar little chirp, and the other birds lift into the air, fanning out around me.

I pull from Lissa's grip. "Run," I say, but she's already pulling out her knife, shaking her head.

"Mog," I whisper, and the blades slide like smoke from beneath my jacket, wind around each other, curl and extend until they are the scythe.

I lash out at a bird, but it's swifter than my strike. Its dark eyes mock me, as it flutters just out of my reach. Ink spatters the ground with every beat of its wings.

I swing at the sparrows streaming around me, and the blade does nothing to stop them. They swoop around my head, then one by one jab their little beaks into my flesh. When they have supped upon my blood, they crash into the first bloodthirsty little sparrow, hovering before me. There's a burst of wings, a muddy flash.

I throw an arm in front of my face. Reality shrieks, the air burns. A familiar smell of cologne.

I lower my arm. My knuckles bulge around the scythe.

The sparrows are gone, and he is there.

My skin grows tight around me. HD rages. *Kill him. Kill him.*

But I can't, I can hardly move. I see ghosts all the time, but not this one. Never this one. My fingers loosen their grip on the scythe. This isn't fair! This was dealt with. I dealt with it!

Morrigan stands in front of me, dressed immaculately in the suit he wore when last I saw him. His jaw marked with just a hint of stubble, eyes as steely as Clint Eastwood's Harry Callahan. All he's missing is the .44 Magnum, though he doesn't need it.

He straightens his tie, checks his cufflinks, as though he's going to a funeral. The rain doesn't touch him, even as I'm drenched to the bone, clothes hanging off me like a wet dog. And somehow, that releases me from my shock. Morrigan looking neat as a pin, looking like he experiences resurrection as a matter of course.

I tighten my grip on Mog and, again, prepare to swing. Happy fucking birthday, Morrigan.

A couple of shoppers look on as though they can't help themselves, umbrellas open, eyes wide. HD suggests we take them out first. I lower the scythe, my heart pounds in my ears.

Morrigan stretches, cracks his neck, most ungodlike but very Morrigan. "Thank you for your blood, I needed that, a drop or two of Death for a bit of life. I have to say, Steven, that you've done all right for yourself. I'm very impressed, honestly. Shame it's all got to end."

Something's not quite right about Morrigan. And it's not that he shouldn't be here at all.

It's him, but there's an insubstantial quality to him, for all his debonair stylings, as though he might fall apart in a moment. This I have to take as a good thing. There's a burst of lightning directly behind us. I can almost see the bones through his suit. The shoppers hurry on. But this is Queen Street Mall. There are always more shoppers.

Lightning diminishes my senses, I don't catch the movement but Morrigan is suddenly just out of reach of my scythe. I have to grab Lissa by the wrist to stop her stepping in front of me. She's got two knives now. But this requires more than knife work.

"I like your stick, Steven," Morrigan says. "Pity no one's taught you how to use it, but who would? Mr. D is far too incompetent, and that thing inside you, it knows nothing of finesse."

"You were dead, more than dead, nothing but a stinking memory, and if I could I would have had that removed. Your soul, if it ever existed in the first place, was destroyed."

"Death, souls, both are so intangible."

His voice takes on an avuncular tone, and I know I'm going to get a lecture. Now, maybe now it's time to attack, but he's just too far away.

"How do you catch the wind, Steven? How do you destroy someone who has made deals with things older than time?" Morrigan chuckles. "You, like all your family, have always been focused on the narrow little world that is Mortmax: the good death. The soul pomped. The Stirrer stalled. The stockholders happy. You were never about the big picture. It was always 'this is impossible,' or 'I can't do that'—never 'how can I achieve my objectives?' And yet, here you are, Lord Orcus." He dips his head in Lissa's direction. "Ms. Jones. I can honestly say what an absolute pleasure it is seeing both of you, and a couple too, I'm surprised. I can't say that I took you as the sort to stick around, my dear. I mean, you and Eric Tremaine? What a travesty!"

"Can't I cut him, please?" Lissa growls.

"No," I say. "He's too dangerous."

Morrigan waves a finger in my direction. "Dangerous doesn't even begin to describe what I am, Steven."

"You might sound like Morrigan, but you're not him."

"Oh, I'm very much Morrigan," he says, warmly. "When I discovered what was going to happen, what was going to come, that out of the Deepest Dark a god was rising and the End of Days was a *fait accomplis*, I chose my side. I had been having visions for years. Of an end that was definite. Not long after that the god started whispering, and I listened.

"Before my... epiphany, I won't deny that I was ambitious, but Ankou was enough for me. To be RM, it was a power tempered with such awful costs—I'd not wish it on my worst enemy, which would be... you, I guess."

He chuckles, there's a giddy quality to the laugh that almost completely belies his comments. Morrigan was anything but giddy.

I take a step towards him, and he takes a step back, light on his feet, almost dancing, keeping out of reach of my scythe.

"So you were never trying to become RM?"

"What part of me saying I'd not wish it on my worst enemy did you not understand? For this to work I had to not only die, but be obliterated. Sent to a non-space that only the Stirrer god could navigate."

"All your plans, all your efficiencies, they were just a scam?"

Morrigan scowls. "Not at all. I don't deny I would have made a fabulous RM. Mortmax would have run most smoothly. And it will, just in one glorious burst: the world's death. I'll achieve what the Orcus was working toward without the spread of eons. Everything must go, and I'll be the one to see it out." He lifts a hand and looks at it, as though seeing it for the first time. "Years ago, I made my deal. I never expected you to help me."

"And what happens then? What do you get out of it?"

"I get forever. I get worshippers. I get to remake the world in my image, and it will be a far better place for the absence of you and your ilk."

More crows arrive, raucous and itching for a fight. Morrigan tilts his head and gives me such a recriminating smile. "Really, Steven, how quickly you pick up bad habits. The Orcus and their silly little black birds!"

"And this is coming from someone who uses sparrows?"

"Believe me, they are neither silly nor little." Morrigan shakes his hands, two slender birds slip from his fingertips.

The inklings swell, in the blink of an eye they're twice their normal size and they keep growing. Fangs curve in wicked rows from their beaks. With every thrashing wing beat they expand, drawing mass from the night itself, or the light of the comet, doubling until they are larger than any crow.

They rise into the sky, growth slowing, and they're upon my birds, tearing them out of the air.

"Call off your crows, or I will let my pets devour every single one of them," Morrigan says.

The sparrows circle above us like great malevolent bats. Around them weave my crows warily, warily. Blood and feathers tumble down. There's a rage in the sky that is palpable. HD echoes with it inside of me, a wild and bitter reflection of my poor stymied Avians.

"Run," I whisper at Lissa.

"No," she says.

"Then stay behind me please." I need to end this quickly. I know what I am doing, I think.

A swift strike, and the bloodshed will be over. The god will be dead, and we can deal with the aftermath. I run at Morrigan, and he doesn't move. All the better to chop off his head.

I swing Mog at his neck. I've never been faster or more certain in my strike.

Morrigan drops, and catches the snath of the scythe neatly. I feel the shock of contact as it connects with his palm. He closes his fingers around the stony curve. I try and yank it free. It might as well be stuck in concrete.

Morrigan grins. "This is no bloody carnival and dance on the top of the One Tree. Nor is it a Negotiation with RMs looking hungrily on. This is you and me. Forces incarnate, and I am stronger."

Mog screams. I try and change it to the blades, to free it from his grasp that way, but Mog is immutable. I've no power over my scythe.

"I'll be having that, thank you," Morrigan says, and pulls Mog from my grip.

Mog moans, it struggles, but it can't work its way free.

I rush at him and he jabs the handle of the scythe dismissively into my chest. It is a single easy movement, but one all too persuasive. I tumble back and land hard on my rear, winded. I flick my head around, where's Lissa?

Then I see her, circling around behind us. Morrigan's seen her too.

"I wouldn't try that, Ms. Jones. Not if you want to keep your head. Unlike your boyfriend, I know how to use a scythe."

Lissa steps backwards, hurls her knife at his head. He casually bats it out of the air and tsks. Morrigan turns back to me, still on my arse trying to get air into my lungs.

"She never listens does she?"

"Leave her alone," I manage, barely a whisper.

"She's nothing to me," Morrigan says knocking another knife out of the air. "I've no time for this, and we've chatted enough. Far too much, in fact, but it gets that way when you've been dead a while, loosens the tongue."

There are more crows, certainly enough, now, to keep his two sparrows in check. A swift battle's being fought in the sky directly above, and they prove themselves far more capable than me. Crows collide, one after another, with an inkling. Clutching at wings, back and legs. The weight of their numbers brings the inkling down. It lands with a loud and very wet slap. Black ink stains the pavement.

Enough of my Avians get past the remaining bird to harry Morrigan. The rest bring the other inkling down. They're angry, mad at this monster that corrupted my sparrows. I've never seen them more focused in their rage. And it means nothing.

Morrigan cuts them out of the air, blood and feathers, sections of dead and dying birds crash into the earth. I can taste their deaths; feel their shocked entry to the Underworld. There's been too much of that today. I call them off.

"Wise decision, Steven. Live to fight another day, and all that. Pity there aren't any days left."

He swings the scythe in a circle before him. The air crackles, seems to peel away. And where the blade goes a flap of... reality opens. A ruddy light spills through, everything it touches glows faintly blue. The color of the dead.

"Bet you didn't know you could do that," Morrigan says.

My biceps burns. Wal pulls himself free. "Fuck me," he says. "Isn't that Morrigan?"

"Not now!" I drive him back onto my arm, as I get up. I sprint towards Morrigan, running to knock the legs out from under him, trying not to think of Mog's blade slashing into me. I don't even see the scythe's handle hit me again. I'm just back on my arse, Morrigan looking down at me with that disapproving gaze.

"Time, as they say, to unleash hell. But first, this." He draws a symbol in the air. A fiery circle that is at once the most circular circle I have ever seen and the least, as though it's angular as well as curved.

It hovers a moment by his hand, offending my eye with its off geometry, then with a flick of his wrist the circle is flung at me. The flame pulses through my being, like the roughest, most horrible of pomps. I scream, thrash on my back. Something inside me chortles. I've a vision of blood and fire. A terrible pressure builds deep in my skull.

Am I having a stroke? Could I be having a stroke? I clutch at my head.

See ya, a voice whispers, and it isn't Morrigan's.

The pressure goes. I open my eyes, in time to see Morrigan step through the hole he's made.

He's gone. But he's not the only one.

The crows are scattering, ignoring me.

And I can't feel them.

I can't feel anything, but what my regular senses tell me. The rain is cold as it strikes my face. I start to shiver. I look at my hands. Close my eyes. It's gone. All of it is gone. No, not quite. Something remains. A fragment. Small and wounded. But it isn't enough. I can't even pretend that.

An arm slides under mine.

"Steve, are you OK?" Lissa says as she helps me to my feet, and we both stare at that shimmering portal, it's already spreading, reaching slender but thickening fingers into the sky. The air stinks of fire. As though Hell and the living world can't handle the friction of their contact. I can hear the creaking of the One Tree, as raw and naked as if I were dead.

Morrigan has cut a doorway to Hell, and there's no way I know of to close it.

"It's gone," I say.

"Yeah, he's gone."

"Not Morrigan. Not just Morrigan. HD is gone. The Hungry Death is free of my body. We have to get to Number Four," I say pulling her towards me, and shifting.

Only I don't shift. I'm standing there, still on Queen Street Mall, in the rain. Of course I can't shift, I don't have that power anymore. I don't have any power; in fact I can hardly stand.

There's a sound coming from the portal: part electric buzz, part growl. Both Lissa and I turn towards it.

"I think we better run," I say.

And a Stirrer comes charging out of Hell.

PART TWO

THE WAVE

The wave—there is a movement there!

"The City in the Sea"—Edgar Allan Poe

20

The Stirrer stands there a moment, sniffing at the air like a dog seeking a new scent. Its head swings on its long neck, its eyes focus on us.

"So that's what they look like in the flesh," Lissa says. "Now I've another reason not to like them. Too many teeth for one thing."

The Stirrer isn't bound in human skin and bones. It's the real deal. Tall, long-limbed and sharp-toothed. Someone in the mall screams, and I remember at last that we are not alone, that this has played out in front of an audience, most of whom are suddenly deciding it's better to be anywhere but here.

The Stirrer makes a swift and predatory movement towards the screamer: a man backing slowly away, two bags of shopping held in front of him like a shield. The Stirrer smacks its toothy mouth, hunches down as though ready to spring.

So here it is, the end of the world, and it happened so easily. I can barely move. What can I do to stop it now? Does it even matter?

"Steven!" Lissa grabs my arm. "Get a fucking grip, OK." I look at her blankly.

Lissa sighs and steps in front of me, holding her knives loosely in both hands. "Hey you," she shouts. "Hey, dickhead."

Screamer and Stirrer both turn to face her.

The Stirrer bounds towards her, but Lissa's ready. Then again, she was born ready.

Her movements are fluid, and no less predatory than the Stirrer's.

She takes a step back, feet splashing in the rain, feints with her left knife then kicks her attacker in the stomach with all the persuasion a pair of Docs can provide.

The creature goes down.

She slices open her hand. Blood flows, and she punches out, catching the Stirrer in the mouth just as it's getting groggily to its feet. The Stirrer growls, shudders, falls dead to the ground.

"That's new," she says. "Easier than I thought. Blood still works."

"Yeah, if you can bleed, it can die," I manage.

"Good to know."

There's another Stirrer coming through, and another. Someone else screams, more shoppers who have just walked onto the scene. It's not the sort of thing you expect to see on exiting the Myer Center.

Lissa groans. "Screamers, I've never understood screamers. All it does is draw attention to yourself. You come across a monster, surely you keep quiet. Nothing else makes any sense!"

She turns to address the crowd. "All of you!" Lissa yells. "Get out of here! Now. Fuck it! Now!" She sheathes her knives and grabs my hand, keeping one hand blood-slicked and ready.

All down the mall, doors close, roller doors to shop fronts clattering down. People aren't stupid, even the screamers are running for it.

A Stirrer comes at us, it stumbles, straightens, and stands unsteadily on its feet, and Lissa punches it in the head. Another successful stall, but there are more, and we're still not moving, and that's my fault.

"We have to go." Lissa tugs on my hand. "They're still acclimatizing to our reality, or something, but I suspect they're going to get faster, and soon. We need to mobilize, and we don't want to be pinned down here. And you, you need to move. Right this instant, lover." I let her lead me.

We reach the edge of Queen Street and George, where the buildings obscure the mall, and I look back one last time at the beginning of our battle against the Stirrers on earth. I'd been so confident after my confrontation with Water. The way I'd handled that, finally facing my fear. And the love Lissa had shown in bringing me back had helped too. I thought I could take on anything.

And now this.

Three Stirrers. Four. Five. More keep coming through the portal, and it keeps growing. And I can't stop them. I've no HD inside me, I'm as powerless as any punter.

I didn't expect it to be easy. But this is something altogether different. How did we end up here? Total fucking Steve Fail.

Lissa drags me along, holding my hand. Already on the phone, I catch snippets of her conversation.

"Tim, we need everybody in the... Everybody. Stirrers in the mall, and they're the toothy variety. I know. I know. He's with me. He can't... Mobilize."

We make it to the front door of Number Four just as the first of my Pomps come through. They look to Lissa, and she doesn't disappoint them.

"The mall," Lissa says. "Don't do anything stupid until reinforcements arrive. They look scary, but they're not so tough. Cut shallow, move swift, these things won't know what hit them."

The Pomps nod, they barely spare me a glance. Am I that diminished? Lissa gives my hand a squeeze.

"Almost there," she says.

The door opens for us. I grip the handle to steady myself then yank back my palm in agony. The door's taken its price in blood. That's not supposed to happen. I'm meant to be able to enter this space without cost: I already pay enough. I'm the Orcus.

Except, I'm not anymore. Not in any way that counts. The mere sliver of power I can feel within me is just that and nothing more.

And everything that I had taken for granted is telling me so.

It's the slowest lift ride in history. But Lissa tidies me up a little. She positively fusses. "You don't want them seeing you like this in there. You're going to be OK," she says. "Deep breaths."

The lift stops. I do as she says. Breathe deep, and the door opens to anarchy.

Phones are ringing off the hook.

The moment we've dreaded has arrived. Alarms sound, some echoing down from Neti's rooms. People are walking around, handing out knives. Lissa seems to appreciate that.

Tim strides towards the door, jacket off, sweat rings under his armpits, he has blades buckled to his waist. It just doesn't look right. He looks about as comfortable as a cat dangling over a swimming pool.

"Shit," he says. "It's happening then."

Lissa steps in front of me, I can't see Tim's reaction. "Yes it is," she says.

I look at a Pomp cradling his stitches. "You're going to need to bleed today," I say. "We all are." The Pomp nods his head. I'm trying to remember his name, but I can't. "It's started."

I walk away from Lissa's talk, straight to the bathroom. I lock the door behind me, and I cry. Everything I needed to win this fight has been taken away. What the fuck kind of man am I?

Then it strikes me. I'm just a man now. That's all I am.

I wipe my eyes, take a deep breath. I suppose that it's going to have to do.

I've washed my face a little, and am ready to face the world, when there's a knock at the door.

"You in there?" Brooker asks.

"I'm here."

"Open the bloody door."

I'm shaking, teeth chattering uncontrollably. I don't want anyone to see me like this, but I can't stay here forever, I have to face up to what is going on. I get a good grip on the door, and push it open to Lissa and the doctor.

Dr. Brooker grabs my shoulders. "You're in shock, Steven. I'd have thought the Hungry Death would have shielded you from it. But obviously not."

"Maybe that explains it. Why I'm so weak."

"You've always been a bit weedy," Lissa says. "I was just about to knock that door down you know."

I grin up at her. "Would have liked to see you try."

She bears my weight, slides an arm around my shoulder.

"Get him to his throne," Dr. Brooker says.

Lissa carries me to the throne. I fall into it, and it's uncomfortable, as though the throne, like the door, doesn't recognize who I am. But there must be enough residual... something, because my dizziness fades away, a little, not a lot, and that could just be from the act of sitting, not the chair itself.

"How you doing?" Lissa asks softly.

"Not good," I say.

"You're going to be OK. There are forty Pomps heading towards Queen Street Mall. Half of Sydney and Melbourne's active staff are on their way and the Ankous are starting to arrive with their staff in real numbers now."

"What have I done?"

"Nothing, this isn't your fault."

"You saw Morrigan. You saw how easily he took the scythe from me. I've stumbled from one defeat to another today. And they're costing lives. How do I do this, Lissa? How do I lead this battle if I'm not Death anymore?"

"Well, for one, we don't know if it's permanent. Two, you did all right against Stirrers before you were Death. It's what you know as much as what you are. We're all here, we'll all follow you, and don't discount your advisors, I'd like to think we are pretty good in the field."

"HD's gone. I just didn't think I'd miss it so much. This is what I've yearned for. But I wanted to give it away, not have it taken from me."

"And, yes, the timing could be better," Lissa says.

"No one can know about this. I've lost my power, but the threat remains."

"If you don't have HD's power, just where is it? Where's the Hungry Death running free?"

Bugger! The thought hadn't even occurred to me. I close my eyes, and I can feel it. HD is out there. Not far away. I get flashes of its vision.

For a heartbeat, it's staring at the widening gash in reality on Queen Street Mall. Alarms are ringing, Pomps are already stalling the creatures.

The Hungry Death shifts away and I lose sight of the battle.

Sitting on the throne, I'm slowly waking. Slowly energizing to be honest, with Lissa here, I'm starting to feel much better.

In fact, everything is becoming all that much clearer now. Ridiculously clear, the sort of clarity that washes over you in an instant and is gone just as quickly. I need to act, while I have it.

There's a knock on the door, Tim.

"Sorry to interrupt," he says. Tim's looking oddly energized now too. As though, finally, with the end of the world happening he can just move with it. He looks from me to Lissa and back again. "The office is filling up, we're going to need some leadership, and maybe a certain scythe, and soon."

"That might be a problem," I say. "How do I put this..."

"He's lost his powers," Lissa says. "And the scythe."

"What!"

"Sh!" Lissa and I say simultaneously.

"This is something of a problem." Tim's face has paled; he grabs a chair and drops into it.

"Yeah," I say. "The Stirrer god is manifest, and something just as horrible has fled its bloody cage." I grin at them both manically. "But on the upside, I feel really good." And I do. I feel human again. Not Death at all, pretty much one hundred per cent de Selby. No heart beat, but my own. No World Pulse.

When am I ever likely to feel this way again?

I plant a loud kiss on Lissa's cheek, pull away and she lifts a hand to the spot, and blushes.

"So why the hell are we still Pomps, if you're not Orcus?" Tim asks.

"I guess it's because HD still exists, his power remains, it's just not in me." I look over at Lissa; push myself up from my chair. "But I'll get it back." I hope. "Get Cerbo here, we're going to need to organize some sort of war meeting."

"And the other Ankous?"

"Right now I don't care about them as much, and I think that if we have too many Ankous together in the room they might understand what it is that I am. Just Cerbo for now. Keep the rest with their crews."

He's here a few minutes later, dressed all in black, knives belted up both his thighs. I want to ask if this is his apocalypse get-up, or whether it's just his usual pomping gear, but I can't quite bring myself to. Like Tim, like Lissa, like everybody in Number Four, he doesn't look scared, just ready to roll.

I've spread out a map of the city, marking the position of Morrigan's portal on the edge of Queen Street Mall.

"We're going to need to mount some sort of defense," Cerbo says. "Try and contain them to the mall between Albert Street and George."

"Already on it," Lissa says, she's been constantly on the phone with our Pomps on Queen Street. There have been deaths, but the Stirrers haven't made any progress out of the mall.

"The Stirrers can be beaten, their presence here is tenuous at best."

"But it won't be when that comet hits. We have to make sure that never happens," Cerbo says.

"And how do we do that?"

"Like we've discussed, we have to kill the human form of the Stirrer god."

"That may be easier said than done. He has Mog."

Cerbo almost drops his coffee. Almost but not quite, he overcompensates for it by taking another sip before replying. His hands shake, though.

"There are things a man wants to hear and there are those he dreads. At least we have you on our side, and the Hungry Death."

I grin as broadly as I can.

"Of course. Absolutely." Lissa squeezes my hand. "What do you suggest we do?"

"Wage war on Hell itself," he says. "We arm up and lay siege to the city of Devour."

"You can't just march into the Underworld like that," Lissa says. "We'd need an army, siege craft, everything."

Cerbo nods his head in agreement. "We have all those things in you, Steve! Through the Hungry Death you rule Hell, all its resources are at your disposal, you can summon a hundred thousand crows, you can change the very nature of the air if you will it."

"Yes, of course I can. Let's take this to them, it's our best hope." Yes, if I still contained HD. But it's out there somewhere. "You, Lissa, and Tim mobilize the troops. Every Pomp we can bring here, and as swiftly as we can."

"And what of you?" Cerbo says.

"I have an old friend to see," I say. "Someone who we are going to need on our side if we're to win this fight."

"Who?"

"Trust me." Cerbo looks at me peculiarly.

Rule number one of Mortmax: never trust someone who says "Trust me."

I have to get out of there fast before he realizes.

I walk out of my office and straight into Ari. Britain's Ankou grins, and I match it, trying for as ballsy a smile as possible.

She grabs my arm and squeezes. For the first time she seems almost happy to see me. Nothing Pomps like more than a crisis.

"I know Tim said to wait, but fuck it, we're here to fight, and I don't really care what you think about that, young man."

"Well, I think it's a great idea. We need you."

With her are thirty Pomps, all veterans of the trade. Finally, some experienced workers to backup my Pomps. They're all armed. Brace paint marks their wrists. Bottles of the stuff are strapped to their belts. All bear the cicatrices of our trade on their palms. Stirrers may have been focusing their attentions on Australia, but all of these Pomps have stalled more than their fair share over the years.

"Tim's apprised me of the situation," Ari says. She turns to the Pomps behind her. "These are my best."

They give a rather sarcastic cheer. "Fucking oath, mate," one of them says.

"I think you're going to need someone that knows what they are doing down at Queen Street," Ari says.

No arguments there. Ari's knife is belted to her waist, she's more than capable of taking on Stirrers. "So, if you don't mind, Mr. de Selby. Please let me at these monsters."

"Absolutely," I say, though her Pomps are already heading for the stairwell, no point in waiting for the lift, or for the say-so of the Orcus, obviously.

"Don't mind them, they're just enthusiastic. Oh and if you could send that fabulous girlfriend of yours along too, there'll be no complaints."

Of course not. In the last few months Lissa's racked up more stalls than any living Pomp, other than me.

"Get to it, and try not to leave any for us. I'm rather tired of stalling Stirrers."

"Familiarity breeds contempt." Ari grins. "Be seeing you." She races after her Pomps. If anyone can keep Queen Street Mall contained it's her.

I head towards the fire escape, not sure where the hell it is I am going once I get out onto the street, and relieved that no one has decided to ask me why I am not shifting.

Lissa catches me up before I reach the stairs.

"You can't go after it alone," she says. "You're weaker than any of us now. Sorry, but it's true."

I smile. "It's OK. I have to do this alone, and you're better off being here. People need you, as much if not more than I do, right now. HD will face me, I'm sure of it. Without him inside me, I'm seeing everything so clearly now."

"Then don't. Don't go after it."

"I have to. You know I have to. I don't do this, then the whole world goes somewhere worse than Hell. I wish I could have you watching my back, but I need you here. I need you helping Tim and Cerbo." I kiss her hard. "We've overcome some terrible stuff together. I know we'll succeed."

Lissa grabs my wrist. Pulls something from her pocket. Brace paint. She quickly traces my wrist with the triangular brace symbol. Despite staring at the Brits with their brace paint bottles it had completely gone out of my head.

"What would I do without you?" I ask, sliding what's left of the paint into my pocket.

"I often wonder about that." Lissa steps back to check out her work. "Should give you a little protection from Stirrers at least."

"Thank you."

"Steven," she says as I push the fire-escape door open.

"What?" I say, sounding more abrupt than I mean

"I do love you, you know."

"Yeah, I know." I flash her a wicked smile. Lissa's lips thin. I push through the door and let it slam behind me.

I sprint down the stairs to the ground floor, enjoying the lack of HD in my skull.

It's magnificent and freeing all at once. I've never felt so clear headed. I push the front doors open and walk out onto the street. Sirens are sounding. Traffic is backed up along George Street. The air is chilled with the presence of the hole into Hell. I don't know what I'm going to do. Or how I am going to do it.

Then I feel HD, almost as intensely as I did on the throne.

It's time I faced my other half. Even if all it wants to do is kill me, it's the only hope I have. The only hope any of us have.

21

Walking down George Street, HD is an absence and a calling, my magnetic North. It's everywhere, shifting around the city.

I'm given impressions of a confusion of suburbs. Toowong one moment, Eight Mile Plains the next, then New Farm, West End and Kangaroo Point. But never further than a few kilometers from the city, and always, briefly, between each shift, somewhere nearby. Its movements don't make any sense to me. But I know I will find it, if I just keep walking. I know that it will come back to me, because it has to.

I pass Queen Street Mall. Barriers are being quickly erected, and Pomps stall whatever comes through. So far I can see no casualties. The cops stationed there are in full riot gear, brace symbols painted over their vests.

I'm not used to seeing this. They hold their weapons with a casual seriousness, I've no doubt they're good at what they do. But it alarms me to see rifles in Queen Street Mall. It isn't the eighties anymore. I feel like we've stepped back in time. Alex is talking to one of the men. They're both staring at the crack between the worlds, and I've no time to chat so I leave them be.

Ari's got her crew fanning through my ranks. They nod at me, as I walk by. Ari gives me an odd look, but I don't linger. I know I should be leading this, but I can't. Doesn't mean I don't feel guilty about it.

I leave her with my Pomps, and run straight into another bunch of my recruits walking with a couple of cops. Danni and Max, two of my newest Pomps. They're usually stuck behind the desk, helping interpret the schedule. I can see why they've been given George Street to patrol: they're not ready to face Stirrers one-on-one.

They're happy, and a bit nervous to see me. I slow but I don't stop. If I stay with them too long they'll notice—though I'm not sure they'll understand that they're sensing my lack.

Danni nods over at the cops. "We'll keep these guys safe," she says.

"I know you will." I pat her on the back as I pass. "Good to see you both in the field."

She frowns. *God, can she tell what I am, or what I'm not?*

I gesture down the street. "I'm chasing something. But I will be back."

"Good luck," Danni calls.

I wish I could get to know them all better, these people who are going to die for me and this world. Jesus, I don't know even a tenth of their names. It fills me with a bitter fury and a sadness that could stop me from moving at all if I let it. But I don't.

I refuse to.

These people are counting on me.

I keep heading down George Street. Pushing my way through the barricades, and more cops and Pomps. Hoping that no one will ask why I'm not just shifting. The sky above is lit with the blue light of the comet; the portal in reality is similarly colored and slowly rising in the sky, and heading south and east. But none of that concerns me now. All I can focus on is the slight fluttering sensation directing me toward my quarry.

The presence of the Stirrers beyond is a crushing one to me now I have none of HD's power in me. I can feel the brace symbol that Lissa painted on my wrist growing warm. It's being pushed to its limits.

I pass a drunk sobbing in the gutter. His stench wafts over me: stale beer and fresh vomit. I can understand the inclination to drink, but the Death of the Water has drawn the desire from me like a poison, and I'm not that anxious to let it back into my life. Two cops, faces bored and concerned at once, hover—watching him, watching the traffic. The poor bastard's producing the full-body sort of sobs that only a serious bender can coax out of most men.

I feel like he's crying for me: crying for this world where death is king, and it's a mad king at that. I crouch down, wincing at the smell of him. Is this what I'm like? Is this me? I pull the brace paint from my pocket, carefully mark his wrist with the triangle and the line.

"You're right, mate," I whisper. "You're right." He looks at the symbol, then up at me. "Leave that on your arm and you'll be OK."

I drag him to a bench and sit him down. He settles there wearily, the sobs have passed. "It's so alone," he whispers and falls asleep.

If the world doesn't end tomorrow, he's going to wish it had.

Where do you find Death?

This I can tell you. You search bus stations, train stations, taxi ranks. Places in the nowhere between somewhere, where minutes count down. Boredom and despair are closely aligned, and they live at these stations of waiting, where you think you're only waiting to go somewhere, but you're really waiting to die.

It's the waiting that kills you. Here as much as any emergency ward, or hospital bed. Few people go out in a blaze of glory. Most just wait to die. Maybe that's all we're ever doing.

My phone rings several times, but I ignore it. I need to concentrate on HD. And that's hard enough with the portal in the earth-Hell interface and all those Stirrers running so much interference.

But the thin thread of connection between HD and me never wavers. We've shared intimacies so deep that in many ways I'm still HD in part and it is still me.

I check Roma Street Station. Nothing. I search the bus stops beneath King George Square, feet aching, missing my ability to shift, but hurrying fast, despite the blisters building against the backs of my heels. Everywhere people are trying to get out of the city, catching taxis, trains, the few buses left.

And all of them wear that dazed expression that too much exposure to Stirrers engenders. If the commute home wasn't habitual, if my Pomps weren't helping enforce the evacuation: a lot of them would be staying put.

And there will still be those who do.

I can imagine people, unbraced, falling asleep in offices and never waking again; though their body will walk, their minds will plan, their hands will search out weapons.

Stirrers drain will as much as life. They've a gravity that's hard to escape and I know that more intimately now than I ever really wanted to. The brace symbol keeps getting hotter, but it's still bearing the bulk of the load.

Anyone I pass I brace, until I've no more paint.

It's easy work, people hardly seem to notice. The last person I paint, a woman on the corner of Turbot and George whispers in my ear, "It's so alone, that I could cry."

Then the brace kicks in and she blinks, shakes her head and quickly walks away.

I keep down George Street, where it becomes Roma Street, the blocky building of the Transit Center not far away. I pass the spot where I last saw my parents on this earth, and where their spirits fled after telling me they loved me and that it was all going to be all right, even if they didn't believe it.

It still hurts me a little. I'd been so alone, and I would have been dead too, if it wasn't for Lissa. She'd pulled me past that and kept me alive. Though, as I'd found out, all of that was part of Morrigan's plan. It didn't matter, without Lissa I think I would have given up. I would never have had the strength to go on.

The flashes of HD continue, moments of clarity, jumbled between headache-inducing shifts. Everywhere it goes it sets the Avians flying—spiralling above it as though it's the choicest carrion. They sing, calling to it with throat-tearing longing. HD unleashed suits their predatory tendencies. They adore its messiness far more than mine, and I can't say that I don't feel a little hurt by that. But I don't let it stop me.

I catch a glimpse of Teneriffe, the water serene, but that's not where HD's attention is focused. The 470 bus rumbles past on its way to the CityCat. Somewhere in the shadows, HD crouches. It's not right. There's a hesitation that undercuts what should be typical predatory behavior. A red SUV pulls in beside it, throbbing with music, and HD shifts as though startled by the sound. Why isn't HD letting rip, now it has its chance? I was expecting wholesale slaughter, not this timidity.

It slides beneath the metal seats at the Springwood bus station. This is as far south as it has moved. I hope this isn't a trend, an expansion of its territory. I've no chance of following it there in time.

The 555 bus disgorges its passengers. Here is the usual gaggle of tired workers and kids back from the Hyperdome. It may be the start of the end of the world, but word doesn't spread that quickly, and even with the comet in the sky, folk get on with their lives.

I feel HD tense, then he's gone.

The bus stop outside Royal Brisbane Hospital. People waiting, caged in grief or weariness so deep that they don't even see the chasm in the sky.

A small stop behind the CityCat terminal at West End, here the shadows are deep, delineated by hard sulphurous lights. A drunk stumbles towards the toilets, but HD doesn't follow.

What the fuck is going on?

I stop and think.

When it dawns on me I can't help but smile.

"You're mine," I whisper. "I'm onto you."

That gets its attention.

The Hungry Death's shifting slows.

The point around which it is moving is coming into focus. For a moment, HD is nearby, then it's at the Cultural Center Bus Station. Then a small park near the Kurilpa Bridge. It stops there. And I know that HD is waiting for me. I'm still on George Street. And I run. How many times have I run down this street? How many times have I fled my doom? Now I'm racing toward it. The running's hard work, I'm not the immortal creature I was a few hours ago.

I run hard, even as a stitch tears across my stomach. Not as fit as I used to be. I reach the bridge and the edge of the river and I stop, and not just to catch my breath. I should be able to feel the water below, its connection to the Styx and the Underworld, but I can't. It's nothing but a bridge to me.

I glance back towards the heart of the city. Alarm bells ring out from a hundred different buildings. And for a moment, I feel that they're ringing for me. I can't run anymore, but I'm nearly there.

I step onto the bridge reflecting how just a few months ago my colleagues all sacrificed themselves here to give me HD undiluted. How would Suzanne feel about that? Here I am just a man again. There are a few people with me, staring back at the city. They don't acknowledge me as I pass. That's how unremarkable I have become. A man gasps, perhaps . . . no, he is pointing in the direction of Mount Coot-tha. This is not good. Old One Tree Hill is slickly luminous.

And, while I may not be able to feel it I can see it, just as any regular punter can, though they won't understand its significance. The branches of the One Tree are beginning to reveal themselves.

Stitch or no stitch. I run. Fast as I can.

Halfway over the bridge a force tugs at my back. I spin on my heel, lashing out with my hands. Something snags on my little finger. I yank my arm back, and my finger breaks.

There's a deep-throated chuckle, low and menacing. And I begin to wonder just what it was I was hoping to achieve. My head is throbbing with the presence of HD.

For a moment there's a breath against my neck.

"I don't have time for these games," I gasp, the breath is icy, my skin crawls.

"Games are everything," it whispers, and I'm shocked, I've never heard HD outside of my skull. Just like the vision of the One Tree, it's a moment that has me reeling. I have to concentrate not to bow down before this force. But I do not, even though I know how powerful it is.

"Look what's happening," I say.

"I don't need to look. It is everywhere. The earth is full of death. And more is coming."

"But it isn't yours."

"What of it?"

"Aren't you the Death of this world?"

"I have always been," it mumbles.

"Not for much longer. What have you done in the last hour?"

"I've—"

I know exactly what it has done. Nothing at all. "Your chaos is the merest trifle to what the Stirrer god is capable of. Morrigan let you free, and you couldn't be fast enough to escape me. But now, look at you, so bloody pathetic."

A wind blows in from across the river. It's almost as cold as HD's breath, and I feel it now, for all my running. The wind lifts papers, plastic bags and dust. It makes the whole mess dance, and in the middle of it all HD stands—not a hint of rhythm about it. It's humanoid, hunched over. I can't make out a face. Just the shadow. This is the Hungry Death—formless and, well, hungry.

"I'll claw the flesh from your bones," HD spits. "I'll chew and grind and crush–"

"You're nothing without me," I say. "A Death brought so low that it is little more than a minor irritant. Do you think Water would laugh? Me, I don't know whether to laugh or cry."

"You need me," HD says.

"Perhaps," I reply. "But you need me even more. How can you be Death when all you are is detritus?"

It shifts.

But not far. I can feel it, in the park beyond the bridge. The Gallery of Modern Art, just behind it. The gallery's great square structure rising like some temple to a god of sharp angles, iron and glass.

The lights on the bridge flicker. Bringing us in and out of shadow. But I don't need vision. HD's presence is so loud in my head, so magnetic, that I can't help but be drawn to it.

HD slouches there in the middle of the park. Standing still, crows circling above it. This time I don't run. I don't need to.

Death waits for me, and it won't need to wait for long.

22

The lights that border the park are strobing in time with the throbbing of my broken finger.

HD has moved again. Further into the shadows, I can feel its gaze upon me. I get intense and thankfully brief flashes of myself from his perspective. I know that I am either going to win this monster back, or it's going to kill me.

"I'm here," I say.

HD shifts around me. First to my left, then to my right. Shadow things dart down from the sky. There's a detonation of darkness, a shifting night-bound form rises before me.

I am looking into my own eyes. A shade, a mirror thing.

Crows line his limbs, they cover his body like a cloak. They caw and they click and they groan. I stare into hundreds of beady eyes. It's impressive, this living cloak of Avians, but also remarkably empty. Is this all HD is capable of?

"You need me," I say.

The crows lift from its limbs. "No I don't."

"Yes you do. Without my form you're just a concept. You're too used to operating through others, generation after generation, we've bound you. And now," I grin, "now you can't handle being free. Look at you here, you desired this with all your heart. You tried your hardest to break free and, when it is finally given to you, you're cowering in the dark. You're the Hungry Death. You're the nightmare, and yet you hide."

Crows strike me, drawing blood, but I keep going. HD and I are wrapped too tightly around each other, it can't hurt me as much as it would like. A bird strikes my eye. Something bursts, my vision darkens. But I don't need sight. All I require is will. "You need me."

I keep moving. Fluid runs down my face.

Fingers grab at me, and suddenly I'm being lifted into the air. I struggle in that grip, but can't get free. The Hungry Death walks to the riverside and throws me in. Cold water closes above my head. I splutter, break the surface, and gasp for breath. I'm bleeding all over, I can only see out of one eye, at least a couple of my fingers are broken. My lungs burn in my chest. My clothes grow heavy, pulling me down. I struggle out of my jacket and swim to the shore.

HD hasn't moved.

"Is that all you've got?" I snarl as I drag myself from the water.

He grabs me again, throws me back into the river.

I'm slower coming out this time, shivering and cold, but I still manage it.

"I'm going to keep coming," I say. "I'm going to keep coming because I need you. I need you to stop Morrigan. And you need me. The world is ending, but it's not your end. People are dying, but it's not your death. You need me because your enemy is burning in the sky, and without me you are nothing but dust and shadows and bird shit."

HD strikes out at my face, I duck beneath it, then spring up fists clenched and hit back hard as I can. It's not ready for it. Its nose crunches beneath my knuckles. I'm shivering and frail, but I've just broken HD's nose. The smile I'm grinning isn't Death's rictus. It's mine, fuck it. It's mine.

"You need me," I growl, and punch HD in the face again, hard enough that its neck snaps back. "You fucking need me."

HD tries to grab me, to hold me. But I punch it hard in the stomach, dancing out of its reach.

Crows swarm around us, like a cloud of gigantic mosquitoes.

I can sense their hesitancy, their unwillingness to come down in support of either side now I've shown that I'm prepared to fight, that I'm not done with yet. But this hesitation is only going to last so long.

HD kicks out with its long legs. It's a movement almost too fast to see, but I manage to evade its clawed foot. With the punches that follow I'm not so lucky, but I've realized that it doesn't matter. HD's blows rain down on me, but they do not hurt. Not much. Not as they should when Death is arrayed against you. I swing out again, and knock the Hungry Death under its chin. It's like punching a child. HD falls flat on his arse.

It weeps, the huge gasping tears of a drunk.

"Ape. Ape. You stupid fucking clever apes. I was DEATH! I devoured. But then you devoured me, your thirteen. So reckless, so mad. I was meant to devour. I am meant to devour!"

The sight shocks me. I step back a little. The crows circle us, a great dark mass blocking out the comet, and obscuring the city.

"You need me."

"All right. All right. I need you. I am you. AND I HATE IT! Inside you I am all potential power even if it is constantly checked. Here... here, I am nothing." He scrambles back against the low retaining wall. Garden plants behind him. "The sky's too big. How did it get so big?"

I reach out. "Give me your hand."

He does, without hesitation, holding mine with a desperation that I didn't quite expect.

The air shimmers. I feel his presence enter me, the merest nail point of pressure. Then another. And another. A thousand tiny slivers, a million, and more. He slides roughly into every cell of me. HD doesn't make it easy, but perhaps there is no other way.

Then those tiny slivers burst. The sensation's worse than the roughest of pomps. Imagine every cell of your body being sliced open by the edge of a sheet of paper: slow and long. Last time this process occurred in increments and even then it brought down a plane. This time it's all at once and it's horrible.

The lights that line the park flare then shatter. Glass tumbles — a brittle fractured rain. I fall to my knees and howl.

The cry that tears from my throat, raw and loud, stills the earth. It echoes back at me down from One Tree Hill, from the sky and the ground. It runs through my body like the memory of thunder. I gasp, one last weary gasp.

All is still. I can breathe again.

When I look up, I can see with both eyes. I'm whole once more — how did it ever come about that I required the madness of HD inside me to be whole? Crows cover the park around me, and there's something unapologetically regal in their bearing.

"Awcus. Awcus," they say.

I spit blood onto the grass, it sizzles there, as thought it were alive. "We've a war to fight," I say. They lift into the air, a storm of wings and caws.

And I hear it. That familiar rhythm, the one that nearly drove me mad, but is now so welcome because it means we still have a chance.

The World Pulse beats in my ears. I'm Death again.

And people are dying nearby.

Pomps, my people.

23

I shift into Queen Street Mall. Screams and shouts, gunfire and smoke, and all of it lit with the cold blue light of Hell and the comet.

The battle isn't going well. Stirrers have taken control of Queen Street Mall, from the portal all the way up to the edge of George Street. Lissa's at the front, her bloody hands closing around a Stirrer's throat. I kick its legs out from behind.

"Their heads," Lissa says. "Touch alone doesn't do it anymore, you have to mark their heads it's the only thing that works. It's a bitch of a job though!"

Someone sighs, soft and sad, nearby. I turn my head. Catch a glimpse of one of my Pomps—Gale, North Sydney—having her throat torn out.

Lissa slaps her palm against the Stirrer's head and it drops to the ground, just as Gale rises clumsily, a Stirrer now. Lissa's ready. She brushes Gale's brow and stalls her too.

I shift to her side—already people have come between us—and without a word, Lissa passes me a knife from her belt. I slide it fast across my hand. And I fight as I've never fought before. I shift and strike at the nearest Stirrer, then shift on to the next. I'm stalling them as swiftly as I can, and each stall is horrible and hard. But my appearance has made a difference. The tide of the battle turns.

I lift my hands, and a hundred crows sweep over my shoulder and into the melee. I follow, bloody fists swinging. The Stirrers fall back.

I can hear Ari yelling in the distance, her Welsh accent booming across the mall.

We fight and time passes in blood spilt and Stirrers stalled. I can't tell how long, except that it feels both endless and over all at once, until there are no Stirrers left, just the remnants, their corpses bubbling. My Pomps let out a ragged cheer.

Lissa hugs me. "We could have done with that sooner," she says.

"I came as fast as I could."

"HD?"

"We've come to an agreement. Whatever Morrigan did won't happen again."

"So, you're stuck with him?"

"Yeah, and I can deal. What happened here?"

"About half an hour after you left there was a rush of them through the portal." Lissa sighs. "We weren't ready for their numbers. Didn't help that our dead ended up . . . you know."

"Yeah, fighting for the other side."

"Steve, it was horrible, I never thought I would have to do that again."

It always is when it's a friend. I kiss her gently.

"And it's only going to get worse," she says.

About a hundred Pomps stand by the rift in Queen Street Mall. Alex is there too. The whole mall has been cordoned off. Brace symbols glowing and marking every exit point. There are camera crews everywhere. A rift in reality is somewhat newsworthy, and rather hard to cover up. Though I've heard it's playing havoc with their electrical equipment.

"Where did all the cops come from?" I ask.

"We've a response unit for this sort of thing," Alex says.

"So you're telling me you've had systems in place for this?"

Alex grins. "We've always had emergency response protocols—call 'em ERPS."

"And I didn't know about this because..."

Alex clears his throat. "Because we were a little worried that the emergency might be you."

"Fair enough."

"So... Morrigan's back," Alex says.

"Yeah, I'm sorry."

"Not your fault, Steve. Besides, it means I get a chance to kill him." He slaps a round into the magazine of his gun.

"Get me everyone you can, Alex. I need to make as many Pomps as possible."

"Yeah, there'll be no shortage of volunteers. Morrigan's little Schism, and the whole Rillman-Solstice thing. People are itching to strike back at that."

"Tell them it's bigger than that, tell them they're fighting for the world."

"I'll get as many here as I can."

An hour later I've doubled the number of Pomps on the ground and the Stirrers have stopped their assault on the breach. I peer through the portal, there's nothing but the Underworld, not a Stirrer in sight, not even a soul. I'd feared that the dead might flood the living world, I guess they're too busy escaping it.

Even more news cameras are among us now, it seems ridiculous that I have to waste a good twenty people to keep them back, and shielded with brace symbols. The triangle and the line are getting a good workout today.

"We were never going to keep this one quiet. It's all over Twitter—#Queenstmaul," Alex says.

"Do you really think you kept the Regional Apocalypse quiet?"

He smiles. "At least we could pretend about that one. This, well, this is pure spectacle!"

I look at that glowing deadly portal stretching up into the sky, reaching towards the comet, I wonder what will happen if they meet. "It is, isn't it?"

Standing here, I can feel Mog somewhere beyond the portal. HD stirs within me, Morrigan can't be too far away in the Underworld.

Cerbo taps me on the shoulder, he's quite pale, sickly even, and I guess it has nothing to do with the splashes of blood across his face. "When were you going to tell me?"

"If it became necessary."

"Losing control of the Hungry Death, that wasn't high on your list of things to inform me?"

"Look, it's back where it belongs. HD is under control." It grumbles a little inside me, but nothing more, and for that I'm extremely grateful.

Cerbo sniffs. "HD, indeed...we've contained the rift, for now, nothing can come out. The braces are holding, even if they cost us a lot of blood."

"But..."

"It still doesn't help us in the long term. If the incarnation isn't destroyed that comet will plow into the earth, and life, death, everything as we know it will come to an end. You're going to need to go in there. We can't waste any more time. We're going to need to bring the fight to the Stirrers."

24

We've around two thousand Pomps gathered around us. Women and men armed with their knives and a determination to stall Stirrers. Not nearly enough, even though packed into the end of Queen Street Mall, with Brisbane Square lit behind us, it seems like a lot.

There's a hum of chatter in the air. Even a little laughter.

"This is it," I say. "We need to take this to the Underworld."

Ari nods her head, and the other Ankous follow her lead. I've never seen such unity in my crew.

Tim grimaces at me. "We can be ready to move in whenever you are," he says.

"No, let the numbers build a little more. Are Sally and the kids safe?" I ask.

"Is anyone really safe now?" He points back down George Street. "They're at Number Four, they're guarded. Not that Sal needs protection. You ever seen that woman handle a sawn-off shotgun?"

"Really?"

Tim slips out his phone, taps open a photo. The camera's looking down the barrel of a shotgun, and Sally's at the other end. There's a grin on her face that I'd find scary if I didn't know her so well.

"Took it half an hour ago," Tim says with some pride. "The ammos infused with my blood. Mightn't kill a Stirrer, but it does the next best thing."

"I have a better idea," I say.

"What?"

"Trust me."

Tim shakes his head frantically. "No... I mean, do you think that's wise?"

"Pomping was a family business, and Sally's family."

"I don't think she'll go for it."

"If she doesn't, she doesn't, but I think that's up to her."

I focus on Sally's heartbeat, picking it out of the vast stream of the World Pulse. It's recognizable, and close. In fact, I know exactly where in Number Four she is.

I shift to my office, and am confronted with almost exactly the same image as Tim's photo. The shotgun's shoved in my face.

"It's all right. It's all right. Just me!"

She lowers it quickly enough. "Sorry," she says. "You just took me by surprise."

"Yeah, I probably should have knocked."

Tim's chosen wisely. I suppose this may well be the safest place on earth right now. Sally's taken down "The Triumph of Death," and turned it to face the wall. I don't know if it's to spare her or the children from looking at it.

"Your office, your rules."

I give her a hug. I get down on my knees and hug the kids, both of them are happy to see me. It's something of a rare event for them to get a visit these days. I must look a sight, but they don't seem to mind.

They're in their pajamas, coloring books and crayons spread all over the floor. And they actually look excited by the adventure they're having. Early days yet.

"They're growing aren't they?" I say, getting slowly to my feet.

I open the blinds to Hell, I can see the reflection of the tear in reality here. It's weird to watch those earthly colors entering Hell.

Without death to filter it, the lights of a living world wash through the portal all too gaudy and bright.

"So this isn't a social visit?" Sally says.

"No, and I'm not here to just say goodbye. But we're going into Hell, and I have few people to spare to keep you safe."

"So the End of Days, everything you and Tim have been dreading, it's coming true."

"No, you're still alive, and Tim and Lissa. But it's going to get worse. I want you to be able to keep the kids and yourself safe."

She smiles grimly. "You want to turn me into a Pomp?"

I nod. "But only if you accept it, this isn't something I would force on anyone, even now."

"But I think you'd judge me if I knocked it back," Sally says.

"Of course I would, but that's beside the point."

Sally laughs. "I'd expect nothing less of you, Steve." She squeezes my hand. "You know that we were a good stable Black Sheep family before all this came along. Your Aunt Tegan would be horrified, she was always so resolutely anti-Pomp. Steve, anything that helps keep Stirrers at bay is a good thing. Do it."

The process is swift, there's no time for ceremony. Sally holds my gaze for the whole thing, and when I am done: she kisses me on the cheek.

"Not so bad at all," Sally says. "Actually, a bit of a fizzer."

"What were you expecting?"

"I don't know, lightning, thunder. The ancient energies of a primal force."

"You've been reading too many horror novels."

"It's got me ready for this hasn't it?" Sally snorts."You look after my Tim now, won't you?"

"Yeah, I will." I walk around my desk, I slide open the middle drawer and pull out a silver knife.

"You know the process don't you?"

Sally nods her head. "Of course I do."

"The trick's not to cut too deep. You're a Pomp now, you'll heal faster, but only a little. You probably won't need to use what I've given you, but if you do . . ."

"I'll be ready," she says.

"I know you will. I have to go."

Sally grabs my hand.

"The two of you, and Lissa, you're going to save the world."

"Yeah."

"Steve," she says. "Did you ask her to marry you?"

"No. It just doesn't seem right."

Sally laughs. "You ask her and she'll answer, and it will be a yes."

I feel my face burning.

"When Robyn left you, I knew someone better would come your way. I just didn't suspect she would be so wonderful." Sally holds my hand. "Steve, I think your parents would be very proud of you. Tim and I are. You've grown. Believe me, you've grown."

I hug her tight. "You're going to make me cry," I sniff.

"No time for crying. You go and save the world, and keep my Tim safe."

I nod, even knowing that I can't keep that promise, that I can't keep anyone safe, if anything I'm pushing them squarely in danger's way. But, both of us understand that. I want to say goodbye. I want to explain just why I haven't asked Lissa. But I can't.

Instead, I smile one last time at Sally and the kids, and shift back to Queen Street Mall and the portal into Hell.

25

Over the last hour our numbers have built on that George Street edge of Queen Street Mall. I'm waiting for them to grow a little more before we begin our assault on Hell, maybe another hundred if I can get them here in time. Each has their wrist pained with brace paint for added protection. The air's cold, but someone's dragged an espresso cart to one side of the mall. Even at the End of Days coffee proves essential.

My hands close around a cup filled with the pitch-black stuff, and I breathe in the beautiful steam. My body feels raw with the effort of containing HD. We've made our peace, but the Death's sullen and ragged around the edges, it's like holding a piece of glass in your hands, and squeezing gently. And I know it'll grow in strength again, once it gets over the shock of its brief freedom.

A few of my Pomps are still brushing spiders from their suits. None had gotten it as bad as me, but the spiders certainly hadn't appreciated us using Neti's rooms as a thoroughfare.

Alex approaches me, face creased with concentration as he speaks into his phone. Just looking at him has me worried.

He hangs up, drops his phone into his pocket. "You're not going to believe this. There're dogs coming into the city."

"Dogs?"

"Rabid, or something like it. They're savaging anyone they come across, killing them, and the bodies are stirring."

Of course. The dogs that I'd encountered in the pit trap and in Dubbo were only the beginning. "How many? Where?"

"Captain Cook Bridge and down Coronation Drive. Hundreds, they've already attacked the cops stationed there. We get our share of wild animals, but this is ridiculous."

"They have any Pomps with them?"

"Yeah, I sent some of them there."

"Tell them to deal with them like any other Stirrer. Blood."

"No! You're telling me there's such a thing as Stirrer-dogs?"

"Deal with it," I say.

Alex gets back on the phone and makes some calls.

"Yes, I understand, sir," he's saying. He hangs up and turns towards me. "They're going to have to fall back. They're pomping them all right, but only after being bitten. We've had casualties."

"You're right, bring them back here. This is where the action is. This is where everyone should be."

Alex smiles grimly. "I'm not right, that wasn't my decision. There's a whole chain-of-command thing you realize."

"After all this, trust me, you'll be a lot higher up that chain, or you'll be sacked. Don't worry, you can always work for me."

Alex chuckles. "Join the Mortmax cult. Not a chance in fucking hell."

I smile with him (he's closer to joining than he realizes) though my attention is focused on the sky and what I can see from there. I'm high right now with my Avian Pomps, circling the city. I can see the dogs approaching from every route. Every breed that you would expect to find in a big city, I imagine this plague of Stirrers spreading across the suburbs.

This is innovative thinking. Much easier to inhabit dogs, and bring down the household from within.

The closest pack is maybe a minute or two away, sprinting up the Mary Street exit. I hear machine-gun fire. The first few dogs explode in gouts of stale blood and bone, but the ones behind keep coming.

The gunner turns and runs, but is knocked over by a greyhound, his throat neatly torn out by a poodle. A few moments later he's rising, running clumsily with the pack.

But we've got animals of our own.

I send my crows down.

A thousand beaks against two hundred dogs. Wings and fur clash. Souls are stalled and devoured. The pack is halted in screams and caws and blood. The corpses are picked over by my Avians. Gah! All that dog meat.

I've given us maybe an extra fifteen minutes.

I draw my Ankous around me. Word has already spread out about the battle being fought nearby. I'd feel more persuasive if I had my scythe with me, but I don't. "Right, then. Everybody we don't have much time, we're going to have to enter Hell now. We waste time fighting these dogs when the major battle is beyond, we risk losing this altogether."

HD creaks inside me. I feel myself broaden across the back, feel myself grow taller, and slightly wider. My voice deepens.

"We let Hell come to us we might as well give up now. It's time."

Ari slaps her knives into their sheaths. The other Ankous follow. "Hell it is then."

I look over at Alex. "Sorry mate, you're not coming with us."

Alex scowls. "No way I'm missing this."

"Only Pomps, I'm afraid."

He grins. "I should have known. Join me up, mate."

"You really want to go to Hell?"

"Not so much, but I do want to see that bastard Morrigan pay."

There's one more thing I need to do, to get. I shift home and find it: Dad's old duffle coat. I slip it on. It's cold where we're going, and wearing Dad's coat, the one he'd passed on to me, I feel like I have a bit of him with me, too.

There's a red velvet box in my jacket pocket, I look at it once, then place it on the dressing table. Maybe Lissa will find it, maybe she won't. Or perhaps it won't matter at all. I hope it does.

I straighten the lapels of my coat then shift back to the mall.

I stand with Lissa and Tim, the others are arrayed behind us, starting with Alex and my Ankous. More Pomps are arriving, cops in riot gear, too.

Knives flashing, guns held cautiously, everyone looking at me.

Here are as many Pomps as we can gather without crippling the work that still needs to be done; the world's living and dying goes on regardless. But that is no longer these Pomps' concern. Kit bags ring, tents dragged from nearby stores rest heavily on backs. There are even a few people carrying ladders.

We look less like an army, more like a business convention that's spontaneously decided to go hunting and camping. The only thing missing are the nametags.

"Ready now?" Lissa says.

"Yeah," I say—HD shivers with anticipation.

"Then let's get it over with, eh, love," Lissa says.

The portal shimmers and crackles, a cold wind roars through it. For a moment I hesitate. I reach down, slide my fingers around Lissa's hand and squeeze. How many more times will I get the chance? Can't think of that. I take a deep breath.

"Now, I'm ready," I say.

"This time won't be so bad," Lissa says.

"Why's that?"

"Because this time we're doing it together."

I kiss her quickly. "I love you."

"Of course you do," she says.

And we walk into the darkness of Hell, leading our small army behind us.

26

"I don't remember it being like this." Lissa's breath comes in plumes. Our footsteps crackle in the ice. I can feel the cold running up my legs.

"It's a bit of an anticlimax," Tim says from behind us.

Maybe for him. "I don't know what to say. It's not normally this cold."

We're in Queen Street Mall's Underworld equivalent. For a moment the shock stops me. This is no Underworld I'm familiar with. Ice rimes the mall, there are no milling souls. No activity at all.

"It's never like you remember it, and I was only here yesterday. But this, this isn't how it should be at all."

The One Tree's branches hang almost silently above us, I'd even venture to say they look limp, if such a thing is possible. What has Morrigan done?

All my Pomps' wrists glow. It's an oddly reassuring sight, the brace paint doing its job. There's a little warmth here, even as more of them crowd into the Underworld, the ice is melting, the darkness lifting.

I watch with amusement, as those with tattoos suddenly have to deal with them coming alive and vociferous. Wal slides from my arm and gives me a quick wink. There's all manner of chatter. Inklings like to talk. Cerbo is having an animated chat with a python that's wrapped around his wrist. Even in this dark time there's a little enchantment.

You've gotta like that.

"So where are we heading?" Wal says, taking in the whole Pomp army thing as though it's an everyday sort of occurrence.

I'm not sure... towards Mount Coot-tha? That's where my heart is drawing me.

"Forward," I say. "We go forward."

And Lissa, Tim, Alex and my little army stride deeper into the urban spaces of the Underworld.

A few streets along, a dark shape walks toward us from behind a column that is coated with crackling ice. A Stirrer. There's a collective growl from my ranks, knives out, blood ready to flow. The Stirrer wilts, waves its hands furiously. Alex steps around me. His pistol is out, he lifts it towards the Stirrer. Lissa's by his side with her knife.

"Don't shoot," it yells in a voice that is liquid and deep, far too deliquescent to pass as human, there's a bit of bird song in it, and a touch of throat gargle. "Don't!"

Alex looks to me: his gun is raised, pointed at the Stirrer's narrow head.

I nod.

Alex sighs, shakes his head. "Does that nod mean shoot or don't shoot?"

"Don't," I whisper.

"Steve, a nod's not really that specific, and if it is, well it's normally in the affirmative, as in shoot the fucking bastard. Now, a shake on the—"

I glare at him. "You've made your point, Pomp." Alex scowls when I say that word. "Put down the gun."

Alex lowers the pistol, and the Stirrer relaxes. Well as much as you can when you are one against an army that is staring at you with bloody hands and tooth-grinding hatred. I fix a smile on my face.

"I've been sent to guide you." The Stirrer's hands are out, palms forward. It's unarmed, though the inch-long claws it's sporting are weapon enough, as are the rows of sharkish teeth. Get those around your neck and you'll be spraying your life's blood all over the place.

"Into a trap?" Wal says. I glare at him, he's only saying what I'm thinking.

The Stirrer smacks its lips concealing and revealing all those teeth. Takes me a moment to realize that it's laughing. Alex lifts his pistol again, I wave it down absently.

"Lon said you would say that," the Stirrer says. "But he also said that if we cannot trust each other all is lost, and the abyss and torment waits for you. I can guide you along the fastest routes to Devour. The god is yet to arrive."

"You telling me that Morrigan hasn't reached the city yet?"

"No, he has been somewhat, distracted, all our reports suggest he is on the One Tree."

"Why the One Tree? Why now?"

"We don't know, but it will make your approach to Devour much easier."

I grab Tim, Lissa and Alex, pull them into a huddle, Wal joins us, not bothering to wait for an invitation.

"I'm going to have to go after Morrigan."

"No," Tim says. "He probably wants us to separate. We need you. And what if this Stirrer's spinning shit?"

"Look at you. The finest Pomps of your generation. If you can't deal with a few Stirrers without me, we might as well give up now."

"And what about you?" Lissa says. "You'll be on your own. Without Mog. Christ, Steve, Morrigan has your scythe, he drove HD from your body, what if he does it again."

"He won't and this might be my only chance to face him. Besides, I won't be alone, I have Wal here." The cherub puffs up his chest, he's looking decidedly, almost aggressively, chipper. "Who's going to go up against Wal?" I say.

Lissa snorts. And Wal grimaces at her. "She's really not worth it," he says.

"I could come with you," Lissa says.

"No... you're better off here. They're going to need you, even more than I do."

Lissa shakes her head. Not buying it at all. Yeah, I could do with her help, yeah, I'd love to have her with me. But I can't stand the thought of her on that tree, I can't see her there again. And damned if I am going to lose her another time.

"I'll be back as quick as I can," I say. "Hopefully with my scythe."

I leave them as they head to Devour, led by the Stirrer. Alone, at last, but for Wal. I punch a number into my phone.

Silence, but I can feel it down the other end of the line.

"The time is coming," I say. "I'll bring him to you if I can."

"I will be waiting." The voice makes me jump, sounds like it's scratching around in my ear canal rather than my phone. "Even now, all my energies are focused upon the task of drawing that doorway to me and keeping it with your Pomps. It is a mighty endeavor, but all of it depends on you."

"If I fail—"

"Everything ends for a while."

"Then what happens?"

"Something else begins," the voice is warmer than I've ever heard it. "New doors are made and new doors are opened."

"We'll just never be around to see it."

"We never are."

"I'll bring him to you if I can."

"I know you will, because we have a deal."

"I haven't forgotten."

I hang up the phone. I've a god to find.

27

The Underworld surrounds me. Though the One Tree is silent. I stand in the shadow of one of its mighty root buttresses, at the top of Mount Coot-tha. Brisbane's Hellish clone extends below me, out to the Tethys and the black mountains of Hell.

I'm buying a coffee from a barista with a crow growing from his shoulder. I hate wasting my time this way, with my friends approaching Devour, but there are things I have to find out here. And this barista sees most of what happens on the Hill. He may not be the most trustworthy source of information I have, but he has four sets of eyes.

I just wish he was a little faster, I'm about the only customer. Sure, there are more people here than in the icy heart of the city, but it's all far too quiet.

"Your coffee, Mr. Orcus," he says, and pushes the long black across the counter. Wal has ordered a chai latte with some sort of creamy froth.

"Now, you can do me a favor. Have you seen this man?"

I show the barista the photo of Morrigan I have in my phone, and he nods. Points up toward the branches of the One Tree.

"He came through here, about eight hours ago. Bought a flat white. Seemed pissed off at something."

"Morrigan always does." Wal and I exchange looks. Morrigan

can't even be satisfied becoming a god, and what the hell was he doing buying a coffee?

The barista snorts. "Wait a minute, that's *the* Morrigan?" he says. "Oh, but you've fucked up if *the* Morrigan is back."

"It wasn't my fault."

Both barista and crow cackle. "Mate, if *the* Morrigan's walking around Hell it's your fault."

I ignore them. "When are you due to walk the Tree?"

The barista stops laughing.

"Surely it must be hard. This close to the tree, feeling its call."

"I manage."

"Yeah, but I don't envy you."

The crow's still chuckling away, and the barista stops it with a glare. "Do you want sugar with that LB?"

I shake my head. "It's fine how it is."

I leave the barista to his espresso machine and walk toward the tree, and the stairs that wend their way up its trunk.

"Now that was just cruel," says Wal, a frothy mustache covering his upper lip.

"The bastard pissed me off."

"Still... to draw attention to it..."

Here, where the One Tree is all, a creaking, drawing presence. I'm sure the barista can resist its call but I have made it harder for him. Unless he wants to leave the tree altogether and head to Charon's Ark.

I feel a little bad until I sip my coffee. Cold, and far too weak. Sympathy slips out the window and I drop the coffee in the bin.

"He deserved it," I say emphatically, and shift just a little further up to the base of the trunk and the stairs that wind around it. I remember running up these once, well, running part way up before being sick. At least this time I can shift. Need to keep the shifts small though, Mog and Morrigan are nearby but I can't quite work out where.

I stride towards the stairs, and around me the dead part, those who have managed to hold onto a little of the urgency of life glower at me. I'm not the most popular person here. Can't blame them. The Hungry Death inside me takes some delight in their reaction.

At the bottom of the stairs I turn around and look back at my kingdom. There's still a huge disconnect whenever I consider Hell. I don't feel like I have any true dominion over this place. The busy rush of the dead, though that is absent today, the city echoing my city, the tree above and around me. None of it is mine. If anything I'm a caretaker. I've no kingly ways about me, I'm not that great at the business of death.

I remember one of my dad's favorite lines: pomping is for Pomps, and business is for arseholes. Of course, Dad had proven remarkably good at business, too. Didn't stop him saying that though.

I wonder what he would think of me now. Mum would have been proud, but Dad, well he was always a little bit prickly.

Nah, he would have been proud: even if he called me an arsehole.

I take the first step that will lead me on a steep circuit of the One Tree, and almost at once I can sense Morrigan.

It affects me more than I anticipate.

"You right?" Wal asks.

"Yeah," I say, unconvincingly.

"You're a constant worry, Mr. de Selby," Wal says.

There's a murmur behind me. I turn. There may not be as many of them as usual, but people are already waiting to climb the tree, and find their resting place. They're going to have to wait a little more.

I close my eyes. Feel Morrigan's rage, and something more, a sadness or a fear.

"He isn't happy."

"This isn't a happy place."

The tree has obviously brought back memories for Morrigan as well.

I start taking the stairs two at a time, then shifting, moving by degrees, closer to my enemy. I pass a clump of Pomps, and they hardly notice my passage. I don't push it, just move on. They have their journey to make now, and I have mine. There's no rage or sadness there for them, just a steady stepping.

The dead don't hold onto their feelings for very long. For most it's only a few hours, sometimes much less. For those of us familiar with the business, it's quite often longer, particularly if there is something or someone to remind us. Lissa had managed to stay passionate, and distinctly Lissa-esque, for days. I'd said goodbye to my parents on this tree, I'd drawn Lissa back from the Underworld from here too. All of them had contained enough emotion to react to me.

I follow the winding stairs, stopping at every branch, seeking Morrigan out. Here, among the branches, people settle down, stretch out and become one with the tree. Various stages of that absorption process present themselves to me. People bound in the barest fingertips of the One Tree, others little more than lumps in the wood.

Every time I place my hand on the tree trunk the bark responds to my touch. Hums with an alarming electricity. It recognizes me, though that doesn't stop it from trying to tempt me to rest, to lie down and let it do its job.

There's a quiet desperation in its call that I've never noticed before. The souls fleeing to Charon and his Ark are having an effect. The One Tree is starving, I'd even go so far as to say the One Tree's dying.

It's no challenge to ignore the One Tree's call, but I can't help but be impressed by its single-mindedness. I recognize the Hungry Death in it. A vaster more organic Hungry Death, sure, but one still very much focused on a single outcome. How humans must irritate it, all that indecision.

But I'm anything but indecisive today, as I climb its trunk.

"I don't like the look of this." Wal says. "Or the smell, the smell in particular, it's all too bloody burny for my liking."

Smoke wafts down from above, driven by a wind from the sea. A peculiar cologne-scented smoke, and lots of it.

"Check the branches above," I say.

Wal, looks up. "There's not that many of them left."

All of a sudden, I know where Morrigan is. It's so damn obvious. After all, I gave the poor bastard Morrigan's book.

"Get to Mr. D," I say. "Warn him." Wal shoots up into the air.

But I know it's already too late.

28

The uppermost branch of the One Tree is hard beneath my feet, shuddering in time with the energies of a god. A big, angry god. One that likes throwing its fists around.

I have to stop to take in the sight before me. I don't know whether to be reassured or sickened. If Morrigan is trying to sort out grudges, his eye can't be as closely focused on the prize as it should be. Or maybe he just knows that he can't lose and is having some fun with it.

Morrigan punches Mr. D in the face: over and over. My old boss shudders, his head snapping back with every wince-inducing blow. I know Mr. D's dead, that this Underworld body is merely a psychic equivalent, but it's all about the verisimilitude. Looking at Mr. D, it's hard to believe that nerves aren't firing in his body. Or that the blood running from his face isn't blood. But maybe the difference between the two is so subtle that it really isn't a difference at all. Just as Morrigan is a god and is still just Morrigan. Angry and wanting to take it out on whomever crossed him.

The book I gave Mr. D to guard is open and burning. Dark shapes are rising from it and colliding with Morrigan.

A flood of flitting sparrows. Each moment Morrigan seems more . . . whole. Not bigger, but there's a mass to him. A definite solidity that he hadn't had when I'd last seen him, which is disturbing: he'd so easily snatched the scythe from my grip even then.

A final sparrow melds with him. The book turns to ash.

Mr. D takes each punch with admirable silence for one who's having the shit beaten out of them.

Morrigan's doing something that I've wanted to do to Mr. D on more than one occasion. But there's an intensity to the violence that is most unlike Morrigan. The guy was a planner, he worked hard, didn't give in to his feelings, and yet here he is letting go.

I'm all manner of control and silence as I run behind him, clench my fist and swing at the back of his head. Only Morrigan isn't there anymore, the bastard's dropped to my left. I almost end up striking Mr. D instead, my fist falling short.

Not that I have much time to register because Morrigan's punching me in the stomach. He's quick on the tail of that with a roundhouse to my jaw that has me stumbling back, arms flailing.

"Hardly fair that," Morrigan says.

I rub my jaw. "Use whatever advantage you have," I say, taking a few steps backwards along the branch. "You taught me everything I know."

"You still don't know how to fight," he says.

"I make do."

At least he's not focusing on Mr. D anymore. That's something. I hope the guy's trying to get as far away as possible.

Morrigan squints at me. "I see you have your old parasite back inside you."

"No thanks to you."

"Pathetic really, the thing you have become." I'm not sure who he's talking to, me or HD. But at least he's talking and not throwing punches.

"And, this is coming from a god in a ghost."

"Oh, I'm much more than that," Morrigan says.

"What will you be once the world is dead, a cinder inhabited by the last of the Stirrers?"

"I don't need much. I'll have an eternity to keep myself occupied." He smiles. "I really do hate you, Steven. You've made a habit of having people hate you. Me, the god inside me, we'll destroy this little world just for conceiving of you."

"What did I ever do to deserve that?"

"See, typical Steven de Selby. Always with the 'I didn't deserve this', or 'it wasn't my fault'."

It wasn't.

"And yet the universe folds around you. Your capacity to stay alive and to piss me off knows no bounds."

"Surely you were fond of me once." *Where's Mog? Where's my scythe?* I can feel it, so close, HD's hunger for it burns inside me like a star.

"I couldn't stand you, or those overindulgent parents of yours."

Ah, there it is! A few meters from Morrigan.

"Say what you will about me, but don't bring my parents into it."

I gesture toward Mog. It lifts into the air, streaks toward me. Morrigan's arm flashes out, in a movement too fast for my eyes to really comprehend, only now, Mog is back in his hands, and he has a good grip on it. I can see it struggling there, but it seems no effort for him to swing it about his head. Morrigan was always an awful show-off.

"No, this is mine now." He slices the scythe up at my belly. I scurry backwards, a clumsy move, but effective. In my book, any move is effective if it doesn't lead to loss of blood. But now I'm dangerously close to the edge of the branch.

Morrigan frowns. He stomps toward me across the branch and kicks me once in the chest, following through with a boot to the head. My teeth crack together, I blink back waves of red. HD rages inside me. Morrigan kicks me again.

I try to catch his boot, and I catch it all right, in the face.

"You're nothing to me," says Morrigan.

I spit out a tooth, that's going to make my dentist happy. "Same old fucking Morrigan."

Morrigan snorts. "I am and have always been far superior to you."

"Rillman thought that too."

"He was a hack. Nothing but a brilliant hack, and really not that brilliant. He could never look beyond his heart. He would have been a failure as an RM."

"You had no heart and he had too much. Maybe I'm just right."

"Would you just shut up and die!"

He kicks at my face again. This time I get a good grip on the boot. He yanks his leg back, but I do not let go. I've seen something he hasn't.

Mr. D throws just about the most perfect punch I have ever seen. Follows it with a left hook. Morrigan stumbles backwards. "You forget that Steven has allies," Mr. D says. "And you forget that at your peril."

Morrigan is momentarily unbalanced, just on the edge of the One Tree. Wal shoots past me, wings a blur, and strikes Morrigan hard in the chest. It tips things in favor of gravity.

Morrigan scrambles at the air, but it's too late. Morrigan and Mog topple off the One Tree. I try and call the scythe to me, but Morrigan has a firm grip on it.

"You took your time," I say to Wal as Mr. D shuffles over and pulls me to my feet. Wal jumps onto my shoulder. We hurry to the edge of the tree branch and peer down.

"Nah, I was just waiting for the right moment," Wal says too glibly for my liking—I really could kiss the bugger though.

We both watch Morrigan fall. Long before he hits bottom he shifts and is gone. Ah, if only it was that easy to kill the Stirrer god manifest.

"Do you remember the time he tried to kill us all in the Negotiation?" I say, though it turned out that he wasn't really trying to kill us at all.

Mr. D laughs. "What, with the machine guns and the choppers? Had to give him points for trying."

"I'm so tired of people beating the shit out of me," I say. "Morrigan, Francis, now bloody Morrigan again."

"You keep getting up, they're going to keep hitting," Wal says. "It's a good sign."

"He'll be heading toward Devour," Mr. D says, breathing heavily. His face is still, not the all-singing, all-dancing cavalcade I'm used to. Blood tracks from a nostril to his lip. I didn't think dead people could be so badly hurt. For a moment I feel bad complaining about my own beating.

He catches me looking at him. "Like I said, rules are changing again, Steven." He wipes his hand across his face, then considers the mess. "When the dead bleed Hell is in a lot of trouble."

"You said he was gone for good. That he couldn't come back."

"I know. I know. I was wrong. Who would have thought you could make such a deal with Stirrers. Such a very, very attractive deal."

I narrow my eyes.

"Of course, I would never consider such a thing myself. Not in a thousand years. But still . . . Now tell me, we didn't talk of this when you brought the book, just how did you settle things with Water?"

I tell him just what I've done and his eyes widen at that. He smiles a little sadly, and shakes my hand. "My, how you've grown, Mr. de Selby. Let me tell you, that really impresses me. But it may not be enough."

"What do you mean?"

"Regardless of your peacemaking, you're still going to have to bring Morrigan out, draw him back to the real world. The Stirrer god has used him to take form, which means that it is both god and Morrigan, but here it is mainly god. It has its memories and its hatred/disgust of you and of me—why else would it waste time coming up here to beat up on me? The Stirrer's rage is being blown through the prism of Morrigan's. I believe that it has made a mistake. And you will have to use that mistake to your advantage."

"I'm not a tactician," I say.

"The tactic is a simple one. You should be able to get the job done. You proved yourself an exemplar of the art—Tremaine and Derek certainly thought so."

"They didn't think I was good at anything."

"Steve, you know how to piss people off. Morrigan got that right. Sure you have people who love you, but you can drive them mad. You're brilliant at it. You need to get Morrigan mad, and keep him mad. And I know you can do it." Mr. D squeezes my hand. "It has been a pleasure working with you, son. I want you to know that. You've delighted and surprised me."

I don't know what to say to that. There's a tightness in my throat.

"Thank you," I say at last.

I shift and something goes wrong. I'm falling, Wal by my side trying his darndest to keep me in the air, but his wings aren't up to the task.

I try and shift again.

Nothing. The ground's coming up fast.

29

I'm falling, Wal looping around me shouting encouragements. Falling and spinning. I cut through thin clouds. Catching glimpses of the One Tree, and the city beneath. The ground rears up. Ground. Tree. City. Ground. Tree—soon it's going to be nothing but ground.

The air of Hell whistles deafeningly in my ears. For a moment I regret that I never really got to know my kingdom that well, that other external threats stopped me from appreciating this part of my job. What wonders did I miss? Maybe I'll get a chance to find out. Maybe not. Things just always seemed to escalate.

Above the noise of my falling, and the creaking of the One Tree, there's another shriller creak. A hand grabs me. Flings me over the central bar of the bike, and Mr. D's doubling me, and cheering like a fool, as we loop back up into the sky and around.

"Sorry," Mr. D says, as we rush towards the ground again. "I thought my bike would appear a little sooner, but no. It had to wait until the last minute."

We're facing toward the ground. Rushing, faster and faster toward it. A dead man looks up, and for a moment his deathly disinterest passes. He points up at us. I wave.

And the bike crashes into the ground.

We're through.

Into the Deepest Dark. For once there is air here. Not the weird absent substance that RMs can breathe, but real air, and it's lifting up the dust of the plain and sending it in great clouds away from the city.

The sky above and below us is darker than I have ever seen it, no souls glitter there. The Stirrer god is all. Mr. D brings his bike to a halt. I look from that dark sky along the dusty plain before us. There is the city of Devour, and before it is my army. Here are my Pomps.

Just to the east of the city is the portal. I can see bits of Brisbane through it, though it's no longer the mall, it's moving south and east, toward the sea. The Death of the Water's engines are working, or it's just getting bigger, either way it seems to be moving in the right direction.

"I'm going to have to leave you here," Mr. D says. "There's a few things I need to attend to."

Before I have a chance to ask him what, he's off on his bike riding frantically, and I get to feel how most people must feel when I run off on them. It's bloody irritating.

"Curious fellow isn't he?" Wal says.

I nod my head. A few hundred meters away from us my Pomps have gathered, and beyond them the walls of Devour.

Their numbers seem so insignificant against those walls. How did I ever think this was going to work? But as I near them, take in the row after row of men and women in suits, looking like the agents from the *Matrix,* only better dressed, I can't help but feel a burst of pride. Here we wait to take on our ancient enemy and we couldn't be any more fabulous.

My crew doesn't look defeated. They look ready and hungry to fight. They look pissed off and fired up.

I reach the rear of my little army, where tents have been set up. There are rows of tables, and kitchens preparing food. Here the mood is more like a carnival. People are eating and chatting, taking the Deepest Dark in their stride. And I can see the police mixed with my crew.

There's a small part of me that is offended by it all, this one place where I was granted solitude, now so crowded. But it's only a sliver of discontent.

They part to let me through to the front, where I can sense Lissa and Tim's heartbeats, and those of my Ankous. I get the feeling people were waiting for me to arrive. Well, it is my party I guess.

Lissa, Tim and Alex stand with the Ankous. Lissa looks up as I approach, and she grins. Every time I see that smile it hits me just how lucky I am. And how pleased I am to see her.

"Hey, it's the old gang," I say.

"Did you get it?" Tim asks.

"No, but it was worth a try." I wave my empty hands in front of his face. "I did learn something though."

"Something worthwhile?" Cerbo asks.

"Yeah, I think so. Morrigan isn't thinking this through. He's letting his emotions muddy everything."

"So he's still a dickhead then?" Tim says, lighting a cigarette.

"Yeah, he's still a dickhead. And this isn't the methodical work-everything-through-to-the-nth-degree Morrigan. This is the crazy-with-power, I'm-going-to-waste-time-beating-up-Mr.-D Morrigan. And that's the sort of enemy we have a chance against." I look at my Pomps out on the field. Food is being handed out, sentries have been set at the edges of my army, knives at ready. "How are you lot coping?"

"OK. Waiting mainly. The Stirrer that led us here is gone, just walked through the walls. We couldn't follow, but nothing's attacked us yet. We'd all be considerably more confident if we knew that you had the scythe."

"Yes, things would be easier, I know. But I don't have it. Anything else?"

"The air's thin down here, but it's breathable," Alex says, then coughs. "If a little dusty."

The air's whistling through the gash in reality, bringing with it all sorts of rubbish, and bird life. It's startling to see chip packets, and plastic bags dancing around the dust of the Deepest Dark.

"The longer that stays open," I say, nodding to the portal, "the more air you'll have to breathe."

"Is anyone else freaking out here?" Tim says.

"Yep," murmurs Alex. "Not a big fan of the sensation."

Lissa and Cerbo say nothing, and I'm truly grateful for that.

Tim looks at the wall. "Morrigan in there, you think?"

"Yeah, I can feel him, and I have no doubt that he can feel me."

"So how do we get the bastard to engage with us?"

"You've been in siege-type situations before, right?" I ask Alex.

"A guy with a gun in a two-story, brick, suburban house does not equal a fortress." He nods over toward a bunch of very organized-looking cops. "They're part of the CT unit," he glances back at me, "Counter Terrorism. But I'd say this is well beyond their remit too. You've dragged us all down to Hell. You're the only one who really understands the conditions here. The city has, what, maybe a few thousand Stirrers? Well we've got about three thousand people here, ready to fight." I want to correct him, to tell him that no one really knows how many Stirrers there are left. "What I'd like to know is why none of you lot ever thought to bring the fight down here before?"

"Actually," Cerbo says. "Once, long ago, we did. When the Stirrers were regarded as a spent force. A particularly industrious RM decided it was time to strike a final blow against the enemy. A thousand Pomps breached the gates of Hell, and laid siege to the city. That was before Devour grew walls. But it didn't make any difference. None of them returned. Led to a period of… uncertainty among the RMs. Three were destroyed in Schisms. After that, you can understand why it was never attempted again."

"We don't need to destroy Devour, or conquer it," I say. "We need to draw Morrigan out." I nod toward the great shimmering streak of the portal. "Morrigan can't be defeated here, but if we can bring him back to the living world, then we might just stand a chance."

"Is anyone freaking out here?" Tim says again.

I look at him severely. "So what do you think we should do?"

"Oh no," Tim says, "no, this... this is your call. I've never really had to lay siege to anything before."

"And you think I have?"

"Well, you're the one who's seen *Lord of the Rings* a dozen times."

"Twice all the way through, and the extended editions." I look over at Lissa. "It's the only way to see them. Still, that's hardly a sieging primer, and none of theirs were successful."

Tim waves a finger in the air. "But they were almost successful! Almost!"

"Would you two shut up," Lissa says.

"I know how to take a fortress," Wal says.

We all turn to look at him.

He shrugs. "Hey, I've lived." He flies onto my shoulder, gestures out at my Pomps. "What you've got here is an army—of sorts." He gestures toward the fortress. "What you've got there are walls. What you need is something to break down those walls. An army attacking a walled city without a siege engine, without ladders, or cannons, is like a starving man with a tin of beans and no can opener... if the tin could drop stones on his head... might as well be staring at Warhol's paintings of Campbell's soup."

"Where the hell am I going to get a siege engine?"

"Think about it. I've seen you, I know what you can do. You may not have a catapult, but you have control of millions of tiny ones, and that adds up to one powerful force."

I nod my head. I can control the dust, I used it in my fight against Rillman, before I killed him. But this is on an entirely different scale.

"Do you think it will work?" I ask.

"It might, but there's only one way to know for certain."

We call everyone back from the walls. Once they're clear I hurl dust against them.

Not handfuls, but great waves. The earth shakes with my power and the dust crashes against the walls with such force that my ears ring with it. But the walls don't fall.

I think about it.

I send my thoughts into the cracks in the stone, or try to. Every rock has faults, cracks, weaknesses. I find them out, I guide the dust into them. I close my eyes and let it expand.

The walls shudder, they tumble.

There's a sound, louder than the creak of the One Tree or the howling of HD. It's the beat of the billions of hearts that I am fighting for, it's the beating of the single heart in my chest, it's the beating of Lissa's heart in the near distance.

There's a bone-shaking rumble and the earth rolls beneath my feet. A gale slams into me, throwing me backward. There are distant echoing detonations, a great big stone—ashlar, I remember, it's called ashlar—comes hurtling out of the dust.

Before I can get out of the way it strikes me. Hard, in the face.

Well, that's just great. The stone's rumbled on past me. I can't see. I take a couple of steps forward, then decide I need to sit down. Lissa's coming towards me. I can hear her racing heartbeat drawing near. Surely I can't look that bad.

One moment I'm sitting upright, the next I'm in the dust. Half choking. *Is this how Francis felt?* I remember my hands closing around his throat. I remember the way he shuddered as I squeezed.

HD chuckles with the blackest delight. All I can taste is my own blood.

Justice, I suppose. Justice. Then I can't breathe at all.

30

The speed at which you heal is frightening," Dr. Brooker says.

"What?" I'm looking up into his face. I really have to stop waking up like this. At least I'm not blind, that counts for something, surely. Wal's sitting next to me, eyes shining (has he been crying?)

"Believe me, mate, you were a mess," the cherub says.

I'm lying on a stretcher in a tent. Still in the Deepest Dark, I can feel it around us.

Dr. Brooker clears his throat. "I thought dealing with RMs made me a bit blasé, but then you go and top it. Steven, you came in here three hours ago, all your major organs, your eyes. All of it crushed, I've seen paste with greater consistency than parts of you. You looked like you'd been hit by a truck, then crushed under a steamroller. There's no way anyone can survive that."

"But I'm not anyone," I sit up and wince with the effort. To say I still feel a bit sore is like saying Mars Bars are a bit sweet or a bit fattening.

"No, you are definitely not. Hell must accelerate your healing processes incredibly."

"Of course it does, how else could you suffer endlessly?" I say.

Dr. Brooker grunts. "Don't be so glib."

"The siege." I slide out of the bed. "I have to."

"Don't worry, you haven't missed much."

But, yes, I have. There are dozens of wounded. I can smell blood and death and the chemical odors of a hospital at work. Doctors from all across Mortmax are tending to them.

"I need to—"

"You need to put on some pants."

He throws me my coat, torn in several places but still serviceable, and my underpants and trousers. I realize that I'm standing there naked. I dress quickly, and, even as I do, the pain melts from me.

"What's happening?"

"We're winning, I think," Dr. Brooker says, he slips on a pair of surgical gloves. "Get out of here, I have real patients to attend to."

I nod.

"And make sure you don't come back."

There's a gap in the city's walls of about a hundred meters. Tim's walking out of it, with a guard of twenty Pomps. His hair is covered with dust, and for the first time I'm glad that my scalp is little more than stubble.

He looks at me wide-eyed. "Jesus, you look good for a—"

"Where's Lissa?"

"She's in the city. She was with you, but they needed her, your Pomps. You going to find her?"

I nod. "What have I missed?"

"I don't get it," Tim says. "We've faced almost no resistance at all. When the wall fell, Stirrers rushed out. For a moment I thought, here it is, we've kicked the fucking ants' nest, but there really wasn't that many of them." He nods toward a pile of Stirrer corpses. "We'll give them a proper burial when we can."

"And Morrigan?"

Tim shakes his head. "Nowhere."

I grimace. "But I can feel him."

"Yeah, and where are the rest of the Stirrers?"

"Maybe we've always over-calculated their numbers. If you're going to make a mistake that's how it should go, right?"

Devour is as I remember it, buildings empty of anything, mere parodies of our own. I can't really imagine Stirrers living here, working here. Their sole focus through the eons has been to enter our own world. They've a severe case of the grass-is-greener syndrome.

A small marquee has been set up by the wall, the Ankous and Lissa are arguing.

Lissa turns as Tim and I approach. She grabs me hard and squeezes. "God, it's so good to see you back." She glares at the Ankous. "Look, he'll tell you," she says heatedly.

"Tell them what?"

"That we're wasting our time here, that we need to get deeper into the city."

"No," Ari says. "Not even Steven is that stupid."

Wal chuckles from behind me. HD's not impressed.

"Yes, I am that stupid. Morrigan *is* deeper in the city, and it's Morrigan I need. If we don't engage with him then everything is pointless, the world still ends and we've only set up camp in its ruins."

"It's not too late to follow my plan, you know," Cerbo says.

I give him a withering look. "Christ! Always with the bloody death plan! We've managed so far with few casualties." As long as I don't think about those I lost this afternoon across Brisbane, or those who have died in the battle since. "We're obviously wearing away at the Stirrers, or we wouldn't be here. But we need to draw Morrigan out, and I think we can."

"I am not going any further into the city," Ari says, and the other Ankous nod. I'm not surprised, I wouldn't want to either, and they've already followed me so far.

"None of you are," I say. "Just me, I've a plan."

"No," Lissa snaps. "You're not going anywhere without me."

"Or me," Tim says.

"Yeah, goes for me as well," Alex says.

"I'd rather if you didn't," I say, but I can't sound convincing, because it's an absolute lie.

All four of us have been hurt by Morrigan, all of us have a personal stake in his defeat that goes beyond saving the world. I can't deny any of them. Besides, the company would be good.

"I'd rather not go if you don't mind," Wal says, and grins grimly. He's the only one who has no choice in the matter.

I straighten my tatty coat and clear my throat. "Then if you're coming with me, I don't want to waste time. We go now."

"And if you don't come back?" Ari demands.

"If we're not back in twenty-four hours, go home," I squeeze her hand, "walk through the portal, and spend time with your loved ones. You've all worked so hard, and if it wasn't enough, then that is no fault of yours. I'm proud of each and every one of you. Thank you."

"Oi," Tim says, "we haven't failed yet."

And we're not going to.

Hell is my kingdom, and it shall bend to my will. And no dark god is going to change that.

The city towers around us. We have been walking for hours, silently but for the occasional tune that Wal whistles, until he is hissed down. He's good, but old show tunes seem wildly inappropriate. The city is cold and dark and empty.

But somewhere ahead Morrigan waits.

My wrist burns, I've marked it not with the triangle and the line, but with the Stirrer's own mask symbol, in the hope that it will shield me from Morrigan. That he won't feel me until it's too late.

I'm walking at the front with Alex, Lissa a little behind, our footfalls echoing quietly ahead of us. Alex passes me a pistol.

"I think you need a weapon," he says. "It's a Glock, standard issue."

"I'm familiar with it," I say—meaning I know which end to point. "You ever had to use it?"

"There're thirteen rounds in there," he says not looking me in the eye.

OK, we'll leave it at that, then.

"Point, squeeze and kill. The bullets have been braced with my blood." Alex smiles. "Being a Pomp and everything, it should make a Stirrer stop and have a serious think."

I hold the pistol, speculatively, it's heavier than I expect: this kind of death always is. "You don't need it?" I ask him.

"No, I've got the rifle." Alex gives me a pained look. "Who'd have thought I would end up down here. This was Dad's territory. But I wonder what he'd think of what we're doing... I miss the old bastard, you know. Still got half a carton of his beer in the fridge."

"You keeping it in his memory?"

"Nah, it's terrible shit. I open a bottle now and then, just smell it to remind me of him."

"Dad's got a set of golf clubs," I say. "When Lissa's not around I get out the five iron, talk to it like it's him. Stupid, huh?"

"Yeah, fucking stupid."

It's easy grieving the loss of your mum, easier to cry or something. But dads... dads are problematic. This is about as close to tears as I'm going to get.

"Could murder one of those beers now," Alex says.

"You and me, both."

"What are we going to do once we find Morrigan?"

"That's the tough part," I say. "I need to get him back to the living world. You see, I've made a deal."

"What sort of deal?"

"Trust me, a good one. I'm not talking a Lando Calrissian chatting with Vader sort of deal. This one will end this. But I can't do what I need to here."

A soft shuffle of feet, a movement in the air, alerts us to a presence. Alex raises his rifle.

"Always with the gun," the Stirrer says, stepping out from the shadows.

"What do you want?" We say almost simultaneously

"You're almost there," it says. "Morrigan has called a moot. The Stirrers have gathered, all but the most stupid of creatures have resisted the call—those which your Pomps met at the wall. Hurry, follow me."

"How many Stirrers?"

It turns back to me and smiles. "A lot. A lot of Stirrers, too many for my allies to make a difference right now. But you, I'm sure you have a plan."

"Yeah, I've got a plan." Tim and Lissa have moved in close, Wal is resting on my shoulder. "Nearly there," I say.

We follow it down winding streets, and it whispers, whispers, and I feel Morrigan's presence grow. HD shifts angrily inside me.

"The city, how the hell do you live here?" I ask, more to distract myself than anything else.

The Stirrer stops, looks at me, shocked. "You do not see it?"

"What?"

"The splendor."

"No, all I see is gray and stony and cold."

"Ah, Mr. de Selby, your kind do not have the eyes for this. It makes sense I suppose. Everything is glorious here. The colors vibrant and warm, the boulevards broad. Right now a gentle wind is blowing, and I can smell the sea, rising up from a distant place, but no less delightful for it. It is your world that is all gray and cold, and awful."

"Then why do you want it?"

"Worlds are infinitely malleable. Our god promises to make it in the image of our dreams. But this dream," the Stirrer gestures at the walls, weeping and sullen, "this dream is just as vast, just as wonderful, it does not need to be any bigger."

Unless you have a god to fill it, I think. *Then a world, a universe, is never big enough.*

We reach a broadening in the road, and there at last I see the extent of what we face.

"Perhaps, Ari was right," Lissa says quietly.

There must be ten thousand at least. But what is more frightening than that is their silence. There is no snuffling, no howling, just quiet, stillness. An ocean, glassy and flat with not a breath of wind.

And at their heart stands Morrigan. I don't ask the Stirrer what it sees, I can recognize the rapture in its face—and this is one of the rebels.

I look over at Morrigan. He's standing there, eyes closed, arms out. The scythe must be nearby, yes, a Stirrer holds it with such reverence you would think it were some sort of holy vessel. I guess it is in a way.

Now's my chance. Before anyone can protest, I slide the Glock from my belt, unclick the safety. I shift right beside Morrigan. The Stirrer turns toward me, Mog clutched to its chest.

I kick it hard in the stomach. Mog clatters to the ground. Morrigan turns towards me, and I shoot him in the face, the kick of the gun's a bit more than I expect, but maybe my aim was off because it's a great shot. Morrigan stumbles back, not really hurt. Just stunned by the force of the bullet.

It's all I need.

The scythe recognizes me at once, I reach towards it, it hurtles towards my palms. My fingers close around the snath.

And I shift.

Back to Lissa, Tim and Alex. The Stirrer has left, I don't blame it.

"Well, there we go, easy," I say. "But we really better start running."

Lissa slaps my head. "That was your plan?"

"Got my scythe back, didn't it?"

Morrigan howls. He pulls his hand from his face and there's not even a welt. His eyes open and I swear he is looking into my soul. I give him the finger.

In a single movement, the Stirrers turn. And twenty thousand eyes filled with hatred are focused upon us. All stillness, all quiet is gone, and only hunger remains.

"Guys, I think we need to run," I say, and they already are.

"This what you call drawing Morrigan out?" Alex says.

"It might be."

"It's certainly got a reaction," Lissa says.

"Less chat, more run," I say.

And the race is on. We run so hard we throw dust up behind us. The air's heavy with it. It gets in our hair, our lungs. We're all coughing and snorting, but none of us stop.

I call Wal to me.

"Yes," he says, blinking dust out of his eyes. His wings dark with the stuff.

"I need you to fly ahead. Warn them of what's coming."

Wal nods, looks back at the approaching Stirrers. "You're not going to make it. They'll wash over you like a wave."

"Leave that to me. You just go."

He doesn't hesitate a moment longer, he's off.

"You shift," Lissa says. "Leave us."

"I can't," I say. I need to know that he is following, I need him to think that I'm such an idiot, and maybe I am. I certainly didn't expect so many Stirrers. I lift dear old Mog above my head. "At least I have this now."

We round a corner, into a narrowing street, and Alex stops running, I stop with him.

"You keep moving," he says. He doesn't sound winded.

"You right?"

"Fine, couldn't be better." His face is flushed, his eyes shine.

"We've got to keep going," I jerk a thumb towards the others.

Tim and Lissa sprint ahead of us, not yet aware that we're no longer with them. The approaching Stirrers are growing louder, their footfalls thunderous. Dust tumbles from the roof above.

"I'm done running," Alex says.

"What the fuck?"

"Blood's good for some things," Alex says. He reaches beneath his jacket pulls out a belt of round objects, I take a step back. "But sometimes you really need grenades." He yanks out the pin and tosses the first grenade around the corner.

In an eye blink, before the first one goes off, he hurls another two. "Always played Deep Field in cricket, out the back. Got a bloody good arm, Dad used to say. You keep running," he shouts at me. "I'll hold them off here where the street narrows. It's a good position."

The Stirrers are quiet behind the corner. Then I hear Morrigan shouting something unintelligible.

"You can't. I can shift, I can do this."

Alex snorts. "Shit! Mate, you and grenades? I think not. They'd be picking pieces of you out of the walls. Too fucking risky."

"You can't."

"I can," Alex says. "Don't you go telling me how I can or can't die." He reaches out a hand, and I shake it. "You never know, I might get lucky. But saving the world—what better way to go? I always worried I'd get shot in the head by some stupid kid high on fucking meth. This I can deal with. Regardless, Steve, it's been a pleasure." The Stirrers shuffle cautiously around the corner. It would be almost comedic. In fact, Alex is smiling.

I don't know what to say. Nothing wants to come out of my mouth.

Alex lets go of my hand and casually lobs another two grenades in their direction: one strikes a Stirrer in the face before exploding. It's a bit messy, and Alex winces.

"Hope that wasn't one of your mates. Morrigan better put in an appearance soon, fucking prick," he says. "Now, you run."

And I do, I shift to Lissa's side.

"Where's Alex?" Lissa demands, and I have to hold her to stop her turning back.

"Grenades," I answer. There's another burst of explosions. "To give us more time."

"He can't."

"But he has," I say, and Lissa nods her head.

A few blocks further on, Alex's soul appears beside us.

"Run," he says, to all of us. "Run and run."

And he runs with us. "Slowed them a little," he says, and I can almost imagine that he's still alive. Only he's moving the way the dead move, in rapid bursts, sliding easily between one point in time and the next. Not quite fixed in any. It breaks my heart to see it.

The trip back is at once interminable and swift. Down roads that narrow and widen and curl so that sometimes it feels that we're not running away from the Stirrers, but drawing closer to them. There are side streets, and any moment I expect to see the enemy come flooding out of them. Any moment.

Alex, I don't know how he does it, keeps up with us, and he's cracking jokes. It's an Alex I've never seen before, one free of worry. Death almost suits him. All it does though, is show what could have been. *Fuck. Fuck. Fuck. All this decisiveness, all this strength and I still let my friends down.*

Twice Tim stops to vomit, Lissa patting his back. "Have. To. Get into shape," he says, the second time, wiping his mouth.

We're near the edge of the city, dust hazing the air, and just a hint of something else—life force, the living world beyond—when Wal catches us, coming the other way.

"They're ready," he pants, landing on my shoulder. "Waiting." He peers over at Alex, and frowns. "Sorry, mate."

"It's all right," Alex says.

No, it's not.

The Stirrers are getting closer, at this rate they're going to catch us before we reach my Pomps.

I stop. "You lot, keep running. Gonna bloody a few noses."

Lissa hesitates.

I shake my head, "I'll be all right, I promise."

For another moment I think she's not going to go, but she does, following Tim's lead.

Wal drops onto my shoulder. "I really need to get in shape," he says, shaking his head and showering me in cherub sweat.

"You, too," I say to him. "I need to do this alone."

"Right, right, we'll be waiting by the wall." Then he's off too, darting back toward my Pomps. Just me and Alex now, and the Stirrers drawing nearer.

"I'm so sorry," I say.

Alex shakes his head. "What the fuck for mate? Trying to save the world? You ready?"

"Yeah."

I spin to one side and swing Mog. It's time to make a mess.

Mog arcs around me cutting and cutting. It's not as smooth or as neat as I would like. But the Stirrers, hemmed in by the narrow streets have trouble getting close enough to stop me. I keep them clear for seconds. And seconds more, shifting in and out of the mass of them. Always hoping that enough time has passed, that Lissa and Tim are close to the ranks of my Pomps.

But even with Mog I know that they can wash over me if I move too slowly.

They catch on quickly and start grabbing me, grabbing the snath of the scythe en masse. Sharp-toothed faces snap at me.

"Morrigan's coming," Alex whispers in my ear. He touches my shoulder, inadvertently pomping himself. He blinks, then he's gone.

I don't even get to say goodbye. But I've no time to react.

I've done what I can. Enough of them get a good grip and I'll be torn apart. I shift out of there.

Lissa and Tim have almost reached the others, and Wal has slowed his flight to keep pace with them.

"I told you I wouldn't be long," I say.

We turn another corner, and there they are. A hundred meters away from us, down the last laneway. The wall that I tore asunder is behind them. Behind us run the Stirrers. I've not slowed them by much, I'm not sure it will be enough.

My Pomps are waiting, Ari's experienced fighters at the front, but I can see the terror in their eyes as they take in our pursuers.

Tim, Lissa and I crash through their ranks.

"They're here," Ari yells. "Retreat. Retreat."

And they actually move backwards at a steady pace. Until the Stirrers meet our front. There are screams of rage and fear coming from both sides. But it is no rout, we move back slowly, slowly. I kiss Lissa who is still catching her breath, surrounded by the mass of our Pomps passing through the gap in the wall.

"I have to deal with this," I say and shift back to the front.

It's a desperate fight, but I know my presence, my ability to shift lightning quick, stops us from becoming overwhelmed. The air stinks of blood and ash, and just the mildest hint, again, of the sea.

We are all through the walls. Crashing back: fighting so as not to be consumed in our retreat.

We're out and on the plain of the Deepest Dark when I realize that Stirrers are closing around us from east and west, having poured out from secret exits (or really obvious ones that we failed to notice) further along the walls, sealing us against the wall. We've been trapped outside the city, which I fought so hard to break.

We're being attacked on all sides. Morrigan is aiming to end this now.

I shift back to Lissa and Tim.

"Classic pincer movement," Tim says, still gasping from all that running, suddenly getting all strategic. I glare at him.

"So how did we fall for it?"

"That's why it's a fucking classic."

"There I thought we were drawing Morrigan out, and he was driving us towards this."

Before us the portal shimmers, glowing with a coastal light just beyond reach, thousands of Stirrers stand in the way. We're going to be consumed here. There's a moment of pause, the Stirrers pull back a little and look towards the ranks of our enemy that cram the gap in the wall.

They're waiting for something. We all are.

Cerbo isn't too far from the wall. Ari stands with him, both are as bloody as me, I shift to them. Cerbo looks up at me, and smiles grimly.

"Well, Mr. de Selby, we did our best."

"It's not over yet," I tell him.

"Not until our hearts stop beating, eh? Not until the comet falls from the sky?" He looks at his bloody hands. "What in blazes are they waiting for?"

"Not a what but a who!" Wal says, landing in our midst. He nods at Cerbo's inkling. "Hello, Stuart," he says. The cobra dips its head. Wal flies to my side, drops on my shoulder again.

"He's almost at the front."

The Stirrers part and Morrigan stands there, cocky as all hell, even without the scythe. He's holding what looks like a bloody big broadsword. I want to tell my Pomps nearest to pull back, but there is no room: nowhere to go. We're hemmed in.

"Let the harvest begin," he roars, "let death in all its glory reign."

"Pompous prick," Ari moans from behind me. "I never could stand him."

Morrigan swings the sword before him with all the strength of a god, heads and limbs fly.

"That wasn't meant to happen," Wal says, his face aghast. He beats his wings frantically, gets some elevation, before dropping back down beside my face. "We're kind of surrounded, kiddo."

We're in trouble, serious trouble. I shift back to Lissa and Tim. Wal follows.

"Good enough day to die as any," I say, and it is.

Lissa kisses me. "Always a good day to die with you," she says, then grimaces. "Christ, how emo was that?"

"I knew an emo once," Wal says. "It didn't end well. It never does."

We slide our knives across our palms, and prepare to fight.

There's a sound like a great wind or a rising conflagration. I turn towards its source. Behind us the root-tips of the One Tree sway. A bluish light burns hotter for a few moments. The air rings. And hands claw their way through the dirt. What new thing is this?

Mr. D on his bicycle shoots around the front towards me. "Sorry I took so long. Charon sends his regards and these souls from the Ark."

Finally the dead have risen, Mr. D at their fore, and they're not as I know them. Instead of dull and uncaring, or maybe a little scared, the dead have risen and they look pissed off. But it isn't the only change, guided by a signal I neither hear nor feel, a thousand or so Stirrers from Morrigan's own ranks turn on their own kind.

The Stirrer rebellion has begun.

And as one we rush into that darkness, me at the front. All of my Pomps behind me. Here we are fighting not for a cause, not for a country, but for life and death itself.

Here is the triumph of Death. Here is Breughel's painting: a last-ditch battle of the dead.

Lissa stands to my left. Tim to my right. Their hands are bloody as they grapple with the Stirrers. People scream, howl, yell. Stirrers roar, but they do not stop.

And there is death. Everywhere there is death.

Morrigan strides towards us, ignoring the fight, and I know that he's coming for me.

"We can't win here," Cerbo yells at me. "You need to draw him out."

"I know," I shout back. "He has to go through that portal. Out there, out in the real world we have a chance at stopping him. Here we can't. The rules are different here. We're lacking one thing."

"What?"

"Trust me."

Morrigan, holding the great sword casually in one hand, steps neatly over the corpse of a Pomp. He has a bag around his waist, and seeing me now he reaches into it, and yanks out Alex's head.

I'd kill him now if I could. I'd rip the heart right out of him.

"Alas, poor Alex. I knew his father well, the drunken fool," Morrigan says. "Any other friends you would like me to kill? Where's that bitch girlfriend of yours?"

I'm trying to speak. I can't. HD pushes at me.

"Oh, it looks like you're in shock," Morrigan says. "Look at that!" he chuckles. "I've shocked the Orcus. I don't know whether or not to be honored or horrified. It's going to be all right, Steven. You have to believe me. I'm just here to make your job easier, get rid of those you love sooner, cut out as much of the dread as I—"

Lissa hits him in the back of the head with an impressive bone-crunching sort of whack. He jerks forward and I swing Mog at his throat.

Morrigan's hands fly out, and he grips the snath of the scythe as though it had never left his hands. There's a gravity to those palms that I can't even hope to match.

Lissa punches away, as I yank at the scythe. But it's no good, we've been here before. I can't pull it from his grip. Morrigan's lips curl into the darkest, most dreadful rictus.

"Shall I kill Ms. Jones now?" The voice is barely a whisper, an intimate breath in my ear, but not lacking in threat. I get the feeling that if he could, he'd bite the side of my face and spit the bloody mess back at me.

He wrenches Mog out of my hands and swings neatly around in a circle, dancing backwards as he does: the scythe high and whistling towards Lissa's head.

I shift.

The snath of the scythe strikes my back. Nearly snaps me in two, ribs creak, maybe break. I can't tell. But I clap my arm over the snath: draw the shaft tight and close to my body, the blade curled towards me. It's a clumsy move, but effective. I stand there, panting, looking at Lissa: her hands bloody, dust streaking her face.

Her chest heaves. I can feel her hurt. Still, she's all but ready to start swinging again. I shake my head.

"Run," I say, nodding towards the portal.

Her jaw is set. Her eyes burn stubbornly, no mockery there now, just rage.

"Run, if you love me. Run."

And she does, just as Morrigan drives a boot into my lower back, cracking something. A howl escapes my lips and he cuts down with the scythe. I shift, moments before it strikes my flesh. Only a few meters away, but it's enough. I get unsteadily to my feet, standing between Morrigan and Lissa, waiting to repeat it over again.

"Things aren't going as you hoped are they?" Morrigan says. "I feel for you. It's terrible when plans go awry, when the reins start slipping no matter how tight a hold you have. It burns the fingers, stings the soul."

My chest and back are sticky and bruised. They're healing quickly but the hurt is deep enough that I can't speak. I try for a snarl instead. Not a good idea, it only comes out as a wheeze.

"There's only so many times you can get between her and the inevitable," Morrigan says, leaping towards me and flipping the bottom of the scythe at my head. I fling up my hands. Too late, it connects. Hard. Teeth loosen in my mouth, my ears ring. I almost drop to my knees. "Perhaps we should just get it over with, eh?"

At least I am still between him and Lissa.

He gets a good grip on the shaft, takes a swift backswing and there's a peculiar thunder like someone's slamming two bags of machine parts together.

Morrigan lowers the scythe, looks up, and catches a bicycle in the face. He hits the ground hard in a cloud of dust.

"I told you I still had a few tricks up my sleeve," Mr. D says from behind me. How long has he been standing there? He grabs my arm and starts dragging me away from Morrigan.

Morrigan rises to one knee, dark blood streams from his face. He looks to Mr. D. "This all you got?" he demands, Mog arcing above his head. It catches another bicycle, an old Malvern Star like the one I used to ride as a kid, and sends it hurtling into the ground.

"I thought it was pretty good, actually," Mr. D says, dragging me faster. "Bikes, I've always had an affinity for them. And I've been here long enough to know how to fiddle around with reality a little."

I know this. Here at last is my dream. I can't help but smile.

And the bikes plummet, a downpour of bicycles. A penny-farthing takes out a Stirrer nearby with an explosion of gears and wheels. A Stirrer tumbles. Blood flows. But the Stirrers aren't the only casualties.

"No!" Mr. D pales. "No, that wasn't—"

But it is.

The bicycles fall, and they strike Stirrers and Pomps indiscriminately where the fighting is thickest. We don't miss out though. A ten-speed racer crashes down between us. Knocking a chunk out of my arm, and driving Mr. D to the ground. Dust is thrown up into the air with each fall, so that I can't see more than a few meters in front of me.

"Pull back," I yell. Not that it's really necessary, everybody's already getting out of the way, until there's only Morrigan standing in the middle of the downpour, laughing and cutting bicycles from the air.

"Really. That wasn't meant to happen," Mr. D moans. There's a bloody gash along one of his cheeks. I can see bone beneath.

We've managed to escape the main fall. Lissa and Tim aren't that far away, their heartbeats loud in my head. I want to be with them. I don't want to be here consoling this buffoon. Even if he did just save my life.

"When will they stop falling?"

Mr. D looks at his watch. "A few minutes—no more. I'm so sorry."

"You do realize that we're winning don't you?"

Mr. D is silent.

And we are. We're winning here. I can see that. The bicycles, the dead army and the betrayal of the Stirrer rebels have shifted our fortunes, but this, all of this is meaningless unless I defeat Morrigan himself.

Just once I'd like to do something that doesn't come to a battle to the death. That people hunger for this role: it strikes me as crazy.

"Why are you smiling?" Wal asks me.

"Things are working out."

"It's not that sort of smile." But yes it is.

The wind has changed in the world beyond, it's no longer the metallic rot of the city. This is all brine, all cold ocean winds with a hint of traffic fumes.

The sea is life, and here is life knocking on Hell's door. I'm not surprised when half a dozen seagulls break the surface of the portal, calling mournfully as they do. I've no doubt they'll make a living on the scraps of the Underworld, they'll mark the sky above the sea of Hell.

Yet I can't help feeling sorry for them.

They're quickly gone into the Deepest Dark, but the battle remains. And the wind lifts more dust into the air. Choking clouds of it, disadvantageous to both sides. My eyes sting, my lungs burn. I try to hurl it all away, but the dust has grown fickle, the world beyond has enchanted it—or I've just lost my knack.

Morrigan gazes curiously toward the light, anything I suppose must be more attractive than here. I can see that he is weighing up his options, making a decision.

Then he acts.

He strides toward the portal, his Stirrers providing cover. There are fewer and fewer of them now, maybe thirty, perhaps forty at most. But they are fighting furiously, fanning out around Morrigan. Not that it matters: Morrigan has the scythe. No one can stop him with that weapon in his hands, not even me. The Pomps move out of his way.

And it's then that I realize who stands between him and the gateway.

Lissa.

Stirrers hem her in. There's nowhere for her to go.

Mr. D pats my back. "Get her. End this. Do what needs to be done."

I try and shift. Nothing. Morrigan waggles a finger in my direction, his face a picture of pure delight.

So, instead, I run.

Morrigan clears a path through my Pomps. He heads straight toward Lissa. My people are being killed trying to protect her. And she's pushing past them, calling them back. Lissa refuses to let people put themselves in front of her. She's swearing, snarling, and I've never seen her so mad. I'm crashing through Stirrers, trying to get to her.

My blood boils from my fingers. Stirrer after Stirrer I hurl back with my touch. My body shudders with the effort, after all this running, all this fighting. And I'm moving fast, but not fast enough. A Stirrer takes me around the legs and I'm on my belly, winded. I lash out a hand, and the Stirrer screams. I get to my feet. Unsteady, but I have to reach Lissa.

And I make it.

I stand in front of him.

"Just you and me, prick."

Morrigan grabs me with a free hand, and throws me away easily. I land on my face, twenty, thirty meters away. I get shakily to my feet, helped by a Pomp I don't recognize. No time for thank yous, I turn back towards Lissa.

The space between her and Morrigan opens. Morrigan says something. Lissa pulls a knife from her boot and growls at him. Her throw is accurate, takes him in the throat.

Morrigan stands there a moment, knife lodged just under his Adam's Apple. He tugs it free, and smiles.

I try and shift. Morrigan grins at me, shakes his head. Wal shoots from my side straight at Morrigan who, without even looking, knocks him out of the air with the end of the scythe.

Almost casually, Morrigan hurls the knife back at Lissa. As though it's the easiest thing in the world.

I'm sprinting, crashing past Stirrers, leaping over the bodies of my comrades desperate to get between her and that blade. I'm not fast enough. The knife juts from her belly.

Lissa shivers, her mouth works at words I cannot hear. She presses a hand around the wound, takes a step forward, and throws her other blade. This one Morrigan snatches out of the air, and flicks back, lightning fast. It strikes her a few inches from the other knife, hilt buried deep.

Blood's already seeping from the wounds. She drops onto her backside as though someone's just pulled the legs out from under her.

I reach her a moment later.

Morrigan is already turning away, walking towards the light.

It's working. It's working too well.

"Not so bad," Lissa says softly, her hands are sticky with blood. I can smell the death on her. She shakes. Her whole body shakes, and there's nothing I can do to still it. "Look, the prick's doing what you wanted him to do. Follow him, take me with you. Get me to the sun, if I'm going to die. Let me die with the sun on my face."

"You can have the sun," I tell her, "but you are not going to die. I won't let you. And I have some say in the matter."

I lift her gently, and walk with her from Hell to earth. But I am not bringing her home to die.

All around me the Stirrers run toward the portal, Mr. D's dead soldiers are gone, pushed back by this light, this living world in which they can no longer have any part. Tim runs toward me. Dr. Brooker by his side.

We walk out into the sun.

Waves thunder. The light is briefly blinding. The smell of life so strong that I almost choke on it.

Wal pulls the hair from Lissa face, letting the light shine onto her cheeks. And for a moment there's color there, beneath the dust and blood, enough that I could almost convince myself that she's all right. But she's not.

"Put her down," Dr. Brooker says, he rests a hand gently on my shoulder. "I'm begging you, Steven. Put her down. You're killing her."

He throws a thick blanket on the ground, I lay her gently there. She's shivering. The fight is on behind me. But I can't go to it. Lissa's wounded, I can't leave her. She wouldn't leave me.

"Steve," she whispers.

I lean in close. "I love you," she says. "I really love you, but you can't stay with me. You have to finish this. Please..."

And I know she's right, but still, I hesitate.

Dr. Brooker pushes me away, gently but no less forcefully. "I need space," he says. "Let me do my job and you do yours."

"Her bowel," I say. "It's—"

"Go," Dr. Brooker snarls, and I catch a glimpse of the doctor of old, the one that wouldn't think twice about clipping me around the ear.

"Don't you let her die."

"Finish this," Dr. Brooker says. "Whatever you have planned, get it done. Or what I do here won't matter."

I turn, there is Morrigan, surrounded by his Stirrers. He looks over at me, eyes positively twinkling.

"Ladies and gentlemen," he yells, bowing deeply. "Welcome to the end of the world."

31

The world isn't over yet. I walk across the sand toward Morrigan. HD swells within me. And I let it. I've no resistance to it now, no desire but to see Morrigan and the Stirrer god destroyed.

Time to shine, it whispers.

"See, see how I fill the sky!" Morrigan stands there, the comet over his shoulder, the bright blue waters of the Coral Sea gleaming. Truly a moment of triumph. He looks over at me, and winks. "Death, thou shalt die."

"Tosser," Wal whispers in my ear.

The few remaining Stirrers give a ragged cheer, but I'm stalling them as I come, around me my crew have gathered.

My Pomps and my Ankous are covered in dust and blood, like miners that have just dug themselves out of a cave-in with nothing but their bare hands. All of them look on the edge of despair, but they follow me. And they fight.

And the Stirrers are banished, one by one. And somewhere behind me, Lissa lies dying.

At last Morrigan stands alone, waiting. He looks bored. And we have him surrounded. He twirls the scythe in his hands like a baton, then rests it in the crook of his arm and claps.

"Great team effort on your part," he says. "But me, I don't need a team."

Neither do I. Not now.

I send my crew away, back to the edge of the beach, none of them want to argue the point. Tim is the last to go. I shake my head at him. Wal hovers in the distance, midway between Lissa and me. I signal for him to stay there. He has no role in this now.

I stand before Morrigan, my hand slick with my own blood. My body filled with rage and despair. If Lissa dies . . . but she isn't going to die. I won't let her, and I know I have it in my power to stop that death.

Morrigan has the towers, the high rises and shops of the Gold Coast behind him, and that great tear in reality of the world. He's the boss from Hell, literally. All I have is the sea, and its song to my back, the great distances to the horizon.

And it better be enough.

I shrug off my duffel coat: let it drop to the sand.

"Haven't we been here before?" Morrigan says.

"I guess that's just how it is with us."

Morrigan shakes his head. "No. I mean, *here*." He points behind him, at a restaurant on the strip along the beach. "I'm sure we had a staff party there."

"Maybe. I—"

"Oh, you wouldn't remember. You got royally pissed." He grimaces, leans on the scythe and for a moment he just looks like a tired old man and, despite himself, despite what he is certain is victory, there's bitterness there, too. "You always drank so much. I'm sure it won't surprise you to know that your parents were worried. I told them that it was just a stage you were going through. That you'd grow out of it. What the fuck did I care? You were all going to be dead soon anyway."

"Don't you ever bring up my parents again."

"Why? They were a part of my life, too. I have just as much right—"

"You killed them, you prick."

"Yes, yes I did. But it was all for a good cause. I mean, look at you, my boy. Wouldn't they be just so proud? I'm proud, despite myself."

I feel my face flush. Enough. He's just drawing this out, surely. But I can see the surprise on his face—the genuine shock of his pride.

"Doesn't matter. None of that matters. This is what is important. This moment. All those other more... questionable times, those defeats, none of it matters, all of it led here." Morrigan grins. "You've cast the toothy fuckers out, but that means nothing. I'll resurrect them from the Deepest Dark myself, and we'll dance on this world's bones."

The comet is a second sun in the sky. There's a hush in the air that's electric, that whispers just beneath hearing with the weight of the end of the world.

But I've my own argument, and I do not doubt its persuasiveness.

Now!

My Avians attack, coming from dozens of directions at once, and he cuts them easily out of the sky. I call them to a halt. The birds circle above us, and I can feel their hatred for this man. It almost matches my own.

"So that was your plan, eh," Morrigan says. "To peck me to death."

"No."

He jabs out at me with Mog's blunt end. Straight into my face. I go down. Drop to the sand. Skull ringing, nose broken I think. He swings the scythe at my head, point first. I scramble backwards, frantically. Arms flailing. The point nicks the skin of my left hand.

"I'm going to cut you into little pieces," Morrigan chortles. "There will be no end to the fire and death that I am bringing. I'll resurrect and burn you to screaming ash a thousand thousand times, and that will just be the beginning."

I stagger to my feet. The scythe misses my chest by millimeters. I step back, boots sinking in the wet sand. I'm running out of room, the water's lapping at my heels. A decent wave and I'll be knocked into the blade. I wipe the blood from my nose. "You've got a lot of fun planned then," I say.

Morrigan nods. "And an eternity to fulfil it. That's the thing with eternity, you really need to pace yourself."

He connects with Mog this time, takes a flap of skin from my forearm, it hangs with the shirtsleeve, I can see bone and meat beneath. I choke down a scream. It heals quickly but it doesn't stop the pain. Morrigan's grin threatens to split his face.

Waves crash against my thighs now, but they don't topple me, it's almost as if the water holds me up. Morrigan's followed me, the water above his ankles.

He has me beaten, and he knows it. I lift my head high.

"Might as well get the first death in, then," I say. "You boring old prick."

Morrigan's eyes widen, he draws back the scythe, and I take a deep breath. Mog curves towards my head, and stops.

A hand. A hand grips it beneath the blade, halts the edge just inches from my neck. Morrigan isn't smiling anymore.

Another hand grabs his leg. And another, and another. Water given form, to halt a god. The limbs strain against his strength, but they hold.

"Always have a backup plan," I growl.

Morrigan struggles, wrenching his shoulders from left to right. And he almost breaks free. The ocean behind me groans. But almost isn't enough.

I close my fingers around the scythe haft. "I believe that's mine," I say.

I pull Mog from his grip, yank so hard that I almost fall on my arse into the water, and I would, but the sea won't let me fall.

Not yet. Not until this is done. We have a deal.

The scythe is mine again. Mog croons. Glad to be home. Home.

Home. Perhaps embarrassed by what it was made to do. My fingers tighten around the familiar icy grips, and God help me: it's never felt so good.

"You can't stop this," Morrigan growls. "This world is mine. I deserve it."

"You certainly deserve something, mate."

Morrigan's face strains and the muscles beneath begin to... bubble. Something is coming through.

Here, at last, the Stirrer god is asserting itself.

He/it struggles in Water's grip, just as Mog had once struggled in Morrigan's. But there is no escaping the Death of the Water. Not this time. Those vast stony engines of the Water are working furiously. I can feel them: a distant throbbing, tides churning.

I tighten my grip on the scythe, and I know at last what it was made for.

Not to cut away at the threads of the universe, not to reap the souls of the living. No, those jobs sullied it. This scythe has one true function. Just as I, as Orcus, have one true role. And I understand that now.

I am Death, without me life would have nothing to quicken it, without me, there would be nothing but Morrigan's cruel endlessness. And how fucking dull is that?

I swing Mog with everything I have.

HD rides along that swing, his glee setting my teeth to such a grinding, awful rictus that a molar cracks, shatters in my mouth. HD, Mog and me: together again at last.

Mog strikes Morrigan's neck with absolute precision. The blade shearing through muscle and bone, and far more than that—it cuts away the god. Tears it open and devours it.

Aunt Neti once talked about cutting a vast crack in the world, and now I know what she means.

There's a sound like reality's lungs imploding. Morrigan manages a sneer before his head tumbles to the sand.

Sparrows burst from the wound. But the instant they hit the air they shudder and die and drop. Staining the water with ink that fades away to nothing almost at once.

A pulse of light builds out at sea, eye-searingly intense. I feel it rather than see it. Shadows thin and lengthen, impossibly long. The light passes. A great beating rumble follows it, sonic booms crashing into each other, rising and building like cosmic nails being scraped down a cosmic blackboard.

All the windows in the shops and apartment buildings facing the sea shatter.

Morrigan's headless body quakes, expands and contracts. No more of his sparrows seek the sky. He lurches forward. The air heats up. The hands that grip him shudder, some of them are smoking, but they do not let go, and Morrigan vanishes.

All at once. There is no deathly howling, no rage, just a sudden, silent absence.

And with him goes the comet in the sky. The portal claps shut like a gunshot a moment later. The man who killed my friends and family, and the god that drove its creatures to rage against our world, are gone.

Here on the shore it ends.

Wal hovers beside me. "You did it," he says. "You bloody did it!"

"Yeah, I . . . we did."

Wal smiles. "Look at you, all gro—"

Then he's torn from reality too, resituated back on my arm. Earth and Hell are realigned. I didn't get a chance to thank him, or to say sorry.

32

Waves crash against my thighs, no longer concerned with holding me up or holding a god back.

The sand sucks at my boots. Mog is all that's steadying me. I lean on it heavily.

"You did good," I tell it. "You did good."

The scythe croons in my grip, radiates pride. I look to the shore, and Tim's running toward me. He splashes through the water up to his thighs and nearly gets knocked over by a wave himself.

"Hey," I say.

Tim slides an arm under mine. "Let's get you out of here before you drown, eh." He pulls me from the sea.

"It's done," I say. "Can you feel it?"

The schedule will have changed. The world's started breathing again. Even now I can feel people dying, but no more than any other day. The heartbeat of the world is loud inside my head, and it is strong and there is no end to it in sight.

"Yes. It's done. The Gold Coast, though," he grins. "Why the Gold Coast of all places?"

I don't have time for this. I have to get back to Lissa.

I'm on the verge of pushing past him when I realize the grin has died on his face. He points up at the sky. Above us seagulls hurtle from the water, thousands of them, rushing west, toward the hinterland, toward anywhere that isn't this beach.

"What's that all about?" Tim says.

Somewhere nearby, dogs howl.

"Things are about to get interesting," I say. Why now? Why does this have to happen now? Lissa's in trouble, I know she doesn't have much time left. But there should be enough. If only—

"What have you gone and done?" Tim demands.

"Only what needed to be done, because I was the only one to do it."

There's a great hissing as the water slides away from the coast, revealing the sand beneath, the rock and the slimy undercarriage of the sea.

The water draws back, grows, until it has reached some sort of critical mass, then advances. And all of a sudden there is a wave crashing toward the shore with the roar of a dozen freight trains. A bloody big one, a tsunami of Roland Emmerich disaster movie proportions. It towers over all of us.

"So, how do we stop that?" Tim says.

"We don't," I say stepping in front of him. "I do."

I was hoping that debts would be called in later, that I would have more time to get everyone used to the idea.

As if that was ever going to happen! When do I ever get enough time to do anything?

I walk back toward the water, lean on my scythe, stare at the coming wave and say, "Yeah, I know we have a deal."

The wave continues its hurtling approach, there's the vastness of the Pacific Ocean behind it and the will of a Death with whom I have made an agreement. I wave my hands frantically at it. So much for being cool. HD prickles inside me, I resist the urge to run or to shift, what would be the point anyway?

"We have a deal!"

The wave obscures the sun. Birds continue to hurtle west, away from the shore. Only my crows remain, and they're anxious and squawking. They circle high above my head, but the wave is higher.

"WE.

"HAVE

"A

"DEAL!"

It stops, just stops, inches from my chest, water towering impossibly over us and frozen on the edge of breaking. I stab a finger into the wave. "We have a deal!"

A familiar face pushes through the water. It's too smug by far. For a moment I think it will let me off, and that this is just one last big: BOO!

My hopes lift, no matter how I try not to let them.

"Yes, and you will keep it," it says. No luck there then, was at best a slim chance. When I'd made the deal I really hadn't expected to survive.

"What's all this?" I can't help myself; I slap my hand against the surface of the water. That it's just water, that it's not hard, or viscous or something magicked solid surprises me.

The Death is showing off. I may have torn asunder a city's walls with little more than dust but that was nothing compared to this.

"This is insurance," the Death of the Water says.

A cold rage fills me. "You don't need it. I'm a man of my fucking word. Jesus, it's all about theatrics with you types."

The Death of the Water dips its head. "There's a long history of it, yes. What else could make the eons tolerable? Little deaths, drownings, minor tragedies. But once in a while, one has to let oneself go." A hand snatches out, grabs my arm and pulls me into the wave.

"Not yet." I yank my arm back. "That's not how this works." Lissa's dying behind me, and it expects me to just walk away. Lissa dies and the whole world drowns as far as I'm concerned.

"You said it yourself, we have a deal."

"Not yet. They need to know. We stopped a god today, you think if you snatch me into the water that they won't try and come after me? Do you really want to fight a war? Besides, the deal can't be done until I'm finished here, and I'm not finished. I'm not quite the letter of our agreement."

The hand grips me tighter. I feel the limits of Water's restraint, and I know I'm at the edge of them. But then it's as if the ocean itself takes a deep breath. The wall of water shivers then stills.

It lets me go. "You can have your goodbye."

"Nothing good about it," I murmur. Except, well, we've just saved the world.

A cold wind howls across the wall of the wave. Its top tips ever so slightly, water tumbling like rain. There's a rainbow on the southern end of the beach.

I walk back towards Lissa, Tim hovering at a distance. The beach is packed with the dead, souls of those drawn to this End of Days, this meeting of the Deaths various. I can't help it, I pomp some as I go almost without thinking. They're quick to get out of the way. Something new, I guess, but I've no time to consider it.

She lies there, Dr. Brooker leaning over her. There's a blanket beneath her, but nothing hiding her injuries, I look at them, as much as it hurts to do so. Two wounds already dark and swollen, already open to death. I remind myself why I am here. I'm responsible for those injuries, and I will be responsible for their healing.

Dr. Brooker doesn't look like he's seen anything of what has just gone on. And that takes real concentration. He doesn't even see me approach.

He's working swiftly, efficiently. He's already got a drip in one arm, and he's packing something into the wound.

"You're going to have to move aside," I say.

"Steve, are you sure that—"

"I know what I'm doing."

"Steve," Lissa says, her eyes are glazed over, but she manages to focus them on me. My girl is so strong. "You finished it?"

"Yeah, well, not quite. There's something I have to do. Something so you'll survive."

Lissa frowns. Her eyes widen. She knows. She's not stupid.

"Don't you come near me," Lissa says. "You can't do this."

"I don't do this, and you'll die. Trust me, I know. I have to."

She lifts her legs to her chest, or tries to at any rate. Just watching her hurts, but it doesn't stop me. She can hate me all she wants, as long as she lives.

"You were never meant to die," I say. "Remember, I brought you back. You can't die now. You're the best of me. Don't you know what sort of monster I would become without you."

I can't stop the tears that slide down my cheeks. They're as deep and powerful a force as the Death of the Water. And God help me, she's the one that tries to offer me comfort.

"You think too little of yourself," Lissa says, touching my face. Her fingers are so warm. Here is that last burst of life before death. I don't know if what I am giving her is much better, but it's all I have.

I brush my thumb across her face, gently, gently. Slide a strand of hair from her brow. I kiss her softly then harder, and she's kissing me back.

Swift, without hesitation, I pull from the kiss, and holding Lissa tight, release a thirteenth of the Hungry Death into her.

There is fire. A blazing heat, as though I've closed my body around red-hot barbed wire. I bite my tongue against the agony of it.

I will not scream: not now.

The air turns electric, and she shudders with this shared pain. It passes quickly, though. That's something, surely. I tell myself that has to be enough.

When I am finished Mog is gone, and I'm holding the Knives of the Negotiation again. The Orcus is no longer wholly inside me. Mog cannot form. The knives mumble contentedly like homicidal babies. They feel a little heavier, or it's just that I am a little weaker.

She blinks at me. Already there is color in her cheeks and the wounds are closing. It's always swift that first time, with the flush of power that comes with becoming an RM. "What have you done?" Lissa demands, she's still a little a woozy, but she won't be for long. "It's not over yet, is it?"

I can't face her. I have more work to do.

"I'll be back soon," I say, not looking her in the eyes, talking to the wounds so swiftly closing. "Rest, just a little longer. I'll explain everything."

Tim walks towards me. "Lissa's OK," I say.

"Good, thank Christ. What the hell is all that about?" Tim demands jabbing towards the wall of water. His voice is low, but no less vehement. "What sort of deal leads to a massive tidal wave?"

"One that's not so good for me, but good for everyone else."

"What the fuck?"

"I don't have time to discuss it. I've still got things to do."

"Yeah, like run Mortmax. Like being my cousin."

"I'll always be your cousin, Tim," I say softly. "But I have to give up Mortmax."

"What?"

"I'm getting rid of all this power."

"You can't be serious, and what, give it to them?" He gestures at the assembled Ankous. All of them bloody, and tired, and alive.

"Why not? They're the most qualified. They've all worked so hard to stop the Stirrer god. I couldn't have done it without them, and you, and Lissa. Look, the Orcus was always meant to be thirteen. One person shouldn't be responsible for the world, and certainly not me. Christ, the number of times I nearly killed you, trust me, you don't want all of this thing inside me."

"You haven't discussed it with anyone," Tim says. "Surely this sort of thing should be negotiated, talked out."

"I don't have time. And really, if I did, maybe I'd convince myself that it was a bad idea. Maybe I'd let the Hungry Death have more control. We've won after all. This is the best way. No one discussed it with me when I became what I am. Believe me, they're all much more ready for the responsibility than I ever was."

"I thought you needed the blood of a Negotiation to make an RM." The poor bugger's grasping at straws now. I want to tell him that everything is OK, but it isn't, I can't even pretend that. I'm too frightened. It was much easier to deal with when the end of the world loomed, kind of provided a stark context that is now seriously lacking.

I shake my head, there's been blood enough. "That was in the old regime. Things have changed, and considerably. I'm Orcus. The Stirrers are defeated. I think I can decide how this is done."

HD rails inside of me. I feel it rattling the cage, it's never liked this decision. But I know it for the wind and bluster that it is. We've had that fight. And I won.

And, while everything is in flux, I need to act.

Right now it isn't strong enough to do anything, but in a year or two that strength might grow again. In a year or two it might start to work at the weaknesses I know I possess and the ones I don't have a clue about.

HD only ever came back to me because it was frightened and it knew that it could eventually bend me to its will again. I'm not going to let it.

I'm playing my game this time.

I close my eyes and release HD into each of my Ankous, it's a sensation akin to pulling the finger bones from your flesh. And each time I do it, like pomping, it gets worse. I'm tearing something integral from me. And as I pass that power onto each I am diminished.

So I do it as quickly as I can. Rip the bloody bandage off. Doesn't make it any less painful for anyone though.

As the last of it goes, I look over at Tim. The beach seems emptier than I remember it, and I realize that I can't see the dead anymore.

Tim looks at me hesitantly and takes a deep breath. I shake my head.

"This isn't for you," I say. "You have a family. You never wanted this." And I don't want to say it, because I love him, but I don't quite trust what he might become. "And Lissa needed it."

"I know," Tim says, and he sounds relieved but that relief quickly shifts to anger. He jabs a finger into my chest. "I told you to negotiate with the Water. But this, Steve. This!"

Tim looks over at Lissa. I can't read his expression, sorrow maybe, pity perhaps, but when he turns back to me, the look is nothing but despair and rage.

"She's going to need your help," I say.

Tim's lip quivers. "So, you're gonna leave us to clean up this mess, it's... Christ, I've lost my mum, my dad, and now..."

"Shit, mate... Tim. I don't want to go. But I have to. You see that wave? The only thing that's stopping it is the deal I made. The deal I have to follow through with. I know you thought that when this was over we'd all grab a beer, and everything would be like it was. But that was never going to happen. I'm lucky that I'm even getting this moment."

I'm running out of time, I gently push him away. "Look after my... just look after her." Lissa, leaning on Brooker's shoulder, is already walking towards us, across the beach, sick of waiting. It's hard to tear my gaze from her, but I do because I need to see that Tim is getting this, that he understands how hard this is for me. And I think he does.

"I will. Not that Lissa... she'll be OK," Tim says, wiping at his eyes.

I shake my head. "We all need help from time to time." I hand him the Knives of the Negotiation. "And these. Guard these. They've been nothing but trouble."

Letting them go, I realize how heavy they were. I feel my shoulders lift, and for a moment guilt rises in me, passing these blades on to a man I love like a brother. But that's what we all do in the end: we pass everything on.

"You're never going to let me leave this job are you?"

"Not likely, mate. You're too good at it."

Tim holds the knives warily. "Yeah, I'll make sure they're safe."

"Hide them," I say. "Hide the bloody things as cleverly as you can. You say goodbye to Sally for me, and the kids. Tell them that we won, and that we were all very brave."

I hug him then, tight. I fight back a sob, and hold him. For a second, Tim's motionless, and I think he's never going to forgive me.

But then he hugs me back, nearly crushes me.

Behind him the Ankous, Regional Managers newly instated, look more confused than ever. Promotions are usually much harder in this business. Only Cerbo seems happy. He grins at me. I know the bastard will do Suzanne proud.

I'm just a man now.

Not a Pomp. Nothing beyond the human I was when I came into this world, and I feel as naked, as powerless as a baby. I wish I was as ignorant.

But I know what lies ahead. I walk to Lissa. She stands, leaning on Dr. Brooker. Her fingers touch her stomach, with an almost endearing hesitancy, feeling for the wounds that are no longer there. Her face is flushed with new power. There'll be a soft voice whispering darkly within her.

I remember how Suzanne once talked about sacrifice. What it takes to become an RM. I think I finally understand her, and maybe why they chose me for this. Maybe they gave up everything because they knew that when it came to it, I'd be able to give this greater power away.

The things I know about Death are this:

Death can never be one person, one thing. When the Hungry Death ruled there was only madness and blood. Leave it for too long lodged inside me and that was where we were headed. Despite my deal, I think I would have given this up anyway.

Lissa blinks. "I can hear the heartbeats of the . . . this was in your head?" She touches my brow. Her fingers are warm, electric. My throat tightens.

"Yes, but it was louder. I had the World's Pulse to contend with." Even now I can't resist being a show-off. Why do I always need to impress this woman?

"It's terrifying isn't it?" she says.

"Terrifying and wonderful." I grab her hand, push it against my chest. "There, you can feel mine. Can you hear it?"

She frowns, then smiles. "Yes."

"Don't forget it."

"I won't."

There has always been a wall between us. When she was dead and I was alive. When she was mortal and I was RM. Same wall, we've just swapped sides. She has countless days ahead. Mine are gone.

"Mr. D will help you," I say in a rush. "One thing I've learned is to never leave a power vacuum. You'll be better than me, I know that."

"Leave?" Lissa pulls her hand from mine. "Where are you going?"

"I'm so sorry," I say.

And, for the first time, I think she notices the wave. "What in all fuck is that?"

The wave top keeps spilling over and it's getting worse. I realize that, as I've walked up the beach, it's followed me.

The wave higher than the Gold Coast Towers thrums like a three-hundred-meter tall guitar string. Its tip, on the verge of breaking, reaches over us. Those who aren't Pomps or RMs, regular folk like me, have already run for cover. Pointless, of course. If this wave breaks, the whole city, and those glass and steel citadels within it, will be ground out, drowned in sea and rage. But all of us cling onto whatever extra moments of life we can manage. I understand that as well as anyone.

And this is imposing in a truly terrifying way. It's an effort not to cower beneath the wave, but I refuse to.

All this spectacle for one man.

"Please excuse me," I say to Lissa. "I have to sort this out first."

"You don't need to be so threatening," I say to the Death of the Water. "I keep my promises."

Water's voice is a whisper in my ear. Its actions are loud enough. "You're done. You're just a mortal now. You don't come with me, calamity will prevail and death and death and death."

HD would have loved this, it's probably grinning like mad in his thirteen new hosts. I resist checking the faces of my old Ankous.

"Now that's just nasty," I say. "I need ten minutes, you can't want more trouble with my people."

I turn back and survey the beach. All my Pomps are there. Not one of them has fled. They might look as terrified as I feel, but they haven't deserted me.

"Ten you shall have, for I am patience. I am cold and measured in my waiting, the steady engine of the currents and the slide of—"

"That better not be part of my ten fucking minutes," I say.

"What's he talking about?" Lissa says.

"I'm saying goodbye, my love."

Lissa's eyes widen. For a moment I think she's about to throw a punch at my head. Her hands clench and unclench, fury and grief vie for dominance.

"You prick, you made a bloody deal?" she says. "You went and made a deal with the sea?"

"I had no choice. Life came from the sea, and death. I needed it." I sound stronger, braver than I feel. How can I let the mask slip now?

"And look what it's done," Lissa demands.

"Yes, look," I say pointing at a sky no longer lit by a comet, the Gold Coast almost as quiet as New Year's morning. Crows are singing in the distance. I don't know what they see, but I can imagine it. "We've won. That's all that matters."

I reach out and take Lissa's hand. "Will you walk with me along the shore?" I glance over at Tim, but his back is to me. The Ankous, RMs I mean, are looking on with amazement. They're weary, all of them. Tired, blood-spattered, shocked by the force of HD inside them. Each blinks as though newly dead. Most of them know more about Death than me, about the role of an RM, but none of them have experienced this.

Some try and come over to me and Lissa. Tim stops them with an arm wave.

"Not now. Later," I hear him say. "Not now."

He knows how to manage ministers, he knows how to manage RMs. I feel a momentary burst of pride. Tim herds them away from the water, but he doesn't turn to me.

We've said our goodbye.

"You can't," Lissa says at last. I can see her trying to process this on top of everything else, our victory, her new power.

"I have to."

I knew it was heading this way. That was the deal that I had made. The plan I had planned. Sure, part of me had hoped otherwise, but everyone does when they're dealing with Death, no matter what Death it is.

I don't like seeing my girl cry. I don't. I don't want to say goodbye. But she's got part of me inside her now, part of what I was, and if she's more wicked as a result, she's stronger, too.

And she always was stronger than me. I saved her once, pulled an Orpheus Maneuver, but only because she was resolute enough for the both of us. Lissa will be better than me. I gave it to her, just as I was given the Orcus: because she will do what is right.

"You knew this was coming," I say. "Some time, sooner or later. You had to. Listen, please, you have to hear this out, because I don't have much time. You can't bring me back. You'll tear the world down if you do, the world we've just saved."

"You stupid, stupid man," Lissa whispers, but there's no hatred there, just shock, and she kisses me. And the kiss doesn't feel quite real, because I'm desperately trying to take it all in. Store the memory as deeply and clearly as I can.

The feel of her lips.

The taste of her mouth. The tongue that searches for and meets mine. It should be a perfect kiss, but it can't be.

Longing, exhaustion and fear ruin it.

I want to hold her, and hold her and hold her. I want to devour and be devoured. And to laugh and to make a life with her. I want these things forever. But I can't have them. No one gets that. Not even a man who was Death.

I have to stop.

Why are there always more words to be said? Why can't I just leave it at a kiss? "Look after Tim for me. Don't know what he's going to do now that I'm not around."

And it's as though I've summoned him. Tim's walking in our direction, almost breaking into a run. So much for last goodbyes.

Hands tug at me, pull me back towards the face of the water. I look from Tim to Lissa.

"We'll get you back," Tim shouts, eyes frantically searching the shoreline as though the answer might lie along the water's edge. "I swear, we'll get you back."

"I don't think you can," I say. Lissa's perfectly still, caught between moments on the cusp of a despair she didn't see coming.

There's rage there too, and I can't blame her. I'm familiar with that pain. Living is pain as much as it is anything. I guess it's remarkable that we find any happiness at all.

But we do.

"Here, I am," I say to the Water. "Here I am, the last one. The balance that undoes all that I've ruined."

"It will hurt," the Death of the Water says.

"I am familiar with hurt." I wish the words didn't catch in my throat, that I didn't stumble over them, that I sounded less frightened.

"Wait!" Lissa cries and I struggle from the water's grip, grab Lissa's face and kiss her, hard, harder than I ever have. "Sorry," I breathe. "I'm so sorry."

"Don't be. Don't. And Steven, it's a yes."

"What?"

"It's a yes."

"You mean—"

"You know what I mean. It would have been a yes."

I kiss her again. I have to. How can I ever stop? Everything is in that kiss, but it's not enough, and it has to end.

"You were right," I say. "You and me, we always suffer for our love. I'm so sorry."

I know she feels my fear, my racing heartbeat, and understands what it is, and it kills me to see what that does to her. But I can't undo this. If it were that easy, if I could be so cruel, so careless of another's life, I don't believe she would love me.

I stand a little taller.

Lissa reaches to touch my face again and I strain toward her, but Water has lost its patience. Hands yank me backwards and I've no strength to resist the force of that vast Death.

Not anymore.

I made a deal and I will honor it.

Lissa's eyes shine bright and fierce. She doesn't say anything. She doesn't need to. She doesn't look away.

The water's cold.

Whales sing in the deep places of the sea. The currents grind and waves break against a thousand shores, but this vast one doesn't. Water honors its deal too. This wave recedes and I recede with it.

All I'm seeing are her eyes, green and wild, flecked with gray. All I'm feeling is her kiss.

"Do your fucking worst," I say with my last breath.

And it does.

ACKNOWLEDGMENTS

So, book three. Can't believe we made it this far. I feel like Steve's journey has been my own somewhat, and I've been just as reliant on the people around me to help get me to the end of it.

And, once again, for the last stages a huge thank you to my publisher Bernadette Foley, my structural editor Roberta Ivers, copy-editor Kate Stevens, and Emma Whetham for keeping things together. Your faith in these books has helped buoy me through some pretty rough seas.

Thanks again to everyone at Avid Reader Bookstore for being amazing, and for *still* putting up with the least available casual staff member ever. Particular word must go out to the Sunday crew—Helen, Melina and Sophie.

Thanks again to Paul Landymore and Alex Adsett, SF Sunday stalwarts, as well as all the SF Sunday regulars.

And a big thank you to the bands and musicians whose music has kept me focused through this whole series. Gotye, Spoon, and Okkervil River in particular, oh and to a band called Frankie and the Moon whose song "Everything" got me through the final scene in this book. Listen to it, and you'll know what I mean.

Thanks to Diana, there's a reason these books are dedicated to you, my darling.

And thanks to you, who have followed me onto book three.

All done now.

extras

meet the author

Diana Jamieson

TRENT JAMIESON has had more than sixty short stories published over the past decade, and, in 2005, won an Aurealis Award for his story "Slow and Ache." His most recent stories have appeared in *Cosmos Magazine*, Zahir, Murky Depths, and Jack Dann's anthology *Dreaming Again*. His collection, *Reserved for Travelling Shows*, was released in 2006. He won the 2008 Aurealis Award for best YA short story with his story "Cracks."

Trent was fiction editor of *Redsine* magazine, and worked for Prime Books on Kirsten Bishop's multi–award winning novel *The Etched City*. He's a seasonal academic at Queensland University of Technology, teaching creative writing, and has taught at Clarion South. He has a fondness for New Zealand beer and gloomy music. He lives in Brisbane with his wife, Diana. Trent's blog can be found at www.trentjamieson.com.

interview

Have you always known that you wanted to be a writer?

Pretty much. I've wanted to write since I was about five, and it was always fantasy or science fiction. It only took me three decades to sell my first book, but I've been writing in all that time. The only thing I ever really thought I might like to do is be a stage magician, but I don't have the eye-hand coordination for that nor the patter.

When you aren't busy writing, what are some of your hobbies?

I like walking—I live next to a fair bit of brush, we have wallabies and koalas in there, and right now the young Kookaburras are learning to laugh, it's a really really horrible sound, until they get it. I love reading, of course, and, occasionally, I'll sketch one of my pets. But I don't really have a hobby, it's that lack of eye-hand coordination, I think. When I stop writing I sit in a corner and power down.

Who or what inspired you to write about Death?

Fritz Leiber's Death in the Lankhmar books for starters. The depiction of Charon in the old *Clash of the Titans* movie. There's a bit of Neil Gaiman's Death in there as well as Pratchett's. Though in my world there are thirteen deaths, collectively called the Orcus, and none of them get along all that well.

I've always had an interest in death, and the brevity of life. It's the wall we all end up hitting. It's fun to imagine various scenarios for what might come after.

I've thrown in a lot of Death folklore as well, though I've mixed it up. Terms like Ankou and Orcus hold slightly different meanings in different cultures' folkstories—an Ankou for instance, is Death's helper, but is sort of death as well.

***How did you develop the world of* DEATH MOST DEFINITE?**

It all started with that first scene. I had no idea what was going on, but it made me want to find out. Pretty quickly in I had the idea of people working for Death, and what might happen if someone starts murdering them.

Of course, at its heart it's still a love story. And Steven always fell in love at first sight.

If death really was run like a corporation, how well do you think it would succeed?

Like any corporation. Really well when everything's working, and utterly terribly when it's not. Oh, and someone would always be stealing the paper clips and pens. And the phones would never work, and we'd all be crashing toward some sort of apocalypse.

Hmm, kind of like the DEATH MOST DEFINITE, I suppose.

Do you have a favorite character? If so, why?

Other than Steven and Lissa, whom I see as the heart of the story. I think it's Wal. I never expected to have a plump Cherub show up at all, until, well, until he did. He's part conscience part troublemaker, and quite tolerant for a creature stuck on someone's arm most of the time.

Oh, but I also love Tim, Don and Sam, Mr D, and Charon. And, in book two there's Aunt Neti. She guards the stone knives of Negotiation, and the secret back ways into hell, and has many eyes and many arms and likes to cook scones—they're delicious, just don't ask what's in them or the jam. (You can tell that I'm deep in edits for book two can't you?)

What can we look forward to in Steven's next outing, **MANAGING DEATH?**

Well, Steven has to learn how to be Death while organizing a meeting of the Regional Managers called a Death Moot.

You'll meet Aunt Neti, the mysterious Francis Rillman, and the even more mysterious and disturbing Hungry Death. There's betrayals, great battles, an approaching evil god, and scones and jam to be had.

And Steven still has a lot of growing up to do: lucky he's got Lissa and Tim by his side, and Wal, stuck on his arm. This book is a good deal darker, but I suppose that's what happens when you move up the ladder at Mortmax Industries.

Finally, what has been your favorite part of the publication process so far?

I may sound like a glutton for punishment, but so far it's been the editing. I've loved reworking these stories, making them as tight as I can. I've learned a lot—the publication process is such a team effort—and I think that's going to really show in book three—but you'll just have to wait and see.

I'm dying to see the books in print. I know how hard I've worked on them, as have my editors at Orbit, and, after thirty years of waiting and writing, it'll be great to finally see one of my own novels in a bookstore!

introducing

If you enjoyed
THE BUSINESS OF DEATH,
look out for

A MADNESS OF ANGELS

by Kate Griffin

Two years after his untimely death, Matthew Swift finds himself breathing once again, lying in bed in his London home.

Except that it's no longer his bed, or his home. And the last time this sorcerer was seen alive, an unknown assailant had gouged a hole so deep in his chest that his death was irrefutable… despite his body never being found.

He doesn't have long to mull over his resurrection, though, or the changes that have been wrought upon him. His only concern now is vengeance. Vengeance upon his monstrous killer and vengeance upon the one who brought him back.

Not how it should have been.

Too long, this awakening, floor warm beneath my fingers, itchy carpet, thick, a prickling across my skin, turning rapidly into the red-hot feeling of burrowing ants; too long without sensation, everything weak, like the legs of a baby. I said twitch, and my toes twitched, and the rest of my body shuddered at the effort. I said blink, and my eyes were two half-sucked toffees, uneven, sticky, heavy, pushing back against the passage of my eyelids like I was trying to lift weights before a marathon.

All this, I felt, would pass. As the static blue shock of my wakening, if that is the word, passed, little worms of it digging away into the floor or crawling along the ceiling back into the telephone lines, the hot blanket of their protection faded from my body. The cold intruded like a great hungry worm into every joint and inch of skin, my bones suddenly too long for my flesh, my muscles suddenly too tense in their relaxed form to tense ever again, every part starting to quiver as the full shock of sensation returned.

I lay on the floor naked as a shedding snake, and we contemplated our situation.

runrunrunrunrunRUNRUNRUNRUN! hissed the panicked voice inside me, the one that saw the bed legs an inch from my nose as the feet of an ogre, heard the odd swish of traffic through the rain outside as the spitting of venom down a forked tongue, felt the thin neon light drifting through the familiar dirty window pane as hot as noonday glare through a hole in the ozone layer.

I tried moving my leg and found the action oddly giddying, as if this was the ultimate achievement for which my life so far had been spent in training, the fulfilment of all ambition. Or perhaps it was simply that we had pins and needles and, not entirely knowing how to deal with pain, we laughed through it, turning my head to stick my nose into the dust of the carpet to muffle my own inane giggling as I brought my knee up towards my chin, and tears dribbled around the edge of my mouth. We tasted them, curious, and found the saltiness pleasurable, like the first, tongue-clenching, moisture-eating bite of hot, crispy bacon. At that moment finding a plate of crispy bacon became my one guiding motivation in life, the thing that overwhelmed all others, and so, with a mighty heave and this light to guide me, I pulled myself up, crawling across the end of the bed and leaning against the chest of drawers while waiting for the world to decide which way down would be for the duration.

It wasn't quite my room, this place I found myself in. The inaccuracies were gentle, superficial. It was still my paint on the wall, a pale, inoffensive yellow; it was still my window with its view out onto the little parade of shops on the other side of the road, unmistakable: the newsagent, the off-licence, the cobbler and all-round domestic supplier, the launderette, and, red lantern still burning cheerfully in the window, Mrs Lee Po's famous Chinese takeaway. My window, my view; not my room. The bed was new, an ugly, polished thing trying to pretend to be part of a medieval bridal chamber for a princess in a pointy hat. The mattress, when I sat on it, was so hard I ached within a minute from being in contact with it; on the wall hung a huge, gold-framed mirror in which I could picture Marie Antoinette having her curls perfected; in the corner there were two wardrobes, not one. I waddled across to them, and leant against the nearest to recover my breath from the epic distance covered. Seeing by the light seeping under the door, and the neon glow from outside, I opened the first one and surveyed jackets of rough tweed, long dresses in silk, white and cream-coloured shirts distinctively tailored, pointed black leather shoes, high-heeled sandals composed almost entirely of straps and no real protective substance, and a handbag the size of a feather pillow, suspended with a heavy, thick gold chain. I opened the handbag and rifled through the contents. A purse, containing £50, which I took, a couple of credit cards, a library membership to the local Dulwich Portakabin, and a small but orderly handful of thick white business cards. I pulled one out and in the dull light read the name—"Laura Linbard, Business Associate, KSP." I put it on the bed and opened the other wardrobe.

This one contained trousers, shirts, jackets and, to my surprise, a large pair of thick yellow fisherman's oils and sailing boots. There was a small, important-looking box at the bottom of the wardrobe. I opened it and found a stethoscope, a small first-aid kit, a thermometer and several special and painful-looking metal tools whose nature I dared not speculate on. I pulled a white cotton shirt off its hanger and a pair of grey trousers. In a drawer I found underpants which didn't quite fit comfortably, and a pair of thick black socks. Dressing, I felt cautiously around my left shoulder and ribcage, probing for damage, and finding that every bone was properly set, every inch of skin correctly healed, not even a scar, not a trace of dry blood.

The shirt cuff reached roughly to the point where my thumb joint aligned with the rest of my hand; the trousers dangled around the balls of my feet. The socks fitted perfectly, as always seems the way. The shoes were several sizes too small; that perplexed me. How is it possible for someone to have such long arms and legs, and yet wear shoes for feet that you'd think would have to have been bound? Feeling I might regret it later, I left the shoes.

I put the business card and the £50 in my trouser pockets and headed for the door. On the way out, we caught sight of our reflection in the big mirror and stopped, stared, fascinated. Was this now us? Dark brown hair heading for the disreputable side of uncared for—not long enough to be a bohemian statement, not short enough to be stylish. Pale face that freckled in the sun, slightly over-large nose for the compact features that surrounded it, head plonked as if by accident on top of a body made all the more sticklike by the ridiculous oversized clothes it wore. It was not the flesh we would have chosen, but I had long since given up dreams of resembling anyone from the movies and, with the pragmatism of the perfectly average, come to realise that this was me and that was fine.

And this was me, looking back out of the mirror.

Not quite me.

I leant in, turning my head this way and that, running my fingers through my hair—greasy and unwashed—in search of blood, bumps, splits. Turning my face this way and that, searching for bruises and scars. An almost perfect wakening, but there was still something wrong with this picture.

I leant right in close until my breath condensed in a little grey puff on the glass, and stared deep into my own eyes. As a teenager it had bothered me how round my eyes had been, somehow always imagining that small eyes = great intelligence, until one day at school the thirteen-year-old Max Borton had pointed out that round dark eyes were a great way to get the girls. I blinked and the reflection in the mirror blinked back, the bright irises reflecting cat-like the orange glow of the washed-out street lamps. My eyes, which, when I had last had cause to look at them, had been brown. Now they were the pale, brilliant albino blue of the cloudless winter sky, and I was no longer the only creature that watched from behind their lens.

runrunrunrunrunrunRUNRUNRUNRUNRUNRUNRUNRUN!

I put my head against the cold glass of the mirror, fighting the sudden terror that threatened to knock us back to the floor. The trick was to keep breathing, to keep moving. Nothing else mattered. Run long and hard enough, and perhaps while you're running you might actually come up with a plan. But nothing mattered if you were already dead.

My legs thought better than my brain, walked me out of the room. My fingers eased back the door and I blinked in the shocking light of the hundred-watt bulb in the corridor outside. The carpet here was thick and new, the banisters polished, but it was a painting on the wall, a print of a Picasso I'd picked up for a fiver—too many years ago—all colour and strange, scattered proportions—which stole our attention. It still hung exactly where I'd left it. I felt almost offended. We were fascinated: an explosion of visual wonder right there for the same price as a cheap Thai meal, in full glory. Was everything like this? I found it hard to remember. I licked my lips and tasted blood, dry and old. Thoughts and memories were still too tangled to make clear sense of them. All that mattered was moving, staying alive long enough to get a plan together, find some answers.

From downstairs I heard laughter, voices, the chink of glasses, and a door being opened. Footsteps on the tiles that led from living room to kitchen, a *clink* where they still hadn't cemented in the loose white one in the centre of the diamond pattern; the sound of plates; the roar of the oven fan as it pumped out hot air.

I started walking down. The voices grew louder, a sound of polite gossipy chit-chat, dominated by one woman with a penetrating voice and a laugh that started at the back of her nose before travelling down to the lungs and back up again, and who I instinctively disliked. I glanced down the corridor to the kitchen and saw a man's back turned to me, bent over something that steamed and smelt of pie. The urge to eat anything, everything, briefly drowned out the taste of blood in my mouth. Like a bewildered ghost who can't understand that it has died, I walked past the kitchen and pushed at the half-open door to the living room.

There were three of them, with a fourth place set for the absent cook, drinking wine over the remnants of a salad, around a table whose top was made of frosted glass. As I came in, nobody seemed to notice me, all attention on the one woman there with the tone and look of someone in the middle of a witty address. But when she turned in my direction with "George, the pie!" already half-escaped from her lips, the sound of her dropped wineglass shattering on the table quickly redirected the others' attention.

They stared at me, I stared at them. There was an embarrassed silence that only the English can do so well, and that probably lasted less than a second, but felt like a dozen ticks of the clock. Then, as she had to, as things probably must be, one of the women screamed.

The sound sent a shudder down my spine, smashed through the horror and incomprehension in my brain, and at last let me understand, let me finally realise that this was no longer my house, that I had been gone too long, and that to these people I was the intruder, they the rightful owners. The scream slammed into my brain like a train hitting the buffers and tore a path through my consciousness that let everything else begin to flood in: the true realisation that if my house was not mine, my job, my friends, my old life would not be mine, nor my possessions, my money, my debts, my clothes, my shoes, my films, my music; all gone in a second, things I had owned since a scrawny teenager, the electric toothbrush my father had given me in a fit of concern for my health, the photos of my friends and the places I'd been, the copy of *Calvin and Hobbes* my first girlfriend had given me as a sign of enduring friendship the Christmas after we'd split up, my favourite pair of slippers, the holiday I was planning to the mountains of northern Spain, all, everything I had worked for, everything I had owned and wanted to achieve, vanished in that scream.

I ran. We didn't run from the sound, that wasn't what frightened us. I ran to become lost, and wished I had never woken in the first place, but stayed drifting in the blue.